THE WORKS OF TOBIAS SMOLLETT

The History and Adventures of an Atom

THE WORKS OF TOBIAS SMOLLETT

Jerry C. Beasley, General Editor
University of Delaware

O M Brack, Jr., Textual Editor
Arizona State University

Jim Springer Borck, Technical Editor
Louisiana State University

This edition includes all of the works by which Tobias Smollett was best known in his own day and by which he most deserves to be remembered. The edition conforms to the highest standards of textual and editorial scholarship. Individual volumes provide carefully prepared texts together with biographical and historical introductions and extensive explanatory notes.

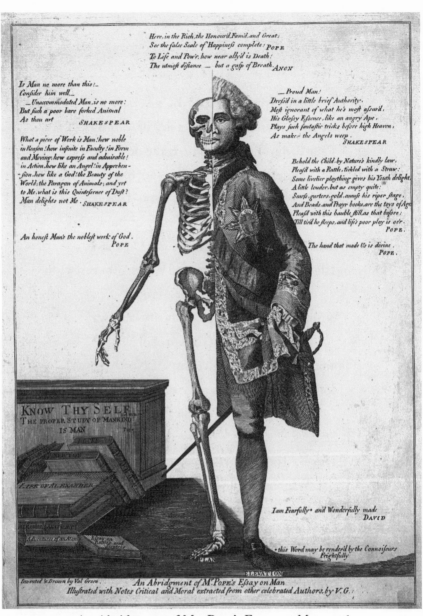

An Abridgment of Mr. Pope's Essay on Man, 1769.
(Reproduced by permission of the Huntington Library, San Marino, California.)

The History and Adventures of an Atom

TOBIAS SMOLLETT

Introduction and Notes by

ROBERT ADAMS DAY

The Text Edited by

O M BRACK, JR.

The University of Georgia Press
Athens and London

© 1989 by the University of Georgia Press
Athens, Georgia 30602
All rights reserved

Set in 10/13 Linotron 202 Janson
Typeset by The Composing Room of Michigan, Inc.
Printed and bound by Thomson-Shore, Inc.
The paper in this book meets the guidelines for permanence
and durability of the Committee on Production Guidelines for
Book Longevity of the Council on Library Resources.

Printed in the United States of America

96 95 94 93 92   C   6 5 4 3 2
96 95 94 93 92   P   5 4 3 2 1

Library of Congress Cataloging in Publication Data

Smollett, Tobias George, 1721–1771.
The history and adventures of an atom / Tobias Smollett;
introduction and notes by Robert Adams Day;
text edited by O M Brack, Jr.
p.   cm. — (The Works of Tobias Smollett)
Includes index.
ISBN 0-8203-1073-5 (alk. paper)
ISBN 0-8203-1437-4 (pbk.: alk. paper)
1. Great Britain—Politics and government—18th century—Humor.
I. Day, Robert Adams, 1924– . II. Brack, O M. III. Title.
IV. Series: Smollett, Tobias George, 1721–1771. Works. 1988.
PR3694.H5 1989   88-30705
823'.6—dc19   CIP

British Library Cataloging in Publication Data available

FOR MILTON, WHO HELPED

NOTE

This edition of *The History and Adventures of an Atom* is in every way identical to the original clothbound edition except that the editor has taken the occasion of its preparation to correct certain inaccuracies; he wishes to thank Professor Pat Rogers for pointing these out. The list that follows gives page and line references to these corrections for the convenience of the reader: xxix.21–23, 215.37–38, 215.42, 227.1–2.

R.A.D.
November 1991

CONTENTS

Contents

ILLUSTRATIONS

Numbers in parentheses following the titles of most prints direct the reader to the annotations in volumes 3 and 4 of the *Catalogue of Political and Personal Satires in the British Museum*, compiled by Frederic G. Stephens and Edward Hawkins (London, 1877, 1883). The notes to the text make frequent reference to prints not listed below; in the notes, a print number marked with an asterisk (*) indicates that the print in question has been included in the present volume.

Unless otherwise indicated in captions, all illustrations have been reproduced, with permission, from the holdings of the British Library.

PREFACE

The History and Adventures of an Atom has never before been edited, though it has been reprinted in some of the collected editions of Smollett's fiction. The only annotation heretofore provided has been the reproduction of one of the several early "keys." None of these keys gives more information than the identity (and sometimes the dates) of the persons referred to, and none is completely accurate. The editor's task has therefore been virtually to start from scratch; and since the *Adventures of an Atom* is more densely and complexly allusive than any other work by Smollett, the notes to the text have had to be correspondingly minute. The body of major scholarship devoted to the *Atom* is very small, but the pioneering work of Arnold Whitridge, Louis L. Martz, James R. Foster, and Lewis M. Knapp must be mentioned with gratitude, since it has contributed greatly to the present edition. Paradoxically, the most important source of information has been the nonfictional writings of Smollett himself, as will be seen from the editor's introduction.

Unique among Smollett's works, the *Atom* presents its reader (and its annotator) with a set of problems also unique. Smollett's familiar linguistic exuberance is in this work given its freest rein: Scotticisms, archaisms, vulgarisms, and learned terms abound, and many common words are used in senses obsolete or obsolescent even in Smollett's own day, yet in contexts where the modern sense more or less fits, and may thus mislead the reader. Smollett constantly refers to the minutiae of historical events familiar enough in his time but now completely forgotten; and he sometimes makes much of matters which his contemporaries in general did not consider very significant.

Although a satirist is of course not upon oath, the modern reader needs to be told when Smollett is merely exaggerating a fact, when he is fantasticating, when his information is mistakenly erroneous, and when—though rarely—his animus leads him into direct accusations that he must have known to be unjustified. His inflated digressions, with their parade of obscure learning, are (virtually always, perhaps invariably) *not* fabrications, and annotation gives an impressive picture of the wealth of "useless knowledge" that Smollett had accumulated for his purposes. His discourse in the *Atom* is enriched with allusions to ancient and modern literature (some of it very recondite) far more frequently than it is in the novels. The "Japanese" material is not arbitrarily applied, and the ingenuity that Smollett showed in its selection and use is eminently worth demonstrating. Finally, the *Atom* is unusual, if not unique, in two other respects: the degree to which it is a tissue of echoes and allusions to, almost a reworking of, Smollett's earlier works— fictional, polemical, and historical; and the heavy reliance of its imagery on the political cartoons of his day, often to the extent that the text cannot be properly understood without detailed reference to them.

The explanatory notes included in this edition are intended to provide the serious reader with the information necessary to an understanding of all these many complications of Smollett's text. The notes furnish full documentation of their sources, primary and secondary, except that the editor has relied very broadly on the following general works of reference, not mentioned in the notes:

George H. Cunningham, *London* (London: J. M. Dent, 1927)
The Dictionary of National Biography
N. G. C. Hammond and H. H. Scullard, *The Oxford Classical Dictionary*, 2d ed. (Oxford: Oxford University Press, 1970)
Henry A. Harben, *A Dictionary of London* (London: Herbert Jenkins, 1918)
Thomas B. Harbottle, *A Dictionary of Battles*, rev. George Bruce (New York: Stein & Day, 1975)
The Oxford English Dictionary (*OED*)
W. G. Smith and J. E. Heseltine, *The Oxford Dictionary of Proverbs*, 3d ed., rev. F. P. Wilson (Oxford: Clarendon Press, 1970).

Translations from Greek and Latin are the editor's own unless otherwise indicated. References to Shakespeare cite the texts as presented in *The Riverside Shakespeare*, ed. G. Blakemore Evans et al. (Boston: Houghton Mifflin, 1974).

An unusual feature of the present volume is a "Key," separate from the notes, which identifies in alphabetical order the many personages (and certain places) presented in the text under "Japanese" names. The key provides the reader, who may wish to proceed rapidly through the narrative while avoiding constant reference to the notes, with a means of readily identifying the characters. It is based on a collation of the existing keys, printed and manuscript, but these have been carefully checked for errors and inconsistencies.

The editor's introduction is intended to furnish the reader with general information essential to a full understanding of Smollett's satire. It briefly sketches the political structure of Great Britain as Smollett knew it and provides a succinct review of the principal events of the Seven Years' War, the foundation or framework on which the narrative of the *Atom* is constructed. This review is followed by an outline of Smollett's opinions concerning British politics and political figures, the conduct of the war, and the nature of what he regarded as a decaying society. Subsequent sections discuss the sources of the *Atom* and the literary influences upon it; the actual circumstances of the work's composition; the evidence for Smollett's authorship (a question on which some scholars have even recently been hesitant to pronounce, but which the editor trusts may now be regarded as settled); and lastly, the curious circumstances of the work's first publication, the nature of its early reception, and its several reprintings. Following the introduction is a chronology of dates and events pertinent to the *Atom*, and to the events in Smollett's life and career bearing upon its sources and composition.

ACKNOWLEDGMENTS

Anyone who attentively reads all of the pages that follow will readily admit that nowadays only a polymath of formidable proportions could have dealt adequately, unassisted, with the problems posed by the text of Smollett's *Atom*. When faced with such a task it is good to have friends; and it is even better to have arrived at the point where one is faced with the more agreeable task of thanking these friends for their generosity and kindness.

I have worked at the British Library, the London Library, the Bodleian and several college libraries at Oxford University; at the Cambridge University Library and at the Wren Library, Trinity College, Cambridge; at the Bibliothèque Nationale; at the Henry E. Huntington Library, the William Andrews Clark Memorial Library, and the libraries of Harvard, Yale, and Princeton universities. I cannot number, and probably do not even remember, all the instances of kind and painstaking help I have received from the staff members of these libraries, but I want to single out for special thanks Mrs. Lillian Brocklebank of the North Library staff in the British Library.

The problems of dealing with Greek and Japanese (or, rather, Smollett's versions of Greek and Japanese) were turned into pleasures by Dr. Judith Binder of the American School of Classical Studies in Athens; Professors Jacob Stern and John Van Sickle, City University of New York; Professor P. G. O'Neill of the University of London; Dr. Glen Baxter, Mr. Shimizu Akihiko, Professor Alan Cranston, and Mrs. Kazuko Cranston, all of Harvard University; and Professor Earl Miner of Princeton University, who cracked a Japanese nut which had resisted the efforts of everyone else.

An American literary scholar is apt to quail at the difficulties of educating himself in the intricacies of British political, administrative, and military history; but he is equally apt to pass blithely over complexities whose existence he does not suspect. Donald Greene, Leo S. Bing Professor Emeritus of the University of Southern California, John Brewer, Professor of History and Literature at Harvard University, and Paul-Gabriel Boucé, Professor of English at the Université de Paris III, Sorbonne Nouvelle, spent many hours which they could ill spare from their own work in examining my annotations. They have prevented me from letting embarrassing errors get into print, and my gratitude to them is as profound as it is heartfelt. I am grateful to Professor James G. Basker of Barnard College for providing timely assistance in checking some points of documentation, and to Professor Nicolas Gross of the University of Delaware for assistance in the transcription of eighteenth-century Greek type. Lastly, I wish to thank Professor Jerry C. Beasley of the University of Delaware and Mr. Milton C. Malkin for their generous, patient, and thorough scrutiny of the manuscript for mistakes and inconsistencies as it went through successive versions.

Part of my work was completed with the support of research grants from the City University of New York (1978–79) and from the National Endowment for the Humanities and the Henry E. Huntington Library (1984). I am most grateful for this support. Finally, I wish to acknowledge with thanks that publication of this volume was assisted by a grant from funds administered by Helen Cairns, Dean of Graduate Studies and Research at Queens College, City University of New York.

ABBREVIATIONS

Asprey
: Robert B. Asprey, *Frederick the Great: The Magnificent Enigma* (New York: Ticknor and Fields, 1986).

Basker
: James G. Basker, *Tobias Smollett: Critic and Journalist* (Newark: University of Delaware Press, 1988).

Brewer, "Misfortunes"
: John Brewer, "The Misfortunes of Lord Bute: A Case-Study in Eighteenth-Century Political Argument and Public Opinion," *Historical Journal* 16 (1973): 3–43.

Brewer, *Party*
: John Brewer, *Party Ideology and Popular Politics at the Accession of George III* (Cambridge: The University Press, 1976).

Briton
: Tobias Smollett, *The Briton* (38 weekly numbers, May 1762–February 1763).

Brooke, *Chatham*
: John Brooke, *The Chatham Administration* (Westport, Conn.: Greenwood Press, 1976).

Brooke, *George III*
: John Brooke, *King George III* (New York: McGraw-Hill, 1972).

Browning
: Reed Browning, *The Duke of Newcastle* (New Haven: Yale University Press, 1975).

Chambers
: Ephraim Chambers, *Cyclopædia: Or, An Universal Dictionary*, 2 vols. (London, 1751).

Compendium of Voyages
: Tobias Smollett, ed., *A Compendium of Authentic and Entertaining Voyages*, 7 vols. (London, 1756).

Complete History
: Tobias Smollett, *A Complete History of England*, 4 vols. (London, 1757–58).

Continuation
: Tobias Smollett, *Continuation of the Complete History of England*, 5 vols. (London: 1760–65).

Corbett
: Sir Julian S. Corbett, *England in the Seven Years' War*, 2d ed., 2 vols. (London: Longmans, 1918).

CR
: *The Critical Review* (London, 1756–).

Davies	J. D. Griffith Davies, *A King in Toils* (London: Lindsay Drummond, 1938).
Fortescue	The Hon. J. W. Fortescue, *A History of the British Army*, vol. 2 (London: Macmillan, 1910).
Gipson	Lawrence H. Gipson, *The Coming of the Revolution* (New York: Harper & Row, 1954).
Hatton	Ragnhild Hatton, *George I: Elector and King* (London: Thames and Hudson, 1978).
JEGP	*Journal of English and Germanic Philology.*
Knapp	Lewis Mansfield Knapp, *Tobias Smollett: Doctor of Men and Manners* (Princeton: Princeton University Press, 1949).
Letters	*The Letters of Tobias Smollett*, ed. Lewis M. Knapp (Oxford: Clarendon Press, 1970).
Mack	Maynard Mack, *The Garden and the City* (New Haven: Yale University Press, 1969).
Martz	Louis L. Martz, *The Later Career of Tobias Smollett* (New Haven: Yale University Press, 1942).
Namier, *England*	Sir Lewis B. Namier, *England in the Age of the American Revolution* (London: Macmillan, 1930).
Namier, *Structure*	Sir Lewis B. Namier, *The Structure of Politics at the Accession of George III*, 2d ed. (London: Macmillan, 1957).
Nobbe	George Nobbe, *The North Briton: A Study in Political Propaganda* (New York: Columbia University Press, 1939).
PBSA	*Papers of the Bibliographical Society of America.*
PH	*The Parliamentary History of England . . . to the Year 1803* (London: Hansard, 1812). Numbers refer to volumes and columns, not pages.
Present State	Tobias Smollett, ed., *The Present State of All Nations*, 8 vols. (London: 1768–69).

Rudé	George Rudé, *Wilkes and Liberty* (Oxford: Clarendon Press, 1962).
Sedgwick	Romney Sedgwick, ed., *Letters from George III to Lord Bute* (London: Macmillan, 1939).
Sekora	John Sekora, *Luxury: The Concept in Western Thought, Eden to Smollett* (Baltimore: Johns Hopkins University Press, 1977).
Speck	W. A. Speck, *Stability and Strife: England, 1714–1760* (Cambridge: Harvard University Press, 1977).
Travels	Tobias Smollett, *Travels Through France and Italy*, ed. Frank Felsenstein (Oxford: Oxford University Press, 1979).
UH	*Universal History*, octavo edition (London, 1759), vol. 9 of the "Modern Part," pp. 1–169, from which Smollett derived virtually all of his information on Japan. (In a few instances, notes refer to other volumes, and the appropriate volume and page numbers are given.)
Voltaire	*The Works of Mons. de Voltaire*: The Prose Works, annotated by Smollett, 25 vols. (London, 1761–65).
Walpole, *Correspondence*	*The Yale Edition of Horace Walpole's Correspondence*, ed. W. S. Lewis et al., 48 vols. (New Haven: Yale University Press, 1938–83).
Walpole, *George II*	Horace Walpole, *Memoirs of the Last Ten Years of the Reign of George the Second*, ed. John Brooke, 3 vols. (New Haven: Yale University Press, 1985).
Walpole, *George III*	Horace Walpole, *Memoirs of the Reign of King George the Third*, ed. G. F. R. Barker, 4 vols. (New York: Putnam, 1894).
Williams	Basil Williams, *The Life of William Pitt, Earl of Chatham*, 2 vols. (London: Longmans, 1913).
Wright	Joseph Wright, *The English Dialect Dictionary* (London: Henry Frowde, 1898).

INTRODUCTION

It is safe to say that no lengthy work by a major British author (if we except their juvenilia) is so little known, or has been so little studied, as Tobias Smollett's *History and Adventures of an Atom* (1769). Only a handful of living persons have read it through; and the scholarship devoted to it, aside from brief mention in books or essays and a few short notes in learned journals, consists of three articles, a single chapter or section in each of three books, a recent American dissertation, and a chapter of another.[1] It may not be inappropriate, then, to begin by telling the reader, as Fielding did with *Tom Jones*, what the *Atom* is like and what it is not like.

In intention the *Atom* is a savage satirical attack by a son of Pope, Swift, and Rabelais who has been "traduced by malice, persecuted by faction, abandoned by false patrons, and overwhelmed by the sense of a domestic calamity,"[2] in which Smollett looks back over the previous fifteen years and lashes English conduct of domestic and foreign affairs, English politics and politicians, and "the whole body of the people . . . equally and universally contaminated and corrupted."[3] In execution, the *Atom* is an allegorical narrative of fantastic events that had taken place in Japan a thousand years previously, dictated to a London haberdasher named Nathaniel Peacock by an all-knowing atom that has resided in the bodies of the greatest figures of the state; the story is interrupted by irrelevant digressions that pour out floods of obscure erudition, couched in a relentlessly helter-skelter style; and it is sauced with imagery that makes it by far the most scatological work in English literature.[4] It is also (in execution) a rewriting of all those works of Tobias Smollett that had dealt with recent history and (in intention) a release of personal spleen and indignation; it is likewise a turning of his enemies' weapons against them by a man totally freed from the restraints of the historian or the pretended good manners of the polemicist, governed entirely, as he now is, by the desire to destroy through words and by the satirist's savage delight in his own powers.

These last characteristics, as we shall see, somewhat impair the *Atom*'s artistic achievement and blunt its impact on its victims. If the coarseness of its imagery has repelled some readers, more have in all likelihood been daunted by the complexity of the events and the obscurity of some of the persons satirized, as is evident from the "keys" that were appended in manuscript to early copies and in print to modern editions, together with the disconcerting fact that no two keys are perfectly in agreement.

The *Atom* nevertheless offers its rewards. One of its earliest reviewers complained of "a mixture of indelicacy which though it cannot gratify the loosest imagination, can scarce fail to disgust the coarsest," yet had to concede "great spirit and humour."[5] The modern reader will be less distressed by the coarseness than by the necessity, if he is to relish the satire, of becoming something of an expert on the history of the Seven Years' War and the personages involved in it. He will be rewarded by discovering anew the extraordinary vigor and fertility of Smollett's comic invention; by the robust enjoyment of knockabout satire; and by the endless variety and richness of the *Atom*'s verbal texture. Smollett wrote the *Atom* with a *saeva indignatio* at least equal to Swift's and with more than a little of his genius. Far duller works have been far more admired.

THE SEVEN YEARS' WAR AND ITS BACKGROUND

The modern reader, especially if American, may benefit from general information on a few political and historical facts which Smollett and his audience took for granted, but which have been changed or obliterated by the passage of time. These relate to the structure of British politics in Smollett's day, and to the principal events of the Seven Years' War.

The administrative and parliamentary structure of the British government has been greatly modified since the mid-eighteenth century. As Donald Greene has observed: "The modern student of eighteenth-century British politics would do well, if he wishes to understand what was actually going on, to think in terms of twentieth-century Washington rather than of twentieth-century Westminster."[6] In short, if the American president and most of the Senate held hereditary office for life, we should now have in the United States a very close approximation in structure of the government that Smollett knew;[7] making these offices elective was perhaps the principal innovation of the Founding Fathers when drafting the Constitution, which built upon and reformed the British system.

The British monarch, in the first place, was both technically and in fact far more powerful and independent than would be the case even in Victoria's day. He could and often did conduct foreign policy entirely on his own (as with secret treaties), or relying only on the advice of a very few trusted subordinates. All state functionaries were in theory his servants, and could be appointed and in most cases dismissed as he thought fit. The award of all honors, peerages, bishoprics, pensions, commissions and promotions in the army and navy, and lucrative appointments or sinecures, together with all acts of Parliament, required the sovereign's consent to become valid, and could except for the last be made entirely on his own initiative. This fact—as with the young George III's ill-judged sponsorship of his favorite Lord Bute as first minister, or his grandfather's stubborn reluctance to part with *his* favorite Carteret or to give Lord Temple a Garter or Pitt a cabinet post[8]— might be disastrous to the point of bringing government activities to a halt. The king might call and preside at cabinet and privy council meetings as he chose, and he had frequent, sometimes daily, private audiences in the "Closet" with several of his most important ministers. While the pressure of circumstances or the persuasion and threats of powerful ministers could eventually bully him into abandoning a favorite project or accepting a distasteful measure or man, there was no absolute guarantee of this; everything (short of a flat contradiction of the expressed will of Parliament, which held the power of the purse) ultimately depended on the monarch's personality and his opinions.

It has long been taken for granted that George II was "a king in chains," with powers and prerogatives vastly diminished from those enjoyed by his predecessors; that the first minister most frequently in power after the mid-1740s, Thomas Pelham-Holles, duke of Newcastle, was an impotent ditherer, chiefly concerned with meddling in patronage and with petty manipulation of Parliament; and that William Pitt, universally acknowledged as the savior of the nation and thus the Winston Churchill of his day, virtually governed Britain in all respects. (Such certainly was Smollett's view, both in the *Atom* and in his other writings.) But some recent studies have powerfully argued that in fact the king and Newcastle were far better informed than Pitt on a good many important matters; that they constantly manipulated him, overtly and covertly, controlling the information that was made available to him; and that both in general policies and in specific decisions George II, together with Newcastle and Lord Chancellor Hardwicke, very effectively ruled Britain, while Pitt was the servant of the cabinet.[9]

But whatever the truth may be, the image of a Pitt of heroic stature surrounded by weaklings and incompetents prevailed with the general public and with Smollett as well, just as the genuinely erroneous notion of Lord Bute as the power behind the throne from his resignation in 1763 until as late as 1780 was almost universally believed.[10] Pitt, however, was not "prime minister," since there was no prime minister in the modern sense; and in fact the idea of such an office was generally agreed to be abhorrent, as Sir Robert

Walpole and the duke of Newcastle had often been forced to remember. That minister who in fact had the surest control over votes in the Commons and at the same time enjoyed the king's confidence or at least his cooperation was, while he retained these, the head of government; but he might lose either or both for a variety of reasons. Usually, however, the office of first lord of the treasury was associated with supreme power, since the person holding it bore the ultimate responsibility both for securing revenues, by means of taxation, and for disbursing government funds. Pitt never held this office. From 1757 through 1761 he was secretary of state for the southern department, which included the colonies, and whatever his actual powers and responsibilities might have been he gladly left fiscal matters, the management of Parliament, and the distribution of patronage to Newcastle, who was first lord of the treasury. At the time of his resignation in October 1761, Pitt aroused much resentment by a tactless remark indicating that he saw himself as "directing" the government.[11]

What are now stigmatized, hypocritically or not, as bribery, corruption, and patronage were in Smollett's time regarded at all levels with much greater realism. Officials routinely accepted presents to assure the performance of specific services included in their regular duties; many high officials received large salaries while paying small sums to clerks to do most of the actual work involved. Many obsolete offices, as in the royal household, involved honor and money, but (except for attendance at court) no duties whatsoever, and this continued to be mainly the case until Prince Albert's day. Substantial pensions, or titles, might be awarded after notable military or political service, or as a sop when a functionary who had become obnoxious for whatever reason was relieved of office. Such rewards, as a matter of course, were to be expected in return for the trouble and expense of pursuing a career in Parliament, and indiscriminate opposition to the administration (William Pitt being the most eminent example) was a recognized method of obtaining them—though Pitt at first, to the astonishment and delight of all, was interested purely in power.[12] Repeated legislative attempts to keep "placemen" out of Parliament met with little success. And anyone rewarded with high office expected also that various places and awards would be put at his disposal for friends, relatives, and adherents, the former incumbents being turned out; this occurred wholesale when a new administration came in, as in the celebrated "Massacre of the Pelhamite Innocents," when the incoming Bute administration removed the allowances of many who had been enjoying them since the beginning of Newcastle's long tenure at the treasury.[13] The permanent civil servant with tenure guaranteed was unknown, though a few indispensable people in effect achieved permanence.[14]

Rotten and pocket boroughs had not yet come to be called so. The ancient borough charters limited the franchise in an infinity of ways, ranging from virtual manhood suffrage (for persons of some landed property) to the seven electors of Old Sarum who first put Pitt in Parliament. The buying or owning of votes was taken completely for granted and was denounced only by those who were not able to practice it or who had lost an election. On a higher level, a reliable or powerful M.P. might be made a peer to continue his voting record or reverse it; bishops, who usually voted pro-administration without question, were often appointed for their political views and efforts rather than for any achievements in spiritual leadership or theological learning.

The tax structure that Smollett knew also requires explanation for the modern reader. Revenue was derived chiefly from five sources: customs duties; excise taxes on various commodities and luxuries, such as beer, imported textiles, tobacco, tea, and so on; taxes on assessed income from landed property, and on stamps and stamped paper; and such minor taxes as that on windows and the duties on pensions and offices. By far the largest revenue came from customs and from the excise taxes (£5,440,000 at the start of the Seven Years' War).[15] These latter were universally disliked and were kept as few and as low as circumstances permitted; new ones were introduced only with great effort and over much protest. (An attempt to create a new excise tax had threatened to cause the downfall of Walpole in the 1730s, and the controversy over a new tax on cider precipitated that of Bute in 1763.[16]) But the established excise taxes, since they were reflected in the prices of goods and thus were universally applied, were less obtrusive than the land tax. This ranged at various times in the century from ten to twenty percent ("four shillings in the pound"), and was thus directly felt by the nobility and the landed gentry; at the commencement of the Seven Years' War it stood at two shillings in the pound but was immediately raised to four, doubling the current revenue of £1,000,000.[17] But there was no tax whatever on ordinary wages and salaries, business profits, or dividends and interest; this fact contributed fundamentally to most of the enormous fortunes made during the century, to the equally enormous power and influence of the London merchants and bankers, and to the hatred they generated among the older landed families, with whose views Smollett tended to identify.

Today's reader must make a constant effort to remember that in the minds of the cultivated public during Smollett's time, the people who counted (except in the matter of voluntary charity, which as a religious duty was often surprisingly generous[18]) did not include the great bulk of the population. The nobility and gentry, prosperous merchants, small landowners, the clergy, a few eminent artists and writers, doctors and lawyers, and perhaps a few small entrepreneurs of one kind or another were the British public. The lower orders, or the "meaner sort" of people—servants, laborers, tenant farmers, soldiers and sailors, clerks and craftsmen, the disenfranchised in general—went unnoticed, except when they rioted or were involved in crime. When Smollett speaks in the *Atom* of "the mob" or "the many-headed beast," he usually means the House of Commons.

Although many short-lived issues generated intense heat, the principal problems of the century for the British government were few but long-lasting. First was the threat of the Catholic Stuart pretenders to the throne, which was justly considered a serious danger until the second half of the century.[19] Second was the fact that the king was also the elector of Hanover. Richard Pares says of matters at the outbreak of the Seven Years' War: "The most prominent single issue was what one might call the 'German question'—that is to say, the expediency of opposing France in Germany, the choice of a German ally, the terms of the alliance, and, above all, the relation of British policy to the interests of the Elector of Hanover."[20] The Continental connection made isolationism simply not possible until late in the century. A third important problem was the series of commercial and political rivalries and alliances among Britain and the other nations of Europe which inevitably led, between 1700 and 1800, to four major wars: those of the Spanish Succession (1702–13) and the Austrian Succession (1740–48), the Seven Years' War, and the American Revolution (the last also involving Britain in war with France and Spain). Domestic problems relating to taxation, food supply and economic controls, and social unrest and welfare made a fourth area of broad concern in peacetime, though war might abruptly increase their significance. What may have been the most important matter of all—the fostering, retention, or loss of the American colonies—was not seen as a vital issue until late in the period with which we are concerned.[21]

The Seven Years' War (1756–63, if we omit the earlier skirmishes that preceded the formal declaration of hostilities) arose, in the larger sense, as an expression of British efforts to contain French territorial and commercial expansion and, in the smaller, as a result of French encroachments by land and British by sea. The history of the war may be divided into three phases: a series of military debacles for which the Newcastle administration was largely responsible, and which resulted in its downfall; Pitt's war, which included land operations on the European continent and which, though it also began disastrously, ended in a spectacular series of victories; and Bute's war, largely a continuation of Pitt's campaigns and victories but also involving war with and victories over Spain, ending with the Peace of Paris. The war's aftermath, with the fall of Bute, with the weak performance of the Grenville and Rockingham ministries and the attendant domestic and political confusion, coupled with the greatest national debt in Britain's history, led directly to the American Revolution.

The Seven Years' War (often called the "Great War for Empire," but usually thought of by Americans under the less comprehensive and less accurate rubric of the French and Indian Wars) was a conflict which pitted France, the Austrian empire, Russia, and Spain against Great Britain, Prussia, and mercenary troops of other German states. But from our point of view it was primarily a struggle for world domination between France and Britain, with Britain also bound by treaties to support Frederick the Great of Prussia (who was the nephew of George II) in his wars against France, Austria, and Russia by providing troops and a huge annual subsidy. These treaties chiefly owed their existence to the king's natural anxieties as elector of Hanover (which could either be defended by Frederick or, if he pleased, easily overrun and taken) and to the duke of Newcastle's never-surrendered project of establishing a Continental balance of power.[22]

The precarious truce established by the Peace of Aix-la-Chapelle in 1748 was broken in Europe when Frederick conquered Saxony (1756) and in America when, in the summer of 1754, Major George Washington was defeated in an expedition against the French forts on the Ohio, built in contravention of the Peace.[23] The British were ill-prepared for war, and a series of military and naval disasters followed: General Braddock's defeat, Admiral Boscawen's abortive naval expedition against Canada, Admiral Byng's equally abortive engagement with the French fleet and the consequent loss of Minorca. The resulting crisis led in 1756 to the formation of Pitt's first, short-lived administration. In the following year the Army of Observation, a mixed German and British force led by George II's second son, the duke of Cumberland, was encircled by French forces in Germany; Cumberland agreed to disband his troops and returned to England in disgrace. An enormous fleet, intended for an amphibious assault on the French coast in the autumn, reached its target but returned to England without even putting troops ashore.

Meanwhile Pitt, returned to office in June 1757 (he had been dismissed, and for eleven weeks the king had tried in vain to form a government without him), concluded an alliance with Newcastle, continued (at least in his own eyes and those of the general public) to direct the war until his resignation in October 1761, and was regarded as the savior of the nation. The train of disasters was now followed by a series of triumphs. On the Continent Frederick, now aided by British and German troops under Ferdinand, duke of Brunswick, was repeatedly though not always victorious over the French, Austrians, and Russians; in India British naval victories were accompanied by Robert Clive's total defeat of the French on land; British fleets conquered islands in the Caribbean held by the French and took Senegal in west Africa; and the French in Canada were finally and thoroughly defeated in a series of operations culminating in General Wolfe's capture of Quebec.

The aged George II (he was seventy-seven) died in October 1760 and was succeeded by his twenty-two-year-old grandson. The new king, dominated by his tutor, bosom friend, confidant, and father-figure, John Stuart, the earl of Bute, wished to end hostilities as soon as possible; he regarded Hanover as "that horrid electorate"[24] and opposed the costly subsidies to Frederick. Accordingly, tentative (but abortive) peace negotiations began; but meanwhile the French naval forces had been virtually neutralized or destroyed by British fleets. At this point, however, war broke out with Spain (Pitt had resigned in a cabinet dispute over whether Britain should strike first), and the British took Manila and Havana. Frederick, who had seen his British subsidies end and Russia withdraw from the war on the death of the empress Elizabeth, now underwent serious defeats, and a series of inconclusive campaigns under Ferdinand in Germany seemed destined to be endless. Under Bute, now effectively first minister, peace preliminaries were signed late in 1762; the Peace of Paris was ratified early in 1763; in April Bute resigned (as he had in any case wished to do as soon as peace could be established), and Britain was left to cope with the economic consequences of having successfully waged a "bloody and expensive war."[25]

Such, in very broad outline, are the vastly complicated events with which Smollett is chiefly concerned in the *Atom*. These may be said to run from the death of first minister Henry Pelham in 1754, and the general election of the same year, to the election of 1768 and the ominous rioting on behalf of John Wilkes. The *Atom*'s chronicle covers the political ascendancy, greatness, and virtual eclipse of William Pitt, and the rise and fall of Lord Bute.

SMOLLETT AND CONTEMPORARY POLITICS

While Smollett's political opinions are made abundantly clear by himself in the narrative that follows, certain clarifications are in order. The most important of these concerns the terms Whig and Tory. On the one hand it has been firmly demonstrated by Sir Lewis Namier and his followers that party discipline and party platforms as known in the nineteenth century, not to mention present-day Britain, simply did not exist in Smollett's time.[26] On the other, there is no question that many politicians sincerely thought of themselves as Whigs and their opponents as Tories, or the reverse.[27] Yet the principles designated by party names might and did change almost from year to year, even while those who used the terms might honestly believe in their consistent meaning. Thus the duke of Newcastle thought of himself throughout his long career as a Whig; yet his political behavior was chiefly consecrated to staying in power, manipulating domestic politics to ensure support for the administration, and attempting to regulate and control an archaic system of Continental alliances which was perpetually going awry. Pitt (who, though at the time he was in uneasy alliance with Newcastle and therefore with the Whigs, urged the newly enthroned George III to make Tory appointments[28]) was also principally concerned with gaining and keeping power, but by means of brilliantly opposing the measures of any administration in which he was not preeminent. He has been characterized politically as a perpetual Patriot, this term meaning simply "one dedicated to opposition."[29]

By the time Smollett wrote the *Atom* he was undoubtedly quite sincere in denouncing both parties, or more properly for him, "factions," as equally knavish and foolish. The old stereotype of Smollett as a bigoted and unreconstructed Tory has been thoroughly demolished;[30] it certainly will not stand up against what he says in the *Atom*.

It is surely off the mark to require that a satirist be fair and objective in his treatment of those whom he attacks. Yet with a very few exceptions Smollett remained faithful to the facts in the *Atom*; for most of the views expressed therein he could have found substantial support in various areas of British public opinion,[31] and history has largely vindicated him. Aside from the slaughter and impoverishment of thousands and the weakening of the French armies, the campaigns on the European continent had virtually no result for Britain or anyone else beyond the restoration of the *status quo ante* as to the boundaries and power of nations. The burdens of the war brought to England a national debt and an economic depression which led to the imposition of the taxes that, together with the permanent removal of the French threat to the American colonies, made the American Revolution possible. The widespread opposition to the lenient terms of the Peace of Paris, and the desire to annihilate France, can be seen from two hundred years' perspective (especially considering the economic and political sequels to World Wars I and II) to be the effects of shortsighted jingoism. The defeat of Braddock, and of Abercromby at Ticonderoga; the failure of Boscawen to intercept the

French fleet; the loss of Minorca and the making of Admiral Byng into a scapegoat; the disastrous expeditions of Saint Cas, Saint Malo, and Rochefort; the humiliating defeat of Cumberland's troops at Stade and his signing of the ill-considered Convention of Klosterseven: these events provoked criticism from all quarters. Where Smollett is less than fair is in his slanted accounts of the campaign for Quebec and the battle of Minden, together with some other Allied successes; in his playing down of Frederick's victories; and in his real or pretended assumption that Pitt had little or nothing to do either with selecting successful officers or with the immediate direction of military operations.[32]

Pitt and Frederick became national heroes who could do no wrong, though Pitt's acceptance of a pension in 1761 and a peerage in 1766 seriously undermined his popularity.[33] But few sincere voices could be found to defend George II or the duke of Newcastle. Most of the minor characters included by Smollett in the cast of the *Atom* were equally open to criticism. It is notable that Smollett gives a balanced portrait of Lord Bute; earlier he had intemperately defended Bute in his weekly propaganda paper, the *Briton*, and then later came to feel that Bute had callously abandoned him (which, in fact, was probably the case).[34]

Whatever their precise shape in a given controversy, Smollett's general views were simple and were consistently maintained. He was in principle opposed to the more recently established elements in the English political equation—the power of the City merchants and bankers, or the financial forces in general, as against the older landed interest and the aristocracy; the increasingly powerful voice of "the mob" (which for him included small tradesmen and artisans as well as the genuine rabble); the ability of a small political oligarchy to take and hold power for lengthy periods by manipulating the crown, the Parliament, and the people; and above all he opposed the "Continental connection," which, as Richard Pares has said, was perhaps the thorniest political problem that England faced in Smollett's time.[35] It is true that he occasionally hedged with regard to those currently in power, out of deference to their position—or more likely out of caution, especially after Admiral Knowles won a libel suit against him in 1759;[36] but in general he stuck to his guns.

The principal question that Smollett's views in the *Atom* pose for a reader today arises from his devastating attack on Pitt. It is perhaps best answered by reflecting that there were, so to speak, two Pitts—the Great Commoner who galvanized the British war effort and won the "Great War for Empire," who earned the admiration and love of the colonies by opposing the Stamp

Act in 1766, and who later as Lord Chatham the elder statesman dominated Parliament whenever he chose to appear; and the preeminently skillful politician who required supreme power before he would perform and who would do almost anything to get it, not merely cowing his opponents with his rhetoric but also adroitly and nimbly changing sides, if there was need, when his opposition was rewarded with office.[37] It is the latter Pitt whom the *Atom* attacks, and who has lately been painted by historians in very much the same colors as Smollett's. If one asks how Smollett could have been so stubborn or so foolish as to fly in the face of the popular consensus regarding Pitt, he may consider that not only Bute but both George II and his grandson detested Pitt heartily until he had made himself indispensable to each;[38] that Newcastle lived in perpetual fear of him; that Cumberland refused to take charge of the Army of Observation on the Continent until Pitt was dismissed;[39] and that almost every politician who allied himself with Pitt ended by breaking with him. When Pitt resigned in 1761 over the issue of war with Spain, the entire cabinet, with the exception of his brother-in-law Lord Temple, was against him.[40] He might have been admired and respected, but he was not loved by those who knew him.

Moreover, Smollett was far from being in favor of war in general. Throughout his writings his detestation of cruelty is apparent (even the cruel practical jokes in his novels may be seen as a deliberate choice of the vilest possible punishment for offenders). But we cannot say that he went as far as Samuel Johnson, for instance, in his abhorrence of war and bloodshed.[41] Smollett seems to have been convinced that France was so dangerous an enemy that it must be weakened even at great cost, and he apparently applauded Britain's acquisition of an overseas empire.[42] Yet he saw no gain whatever in the costly and bloody campaigns in support of Frederick the Great, conducted, as he regarded them, merely for the sake of Hanover; and indeed (though here we may suspect that he felt he was going out on a limb) he sometimes proposed in the *Briton* the amazingly sophisticated idea, far ahead of its time, that Britain might extend its possessions too far and sink like the Roman Empire under its own weight.[43] But since he advanced this notion in defense of the concession of certain conquered territories to France, as required by the conditions of the Peace of Paris, it may well be that he was merely grasping at straws in favor of Bute and his policies.

Historical scholarship has now weaned us away from the belief that the young George III, his mother (the dowager princess Augusta), and Lord Bute were blindly infatuated with the idea of a "Patriot King" associated with the writings and the posthumous image of Lord Bolingbroke. They were considerably more eclectic in their thinking, far less ideologues, than that; and in any case it is very doubtful that Princess Augusta had much influence on her son immediately before or after he came to the throne.[44] Pitt himself, in fact, advised the new king to make appointments that would lead to a representation of both parties in significant numbers.[45] But with Smollett the case is perhaps different. In the *Briton* he may make an exaggerated case for the sanctity of the crown and the importance of the royal prerogative; in theory, however (as has now been adequately demonstrated by various studies), scarcely anyone would have disagreed with him.[46] The practical problem was that Lord Bute was a Scot, that he had virtually no parliamentary experience, and that he had never built up an adequate body of supporters from any level of society. But while it may be argued that in the *Briton* Smollett is far more interested in defending his fellow Scot and his policies than in any theoretical point whatever, the case is not the same in the *Atom*, where he has no one but himself to satisfy.

Smollett's views in the *Atom* on politics, foreign policy, and society are consistent with those which he maintained more cautiously in the *Complete History of England*, in its *Continuation*, and (still more cautiously) in the *Critical Review*.[47] In his judgment the attrition of royal prerogative since the Glorious Revolution (at least from the perspective of 1764) has gone too far; ministers should be appointed purely for virtue and ability, without regard to party affiliation; both houses of Parliament are shamefully confused, ignorant, venal, and are constantly manipulated by selfish oligarchs; persons without birth or breeding have engrossed most of the effective power in the realm, while the old aristocracy is weak and decadent; the moneyed interests have virtually obliterated the traditional power of the landed gentry; "luxury" has corrupted the fabric of society from top to bottom; and (worst of all) the "mob," comprising almost all persons below the nobility—cowardly, selfish, fickle, stupid, easily led—has been weakly allowed to assert, through sheer force of numbers, a power it ought never to have had.[48] On the level of specific evils, George II is the next thing to an idiot; his natural tendency to sacrifice the welfare of England to that of Hanover, which has resulted in a wasteful war and a crushing burden of debt and which should have been repressed by all lawful means, has been encouraged as an avenue to power, first by the unspeakably silly and inept Newcastle and next by the able but opportunistic and totally unprincipled Pitt, who also relies on the support of the vile "mob." Nearly all the high officials of government are knaves or fools or both. The wise (such as Lord Granville, lord president of the council) choose to do nothing.[49] Foreign policy is largely concerned with neglecting important matters, wasting money on subsidies to protect Hanover, and supporting the unspeakable Frederick in his wars. Generals and admirals are chosen at random, and are nearly always incompetent; the effective few (such as Wolfe, Clive, Cumming, Hawke, Elliot) are promoted by accident or through influence, and later are often either neglected or ignored, or die in action. George III is amiable but ignorant and inexperienced, Bute is virtuous but foolishly idealistic and conceitedly oblivious to practical politics; the war is ended by bribery (the ratification of the Peace of Paris), and domestic policy has degenerated into a ridiculous tug-of-war between Whigs and Tories, both equally stupid and equally obsessed with personal vanity and vengeance, while Bute, driven out of office, vainly tries to put together a stable government from behind the scenes. Such, in essence, is the *Atom*.

As we have seen, there were many to agree at the time with Smollett's opinions concerning the political and military figures of his day. And after mid-1760 the desire to give up the German war, indeed to put an end to all hostilities, rapidly grew in strength. By 1766 most perhaps would have agreed with Smollett's opinions of Pitt and of Frederick, now that Prussia was at peace and Pitt had taken a peerage. Modern thought has repudiated as archaic such ideas as Smollett's on economics and especially on "luxury," since deficit funding (which, after all, had begun in the 1690s) and what he would have considered outrageous extravagance have come to be matters of course in our consumer society. But the basic ideas, three in number, which he enunciated in his nonfictional writings and in the *Atom* are of another order. Unpopular in his time they unquestionably were, but we may view them differently. First was the issue of Britain's commitment to the German war: was it an absolutely essential ingredient in bringing France to the peace table? Despite the saying that Pitt "had won the American war on the plains of Germany,"[50] the truth about this matter is still far from clear. Second, the question of whether Bute's peace was not on the whole as good as that which Pitt might have made (and even Smollett admitted that Bute's peace might have been better if less hasty and undigested[51]) is even less firmly agreed upon by modern historians. And finally, Smollett's most hesitantly advanced, controversial, and forward-looking idea—that Britain might have overreached itself, acquiring more possessions than it could well control—was taken very seriously in his time by a few farsighted persons, among them the duke of Bedford, by no means a naive or ignorant negotiator in the peace settlement.[52]

What we might call an adequate total picture of Tobias Smollett's intellectual development and of the furniture of his mind has not yet been provided by those who have written about him. Certain points, however, have been made clear. In politics he was certainly not the hidebound "Tory" or reactionary who has sometimes been presented, and it is doubtful that the image of "Radical Dr. Smollett" will bear prolonged and detailed inspection.[53] But three basic characteristics of his thought are beyond dispute. He was, at least by his own definitions, an enlightened Scot, a gentleman, and a satirist. Always ready to defend his countrymen, he was not, whatever his pugnacity and irascibility, desirous of turning the clock back; he was no Jacobite. As a gentleman, the descendant of generations of landowners, small though their holdings might have been, he was perhaps unduly prone to scorn "new men," whatever their eminence or attainments, who could not trace their pretensions to gentility beyond their fathers or grandfathers.[54] Above all, he saw himself as a satirist in the tradition of Rabelais, Swift, Cervantes, and Pope. Though written of Samuel Johnson, the following words accurately sum up Smollett's character as well. He had "a quickness to sense incongruity and pretense, a well-developed aggressiveness, a temperamental irritability and dissatisfaction aggravated by personal suffering, an instinctive reductionist talent not unlike Swift's, and . . . a certain violence or immoderation of character combined with a desperate attachment to the disciplines of moderation and good sense."[55]

Such was the man who, in 1764, had withdrawn from the political turmoil of London to the mild climate of Nice. There, during a leisure earned by the unaided efforts of his pen rather than by political patronage, he purged his spleen by beginning to compose *The History and Adventures of an Atom*.

SOURCES AND INFLUENCES

The *Atom* is a unique literary work, but it is so in the restricted sense that it is a unique synthesis of ingredients that were far from unique or rare—readily available, in fact, and known to many. The chief strands that form its fabric are these: the narration of the story by an omniscient being that has also been virtually omnipresent; satire handled as "secret history," purporting to reveal the hidden springs and sordid motivations really governing famous persons in happenings known to the public; the narrative placed in a remote country, made to seem verisimilar if fantastic by a wealth of specific detail regarding persons, places, and objects; allegory in which historical events are made ridiculous by reducing them into outlandish or contemptible imagery; irrelevant digressions on esoteric or absurd subjects, involving torrents of obscure pedantry; and ubiquitous scatology.

Identification of the exact sources of these satiric strategies must rest upon conjecture, but Smollett left abundant traces of his working methods as he composed the *Atom*. The notes to the present volume make it clear that the *Atom* may justly be seen as a vast patchwork of quotations from, versions of, and allusions to passages in the later works of Smollett's career, running from the time when he launched the *Critical Review* in 1756 to the publication, in 1765 and 1766, respectively, of the fifth volume of his *Continuation of the Complete History of England* and of his *Travels*. Smollett had also translated *Don Quixote*; and he may well have been thinking, as he composed his satire, of Cervantes' famous simile of the back side of a fair tapestry, seemingly ugly and distorted with its knots, lumps, projecting threads and grotesque figures, but nevertheless revealing how the tapestry (in this case, Britain 1754–68) is really put together.[56]

Smollett's work during this period, with the single exception of his novel *The Adventures of Sir Launcelot Greaves*, was as an editor, historian, compiler, and polemicist, and his duties obliged him to read and absorb an enormous mass of heterogeneous material on every conceivable subject from patristic theology to snuff. He could not have written more than a portion of the reviews in the *Critical*, but he must at least have skimmed every page of it; and if a given review deals with history, science, medicine, or fiction we are safe in assuming that Smollett wrote it, or carefully checked it if he did not write it. Thus, by invoking Occam's razor and discarding farfetched explanations in favor of the simplest and most obvious ones, we may reliably account for the materials generating Smollett's distinctive forms of satire in the *Atom*.

The successive volumes of *Tristram Shandy* were reviewed with scant charity in the *Critical*, in at least two instances by Smollett.[57] But these reviews, taken together, share an interesting and seemingly obsessive theme. *Tristram Shandy* is seen as little more than an imitation of Rabelais; and the ingredients of "Rabelaisian" humor seem to be but three—lewdness, especially of the scatological variety; a pert, self-centered style, impudently buttonholing the reader; and frequent gratuitous digressions that pile up arcane learning on ridiculous topics:

we see . . . the most evident traces of Rabelais . . . the same sort of apostrophes to the reader, breaking in upon the narrative, not infrequently with an air of petulant impertinence; the same *sales Plautini*; the *immunda* ignominiosaq: dicta; the same whimsical digressions; and the same parade of learning.[58]

. . . petulance, pruriency, and ostentation of learning.[59]

Rabelais dealt in the same kind of haberdashery [the reader will remember that the "writer" of the *Atom*, Nathaniel Peacock, is a haberdasher]. . . . He had his extravagant rhapsodies, his disquisitions on arts and sciences, theology and ethics; his Hebrew, Greek, Latin, Italian, Spanish, High Dutch, Low Dutch . . . his decent allusions to the parts that distinguish the sexes; and his cleanly comments upon intestinal exoneration.[60]

. . . "tes paroles sont brayes." That is, not a language spoken *ab anteriori*.[61]

Another review, of *Yorick's Meditations*, an imitation of *Tristram Shandy*, lists its many digressions, including one on the close-stool.[62] The review of volumes 7 and 8 of *Tristram Shandy* takes the form of a parody "by the Reviewers of Breeches," and we may note that the *Atom* contains a digression on breeches.[63] Interestingly, the *Critical* later says in its review of the *Atom* that it "unites the happy extravagance of Rabelais to the splendid humour of Swift," while the *Town and Country Magazine* also finds Smollett imitating Rabelais and Swift.[64]

On the basis of this quantity of evidence, with its repetitive (or obsessive) opinions, it is hard to avoid surmising that Smollett as early as 1761 had been inspired with the project of giving his stunningly popular rival, the author of *Tristram Shandy*, a run for his money with a work of Rabelaisian humor, featuring digressions, kaleidoscopically polyglot style, impertinence, learning, and scatology. (It is worth pointing out here that Smollett's own hobby-horse seems to have run away with him. Rabelais is certainly scatological and so is Smollett; but Sterne's lewdness is several times as prone to dwell upon "the parts that distinguish the sexes" as it is to treat of "intestinal exoneration." "Misprision of a precursor by a strong ephebe" did not have to wait for the Romantic poets and the theories of Harold Bloom.[65])

Reviews in the *Critical* likewise furnish evidence for the probable source of the atom-narrator. Louis Martz once suggested that Smollett may have been inspired by John Hawkesworth's *Adventurer* paper number 5 (1752), in which a transmigrating soul (at the time lodged in a flea) dictates its adventures in a "small shrill voice."[66] But Hawkesworth's flea does not narrate a secret history of Britain; his paper is a playful miniature. The *Atom* in fact relies on, and must be an amalgamation of, three traditions.

The first tradition is that of the "spy" novel, in which an alien of some sort reports secretly on the absurd beliefs and customs of one's own country. Originating in the popular *L'Espion turc* of Giovanni Paolo Marana in the seventeenth century, this species of narrative had as its most noted practitioners Montesquieu in the *Lettres persanes* (1721) and Goldsmith in *The Citizen of the World* (1762). The second tradition is found in the "secret history," "key-novel," or *chronique scandaleuse*, again with a seventeenth-century French origin in Bussy-Rabutin's *Histoire amoureuse des Gaules*, and made notorious by such English writers of the early eighteenth century as Delarivière Manley and Eliza Haywood. In this the allegedly sordid "true stories" behind noted events are enacted under feigned names, the persons meant being revealed in a "key," either provided by the author or laboriously assembled in manuscript by one or more readers for the enlightenment of posterity.[67] Of such works Smollett certainly knew at least Lesage's *Le diable boiteux* ("The Devil upon Crutches")[68] and the anonymous *Mémoires sécrets pour servir à l'histoire de Perse*, in which England is represented as Japan and Spain as China.[69] The third tradition is that of the tale with a nonhuman narrator, who (or which) has the advantages of being rapidly bandied about by various owners and of being able to overhear secrets with impunity. Such fictions go back as far as the "golden" *Ass* of the Roman Apuleius, and the device was employed by Cervantes in the *Colóquio de dos perros*, one of the *novelas ejemplares*; among the contributors to their sudden vogue in the eighteenth century were *Le sopha* (1740), by Crébillon *fils*, and Francis Coventry's *Pompey the Little* (1751), in which the adventures happen to a lapdog.[70] If one wishes to follow those critics who see Smollett's work as artistically dominated throughout by the picaresque mode, he may find in the *Atom* the picaresque pushed to its utmost logical possibility: the protagonist has no characteristics whatever beyond arrogance and a good memory, while the adventures may be as rapid, numerous, and various as the author's imagination will allow, with no requirements of realism to interfere.[71]

All three of these narrative traditions, however, were united in a book which the *Critical* reviewed with enthusiasm, Charles Johnstone's *Chrysal* (1760, 1765).[72] In this tale the spirit of gold, temporarily embodied in a guinea, recounts to an emaciated alchemist at the end of his tether its recent adventures in the hands of George II, his mistress the countess of Yarmouth, Frederick the Great, Lord Chesterfield, and assorted fools, knaves, and monsters, including (in the expanded four-volume edition of 1765) Sir Francis Dashwood and his rakish cronies of the "Hell-Fire Club" at Medmenham Abbey. At the conclusion, just as Chrysal is about to reveal the secret of making gold, the alchemist farts, and the spirit, "with a look of ineffable disgust," disappears. The reviews in the *Critical* speak of *Chrysal's* "good sense and merit," but hesitate to allow it a rating above the mediocre because of the distorted evil of some characters and the lack of external safeguards or guarantees against the author's maliciously mingling the false with the true.[73] The modern reader who compares *Chrysal* with the *Atom* will find them astonishingly similar in skeletal structure, and indeed as to the events described. The chief differences are that Pitt, King George, and Frederick are presented in *Chrysal* as near-divinities, that Johnstone introduces wholly imaginary type-characters to illustrate private vices as juicily as possible, and that Smollett is incomparably the better writer, both in style and in the handling of scenes. The political stand taken in *Chrysal* is firmly "Whig," insofar as that very inaccurate term may be used, or better, "pro-administration," if we take the latter term to mean the Pitt-Newcastle coalition that was in power when the first version of the novel appeared.

Such is not the view of one of Smollett's two principal sources for the Oriental setting of the *Atom*, John Shebbeare's *History . . . of the Sumatrans* (1762–63, although a version was apparently published in 1760).[74] This work, under the transparent disguise of the detailed political history of a remote kingdom, is an all-out attack on the British government in the last years of George II; the new reign, with its benevolent minister (Lord Bute), is represented as a heaven-sent era of reformation and virtue. Shebbeare, a political hack-writer, had already been severely punished for libel, and his violent prejudice against everything Scottish (to say nothing of his personal attacks on Smollett and his works) had already aroused Smollett's ire on more than one occasion.[75] Despite his antagonism, a convincing case has been made for Smollett's use of Shebbeare's *Lydia* (1755) in *The Expedition of Humphry Clinker*, and the *Atom* certainly echoes several of *Lydia*'s features— digressions that interrupt the narrative, together with the depiction of the duke of Newcastle's alleged ignorance of elementary geography, his silly mannerisms, and his (also alleged) incontinence when terrified or baffled.[76]

The Sumatrans was clearly written either to order or in the hope (rewarded, as it turned out) of securing remuneration.[77] The *Critical* nevertheless praises it highly, demurring only with respect to its extremely rough handling of that formidable demagogue and arch-Pittite, Alderman William Beckford; Smollett, the reviewer, was willing to sink his personal animosity in favor of the political position he had espoused in 1762, when he undertook to write the *Briton* as a champion of Bute and foe to his predecessors and opponents.[78] In *The Sumatrans*, however, Smollett found a crude model for the *Atom*; Shebbeare's work was reviewed, we may note, just before Smollett's departure for France, where most of the *Atom* was probably written.[79] In spite of his uncouth prose, Shebbeare had shown how the policies and personalities of the British government could be dealt with from the point of view of an

English (or superhuman) historian writing about the intrigues of an Oriental kingdom.

But this vague though ingenious notion of an "Oriental" setting—Shebbeare evidently knew almost nothing of southeast Asia, and his account does not pretend to use "Sumatra" as anything more than a *pro forma* disguise for Britain—was given focus and point by another work with which Smollett was intimately connected and which he almost certainly reviewed for the *Critical*. Louis Martz long ago pointed out some of Smollett's detailed borrowings for the *Atom* from the account of Japan in the *Universal History*, a huge compendium ultimately in sixty volumes, which had begun to appear in 1730. For some years Smollett had done extensive editorial work on the "Modern Part" of this compilation, which, despite its bulk, he took with him in its entirety when he traveled to France in 1763.[80] The opening paragraphs of his review, which appeared in September 1759, seem almost to show us Smollett's plan taking shape in his mind. They are therefore worth quoting at length.

The ninth volume opens with the history of Japan, a subject . . . curious [deserving careful attention], whether we consider the genius and acquired knowledge of the people, or the nature of their situation, which is, in many respects, analogous to that of Great Britain. Japan . . . is but small in point of extent. It consists of three . . . islands, on the most eastern verge of Asia. . . .

. . . if England and Scotland were divided from each other by an arm of the sea, Japan might be aptly compared to Britain and Ireland . . . subjected to the domination of one monarch. . . . The coasts of Japan are dangerous and rocky; so are those of Great Britain. The climate of Japan is wet, stormy, and variable; so is that of Great Britain. Both countries produce great quantities of corn.[81]

. . . There is, moreover, a resemblance in the genius and disposition of the people: the Japanese, like the English, are brave and warlike, quick in apprehension, solid in understanding, modest, patient, courteous, docile, industrious, studious, just in their dealings, and sincere in their professions. The resemblance will likewise hold in their vices, follies, and foibles. The Japanese are proud, supercilious, passionate, humourous, and addicted to suicide; split into a multitude of religious sects, and so distracted by political factions, that the nation is at last divided between two separate governments.

Perhaps the analogy is still more remarkable . . . with respect to their neighbours. The next continent to Japan is China, which, in divers respects, may be compared to France . . . . China is more populous, powerful, and extensive . . . its palaces are more grand . . . its armies are more numerous . . . . But what the

Chinese have invented, the Japanese have improved. . . . The Chinese are more *gay*, the Japanese more *substantial*. . . . The Chinese are remarkable for *dissimulation*, *complaisance*, and *effeminacy*; the Japanese are famous for their *integrity*, *plain-dealing*, and *manly vigour*. Finally, they are rivals, consequently jealous of each other.[82]

The enthusiastic review goes on to give a lengthy account of acupuncture and to quote several instructive anecdotes relative to the current Japanese policy of rigorously excluding foreigners.

In the preface to the *Atom* Smollett virtually confessed to his reliance on the *Universal History*,[83] but he did not confine himself to the details mentioned in his review of the work. The history of Japan, with its emperor no more than a cipher for the past six hundred years while the powerful *shōguns* ruled in fact, seemed to him a close parallel to what he regarded as the shameful and dangerous impotence of the British crown in his own day,[84] subordinated to ministers who in turn were the leaders of rival political parties (or "factions," as Smollett preferred to see them and as modern research has shown them to have been). "Taycho," an upstart who achieved supreme power and was the only ruler ever to attempt foreign conquest, who exhausted Japan's treasure by wars on the Chinese mainland, admirably fitted the view Smollett had come to hold concerning William Pitt. On a much pettier level he could find such figures as the woman emperor Syko, who could be equated with Queen Anne; a god of war called "Fatzman," who suggested the grotesquely obese duke of Cumberland, commander-in-chief of the armed forces; and many others. These characters—137 of them—he adapted with remarkable ingenuity to compile a catalogue of "Japanese" persons, places, and things, fleshing out his political narrative and enriching his satire with concrete detail, fascinating because exotic, yet tempting the reader to investigate parallels and similarities.[85] One is reminded of the factually detailed "biographical" dossiers which such modern writers as Joyce compiled for their personages, to furnish scaffolding, as it were, to keep their fancy under perpetual control and prevent its straying too far from the point.

Yet fancy there had to be in the *Atom*, and Smollett found a rich and exciting model for satire of current politics in Swift's *Gulliver's Travels*, *A Tale of a Tub*, and *A Modest Proposal*. Thus he suggests that the vengeful English after the battle of Culloden, which crushed the Jacobite rebellion of 1745–46, might have subsisted on the flesh of the Scots; satirizes Pitt in imagery borrowed from the religious demagogues or Dissenting preachers in the *Tale*; and in general reduces political to physical action in the manner of Gulliver's

experiences in Lilliput.[86] Even closer perhaps to the kind of satire Smollett
would write, and to the objects of his satire as well, were the five "John Bull"
pamphlets by his fellow Scot and fellow physician John Arbuthnot, which
had appeared in 1712.[87] Chief medical attendant to Queen Anne and intimate friend of Pope, Swift, and Bolingbroke, Arbuthnot anticipated Smollett
by satirizing the conduct of the costly War of the Spanish Succession, with
its ruinous drains on England in men and money, and the generals and politicians who wanted to prolong it for their own purposes. Like the *Atom*, but
unlike the works of Swift (at least his major prose satires), the John Bull
pamphlets go into the greatest detail in lampooning specific persons and
events; they reduce political chicanery and military or diplomatic exploits to
the level of neighborhood squabbles in the most ridiculously homespun
imagery; their language oscillates wildly between highflown legal or medical
jargon and the coarsest slang or thieves' cant. England is John Bull, the
Netherlands are Nic. Frog, Louis XIV is Lewis Baboon, the duke of Marlborough is Hocus. Throughout, one can find scenes and turns of phrase
which might have offered valuable suggestions to Smollett, though possible
direct borrowings seem to have been few indeed.

The style and method of the Arbuthnot pamphlets are, on the other hand,
remarkably similar to those of the *Atom*, an affinity perceived by Smollett's
earliest biographers in editions of his works before 1800.[88] Moreover, Smollett did not have to be a collector of old curiosities to know *John Bull*; in 1755
John Hawkesworth assembled a new edition of Swift's works which included
Arbuthnot's pamphlets; this edition was reprinted for years in various for-
mats.[89] In December 1760 the *Critical* reviewed with enthusiasm *Sister Peg*,
an anonymous satirical narrative concerning the Scottish Militia Bill, which
in that year had been defeated in Parliament. Generally attributed to Adam
Ferguson (though possibly by David Hume), this pamphlet took over the
characters of Arbuthnot, adding such figures as "Jowler" (Pitt as a loud-
mouthed foxhound), Lord Chancellor Hardwicke as an old nurse, and Newcastle as "Hubble-bubble," a vapid sputterer. Further, the attitudes expressed regarding Continental connections were exactly those of Smollett in
the *Atom*. The *Critical* found the author of *Sister Peg* to be "satyrical, intelligent, and public-spirited," with a genius in portraiture (as shown by Jowler
and Hubble-bubble), though "sometimes indecent in his expression," and
concluded that had not Arbuthnot come before and thus acquired partisans,
this production would have to be allowed supremacy in its particular mode of
satire.[90] It is relevant to note that Smollett corresponded with Hume and
greatly respected and admired him; if he believed *Sister Peg* to be Hume's

work, he certainly did not allow professional rivalry to cloud his estimation of his countryman and fellow historian of England.[91]

With all of these precursors of the *Atom* in view, demonstrably known to Smollett and examined by him, we need not marvel at his originality in conceiving the satirical devices of the *Atom*. We may rather conclude that, given the inclination to produce a political satire, he would have had to be rather obtuse not to gather up the many hints available to him. His genius was demonstrated in the particular way in which he chose to fuse and synthesize them.

It is unnecessary to seek a particular source for the *Atom*'s egregious scatology. Sterne and Sterne's master Rabelais, to say nothing of Swift, were (as Smollett chose to see them) the sources he admitted, so to speak; but scatology had been an obsession with him throughout his career in letters, and would continue to be so until its end.[92] It is not astonishing that, given this unsavory preoccupation and the wish to attack with the utmost violence, he should have chosen scatology as a weapon, nor that he should have tossed his dung about with such frequency; rather, the remarkable fact is perhaps that although he did not toss it, like Addison's Virgil, with "an air of gracefulness,"[93] he allowed no scatological Anglo-Saxon monosyllable to sully his page.

The basic narrative line of the *Atom*, however fantastic its elaborations in imagery, was dictated by the political and military history of the Seven Years' War and its aftermath. For this Smollett had only to turn to his own accounts of these events in the *Continuation of the Complete History of England* (which runs from the peace of Aix-la-Chapelle in 1748 to the summer of 1765), and in the thirty-eight issues of the *Briton* (29 May 1762–12 February 1763). Scores of passages in the *Atom* echo arguments, figures, sentences, or phrases in the *Briton*, often verbatim; Smollett seems to have felt that these were too good to waste in an ephemeral publication. Moreover, rather than being merely sources of the raw materials of satire, these passages, to pursue the metaphor of manufacturing, were semi-fabricated; for in writing the *Briton* Smollett was conducting pro-Bute polemic in the no-holds-barred manner of the mid-eighteenth century, including a nautical allegory, an "Arabian tale," and a pseudo-Shakespearean fragment.[94] He spared no pains in attacking the behavior and views of Pitt, Newcastle, Pitt's brother-in-law Earl Temple, John Wilkes, and others, even though he and Wilkes had been firm friends just prior to the beginning of the pamphlet war, and though as late as December 1759 he had characterized Pitt in a letter as, barring the Continental connection which even he could not break, "the greatest man that ever lived."[95]

Yet in most instances, Smollett even in the *Briton* does not distort the *facts* of recent history; he merely, by every means he can contrive, puts the most unfavorable interpretation on some of those facts. And if we compare Smollett's handling of a given incident in the *Continuation*, the *Critical*, the *Briton*, and the *Atom*, we discover (with negligible exceptions) the same to be true. Smollett's opinions on such matters as, for example, the heartless treatment of Admiral Byng, the military disaster at Saint Cas, the British subsidies for Frederick the Great, the British ignorance of Louisiana's strategic importance, or the conduct of Frederick toward the royal family of Poland and Saxony are uniform throughout. The difference lies merely in the fact that in the *Critical* and the *Continuation* he is restrained by considerations of prudence or by his own rather exalted idea of himself as an impartial historian.[96] Yet even as early as 1760, in the *Continuation* (discussing the opening of Parliament in November 1759), he could allow his indignation to carry him so far as to write the following passage concerning the king and Pitt:

> Very great reason, indeed, had his majesty to be satisfied with an address of such a nature from an house of commons, in which opposition lay strangled at the foot of the minister [Pitt]; in which those demagogues, who had raised themselves to reputation and renown, by declaiming against continental measures [Pitt again], were become so perfectly reconciled to the object of their former reprobation, as to cultivate it with a degree of enthusiasm, unknown to any former administration, and lay the nation under such contributions in its behalf, as no other m[inistr]y durst ever meditate. Thus disposed, it was no wonder they admired the moderation of their sovereign, in offering to treat of peace, after above a million men had perished by the war, and twice that number been reduced to misery; after whole provinces had been depopulated, whole countries subdued, and the victors themselves almost crushed by the trophies they had gained.[97]

At no point, for example, does Smollett excuse Pitt for his sudden reversal of principle in supporting the wars on the European continent; but when he wishes to express disapproval in the *Continuation* he will usually resort to some such locution as "persons ill-disposed towards Mr. Pitt did not scruple to maintain," and so on. One could say, in short, that the basic narrative of the *Atom* represents a rewriting of the *Continuation* in which Smollett takes a gleeful delight in the opportunity to say exactly what he thinks, with no restraint whatever.[98]

One further source of satiric material for the *Atom* must be noted, though it cannot be discussed in detail in any form short of a monograph. The *Atom* represents what appears to be a unique instance in English literature of the wholesale borrowing of imagery from a particular nonliterary source, and a very sordid one at that: the hundreds of scurrilous prints (we should now call them cartoons) in which the events and personages of the day were ruthlessly denigrated. In these the fundamental satiric strategy of rendering an abstraction ridiculous by making it concrete is pursued to a length that our age does not often duplicate. In one print, for example, George II is a farting satyr to whom the queen is about to administer an enema of gold; in another, Pitt blows bubbles to delude the mob. Smollett himself is represented as a quack doctor and a mountebank's zany; and Lord Bute is shown astride a broomstick, guiding it toward a broom sprouting from between the thighs of the dowager princess of Wales.[99] In scores of instances, as the notes to the present edition show, it is clear that Smollett has borrowed the imagery concerning a particular target of his satire from one or more of these prints, and often indeed his satire is hard to grasp unless one refers to the print in question.

Smollett's burning interest in these prints is no mystery. The steady stream of political pamphlets and prints attacking the ministry in power had fluctuated in intensity since the two forms first became major instruments of propaganda during the early years of Walpole's long administration; the stream suddenly grew into a raging torrent with the advent of Bute as first minister. Horace Walpole wrote on 20 June 1762 to Sir Horace Mann: "The new administration begins tempestuously. My father was not more abused after twenty years than Lord Bute is in twenty days. Weekly papers swarm, and like other swarms of insects, sting."[100] And when Smollett took up the cudgels for Bute with the *Briton*, he himself was frequently lampooned in a way that, given his sensitive irritability regarding his own status and that of the hated Scots in general, he must have found intolerable. Turning the satirists' own weapons against them was a logical form of revenge.[101]

Lastly, in constructing the *Atom*'s nine arias (as we might call them) or virtuoso digressions on topics of absurdly recondite erudition, Smollett had recourse chiefly to the pages of his own *Critical Review* and to the sources he had to consult during his lengthy editorial labors on the *Universal History*. In the *Critical* he could find (and in many cases surely had himself written) summaries of and quotations from books on ancient music, chemistry, alchemy, witchcraft, medicine, law, church history, and a host of other subjects both obvious and obscure. These he pillaged, often verbatim (very occasionally slipping into conflation or errors when copying), for the *Atom*'s breathless catalogues of arcane facts and authorities, not one of which, apparently, is fabricated.

COMPOSITION

In attempting to reconstruct and date the composition of the *Atom* we must resort entirely to conjecture, but clues are not lacking. The absolute *termini a quo* and *ad quem* are of course the Marriage Act and the Jewish Naturalization Bill of 1753 (the earliest contemporary events incorporated into the narrative) together with the death of Henry Pelham in March 1754, which left his elder brother the duke of Newcastle at the helm of state; and a period in the autumn of 1768, between 31 August—the date of Smollett's last preserved letter written in England, to David Hume—and about the first of November, by which time the printer John Almon must have begun setting up the book in type.[102] We can be considerably more precise, however, in dating Smollett's work on the manuscript.

Smollett could hardly have cherished all the attitudes and opinions that galvanize the *Atom* until about the middle of the year 1760. At that time he, like many others, was powerfully affected by Israel Mauduit's anti-war pamphlet, *Considerations on the Present German War*, which he praises and summarizes at length in the *Continuation*, saying that his own opinions are "exactly conformable" to those it presents.[103] We should, incidentally, bear in mind that at no point does Smollett condemn the vigorous prosecution of the war in America, Africa, or India; it is only the German campaign, which can give no profit to Britain except insofar as it exhausts France, that he execrates; and he often maintains that France can keep the European land war going on forever.[104] Smollett, like many others, despised the duke of Newcastle, first lord of the treasury, for a variety of reasons; and he abhorred Frederick the Great (a view shared by few at the time) as a general enemy of the human race and an agent of limitless destruction. But as late as January 1760 his new venture, the *British Magazine*, opened with a florid dedication to Pitt, to whom the *History* had also been dedicated. It is hard to believe that Smollett could have simultaneously written that dedication and entertained the sentiments that dictate the portrait of Taycho in the *Atom*. On the other hand, the *Atom* certainly contains several passages lifted from the early issues of the *British Magazine*, as well as from *Sir Launcelot Greaves*, which first appeared in the issues of its earliest eighteen months.[105] It is at least possible that at this time Smollett was assembling materials for a humorous or satirical work, perhaps only dimly conceived; and we have seen that in 1761 and later he was profoundly struck by the "Rabelaisian" Sterne of *Tristram Shandy*.

By 1762, however, the situation was quite different. Pitt was out (he had resigned in October 1761), Lord Bute was in, and Smollett was energetically defending his fellow-Scot and his policies in the *Briton*. Although we may find his open letter of 3 October 1762 (printed on 7 October in *The Gazetteer and London Daily Advertiser*) lacking in candor when he virtually denies without denying in so many words his authorship of the *Briton*,[106] there is no reason to doubt the accuracy of what he says in the letter concerning his opinions on Pitt, since his statement entirely agrees with what we find in his other works. He had admired Pitt for his probity with regard to the financial perquisites of office, virtually unique at the time among political figures,[107] and for his vigorous opposition to Hanoverian entanglements. He had begun to change his views when Pitt, who won cabinet office in 1756–57, warmly espoused the German war and the attendant subsidies; and now that Pitt was no longer the most powerful man in England (though Smollett prudently does not say this), he could safely point out that in the *Briton* and the *Continuation* he had done no more than thoughtfully and sorrowfully to decry Pitt's reversal of principle. By the middle of 1762 Smollett was fully equipped both with the materials and with the opinions necessary to write the *Atom*.

But had he the time or the health? Lewis Knapp has abundantly shown that Smollett was virtually an invalid throughout the year 1762; his letters complain of emaciation, catarrh, exhaustion; he spent at least part of the year at Southampton and at Bath to take the waters and was trying frantically to obtain a consular post in a warm climate; he was writing a *Briton* a week, continuing to edit the *Universal History*, at least supervising the *British Magazine* and the *Critical Review*, and no doubt working on his edition of Voltaire, begun in 1761, which would reach twenty-five volumes by 1763.[108] We may reasonably doubt that these exertions left him much time, whatever his inclinations, for satire. And early in 1763 the *Briton* was discontinued, no pension or consulship seemed forthcoming, and Smollett and his wife were prostrated by the sudden death in adolescence of their beloved only daughter.[109]

From June 1763 until early 1765, however, Smollett was isolated from England and its affairs in Boulogne and Nice (with a brief journey to Italy). The year 1764 he spent largely in a comfortable house at Nice, and during this time he evidently assembled the materials which became his *Travels* and most of volume 5 of the *Continuation* (the first four volumes had appeared in thirty-nine numbers, running through February 1762).[110] He had with him his own complete works as author and editor of both books and periodicals, together with the *Universal History*.[111] The innumerable parallels between the *Continuation* and the *Atom*, the *Atom*'s use of several passages from two letters in the *Travels*, and its reflection or outright lifting of a multitude of passages from the *Critical* and the *Briton* which could hardly have been reproduced from memory, lead to the conclusion that much of the *Atom* must have been composed at Nice as Smollett reflected with bitterness and at leisure on how he had been "traduced by malice, persecuted by faction, and abandoned by false patrons [Bute]," amid "illiberal dispute and incredible infatuation."[112]

At this point we should consider some facts concerning the *Atom*'s structure. The occurrences it covers run from shortly before the outbreak of hostilities in America in the summer of 1754 to the preparations for the dispatch of British troops to rebellious Boston in 1768, the "Wilkes and liberty" riots in the spring of 1768, and (perhaps) Bute's departure for France in August and Pitt's resignation in October; but the narrative is by no means uniform in its density of texture or thoroughness in reflecting events. In its first edition it totals 412 duodecimo pages. These may be divided as follows:

1. Preliminary matter, including the frame story and lengthy portraits of George II and the principal members of the cabinet, 1754–57. This occupies pages 1–74 of volume 1.

2. The remainder of volume 1 and the first 161 pages of volume 2 are taken up with a narrative of events from the first military skirmishes in America of 1754–56 to the resignation of Bute in 1763. These include Pitt's coming to power; Frederick's activities on the Continent; the principal campaigns and battles, naval and military, of the global war; the death of George II and the accession of his grandson; the resignations of Pitt and Newcastle; and the Peace of Paris. The texture is uniform throughout. Eight of the nine arias or digressions occur in this portion of the work (the first of these is in the preliminary matter); the narrative is thoroughly detailed and filled with embellishments of all kinds; and it closes with a balanced portrait of Bute and a summary of his achievements.

3. Domestic crises from May 1763 to the spring of 1765, which is the terminal date of the events covered in volume 5 of the *Continuation*; these occupy pages 162–67 of volume 2. The coverage is selective, to say the least: the narrative is confused and hard to follow; Bute is given a prominence he did not in fact have; and the principal personalities of the period are only glanced at.

4. The remaining pages of volume 2 (168–90) refer to happenings of the next three years. Very little is discussed except the Stamp Act and the tumults in the colonies; the narrative breaks off abruptly, seemingly at the beginning of a new episode. There is no pretense of a conclusion.

Thus we find that the *Atom* in its first published state consists of a smoothly finished narrative containing 384 pages devoted to the transactions of nearly

ten years; five pages treating the next two years, quite as laden with important matters but perfunctorily dealt with; and twenty-three pages on the subsequent three years, breaking off with no indication that a proper conclusion
is possible nor yet any attempt to sum up.

One other item of internal evidence, however, is worth noting. The gar-
rulous Atom's private revelations about the life and character of Richard III,
totally at variance with Smollett's view of that monarch in the rest of his
works,[113] occur early in volume 2, just before the taking of Quebec in 1759,
and are clearly a parody of Horace Walpole's *Historic Doubts on . . . Richard
III*. This work appeared early in 1768 and was severely handled by the *Critical* in its February issue.[114] Evidently, then, Smollett must have been
adding various materials to his manuscript in 1768 as well as attempting a
continuation.

Taking all of this information together, the most plausible (though of
course arguable) chronology for the composition of the *Atom* must be as follows. Smollett, with abundant leisure at Nice but denied detailed or up-to-
date information on current events,[115] worked there on the *Travels*, volume 5
of the *Continuation*, and the *Atom* up to the point of Bute's resignation and his
own departure from England. Back in England in 1765, he completed and
published the first two of these works and may have continued writing the
Atom, but doubtless either did not dare or at least hesitated to publish it,
especially since Pitt might at any moment return to power (and shortly thereafter did so).[116] As the months passed, however, Smollett's views of the
nation's future and his own must have become increasingly gloomy. His
health continued to deteriorate in England's damp and chilly weather, far
away from the beneficial effects he had experienced by the Mediterranean;
the possibility of a consulship or residency in a place with a congenial climate
began to seem hopeless; and the political situation, given his opinions on the
threat of mob rule, must have given rise to his greatest indignation and his
worst fears. He may even, as a Scot of some fame (or notoriety), have begun
to fear for his personal safety: "In 1768 . . . anti-Scots feeling had especially
focused on the Wilkite cause, with some harassment of Scots in the streets by
'Wilkes and Liberty' mobs and with the trials in August of three Scots soldiers for having killed a man during the Wilkite riots and the consequent
'massacre of St. George's Fields' (10 May 1768)."[117] And so in the summer of
1768, perhaps having already decided to leave England forever in the
autumn, he must have made final revisions and sketched out a "treatment" of
the years 1765–68, but for one reason or another (perhaps having lost the
direct commitment of personal indignation that he had nourished some years

before) did not see fit to conclude the work. Unwilling, however, to forsake the opportunity to fire this Parthian shot at his enemies, he had it conveyed to the hands of the bookseller John Almon (under circumstances which probably can never be clarified) and washed his own hands of it.

ATTRIBUTION

So far as can be determined from the documents that have been preserved, Smollett never acknowledged that he had written the *Atom* and never referred to it in his correspondence. This fact has led to a certain amount of confusion concerning its attribution to him, since scholars are often chary of proceeding in such cases without the firmest evidence, and since, perhaps because of its outrageous tone and ubiquitous scatology, the *Atom* has been given very little detailed study. Thus Lewis Knapp, the leading Smollett scholar of our time, was hesitant to pronounce unequivocally for Smollett's authorship; thus several decades ago a fabricated "Smollett letter" asserted that he had *not* written it; and thus the only extensive study of the question, at about the same time, ventured only to say that it "seems reasonably safe to conclude" that Smollett wrote the *Atom*.[118] But the firmest evidence is not wanting. It is both internal and external; and while we still lack an affidavit of authorship in Smollett's hand, nothing further remains to be desired to corroborate the attribution of the *Atom* to him.

The absence of an assertion by Smollett that he had written the *Atom* is not at all difficult to explain. The work is unfinished, for one thing; but the anxiety about the danger of prosecution for libel mentioned in its preface, and in the preface to *Humphry Clinker* as well, should not be read as entirely ironic or playful.[119] Smollett had been fined and imprisoned for libel in 1759–60; there was no reason why he might not return to England from Italy for a longer or shorter stay in the near future; though many of the most noted personages lampooned in the *Atom* had died by 1769, Pitt, Bute, and George III were either in fact or very possibly might soon again be in positions of the highest authority.[120] And even though George II had been dead for nearly a decade, *lèse-majesté* was a far graver offense than mere libel.[121] Wilkes had been condemned for seditious libel and expelled from the Commons for his treatment of George III in the *North Briton*'s famous Number 45; and, what was worse, John Shebbeare had stood in the pillory in 1759 for, among other things, satirizing the long-dead George I. The principle that satire of a dead monarch was punishable had been laid down on that occasion by none other than Smollett's nemesis in his own libel trial, Lord Chief Justice Mansfield.[122]

The one document we have that may perhaps bear on all these matters is a letter written to Smollett in Leghorn by his good friend Dr. John Armstrong on 28 March 1769, three days before the *Atom*'s long-delayed publication.

London March 28th 1769

O, my dear Doctor, I should severely reproach myself for having so long delayed answering your Letter, which gave much pleasure and Entertainment not only to me, but to all our common Friends—if it was not that I waited for some News that might please you. I have none to send you at last; except you are as I am upon the Douglas side.[123] But this is treating you with stale Intelligence.

It is needless to say how much I rejoice in your Recovery—but I have all along had great Confidence in the vigorous Stamina with which Nature has blest you. I hope you may within a year or two be able to weather out if not an English winter at least an English summer. Meantime if you won't come to us, I'll come to you; and shall with the help of small Punch and your Company laugh at the Tuscan dogdays.

I enjoy with a pleasing Sympathy the agreeable Society you find amongst the professors at Pisa. All countries and all Religions are the same to men of liberal minds. [page 2] And the most contemptible, sometimes even the most dangerous of all Animals, is an ill-natured Blockhead who affects to despise his Neighbours, because he secretly envies their superiour abilities, and regards them with a jealous Eye.

The daily, industrious, indefatigable operations of the most pernicious Lyes— The most impudent audacious Quackeries that were ever practised upon a blind stupid ignorant profane populace, still continue to prosper. The London mob have long every hour of the day *damn'd their Eyesight*—and they happen to have good reason for it. I will not at once disgust and shock you with the Recital of such seditious and treasonable Insolencies as never durst before Wednesday last brow-beat a Throne—at least never with Impunity. Your Friends at Pisa envy our Constitution—I'm afraid we may in a short time be reduced to sigh after theirs. For the View at present all around us is an object of the most extreme Indignation Contempt and Horror.

Meantime the infernal Spirit of the most absurd Discord, Erynnis blind and blundering in Dotage, has not yet so universally poysoned the *noble* mind of the publick as to engross it entirely to the clumsey dirty black-guard amusements and Exercises. For History still makes a Shift to waddle on, tho' it grows rather a *lame Duck*; And there are still Jack-daws [page 3] [tear in text] swallow the green cheese of Tragedy, and the no less insipid curd of your *new Comedy*. So much the better—all Trades would *live* they say—

But talking of some recent publications puts me in mind of something I had almost forgot to tell you—That several people who have a particular regard and esteem for the reputed Author of the present State of all Nations are sorry to find that he has too much exposed the posteriors of our Brothers in the North; and made some undeserved Compliments to their Neighbours in the South, who already have a comfortable enough share of self-conceit; and that amongst other perfections he allows them to be the handsomest people in Europe, which they think a very disputable Opinion.

All the Friends you have mentioned are well, and desire to be kindly remembered to you. Your Health is never forgot in our Compotations. I am sorry to tell you that our Society has lost one worthy member in Doctor Russel who died some Months ago of a malignant Fever. I beg you'll let me hear from you soon; and am, with my best Compliments to Mrs Smollett, at the same time never forgetting Miss [blank] and Miss Currie

my dear Sir
Your ever affectionate Friend and
faithful humble Servant
John Armstrong[124]

The cryptic and incoherent passage in the middle of this otherwise very lucid letter, followed by "talking of some recent publications" and a reference to Smollett's *Present State of All Nations* (1768–69), raises at least the possibility that Armstrong is attempting to tell Smollett something, in code as it were, about the appearance of another work which cannot be referred to directly, but which is called "your *new Comedy*." The *Atom* clearly fits the description; but we must certainly admit that this reading of the passage cannot be more than conjectural. In any case, the bleak picture painted of the state of London intellectual life, with the letters of Junius attacking the throne itself, agrees with what we know of Smollett's own views of the England he had just quitted.[125]

When the *Atom* appeared it was promptly reviewed in at least nine periodicals. Of these, three did not raise the question of authorship at all; five remarked that the *Atom* was "said" or "reputed" to be by Smollett; and the *Critical* (in a review which the marked copy at University College, London, assigns to Smollett himself) said, after lavishly praising the book, "we are unwilling to be more particular . . . for reasons that may be easily guessed."[126] The *Monthly Review*, the *London Chronicle*, and the *Whitehall Evening Post* all listed "Smollett's Adventures of an Atom" among works reviewed or published.[127] But most significant of all, *The Political Register* and *Critical Memoirs of the Times* clearly and directly attribute the *Atom* to Smollett. Their editors were the booksellers John Almon and George Kearsly. Politically, both Almon and Kearsly were opponents or enemies of Smollett; both reviewed the *Atom* in such a way as to suggest that they were hinting at the presence of materials for a libel action; and, most importantly, both had somehow or other undertaken to publish the *Atom*, withdrawing it only when the nature of its contents became apparent to them.[128]

The external evidence, then, is abundant enough to establish Smollett's authorship beyond question. The internal evidence has already been studied in some detail by several scholars.[129] But, as the notes to the present volume indicate, this evidence consists of literally hundreds of items. Detailed commentary on these would require a book in itself, and is in any case unnecessary, since all internal evidence tends to three unmistakable points:

1. If Smollett did not write the *Atom*, its author was a person unknown who devoted himself to plagiarizing the works of Smollett with unexampled pertinacity and thoroughness.

2. The political and personal opinions of the *Atom* are perfectly conformable with those of Smollett at all points, including even such anomalies as the conduct of Lord George Sackville at Minden. Smollett was almost alone in defending Sackville; he is not even mentioned in the *Atom*, despite the fact that his behavior would have been an admirable means of strengthening Smollett's denigration of that action. Smollett's views on such minor matters as the importance of Louisiana and Pitt's alleged neglect of the "fighting Quaker" Thomas Cumming are other cases in point.[130]

3. Lastly, the "profile" of the *Atom*'s author must be considered. The style of the *Atom* is thick with Smollettisms: "understrapper," "brought on the carpet," "certain it is," "big with" (in the sense of "pregnant or fraught with"), "blood and treasure," "incendiary." Numerous examples of Scotticisms are found: words used in their French sense, as "assist" for "be present at" or "actually" for "at this or that time," and archaisms used in Scotland that had vanished from standard English. The author is a rarity in English writing of his time in his indignation at the prevailing English prejudice against the Scots (remarkably resembling certain recent varieties of anti-Semitism in England and America) as hungry, rapacious, clannish, dirty, uncouth, threatening competitors.[131] And finally, the *Atom* was written either by a physician or by a man preoccupied with medicine and science. Not only is the imagery often medical (Hanover is an "ulcerated boil" on the rump of Great Britain), but references to bodily tissues and fluids, anatomy, diseases, remedies and treatments, all couched in medical or technical termi-

nology, occur by the dozen; seldom do more than four or five pages pass without a "sternutatory" or a "viscus."[132] It was not only with reference to scatology that Smollett thought himself a disciple of Rabelais.

The reader may wonder that so much evidence seemingly needs to be adduced in a matter which may now appear rather obvious, especially since many writers on Smollett have taken his authorship of the *Atom* for granted. But arguing in a circle is never defensible; and since much of the information here presented is new, while at the same time doubts on Smollett's authorship have been expressed in the recent past, it seems advisable to have the ascription of a lengthy and not unimportant work to a major author settled beyond question in the first serious scholarly edition of that work. Smollett's reputation will not suffer from the firm placement of this satire in his canon.

PUBLICATION AND RECEPTION

The curious circumstances surrounding the publication of the *Atom* have been deduced from bibliographical evidence by O M Brack, Jr.[133] Briefly, it appears that in the late autumn of 1768 the printer and bookseller John Almon printed the work in two duodecimo volumes, advertised it for sale, and distributed a certain number of copies, presumably in early December. Almon was a zealous promoter of the causes of both Pitt and John Wilkes, and he was a close friend and constant advisor of Wilkes both before and after the publication of Number 45 of the *North Briton*, which led to Wilkes's arrest and to the "Wilkes and Liberty" movement, soon to reach an almost insurrectionary force on both sides of the Atlantic.[134] The modern reader may find it hard to believe that such a person could have printed a work so diametrically opposed to his own views and so violently attacking his two heroes, but such was the case.[135] We are forced to suppose that Almon must have been ignorant of the *Atom*'s contents when he offered it for sale, since it evidently was hastily withdrawn, but only after at least a few copies had been sold. The work was advertised again in February 1769, this time by George Kearsly (or Kearsley), whose views and activities corresponded with or even exceeded Almon's;[136] and we may again suppose initial ignorance of the *Atom*'s contents, for there is no evidence that Kearsly ever distributed it. Finally the work was advertised again by Robinson and Roberts, who had published and were publishing other works of Smollett;[137] and it appeared, perhaps with deliberate timing, on 1 April 1769.

We can only conjecture as to just what had happened among the booksellers. We have seen from their published notices that Almon and Kearsly must (at least eventually) have known the *Atom* to be Smollett's. Almon doubtless thought on receiving the manuscript that in any case he had a salable property; and on discovering that he had been ideologically "bitten," as he would have termed it, he unloaded the sheets of the *Atom*, or the bound copies, or both, on Kearsly. Kearsly in turn either discovered the nature of what he had acquired, or, if he already knew, changed his mind about the advisability of publishing it. Robinson and Roberts either decided that the *Atom* was relatively harmless or that distributing it was worth the risk.

It is unfortunately impossible to come any closer than this account can take us to the facts of the *Atom*'s publication. The two audaciously anti-administration booksellers who thought better of publishing the book after they had acquired it could have felt so only if they feared prosecution or, more probably (since both had been in very hot water without lasting ill effects), if they declined to be parties to the promotion of anti-Pitt, anti-Wilkes, pro-Bute satire. And both attacked the *Atom* in print after it was published.

Book reviews in Smollett's day, if lengthy, tended to consist of a few sentences characterizing the work, one or more quoted passages from it, often very long, and a few concluding sentences of evaluation. Such was the case with the *Atom*, which was promptly noticed in the leading London periodicals. The *London Magazine* said: "This very shrewd and very entertaining history of the present times, is attributed to the ingenious Dr. Smollett. . . . such an account . . . must give much amusement to the public."[138] The *London Chronicle* review appeared in two parts in successive issues, and began: "This work, which is attributed to the Author of Roderick Random, is a satirical political history of the public transactions, and of the characters and conduct of some great men in a certain kingdom, to which the author has given the name of Japan, during the late and present reigns."[139] The *Town and Country Magazine* found the *Atom* to be "a sarcastic production in imitation of Rabelais and Swift, meant to lash the m[inister]s, politics, and parties of a certain island; and [it] is executed with much genuine wit, and original humour."[140] The *Gentleman's Magazine* made no mention of the author, and found the book to be written with "great spirit and humour; but there is a mixture of indelicacy and indecency which though it cannot gratify the loosest imagination can scarce fail to disgust the coarsest."[141]

The *Monthly Review*, which carried on a running political and literary feud of fluctuating intensity with Smollett's *Critical*, its chief rival, was surprisingly mild (its review was by the esteemed John Hawkesworth, whose relations with Smollett were generally amicable): "There is much spirit, humour, and satire in this piece; but there is also much nastiness and obscenity: of that kind, however, which is disgusting, and consequently not pernicious. There are also some inconsistencies. . . . There are many inaccuracies of style and expression; but it would be treating a hasty performance of this kind too severely to point them out."[142] Smollett's own *Critical* (in a review almost certainly written by him) was predictably enthusiastic: "This satire unites the happy extravagance of Rabelais to the splendid humour of Swift. . . . [Anyone who knows what life is like must think] the author's pencil if it has a fault, errs on the side of delicacy. More characteristically true than any picture ever drawn of a certain people . . . ridicule and reality are here blended together with inimitable art and originality." The reviewer "disapprove[s] of the severity with which a certain respectable character" (probably meaning Pitt) "is drawn," but finds the pictures of Newcastle and Hardwicke to be particularly good. The notice ends: "We are unwilling to be more particular in our account of this piece, for reasons that may be easily guessed; but we must conclude, by saying as Shakespeare does of music, that the man who does not love and relish this performance has no wit in his own composition."[143]

In striking contrast to this luscious praise is the notice in the *Political Register*. Almon was the editor of this journal, and if we may indulge in conjecture we can see him taking revenge for having been tricked into printing what he now reviews.

[The *Atom*] falls so short of the graceful simplicity and lively entertaining humour of his [Smollett's] other performances of the same kind, that we could not give credit to it did we not perceive a political transformation . . . which points out the author to those that are in possession of the list of ministerial writers.

The foul, abusive, degrading character of the late k--- . . . is mean, malevolent, and unpardonable; but be it remembered that the supposed author was a prisoner in the king's bench during the k---'s reign, which he will never forget; nor forgive the ministry at that period, whose characters are vilely mangled in this work, to gratify keen resentment.[144]

The notice of the *Atom* in George Kearsly's *Critical Memoirs of the Times*, whether or not by Kearsly himself, gave it the most thoughtful attention found in any contemporary account. The political animus of this review is obvious—alone among the criticisms it takes the trouble to complain of the *Atom*'s treatment of Wilkes, though in fact Wilkes (in comparison, say, with

Newcastle or Frederick the Great) is rather gently treated. It contains the
highest proportion of comment to quotation among all of the reviews.

> This performance is said to come from the pen of the celebrated author of
> Roderick Random. It is, however, a very gross and inelegant production, very
> unworthy of such a writer. Add to this that the share of merit, which might have
> been attributed to it on the score of its satirical and characteristical descriptions,
> is in a great measure evaporated by the delay of its publication: the most remark-
> able personages in it, being either naturally or politically dead since their por-
> traits were drawn. Portraits indeed they should not be called, but rather vil-
> lainous caricatures, not more disgraceful to the objects than the painter.
>
> The Atom is supposed to give the following account of the people of the
> empire of Japan; under which name we presume we need not inform the reader
> the author means an island with which he is much better acquainted.

The review then quotes in its entirety a lengthy passage from the text, beginning on page 8, below ("The empire of Japan consists . . .), and concluding
on page 9 (. . . chaos of their absurdities"). After the quotation it continues as
follows: "There are some touches in the above picture, not ill-designed, and
which in general sketches may pass for the pencilling of a masterly hand.
They are too strong, nevertheless, to be made use of in the delineation of the
particular features of individuals. There is indeed, too much truth in the
writer's observation that 'while the constitution of human nature remains
unchanged, satire will be always better received than panegyric . . . .'" The
review next quotes fully the paragraph on satire beginning with this sentence, page 38, below. And it then goes on:

> Admitting all this, however, it is beneath the character of a man of genius, to
> employ his talents to such an infamous purpose as that of gratifying only the
> malignity of mankind. Yet this seems to be the sole purpose of our malignant
> atom; who takes up the history of his pretended Japan, at the beginning of the
> last war, and closes it soon after the peace. The characters that figured, and
> events that happened during that interval, are here depicted and related under
> fictitious terms and appellations; very easily decyphered by those who are in the
> least acquainted with the public transactions during that period.
>
> Of the personages and conduct of the *late* emperor or dairo of Japan and his
> ministers, the Atom has drawn the most disgusting and odious picture imagin-
> able; we shall select a specimen or two of the work, therefore, from his descrip-
> tion of the *present*.

There follows a complete quotation of the passage describing George III, Bute, and the latter's philosophy of government, beginning (page 96, below) with "Gio-gio was a young prince . . ." and concluding (page 97) with ". . . dragging in opposite directions." The quotation completed, the discussion continues with a complaint: "The historian's further illustration of this example is gross, vulgar and puerile; we pass it over, therefore, to come to the subsequent conduct of Yak-Strot with regard to his royal pupil." The review then repeats in full the passage treating Bute's economies in the royal household and his plans for patronage of the arts and letters: "He dismissed from the Dairo's service . . ." (page 101, below), concluding with ". . . not above four or five men of genius could be found in the whole empire of Japan" (page 102). Following this passage the author turns his attention to the *Atom's* treatment of Pitt: "The various tergiversations of our late great commoner are here ludicrously repeated, as the conduct of the orator Taycho; and the famous exploit of Number 45, by our present popular patriot, recorded in the same strain, as that of the dirtmonger Ian-ki-dtzin; whom he leaves beyond sea making ineffectual appeals to the people at home. What a field has since opened for our atom to display his adventures in! But we shall take leave of this very partial and illiberal performance with the full eulogium to Lord B---." The review concludes by quoting the *Atom's* most extended and sustained expression of praise for Bute, pages 123–24, below: "As for Yak-strot, he was every thing but a down-right martyr to the odium of the public . . . . There was very little vicious in his composition; and as to his follies, they were rather the subjects of ridicule than of resentment."[145]

We may conclude that the *Atom*, though its impact on the London literary world was far from sensational, received as much attention from the reviewers as might reasonably have been expected. Had Smollett cared or dared to publish it in 1765, it would surely have created a greater stir and perhaps landed him in hot water; but the fact that "the most remarkable personages in it" were "either naturally, or politically dead," together with the complexity and minute detail of its texture, could not fail to militate against its success. The book did not, however, escape the notice of so discriminating a critic as Edmund Burke. He reprinted in its entirety the digression on surnames from volume two, with a complimentary remark on its wit, in the *Annual Register*, of which he was editor at the time; and thus he obliquely testified that in his opinion one passage at least from Smollett's satire merited preservation for posterity among the notabilities of 1769.[146] The *Atom* was not mentioned in the Baron Grimm's influential *Correspondence littéraire*, which in elegant scribal copies kept the crowned heads of Europe abreast of current developments in letters; nor, so far as is known, was it noticed in other Continental reviews. Though Clara Reeve mentioned it briefly but favorably in *The Progress of Romance* (1785),[147] there seems to be little or no further documentation of its immediate popularity. However, a print which appeared in May and August 1769, shortly after the *Atom's* publication, would seem to indicate that the artist expected Smollett's work to be fairly familiar to his customers. This print, entitled *An Abridgment of Mr. Pope's Essay on Man*, features a pile of volumes with titles on their spines, such as "Locke," "Newton," and "Life of Alexander"; at the bottom of the pile is "Adventures of an Atom," surmounted by "An Essay on Rattles and Sceptres."[148]

The most notable comment on the *Atom* between its first reviews and the observations of scholars in our own day appeared in the "Life of Smollett" prefacing the six-volume collection of *Miscellaneous Works* brought out in Edinburgh in 1796–97 and reprinted in 1800. The author of this "Life," Robert Anderson, M.D., is anxious to praise Smollett wherever possible, but his account of the *Atom* at least shows that he had read it carefully:

His *Adventures of an Atom* belong to the class of compositions in fictitious history, in the form rather than the substance of the work, which consists of real characters and historical incidents, aggravated and embellished by humour and fancy, and tinged by the dark hues of political prejudice. This species of romance was first introduced into the English language by Mrs. Manley, in the "Memoirs of the New Atlantis," to stigmatize the whig administration in the reign of Queen Anne. It was afterwards improved by Swift, who blended in his political allegories, humour and satire, ridicule and reality, with inimitable art and originality, and advanced to perfection by Dr. Arbuthnot, in the "History of John Bull." The plan of this performance combines the wild extravagance of Rabelais, and the broad caricature of Mrs. Manley, with the splendid humour of Swift, and the brilliant wit and profound erudition of Dr. Arbuthnot. He takes the advantage of the Pythagorean doctrine of transmigration to endue his atom with reason and the organs of speech, which he excites in the brain of *Mr. Nathaniel Peacock*, who writes down what it dictates of the history of one period, during which it underwent some strange revolutions in the empire of *Japan* (England); and was conscious of some political anecdotes, to be divulged for the instruction of British ministers. He professes to give a plain narrative of historical incidents, "without pretending to philosophize like H--e, or dogmatize like S-----tt." The characters of the chiefs who disputed the administration of Japan, are drawn in the high style of recognizable caricature. The portraits of King George II, and the Duke of Cumberland are aggravated with strokes of satire; and the leaders of the whig party, with the exception of the Earl of Hardwick, "the wisest man, and the greatest cypher," are stigmatized as a set of sordid knaves, utterly devoid of sentiment and integrity. Even the Earl of Bute and Lord Mansfield, the favourite subjects of his panegyric, are exposed to the virulence of his satire, and the keen shafts of his ridicule. From our knowledge of Smollett's character, we expect, what we find, in this work; ideas that indicate a firm and lofty mind, and a diction ardent and energetic, correspondent to the feelings of his heart. Though it is inferior, upon the whole, to his other novels, for ingenuity and contrivance in the composition, and for observation of life, it is written, for the most,—with his usual humour, animation, and felicity of expression. His comparison of the *Council Board* to the allegorical *table of Cebes*, is well managed; and his digressions on *surnames, breeches, alchemy, magic, necromancy,* and *sorcery,* display that peculiar combination of profound learning and genuine humour, which forms the basis of ludicrous composition. In his representation of personal characters, he is most liable to censure. Political prejudice never appears more justly reprehensible, than when it attempts to cast a veil over distinguished merit, and loads exalted characters with obloquy. There can hardly be any contemplation more painful than to dwell on the virulent excesses of a man of genius; and yet the utility of such contemplation may be equal to the pain. The strength and the acuteness of sensation which partly constitute genius, have a great tendency to produce virulence, if the mind is not perpetually on its guard against that subtile, insinuating, and corrosive poison, hatred against all whose opinions are opposite to our own.

"In this performance," Dr. Moore justly observes, "Smollett combines the manner of Swift and Rabelais; while in many parts he equals their humour, he has not always avoided their indelicacy, and has sometimes followed the wild extravagance of the latter. Prejudice has certainly guided his pencil in drawing the portraits, or rather caricatures, interspersed through this work, some of which do the greatest injustice to the originals for whom they were intended; yet the performance, on the whole, affords new proofs of the humour, wit, learning, and powerful genius of the painter; and it may be asserted with truth, that no political allegory has been executed with equal wit and pleasantry, since the days of Arbuthnot."[149]

Though Anderson's commentary may seem to us somewhat too tender of Pitt and others, and somewhat too inclined to equate the *Atom* in merit with its most distinguished predecessors, it is nevertheless not distorted in its total view of the work. It was a fitting vehicle for preserving whatever limited reputation and esteem the *Atom* might enjoy among the curious during its long period of eclipse during the nineteenth and early twentieth centuries, when most lovers and admirers of Smollett were hardly aware of its existence.

In the Robinson and Roberts edition of 1769 the two volumes of the *Atom* sold for the sum of five shillings sewed and six shillings bound,[150] a price which can hardly have helped the sales of so small a book. A Dublin edition appeared in the same year.[151] A London edition of 1778 was called the "tenth," though anyone familiar with the practices of eighteenth-century booksellers will be skeptical of this claim; there was an Edinburgh edition in 1784 and a London edition in 1786. In 1795 the work appeared as No. 50 in *Cooke's Pocket Edition of Select Novels*. It was also included, but with no critical apparatus beyond the reproduction of one or another of the several "keys," in the numerous collected editions of Smollett's works published in Edinburgh, London, Oxford, New York, and Philadelphia from 1796 through 1926. These were at least fourteen in number; but although the most notable bore the names of Sir Walter Scott, George Saintsbury, William Ernest Henley, Thomas Seccombe, and Gustavus Maynadier, these eminent men of letters had little or nothing to say about the *Atom*, and their "editions" of it were merely reprints of earlier ones.[152] The present edition of Smollett's satire is thus not only the first to appear since 1926, but also the first ever to provide both a carefully edited text and a full apparatus of historical annotation.

Notes

1. These are: James R. Foster, "Smollett and the *Atom*," *PMLA* 68 (1953): 1032–46; Martz, 90–103; Arnold Whitridge, *Tobias Smollett* (Brooklyn: privately printed, 1925), 56–79; Damian Grant, *Tobias Smollett: A Study in Style* (Manchester, Eng.: Manchester University Press, 1977), 56–59, 175–77; Henry B. Prickett, "The Political Writings and Opinions of Tobias Smollett" (Ph.D. diss., Harvard University, 1952), 308–37; Wayne J. Douglass, "Smollett and the Sordid Knaves: Political Satire in *The Adventures of an Atom*" (Ph.D. diss., University of Florida, 1976). See also two more recent articles by the editor of the present volume: "The Authorship of the *Atom*," *Philological Quarterly* 59 (1981): 183–89; "*Ut Pictura Poesis?* Smollett, Satire, and the Graphic Arts," in *Studies in Eighteenth-Century Culture*, vol. 10, ed. Harry C. Payne (Madison: University of Wisconsin Press, 1981), 297–312.
2. Smollett's words at the opening of his first letter in the *Travels* (p. 2).
3. Lismahago's words in *Humphry Clinker*, as repeated in a letter from Matthew Bramble to Dr. Lewis, Tweedmouth, July 15.
4. This statement is made with full knowledge of the poems of Swift and Pope and of Sir John Harington's earlier *Metamorphosis of Ajax* (1596), and of Norman Mailer's *The Naked and the Dead* (nominated for that honor by the London

Times Literary Supplement, 5 May 1978, p. 493, col. 2), to say nothing of Mailer's *Ancient Evenings*.

5. *Gentleman's Magazine* 39 (April 1769): 205.

6. Introduction to *The Politics of Samuel Johnson* (New Haven: Yale University Press, 1960), 5–6.

7. In eighteenth-century England the twenty-six members of the bench of bishops, or lords spiritual, were appointed for life by the crown; the Scottish peerage was represented by sixteen members who were elected for the seven-year duration of a given Parliament, but might or might not be re-elected; the crown (persuaded by the incumbent ministry) might alter the political complexion of the House of Lords by creating new peers.

8. See below, vol. 1, nn. 287, 494; and see Williams, 2:36.

9. See J. C. D. Clark, *The Dynamics of Change: The Crisis of the 1750s and the English Party Systems* (Cambridge: The University Press, 1982); Stephen B. Baxter, "The Conduct of the Seven Years' War," in *England's Rise to Greatness, 1660–1763*, ed. S. B. Baxter (Berkeley: University of California Press, 1983), 323–48; and Richard Middleton, *The Bells of Victory: The Pitt-Newcastle Ministry and the Conduct of the Seven Years' War, 1757–1762* (New York: Cambridge University Press, 1985).

10. See Brewer, "Misfortunes," 3–4, and below, vol. 2, nn. 399, 407, 408, 410, 412, 452, 462, 463. So acute and well informed an observer as David Hume thought that Bute was all-powerful behind the scenes as late as 1771; see Duncan Forbes, *Hume's Philosophical Politics* (Cambridge: The University Press, 1975), 132. In 1770 the young Thomas Chatterton wrote two lengthy verse satires, "Kew Gardens" and "The Whore of Babylon," describing what he believed to be the sinister, hidden influence of Bute and the king's mother. See Donald S. Taylor, *Thomas Chatterton's Art* (Princeton: Princeton University Press, 1978), 210–17. The texts of the two poems may be found in Donald S. Taylor and Benjamin B. Hoover, eds., *The Complete Works of Thomas Chatterton* (Oxford: Clarendon Press, 1971), 1:452–67, 512–42. On 2 March 1770 Pitt, who certainly knew the contrary, spoke in the House of Lords of "an invisible power . . . who notwithstanding he was abroad, was at this moment as potent as ever"; see Brooke, *George III*, 391.

11. See below, vol. 2, n. 246.

12. On this aspect of Pitt's career see Brewer, *Party*, chapter 6, "Pitt and Patriotism: A Case Study in Political Argument," and the listing of pro-Pitt and anti-Pitt pamphlets (pp. 336–60); see also the list in Marie Peters, *Pitt and Popularity* (Oxford: Clarendon Press, 1980), 282–91.

13. A detailed account of the "Massacre" may be found in Namier, *England*, 468–83.

14. An example of such a career is that of John Clevland, secretary of the admiralty. See below, vol. 1, n. 244, and the references cited therein. Even more notable in this way was Charles Jenkinson (1727–1808), M.P. and secretary to Lord Bute,

who became the confidant and political agent of George III and was created earl
of Liverpool in 1796. See Ninetta S. Jucker, ed., *The Jenkinson Papers: 1760–1766*
(London: Macmillan, 1949).

15. This figure is taken from the detailed discussion of taxation during the Seven
Years' War in Stephen Dowell, *A History of Taxation and Taxes in England* (London: Longmans, Green, 1884), 2:130–43.

16. See J. H. Plumb, *Sir Robert Walpole: The King's Minister* (London: Cresset Press,
1960), 1:233–83; and on Bute see below, vol. 2, n. 393.

17. See Dowell, *A History of Taxation*, 2:130–43.

18. For examples see Roy Porter, *English Society in the Eighteenth Century* (Harmondsworth: Penguin Books, 1982), 309–19. For more general accounts of the structure of English society at the time see J. C. D. Clark, *English Society, 1688–1832: Ideology, Social Structure and Political Practice During the Ancien Regime* (New York: Cambridge University Press, 1985); and H. T. Dickinson, *Liberty and Property: Political Ideology in Eighteenth-Century Britain* (New York: Holmes and Meier, 1977). See also J. A. W. Gunn, *Beyond Liberty and Property: The Process of Self-Recognition in Eighteenth-Century Political Thought* (Kingston and Montreal: McGill–Queen's University Press, 1983).

19. See Basil Williams, *The Whig Supremacy* (Oxford: Clarendon Press, 1962), 157–63, 251–57; Paul S. Fritz, *The English Ministers and Jacobitism between the Rebellions of 1715 and 1745* (Toronto: University of Toronto Press, 1975); and Eveline Cruickshanks, ed., *Ideology and Conspiracy: Aspects of Jacobitism, 1680–1759* (Edinburgh: John Donald, 1982).

20. *King George III and the Politicians* (Oxford: Clarendon Press, 1954), 4. For an extensive treatment of Britain's Continental problems see Richard Lodge, *Great Britain and Prussia in the Eighteenth Century* (Oxford: Clarendon Press, 1923; reprint, New York: Octagon Books, 1972).

21. For example, the vital office of secretary of state for the colonies was not created until January 1768 (with Lord Hillsborough filling the post). On colonial policy see Williams, *The Whig Supremacy*, 307–24. A thorough and useful survey, both of the political and economic situation in this period and of the Seven Years' War and the events that led to the American Revolution, is I. R. Christie, *Crisis of Empire: Great Britain and the American Colonies, 1754–1783* (New York: W. W. Norton, 1966). For more detailed studies of the political errors and ideological attitudes that promoted the Revolution see Gipson, and see also Robert W. Tucker and David C. Hendrickson, *The Fall of the First British Empire: Origins of the War of American Independence* (Baltimore: Johns Hopkins University Press, 1982); Bernard Bailyn, *The Ideological Origins of the American Revolution* (Cambridge: Harvard University Press, 1967); Edmund S. and Helen M. Morgan, *The Stamp Act Crisis: Prologue to Revolution*, rev. ed. (New York: Collier Books, 1976); John L. Bullion, *A Great and Necessary Measure: George Grenville and the Genesis of the Stamp Act* (Columbia: University of Missouri Press, 1983). The

most extensive and detailed study of the colonies, and of British imperial and colonial policy, is Lawrence Gipson's monumental fifteen-volume work, *The British Empire before the American Revolution* (New York: Alfred Knopf, 1936–70).

22. On the disastrous effects of Newcastle's persistent attempts see Reed Browning, "The Duke of Newcastle and the Imperial Election Plan," *Journal of British Studies* 7 (1967): 28–47.

23. All of the events mentioned in this general account are taken up in the *Atom*; treatments of them in Smollett's other works and in standard historical sources are acknowledged in detail in the notes to the text, below.

24. Sedgwick, 28.

25. The phrase, "a bloody war," included by Bute in George III's first speech to the privy council on his accession, was altered at Pitt's insistence to "an expensive but just and necessary war." See Brooke, *George III*, 75, and Williams, 2:64.

26. The classic discussion and demonstration of this thesis is Namier, *Structure*. See also John Brooke, "Namier and Namierism," *History and Theory* 3 (1964): 331–47.

27. The significance of party ideology is examined in great detail by Linda Colley, *In Defiance of Oligarchy: The Tory Party, 1740–1760* (Cambridge: The University Press, 1982). See also Brian W. Hill, *British Parliamentary Parties, 1742–1832* (Boston: Allen and Unwin, 1985), and *The Growth of Parliamentary Parties, 1689–1747* (Hamden, Conn.: Archon Books, 1976).

28. See Brewer, *Party*, 47.

29. The reader is referred to the analysis of Pitt's motivations in Brewer, *Party*, 96–111; but Peters, *Pitt and Popularity*, modifies this analysis and shows it to be in need of qualification.

30. See Robin Fabel, "The Patriotic Briton: Smollett and English Politics," *Eighteenth-Century Studies* 8 (1974): 100–114.

31. For examples see the lists of pamphlets given in Brewer, *Party*, 336–60.

32. See below, vol. 1, n. 755, and vol. 2, nn. 94, 114.

33. See below, vol. 2, n. 259; and see Brewer, *Party*, 107–8, and Peters, *Pitt and Popularity*, 205–39.

34. The problems of who recruited Smollett for the *Briton*, what he received or expected for writing the journal, and how Bute regarded its usefulness remain unsolved; the evidence is largely conjectural. Dr. John Campbell, historian, co-editor with Smollett of the *Universal History*, one of Bute's closest advisors and a principal propagandist for his administration, may well have been the intermediary between them; see Martz, 8, and Brewer, *Party*, 222, 224–26. Prickett, "Political Writings," concludes (pp. 270–78, 309–10) that Bute, finding the *Briton* ineffective, simply ignored it. See also Peters, *Pitt and Popularity*, 241–61; and see below, vol. 2, n. 369.

35. *King George III*, 4.

36. In the May 1758 issue of the *Critical Review*, Smollett vituperatively reviewed a

pamphlet in which Vice-Admiral Charles Knowles had defended his conduct during the abortive expedition of 1757 against Rochefort. Denigrating Knowles's entire career, Smollett called him "an ignorant, assuming, officious, fribbling pretender; conceited as a peacock, obstinate as a mule, and mischievous as a monkey" (*CR* 5:439). Knowles sued the printer and Smollett for libel. The former was acquitted in June 1759 after Smollett had come forward to declare himself both author and publisher of the offending words; in November 1760 Smollett was fined £100, sentenced to three months' imprisonment (which he served in the King's Bench Prison from the end of November through mid-February), and required to give security for his good behavior for seven years. See Knapp, 213–14, 218, 230–36.

37. The most spectacular instance of Pitt's changeability was his instant and complete reversal of attitude on the German war and on aid to Frederick. For a recent summary of the scholarship on this point, see Baxter, "The Conduct of the Seven Years' War," 341.

38. See below, vol. 1, n. 435; and see Sedgwick, 57, 60: Pitt is "that snake in the grass" and "the blackest of hearts." Bute and the king may be exonerated of prejudice if we consider certain opinions of Samuel Johnson and David Hume on the "feudal gabble" of the "great actor," who is "our Cutthroat"; see Donald Greene, ed., *Samuel Johnson: Political Writings*, The Yale Edition of Johnson's Works, vol. 10 (New Haven: Yale University Press, 1977), 347–48, 367–68 and n. 9. But see also Romney Sedgwick, "Letters from William Pitt to Lord Bute, 1755–1758," in *Essays Presented to Sir Lewis Namier*, ed. Richard Pares and A. J. P. Taylor (New York: St. Martin's Press, 1956), 108–66.

39. See below, vol. 1, n. 469.

40. See below, vol. 2, n. 246, and the references cited therein.

41. See, for example, Johnson's savage satire, "[The Vultures]," written at the height of the Seven Years' War. Published as *Idler*, no. 22, in the *Universal Chronicle*, 9 September 1758, this satire was omitted from the collected edition of the *Idler* in 1761. See also the references cited in n. 38, above; and for a general discussion of Johnson's views see Donald J. Greene, "Samuel Johnson and the Great War for Empire," in *English Writers of the Eighteenth Century*, ed. John H. Middendorf (New York: Columbia University Press, 1971), 37–65.

42. Smollett's approving views of Britain's acquisition of an overseas empire and the successful attempts to weaken the power of France are studied and summarized in Prickett, "Political Writings," 184–85, 195, 205.

43. See *Briton*, no. 6 (3 July 1762) and no. 22 (23 October 1762).

44. For a judicious summary of the evidence concerning these points see Sir Lewis Namier, "George III and Bute," *Avenues of History* (London: Hamish Hamilton, 1952), 118–21. Brooke, *George III*, 46, 49, 50, 266, argues that the widespread belief in Princess Augusta's influence over her son was pure myth. See James L.

McKelvey, *George III and Lord Bute: The Leicester House Years* (Durham, N.C.: Duke University Press, 1973). A useful discussion of Bolingbroke's theories and his posthumous influence is Isaac Kramnick, *Bolingbroke and His Circle: The Politics of Nostalgia in the Age of Walpole* (Cambridge: Harvard University Press, 1968).

45. See above, n. 28.

46. See Brewer, *Party*, 112–17, for summary and discussion of contemporary views on this point.

47. The evidence for this statement is carefully analyzed and discussed in Prickett, "Political Writings," 318–28.

48. For examples of these opinions in Smollett's works see Sekora, 146–53.

49. John Carteret became Earl Granville in 1744 on the death of his mother, who was Countess Granville in her own right. On Granville's career see Basil Williams, *Carteret and Newcastle* (London: Frank Cass, 1966).

50. The saying originated with Pitt himself, in a speech of 9 December 1762 against the Peace of Paris; see *PH*, 15:1267.

51. See below, vol. 2, n. 351.

52. Ronald Hyam, "Imperial Interests and the Peace of Paris (1763)," in *Reappraisals in British Imperial History*, ed. R. Hyam and G. Martin (London: Macmillan, 1975), 26.

53. The most reliable accounts of Smollett's political views are those of Robin Fabel, "The Patriotic Briton"; Donald Greene, "Smollett the Historian: A Reappraisal," in *Tobias Smollett: Bicentennial Essays Presented to Lewis M. Knapp*, ed. G. S. Rousseau and P.-G. Boucé (New York: Oxford University Press, 1971), 25–56; and W. A. Speck, "Tobias Smollett and the Historian," in *Society and Literature in England, 1700–1760* (Atlantic Highlands, N.J.: Humanities Press, 1983), 167–85.

54. The best and most balanced summary of Smollett's views in general is that of Ian Campbell Ross, "Tobias Smollett: Gentleman by Birth, Education, and Profession," *British Journal for Eighteenth-Century Studies* 5 (1982): 179–90.

55. This estimate of Johnson is from his biographer Walter Jackson Bate, as summarized by C. J. Rawson, "Jobswell: A Short View of the Johnson-Boswell Industry," *Sewanee Review* 88 (1980): 106.

56. In reviewing *The Peregrinations of Jeremiah Grant, the West Indian*, *CR* 15 (January 1763): 18, Smollett remarks: "We cannot call it a faithful copy, . . . but submit to the reader, whether the likenesses may not be compared to the wrong side of a tapestry, on which the figures do not appear to the best advantage. . . ." See Basker, 228, 271. The image is from the prologue to part 2 of *Don Quixote*; see the translation of Samuel Putnam (New York: Viking, 1949), 1028, n. 29. We should number among those works relevant to the *Atom* large portions of the *Universal History* (discussed below), for which Smollett's editorial effort involved

much rewriting—perhaps as much as one-third of the "Modern Part," including the sections on the German Empire and Japan; see Martz, 8, and Martz, "Tobias Smollett and the *Universal History*," *Modern Language Notes* 56 (1941): 1–14.

57. Philip J. Klukoff, "Two Smollett Attributions in the *Critical Review: The Reverie* and *Tristram Shandy*," *Notes & Queries* 211 (1966): 465–66; Basker, 263.

58. *CR* 11 (April 1761): 315. The Latin phrases signify "jokes of Plautus" (therefore coarse), and "unclean and shameful expressions." The text contains an error; "ignominiosaq: dicta" should read "ignominiosaque dicta."

59. *CR* 13 (January 1762): 66.

60. *CR* 13 (January 1762): 67.

61. *CR* 13 (January 1762): 68. The quotation is from the review of volumes 5 and 6 of *Tristram Shandy*. The Latinate circumlocution for farting is echoed in the *Atom*; see below, p. 35. The word *braye* is from medieval or early Renaissance French and refers to underdrawers, or a loincloth.

62. *CR* 10 (January 1760): 70; see Basker, 226, 259.

63. *CR* 19 (January 1765): 66; see below, the text, pp. 33–34. The significant portions of all of these reviews of *Tristram Shandy* are reproduced in *Sterne: The Critical Heritage*, ed. Alan B. Howes (London: Routledge and Kegan Paul, 1974), 52, 62, 125–27, 138–40, 159–60, 179.

64. These reviews are quoted below, pp. lix and lviii. The similarity in wording of the two reviews may be accounted for by the fact that *Town and Country* had been founded by the son of Archibald Hamilton, co-proprietor and printer of the *Critical Review* and the *British Magazine*; see Basker, 32, 189, 207.

65. See Bloom, *The Anxiety of Influence* (New York: Oxford University Press, 1973), and Huntington Brown, *Rabelais in English Literature* (Paris: Les Belles Lettres, 1933), 184–88.

66. Martz, 91.

67. For Marana's work see Arthur Weitzmann, ed., *Letters Writ by a Turkish Spy* (New York: Columbia University Press, 1970). On Manley and Haywood see Paul B. Anderson, "Delarivière Manley's Prose Fiction," *Philological Quarterly* 13 (1934): 168–88; Robert Adams Day, *Told in Letters* (Ann Arbor: University of Michigan Press, 1966); John J. Richetti, *Popular Fiction Before Richardson* (Oxford: Clarendon Press, 1969); Jerry C. Beasley, *Novels of the 1740s* (Athens: University of Georgia Press, 1982).

68. Knapp, 104–5, presents virtually conclusive evidence that Smollett had in fact translated *Le diable boiteux*; see also Martz, 91–93.

69. Smollett's knowledge of this last is not firmly established; and it has no real similarity with the *Atom* beyond being a key-novel and calling England Japan. See Martz, 93.

70. See Robert Adams Day, ed., *The History of Pompey the Little* (London: Oxford University Press, 1974); and for a list of such fictions see Toby A. Olshin,

"Form and Theme in Novels about Non-Human Characters, A Neglected Sub-Genre," *Genre* 2 (1969): 43–56.

71. On these points see the discussion of the picaresque mode in Ronald Paulson, *Satire and the Novel in Eighteenth-Century England* (New Haven: Yale University Press, 1967), 190–94.

72. The reviews appeared as follows: *CR* 9 (May 1760): 419; *CR* 11 (April 1761): 336; and *CR* 20 (August 1765): 120–24. *Chrysal* has been edited, with an informative introduction, by Ernest Baker (London: Routledge, 1907).

73. *CR* 9 (May 1760): 419.

74. See James R. Foster, "Smollett's Pamphleteering Foe Shebbeare," *PMLA* 57 (1942): 1090.

75. Foster, "Shebbeare," 1077–86.

76. See Foster, "Shebbeare," 1067–69.

77. Foster, "Shebbeare," 1091.

78. *CR* 15 (March 1763): 210. The review is by Smollett; it contains numerous touches characteristic of his style and opinions. *The Sumatrans* was published anonymously, but Smollett, who had reviewed Shebbeare's polemical series of *Letters to the English People*, recognized him as the author; see Basker, 228, 269, 272.

79. See the discussion below, pp. xlix–lii.

80. See Martz, 96–103; see also the article by Martz, "Tobias Smollett and the *Universal History*," and see Knapp, 248–49. The history of Japan was probably compiled by George Psalmanazar, the impostor and self-styled native of Formosa, who in later life worked for various booksellers, mostly as a historical writer. Smollett knew him well; he is mentioned in *Humphry Clinker* (Jery Melford to Sir Watkin Phillips, London, June 10). On his career see Robert A. Day, "Psalmanazar's 'Formosa' and the British Reader (Including Samuel Johnson)," in *Exoticism in the Enlightenment*, ed. G. S. Rousseau and Roy Porter (Manchester: University of Manchester Press, and Chapel Hill: University of North Carolina Press, 1989).

81. American readers should perhaps be reminded that in British usage "corn" is any sort of edible grain.

82. *CR* 8 (September 1759): 189–90.

83. See below, the text, p. 3: "I likewise turned over to . . . the Universal History, and found . . . many of the names and much of the matter specified in the following sheets."

84. See below, vol. 1, n. 66.

85. See, for example, FI-DE-TA-DA in the key to the present volume.

86. The passages in question are on pp. 9, 24, and 37–38 of the text, below. Smollett almost certainly knew a minor satirical work of Swift, *An Account of the Court and Empire of Japan*, that much resembles the *Atom*. The *Critical* considered this

work "such as would discredit the pen of an author of the lowest class"; see *CR*
19 (May 1765): 350. On Swift's *Account* see below, vol. 2, n. 171.

87. These pamphlets are available in an excellent modern edition by Alan W. Bower
and Robert A. Erickson, *The History of John Bull* (Oxford: Clarendon Press,
1976).

88. See the remarks below, p. lxii; and for a probable direct borrowing from
Arbuthnot by Smollett, see below vol. 1, n. 314.

89. This edition is discussed in Bower and Erickson, *John Bull*, xxvi.

90. *CR* 10 (December 1760): 453, 452, 451. See David R. Raynor, ed., *Sister Peg: A
Pamphlet Hitherto Unknown: By David Hume* (Cambridge: The University Press,
1982). Roger L. Emerson, "Recent Works on Eighteenth-Century Scottish Life
and Thought," *Eighteenth-Century Life* 11 (1985): 104, challenges the attribution
to Hume, pointing out that scholars generally give the pamphlet to Adam Fer-
guson. (Smollett was acquainted with Ferguson; see *Humphry Clinker*, Matthew
Bramble to Dr. Lewis, Edinburgh, August 8.) Richard B. Sher, reviewing
Raynor's work in *Philosophical Books* 24 (April 1983): 85–91, devotes his entire
discussion to questioning the evidence Raynor adduces for Hume's authorship.
The attribution remains unsettled at present. For additional information on
Smollett's close relationships with the Edinburgh intellectuals see Richard B.
Sher, *Church and University in the Scottish Enlightenment: The Moderate Literati of
Edinburgh* (Princeton: Princeton University Press, 1985).

91. See *Letters*, 135–36.

92. On Smollett's scatological preoccupations see Robert Adams Day, "Sex, Scatology, Smollett," in *Sexuality in Eighteenth-Century Britain*, ed. Paul-Gabriel Boucé
(Manchester, Eng.: Manchester University Press, 1982), 225–43.

93. In an essay on the Georgics, first printed in Dryden's translation of Virgil
(1697), Addison remarked that Virgil "delivers the meanest of his precepts with
a kind of grandeur, he breaks the clods and tosses the dung about with an air of
gracefulness"; see *The Miscellaneous Works of Joseph Addison*, ed. A. C. Guthkelch
(London: G. Bell & Sons, 1914), 2:9.

94. These are in *Briton*, no. 38 (12 February 1763), no. 14 (19 August 1762), and
no. 15 (4 September 1762).

95. *Letters*, 87; see also Smollett's letters to Wilkes, pp. 75–79, 82, 102, 104.

96. This idealized portrait of Smollett as historian is found in the general preface to
the *Continuation*, 1:v.

97. *Continuation*, 3:286–87.

98. Prickett, "The Political Writings," 312–29, compares the opinions expressed in
the *Atom* and the *Continuation* in great detail and finds them to be identical
except in some points of emphasis.

99. See Prints 2327, 3913*, 3917, 3853, 3852*. For general accounts of these prints
see Herbert M. Atherton, *Political Prints in the Age of Hogarth* (New York:

Oxford University Press, 1974); and Vincent Carretta, *The Snarling Muse: Verbal and Visual Satire from Pope to Churchill* (Philadelphia: University of Pennsylvania Press, 1983).

100. Walpole, *Correspondence*, 22:42.

101. Three articles on Smollett's use of satirical prints have recently appeared: Robert Adams Day, "*Ut Pictura Poesis?*"; Wayne J. Douglass, "Done After the Dutch Taste: Political Prints and Smollett's *Atom*," *Essays in Literature* 9 (1982): 170–79; Byron W. Gassman, "Smollett's *Briton* and the Art of Political Cartooning," in *Studies in Eighteenth-Century Culture*, vol. 14, ed. O M Brack, Jr. (Madison: University of Wisconsin Press, 1985), 243–58.

102. See *Letters*, 136; and see O M Brack, Jr., "*The History and Adventures of an Atom, 1769*," *PBSA* 64 (1970): 336–38.

103. *Continuation*, 4:155–73. The pamphlet was reviewed with great enthusiasm in *CR* 10 (November 1760): 403–4.

104. See, for example, *Briton*, no. 6 (3 July 1762).

105. See below, vol. 1, nn. 623, 638, 660, 710; and vol. 2, nn. 55, 137, 138, 142, 428.

106. This letter is reproduced in Knapp, 245–46. For a detailed discussion of Smollett's attitudes toward Pitt see Knapp, "Smollett and the Elder Pitt," *Modern Language Notes* 59 (1944): 250–57.

107. Throughout his early career Pitt resolutely eschewed the financial perquisites of office; the most noteworthy instance of this probity was in the matter of the funds entrusted to him as paymaster of the forces. See below, vol. 1, n. 437.

108. Data on the inception and progress of the Voltaire edition are given in Chau Le-Thanh, "Tobias Smollett and *The Works of Mr. de Voltaire*, London, 1761–1769" (Ph.D. diss., University of Chicago, 1967).

109. See Knapp, 246–47. The *Briton* had ceased publication on 12 February; on Smollett's hopes for a pension or consulship see *Letters*, 110–11. Elizabeth Smollett died on 3 April.

110. See Lewis M. Knapp, "The Publication of Smollett's *Complete History* . . . and *Continuation*," *Library*, 4th ser., 16 (1935): 295–308.

111. Knapp, 248–49.

112. *Travels*, 2.

113. See below, vol. 2, n. 52.

114. *CR* 25 (February 1768): 116–26.

115. *Travels*, 233 (Letter 28, from Nice).

116. At the frantic insistence of George III, the duke of Cumberland (his uncle) was acting as intermediary with Pitt, trying to assemble a ministry that would satisfy the exigent Patriot. Only the prima-donna intransigence of Pitt's brother-in-law, Earl Temple, prevented a ministry dominated by Pitt from being formed in late June 1765. In July 1766 the desired administration finally came into being, with Pitt (now earl of Chatham) as lord privy seal. See Williams, 2:171–78; and see

below, vol. 2, nn. 410–26. On the first Rockingham administration in general, see Paul Langford, *The First Rockingham Administration* (London: Oxford University Press, 1973).

117. Eric Rothstein, "Scotophilia and *Humphry Clinker*: The Politics of Beggary, Bugs, and Buttocks," *University of Toronto Quarterly* 52 (1982): 68. In the summer of 1767 Lord Shelburne, then secretary of state for the southern department, had indicated to David Hume, who had approached him on Smollett's behalf, that he could not possibly bestow a consular appointment on a man "notorious for libelling." See Knapp, 271–72. Smollett, though safely in Bath at the time, was well aware of the danger of the Wilkite rioters in 1768; see *Letters*, 134–35.

118. See Knapp, 280–83; see also the review (by Allen T. Hazen and Lillian de la Torre) of a book by Francesco Cordasco, *Philological Quarterly* 31 (1952): 299–300; and see Foster, "*Atom*," 1046.

119. See below, p. 3 of the text; and see *Humphry Clinker*, the prefatory letter to "Henry Davis, Bookseller." Smollett's keen and abiding interest in the matter is evidenced by his review in 1765 of a book on the libel laws; see Basker, 228, 273.

120. On Smollett's trial and punishment for libeling Admiral Knowles see above, n. 36; and for his possible return to England, see the letter quoted above, pp. liv–lv. George II, the dukes of Cumberland and Newcastle, and Lords Hardwicke and Anson had all died by the end of 1768.

121. See Carl R. Kropf, "Libel and Satire in the Eighteenth Century," *Eighteenth-Century Studies* 8 (1974): 153–68.

122. See Rudé, 35, and see below, vol. 2, nn. 377–82; see also Foster, "Smollett's Pamphleteering Foe Shebbeare," 1088, and John Almon, *Biographical, Literary, and Political Anecdotes* (London, 1797), 1:373–74.

123. The Douglas case was the most celebrated lawsuit in eighteenth-century Scotland. Archibald Douglas, duke of Douglas, had died in 1761, leaving no direct heir. His sister, Lady Jane Douglas, had married Colonel John Stewart at the age of forty-eight (presumably therefore long past the age of childbearing), but two years after her marriage reported that she had given birth to twin sons, one of whom had died. The survivor, Archibald Stewart Douglas, laid claim to the duke's estate. The claim was contested on behalf of the young duke of Hamilton, surviving head of the male branch of the Douglas family, on the grounds that the younger Archibald was suppositious. In 1767 the Scottish Court of Session ruled in favor of Hamilton, but in February 1769 the House of Lords reversed the decision.

124. The original document is in the collection of the Philadelphia Historical Society, with whose permission it is transcribed.

125. For these views, vigorously expressed, see *Letters*, 136–38. Dr. Armstrong is probably referring to the most recent letter of Junius (18 March 1769), which was addressed to the duke of Grafton (then first lord of the treasury) and concerned royal pardons, therefore indirectly reflecting on the king's probity. Grafton is bitterly criticized for securing the pardon of a convicted murderer

while Wilkes remained unpardoned. See John Cannon, ed., *The Letters of Junius* (New York: Oxford University Press, 1978).

126. *CR* 27 (May 1769): 369. The marked copy of the earlier volumes of the *Critical*, with reviewers' names added in a contemporary hand, bears the shelfmark "F. H. PERS."

127. The original reviews, notices, and advertisements of the *Atom* are discussed in detail in Robert Adams Day, "The Authorship of the *Atom*."

128. See Day, "The Authorship of the *Atom*," 185–86, and Brack, "*The History and Adventures of an Atom*."

129. Notably Foster, Whitridge, and Martz, in the studies cited above, n. 1.

130. See below, vol. 1, nn. 764–76, and vol. 2, nn. 94, 205; see also Prickett, "The Political Writings," 243. Smollett's attitude toward Sackville was doubtless influenced by the fact that Sackville had been a military advisor and protégé of Bute; see McKelvey, 67–71, 103.

131. See below, vol. 2, nn. 182, 299, 300, 305, 395, 397.

132. For examples of this medical language see below, the text, pp. 15–16, 17, 45, 51, 54, 94, 127, and 128.

133. See Brack, "*The History and Adventures of an Atom*."

134. For an account of the affair see Rudé, 172–90. On the number "45" as inflammatory slogan see John Brewer, "The Number 45: A Wilkite Political Symbol," in Baxter, ed., *England's Rise to Greatness*, 349–80.

135. On the other hand, Almon did not invariably restrict his publishing activities to works whose views he espoused. In October 1768 he issued *The Present State of the Nation*, a controversial and widely discussed work by William Knox, colonial agent and advisor to Grenville, who advocated taxation *and* representation for the colonies and who justified slavery. On Knox and his views see Leland J. Bellot, *William Knox: The Life and Thought of an Eighteenth-Century Imperialist* (Austin: University of Texas Press, 1977).

136. Kearsly printed Number 45 of the *North Briton* and was an ardent partisan of Wilkes. See Rudé, 23–24.

137. In addition to the *Continuation* Robinson and Roberts were currently publishing Smollett's *Present State of All Nations*, which they announced in the *Public Advertiser*, 10, 12, 13 December 1768.

138. *London Magazine* 38 (May 1769): 262.

139. *London Chronicle*, 8–11 April 1769, p. 5, col. 1.

140. *Town and Country Magazine* 1 (May 1769): 269. A favorable notice was to be expected from the *Town and Country*; see above, n. 64.

141. *Gentleman's Magazine* 39 (April 1769): 205.

142. *Monthly Review* 40 (June 1769): 454–55. For the attribution to Hawkesworth see Benjamin C. Nangle, *The Monthly Review* (Oxford: Clarendon Press, 1934), 125.

143. *CR* 27 (May 1769): 362, 365, 369; and see above, n. 126.

144. *Political Register* 4 (1769): 389–90.

145. *Critical Memoirs of the Times* 1, no. 6 (10 April 1769): 505–11. The appearance of

this damaging review only ten days after the official publication date of the *Atom* might indicate either that it had been prepared in advance or that the reviewer was suspiciously eager to perform his task. The index to the bound volume lists "Dr. Smollett" as author of the *Atom*; the reviewer, if not Kearsly himself, may have been William Kenrick; see Basker, 70. (The *New Cambridge Bibliography of English Literature*, col. 1304, queries Kenrick's position as editor of *Critical Memoirs*.)

146. *Annual Register* for 1769, pt. 2, pp. 193–96. For the passage reprinted by Burke see below, the text, pp. 81–83.

147. *The Progress of Romance* (Colchester, 1785): 2:10.

148. This print is reproduced as frontispiece to the present edition from the original in the Huntington Library, with the permission of the trustees. For description and discussion of another copy see Vincent Carretta, "*An Abridgment of Mr. Pope's Essay on Man*: An Uncatalogued Print in the Library of Congress Collection," *Eighteenth-Century Life* 6 (1980), 102–5.

149. *The Miscellaneous Works of Tobias Smollett, M.D., with Memoirs of his Life and Writings*, 2d ed. (Edinburgh, 1800), 1:cxiv–xvi. The reader will note that Anderson confuses Hardwicke, whom Smollett detested, with Granville, and thinks that Smollett admired Mansfield; see below, vol. 1, nn. 213–26, 285–89, 442–45. "Dr. Moore" is Dr. John Moore, a distant cousin and close friend of Smollett, a prominent figure in Edinburgh intellectual circles, and a novelist of note. Moore had no doubts concerning Smollett's authorship of the *Atom*. The life of Smollett that prefaced various subsequent editions of the collected works is in effect a conflation of the accounts of Anderson and Moore; see Fred W. Boege, *Smollett's Reputation as a Novelist* (Princeton: Princeton University Press, 1947), 64–67.

150. The work was advertised at these prices in the *Whitehall Evening Post*, 13–15 April 1769.

151. Under terms of the Copyright Acts of 1709 and 1739, Irish booksellers could legally reprint and sell English books if they did not sell copies in England. See Richard C. Cole, "Smollett and the Eighteenth-Century Irish Book Trade," *PBSA* 69 (1975): 345–63.

152. The 1786 edition was a reprint in *The Novelists' Magazine*, vol. 21. Among editions containing the *Atom* were the six-volume collection by Anderson (1796); the *Works* (1797), edited by Dr. John Moore; the *Miscellaneous Works* (2d ed. of Anderson, 1800); *Miscellaneous Works*, 5 vols. (Edinburgh, 1809); a twelve-volume edition in 1824; the Bohn edition in one volume, 1843; Roscoe's edition, 1844; *Works*, ed. James P. Browne, 8 vols. (London: Bickers & Son, 1872); a six-volume edition prefaced by Sir Walter Scott's life of Smollett (New York: Routledge, 1884); *Works*, ed. George Saintsbury, 12 vols. (London and Philadelphia, 1899–1903); in the twentieth century the twelve-volume editions of Henley, Seccombe, and Maynadier; and lastly the Shakespeare Head Edition, 11 vols. (Oxford: Blackwell, 1925–26).

CHRONOLOGY

The entries below are limited to public events alluded to in the *Atom*, and to events in Smollett's life connected with the sources and composition of the work. For further details of Smollett's chronology consult Robert Donald Spector, *Tobias George Smollett*, rev. ed. (New York: Twayne, 1989), xiii–xvii.

The Atom	Smollett's Life

1740

DEC. Frederick of Prussia invades Silesia; War of the Austrian Succession begins.

1741

APR. Frederick conquers and annexes Silesia.

1745

AUG. Prince Charles Edward Stuart lands in Scotland; rebellion of "the 'Forty-Five."

1746

APR. Rebellion finally crushed at battle of Culloden; duke of Cumberland's punitive measures against the Scots.

1748

Peace of Aix-la-Chapelle ends War of the Austrian Succession.

The Atom Smollett's Life

1753

Lord Hardwicke's Marriage
Act.
The French begin to fortify
posts in the Ohio Valley and
on Lake Erie.

JUNE Jewish Naturalization Act
(repealed in December).

1754

MAR. Death of Henry Pelham, first
lord of the treasury; his
brother, the duke of
Newcastle, succeeds him.

JULY Major George Washington, in
an expedition against French
forts, defeated at Great
Meadows.

1755

JUNE Admiral Boscawen attacks
French fleet at mouth of Saint
Lawrence; captures two ships.

JULY General Braddock's defeat in
the Ohio valley.

SEPT. General Johnson defeats
Baron Dieskau's French
troops at Lake George.

NOV. Britain concludes treaty with
Russia for troops to protect
Hanover.

1756

JAN. Convention of Westminster:
Britain and Prussia unite to
prevent incursions into
Germany by foreign powers.

The Atom   Smollett's Life

MAR. Begins publication of *Critical Review*.

MAY Admiral Byng's inconclusive
     engagement with the French
     fleet off Minorca.

MAY–

JUNE Britain and France declare
     war.

JUNE General Blakeney surrenders
     Port Mahon (and Minorca) to
     the French.

AUG. Forts Oswego and Ontario fall
     to the French.

SEPT. Frederick invades Saxony,
     takes Dresden, Leipzig.

OCT.–

NOV. Newcastle resigns; Pitt-
     Devonshire ministry formed.

1757

JAN. Admiral Byng sentenced to be   Publishes three volumes of
     shot, recommended to mercy.   *Complete History of England.*
     Austrian empire declares war
     on Prussia.

MAR. Execution of Byng.

APR. Pitt dismissed.
     Cumberland goes to Germany
     with the Army of
     Observation.

MAY Frederick takes Prague.

JUNE Pitt-Newcastle ministry
     formed.
     Austrian forces defeat
     Frederick at Kolin.
     Robert Clive defeats the
     French at Plassey (India).

                                                        (continued)

The Atom	Smollett's Life

JULY   Cumberland defeated by the French at Hastenbeck.

SEPT.   Convention of Klosterseven (not honored): Cumberland's forces to be disbanded.
Prince Ferdinand of Brunswick takes command of the Army of Observation.

SEPT.–

OCT.   Abortive amphibious expedition against Rochefort.

NOV.   Frederick defeats Austrian and Imperial troops at Rossbach.

DEC.   Frederick defeats Austrians at Leuthen.

1758

APR.   First subsidy to Prussia under the Convention of Westminster.

                                     Revises *Complete History*; fourth and final volume published.

                                  MAY   Review of pamphlet by Admiral Knowles.

JUNE   Thomas Cumming's fleet takes Goree (Senegal).
Abortive British expedition to Saint Malo.
Frederick defeats the French at Krefeld.

                                  JUNE   Sued for libel by Knowles.

JULY   General Abercromby defeated at Ticonderoga.

AUG.   Frederick defeats the Russians at Zorndorf.

AUG.–

SEPT.   General Bligh demolishes Cherbourg, is routed at Saint Cas.

The Atom	Smollett's Life

OCT. Austrians defeat Frederick at
Hochkirch.

1759

French invasion fleet threatens
England.

Begins editorial work on
"Modern Part" of *Universal
History*; work continues
through 1765.

FEB. General Hopson fails to take
Martinique; dies.

MAY Hopson's troops take
Guadeloupe.

JULY Russians defeat Prussian army
at Züllichau.

JULY–
AUG. French fleet crippled by
British at Le Havre, Lagos.

AUG. Allied troops defeat French at
Minden.
Russians, Austrians defeat
Frederick at Kunersdorf.

SEPT. General Wolfe takes Quebec;
killed in action.

NOV. Final defeat of French fleet at
Quiberon Bay.

1760

JAN. With Goldsmith, starts *British
Magazine*.

FEB. Captain Elliot defeats
remnants of French fleet,
preventing invasion of Ireland.

MAY *Continuation of the Complete
History* begins to appear in
weekly parts.

(*continued*)

The Atom	Smollett's Life
JULY Frederick defeated at Korbach.	
AUG. Frederick defeats Russians at Liegnitz.	
SEPT. Surrender of all French forces in Canada.	
OCT. Death of George II; his grandson succeeds as George III.	
NOV. Frederick defeats Austrians at Torgau.	NOV. Trial and imprisonment for libel.

1761

	Begins edition of Voltaire (25 volumes; to 1765).
JAN.–	
FEB. Final defeat of French forces in India.	FEB. Released from King's Bench Prison.
MAR. Lord Bute appointed a secretary of state.	
JUNE British capture Belle Isle off the French mainland.	
SEPT. George III marries Charlotte of Mecklenburg-Strelitz; their coronation.	
OCT. Pitt resigns; receives pension, title for his wife.	
OCT.–	
DEC. Austrians invade and take much of Prussia.	
NOV. Lord Mayor's feast; king and queen slighted.	

1762

JAN. Empress Elizabeth of Russia dies; Russian hostilities against Frederick cease.	Unsuccessfully applies for consulship.

The Atom	Smollett's Life
Britain discontinues Prussian subsidy.	
Britain declares war against Spain.	
FEB. Martinique surrenders to British.	
MAY Newcastle resigns as first lord of the treasury; Bute replaces him.	MAY First number of *Briton*.
Peace confirmed between Russia and Prussia.	
AUG. Havana surrenders to British fleet.	
SEPT. British capture Manila.	
NOV. Draft of Peace of Paris signed. British-French Continental hostilities cease.	

1763

FEB. Parliament ratifies Peace of Paris.	FEB. Last number of *Briton*.
Peace of Hubertusberg between Prussia and Austria; end of Seven Years' War.	
APR. Bute resigns; Granville ministry formed.	APR. Death of daughter Elizabeth.
Wilkes publishes No. 45 of the *North Briton*.	
	JUNE Departure for France.

1764

JAN. Wilkes, who has fled to Paris, outlawed by Commons.	Residence in Nice; visits Italy at year's end. Work on *Atom*, *Travels*.
MAR. Stamp Act passed.	

(continued)

The Atom	Smollett's Life

1765

JAN.–
MAR. Serious illness of George III.

MAY   Regency Bill.

JULY Administrative chaos;   JULY? Returns to England; travels
      Rockingham ministry formed.   for health to Bath and
                                            Bristol.
                                     OCT. Fifth and final volume of
                                            Continuation appears.

1766

MAR. Pitt attacks Stamp Act; it is   Visits Bath and Scotland
      repealed.

                                     MAY   *Travels* published.

JULY Pitt created earl of Chatham;
      forms ministry.

SEPT. Embargo on export of grain.

1767

MAR. Chatham, in acute depression,   Final and unsuccessful
      quits public life for two years.   application for consulship.

JUNE Townshend Act (import duties
      for colonies).

1768

MAR. General election; Wilkes   *Present State of All Nations*
      elected three times by   appears in weekly parts.
      Middlesex, though Parliament
      declares him incapable of
      sitting.

MAY   Massacre of Saint George's
      Fields; widespread unrest.

                                     SEPT.–
                                     OCT.? Final departure from
                                            England; travels to Italy;
                                            resides in Pisa.

The Atom   Smollett's Life

DEC. *Atom* published by John
Almon.

1769

APR. *Atom* published by Robinson
and Roberts.

OCT. At Leghorn.

1770

Resides at Leghorn.

1771

SEPT. Death of Smollett.

The History and Adventures of an Atom

VOLUME ONE

THE
HISTORY
AND
ADVENTURES
OF AN
ATOM.

IN TWO VOLUMES.

VOL. I.

LONDON:

Printed for J. ALMON, oppofite Burlington-Houfe,
in Piccadilly.   MDCCLXIX.

Title Page of First Edition, Volume 1.
(The Rosenbach Museum & Library, Philadelphia.)

ADVERTISEMENT

FROM THE

PUBLISHER TO THE READER.

In these ticklish times, it may be necessary to give such an account of the following sheets, as will exempt me from the plague of prosecution.[1]

On the 7th of March, in the present year 1748,[2] they were offered to me for sale, by a tall thin woman, about the age of threescore, dressed in a gown of Bombazine,[3] with a cloak and bonnet of black silk, both a little the worse for the wear.—She called herself Dorothy Hatchet, spinster, of the parish of Old-street,[4] administratrix of Mr. Nathaniel Peacock,[5] who died in the said parish on the fifth day of last April, and lies buried in the church-yard of Islington,[6] in the north-west corner, where his grave is distinguished by a monumental board inscribed with the following tristich:[7]

> *Hic, hæc, hoc,*[8]
> Here lies the block
> Of old Nathaniel Peacock.

In this particular, any person whatever may satisfy himself, by taking an afternoon's walk to Islington, where, at the White House,[9] he may recreate and refresh himself with excellent tea and hot rolls for so small a charge as eight-pence.

As to the MS, before I would treat for it, I read it over attentively, and found it contained divers curious particulars of a foreign history, without any allusion to, or resemblance with, the transactions of these times. I likewise turned over to Kempfer[10] and the Universal History,[11] and found in their several accounts of Japan, many of the names and much of the matter specified in the following sheets. Finally, that I might run no risque of misconstruction, I had recourse to an eminent chamber-council[12] of my acquaintance, who diligently perused the whole, and declared it was no more actionable than the Vision of Ezekiel, or the Lamentations of Jeremiah the prophet.[13] Thus assured, I purchased the copy,[14] which I now present in print, with my best respects, to the Courteous Reader, being his very humble servant,

Bucklersbury.[15]   S. ETHERINGTON.[16]

Vivant Rex & Regina.[17]

THE
History and Adventures
OF AN ATOM.

The Editor's Declaration.

I Nathaniel Peacock, of the parish of St. Giles,[18] haberdasher[19] and author, solemnly declare, That on the third of last August, sitting alone in my study, up three pair of stairs,[20] between the hours of eleven and twelve at night, meditating upon the uncertainty of sublunary enjoyment,[21] I heard a shrill, small voice,[22] seemingly proceeding from a chink or crevice in my own pericranium,[23] call distinctly three times, "Nathaniel Peacock, Nathaniel Peacock, Nathaniel Peacock." Astonished, yea, even affrighted, at this citation,[24] I replied in a faultering tone, "In the name of the Lord, what art thou?" Thus adjured,[25] the voice answered and said, "I am an atom." I was now thrown into a violent perturbation of spirit; for I never could behold an atomy[26] without fear and trembling,[27] even when I knew it was no more than a composition of dry bones; but the conceit[28] of being in presence of an atomy informed with spirit, that is, animated by a ghost or goblin, increased my terrors exceedingly. I durst not lift up mine eyes, lest I should behold an apparition more dreadful than the handwriting on the wall.[29] My knees knocked together: my teeth chattered: mine hair bristled up so as to raise a cotton night-cap from the scalp: my tongue cleaved to the roof of my mouth: my temples were bedewed with a cold sweat.[30]—Verily, I was for a season entranced.[31]

At length, by the blessing of God, I recollected myself, and cried aloud, "Avaunt Satan, in the name of the Father, Son, and Holy Ghost." "White-livered caitiff!"[32] said the voice, (with a peculiar tartness of pronunciation) "what art thou afraid of, that thou shouldest thus tremble, and diffuse around thee such an unsavoury odour?[33]—What thou hearest is within thee—is part of thyself. I am one of those atoms, or constituent particles of matter, which can neither be annihilated, divided, nor impaired: the different arrangements of us atoms compose all the variety of objects and essences which nature exhibits, or art[34] can obtain. Of the same shape, substance, and quality, are the component particles, that harden in rock, and flow in water; that blacken in the negro, and brighten in the diamond; that exhale from a rose, and steam from a dunghill.[35] Even now, ten millions of atoms were dispersed in air by that odoriferous gale,[36] which the commotion of thy fear produced; and I can foresee that one of them will be consolidated in a fibre of the olfactory nerve, belonging to a celebrated beauty, whose nostril is excoriated by the immoderate use of plain Spanish.[37] Know, Nathaniel, that we atoms are singly endued with such efficacy of reason, as cannot be expected in an aggregate body, where we croud and squeeze and embarrass[38] one another. Yet, those ideas which we singly possess, we cannot communicate, except once in a thousand years, and then only, when we fill a certain place in the pineal gland[39] of a human creature, the very station which I now maintain in thine.—For the benefit of you miserable mortals, I am determined to promulge[40] the history of one period, during which I underwent some strange revolutions[41] in the empire of Japan, and was conscious of some political anecdotes now to be divulged for the instruction of British ministers.[42] Take up the pen, therefore, and write what I shall unfold."

By this time my first apprehension vanished; but another fear, almost as terrible, usurped its place. I began to think myself insane, and concluded that the voice was no other than the fantastic undulation of a disturbed brain.[43] I therefore preferred[44] an earnest orison[45] at the throne of grace, that I might be restored to the fruition[46] of my right understanding and judgment. "O incredulous wretch, (exclaimed the voice) I will now convince thee that this is no phantasma or hideous dream.[47]—Answer me, dost thou know the meaning and derivation of the word atom?" I replied, "No, verily!" "Then I will tell thee, (said the voice) thou shalt write it down without delay, and consult the curate of the parish on the same subject. If his explanation and mine agree, thou will then be firmly persuaded that I am an actual, independent existence; and that this address is not the vague delirium of a disordered brain. *Atomos* is a Greek word, signifying an indivisible particle, derived from *alpha* privativa, and *temno* to cut."[48]

I marvelled much at this injunction, which, however, I literally obeyed; and next morning sallied forth to visit the habitation of the curate; but in going thither, it was my hap to encounter a learned physician of my acquaintance,[49] who hath read all the books that ever were published in any nation, or language: to him I refered for the derivation of the word atom. He paused a little, threw up his eyes to heaven, stroaked his chin with great solemnity, and hemming three times, "Greek, Sir, (said he) is more familiar to me than my native tongue.—I have conversed, Sir, with Homer and Plato, Hesiod and Theophrastus,[50] Herodotus, Thucydides, Hippocrates, Aretæus,[51] Pindar, and Sophocles, and all the poets and historians of antiquity. Sir, my library cost me two thousand pounds. I have spent as much more in making experiments; and you must know that I have discovered certain chemical specifics,[52] which I would not divulge for fifty times the sum.—As for the word *atomos*, or *atime*, it signifies a scoundrel, Sir, or as it were, Sir, a thing of no estimation. It is derived, Sir, from *alpha* privativa, and *time*, honour. Hence, we call a skeleton an atomy, because, Sir, the bones are, as it were, dishonoured by being stripped of their cloathing, and exposed in their nakedness."

I was sorely vexed at this interpretation, and my apprehension of lunacy recurred: nevertheless, I proceeded in my way to the lodgings of the curate, and desired his explanation, which tallied exactly with what I had written. At my return to my own house, I ascended to my study, asked pardon of my internal monitor; and taking pen, ink, and paper, sat down to write what it dictated, in the following strain.

"It was in the æra of* Foggien,[53] one thousand years ago, that fate determined I should exist in the empire of Japan, where I underwent a great number of vicissitudes, till, at length, I was enclosed in a grain of rice, eaten by a Dutch mariner at Firando,[54] and, becoming a particle of his body, brought to the Cape of Good Hope. There I was discharged in a scorbutic[55] dysentery, taken up in a heap of soil to manure a garden, raised to vegetation in a sallad, devoured by an English supercargo, assimilated to a certain organ of his body, which, at his return to London, being diseased in consequence of impure contact, I was again separated, with a considerable portion of putrefied flesh, thrown upon a dunghill, gobbled up, and digested by a duck, of which duck your father, Ephraim Peacock, having eaten plentifully at a feast of the cordwainers,[56] I was mixed with his circulating juices, and finally fixed in the principal part of that animalcule,[57] which, in process of time, expanded itself into thee, Nathaniel Peacock.

Having thus particularized my transmigrations since my conveyance from Japan, I shall return thither, and unfold some curious particulars of state-intrigue, carried on during the short period, the history of which I mean to

*The history of Japan is divided into three different æras, of which Foggien is the most considerable.

record: I need not tell thee, that the empire of Japan consists of three large islands;[58] or that the people, who inhabit them, are such inconsistent, capricious animals,[59] that one would imagine they were created for the purpose of ridicule. Their minds are in continual agitation, like a shuttlecock tossed to and fro, in order to divert the demons of philosophy and folly. A Japonese, without the intervention of any visible motive, is, by turns, merry and pensive, superficial and profound, generous and illiberal, rash and circumspect, courageous and fearful, benevolent and cruel. They seem to have no fixed principle of action, no certain plan of conduct, no effectual rudder to steer them through the voyage of life; but to be hurried down the rapid tide of each revolving whim, or driven, the sport of every gust of passion that happens to blow. A Japonese will sing at a funeral, and sigh at a wedding; he will this hour talk ribaldry with a prostitute, and the next immerse himself in the study of metaphysics or theology. In favour of one stranger, he will exert all the virtues of hospitality; against another he will exercise all the animosity of the most sordid prejudice: one minute sees him hazarding his all on the success of the most extravagant project; another beholds him hesitating in lending a few copans* [60] to his friend on undeniable security. To-day, he is afraid of paring his corns; to-morrow, he scruples not to cut his own throat. At one season, he will give half his fortune to the poor; at another, he will not bestow the smallest pittance to save his brother from indigence and distress. He is elated to insolence by the least gleam of success; he is dejected to despondence by the slightest turn of adverse fortune. One hour he doubts the best established truths; the next, he swallows the most improbable fiction. His praise and his censure is what a wise man would choose to avoid, as evils equally pernicious: the first is generally raised without foundation, and carried to such extravagance, as to expose the object to the ridicule of mankind; the last is often unprovoked, yet usually inflamed to all the rage of the most malignant persecution. He will extol above Alexander the great, a petty officer who robs a hen-roost; and damn to infamy, a general for not performing impossibilities. The same man whom he yesterday flattered with the most fulsome adulation, he will to-morrow revile with the most bitter abuse; and, at the turning of a straw, take into his bosom the very person whom he has formerly defamed as the most perfidious rascal.

The Japanese value themselves much upon their constitution, and are very clamorous about the words liberty and property;[61] yet, in fact, the only lib-

---

*Copan is a gold coin used in Japan, value about 43 shillings.

erty they enjoy is to get drunk whenever they please, to revile the government, and quarrel with one another. With respect to their property, they are the tamest animals in the world; and, if properly managed, undergo, without wincing, such impositions, as no other nation in the world would bear. In this particular, they may be compared to an ass, that will crouch under the most unconscionable burthen, provided you scratch his long ears, and allow him to bray his belly-full. They are so practicable,[62] that they have suffered their pockets to be drained, their veins to be emptied, and their credit to be cracked, by the most bungling administrations, to gratify the avarice, pride, and ambition, of the most sordid and contemptible sovereigns, that ever sate upon the throne.

The methods used for accomplishing these purposes are extremely simple. You have seen a dancing bear incensed to a dangerous degree of rage, and all at once appeased by firing a pistol over his nose. The Japonese, even in their most ferocious moods, when they denounce vengeance against the Cuboy, or minister,[63] and even threaten the throne itself; are easily softened into meekness and condescension. A set of tall fellows,[64] hired for the purpose, tickle them under the noses with long straws, into a gentle convulsion, during which they shut their eyes, and smile, and quietly suffer their pockets to be turned inside out. Nay, what is still more remarkable, the ministry is in possession of a pipe, or rather bullock's horn, which being sounded to a particular pitch,[65] has such an effect on the ears and understanding of the people, that they allow their pockets to be picked with their eyes open, and are bribed to betray their own interests with their own money, as easily as if the treasure had come from the remotest corner of the globe. Notwithstanding these capricious peculiarities, the Japonese are become a wealthy and powerful people, partly from their insular situation, and partly from a spirit of commercial adventure, sustained by all the obstinacy of perseverance, and conducted by repeated flashes of good sense, which almost incessantly gleam through the chaos of their absurdities.

Japan was originally governed by monarchs who possessed an absolute power, and succeeded by hereditary right, under the title of Dairo.[66] But in the beginning of the period Foggien, this emperor became a cypher, and the whole administration devolved into the hands of the prime minister, or Cuboy, who now exercises all the power and authority, leaving the trappings of royalty to the inactive Dairo.[67] The prince, who held the reins of government in the short period which I intend to record, was not a lineal descendant[68] of the antient Dairos, the immediate succession having failed, but sprung from a collateral branch which was invited from a foreign country in the person of *Bupo*,[69] in honour of whom the Japonese erected Fakkubasi,* [70] or the temple of the white horse.[71] So much were all his successors devoted to the culture[72] of this idol, which, by the bye, was made of the vilest materials, that, in order to enrich his shrine, they impoverished the whole empire, yet still[73] with the connivance, and by the influence of the Cuboy, who gratified this sordid passion[74] or superstition of the Dairo, with a view to prevent him from employing his attention on matters of greater consequence.

Nathaniel, You have heard of the transmigration of souls, a doctrine avowed by one Pythagoras, a philosopher of Crotona.[75] This doctrine, though discarded and reprobated by christians, is nevertheless sound, and orthodox, I affirm on the integrity of an atom. Further I shall not explain myself on this subject, though I might with safety set the convocation[76] and the whole hierarchy at defiance, knowing, as I do, that it is not in their power to make me bate[77] one particle of what I advance: or, if they should endeavour to reach me through your organs, and even condemn you to the stake at Smithfield,[78] verily, I say unto thee,[79] I should be a gainer by the next remove.[80] I should shift my quarters from a very cold and empty tenement, which I now occupy in the brain of a poor haberdasher, to the nervous plexus situated at the mouth of the stomach of a fat alderman fed with venison and turtle.[81]

But to return to Pythagoras, whom one of your wise countrymen denominated *Peter Gore, the wise-acre* of Croton,[82] you must know that philosopher was a type, which hath not yet been fully unveiled.[83] That he taught the metempsychosis, explained the nature and property of harmonies, demonstrated the motion of the earth, discovered the elements of geometry and arithmetic, enjoined his disciples silence, and abstained from eating any thing that was ever informed by the breath of life; are circumstances known to all the learned world:[84] but his veneration for beans, which cost him his life,[85] his golden thigh, his adventures in the character of a courtezan, his golden verses, his epithet of αὐτὸς ἔφα, the fable of his being born of a virgin, and his descent into hell, are mysteries in which some of the most important truths are concealed.[86]—Between friends, honest Nathaniel, I myself constituted part of that sage's body; and I could say a great deal—but there is a time for all things.—I shall only observe, that Philip Tessier[87] had some reason for supposing Pythagoras to have been a monk; and there are shrewd hints in Meyer's dissertation, *Utrum Pythagoras Judæus fuit, an monachus Carmelita.*[88]

*Vid. Kempfer, Lib. i.

Waving[89] these intricate discussions for the present, (though I cannot help disclosing that Pythagoras was actually circumcised[90]) know, Peacock, that the metempsychosis, or transmigration of souls, is the method which nature and fate constantly pursue, in animating the creatures produced on the face of the earth; and this process, with some variation, is such as the eleusinian mysteries[91] imported, and such as you have read in Dryden's translation of the sixth book of Virgil's Æneid.[92] The Gods have provided a great magazine or diversorium,[93] to which the departed souls of all animals repair at their dismission from the body. Here they are bathed in the waters of oblivion, until they retain no memory of the scenes through which they have passed; but they still preserve their original crasis[94] and capacity. From this repository, all new created beings are supplied with souls; and these souls transmigrate into different animals, according to the pleasure of the great disposer. For example, my good friend Nathaniel Peacock, your own soul has within these hundred years threaded a goat, a spider,[95] and a bishop; and its next stage will be the carcase of a brewer's horse.

In what manner we atoms come by these articles of intelligence, whether by intuition, or communication of ideas,[96] it is not necessary that you should conceive—Suffice it to say, the gods were merry on the follies of mankind, and Mercury[97] undertook to exhibit a mighty nation, ruled and governed by the meanest intellects that could be found in the repository of pre-existing spirits. He laid the scene in Japan, about the middle of the period Foggien, when that nation was at peace with all her neighbours.[98] Into the mass, destined to sway the sceptre, he infused, at the very article[99] of conception, the spirit, which in course of strangulation had been expelled *a posteriori*[100] from a goose, killed on purpose to regale the appetite of the mother.[101] The animalcule,[102] thus inspired,[103] was born, and succeeded to the throne, under the name of Got-hama-baba.[104] His whole life and conversation was no other than a repetition of the humours he had displayed in his last character.[105] He was rapacious, shallow, hot-headed, and perverse; in point of understanding, just sufficient to appear in public without a slavering bib;[106] imbued with no knowledge, illumed by no sentiment, and warmed with no affection; except a blind attachment to the worship of Fakku-basi,[107] which seemed indeed to be a disease in his constitution. His heart was meanly selfish, and his disposition altogether unprincely.

Of all his recreations, that which he delighted in most, was kicking the breech of his Cuboy, or prime minister, an exercise which he every day performed in private.[108] It was therefore necessary that a Cuboy should be found to undergo this diurnal operation without repining. This was a circum-

stance foreseen and provided for by Mercury, who, a little after the conception of Got-hama-baba, impregnated the ovum of a future Cuboy,[109] and
implanted in it a changling soul,[110] which had successively passed through
the bodies of an ass, a dottril,[111] an apple-woman, and a cow-boy.[112] It was
diverting enough to see the rejoicings with which the birth of this Quanbuku* [113] was celebrated; and still more so to observe the marks of fond
admiration in the parents, as the soul of the cow-boy proceeded to expand
itself in the young Cuboy. This is a species of diversion we atoms often enjoy.
We at different times[114] behold the same spirit,[115] hunted down in a hare,
and cried up in an Hector;[116] fawning in a prostitute, and bribing in a minister; breaking forth in a whistle at the plough, and in a sermon from the
pulpit; impelling a hog to the stye, and a counsellor to the cabinet; prompting
a shoe-boy to filch, and a patriot to harangue;[117] squinting in a goat, and
smiling in a matron.

Tutors of all sorts were provided betimes for the young Quanbuku, but his
genius rejected all cultivation; at least the crops it produced were barren and
ungrateful.[118] He was distinguished by the name of Fika-kaka,[119] and
caressed as the heir of an immense fortune.[120] Nay, he was really considered
as one of the most hopeful young Quanbukus in the empire of Japan; for his
want of ideas was attended with a total absence of pride, insolence, or any
other disagreeable vice: indeed his character was founded upon negatives.[121]
He had no understanding, no œconomy,[122] no courage, no industry, no
steadiness, no discernment, no vigour, no retention.[123] He was reputed generous and good-humoured; but was really profuse,[124] chicken-hearted, negli-
gent, fickle, blundering, weak, and leaky.[125] All these qualifications were
agitated by an eagerness, haste, and impatience, that compleated the most
ludicrous composition, which human nature ever produced. He appeared
always in hurry and confusion, as if he had lost his wits in the morning, and
was in quest of them all day.[126]—Let me whisper a secret to you, my good
friend Peacock. All this bustle and trepidation proceeded from a hollowness
in the brain, forming a kind of eddy, in which his animal spirits[127] were
hurried about in a perpetual swirl. Had it not been for this *Lusus Naturæ*,[128]
the circulation would not have been sufficient for the purposes of animal life.
Had the whole world been searched by the princes thereof, it would not have
produced another to have matched this half-witted original,[129] to whom the
administration of a mighty empire was wholly consigned.[130] Notwithstanding all the care that was taken of his education, Fika-kaka never could com-

*Quanbuku is a dignity of the first order in Japan.

prehend any art or science, except that of dancing bareheaded among the Bonzas at the great festival of Cambadoxi.[131] The extent of his knowledge in arithmetic went no farther than the numeration of his ten fingers. In history, he had no idea of what preceded a certain treaty with the Chinese,[132] in the reign of queen Syko,[133] who died within his own remembrance; and was so ignorant of geography,[134] that he did not know that his native country was surrounded by the sea. No system of morality could he ever understand; and of the fourteen sects of religion[135] that are permitted in Japan, the only discipline he could imbibe was a superstitious devotion for Fakku-basi, the temple of the white horse.[136] This, indeed, was neither the fruit of doctrine, nor the result of reason; but a real instinct, implanted in his nature for fulfilling the ends of providence. His person was extremely aukward; his eye vacant, though alarmed;[137] his speech thick, and embarrassed;[138] his utterance ungraceful; and his meaning perplexed.[139] With much difficulty he learned to write his own name, and that of the Dairo; and picked up a smattering of the Chinese language, which was sometimes used at court.[140] In his youth, he freely conversed with women; but, as he advanced in age, he placed his chief felicity in the delights of the table. He hired cooks from China at an enormous expence,[141] and drank huge quantities of the strong liquor distilled from rice, which, by producing repeated intoxication, had an unlucky effect upon his brain, that was naturally of a loose flimsy texture.[142] The immoderate use of this potation was likewise said to have greatly impaired his retentive faculty; inasmuch as he was subject upon every extraordinary emotion of spirit, to an involuntary discharge from the last of the intestines.[143]

Such was the character of Fika-kaka, entitled by his birth to a prodigious estate,[144] as well as to the honours of Quanbuku, the first hereditary dignity in the empire. In consequence of his high station, he was connected with all the great men[145] in Japan, and used to the court from his infancy. Here it was he became acquainted with young Got-hama-baba, his future sovereign; and their souls being congenial,[146] they soon contracted an intimacy, which endured for life. They were like twin particles of matter, which having been divorced from one another by a most violent shock, had floated many thousand years in the ocean of the universe, till at length meeting by accident, and approaching within the spheres of each other's attraction, they rush together with an eager embrace, and continue united ever after.[147]

The favour of the sovereign, added to the natural influence arising from a vast fortune and great alliances, did not fail to elevate Fika-kaka to the most eminent offices of the state,[148] until, at length, he attained to the dignity of Cuboy, or chief-minister,[149] which virtually comprehends all the rest. Here then was the strangest phænomenon that ever appeared in the political world. A statesman without capacity, or the smallest tincture of human learning; a secretary who could not write;[150] a financier who did not understand the multiplication table; and the treasurer of a vast empire, who never could balance accounts with his own butler.[151]

He was no sooner, for the diversion of the Gods, promoted to the Cuboy-ship, than his vanity was pampered with all sorts of adulation. He was in magnificence[152] extolled above the first Meckaddo, or line of emperors, to whom divine honours had been paid; equal in wisdom to Tensio-dai-sin, the first founder of the Japanese monarchy; braver than Whey-vang, of the dynasty of Chew; more learned than Jacko, the chief pontiff of Japan; more liberal than Shi-wang-ti, who was possessed of the universal medicine; and more religious than *Bupo*, alias *Kobot*, who, from a foreign country, brought with him, on a white horse, a book called Kio, containing the mysteries of his religion.[153]

But, by none was he more cultivated than by the Bonzas or clergy,[154] especially those of the university Frenoxena,* [155] so renowned for their learning, sermons, and oratory, who actually chose him their supreme director,[156] and every morning adored him with a very singular rite of worship.[157] This attachment was the more remarkable, as Fika-kaha was known to favour the sect of Nem-buds-ju,[158] who distinguished themselves by the ceremony of circumcision. Some malicious people did not scruple to whisper about, that he himself had privately undergone the operation:[159] but these, to my certain knowledge, were the suggestions of falshood and slander. A slight scarification,[160] indeed, it was once necessary to make, on account of his health; but this was no ceremony of any religious worship. The truth was this. The Nem-buds-ju, being few in number, and generally hated by the whole nation, had recourse to the protection of Fika-kaka, which they obtained for a valuable consideration.[161] Then a law was promulgated in their favour; a step which was so far from exciting the jealousy of the Bonzas, that there was not above three, out of one hundred and fifty-nine thousand, that opened their lips in disapprobation of the measure.[162] Such were the virtue and moderation of the Bonzas, and so loth were they to disoblige their great director Fika-kaka.

What rendered the knot of connection between the Dairo Got-hama-baba, and this Cuboy altogether indissoluble, was a singular circumstance, which I shall now explain. Fika-kika not only devoted himself intirely to the gratifica-

*Vid. Hist. Eccles. Japan. Vol. I.

tion of his master's prejudices and rapacity, even when they interfered the most with the interest and reputation of Japan; but he also submitted personally to his capricious humours with the most placid resignation.[163] He presented his posteriors to be kicked as regularly as the day revolved; and presented them not barely with submission, but with all the appearance of fond desire: and truly this diurnal exposure was attended with such delectation as he never enjoyed in any other attitude.

To explain this matter, I must tell thee, Peacock, that Fika-kaka was from his infancy afflicted with an itching of the podex,[164] which the learned Dr. Woodward[165] would have termed *immanis αιδοίων pruritus*.[166] That great naturalist would have imputed it to a redundancy of cholicky salts, got out of the stomach and guts into the blood, and thrown upon these parts, and he would have attempted to break their colluctations with oil, &c.[167] but I, who know the real causes of this disorder, smile at these whims of philosophy.

Be that as it may, certain it is, all the most eminent physicians in Japan were consulted about this strange tickling and tingling, and among these the celebrated Fan-sey,[168] whose spirit afterwards informed[169] the body of Rabelais. This experienced leech, having prescribed a course of cathartics, balsamics, and sweeteners,[170] on the supposition that the blood was tainted with a scorbutical itch; at length found reason to believe that the disease was local. He therefore tried the method of gentle friction: for which purpose he used almost the very same substances which were many centuries after applied by Gargantua[171] to his own posteriors; such as a night cap, a pillow-bier, a slipper, a poke, a pannier, a beaver, a hen, a cock, a chicken, a calf-skin, a hareskin, a pigeon, a cormorant, a lawyer's bag, a lamprey, a coif, a lure, nay even a goose's neck, without finding that *volupté merifique au trou de cul*, which was the portion of the son of Grangousier.[172] In short, there was nothing that gave Fika-kaka such respite from this tormenting titillation as did smearing the parts with thick cream, which was afterwards licked up by the rough tongue of a boar-cat.[173] But the administration of this remedy was once productive of a disagreeable incident. In the mean time, the distemper gaining ground became so troublesome, that the unfortunate Quanbuku was incessantly in the fidgets, and ran about distracted, cackling like a hen in labour.[174]

The source of all this misfortune was the juxta position of two atoms quarrelling for precedency, in this the Cuboy's seat of honour. Their pressing and squeezing and elbowing and jostling, tho' of no effect in discomposing one another, occasioned all this irritation and titillation in the posteriors of Fika-kaka—What! dost thou mutter, Peacock? dost thou presume to question my veracity? now by the indivisible rotundity of an atom, I have a good mind, caitiff, to raise such a buzzing commotion in thy glandula pinealis,[175] that thou shalt run distracted over the face of the earth, like Io when she was stung by Juno's gadfly![176] What! thou who hast been wrapt from the cradle in visions of mystery and revelation,[177] swallowed impossibilities like lamb's wool,[178] and digested doctrines harder than iron three times quenched in the Ebro![179] thou to demur at what I assert upon the evidence and faith of my own consciousness and consistency!—Oh! you capitulate: well, then beware of a relapse—you know a relapsed heretic finds no mercy.

I say, while Fika-kaka's podex was the scene of contention between two turbulent atoms, I had the honour to be posted immediately under the nail of the Dairo's great toe, which happened one day to itch more than usual for occupation. The Cuboy presenting himself at that instant, and turning his face from his master, Got-hama-baba performed the exercise with such uncommon vehemence, that first his slipper, and then his toe-nail flew off, after having made a small breach in the perineum[180] of Fika-kaka. By the same effort, I was divorced from the great toe of the sovereign, and lodged near the great gut[181] of his minister, exactly in the interstice between the two hostile particles, which were thus in some measure restrained from wrangling; though it was not in my power to keep the peace entirely. Nevertheless, Fika-kaka's torture was immediately suspended; and he was even seized with an orgasm of pleasure, analogous to that which characterises the extacy of love.

Think not, however, Peacock, that I would adduce this circumstance as a proof that pleasure and pain are meer[182] relations, which can exist only as they are contrasted. No: pleasure and pain are simple, independent ideas, incapable of definition;[183] and this which Fika-kaka felt was an extacy compounded of positive pleasure ingrafted upon the removal of pain: but whether this positive pleasure depended upon a particular center of percussion hit upon by accident, or was the inseparable effect of a kicking and scratching conferred by a royal foot and toe, I shall not at present unfold: neither will I demonstrate the *modus operandi* on the nervous papillæ[184] of Fika-kaka's breech, whether by irritation, relaxation, undulation, or vibration.[185] Were these essential discoveries communicated, human philosophy would become too arrogant. It was but the other day that Newton made shift to dive into some subaltern[186] laws of matter; to explain the revolution of the planets, and analyse the composition of light;[187] and ever since, that reptile[188] man has believed itself a demi-god—I hope to see the day when the petulant philosopher shall be driven back to his Categories and the Organum Universale of Aristotle, his οὐσια, his ὕλη, and his ὑποκείμενον.[189]

But waving these digressions, the pleasure which the Cuboy felt from the application of the Dairo's toe-nail was succeeded by a kind of tension or stiffness, which began to grow troublesome just as he reached his own palace, where the Bonzas were assembled to offer up their diurnal incense.[190] Instinct, on this occasion, performed what could hardly have been expected from the most extraordinary talents. At sight of a grizzled beard belonging to one of those venerable doctors, he was struck with the idea of a powerful assuager; and taking him into his cabinet,[191] proposed that he should make oral application to the part affected. The proposal was embraced without hesitation, and the effect even transcended the hope of the Cuboy. The osculation itself was soft, warm, emollient, and comfortable; but when the nervous papillæ were gently stroaked, and as it were fondled by the long, elastic, peristaltic, abstersive[192] fibres that composed this reverend verriculum,[193] such a delectable titillation ensued, that Fika-ka was quite in raptures.

That which he intended at first for a medicine he now converted into an article of luxury. All the Bonzas who enrolled themselves in the number of his dependants, whether old or young, black[194] or fair, rough or smooth, were enjoined every day to perform this additional and posterior rite of worship,[195] so productive of delight to the Cuboy, that he was every morning impatient to receive the Dairo's calcitration,[196] or rather his pedestrian digitation;[197] after which he flew with all the eagerness of desire to the subsequent part of his entertainment.

The transports thus produced seemed to disarrange his whole nervous system, and produce an odd kind of revolution in his fancy; for tho' he was naturally grave, and indeed overwhelmed with constitutional hebetude,[198] he became, in consequence of this periodical tickling, the most giddy, pert buffoon in nature. All was grinning, giggling, laughing, and prating, except when his fears intervened; then he started and stared, and cursed and prayed by turns. There was but one barber in the whole empire that would undertake to shave him, so ticklish and unsteady he was under the hands of the operator. He could not sit above one minute in the same attitude, or on the same seat; but shifted about from couch to chair, from chair to stool, from stool to close-stool,[199] with incessant rotation, and all the time gave audience to those who sollicited his favour and protection. To all and several he promised his best offices,[200] and confirmed these promises with oaths and protestations. One he shook by the hand; another he hugged; a third he kissed on both sides the face; with a fourth he whispered; a fifth he honoured with a familiar horse-laugh.[201] He never had courage to refuse even that which he could not possibly grant; and at last his tongue actually forgot how to pronounce the negative particle:[202] but as in the English language two negatives amount to an affirmative, five hundred affirmatives in the mouth of Fika-kaka did not altogether destroy the efficacy of simple negation. A promise five hundred times repeated, and at every repetition confirmed by oath, barely amounted to a computable chance of performance.[203]

It must be allowed, however, he promoted a great number of Bonzas,[204] and in this promotion he manifested an uncommon taste. They were preferred[205] according to the colour of their beards. He found, by experience, that beards of different colours yielded him different degrees of pleasure in the friction we have described above; and the provision he made for each was in proportion to the satisfaction the candidate could afford. The sensation ensuing from the contact of a grey beard was soft and delicate, and agreeably demulcent,[206] when the parts were unusually inflamed; a red, yellow, or brindled beard, was in request when the business was to thrill or tingle: but a black beard was of all others the most honoured by Fika-kaka, not only on account of its fleecy feel, equally spirited and balsamic, but also for another philosophical reason, which I shall now explain. You know, Peacock, that black colour absorbs the rays of light, and detains them as it were in a repository. Thus a black beard, like the back of a black cat, becomes a phosphorus[207] in the dark, and emits sparkles upon friction. You must know, that one of the gravest doctors of the Bonzas, who had a private request to make, desired an audience of Fika-kaka in his closet at night, and the taper falling down by accident, at that very instant when his beard was in contact with the Cuboy's seat of honour, the electrical snap was heard, and the part illuminated, to the astonishment of the spectators, who looked upon it as a prelude to the apotheosis[208] of Fika-kaka. Being made acquainted with this phænomenon, the minister was exceedingly elevated in his own mind. He rejoiced in it as a communication of some divine efficacy, and raised the happy Bonza to the rank of Pontifex Maximus,[209] or chief priest, in the temple of Fakkubasi. In the course of experiments, he found that all black beards were electrical in the same degree, and being ignorant of philosophy,[210] ascribed it to some supernatural virtue, in consequence of which they were promoted as the holiest of the Bonzas. But you and I know, that such a phosphorus is obtained from the most worthless and corrupted materials, such as rotten wood, putrefied veal, and stinking whiting.

Fika-kaka, such as I described him, could not possibly act in the character of Cuboy, without the assistance of counsellors and subalterns, who understood the detail of government and the forms of business. He was accordingly surrounded by a number of satellites, who reflected his lustre in their several spheres of rotation; and though their immersions and emersions[211] were apparently abrupt and irregular, formed a kind of luminous belt as pale and comfortless as the ring of Saturn, the most distant, cold, and baleful of all the planets.[212]

The most remarkable of these subordinates, was Sti-phi-rum-poo, a man, who, from a low plebeian origin, had raised himself to one of the first offices of the empire, to the dignity of *Quo*, or nobleman, and a considerable share of the Dairo's personal regard.[213] He owed his whole success to his industry, assiduity, and circumspection. During the former part of his life, he studied the laws of Japan with such severity of application, that though unassisted by the least gleam of genius, and destitute of the smallest pretension to talent, he made himself master of all the written ordinances, all the established customs, and forms of proceeding in the different tribunals of the empire. In the progress of his vocation, he became an advocate of some eminence, and even acquired reputation for polemical eloquence, though his manner was ever dry, laboured, and unpleasant—Being elevated to the station of a judge, he so far justified the interest[214] by which he had been promoted, that his honesty was never called in question; and his sentences were generally allowed to be just and upright. He heard causes with the most painful attention, seemed to be indefatigable in his researches after truth; and though he was forbidding in his aspect, slow in deliberation, tedious in discussion, and cold in his address; yet I must own, he was also unbiassed in his decisions—I mean, unbiassed by any consciousness of sinister motive: for a man may be biassed by the nature of his disposition, as well as by prejudices acquired, and yet not guilty of intentional partiality. Sti-phi-rum-poo was scrupulously just, according to his own ideas of justice, and consequently well qualified to decide in common controversies. But in delicate cases, which required an uncommon share of penetration; when the province of a supreme judge is to mitigate the severity, and sometimes even deviate from the dead letter of the common law, in favour of particular institutions, or of humanity in general; he had neither genius to enlighten his understanding, sentiment to elevate his mind, nor courage to surmount the petty inclosures[215] of ordinary practice. He was accused of avarice and cruelty;[216] but, in fact, these were not active passions in his heart. The conduct which seemed to justify these imputations, was wholly owing to a total want of taste and generosity. The nature of his post furnished him with opportunities to accumulate riches; and as the narrowness of his mind admitted no ideas of elegance or refined pleasure, he knew not how to use his wealth so as to avoid the charge of a sordid disposition. His temper was not rapacious but retentive: he knew not the use of wealth, and therefore did not use it at all: but was in this particular neither better nor worse than a strong-box for the convenience and advantage of his heir. The appearance of cruelty remarkable in his counsels, relating to some wretched insurgents who had been taken in open rebellion,[217] and the rancorous pleasure he seemed to feel in pronouncing sentence of death by self-exenteration,* [218] was in fact the gratification of a dastardly heart, which had never acknowledged the least impulse of any liberal sentiment.[219] This being the case, mankind ought not to impute that to his guilt which was, in effect, the consequence of his infirmity. A man might, with equal justice, be punished for being purblind.[220] Sti-phi-rum-poo was much more culpable for seeking to shine in a sphere for which nature never intended him; I mean for commencing statesman, and intermeddling in the machine of government: yet even into this character he was forced, as it were, by the opinion and injunctions of Fika-kaka, who employed him at first in making speeches for the Dairo, which that prince used to pronounce in public, at certain seasons of the year.[221] These speeches being tolerably well received by the populace, the Cuboy conceived an extraordinary opinion of his talents; and thought him extremely well qualified to ease him of great part of the burthen of government.[222] He found him very well disposed to engage heartily in his interests. Then he was admitted to the osculation *a posteriori*; and though his beard was not black, but rather of a subfuscan hue,[223] he managed it with such dexterity, that Fika-kaka declared the salute gave him unspeakable pleasure: while the bystanders protested that the contact produced, not simply electrical sparks or scintillations, but even a perfect irradiation, which seemed altogether supernatural. From this moment, Sti-phi-rum-poo was initiated in the mysteries of the cabinet,[224] and even introduced to the person of the Dairo Got-hama-baba, whose pedestrian favours he shared with his new patron. It was observed, however, that even after his promotion and nobilitation,[225] he still retained his original aukwardness, and never could acquire that graceful ease of attitude with which the Cuboy presented his parts averse to the contemplation of his sovereign. Indeed this minister's body was so well moulded for the celebration of the rite, that one would have imagined nature had formed him expressly for that purpose, with his head and body projecting forwards, so as to form an angle of forty-five with the horizon, while the glutæi muscles[226] swelled backwards as if ambitious to meet half-way the imperial encounter.

*A gentleman capitally convicted in Japan is allowed the privilege of anticipating the common executioner, by ripping out his own bowels.

The third connexion that strengthened this political band was Nin-kom-poo-po,[227] commander of the *Fune*, or navy of Japan,[228] who, if ever man was, might surely be termed the child of fortune. He was bred to the sea from his infancy,[229] and, in the course of pacific service,[230] rose to the command of a jonkh,[231] when he was so lucky as to detect a crew of pyrates employed on a desolate shore in concealing a hoard of money which they had taken from the merchants of Corea. Nin-kom-poo-po, falling in with them at night, attacked them unawares, and having obtained an easy victory, carried off the treasure.[232] I cannot help being amused at the folly of you silly mortals, when I recollect the transports of the people at the return of this fortunate officer, with a paultry mass of silver parading in covered waggons escorted by his crew in arms. The whole city of Meaco resounded with acclamation; and Nin-kom-poo-po was extolled as the greatest hero that ever the empire of Japan produced.[233] The Cuboy honoured him with five kisses[234] in public; accepted of the osculation in private, recommended him in the strongest terms to the Dairo, who promoted him to the rank of Sey-seo-gun,[235] or general at sea. He professed himself an adherent to the Cuboy, entered into a strict alliance[236] with Sti-phi-rum-poo, and the whole management of the *Fune* was consigned into his hands.[237] With respect to his understanding, it was just sufficient to comprehend the duties of a common mariner, and to follow the ordinary route of the most sordid avarice. As to his heart, he might be said to be in a state of total apathy, without principle or passion; for I cannot afford the name of passion to such a vile appetite as an insatiable thirst of lucre. He was, indeed, so cold and forbidding, that, in Japan, the people distinguished him by a nick-name equivalent to the English word Salamander; not that he was inclined to live in fire,[238] but that the coldness of his heart would have extinguished any fire it had approached. Some individuals imagined he had been begot upon a mermaid by a sailor of Kamschatka; but this was a mere fable.[239]——I can assure you, however, that when his lips were in contact with the Cuboy's posteriors, Fika-kaka's teeth were seen to chatter. The pride of this animal was equal to his frigidity. He affected to establish new regulations[240] at the council where he presided: he treated his equals with insolence, and his superiors with contempt. Other people generally rejoice in obliging their fellow-creatures, when they can do it without prejudice to their own interest. Nin-kom-poo-po had a repulsive power in his disposition; and seemed to take pleasure in denying a request.[241] When this vain creature, selfish, inelegant, arrogant, and uncouth, appeared in all his trappings at the Dairo's court, upon a festival, he might have been justly compared to a Lapland idol of ice, adorned with a profusion of brass leaf and trinkets of pewter.[242] In the direction of the Fune, he was provided with a certain number of assessors, counsellors, or co-adjutors;[243] but these he never consulted, more than if they had been wooden images. He distributed his commands among his own dependants; and left all the forms of the office to the care of the scribe, who thus became so necessary, that his influence sometimes had well nigh interfered with that of the president: nay, they have been seen, like the electrical spheres of two bodies, repelling each other.[244] Hence it was observed, that the office of the Sey-seo-gun-sialty resembled the serpent called Amphisbæna,[245] which, contrary to the formation of other animals in head and tail, has a head where the tail should be. Well, indeed, might they compare them to a serpent, in creeping, cunning, coldness, and venom; but the comparison would have held with more propriety, had Nature produced a serpent without ever a head at all.

The fourth who contributed his credit and capacity to this coalition, was Foksi-Roku,[246] a man who greatly surpassed them all in the science of politicks, bold, subtle, interested,[247] insinuating, ambitious, and indefatigable. An adventurer from his cradle, a latitudinarian[248] in principle, a libertine in morals, without the advantages of birth,[249] fortune, character, or interest;[250] by his own natural sagacity, a close attention to the follies and foibles of mankind, a projecting[251] spirit, an invincible assurance, and an obstinacy of perseverance proof against all the shocks of disappointment and repulse; he forced himself as it were into the scale of preferment; and being found equally capable and compliant, rose to high offices of trust and profit, detested by the people, as one of the most desperate tools of a wicked administration;[252] and odious to his colleagues in the m——y,[253] for his superior talents, his restless ambition, and the uncertainty of his attachment.[254]

As interest prompted him, he hovered between the triumvirate we have described, and another knot of competitors for the ad——n, headed by Quamba-cun-dono, a great Quo related to the Dairo, who had bore the supreme command in the army,[255] and was stiled Fatzman,* κατ᾽ ἐξοκὴν, or, by way of eminence.[256] This accomplished prince was not only the greatest in his mind,[257] but also the largest in his person of all the subjects of Japan; and whereas your Shakespeare makes Falstaff urge it as a plea in his own favour, that as he had more flesh, so likewise he had more frailty than other men;[258] I may justly convert the proposition in favour of Quamba-cun-dono, and affirm that as he had more flesh, so he had more virtue than any other Japonese; more bowels,[259] more humanity, more beneficence, more affability.

*Vid. Kempfer. Amænitat. Japan.

He was undoubtedly, for a Fatzman, the most courteous, the most gallant, the most elegant, generous, and munificent Quo that ever adorned the court of Japan. So consummate in the art of war, that the whole world could not produce a general to match him in foresight, vigilance, conduct, and ability. Indeed his intellects were so extraordinary and extensive, that he seemed to sentimentize[260] at every pore, and to have the faculty of thinking diffused all over his frame, even to his fingers ends; or, as the Latins call it *ad unguem*: nay, so wonderful was his organical conformation, that, in the opinion of many Japonese philosophers, his whole body was enveloped in a kind of poultice of brain,[261] and that if he had lost his head in battle, the damage with regard to his power of reflection would have been scarce perceptible. After he had atchieved many glorious exploits, in a war against the Chinese on the continent,[262] he was sent with a strong army to quell a dangerous insurrection in the northern parts of Ximo, which is one of the Japonese islands. He accordingly by his valour crushed the rebellion; and afterwards, by dint of clemency and discretion, extinguished the last embers of disaffection.[263] When the insurgents were defeated, dispersed, and disarmed, and a sufficient number selected for example, his humanity emerged,[264] and took full possession of his breast. He considered them as wretched men misled by false principles of honour, and sympathized with their distress: he pitied them as men and fellow-citizens: he regarded them as useful fellow-subjects, who might be reclaimed and reunited to the community. Instead of sending out the ministers of blood, rapine, and revenge, to ravage, burn, and destroy, without distinction of age, sex, or principle; he extended the arms of mercy to all who would embrace that indulgence: he protected the lives and habitations of the helpless, and diminished the number of the malcontents much more effectually by his benevolence than by his sword.

The southern Japonese had been terribly alarmed at this insurrection, and in the first transports of their deliverance, voluntarily taxed themselves with a considerable yearly tribute to the hero Quamba-cun-dono.[265] In all probability, they would not have appeared so grateful, had they stayed to see the effects of his merciful disposition towards the vanquished rebels: for mercy is surely no attribute of the Japonese,[266] considered as a people. Indeed, nothing could form a more striking contrast, than appeared in the transactions in the northern and southern parts of the empire at this juncture. While the amiable Quamba-cun-dono was employed in the godlike office of gathering together, and cherishing under his wings the poor, dispersed, forlorn, widows and orphans, whom the savage hand of war had deprived of parent, husband, home, and sustenance; while he, in the North, gathered these miserable creatures, even as a hen gathereth her chickens;[267] Sti-phi-rum-poo, and other judges in the South, were condemning such of their parents and husbands as survived the sword, to crucifixion, cauldrons of boiling oil, or exenteration;[268] and the people were indulging their appetites by feasting upon the viscera thus extracted. The liver of a Ximian was in such request at this period, that if the market had been properly managed and supplied, this delicacy would have sold for two Obans a pound, or about four pounds sterling.[269] The troops in the North might have provided at the rate of a thousand head per month for the demand of Meaco; and tho' the other parts of the carcase would not have sold at so high a price as the liver, heart, harrigals,[270] sweet-bread, and pope's eye;[271] yet the whole, upon an average, would have fetched at the rate of three hundred pounds a head; especially if those animals, which are but poorly fed in their own country,[272] had been fattened up and kept upon hard meat[273] for the slaughter. This new branch of traffick would have produced about three hundred and sixty thousand pounds annually: for the rebellion might easily have been fomented from year to year; and consequently it would have yielded a considerable addition to the emperor's revenue, by a proper taxation.

The philosophers of Japan were divided in their opinions concerning this new taste for Ximian flesh, which suddenly sprung up among the Japonese. Some ascribed it to a principle of hatred and revenge, agreeable to the common expression of animosity among the multitude, "You dog, I'll have your liver."[274] Others imputed it to a notion analagous to the vulgar conceit, that the liver of a mad dog being eaten is a preventive against madness; ergo, the liver of a traitor is an antidote against treason. A third sort derived this strange appetite from the belief of the Americans,[275] who imagine they shall inherit all the virtues of the enemies they devour; and a fourth affirmed that the demand for this dainty arose from a very high and peculiar flavour in Ximian flesh, which flavour was discovered by accident: moreover, there were not wanting some who supposed this banquet was a kind of sacrifice to the powers of sorcery; as we find that one of the ingredients of the charm prepared in Shakespear's cauldron was "the liver of blaspheming Jew:"[276] and indeed it is not at all improbable that the liver of a rebellious Ximian might be altogether as effectual. I know that Fika-kaka was stimulated by curiosity to try the experiment, and held divers consultations with his cooks on this subject. They all declared in favour of the trial; and it was accordingly presented at the table, where the Cuboy eat of it to such excess as to produce a surfeit. He underwent a severe evacuation both ways, attended with cold sweats and swoonings. In a word, his agony was so violent, that he ever after loathed the sight of Ximian flesh, whether dead or alive.[277]

With the Fatzman Quamba-cun-dono was connected another Quo called Gotto-mio, viceroy of Xicoco,[278] one of the islands of Japan. If his understanding had been as large as his fortune,[279] and his temper a little more tractable, he would have been a dangerous rival to the Cuboy. But if their brains had been weighed against each other, the nineteenth part of a grain would have turned either scale; and as Fika-kaka had negative qualities, which supported and extended his personal influence, so Gotto-mio had positive powers, that defended him from all approaches of popularity. His pride was of the insolent order; his temper extremely irascible; and his avarice quite rapacious: nay, he is said to have once declined the honour of a kicking[280] from the Dairo. Conceited of his own talents, he affected to harangue in the council of Twenty Eight;[281] but his ideas were embarrassed; his language was mean; and his elocution more discordant than the braying of fifty asses. When Fika-kaka addressed himself to speech, an agreeable simper played upon the countenances of all the audience: but soon as Gotto-mio stood up, every spectator raised his thumbs to his ears, as it were instinctively. The Dairo Got-hama-baba, by the advice of the Cuboy, sent him over to govern the people of Xicoco, and a more effectual method could not have been taken to mortify his arrogance. His deportment was so insolent, his œconomy so sordid,[282] and his government so arbitrary, that those islanders, who are remarkably ferocious and impatient, expressed their hatred and contempt of him on every occasion. His Quanbukuship was hardly safe from outrage in the midst of his guards; and a cross was actually erected for the execution of his favourite Kow-kin,[283] who escaped with some difficulty to the island of Niphon, whither also his patron soon followed him,[284] attended by the curses of the people whom he had been sent to rule.

He who presided at the council of Twenty Eight was called Soo-san-sin-o,[285] an old experienced shrewd politician, who conveyed more sense in one single sentence, than could have been distilled from all the other brains in council, had they been macerated in one alembic.[286] He was a man of extensive learning and elegant taste. He saw through the characters of his fellow-labourers in the ad——n. He laughed at the folly of one faction, and detested the arrogance and presumption of the other. In an assembly of sensible men, his talents would have shone with superior lustre: but at the council of Twenty Eight, they were obscured by the thick clouds of ignorance that enveloped his brethren. The Dairo had a personal respect for him, and is said to have conferred frequent favours on his posteriors in private.[287] He kicked the Cuboy often *ex officio*,[288] as a husband thinks it incumbent upon him to caress his wife: but he kicked the president for pleasure, as a voluptuary embraces his mistress. Soo-san-sin-o, conscious that he had no family interest to support him in cabals among the people, and careless of his country's fate, resolved to enjoy the comforts of life in quiet. He laughed and quaffed[289] with his select companions in private; received his appointments thankfully; and swam with the tide of politicks as it happened to flow.——It was pretty extraordinary that the wisest man should be the greatest cypher: but such was the will of the gods.

Besides these great luminaries that enlightened the cabinet of Japan, I shall have occasion, in the course of my narrative, to describe many other stars of an inferior order. At this board, there was as great a variety of characters, as we find in the celebrated table of Cebes.[290] Nay, indeed, what was objected to the philosopher,[291] might have been more justly said of the Japonese councils. There was neither invention,[292] unity, nor design among them. They consisted of mobs of sauntering, strolling, vagrant,[293] and ridiculous politicians. Their schemes were absurd, and their deliberations like the sketches of anarchy. All was bellowing, bleating, braying, grinning, grumbling, confusion, and uproar.[294] It was more like a dream of chaos than a picture of human life. If the ΔAIMΩN, or Genius[295] was wanting, it must be owned that Fika-kaka exactly answered Cebes's description of TYXH, or Fortune, blind and frantic, running about every where; giving to some, and taking from others, without rule or distinction; while her emblem of the round stone,[296] fairly shews his *giddy* nature; καλῶς μηνύει φύσιν αυτῆς.[297] Here, however, one might have seen many other figures of the painter's allegory; such as Deception tendering the cup of ignorance[298] and error, opinions and appetites; Disappointment and Anguish; Debauchery, Profligacy, Gluttony, and Adulation; Luxury, Fraud, Rapine, Perjury, and Sacrilege: but not the least traces of the virtues which are described in the groupe of true education, and in the grove of happiness.[299]

The two factions that divided the council[300] of Japan, tho' inveterate enemies to each other, heartily and cordially concurred in one particular, which was the worship established in the temple of Fakkubasi, or the White Horse. This was the orthodox faith in Japan, and was certainly founded, as St. Paul saith of the Christian religion, upon the evidence of things not seen.[301] All the votaries of this superstition of Fakkubasi subscribed and swore to the following creed, implicitly, without hesitation, or mental reservation.[302] "I believe in the White Horse,[303] that he descended from heaven, and sojourned in Jeddo, which is the land of promise.[304] I believe in *Bupo* his apostle, who first declared to the children of Niphon, the glad tidings of the gospel of Fakkubasi. I believe that the White Horse was begot by a black mule,[305] and brought forth by a green dragon; that his head is of silver, and his hoofs are of brass;[306] that he eats gold as provender, and discharges diamonds as dung;[307] that the Japonese are ordained and predestined to furnish him with food, and the people of Jeddo to clear away his litter.[308] I believe that the island of Niphon is joined to the continent of Jeddo; and that whoever thinks otherwise shall be damned to all eternity. I believe that the smallest portion of matter may be practically[309] divided *ad infinitum*: that equal quantities taken from equal quantities, an unequal quantity will remain: that two and two make seven: that the sun rules the night, the stars the day; and the moon is made of green cheese. Finally, I believe that a man cannot be saved without devoting[310] his goods and his chattels, his children, relations, and friends, his senses and ideas, his soul and his body, to the religion of the White Horse, as it is prescribed in the ritual of Fakkubasi." These are the tenets which the Japonese ministers swallowed as glib as the English clergy swallow the thirty-nine articles.[311]

Having thus characterised the chiefs that disputed the administration, or, in other words, the empire of Japan, I shall now proceed to a plain narration of historical incidents, without pretending to philosophize like H——e, or dogmatize like S——tt.[312] I shall only tell thee, Nathaniel, that Britain never gave birth but to two historians worthy of credit, and they were Taliessin and Geoffrey of Monmouth.[313] I'll tell you another secret. The whole world has never been able to produce six good historians.[314] Herodotus is fabulous even to a proverb; Thucydides is perplexed, obscure, and unimportant; Polybius is dry and inelegant; Livy superficial; and Tacitus a coxcomb. Guicciardini wants interest; Davila, digestion; and Sarpi, truth.[315] In the whole catalogue of French historians, there is not one of tolerable authenticity.

In the year of the period Foggien one hundred and fifty four,[316] the tranquility of Japan was interrupted by the incroachments of the Chinese adventurers, who made descents upon certain islands belonging to the Japonese a great way to the southward of Xicoco. They even settled colonies, and built forts on some of them, while the two empires were at peace with each other. When the Japonese governors expostulated with the Chinese officers on this intrusion, they were treated with ridicule and contempt:[317] then they had recourse to force of arms, and some skirmishes were fought with various success.[318] When the tidings of these hostilities arrived at Meaco, the whole council of Twenty-Eight was overwhelmed with fear and confusion.[319] The

Dairo kicked them all round, not from passion, but by way of giving an animating fillip to their deliberative faculties. The disputes had happened in the island of Fatsissio:[320] but there were only three members of the council who knew that Fatsissio was an island, although the commerce there carried on was of the utmost importance to the empire of Japan.[321] They were as much in the dark with respect to its situation. Fika-kaka, on the supposition that it adjoined to the coast of Corea, expressed his apprehension that the Chinese would invade it with a numerous army; and was so transported when Foksi-roku assured him it was an island at a vast distance from any continent, that he kissed him five times in the face of the whole council;[322] and his royal master, Got-hama-baba, swore he should be indulged with a double portion of kicking at his next private audience. The same counsellor proposed, that as the Fune or navy of Japan was much more numerous than the fleet of China, they should immediately avail themselves of this advantage. Quamba-cun-dono the Fatzman was of opinion that war should be immediately declared, and an army transported to the continent. Sti-phi-rum-poo thought it would be more expedient to sweep the seas of the Chinese trading vessels, without giving them any previous intimation; and to this opinion admiral Nin-kom-poo-po subscribed, not only out of deference to the superior understanding of his sage ally, who undertook to prove it was not contrary to the law of nature and nations,[323] to plunder the subjects of foreign powers, who trade on the faith of treaties, but also from his own inclination, which was much addicted to pillage without bloodshed. To him, therefore, the task was left of scouring the seas, and intercepting the succours which (they had received intelligence) were ready to sail from one of the ports of China to the island of Fatsissio.[324] In the mean time, junks were provided for transporting thither a body of Japonese troops, under the command of one Koan, an obscure officer without conduct or experience, whom the Fatz-man selected for this service:[325] not that he supposed him possessed of superior merit, but because no leader of distinction cared to engage in such a disagreeable expedition.

Nin-kom-poo-po acted according to the justest ideas which had been formed of his understanding. He let loose his cruisers among the merchant ships of China, and the harbours of Japan were quickly filled with prizes and prisoners.[326] The Chinese exclaimed against these proceedings as the most perfidious acts of piracy; and all the other powers of Asia beheld them with astonishment.[327] But the consummate wisdom of the sea Sey-seo-gun appeared most conspicuous in another stroke of generalship, which he now struck. Instead of blocking up in the Chinese harbour the succours destined to reinforce the enemy in Fatsissio, until they should be driven from their incroachments on that island, he very wisely sent a strong squadron of Fune to cruise in the open sea, midway between China and Fatsissio, in the most tempestuous season of the year, when the fogs are so thick and so constant in that latitude, as to rival the darkness of a winter night;[328] and supported the feasibility of this scheme in council, by observing, that the enemy would be thus decoyed from their harbour, and undoubtedly intercepted in their passage by the Japonese squadron. This plan was applauded as one of the most ingenious stratagems that ever was devised; and Fika-kaka insisted upon kissing his posteriors, as the most honourable mark of his approbation.

Philosophers have observed, that the motives of actions are not to be estimated by events. Fortune did not altogether fulfil the expectations of the council. General Koan suffered himself and his army to be decoyed into the middle of a wood, where they stood like sheep in the shambles, to be slaughtered by an unseen enemy.[329] The Chinese succours perceiving their harbour open, set sail for Fatsissio, which they reached in safety, by changing their course about one degree from the common route; while the Japonese Fune continued cruising among the fogs, until the ships were shattered by storms, and the crews more than half destroyed by cold and distemper.[330]

When the news of these disasters arrived, great commotion arose in the council. The Dairo Got-hama-baba fluttered, and clucked and cackled and hissed like a goose disturbed[331] in the act of incubation. Quamba-cun-dono shed bitter tears: the Cuboy snivelled and sobbed: Sti-phi-rum-poo groaned: Gotto-mio swore: but the sea Sey-seo-gun Nin-kom-poo-po underwent no alteration. He sat as the emblem of insensibility, fixed as the north star, and as cold as that luminary, sending forth emanations of frigidity. Fika-ka, mistaking this congelation[332] for fortitude, went round and embraced him where he sat, exclaiming, "My dear Day,[333] Sey-seo-gun, what would you advise in this dilemma?" But the contact had almost cost him his life; for the touch of Nin-kom-poo-po, thus congealed, had the same effect as that of the fish called Torpor.[334] The Cuboy's whole body was instantly benumbed; and if his friends had not instantly poured down his throat a considerable quantity of strong spirit, the circulation would have ceased. This is what philosophers call a generation of cold, which became so intense, that the mercury in a Japonese thermometer constructed on the same principles which were afterwards adopted by Fahrnheit,[335] and fixed in the apartment, immediately sunk thirty degrees below the freezing point.

The first astonishment of the council was succeeded by critical remarks and argumentation. The Dairo consoled himself by observing, that his troops made a very soldierly appearance as they lay on the field in their new cloathing, smart caps, and clean buskins; and that the enemy allowed they had never seen beards and whiskers in better order. He then declared, that should a war ensue with China, he would go abroad and expose himself for the glory of Japan.[336] Foksi-roku expressed his surprize, that a general should march his army through a wood in an unknown country, without having it first reconnoitred: but the Fatzman assured him, that was a practice never admitted into the discipline of Japan. Gotto-mio swore the man was mad to stand with his men, like oxen in a stall, to be knocked on the head without using any means of defence. "Why the devil (said he) did not he either retreat, or advance to close engagement with the handful of Chinese who formed the ambuscade?" "I hope, my dear Quanbuku, (replied the Fatzman) that the troops of Japan will always stand without flinching. I should have been mortified beyond measure, had they retreated without seeing the face of the enemy:——that would have been a disgrace which never befel any troops formed under my direction;[337] and as for advancing, the ground would not permit any manœuvre of that nature. They were engaged in a *cul de sac*, where they could not form either in hollow square, front line, potence,[338] column or platoon.——It was the fortune of war, and they bore it like men:——we shall be more fortunate on another occasion."[339] The president Soo-san-sin-o, took notice, that if there had been one spaniel in the whole Japonese army, this disaster could not have happened; as the animal would have beat the bushes and discovered the ambuscade. He therefore proposed, that if the war was to be prosecuted in Fatsissio, which is a country overgrown with wood, a number of blood-hounds might be provided and sent over, to run upon the foot in the front and on the flanks of the army, when it should be on its march through such impediments.[340] Quamba-cun-dono declared, that soldiers had much better die in the bed of honour,[341] than be saved and victorious, by such an unmilitary expedient; that such a proposal was so contrary to the rules of war and the scheme of enlisting dogs so derogatory from the dignity of the service, that if ever it should be embraced, he would resign his command, and spend the remainder of his life in retirement. This canine project was equally disliked by the Dairo, who approved of the Fatzman's objection, and sealed his approbation with a pedestrian salute of such momentum, that the Fatzman could hardly stand under the weight of the compliment. It was agreed that new levies should be made, and a new squadron of Fune equipped with all expedition; and thus the assembly broke up.

Fortune had not yet sufficiently humbled the pride of Japan. That body of Chinese which defeated Koan, made several conquests in Fastsissio,[342] and seemed to be in a fair way of reducing the whole island. Yet, the court of China, not satisfied with this success, resolved to strike a blow, that should be equally humiliating to the Japonese, in another part of the world. Having by specious remonstrances already prepossessed all the neighbouring nations against the government of Japan, as the patrons of perfidy and piracy;[343] they fitted out an armament, which was intended to subdue the island of Motao on the coast of Corea, which the Japonese had taken in a former war,[344] and now occupied at a very great expence, as a place of the utmost importance to the commerce of the empire. Repeated advices of the enemy's design were sent from different parts, to the m——y of Japan:[345] but they seemed all overwhelmed by such a lethargy of infatuation,[346] that no measures of prevention were concerted.

Such was the opinion of the people; but the truth is, they were fast asleep. The Japonese hold with the antient Greeks and modern Americans,[347] that dreams are from heaven; and in any perplexing emergency, they, like the Indians, Jews, and natives of Madagascar, have recourse to dreaming as to an oracle. These dreams or divinations are preceded by certain religious rites analagous to the ceremony of the ephod, the urim and the thummim.[348] The rites were religiously performed in the council of Twenty-Eight; and a deep sleep overpowered the Dairo and all his counsellors.

Got-hama-baba the emperor, who reposed his head upon the pillowy sides of Quamba-cun-dono, dreamed that he was sacrificing in the temple of Fak-kubasi, and saw the deity of the White Horse devouring pearls by the bushel at one end, and voiding corruption by the ton at the other. The Fatzman dreamed that a great number of Chinese cooks were busy buttering his brains. Gotto-mio dreamed of lending money and borrowing sense. Sti-phi-rum-poo thought he had procured a new law for clapping padlocks upon the chastity of all the females in Japan under twenty, of which padlocks he himself kept the keys.[349] Nin-kom-poo-po dreamed he was metamorphosed into a sea-lion, in pursuit of a shoal of golden gudgeons.[350] *One did laugh in's sleep, and one cried murder.*[351] The first was Soo-san-sin-o, who had precisely the same vision that disturbed the imagination of the Cuboy. He thought he saw the face of a right reverend prelate of the Bonzas, united with and growing to the posteriors of the minister. Fika-kaka underwent the same disagreeable illusion, with this aggravating circumstance, that he already felt the teeth of the said Bonza.[352] The president laughed aloud at the ridiculous phænomenon: the Cuboy exclaimed in the terror of being encumbered with such a monstrous appendage. It was not without some reason he cried, "Murder!" Foksi-roku, who happened to sleep on the next chair, dreamed of money-bags, places, and reversions;[353] and in the transport of his eagerness, laid fast hold on the trunk-breeches of the Cuboy,[354] including certain fundamentals,[355] which he grasped so violently as to excite pain, and extort the exclamation from Fika-kaka, even in his sleep.

The council being at last waked by the clamours of the people, who surrounded the palace, and proclaimed that Motao was in danger of an invasion; the sea Sey-seo-gun Nin-kom-poo-po, was ordered to fit out a fleet of Fune for the relief of that island; and directions were given that the commander of these Fune should, in his voyage, touch at the garrison of Foutao,[356] and take on board from thence a certain number of troops, to reinforce the Japonese governor of the place that was in danger. Nin-kom-poo-po for this service chose the commander Bihn-goh, a man who had never signalized himself by any act of valour.[357] He sent him out with a squadron of Fune ill manned, wretchedly provided, and inferior in number to the fleet of China,[358] which was by this time known to be assembled in order to support the invasion of the island of Motao. He sailed, nevertheless, on this expedition, and touched at the garrison of Foutao to take in the reinforcement: but the orders sent for this purpose from Nob-o-di, minister for the department of war, appeared so contradictory and absurd, that they could not possibly be obeyed;[359] so that Bihn-goh proceeded without the reinforcement towards Motao, the principal fortress of which was by this time invested.[360] He had been accidentally joined by a few cruisers, which rendered him equal in strength to the Chinese squadron which he now descried. Both commanders seemed afraid of each other. The fleets, however, engaged; but little damage was done to either. They parted as if by consent.[361] Bihn-goh made the best of his way back to Foutao, without making the least attempt to succour, or open a communication with Fi-de-ta-da, the governor of Motao, who, looking upon himself as abandoned by his country, surrendered his fortress, with the whole island, to the Chinese general.[362] These disgraces happening on the back of[363] the Fatsissian disasters, raised a prodigious ferment in Japan, and the ministry had almost sunk under the first fury of the people's resentment. They not only exclaimed against the folly of the administration, but they also accused them of treachery; and seemed to think that the glory and advantage of the empire had been betrayed.[364] What increased the commotion was the terror of an invasion,[365] with which the Chinese threatened the islands of Japan. The terrors of Fika-ka had already cost him two pair of trunk hose,[366] which were defiled by sudden sallies or irruptions from the postern of his microcosm;[367] and these were attended with such noisome effluvia, that the Bonzas could not perform the barbal abstersion[368] without marks of abhorrence. The emperor himself was seen to stop his nose, and turn away his head, when he approached him to perform the pedestrian exercise.

Here I intended to insert a dissertation on trousers or trunk breeches,[369] called by the Greeks βραχοι, & περίζωματα, by the Latins *braccæ laxæ*, by the Spaniards *bragas anchas*, by the Italians *calzone largo*, by the French *haut de chausses*, by the Saxons *bræcce*, by the Swedes *brackor*, by the Irish *briechan*, by the Celtæ *brag*, and by the Japonese *bra-ak*.[370] I could make some curious discoveries touching the analogy between the Περιζωματα and Ζωνιον γυναικεῖον,[371] and point out the precise time at which the Grecian women began to wear the breeches. I would have demonstrated that the *cingulum muliebre*[372] was originally no other than the wife's literally wearing the husband's trousers at certain *orgia*,[373] as a mark of dominion transferred *pro tempore*,[374] to the female. I would have drawn a curious parallel between the Ζωνιον of the Greek, and the *shim* or middle cloth worn by the black ladies in Guinea.[375] I would have proved that breeches were not first used to defend the central parts from the injuries of the weather, inasmuch as they were first worn by the Orientals in a warm climate; as you may see in Persius, *Braccatis illita medis——porticus*.[376] I would have shewn that breeches were first brought from Asia to the northern parts of Europe, by the Celtæ sprung from the antient Gomanaus:[377] that trousers were wore in Scotland long before the time of Pythagoras; and indeed we are told by Jamblychus, that Abaris, the famous Highland philosopher, cotemporary, and personally acquainted with the sage of Crotona, wore long trousers.[378] I myself can attest the truth of that description, as I well remember the person and habit of that learned mountaineer. I would have explained the reasons that compelled the posterity of those mountaineers to abandon the breeches of their forefathers, and expose their posteriors to the wind.[379] I would have convinced the English antiquaries that the inhabitants of Yorkshire came originally from the Highlands of Scotland, before the Scots had laid aside their breeches, and wore this part of dress, long after their ancestors, as well as the southern Britons were unbreeched by the Romans.[380] From this distinction they acquired the name of *Brigantes, quasi Bragantes*; and hence came the verb to *brag* or boast contemptuously: for the neighbours of the Brigantes being at variance with that people, used, by way of contumelious defiance, when they saw any of them passing or repassing, to clap their hands on their posteriors, and cry *Brag-Brag*.[381]——I would have drawn a learned comparison between the shield of Ajax and the seven-fold breeches of a Dutch skipper.[382] Finally, I would have promulgated the original use of trunk breeches, which would have led me into a discussion of the rites of Cloacina, so differently worshipped by the southern and northern inhabitants of this kingdom.[383] These disquisitions would have unveiled the mysteries that now conceal the orgin, migration, superstition, language, laws and connexions of different nations—— *sed nunc non erit his locus.*[384] I shall only observe, that Linschot and others are mistaken in deriving the Japonese from their neighbours the Chinese;[385] and that Dr. Kempfer is right in his conjecture, supposing them to have come from Media immediately after the confusion of Babel.[386] It is no wonder, therefore, that being *Braccatorum filii,* they should retain the wide breeches of their progenitors.[387]

Having dropped these hints concerning the origin of breeches, I shall now return to the great personage that turned me into this train of thinking. The council of Twenty-Eight being assembled in a great hurry, Fika-kaka sat about five seconds in silence, having in his countenance, nearly the same expression which you have seen in the face and attitude of Felix on his tribunal, as represented by the facetious Hogarth in his print done after the Dutch taste.[388] After some pause he rose, and surveying every individual of the council through a long tube,[389] began a speech to this effect: "Imperial Got-hama-baba, my ever-glorious master; and you, ye illustrious nobles of Japan, Quanbukus, Quos, Days, and Daygos,[390] my fellows and colleagues in the work of administration; it is well known to you all, and they are rascals that deny it, I have watched and fasted[391] for the public weal.—By G—d, I have deprived myself of two hours of my natural rest, every night for a week together.—Then, I have been so hurried with state affairs, that I could not eat a comfortable meal in a whole fortnight; and what rendered this misfortune the greater, my chief cook[392] had dressed an olio *a la Chine.*[393]—I say an olio, my Lords, such an olio as never appeared before upon a table in Japan— by the Lord, it cost me fifty Obans; and I had not time to taste a morsel.— Well, then, I have watched that my fellow-subjects should sleep;[394] I have fasted that they should feed.[395]—I have not only watched and fasted, but I have prayed—no, not much of that—yes, by the Lord, I have prayed as it were—I have ejaculated[396]—I have danced and sung at the Matsuris, which, you know, are religious rites[397]—I have headed the multitude, and treated all the ragamuffins in Japan.[398]—To be certain, I could not do too much for our most excellent and sublime emperor, an emperor unequalled in wisdom, and unrivalled in generosity.—Were I to expatiate from the rising of the sun to the setting thereof, I should not speak half his praise.—O happy nation! O fortunate Japan! happy in such a Dairo to wield the sceptre; and let me add, (vanity apart) fortunate in such a Cuboy to conduct the administration.— Such a prince! and such a minister!—a ha! my noble friend Soo-san-sin-o, I see your Dayship smile—I know what you think, ha! ha!—Very well, my Lord—you may think what you please; but two such head-pieces—pardon, my royal master, my presumption in laying our heads together, you wo'n't find again in the whole universe, ha! ha!—I'll be damn'd if you do, ha! ha! ha!"[399] The tumult without doors was, by this time, increased to such a degree, that the Cuboy could utter nothing more *ab anteriori*;[400] and the majority of the members sat aghast in silence. The Dairo declared he would throw his cap out of the window into the midst of the populace, and challenge any single man of them to bring it up:[401] but he was dissuaded from hazarding his sacred person in such a manner. Quamba-cun-dono proposed to let loose the guards among the multitude: but Fika-kaka protested he could never agree to an expedient so big[402] with danger to the persons of all present. Stiphi-rum-poo was of opinion, that they should proceed according to law, and indict the leaders of the mob for a riot. Nin-kom-poo-po exhorted the Dairo and the whole council to take refuge on board the fleet. Gotto-mio sweated in silence: he trembled for his money-bags, and dreaded another encounter with the mob, by whom he had suffered severely in the flesh, upon a former occasion.[403] The president shrugged up his shoulders, and kept his eye fixed upon a postern or back-door. In this general consternation, Foksi-roku stood up and offered a scheme, which was immediately put in execution. "The multitude, my Lords, (said he) is a many headed monster[404]—it is a Cerberus that must have a sop:[405]—it is a wild beast, so ravenous that nothing but blood will appease its appetite:—it is a whale, that must have a barrel for its amusement:[406]—it is a dæmon to which we must offer up human sacrifice. Now the question is, who is to be this sop, this barrel, this scape-goat?— Tremble not, illustrious Fika-kaka—be not afraid—your life is of too much consequence.—But I perceive that the Cuboy is moved—an unsavoury odour assails my nostrils—brief let me be[407]—Bihn-goh must be the victim—happy, if the sacrifice of his single life can appease the commotions of his country. To him let us impute the loss of Motao:—let us, in the mean time, soothe the rabble with solemn promises that national justice shall be done;[408]—let us employ emissaries to mingle in all places of plebeian resort; to puzzle, perplex, and prevaricate; to exaggerate the misconduct of Bihn-goh; to traduce his character with retrospective reproach; strain circumstances to his prejudice; inflame the resentment of the vulgar against that devoted officer; and keep up the flame by feeding it with continual fuel."[409]

The speech was heard with universal applause: Foksi-roku was kicked by the Dairo and kissed by the Cuboy, in token of approbation. The populace were dispersed by means of fair promises. Bihn-goh was put under arrest, and kept as a malefactor in close prison.[410] Agents were employed through the whole metropolis to vilify his character, and accuse him of cowardice and treachery. Authors were enlisted to defame him in public writings; and mobs hired to hang and burn him in effigie.[411] By these means the revenge of the people was artfully transferred, and their attention effectually diverted from the ministry, which was the first object of their indignation. At length, matters being duly prepared for the exhibition of such an extraordinary spectacle, Bihn-goh underwent a public trial, was unanimously found guilty, and unanimously declared innocent; by the same mouths condemned to death and recommended to mercy:[412] but mercy was incompatible with the designs of the ad——n. The unfortunate Bihn-goh was crucified for cowardice, and bore his fate with the most heroic courage.[413] His behaviour at his death was so inconsistent with the crime for which he was doomed to die, that the emissaries of the Cuboy were fain to propagate a report, that Bihn-goh had bribed a person to represent him at his execution, and be crucified in his stead.[414]

This was a stratagem very well calculated for the meridian of the Japonese populace;[415] and it would have satisfied them intirely, had not their fears been concerned. But the Chinese had for some time been threatening an invasion,[416] the terror of which kept the people of Japan in perpetual agitation and disquiet. They neglected their business; and ran about in distraction, inquiring news, listening to reports, staring, whispering, whimpering, clamouring, neglecting their food and renouncing their repose. The Dairo, who believed the Tartars of Yesso[417] (from whom he himself was descended) had more valour, and skill and honesty, than was possessed by any other nation on earth, took a large body of them into his pay, and brought them over to the island of Niphon, for the defence of his Japonese dominions.[418] The truth is, he had a strong predilection for that people: he had been nursed among them,[419] and sucked it from the nipple. His father had succeeded as heir to a paultry farm in that country;[420] and there he fitted up a cabin,[421] which he preferred to all the palaces of Meaco and Jeddo. The son received the first rudiments of his education among these Tartars, whose country had given birth to his progenitor Bupo. He therefore loved their country; he admired their manners,[422] because they were conformable to his own; and he was in particular captivated by the taste they shewed in trimming and curling their mustachios.[423]

In full belief that the Yessites stood as high in the estimation of his Japonese subjects, as in his own, he imported a body of them into Niphon, where, at first, they were received as saviours and protectors; but the apprehension of danger no sooner vanished, than they were exposed to a thousand insults and mortifications arising from the natural prejudice to foreigners, which prevails among the people of Japan. They were reviled, calumniated, and maltreated in every different form, by every class of people; and when the severe season set in, the Japonese refused shelter from the extremities of the weather, to those very auxiliaries they had hired to defend every thing that was dear to them, from the swords of an enemy whom they themselves durst not look in the face.[424] In vain Fika-kaka employed a double band of artists[425] to tickle their noses. They shut their eyes, indeed, as usual: but their eyes no sooner closed, than their mouths opened, and out flew the tropes and figures of obloquy and execration. They exclaimed, that they had not bought, but caught the Tartar;[426] that they had hired the wolves to guard the sheep;[427] that they were simple beasts who could not defend themselves from the dog with their own horns; but what could be expected from a flock which was led by such a pusillanimous bell-weather?[428]—In a word, the Yessites were sent home in disgrace:[429] but the ferment did not subside; and the conduct of the administration was summoned before the venerable tribunal of the populace.[430]

There was one Taycho,[431] who had raised himself to great consideration in this self-constituted college[432] of the mob. He was distinguished by a loud voice, an unabashed countenance,[433] a fluency of abuse, and an intrepidity of opposition to the measures of the Cuboy,[434] who was far from being a favourite with the plebeians. Orator Taycho's eloquence was admirably suited to his audience; he roared, and he brayed, and he bellowed against the m——r: he threw out personal sarcasms against the Dairo himself.[435] He inveighed against his partial attachment to the land of Yesso, which he had more than once manifested to the detriment of Japan: he inflamed the national prejudice against foreigners; and as he professed an inviolable zeal for the commons of Japan, he became the first demagogue of the empire. The truth is, he generally happened to be on the right side.[436] The partiality of the Dairo, the errors, absurdities, and corruption of the ministry, presented such a palpable mark as could not be missed by the arrows of his declamation. This Cerberus had been silenced more than once with a sop;[437] but whether his appetite was not satisfied to the full, or he was still stimulated by the turbulence of his disposition, which would not allow him to rest, he began to shake his chains anew, and open in the old cry;[438] which was a species of musick to the mob, as agreeable as the sound of a bagpipe to a mountaineer of North Britain,[439] or the strum-strum[440] to the swarthy natives of Angola. It was a strain which had the wonderful effect of effacing from the memory of his hearers, every idea of his former fickleness and apostacy.[441]

In order to weaken the effect of orator Taycho's harangues, the Cuboy had found means to intrude upon the councils of the mob, a native of Ximo called Mura-clami,[442] who had acquired some reputation for eloquence, as an advocate in the tribunals of Japan. He certainly possessed an uncommon share of penetration, with a silver tone of voice, and a great magazine of words and phrases, which flowed from him in a pleasing tide of elocution. He had withal the art of soothing, wheedling, insinuating, and misrepresenting with such a degree of plausibility, that his talents were admired even by the few who had sense enough to detect his sophistry. He had no idea of principle, and no feeling of humanity.[443] He had renounced the maxims of his family, after having turned them to the best account by execrating the rites of Fakkubasi or the White Horse, in private among malcontents, while he worshipped him in public with the appearance of enthusiastic devotion. When detected in this double dealing, he fairly owned to the Cuboy, that he cursed the White Horse in private for his private interest, but that he served him in public from inclination.[444]

The Cuboy had just sense enough to perceive that he would always be true to his own interest; and therefore he made it his interest to serve the m——y to the full extent of his faculties. Accordingly Mura-clami fought a good battle with orator Taycho,[445] in the occasional assemblies of the populace. But as it is much more easy to inflame than to allay,[446] to accuse than to acquit, to asperse than to purify, to unveil truth than to varnish falshood; in a word, to patronize a good cause than to support a bad one; the majesty of the mob snuffed up the excrementitious salts[447] of Taycho's invectives, until their jugulars ached, while they rejected with signs of loathing the flowers of Mura-clami's elocution; just as a citizen of Edinburgh stops his nose when he passes by the shop of a perfumer.[448]

While the constitution of human nature remains unchanged, satire will be always better received than panegyric, in those popular harangues. The Athenians and Romans were better pleased with the Philippics of Demosthenes and Tully,[449] than they would have been with all the praise those two orators could have culled from the stores of their eloquence. A man feels a secret satisfaction in seeing his neighbour treated as a rascal.[450] If he be a knave himself, (which ten to one is the case) he rejoices to see a character brought down to the level of his own, and a new member added to his society; if he be one degree removed from actual roguery, (which is the case with nine-tenths of those who enjoy the reputation of virtue) he indulges himself with the Pharisaical consolation, of thanking God he is not like that publican.[451]

But, to return from this digression, Mura-clami, though he could not with all his talents maintain any sort of competition with Taycho, in the opinion of the mob; he, nevertheless, took a more effectual method to weaken the force of his opposition. He pointed out to Fika-kaka the proper means for amending the errors of his administration: he proposed measures for prosecuting the war with vigour: he projected plans of conquest in Fatsissio;[452] recommended active officers; forwarded expeditions; and infused such a spirit into the councils of Japan, as had not before appeared for some centuries.

But his patron was precluded from the benefit of these measures, by the obstinate prejudice and precipitation of the Dairo, who valued his Yessian farm above all the empire of Japan. This precious morsel of inheritance bordered upon the territories of a Tartar chief called Brut-an-tiffi, a famous freebooter, who had inured his Kurds to bloodshed, and enriched himself with rapine.[453] Of all mankind, he hated most the Dairo, tho' his kinsman; and sought a pretence for seizing the farm, which in three days he could have made his own.[454] The Dairo Gothama-baba was not ignorant of his sentiments. He trembled for his cabin when he considered its situation between hawk and buzzard;[455] exposed on one side to the talons of Brut-an-tiffi, and open on the other to the incursions of the Chinese, under whose auspices the said Brut-an-tiffi had acted formerly as a zealous partizan. He had, indeed, in a former quarrel exerted himself with such activity and rancour, to thwart the politics of the Dairo, and accumulate expences on the subjects of Niphon, that he was universally detested through the whole empire of Japan as a lawless robber, deaf to every suggestion of humanity, respecting no law, restricted by no treaty, scoffing at all religion, goaded by ambition, instigated by cruelty, and attended by rapine.[456]

In order to protect the farm from such a dangerous neighbour, Gothama-baba, by an effort of sagacity peculiar to himself, granted a large subsidy from the treasury of Japan, to a remote nation of Mantchoux Tartars, on condition that they should march to the assistance of his farm, whenever it should be attacked.[457] With the same sanity of foresight, the Dutch might engage in a defensive league with the Ottoman Porte, to screen them from the attempts of the most Christian king,[458] who is already on their frontiers. Brut-an-tiffi knew his advantage, and was resolved to enjoy it. He had formed a plan of usurpation,[459] which could not be executed without considerable sums of money. He gave the Dairo to understand, he was perfectly sensible how much the farm lay at his mercy: then proposed, that Got-hama-baba should renounce his subsidiary treaty with the Mantchoux; pay a yearly tribute to him Brut-an-tiffi, in consideration of his forbearing to seize the farm; and maintain an army to protect it on the other side from the irruptions of the Chinese.[460]

Got-hama-baba, alarmed at this declaration, began by his emissaries to sound the inclinations of his Japonese subjects touching a continental war, for the preservation of the farm; but he found them totally averse to this wise system of politicks. Taycho, in particular, began to bawl and bellow among the mob,[461] upon the absurdity of attempting to defend a remote cabin, which was not defensible; upon the iniquity of ruining a mighty empire, for the sake of preserving a few barren acres, a naked common, a poor, pitiful, pelting farm,[462] the interest of which, like Aaron's rod,[463] had already, on many occasions, swallowed up all regard and consideration for the advantage of Japan. He inveighed against the shameful and senseless partiality of Got-hama-baba: he mingled menaces with his representations. He expatiated on the folly and pernicious tendency of a continental war: he enlarged upon the independence of Japan, secure in her insular situation. He declared, that not a man should be sent to the continent, nor a subsidy granted to any greedy, mercenary, freebooting Tartar; and threatened, that if any corrupt minister should dare to form such a connexion, he would hang it about his neck, like a millstone, to sink him to perdition.[464] The bellows of Taycho's oratory blew up such a flame in the nation, that the Cuboy and all his partizans were afraid to whisper one syllable about the farm.

Mean while Brut-an-tiffi, in order to quicken their determinations, withdrew the garrison he had in a town on the frontiers of China, and it was immediately occupied by the Chinese; an army of whom poured in like a deluge through this opening upon the lands adjoining to the farm.[465] Got-hama-baba was now seized with a fit of temporary distraction. He foamed and raved, and cursed and swore in the Tartarian language: he declared he would challenge Brut-an-tiffi to single combat. He not only kicked, but also cuffed the whole council of Twenty-Eight, and played at foot-ball with his imperial tiara.[466] Fika-kaka was dumbfounded: Sti-phi-rum-poo muttered something about a commission of lunacy:[467] Nin-kom-poo-po pronounced the words flat-bottomed junks;[468] but his teeth chattered so much, that his meaning could not be understood. The Fatzman offered to cross the sea and put himself at the head of a body of light horse, to observe the motions of the enemy;[469] and Gotto-mio prayed fervently within himself, that God

Almighty would be pleased to annihilate that accursed farm, which had been productive of such mischief to Japan. Nay, he even ventured to exclaim, "Would to God, the farm was sunk in the middle of the Tartarian ocean!"[470] "Heaven forbid! (cried the president Soo-san-sin-o) for in that case, Japan must be at the expence of weighing[471] it up again."

In the midst of this perplexity, they were suddenly surprised at the apparition of Taycho's head nodding from a window[472] that overlooked their deliberations. At sight of this horrid spectacle the council broke up. The Dairo fled to the inmost recesses of the palace, and all his counsellors vanished, except the unfortunate Fika-kaka, whose fear had rendered him incapable of any sort of motion[473] but one, and that he instantly had to a very efficacious degree. Taycho bolting in at the window, advanced to the Cuboy without ceremony, and accosted him in these words: "It depends upon the Cuboy, whether Taycho continues to oppose his measures, or becomes his most obsequious servant. Arise, illustrious Quanbuku, and cast your eyes upon the steps by which I ascended." Accordingly Fika-kaka looked, and saw a multitude of people who had accompanied their orator into the court of the palace, and raised for him an occasional[474] stair of various implements. The first step was made by an old fig-box, the second by a nightman's bucket, the third by a cask of hempseed, the fourth by a tar-barrel, the fifth by an empty kilderkin, the sixth by a keg, the seventh by a bag of soot, the eighth by a fish-woman's basket, the ninth by a rotten pack-saddle, and the tenth by a block of hard wood from the island of Fatsissio.[475] It was supported on one side by a varnished lettered post, and on the other by a crazy hogshead.[476] The artificers who erected this climax,[477] and now exulted over it with hideous clamour, consisted of grocers, scavengers, halter-makers, carpenters, draymen, distillers, chimney-sweepers, oyster-women, ass-drivers, aldermen, and dealers in waste paper.—To make myself understood, I am obliged, Peacock, to make use of those terms and denominations which are known in this metropolis.

Fika-kaka, having considered this work with astonishment, and heard the populace declare upon oath, that they would exalt their orator above all competition, was again addressed by the invincible Taycho. "Your Quanbuku-ship perceives how bootless it will be to strive against the torrent.—What need is there of many words? admit me to a share of the administration——I will commence your humble slave—I will protect the farm at the expence of Japan, while there is an Oban left in the island of Niphon; and I will muzzle these bears so effectually, that they shall not shew their teeth, except in applauding our proceedings." An author who sees the apparition of a bailiff standing before him in his garret, and instead of being shewn a *capias*,[478] is presented with a bank note; an impatient lover stopped upon Bagshot heath[479] by a person in a masque, who proves to be his sweetheart come to meet him in disguise, for the sake of the frolick; a condemned criminal, who, on the morning of execution-day, instead of being called upon by the finisher of the law,[480] is visited by the sheriff with a free pardon; could not be more agreeably surprised than was Fika-kaka at the demagogue's declaration. He flew into his embrace and wept aloud with joy, calling him his dear Taycho. He squeezed his hand, kissed him on both cheeks, and swore he should share the better half of all his power: then he laughed and snivelled by turns, lolled out his tongue, waddled about the chamber, wriggled and niggled and noddled.[481] Finally, he undertook to prepare the Dairo for his reception, and it was agreed that the orator should wait on his new colleague next morning.— This matter being settled to their mutual satisfaction, Taycho retreated through the window into the courtyard, and was convoyed home in triumph by that many-headed hydra the mob,[482] which shook its multitudinous tail, and brayed through every throat with hideous exultation.

The Cuboy, mean while, had another trial to undergo, a trial which he had not foreseen. Taycho was no sooner departed, than he hied him to the Dairo's cabinet, in order to communicate the happy success of his negotiation. But at certain periods, Got-hama-baba's resentment was more than a match for any other passion that belonged to his disposition, and now it was its turn to reign. The Dairo was made of very combustible materials, and these had been kindled up by the appearance of orator Taycho, who (he knew) had treated his person with indecent freedoms,[483] and publickly vilified the worship of the White Horse. When Fika-kaka, therefore, told him he had made peace with the demagogue, the Dairo, instead of giving him the kick of approbation, turned his own back upon the Cuboy,[484] and silenced him with a *boh!* Had Fika-kaka assailed him with the same syllogistical sophism which was used by the Stagyrite[485] to Alexander in a passion, perhaps he might have listened to reason: ἡ ὀργὴ ου πρὸς ἴσους, ἀλλὰ πρὸς τοῦς κρειττονας γινεται, Σοι δὲ ουδεὶς ἴσος.—"Anger should be raised not by our equals, but by our superiors; but you have no equal."[486]—Certain it is, that Got-hama-baba had no equal; but Fika-kaka was no more like Aristotle, than his master resembled Alexander. The Dairo remained deaf to all his remonstrances, tears, and intreaties, until he declared that there was no other way of saving the farm, but that of giving *charte blanche* to Taycho.[487] This argument seemed at once to dispel the clouds which had been compelled[488] by his indignation: he consented to receive the orator in quality of minister, and next day was appointed for his introduction.[489]

In the morning Taycho the Great repaired to the palace of the Cuboy, where he privately performed the ceremony of osculation *a posteriori*, sung a solemn Palinodia[490] on the subject of political system, repeated and signed the Buponian creed,[491] embraced the religion of Fakkubasi, and adored the White Horse with marks of unfeigned piety and contrition. Then he was conducted to the antichamber of the emperor, who could not, without great difficulty, so far master his personal dislike, as to appear before him with any degree of composure. He was brought forth by Fika-kaka like a tame bear to the stake,[492] if that epithet of *tame* can be given with any propriety to an animal which no body but his keeper dares approach. The orator perceiving him advance, made a low obeisance according to the custom of Japan, that is, by bending the body averse from the Dairo, and laying the right hand upon the left buttock;[493] and pronounced with an audible voice, "Behold, invincible Got-hama-baba, a sincere penitent come to make atonement for his virulent opposition to your government, for his atrocious insolence to your sacred person. I have calumniated your favourite farm, I have questioned your integrity, I have vilified your character, ridiculed your understanding, and despised your authority"—This recapitulation was so disagreeable to the Dairo, that he suddenly flew off at a tangent, and retreated growling to his den;[494] from whence he could by no means be lugged[495] again by the Cuboy, until Taycho, exalting his voice,[496] uttered these words:—"But I will exalt your authority more than ever it was debased—I will extol your wisdom, and expatiate on your generosity; I will glorify the White Horse, and sacrifice all the treasures of Japan, if needful, for the protection of the farm of Yesso." By these cabalistical[497] sounds the wrath of Got-hama-baba was intirely appeased. He now returned with an air of gaiety, strutting, sideling, circling, fluttering, and cobbling[498] like a turkey-cock in his pride, when he displays his feathers to the sun. Taycho hailed the omen; and turning his face from the emperor, received such a salutation on the *os sacrum*,[499] that the parts continued vibrating and tingling for several days.

An indenture tripartite[500] was now drawn up and executed. Fika-kaka was continued treasurer, with his levees,[501] his Bonzas, and his places;[502] and orator Taycho undertook, in the character of chief scribe,[503] to protect the farm of Yesso, as well as to bridle and manage the blatant beast whose name was Legion.[504] That a person of his kidney[505] should have the presumption to undertake such an affair, is not at all surprising; the wonder is, that his performance should even exceed his promise. The truth is, he promised more than he could have performed, had not certain unforeseen incidents, in which he had no concern, contributed towards the infatuation[506] of the people.

The first trial to which he brought his ascendency over the mob, was his procuring from them a free gift,[507] to enable the Dairo to arm his own private tenants in Yesso, together with some ragamuffin Tartars in the neighbourhood, for the defence of the farm. They winked so hard[508] upon this first overt-act of his apostacy,[509] that he was fully persuaded they had resigned up all their senses to his direction; and resolved to shew them to all Europe,[510] as a surprising instance of his art in monster-taming. This furious beast not only suffered itself to be bridled and saddled, but frisked and fawned, and purred and yelped, and crouched before the orator, licking his feet, and presenting its back to the burthens which he was pleased to impose. Immediately after this first essay, Qamba-cun-dono the Fatzman was sent over to assemble and command a body of light horse in Yesso, in order to keep an eye on the motions of the enemy; and indeed this vigilant and sagacious commander conducted himself with such activity and discretion, that he soon brought the war in those parts to a point of termination.[511]

Mean while, Brut-an-tiffi continuing to hover on the skirts of the farm, at the head of his myrmidons, and demanding of the Dairo a categorical answer to the hints he had given, Got-hama-baba underwent several successive fits of impatience and distraction. The Cuboy, instigated by his own partizans, and in particular by Mura-clami, who hoped to see Taycho take some desperate step that would ruin his popularity; I say the Cuboy, thus stimulated, began to ply the orator with such pressing intreaties as he could no longer resist; and now he exhibited such a specimen of his own power and the people's insanity, as transcends the flight of ordinary faith. Without taking the trouble to scratch their long ears, tickle their noses, drench them with mandragora or geneva,[512] or make the least apology for his own turning tail to the principles which he had all his life so strenuously inculcated, he crammed down their throats an obligation to pay a yearly tribute to Brut-an-tiffi,[513] in consideration of his forbearing to seize the Dairo's farm; a tribute which amounted to seven times the value of the lands,[514] for the defence of which it was payed. When I said *crammed*, I ought to have used another phrase. The beast, far from shewing any signs of loathing, closed its eyes, opened its hideous jaws, and as it swallowed the inglorious bond, wagged its tail in token of intire satisfaction.[515]

No fritter on Shrove Tuesday[516] was ever more dexterously turned, than were the hydra's brains by this mountebank in patriotism, this juggler in politicks,[517] this cat in pan,[518] or cake in pan, or κατα παν[519] in principle. Some people gave out that he dealt with a conjurer, and others scrupled not to insinuate that he had sold himself to the evil spirit. But there was no occasion for a conjurer to deceive those whom the dæmon of folly had previously confounded; and as to selling, he sold nothing but the interest of his country; and of that he made a very bad bargain. Be that as it may, the Japonese now viewed Brut-an-tiffi either through a new perspective,[520] or else surveyed him with organs intirely metamorphosed. Yesterday they detested him as a profligate ruffian lost to all sense of honesty and shame, addicted to all manner of vice, a scoffer at religion, particularly that of Fak-kubasi, the scourge of human nature, and the inveterate enemy of Japan. To-day, they glorified him as an unblemished hero,[521] the protector of good faith, the mirror of honesty, the pattern of every virtue, a saint in piety, a devout votary to the White Horse, a friend to mankind, the fast ally and the firmest prop of the Japonese empire.

The farm of Yesso, which they had so long execrated as a putrid and painful excrescence upon the breech of their country, which would never be quiet until this cursed wart was either exterminated or taken away; they now fondled as a favourite mole, nay, and cherished as the apple of their eye. One would have imagined that all the inconsistencies and absurdities which characterise the Japonese nation, had taken their turns to reign, just as the interest of Taycho's ambition required. When it was necessary for him to establish new principles, at that very instant their levity prompted them to renounce their former maxims. Just as he had occasion to fascinate[522] their senses, the dæmon of caprice instigated them to shut their eyes, and hold out their necks, that they might be led by the nose. At the very nick of time when he adopted the cause of Brut-an-tiffi, in diametrical opposition to all his former professions, the spirit of whim and singularity disposed them to kick against the shins of common sense, deny the light of day at noon, and receive in their bosoms as a dove, the man whom before they had shunned as a serpent. Thus every thing concurred to establish for orator Taycho, a despotism of popularity; and that not planned by reason, or raised by art, but founded on fatality and finished by accident. *Quos Jupiter vult perdere priùs dementat.*[523]

Brut-an-tiffi being so amply gratified by the Japonese for his promise of forbearance with respect to the farm of Yesso, and determined, at all events, to make some new acquisition, turned his eyes upon the domains of Pol-hassan-akousti,[524] another of his neighbours, who had formed a most beautiful colony in this part of Tartary; and rushed upon it at a minute's warning.[525] His resolution in this respect was so suddenly taken and quickly executed, that he had not yet formed any excuse for this outrage, in order to save appearances. Without giving himself the trouble to invent a pretence, he drove old Pol-hassan-akousti out of his residence; compelled the domestics of that prince to enter among his own banditti;[526] plundered his house, seized the archives of his family, threatened to shoot the antient gentlewoman his wife,[527] exacted heavy contribution from the tenants; then dispersed a manifesto[528] in which he declared himself the best friend of the said Akousti and his spouse, assuring him he would take care of his estate as a precious deposit to be restored to him in due season. In the mean time, he thought proper to sequester the rents,[529] that they might not enable Pol-hassan to take any measures that should conduce to his own prejudice. As for the articles of meat, drink, clothing, and lodging, for him and his wife and a large family of small children, he had nothing to do but depend upon Providence, until the present troubles should be appeased. His behaviour on this occasion, Peacock, puts me in mind of the Spaniard whom Philip II. employed to assassinate his own son Don Carlos. This compassionate Castilian, when the prince began to deplore his fate, twirled his mustachio, pronouncing with great gravity these words of comfort: *"Calla, calla, Senor, todo que se haze es por su bien."* "I beg your highness won't make any noise; this is all for your own good:"[530] or the politeness of Gibbet in the play[531] called the Beaux Stratagem, who says to Mrs. Sullen, "Your jewels, Madam, if you please—don't be under any uneasiness, Madam—if you make any noise, I shall blow your brains out—I have a particular regard for the ladies, Madam."

But the possession of Pol-hassan's demesnes was not the ultimate aim of Brut-an-tiffi. He had an eye to a fair and fertile province belonging to a Tartar princess of the house of Ostrog.[532] He saw himself at the head of a numerous banditti trained to war, fleshed[533] in carnage, and eager for rapine; his coffers were filled with the spoils he had gathered in his former freebooting expeditions; and the incredible sums payed him as an annual tribute from Japan, added to his other advantages, rendered him one of the most formidable chiefs in all Tartary. Thus elated with the consciousness of his own strength, he resolved to make a sudden irruption into the dominions of Ostrog, at a season of the year when that house could not avail itself of the alliances they had formed with other powers; and he did not doubt but that, in a few weeks, he should be able to subdue the whole country belonging to the Amazonian princess.[534] But I can tell thee, Peacock, his views extended even farther than the conquest of the Ostrog dominions. He even aspired at the empire of Tartary, and had formed the design of deposing the great Cham, who was intimately connected with the princess of Ostrog.[535] Inspired by these projects, he, at the beginning of winter, suddenly poured like a deluge into one of the provinces that owned this Amazon's sway; but he had hardly gained the passes of the mountains, when he found himself opposed by a numerous body of forces, assembled under the command of a celebrated general, who gave him battle without hesitation, and handled him so roughly, that he was fain to retreat into the demesnes of Pol-hassan, where he spent the greatest part of the winter in exacting contributions and extending the reign of desolation.[536]

All the petty princes and states who hold of the great Cham, began to tremble for their dominions, and the Cham himself was so much alarmed at the lawless proceedings of Brut-an-tiffi, that he convoked a general assembly[537] of all the potentates who possessed fiefs in the empire, in order to deliberate upon measures for restraining the ambition of this ferocious freebooter. Among others, the Dairo of Japan, as lord of the farm of Yesso, sent a deputy to this convention, who, in his master's name, solemnly disclaimed and professed his detestation of Brut-an-tiffi's proceedings, which, indeed, were universally condemned.[538] The truth is, he, at this period, dreaded the resentment of all the other co-estates rather more than he feared the menaces of Brut-an-tiffi; and, in particular, apprehended a sentence of outlawry from the Cham,[539] by which at once he would have forfeited all legal title to his beloved farm. Brut-an-tiffi, on the other hand, began to raise a piteous clamour,[540] as if he meant to excite compassion. He declared himself a poor injured prince, who had been a dupe to the honesty and humanity of his own heart. He affirmed that the Amazon of Ostrog had entered into a conspiracy against him, with the Mantchoux Tartars, and prince Akousti: he published particulars of this dreadful conjuration,[541] which appeared to be no other than a defensive alliance formed in the apprehension that he would fall upon some of them, without any regard to treaty, as he had done on a former occasion, when he seized one of the Amazon's best provinces.[542] He publickly taxed the Dairo of Japan with having prompted him to commence hostilities, and hinted that the said Dairo was to have shared his conquests.[543] He openly intreated his co-estates to interpose their influence towards the reestablishment of peace in the empire; and gave them privately to understand, that he would ravage their territories without mercy, should they concur with the Cham in any sentence to his prejudice.

As he had miscarried in his first attempt, and perceived a terrible cloud gathering around him, in all probability he would have been glad to compound matters at this juncture, on condition of being left in *statu quo*; but this was a condition not to be obtained. The princess of Ostrog had by this time formed such a confederacy, as threatened him with utter destruction. She had contracted an offensive and defensive alliance with the Chinese, the Mantchoux, and the Serednee Tartars;[544] and each of these powers engaged to furnish a separate army to humble the insolence of Brut-an-tiffi. The majority of the Tartar fiefs agreed to raise a body of forces to act against him as a disturber of the publick peace; the great Cham threatened him with a decree of outlawry and rebellion;[545] and the Amazon herself opposed him[546] at the head of a very numerous and warlike tribe, which had always been considered as the most formidable in that part of Tartary. Thus powerfully sustained, she resolved to enjoy her revenge; and at any rate retrieve the province which had been ravished from her by Brut-an-tiffi, at a time when she was embarrassed with other difficulties. Brut-an-tiffi did not think himself so reduced as to purchase peace with such a sacrifice. The Mantchoux were at a great distance, naturally slow in their motions, and had a very long march through a desert country, which they would not attempt without having first provided prodigious magazines.[547] The Serednee were a divided people, among whom he had made shift to foment intestine divisions, that would impede the national operations of the war.[548] The Japonese Fatzman formed a strong barrier between him and the Chinese;[549] the army furnished by the fiefs, he despised as raw, undisciplined militia: besides, their declaring against him afforded a specious pretence for laying their respective dominions under contribution. But he chiefly depended upon the coffers of Japan, which he firmly believed would hold out until all his enemies should be utterly exhausted.

As this freebooter was a principal character in the drama which I intend to rehearse,[550] I shall sketch his portrait according to the information I received from a fellow-atom who once resided at his court, constituting part in one of the organs belonging to his first chamberlain. His stature was under the middle size;[551] his aspect mean and forbidding, with a certain expression which did not at all prepossess the spectator in favour of his morals. Had an accurate observer beheld him without any exterior distinctions, in the streets of this metropolis, he would have naturally clapped his hands to his pockets. Thou hast seen the character of Gibbet represented on the stage by a late comedian of expressive feature.[552] Nature sometimes makes a strange contrast between the interior workmanship and the exterior form; but here the one reflected a true image of the other. His heart never felt an impression of tenderness: his notions of right and wrong did not refer to any idea of benevolence, but were founded entirely on the convenience of human commerce; and there was nothing social in the turn of his disposition. By nature he was stern, insolent, and rapacious, uninfluenced by any motive of humanity; unawed by any precept of religion. With respect to religion, he took all opportunities of exposing it to ridicule and contempt.[553] Liberty of conscience he allowed to such extent, as exceeded the bounds of decorum and disgraced all legislation. He pardoned a criminal convicted of bestiality, and publickly declared that all modes of religion, and every species of amour, might be freely practised and prosecuted through all his dominions.[554] His capacity was of the middling mould, and he had taken some pains to cultivate his understanding. He had studied the Chinese language,[555] which he spoke with fluency, and piqued himself upon his learning, which was but superficial. His temper was so capricious and inconstant, that it was impossible even for those who knew him best, to foresee any one particular of his personal demeanour. The same individual he would caress and insult by turns, without the least apparent change of circumstance. He has been known to dismiss one of his favourites with particular marks of regard, and the most flattering professions of affection; and before he had time to pull off his buskins[556] at his own house, he has been hurried on horseback by a detachment of cavalry, and conveyed to the frontiers. Thus harrassed, without refreshment or repose, he was brought back by another party, and reconveyed to the presence of Brut-an-tiffi, who embraced him at meeting, and gently chid him for having been so long absent.[557]—The fixed principles of this Tartar were these: insatiable rapacity, restless ambition, and an insuperable contempt for the Japonese nation. His maxims of government were entirely despotic. He considered his subjects as slaves, to be occasionally[558] sacrificed to the accomplishment of his capital[559] designs; but, in the mean time, he indulged them with the protection of equitable laws, and encouraged them to industry for his own emolument.

His virtues consisted of temperance, vigilance, activity, and perseverance. His folly chiefly appeared in childish vanity and self-conceit. He amused himself with riding, reviewing his troops, reading Chinese authors, playing on a musical instrument in use among the Tartars,[560] trifling with buffoons, conversing with supposed wits, and reasoning with pretended philosophers:[561] but he had no communication with the female sex;[562] nor, indeed, was there any ease, comfort, or enjoyment to be derived from a participation of his pastime.[563] His wits, philosophers, and buffoons, were composed of Chinese refugees,[564] who soon discovered his weak side, and flattered his vanity to an incredible pitch of infatuation. They persuaded him that he was an universal genius, an invincible hero, a sage legislator, a sublime philosopher, a consummate politician, a divine poet, and an elegant historian. They wrote systems, compiled memoirs, and composed poems, which were published in his name; nay, they contrived witticisms, which he uttered as his own.[565]—They had, by means of commercial communication with the banks of the Ganges, procured the history of a Western hero, called Raskalander, which, indeed, was no other than the Memoirs of Alexander wrote by Quintus Curtius,[566] translated from the Indian language, with an intermixture of Oriental fables. This they recommended with many hyperbolical encomiums to the perusal of Brut-an-tiffi, who became enamoured of the performance, and was fired with the ambition of rivalling, if not excelling Raskalander,[567] not only as a warrior, but likewise as a patron of taste and a protector of the liberal arts. As Alexander deposited Homer's Iliad in a precious casket;[568] so Brut-an-tiffi procured a golden box for preserving this sophistication[569] of Quintus Curtius. It was his constant companion: he affected to read it in public; and to lay it under his pillow at night.

Thus pampered with adulation and intoxicated with dreams of conquest, he made no doubt of being able to establish a new empire in Tartary, which should entirely eclipse the kingdom of Tum-ming-qua, and raise a reputation that should infinitely transcend the fame of Yan,[570] or any emperor that ever sat upon the throne of Thibet. He now took the field against the Amazon of the house of Ostrog; penetrated into her dominions; defeated one of her generals in a pitched battle; and undertook the siege of one of her principal cities, in full confidence of seeing her kneeling at his gate before the end of the campaign.[571] In the mean time, her scattered troops were rallied and reinforced by another old, experienced commander,[572] who being well acquainted with the genius of his adversary, pitched upon an advantageous situation, where he waited for another attack. Brut-an-tiffi, flushed with his former victory, and firmly persuaded that no mortal power could withstand his prowess, gave him battle at a very great disadvantage. The consequence was natural:—he lost great part of his army; was obliged to abandon the siege, and retreat with disgrace.[573] A separate body, commanded by one of his ablest captains, met with the same fate in a neighbouring country; and a third detachment at the farthest extremity of his dominions, having attacked an army of the Mantchoux, was repulsed with great loss.[574]

These were not all the mortifications to which he was exposed about this period. The Fatzman of Japan, who had formed an army for the defence of the farm of Yesso against the Chinese, met with a terrible disaster.[575] Notwithstanding his being outnumbered by the enemy, he exhibited many proofs of uncommon activity and valour. At length they came to blows with him, and handled him so roughly, that he was fain to retreat from post to pillar, and leave the farm at their mercy. Had he pursued his route to the right, he might have found shelter in the dominions of Brut-an-tiffi, and this was his intention; but, instead of marching in a straight line, he revolved to the right, like a planet round the sun, impelled as it were by a compound impulse,[576] until he had described a regular semicircle; and then he found himself with all his followers engaged in a sheep-pen, from whence there was no egress; for the enemy, who followed his steps, immediately blocked up the entrance. The unfortunate Fatzman being thus pounded, must have fallen a sacrifice to his centripetal force, had not he been delivered by the interposition of a neighbouring chief, who prevailed upon the Chinese general to let Quamba-cun-dono escape, provided his followers would lay down their arms, and return peaceably to their own habitations. This was a bitter pill, which the Fatzman was obliged to swallow, and is said to have cost him five stone of suet.[577] He returned to Japan in obscurity; the Chinese general took possession of the farm in the name of his emperor; and all the damage which the tenants sustained, was nothing more than a change of masters, which they had no great cause to regret.[578]

To the thinking part of the Japanese, nothing could be more agreeable than this event, by which they were at once delivered from a pernicious excrescence, which, like an ulcerated tumour, exhausted the juices of the body by which it was fed. Brut-an-tiffi considered the transaction in a different point of view. He foresaw that the Chinese forces would now be at liberty to join his enemies, the tribe of Ostrog, with whom the Chinese emperor was intimately connected;[579] and that it would be next to impossible to withstand the joint efforts of the confederacy, which he had brought upon his own head. He therefore raised a hideous clamour. He accused the Fatzman of misconduct, and insisted, not without a mixture of menaces, upon the Dairo's reassembling his forces in the country of Yesso.[580]

The Dairo himself was inconsolable. He neglected his food, and refused to confer with his ministers. He dismissed the Fatzman[581] from his service. He locked himself in his cabinet, and spent the hours in lamentation. "O my dear farm of Yesso! (cried he) shall I never more enjoy thy charms!—Shall I never more regale my eye with thy beauteous prospects, thy hills of heath; thy meads of broom; and thy wastes of sand![582] Shall I never more eat thy black bread, drink thy brown beer, and feast upon thy delicate porkers! Shall I never more receive the homage of the sallow Yessites with their meagre faces, ragged skirts, and wooden shoes! Shall I never more improve their huts, and regulate their pigstyes! O cruel Fate! in vain did I face thy mud-walled mansion with a new freestone[583] front! In vain did I cultivate thy turnep-garden![584] In vain did I enclose a piece of ground at a great expence,

and raise a crop of barley, the first that ever was seen in Yesso! In vain did I
send over a breed of mules and black cattle[585] for the purposes of husbandry!
In vain did I supply you with all the implements of agriculture! In vain did I
sow grass and grain for food, and plant trees, and furze and fern for shelter to
the game, which could not otherwise subsist upon your naked downs! In vain
did I furnish your houseless sides,[586] and fill your hungry bellies with the
good things[587] of Japan! In vain did I expend the treasures of my empire for
thy melioration and defence! In vain did I incur the execrations of my people,
if I must now lose thee for ever; if thou must now fall into the hands of an
insolent alien, who has no affection for thy soil, and no regard for thy interest! O Quamba-cun-dono! Quamba-cun-dono! how hast thou disappointed
my hope! I thought thou wast too ponderous to flinch; that thou wouldst
have stood thy ground fixed as the temple of Fakkubasi, and larded the lean
earth with thy carcase,[588] rather than leave my farm uncovered:[589] but, alas!
thou hast fled before the enemy like a partridge on the mountains;[590] and
suffered thyself at last to be taken in a snare like a foolish dotterel!"[591]

The Cuboy, who overheard this exclamation, attempted to comfort him
through the key-hole. He soothed, and whined, and wheedled, and laughed
and wept all in a breath. He exhorted the illustrious Got-hama-baba to bear
this misfortune with his wonted greatness of mind.—He offered to present
his Imperial majesty with lands in Japan that should be equal in value to the
farm he had lost: or, if that should not be agreeable, to make good at the
peace, all the damage that should be done to it by the enemy. Finally, he
cursed the farm, as the cause of his master's chagrin, and fairly wished it at
the devil.—Here he was suddenly interrupted with a "Bub-ub-ub-boh! my
lord Cuboy, your grace talks like an apothecary.—Go home to your own
palace,[592] and direct your cooks; and may your bonzes kiss your a—— to
your heart's content.—I swear by the horns of the Moon and the hoofs of the
White Horse, that my foot shall not touch your posteriors these three
days."—Fika-kaka, having received this severe check, craved pardon in a
whimpering tone, for the liberty he had taken, and retired to consult with
Mura-clami, who advised him to summon orator Taycho to his assistance.

This mob-driver being made acquainted with the passion of the Dairo, and
the cause of his distress, readily undertook to make such a speech through the
key-hole, as should effectually dispel the emperor's despondence; and to this
enterprize he was encouraged by the hyperbolical praises of Mura-clami,
who exhausted all the tropes of his own rhetoric in extolling the eloquence of
Taycho.—This triumvirate immediately adjourned to the door of the apartment in which Got-hama-baba was seqestered, where the orator kneeling

upon a cushion, with his mouth applied to the key-hole, opened the sluices of his elocution to this effect:

"Most gracious!" "Bo, bo, boh!"[593]—"Most illustrious!" "Bo, boh!"— "Most invincible Got-hama-baba!"—"Boh!"—"When the sun, that glorious luminary is obscured, by envious clouds, all nature saddens, and seems to sympathize with his apparent[594] distress.—Your Imperial majesty is the sun of our hemisphere, whose splendour illuminates our throne; and whose genial warmth enlivens our hearts; and shall we your subjects, your slaves, the creatures of your nod—shall we unmoved behold your ever-glorious effulgence overcast? No! while the vital stream bedews our veins, while our souls retain the faculty of reason, and our tongues the power of speech, we shall not cease to embalm[595] your sorrow with our tears; we shall not cease to pour the overflowings of our affection—our filial tenderness, which will always be reciprocal with your parental care: these are the inexhaustible sources of the nation's happiness. They may be compared to the rivers Jodo and Jodogava,[596] which derive their common origin from the vast lake of Ami. The one winds its silent course, calm, clear, and majestic, reflecting the groves and palaces that adorn its banks, and fertilizing the delightful country through which it runs: the other gushes impetuous through a rugged channel and less fertile soil; yet serves to beautify a number of wild romantic scenes; to fill an hundred aqueducts, and to turn a thousand mills: at length, they join their streams below the imperial city of Meaco, and form a mighty flood devolving to the bay of Osaca,[597] bearing on its spacious bosom, the riches of Japan."—Here the orator paused for breath:—the Cuboy clapped him on the back, whispering, "Super-excellent! O charming simile! Another such will sink the Dairo's grief to the bottom of the sea; and his heart will float like a blown bladder upon the waves of Kugava."[598] Mura-clami was not silent in his praise, while he squeezed an orange between the lips of Taycho; and Got-hama-baba seemed all attention: at length the orator resumed his subject:— "Think not, august emperor, that the cause of your disquiet is unknown, or unlamented by your weeping servants. We have not only perceived your eclipse, but discovered the invidious body by whose interposition that eclipse is effected. The rapacious arms of the hostile Chinese have seized the farm of Yesso!"—"Oh, oh, oh!" "—that farm so cherished by your Imperial favour; that farm which, in the north of Tartary, shone like a jewel in an Æthiop's ear;[599]—yes, that jewel hath been snatched by the savage hand of a Chinese freebooter:—but, dry your tears, my prince; that jewel shall detect his theft, and light us to revenge. It shall become a rock to crush him in his retreat;—a net of iron to entangle his steps; a fallen trunk over which his feet shall stumble. It shall hang like a weight about his neck, and sink him to the lowest gulph of perdition.[600]——Be comforted, then, my liege! your farm is rooted to the center;[601] it can neither be concealed nor removed. Nay, should he hide it at the bottom of the ocean; or place it among the constellations in the heavens; your faithful Taycho would fish it up intire, or tear it headlong from the starry firmament.[602]—We will retrieve the farm of Yesso"—"But, how, how, how, dear orator Taycho?" "The empire of Japan shall be mortgaged for the sake of that precious—that sacred spot, which produced the patriarch apostle *Bupo*, and resounded under the hoofs of the holy steed.—Your people of Japan shall chant the litany of Fakkubasi.—They shall institute crusades for the recovery of the farm; they shall pour their treasury at your imperial feet;—they shall clamour for imposition;[603]—they shall load themselves with tenfold burthens, desolate their country, and beggar their posterity in behalf of Yesso. With these funds I could undertake even to overturn the councils of Pekin.[604]—While the Tartar princes deal in the trade of blood,[605] there will be no want of hands to cut away those noxious weeds which have taken root in the farm of Yesso; those vermin that have preyed upon her delightful blossoms! Amidst such a variety of remedies, there can be no difficulty in choosing.—Like a weary traveller, I will break a bough from the first pine that presents, and brush away those troublesome insects that gnaw the fruits of Yesso.—Should not the mercenary bands of Tartary suffice to repel those insolent invaders; I will engage to chain this island to the continent; to build a bridge from shore to shore, that shall afford a passage more free and ample than the road to Hell.[606] Through this avenue I will ride the mighty beast whose name is Legion.[607]—I have studied the art of war, my Liege:—I had once the honour to serve my country as Lance-presado[608] in the militia of Niphon.—I will unpeople these realms, and overspread the land of Yesso with the forces of Japan."

Got-hama-baba could no longer resist the energy of such expressions. He flew to the door of his cabinet,[609] and embraced the orator in a transport of joy; while Fika-kaka fell upon his neck and wept aloud; and Mura-clami kissed the hem of his garment.

You must know, Peacock, I had by this time changed my situation. I was discharged in the perspiratory vapour from the perinæum[610] of the Cuboy, and sucked into the lungs of Mura-clami, through which I pervaded[611] into the course of the circulation, and visited every part of his composition. I found the brain so full and compact, that there was not room for another particle of matter. But instead of a heart,[612] he had a membranous sac, or hollow viscus,[613] cold and callous, the habitation of sneaking caution, servile flattery, griping avarice, creeping malice, and treacherous deceit. Among these tenants it was my fate to dwell; and there I discovered the motives by which the lawyer's conduct was influenced. He now secretly rejoiced at the presumption of Taycho, which he hoped had already prompted him to undertake more than he could perform; in which case he would infallibly incur disgrace[614] either with the Dairo or the people. It is not impossible but this hope might have been realized, had not fortune unexpectedly interposed, and operated as an auxilliary to the orator's presumption. Success began to dawn upon the arms of Japan in the island of Fatsisio;[615] and towards the end of the campaign, Brut-an-tiffi obtained two petty advantages in Tartary against one body of Chinese, and another of the Ostrog.[616] All these were magnified into astonishing victories, and ascribed to the wisdom and courage of Taycho, because during his ministry they were obtained; though he neither knew why, nor wherefore; and was in this respect as innocent as his master Got-hama-baba, and his colleague Fika-kaka. He had penetration enough to perceive, however, that these events had intoxicated the rabble, and began to pervert their ideas. Success of any kind is apt to perturb the weak brain of a Japonese; but the acquisition of any military trophy, produces an actual delirium.—The streets of Meaco were filled with the multitudes who shouted, whooped, and hollowed. They made processions with flags and banners; they illuminated their houses; they extolled Ian-on-i,[617] a provincial captain of Fatsisio, who had by accident repulsed a body of the enemy, and reduced an old barn which they had fortified.[618] They magnified Brut-an-tiffi; they deified orator Taycho; they drank, they damned, they squabbled, and acted a thousand extravagancies which I shall not pretend to enumerate or particularize. Taycho, who knew their trim,[619] seized this opportunity to strike while the iron was hot.—He forthwith mounted an old tub,[620] which was his public rostrum, and waving his hand in an oratorial attitude, was immediately surrounded with the thronging populace.—I have already given you a specimen of his manner, and therefore shall not repeat the tropes and figures of his harangue: but only sketch out the plan of his address, and specify the chain of his argument alone. He assailed them in the way of paradox, which never fails to produce a wonderful effect upon a heated imagination and a shallow understanding. Having, in his exordium,[621] artfully fascinated their faculties, like a juggler in Bartholomew-fair,[622] by means of an assemblage of words without meaning or import; he proceeded to demonstrate, that a wise and good man ought to discard his maxims the moment he finds they are certainly established on the foundation of eternal truth. That the people of Japan ought to preserve the farm of Yesso, as the apple of their eye, because nature had disjoined it from their empire; and the maintenance of it would involve them in all the quarrels of Tartary: that it was to be preserved at all hazards, because it was not worth preserving: that all the power and opulence of Japan ought to be exerted and employed in its defence, because, by the nature of its situation, it could not possibly be defended: that Brut-an-tiffi was the great protector of the religion of the Bonzas, because he had never shewn the least regard to any religion at all: that he was the fast friend of Japan, because he had more than once acted as a rancorous enemy to this empire, and never let slip the least opportunity of expressing his contempt for the subjects of Niphon: that he was an invincible hero, because he had been thrice beaten, and once compelled to raise a siege in the course of two campaigns: that he was a prince of consummate honour, because he had in the time of profound peace, usurped the dominions and ravaged the countries of his neighbours, in defiance of common honesty; in violation of the most solemn treaties: that he was the most honourable and important ally that the empire of Japan could choose, because his alliance was to be purchased with an enormous annual tribute, for which he was bound to perform no earthly office of friendship or assistance; because connexion with him effectually deprived Japan of the friendship of all the other princes and states of Tartary; and the utmost exertion of his power could never conduce, in the smallest degree, to the interest or advantage of the Japonese empire.[623]

Such were the propositions orator Taycho undertook to demonstrate; and the success justified his undertaking. After a weak mind has been duly prepared, and turned as it were, by opening a sluice or torrent of high-sounding words, the greater the contradiction proposed the stronger impression it makes, because it increases the puzzle, and lays fast hold on the admiration; depositing the small proportion of reason with which it was before impregnated, like the vitriol acid in the copper-mines of Wicklow, into which if you immerse iron, it immediately quits the copper which it had before dissolved, and unites with the other metal, to which it has a stronger attraction.[624]— Orator Taycho was not so well skilled in logic as to amuse[625] his audience with definitions of concrete and abstract terms; or expatiate upon the genus and the difference; or state propositions by the subject, the predicate, and the copula; or form syllogisms by mood and figure:[626] but he was perfectly well acquainted with all the equivocal or synonimous words in his own language, and could ring the changes[627] on them with great dexterity. He knew perfectly well how to express the same ideas by words that literally implied opposition:—for example, a valuable conquest or an invaluable conquest; a shameful rascal or a shameful villain; a hard head or a soft head; a large

conscience or no conscience; immensely great or immensely little; damned
high or damned low; damned bitter, damned sweet; damned severe, damned
insipid; and damned fulsome.[628] He knew how to invert the sense of words
by changing the manner of pronunciation; e.g. "You are a very pretty fellow!" to signify, "You are a very dirty scoundrel."—"You have *always* spoke
respectfully of the higher powers!" to express, "You have often insulted your
betters, and even your sovereign!" "You have *never* turned tail to the principles you professed!" to declare, "You have acted the part of an infamous
apostate."[629] He was well aware that words alter their signification according
to the circumstances of times, customs, and the difference of opinion. Thus
the name of Jack, who used to turn the spit and pull off his master's boots,
was transferred to an iron machine and a wooden instrument[630] now substituted for these purposes: thus a stand for the tea-kettle, acquired the name
of Footman; and the words Canon and Ordinance, signifying originally a rule
or law, was extended to a piece of artillery, which is counted the *ultima lex*, or
ultima ratio regum.[631]—In the same manner the words infidel, heresy, good
man, and political orthodoxy, imply very different significations, among different classes of people. A Mussulman is an infidel at Rome, and a Christian
is distinguished as an unbeliever at Constantinople. A Papist by Protestant-
ism understands heresy; to a Turk, the same idea is conveyed by the sect of
Ali.[632] The term *good man*, at Edinburgh, implies fanaticism; upon the
Exchange of London it signifies cash; and in the general acceptation, benevolence.[633] Political orthodoxy has different, nay opposite definitions, at different places in the same kingdom; at O—— and C——;[634] at the Cocoa-tree
in Pall-mall;[635] and at Garraway's in Exchange-alley.[636] Our orator was well
acquainted with all the legerdemain of his own language, as well as with the
nature of the beast he had to rule. He knew when to distract its weak brain
with a tumult of incongruous and contradictory ideas: he knew when to over-
whelm its feeble faculty of thinking, by pouring in a torrent of words without
any ideas annexed. These throng in like city-milliners to a Mile-end assembly,[637] while it happens to be under the direction of a conductor without
strength and authority. Those that have ideas annexed may be compared to
the females provided with partners, which, though they may croud the place,
do not absolutely destroy all regulation and decorum. But those that are
uncoupled, press in promiscuously with such impetuosity and in such numbers, that the puny master of the ceremonies is unable to withstand the irruption; far less, to distinguish their quality, or accommodate them with partners: thus they fall into the dance without order, and immediately anarchy
ensues. Taycho having kept the monster's brain on a simmer, until, like the

cow-heel in Don Quixote, it seemed to cry, *Comenme, comenme*; Come, eat me, come, eat me;[638] then told them in plain terms, that it was expedient they should part with their wives and their children, their souls and their bodies, their substance and their senses, their blood and their suet, in order to defend the indefensible farm of Yesso, and to support Brut-an-tiffi, their insupportable ally.—The hydra, rolling itself in the dust, turned up its huge unwieldy paunch and wagged its forky tail; then licked the feet of Taycho, and through all its hoarse discordant throats, began to bray applause. The Dairo rejoiced in his success, the first-fruits of which consisted in their agreeing to maintain an army of twenty thousand Tartar mercenaries, who were reinforced by the flower of the national troops of Japan, sent over to defend the farm of Yesso;[639] and in their consenting to prolong the annual tribute granted to Brut-an-tiffi,[640] who, in return for this condescension, accommodated the Dairo with one of his free-booting captains to command the Yessite army. This new general[641] had seen some service, and was counted a good officer: but it was not so much on account of his military character that he obtained this command, as for his dexterity in prolonging the war; his skill in exercising all the different arts of peculation; and his attachment to Brut-an-tiffi, with whom he had agreed to co-operate in milking the Japonese cow. This plan they executed with such effect, as could not possibly result from address[642] alone, unassisted by the infatuation of those whom they pillaged. Every article of contingent expence for draught-horses, waggons, postage, forage, provision, and secret service, was swelled to such a degree as did violence to common sense as well as to common honesty. The general had a fellow-feeling with all the contractors in the army, who were connected with him in such a manner as seemed to preclude all possibility of detection. In vain some of the Japonese officers endeavoured to pry into this mysterious commerce; in vain inspectors were appointed by the government of Japan. The first were removed on different pretences: the last were encountered by such disgraces and discouragements, as in a little time compelled them to resign the office they had undertaken.[643] In a word, there was not a private mercenary Tartar soldier in this army who did not cost the empire of Japan as much as any subaltern officer of its own; and the annual charge of this continental war, undertaken for the protection of the farm of Yesso, exceeded the whole expence of any former war which Japan had ever maintained on its own account since the beginning of the empire:[644] nay, it was attended with one circumstance which rendered it still more insupportable. The money expended in armaments and operations, equipped and prosecuted on the side of Japan, was all circulated within the empire; so that it still remained useful to the community in general; but no instance could be produced, of a single copan that ever returned from the continent of Tartary; therefore all the sums sent thither, were clear loss to the subjects of Japan.[645] Orator Taycho acted as a faithful ally to Brut-an-tiffi, by stretching the bass-strings of the mobile[646] in such a manner, as to be always in concert with the extravagance of the Tartar's demands, and the absurdity of the Dairo's predilection. Fika-kaka was astonished at these phænomena; while Mura-clami hoped in secret, that the orator's brain was disordered; and that his insanity would soon stand confessed, even to the conviction of the people.—"If, (said he to himself) they are not altogether destitute of human reason, they must, of their own accord, perceive and comprehend this plain proposition: A cask of water that discharges *three* by one pipe, and receives no more than *two* by another, must infallibly be emptied at the long-run.[647] Japan discharges *three* millions of obans every year[648] for the defence of that blessed farm, which, were it put up to sale, would not fetch one sixth part of the sum;[649] and the annual ballance of her trade with all the world brings in *two* millions:[650] ergo, it runs out faster than it runs in, and the vessel at the long-run must be empty." Mura-clami was mistaken. He had studied philosophy only in profile.[651] He had endeavoured to investigate the sense, but he had never fathomed the absurdities of human nature. All that Taycho had done for Yesso, amounted not to one-third of what was required for the annual expence of Japan while it maintained the war against China in different quarters of Asia. A former Cuboy, (rest his soul!) finding it impossible to raise within the year the exorbitant supplies that were required to gratify the avarice and ambition of the Dairo, had contrived the method of funding, which hath been lately adopted with such remarkable success in this kingdom.[652] You know, Pea-cock, this is no more than borrowing a certain sum on the credit of the nation, and laying a fresh tax upon the public, to defray the interest of every sum thus borrowed; an excellent expedient, when kept within due bounds, for securing the established government, multiplying the dependants of the m——ry, and throwing all the money of the empire into the hands of the administration. But those loans were so often repeated, that the national debt had already swelled to an enormous burthen;[653] such a variety of taxes was laid upon the subject, as grievously inhanced[654] all the necessaries of life; consequently the poor were distressed, and the price of labour was raised to such a degree, that the Japonese manufactures were every-where undersold by the Chinese traders, who employed their workmen at a more moderate expence.[655] Taycho, in this dilemma, was seized with a strange conceit. Alchemy was at that period become a favourite study in Japan. Some bonzas having more learning and avarice than their brethren, applied themselves to the study of certain Chaldean manuscripts,[656] which their ancestors had brought from Assyria; and in these they found the substance of all that is contained in the works of Hermes Trismegistus, Geber, Zosymus, the Pana-polite, Olympiodorus, Heliodorus, Agathodæmon, Morienus, Albertus Mag-nus, and, above all, your countryman Roger Bacon, who adopted Geber's opinion, that mercury is the common basis, and sulphur the cement of all metals.[657] By the bye, this same friar Bacon was well acquainted with the composition of gun-powder, though the reputation arising from the discov-ery, has been given to Swartz, who lived many years after that monk of Westminster.[658] Whether the Philosopher's stone, otherwise called the Gift Azoth, the fifth Essence, or the Alkahest;[659] which last Van Helmont pilfered from the tenth book of the Archidoxa,[660] that treasure so long deposited in the occiput[661] of the renowned Aureolus, Philippus, Paracelsus, Theophras-tus, Bombast, de Hohenheim;[662] was ever really attained by human adept, I am not at liberty to disclose; but certain it is, the philosophers and alchemists of Japan, employed by orator Taycho to transmute baser metals into gold, miscarried in all their experiments. The whole evaporated in smoke, without leaving so much as the scrapings of a crucible for a specific against the itch.[663] Tickets made of a kind of bamboo, had been long used to reinforce the cir-culation of Japan;[664] but these were of no use in Tartary: the mercenaries and allies of that country would receive nothing but gold and silver, which, indeed, one would imagine they had a particular method of decomposing or annihilating; for, of all the millions transported thither, not one copan was ever known to revisit Japan. "It was a country (as Hamlet says) from whose bourn no travelling copan e'er returned."[665] As the war of Yesso, therefore, engrossed[666] all the specie of Niphon, and some currency was absolutely necessary to the subsistence of the Japonese, the orator contrived a method to save the expence of solid food.[667] He composed a mess that should fill their bellies, and, at the same time, protract the intoxication of their brains, which it was so much his interest to maintain.—He put them upon a diet of yeast; where this did not agree with the stomach, he employed his emissaries to blow up the patients *à posteriori*, as the dog was blown up by the madman of Seville, recorded by Cervantes.[668] The individuals thus inflated were seen swaggering about the streets, smooth and round, and sleek and jolly, with leering eyes and florid complexion. Every one seemed to have the *os magna sonaturum*.[669] He strutted with an air of importance. He broke wind, and broached new systems.[670] He declared as if by revelation, that the more debt the public owed, the richer it became; that food was not necessary to the support of life; nor an intercourse of the sexes required for the propagation of the species. He expatiated on yeast, as the nectar of the gods, that would sustain the animal machine, fill the human mind with divine inspiration, and confer immortality. From the efficacy of this specific, he began to prophesy concerning the White Horse, and declared himself an apostle of Bupo.— Thus they strolled through the island of Niphon, barking and preaching the gospel of Fakku-basi, and presenting their barm goblets[671] to all who were in quest of political salvation. The people had been so well prepared for infatuation, by the speeches of Taycho, and the tidings of success from Tartary, that every passenger[672] greedily swallowed the drench, and in a little time the whole nation was converted; that is, they were totally freed from those troublesome and impertinent faculties of reason and reflection, which could have served no other purpose but to make them miserable under the burthens to which their backs were now subjected. They offered up all their gold and silver, their jewels, their furniture and apparel, at the shrine of Fakku-basi, singing psalms and hymns in praise of the White Horse. They put arms into the hands of their children, and drove them into Tartary, in order to fatten the land of Yesso with their blood. They grew fanatics in that cause, and worshipped Brut-an-tiffi, as the favourite prophet of the beatified Bupo. All was staggering, staring, incoherence and contortion, exclamation and eructation.[673] Still this was no more than a temporary delirium, which might vanish as the intoxicating effects of the yeast subsided. Taycho, therefore, called in two reinforcements to the drench. He resolved to satiate their appetite for blood, and to amuse their infantine vanity with the gew-gaws of triumph. He equipped out one armament at a considerable expence to make a descent on the coast of China, and sent another at a much greater, to fight the enemy in Fatsisio.[674] The commander of the first disembarked upon a desolate island, demolished an unfinished cottage, and brought away a few bunches of wild grapes.[675] He afterwards hovered on the Chinese coast; but was deterred from landing by a very singular phænomenon. In surveying the shore, through spying-glasses, he perceived the whole beach instantaneously fortified, as it were, with parapets of sand, which had escaped the naked eye;[676] and at one particular part, there appeared a body of giants with very hideous features, peeping, as it were, from behind those parapets: from which circumstances the Japonese general concluded there was a very formidable ambuscade, which he thought it would be madness to encounter, and even folly to ascertain.[677] One would imagine he had seen Homer's account of the Cyclops,[678] and did not think himself safe, even at the distance of some miles from the shore; for he pressed the commander of the Fune to weigh anchor immediately, and retire to a place of more safety.—I shall now, Peacock, let you into the whole secret. This great officer was deceived by the carelessness of the commissary,[679] who, instead of perspectives,[680] had furnished him with glasses peculiar to Japan, that magnified and multiplied objects at the same time. They are called Pho-beron-tia.[681]—The large parapets of sand were a couple of mole-hills; and the gigantic faces of grim aspect, were the posteriors of an old woman[682] sacrificing *sub dio*,[683] to the powers of digestion.—There was another circumstance which tended to the miscarriage of this favourite expedition.—The principal design was against a trading town, situated on a navigable river; and at the place where this river disembogued itself into the sea, there was a Chinese fort called Sa-rouf.[684] The admiral of the Fune[685] sent the second in command, whose name was Sel-uon,[686] to lay this fort in ashes, that the embarkation might pass without let[687] or molestation. A Chinese pilot offered to bring his junk within a cable-length of the walls: but he trusted to the light of his own penetration. He ran his junk aground, and solemnly declared there was not water sufficient to float any vessel of force, within three miles of Sa-rouf. This discovery he had made by sounding, and it proved two very surprising paradoxes: first, that the Chinese junks drew little or no water, otherwise they could not have arrived at the town where they were laid up; secondly, that the fort Sa-rouf was raised in a spot where it neither could offend, nor be offended.[688] But the Sey-seo-gun[689] Sel-uon was a mighty man for paradoxes. His superior in command, was a plain man, who did not understand these niceties: he therefore grumbled, and began to be troublesome; upon which, a council of war was held;[690] and he being over-ruled by a majority of voices, the whole embarkation returned to Niphon *re infecta*.[691] You have been told how the beast called Legion brayed, and bellowed, and kicked, when the fate of Byn-goh's expedition was known; it was disposed to be very unruly at the return of this armament: but Taycho lulled it[692] with a double dose of his Mandragora. It growled at the giants, the sand-hills, and the paradoxes of Sel-uon:[693] then brayed aloud *Taycho for ever!* rolled itself up like a lubberly hydra, yawned, and fell fast asleep.—The other armament equipped for the operations in Fatsisio, did not arrive at the place of destination till the opportunity for action was lost. The object was the reduction of a town and island belonging to the Chinese: but before the Fune with the troops arrived from Niphon, the enemy having received intimation of their design, had reinforced the garrison and harbour with a greater number of forces and Fune than the Japonese commander could bring against them. He, therefore, wisely declined an enterprize which must have ended in his own disgrace and destruction.[694]

The Chinese were successful in other parts of Fatsisio. They demolished some forts, they defeated some parties, and massacred some people, belonging to the colonies of Japan.[695] Perhaps the tidings of these disasters would have roused the people of Niphon from the lethargy of intoxication in which they were overwhelmed, had not their delirium been kept up by some fascinating amulets from Tartary: these were no other than the bubbles[696] which Brut-an-tiffi swelled into mighty victories over the Chinese and Ostrog;[697] though, in fact, he had been severely cudgelled, and more than once in very great danger of crucifixion. Taycho presented the monster with a bowl of blood, which he told it this invincible ally had drawn from its enemies the Chinese, and, at the same time, blowed the gay bubbles athwart its numerous eyes.[698] The hydra lapped the gore with signs of infinite relish; groaned and grunted to see the bubbles dance; exclaimed, "O rare Taycho!" and relapsed into the arms of slumber. Thus passed the first campaign of Taycho's administration.

By this time Fika-kaka was fully convinced that the orator actually dealt with the devil, and had even sold him his soul for this power of working miracles on the understanding of the populace. He began to be invaded with fears, that the same consideration would be demanded of him for the ease and pleasure he now enjoyed in partnership with that magician.[699] He no longer heard himself scoffed, ridiculed, and reviled in the assemblies of the people. He no longer saw his measures thwarted, nor his person treated with disdain. He no longer racked his brains for pretences to extort money; nor trembled with terror when he used these pretences to the public. The mouth of the opposition was now glewed to his own posteriors. Many a time and often,[700] when he heard orator Taycho declaiming against him from his rostrum, he cursed him in his heart, and was known to ejaculate "Kiss my a—se, Taycho;" but little did he think the orator would one day stoop to this compliance. He now saw that insolent foul-mouthed demagogue ministring with the utmost servility to his pleasure and ambition. He filled his bags with the treasures of Japan, as if by inchantment; so that he could now gratify his own profuse temper[701] without stint or controul. He took upon himself the whole charge of the administration; and left Fika-kaka to the full enjoyment of his own sensuality, thus divested of all its thorns. It was the contemplation of these circumstances, which inspired the Cuboy with a belief that the devil was concerned in producing this astonishing calm of felicity; and that his infernal highness would require of him some extraordinary sacrifice for the extraordinary favours he bestowed. He could not help suspecting the sincerity of Taycho's attachment, because it seemed altogether unnatural; and if his soul was to be the sacrifice, he wished to treat with Satan as a principal.[702] Full of this idea, he had recourse to his Bonzes as the most likely persons to procure him such an interview with the prince of darkness, as should not be attended with immediate danger to his corporeal parts: but, upon enquiry, he found there was not one conjurer among them all. Some of them made a merit of their ignorance; pretending they could not in conscience give application to an art which must have led them into communication with demons: others insisted there was no such thing as the devil; and this opinion seemed to be much relished by the Cuboy: the rest frankly owned they knew nothing at all of the matter. For my part, Peacock, I not only know there is a devil, but I likewise know that he has marked out nineteen twentieths of the people of this metropolis for his prey.—How now! You shake, sirrah!—You have some reason, considering the experiments you have been trying in the way of sorcery; turning the sieve and sheers;[703] mumbling gibberish over a goose's liver stuck with pins; pricking your thumbs, and writing mystical characters with your blood; forming spells with sticks laid across; reading prayers backwards;[704] and invoking the devil by the name, style, and title of *Sathan, Abrasax Adonai*.[705] I know what communication you had with goody Thrusk at Camberwell,[706] who undertook for three shillings and four-pence to convey you on a broomstick to Norway, where the devil was to hold a conventicle;[707] but you boggled at crossing the sea, without such security for your person as the beldame could not give. I remember your poring over the treatise *De volucri arborea*,[708] until you had well-nigh lost your wits; and your intention to enrol yourself in the Rosicrusian society, until your intrigue with the tripe-woman in Thieving-lane destroyed your pretensions to chastity.[709] Then you cloaked your own wickedness with an affectation of scepticism, and declared there never was any such existence as devil, demon, spirit, or goblin; nor any such art as magic, necromancy, sorcery, or witchcraft.—O infidel! hast thou never heard of the three divisions of magic into natural, artificial, and diabolical?[710] The first of these is no more than medicine; hence the same word Pharmacopola[711] signified both a wise-acre and apothecary. To the second belong the glass sphere of Archimedes, the flying wooden pigeon of Archytus, the emperor Leo's singing birds of gold, Boetius the Consolator's flying birds of brass, hissing serpents of the same metal, and the famous speaking head of Albertus Magnus.[712] The last, which we call diabolical, depends upon the evocation of spirits: such was the art exercised by the magicians of Pharaoh;[713] as well as by that conjurer recorded by Gaspar Peucerus, who animated the dead carcase of a famous female harper in Bologna in such a manner, that she played upon her instrument as well as ever she had done in her life, until another magician removing the charm, which had been placed in her arm-pits, the body fell down deprived of all motion.[714] It is by such means that conjurers cure distempers with charms and amulets; that, according to St. Isidore, they confound the elements, disturb the understanding, slay without poison or any perceptible wound, call up devils, and learn from them how to torment their enemies.[715] Magic was known even to the ancient Romans. Cato teaches us how to charm a dislocated bone, by repeating these mystical words, *Incipe, cantare in alto, S. F. motas danata dardaries, Astotaries, dic una parite dum coeunt, &c.*[716] Besides, the virtues of ABRACADABRA[717] are well known; though the meaning of the word has puzzled some of the best critics of the last age; such as Wendelinus, Scaliger, Saumaise, and father Kircher; not to mention the ancient physician Serenus Sammonicus, who describes the disposition of these characters in hexameter verse.[718] I might here launch out into a very learned dissertation to prove that this very Serenus formed the word ABRACADABRA from the Greek word Αβρασαξ, a name by which Basilides the Ægyptian heretic defined the Deity, as the letters of it imply 365, the number of days in the year.[719] This is the word still fair and legible on one of the two talismans found in the seventeenth century, of which Baronius gives us the figure in the second volume of his Annals.[720] By the bye, Peacock, you must take notice, that the figure of St. George[721] encountering the dragon, which is the symbol of the order of the Garter, and at this day distinguishes so many inns, taverns, and ale-houses, in this kingdom, was no other originally than the device of an abraxas or amulet wore by the Basilidians, as a charm against infection: for, by the man on horseback killing the dragon, was typified the sun purifying the air, and dispersing the noxious vapours from the earth. An abraxas marked with this device, is exhibited by Montfaucon out of the Collection of Sig. Capello.[722] This symbol, improved by the cross on the top of the spear, was afterwards adopted by the Christian crusards,[723] as a badge of their religious warfare, as well as an amulet to ensure victory; the cross alluding to Constantine's labarum,[724] with the motto εν τουτω νικα, "In this you shall conquer." The figure on horseback they metamorphosed into St. George, the same with George the Arian,[725] who at one time was reckoned a martyr, and maintained a place in the Roman Martyrology, from which he and others were erased by pope Gelasius in the fifth century, because the accounts of their martyrdom were written by heretics. This very George, while he officiated as bishop of Alexandria, having ordered a temple of the god *Mythras* to be purified, and converted into a Christian church, found in the said temple this emblem of the sun, which the Persians adored under the name of *Mythras*; and with the addition of the cross, metamorphosed it into a symbol of Christian warfare against idolatry. It was on this occasion that the Pagans rose against George, and murdered him with the utmost barbarity; and from this circumstance he became a saint and martyr, and the amulet or abraxas became his badge of distinction. The cross was considered as such a sure protection in battle, that every sword-hilt was made in this form, and every warrior, before he engaged, kissed it in token of devotion: hence the phrase, "I kiss your hilt,"[726] which is sometimes used even at this day. With respect to the mystical words ΑΒΡΑϹΑΣ ΙΑΩ, ΔΟΩΝΑΙ, which are found upon those amulets, and supposed to be of Hebrew extract, tho' in the Greek character of termination;[727] if thou wouldst know their real signification, thou mayest consult the learned De Croy, in his Treatise concerning the genealogies of the *Gnostics*.[728] Thou wilt find it at the end of St. Irenæus's works, published by Grabius[729] at Oxford.—

But, to return to magic, thou must have heard of the famous Albertus Magnus de Bolstadt, who indifferently exercised the professions of conjurer, bawd, and man-midwife; who forged the celebrated *Androides*, or brazenhead, which pronounced oracles, and solved questions of the utmost difficulty:[730] nor can the fame of Henry Cornelius Agrippa have escaped thee; he, who wrote the Treatises *De occulta Philosophia; & de cæcis Ceremoniis*;[731] who kept his demon secured with an inchanted iron collar, in the shape of a black dog; which black dog being dismissed in his last moments with these words: *Abi perdita bestia quæ me totum perdidisti*; plunged itself in the river Soame, and immediately disappeared.[732] But what need of those profane instances to prove the existence of magicians who held communication with the devil? Don't we read in the scripture of the magicians of Pharaoh and Manasses? of the witch of Endor; of Simon and Barjesus, magicians; and of that sorceress of whose body the apostle Paul dispossessed the devil?[733] Have not the fathers[734] mentioned magicians and sorcerers? Have not different councils denounced anathemas against them? Hath not the civil law decreed punishments to be inflicted upon those convicted of the black art? Have not all the tribunals in France, England, and particularly in Scotland, condemned many persons to the stake for sorceries,[735] on the fullest evidence; nay, even on their own confession? Thou thyself mayest almost remember the havock that was made among the sorcerers in one of the English colonies in North-America, by Dr. Encrease Mather, and Dr. Cotton Mather, those luminaries of the New-England church, under the authority and auspices of Sir William Phipps, that flower of knighthood and mirror of governors, who, not contented with living witnesses, called in the assistance of spectral evidence, to the conviction of those diabolical delinquents.[736]—This was a hint, indeed, which he borrowed from the famous trial of Urban Grandier, canon of Loudun in France, who was duly convicted of magic, upon the depositions of the devils *Astaroth, Eusas, Celsus, Acaos, Cedon, Asmodeus, Alix, Zabulon, Nephthalim, Cham, Uriel,* and *Achas.*[737] I might likewise refer thee to king James's History of Witchcraft, wherein it appears, upon uncontrovertible evidence, that the devil not only presided in person at the assemblies of those wise women; but even condescended to be facetious, and often diverted them by dancing and playing gambols with a lighted candle in his breech.[738] I might bid thee recollect the authenticated account of the earl of Gowry's conspiracy against the said king, in which appears the deposition of a certain person, certifying that the earl of Gowry had studied the black art: that he wore an amulet about his person, of such efficacy, that although he was run several times through the body, not one drop of blood flowed from the wounds until those mystical characters were removed.[739]—Finally, I could fill whole volumes with undeniable facts to prove the existence of magic: but what I have said shall suffice. I must only repeat it again, that there was not one magician, conjurer, wizard, or witch, among all the Bonzes of Japan, whom the Cuboy consulted: a circumstance that astonished him the more, as divers of them, notwithstanding their beards, were shrewdly suspected to be old women; and 'till that time, an old woman with a beard upon her chin had been always considered as an agent of the devil.[740]—It was the nature of Fika-kaka to be impatient and impetuous. Perceiving that none of his Bonzes had any communication with the devil, and that many of them doubted whether there was any such personage as the devil, he began to have some doubts about his own soul: "For if there is no devil (said he), there is no soul to be damned; and it would be a reproach to the justice of heaven to suppose that all souls are to be saved, considering what rascally stuff mankind are made of." This was an inference which gave him great disturbance; for he was one of those who would rather encounter eternal damnation, than run any risque of being annihilated.[741] He therefore assembled all those among the Bonzes who had the reputation of being great philosophers and metaphysicians, in order to hear their opinions concerning the nature of the soul.[742] The first reverend sage who delivered himself on this mysterious subject, having stroked his grey beard, and hemmed thrice with great solemnity, declared that the soul was an animal; a second pronounced it to be the number *three*, or proportion; a third contended for the number *seven*, or harmony; a fourth defined the soul the *universe*; a fifth affirmed it was a mixture of elements; a sixth asserted it was composed of *fire*; a seventh opined it was formed of *water*; an eighth called it an *essence*; a ninth, an idea; a tenth stickled for *substance without extension*; an eleventh, for *extension without substance*; a twelfth cried it was an *accident*;[743] a thirteenth called it a *reflecting mirrour*; a fourteenth, the *image reflected*; a fifteenth insisted upon its being a *tune*; a sixteenth believed it was the instrument that played the tune; a seventeenth undertook to prove it was *material*; an eighteenth exclaimed it was *immaterial*; a nineteenth allowed it was *something*; and a twentieth swore it was *nothing*.—By this time all the individuals that composed this learned assembly, spoke together with equal eagerness and vociferation. The volubility with which a great number of abstruse and unintelligible terms and definitions were pronounced and repeated, not only resembled the confusion of Babel, but they had just the same effect upon the brain of Fika-kaka, as is generally produced in weak heads by looking stedfastly at a mill-wheel or a vortex, or any other object in continual rotation. He grew giddy, ran three times round, and dropped down in the midst of the Bonzes, deprived of sense and motion. When he recovered so far as to be able to reflect upon what had happened, he was greatly disturbed with the terror of annihilation, as he had heard nothing said in the consultation which could give him any reason to believe there was such a thing as an immortal soul. In this emergency he sent for his counsellor Mura-clami, and when that lawyer entered his chamber, exclaimed, "My dear Mura, as I have a soul to be saved!—A soul to be saved!—ay, there's the rub![744]—the devil a soul have I!—Those Bonzes are good for nothing but to kiss my a—se; —a parcel of ignorant asses!—Pox on their philosophy! Instead of demonstrating the immortality of the soul, they have plainly proved the soul is a chimæra, a will o' the wisp, a bubble, a term, a word, a nothing!—My dear Mura! prove but that I have a soul, and I shall be contented to be damned to all eternity!"—"If that be the case, (said the other) your Quambucuship may set your heart at rest: for, if you proceed to govern this empire, in conjunction with Taycho, as you have begun, it will become a point of eternal justice to give you an immortal soul (if you have not one already) that you may undergo eternal punishment, according to your demerits." The Cuboy was much comforted by this assurance, and returned to his former occupations with redoubled ardour. He continued to confer benefices on his back-friends[745] the Bonzes; to regulate the whole army of tax-gatherers; to bribe the tribunes, the centurions, the decuriones,[746] and all the inferior mob-drivers of the empire; to hire those pipers who were best skilled in making the multitude dance, and find out the ablest artists to scratch their long ears, and tickle their noses. These toils were sweetened by a variety of enjoyments. He possessed all the pomp of ostentation; the vanity of levees, the pride of power, the pleasure of adulation, the happiness of being kicked by his sovereign and kissed by his Bonzes; and, above all, the delights of the stomach and the close-stool, which recurred in perpetual succession, and which he seemed to enjoy with a particular relish: for, it must be observed, to the honour of Fika-kaka, that what he eagerly received at one end, he as liberally refunded at the other. But as the faculties of his mind were insufficient to digest the great mess of power which had fallen to his share, so were the organs of his body unable to concoct[747] the enormous mass of aliments which he so greedily swallowed. He laboured under an indigestion of both; and the vague promises which went upwards, as well as the murmurs that passed the other way, were no other than eruptive crudities arising from the defects of his soul and body.[748]

As for Taycho, he confined himself to the management of the war. He recalled the general in chief from Fatsisio,[749] because he had not done that which he could not possibly do: but, instead of sending another on whose abilities he could depend, he allowed the direction of the armaments to devolve upon the second in command, whose character he could not possibly know; because, indeed, he was too obscure to have any character at all. The fruits of his sagacity soon appeared. The new general Abra-moria,[750] having reconnoitred a post of the enemy, which was found too strong to be forced, attacked it without hesitation, and his troops were repulsed and routed with considerable slaughter.[751] It was lucky for Taycho that the tidings of this disaster were qualified by the news of two other advantages which the arms of Japan had gained.—A separate corps of troops, under Yaf-frai and Ya-loff,[752] reduced a strong Chinese fortress in the neighbourhood of Fatsisio;[753] and a body of Japonese, headed by a factor called Ka-liff, obtained a considerable victory at Fla-sao, in the farther extremity of Tartary, where a trading company of Meaco possessed a commercial settlement.[754] The Hydra of Meaco began to shake its numerous heads and growl, when it heard of Abra-moria's defeat. At that instant, one of its leaders exclaimed, "Bless thy long ears! It was not Taycho that recommended Abra-moria to this command. He was appointed by the Fatz-man." This was true. It was likewise true, that Taycho had allowed him quietly to succeed to the command, without knowing any thing of his abilities;—it was equally true, that Taycho was an utter stranger to Yaf-frai and Ya-loff, who took the fortress, as well as to the factor Ka-liff, who obtained the victory at the farther end of Tartary.[755]—Nevertheless, the beast cried aloud, "Hang Abra-moria! and a fig for the Fatz-man. But let the praise of Taycho be magnified! It was Taycho that subdued the fortress in the Isle Ka-frit-o.[756] It was Taycho that defeated the enemy at Fla-sao.—Yaf-frai has slain his thousands;—Ya-loff has slain his five thousands;—but Taycho has slain his ten thousands."[757]

Taycho had credit not only for the success of the Japonese arms, but likewise for the victories of Brut-an-tiffi, who had lately been much beholden to fortune. I have already observed what a noise that Tartar made when the Fatz-man of Japan found himself obliged to capitulate with the Chinese general. In consequence of that event, the war was already at an end with respect to the Japonese, on the continent of Tartary. The emperor of China took possession of the farm of Yesso; the peasants quietly submitted to their new masters; and those very free-booting Tartar chiefs, who had sold their subjects as soldiers to serve under the Fatz-man, had already agreed to send the very same mercenaries into the army of China.[758] It was at this juncture that Brut-an-tiffi exalted his throat. In the preceding campaign he had fought with various success. One of his generals had given battle to the Mantchoux Tartars, and each side claimed the victory.[759] Another of his leaders had been defeated and taken by the Ostrog.[760] The Chinese had already advanced to the frontiers of Brut-an-tiffi's dominions. In this dilemma he exerted himself with equal activity and address: he repulsed the Chinese army with considerable loss;[761] and in the space of one month after this action, gained a victory over the general of the Ostrog.[762] These advantages rendered him insufferably arrogant. He exclaimed against the Fatz-man; he threatened the Dairo; and, as I have taken notice above, a new army was raised at the expence of Japan, to defend him from all future invasions of the Chinese. Already the Tartar general Bron-xi-tic, who was vested at his desire with the command of the mercenary army of Japan, had given a severe check to a strong body of the Chinese, and even threatened to carry the war into the empire of China; but his progress was soon stopt, and he was forced to retreat in his turn towards the farm of Yesso.[763]—But from nothing did orator Taycho reap a fuller harvest of praise, than from the conquest of Tzin-khall, a settlement of the Chinese on the coast of Terra Australis;[764] which conquest was planned by a Banyan[765] merchant of Meaco, who had traded on that coast, and was particularly known to the king of the country. This royal savage was uneasy at the neighbourhood of the Chinese, and conjured[766] the merchant, whose name was Thum-Khumm-qua,[767] to use his influence at the court of Meaco, that an armament should be equipped against the settlement of Tzin-khall, he himself solemnly promising to co-operate in the reduction of it with all his forces.[768]—Thum-Khumm-qua, whose zeal for the good of his country got the better of all his prudential maxims, did not fail to represent this object in the most interesting[769] points of view. He demonstrated to Taycho the importance of the settlement; that it abounded with slaves, ivory, gold, and a precious gum which was not to be found in any other part of the world; a gum in great request all over Asia, and particularly among the Japonese, who were obliged to purchase it in time of war at second-hand from their enemies the Chinese, at an exorbitant price.[770] He demonstrated that the loss of this settlement would be a terrible wound to the emperor of China; and proved that the conquest of it could be atchieved at a very trifling expence. He did more. Tho' by the maxims of his sect he was restrained from engaging in any military enterprize, he offered to conduct the armament in person, in order the more effectually to keep the king of the country steady to his engagements. Though the scheme was in itself plausible and practicable, Mr. orator Taycho shuffled and equivocated until the season for action was past. But Thum-Khumm-qua was indefatigable. He exhorted, he pressed, he remonstrated, he complained; and besieged the orator's house in such a manner, that Taycho at length, in order to be rid of his importunity, granted his request. A small armament was fitted out; the Banyan embarked in it, leaving his own private affairs in confusion; and the settlement was reduced according to his prediction.[771] When the news of this conquest arrived at Meaco, the multifarious beast brayed hoarse applause, and the minister Taycho was magnified[772] exceedingly. As for Thum-Khumm-qua, whose private fortune was consumed in the expedition, all the recompence he received, was the consciousness of having served his country. In vain he reminded Taycho of his promises; in vain he recited the minister's own letters, in which he had given his word that the Banyan should be liberally rewarded, according to the importance of his services: Taycho was both deaf and blind to all his remonstrances and representations; and, at last, fairly flung the door in his face.[773]

Such was the candour and the gratitude of the incomparable Taycho.— The poor projector Thum-Khumm-qua found himself in a piteous case, while the whole nation resounded with joy for the conquest which his sagacity had planned, and his zeal carried into execution.[774] He was not only abandoned by the minister Taycho; but also renounced by the whole sect of the Banyans,[775] who looked upon him as a wicked apostate, because he had been concerned with those who fought with the arm of flesh. It was lucky for him that he afterwards found favour with a subsequent minister,[776] who had not adopted all the maxims of his predecessor Taycho.—The only measures which this egregious demagogue could hitherto properly call his own, were these: His subsidiary treaty with Brut-an-tiffi; his raising an immense army of mercenaries to act in Tartary for the benefit of that prince; his exacting an incredible sum of money from the people of Japan; and finally, two successive armaments which he had sent to annoy the sea-coast of China. I have already given an account of the first, the intent of which was frustrated by a mistake in the perspectives. The other was more fortunate in the beginning.[777] Taycho had by the force of his genius, discovered that nothing so effectually destroyed the oiled paper which the Chinese use in their windows instead of glass, as the gold coin called Oban, when discharged from a military engine at a proper distance. He found that gold was more compact, more heavy, more malleable, and more manageable than any other metal or substance that he knew: he therefore provided a great quantity of obans, and a good body of slingers; and these being conveyed to the coast of China, in a squadron of Fune, as none of the Chinese appeared to oppose these hostilities, a select number of the troops were employed to make ducks and drakes with the obans, on the supposition that this diversion would allure the enemy to the sea-side, where they might be knocked on the head without further trouble: but the care of their own safety got the better of their curiosity on this occasion; and fifty thousand obans were expended in this manner, without bringing one Chinese from his lurking-hole. Considerable damage was done to the windows of the enemy.[778] Then the forces were landed in a village which they found deserted. Here they burned some fishing-boats; and from hence they carried off some military machines, which were brought to Meaco, and conveyed through the streets in procession,[779] amidst the acclamations of the Hydra, who sung the praise of Taycho.—Elevated by this triumph, the minister sent forth the same armament a second time under a new general of his own choosing, whose name was Hylib-bib,[780] who had long entertained an opinion, that the inhabitants of China were not beings of flesh and blood, but mere fantastic shadows, who could neither offend nor be offended. Full of this opinion, he made a descent on the coast of that empire; and to convince his followers that his notion was right, he advanced some leagues into the country,[781] without having taken any precautions to secure a retreat, leaving the Fune at anchor upon an open beach. Some people alledged, that he depended upon the sagacity of an engineer[782] recommended to him by Taycho; which engineer had such an excellent nose, that he could smell a Chinese at the distance of ten leagues: but it seems the scent failed him at this juncture. Perhaps the Chinese general had trailed rusty[783] bacon and other odoriferous substances to confound his sense of smelling. Perhaps no dew had fallen over night, and a strong breeze blew towards the enemy. Certain it is Hylib-bib, in the evening, received repeated intelligence that he was within half a league of a Chinese general, at the head of a body of troops greatly superior in number to the Japonese forces which he himself commanded. He still believed it was all illusion; and when he heard their drums beat, declared it was no more than a ridiculous inchantment. He thought proper, however, to retreat towards the sea-side; but this he did with great deliberation, after having given the enemy fair notice by beat of drum. His motions were so slow, that he took seven hours to march three miles.[784] When he reached the shore where the Fune were at anchor, he saw the whole body of the Chinese drawn up on a rising ground ready to begin the attack. He ordered his rear-guard to face about on the supposition that the phantoms would disappear as soon as they shewed their faces; but finding himself mistaken, and perceiving some of his own people to drop, in consequence of missiles that came from the enemy, he very calmly embarked with his van, leaving his rear to amuse the Chinese, by whom they were, in less than five minutes, either massacred or taken.[785] From this small disgrace the general deduced two important corollaries; first, that the Chinese were actually material beings capable of impulsion; and secondly, that his engineer's nose was not altogether infallible. The people of Meaco did not seem to relish the experiments by which these ideas were ascertained. The monster was heard to grunt in different streets of the metropolis; and these notes of discontent[786] produced the usual effect in the bowels of Fika-kaka: but orator Taycho had his flowers of rhetoric and his bowl of mandragora in readiness. He assured them that Hylib-bib should be employed for the future in keeping sheep on the island of Xicoco,[787] and the engineer be sent to hunt truffles on the mountains of Ximo.[788] Then he tendered his dose, which the Hydra swallowed with signs of pleasure; and lastly, he mounted upon its back, and rode in triumph under the windows of the astonished Cuboy, who, while he shifted his trowsers, exclaimed in a rapture of joy, "All hail, Taycho, thou prince of monster-taming men! the Dairo shall kick thy posteriors, and I will kiss them in token of approbation and applause."

END of the FIRST VOLUME.

The History and Adventures of an Atom

VOLUME TWO

THE

HISTORY

AND

ADVENTURES

OF AN

ATOM.

IN TWO VOLUMES.

VOL. II.

LONDON:

Printed for J. ALMON, opposite Burlington-House,
in Piccadilly. MDCCLXIX.

Title Page of First Edition, Volume 2.
(The Rosenbach Museum & Library, Philadelphia.)

History and Adventures
OF AN ATOM

The time was now come when Fortune, which had hitherto smiled upon the Chinese arms, resolved to turn tail[1] to that vain-glorious nation; and precisely at the same instant Taycho undertook to display his whole capacity in the management of the war. But before he assumed this province,[2] it was necessary that he should establish a despotism in the council of Twenty-eight, some members of which had still the presumption to offer their advice towards the administration of affairs. This council being assembled by the Dairo's order, to deliberate upon the objects of the next campaign, the president[3] began by asking the opinion of Taycho, who was the youngest member; upon which the orator made no articulate reply, but cried "Ba-ba-ba-ba!" The Dairo exclaimed "Boh!" The Fatzman ejaculated the interjection "Pish!" The Cuboy sat in silent astonishment. Gotto-mio swore the man was dumb, and hinted something of lunacy. Foksi-rokhu shook his head; and Soo-san-sin-o shrugged up his shoulders. At length, Fika-kaka going round and kissing Taycho on the forehead, "My dear boy (cried he)!—Gad's curse! what's the matter? Do but open the sluices of your eloquence once more, my dear orator;—let us have one simile—one dear simile; and then I shall die contented.—With respect to the operations of the campaign, don't you think"—Here he was interrupted with "Ka, ka, ka, ka!" "Heigh-day! (cried the Cuboy) Ba-ba-ba, ka-ka-ka! that's the language of children!" "And children you shall be (exclaimed the orator). Here is a two-penny trumpet for the amusement of the illustrious Got-hama-baba; a sword of ginger-bread covered with gold-leaf for the Fatzman, and a rattle for my lord Cuboy.[4] I have, likewise, sugar-plumbs for the rest of the council." So saying, he, without ceremony, advanced to the Dairo, and tied a scarf round the eyes of his imperial majesty: then he produced a number of padlocks, and sealed up the lips of every Quo in council, before they could recollect themselves from their first astonishment. The assembly broke up abruptly; and the Dairo was conducted to his cabinet by the Fatzman and the Cuboy, which last endeavoured to divert the chagrin of his royal master, by blowing the trumpet and shaking the rattle in his ears: but Got-hama-ba-ba could not be so easily appeased. He growled like an enraged bear, at the indignity which had been offered to him, and kicked the Cuboy before as well as behind. Mr. Orator Taycho was fain to come to an explanation. He assured the Dairo, it was necessary that his imperial majesty should remain in the dark, and that the whole council should be muzzled for a season, otherwise he could not accomplish the great things he had projected in favour of the farm of Yesso. He declared, that while his majesty remained blindfold, he would enjoy all his other senses in greater perfection; that his ears would be every day regaled with the shouts of triumph, conveyed in notes of uncommon melody; and that the less quantity of animal spirits[5] was expended in vision, the greater proportion would flow to his extremities; consequently, his pleasure would be more acute in his pedestrian exercitations[6] upon the Cuboy and others whom he delighted to honour. He, therefore, exhorted him to undergo a total privation of eye-sight,[7] which was at best a troublesome faculty, that exposed mankind to a great variety of disagreeable spectacles. This was a proposal which the Dairo did not relish: on the contrary, he waxed exceedingly wroth, and told the orator he would rather enjoy one transient glance of the farm of Yesso, than the most exquisite delights that could be procured for all the other senses. "To gratify your majesty with that ineffable pleasure, (cried Taycho) I have devoted myself, soul and body, and even reconciled contradictions. I have renounced all my former principles without forfeiting the influence which, by professing those principles, I had gained. I have obtained the most astonishing victories over common sense, and even refuted mathematical demonstration. The many-headed Mob, which no former demagogue could ever tame, I have taught to fetch and to carry; to dance to my pipe; to bray to my tune; to swallow what I present without murmuring; to lick my feet when I am angry; and kiss the rod when I think proper to chastise it. I have done more, my liege; I have prepared a drench for it, which, like Lethe, washes away the remembrance of what is past, and takes away all sense of its own condition. I have swept away all the money of the empire; and persuaded the people not only to beggar themselves, but likewise to entail indigence upon their latest posterity;[8] and all for the sake of Yesso. It is by dint of these efforts I have been able to subsidize Brut-an-tiffi, and raise an army of one hundred thousand men to defend your imperial majesty's farm, which, were the entire property of it brought to market, would not fetch one-third part of the sums which are now yearly expended in its defence.[9] I shall strike but one great stroke in the country of Fatsisio, and then turn the whole stream of the war into the channel of Tartary, until the barren plains of Yesso are fertilized with human blood. In the mean time, I must insist upon your majesty's continuing in the dark, and amusing yourself in your cabinet with the trumpet and other gew-gaws which I have provided for your diversion; otherwise I quit the reins of administration,[10] and turn the monster out of my trammels; in which case, like the dog that returns to its vomit,[11] it will not fail to take up its former prejudices against Yesso, which I have with such pains obliged it to resign."—"O my dear Taycho! (cried the affrighted Dairo) talk not of leaving me in such a dreadful dilemma. Rather than the dear farm should fall into the hands of the Chinese, I would be contented to be led about blindfold all the days of my life.—Proceed in your own way.—I invest you with full power and authority, not only to gag my whole council, but even to nail their ears to the pillory, should it be found necessary for the benefit of Yesso. In token of which delegation,[12] present your posteriors, and I will bestow upon you a double portion of my favour." Taycho humbly thanked his imperial majesty for the great honour he intended him; but begged leave to decline the ceremony, on account of the hæmorrhoids, which at that time gave him great disturbance.[13]

The orator having thus annihilated all opposition in the council of Twenty-eight,[14] repaired to his own house, in order to plan the operations of the ensuing campaign. Tho' he had reinforced the army in Tartary with the flower of the Japonese soldiery, and destined a strong squadron of Fune, as usual, to parade on the coast of China;[15] he foresaw it would be necessary to amuse the people with some new stroke on the side of Fatsisio, which indeed was the original, and the most natural scene of the war.[16] He locked himself up in his closet, and in consulting the map of Fatsisio, he found that the principal Chinese settlement of that island, was a fortified town called Quib-quab,[17] to which there was access by two different avenues; one by a broad, rapid, navigable river,[18] on the banks of which the town was situated; and the other by an inland route over mountains, lakes, and dangerous torrents. He measured the map with his compass, and perceived that both routes were nearly of the same length; and therefore he resolved that the forces in Fat-sisio, being divided into two equal bodies, should approach the place by the two different avenues, on the supposition that they would both arrive before the walls of Quib-quab at the same instant of time.[19] The conduct of the inland expedition was given to Yaff-ray, who now commanded in chief in

Fatsisio; and the rest of the troops were sent up the great river, under the auspices of Ya-loff,[20] who had so eminently distinguished himself in the course of the preceding year.

Orator Taycho had received some articles of intelligence which embarrassed him a little at first; but these difficulties soon vanished before the vigour of his resolutions. He knew, that not only the town of Quib-quab was fortified by art,[21] but also, that the whole adjacent country was almost impregnable by nature: that one Chinese general[22] blocked up the passes with a strong body of forces, in the route which was to be followed by Yaffrai;[23] and that another commanded a separate corps[24] in the neighbourhood of Quib-quab, equal, at least, in number to the detachment of Ya-loff, whom he might therefore either prevent from landing, or attack after he should be landed: or finally, should neither of these attempts succeed, he might reinforce the garrison of Quib-quab, so as to make it more numerous than the besieging army, which, according to the rules of war, ought to be ten times the number of the besieged. On the other hand, in order to invalidate these objections, he reflected that Fortune, which hath such a share in all military events, is inconstant and variable; that as the Chinese had been so long successful in Fatsisio, it was now their turn to be unfortunate. He reflected that the dæmon of folly was capricious; and that as it had so long possessed the rulers and generals of Japan, it was high time it should shift its quarters, and occupy the brains of the enemy; in which case they would quit their advantageous posts, and commit some blunder that would lay them at the mercy of the Japonese.—With respect to the reduction of Quib-quab, he had heard, indeed, that the besiegers ought to be ten times the number of the garrison besieged; but as every Japonese was equivalent to ten subjects of China, he thought the match was pretty equal. He reflected, that even if this expedition should not succeed, it would be of little consequence to his reputation, as he could plead at home, that he neither conceived the original plan, nor appointed any of the officers concerned in the execution. It is true, he might have reinforced the army in Fatsisio, so as to leave very little to Fortune: but then he must have subtracted something from the strength of the operations in Tartary, which was now become the favourite scene of the war; or he must have altogether suspended the execution of another darling scheme,[25] which was literally his own conception. There was an island in the great Indian ocean, at a considerable distance from Fatsisio; and here the Chinese had a strong settlement. Taycho was inflamed with the ambition of reducing this island, which was called Thin-quo;[26] and for this purpose he resolved to embark a body of forces[27] which should co-operate with the squadron of

Fune destined to cruize in those latitudes.—The only difficulty that remained was to choose a general to direct this enterprize.—He perused a list of all the military officers in Japan; and as they were all equal in point of reputation, he began to examine their names, in order to pitch upon that which should appear to be the most significant: and in this particular, Taycho was a little superstitious. Not but that surnames, when properly bestowed, might be rendered very useful terms of distinction: but I must tell thee, Peacock, nothing can be more preposterously absurd than the practice of inheriting *cognomina*,[28] which ought ever to be purely personal. I would ask thee, for example, what propriety there was in giving the name *Xenophon*, which signifies *one that speaks a foreign language*, to the celebrated Greek who distinguished himself, not only as a consummate captain, but also as an elegant writer in his mother-tongue? What could be more ridiculous than to denominate the great philosopher of Crotona *Pythagoras*, which implies a *stinking speech?* Or what could be more misapplied than the name of the weeping philosopher *Heraclitus*, signifying *military glory?* The inheritance of surnames, among the Romans, produced still more ludicrous consequences. The best and noblest families in Rome derived their names from the coarsest employments, or else from the corporeal blemishes of their ancestors. The *Pisones* were millers: the *Cicerones* and the *Lentuli* were so called from the *vetches* and the *lentils* which their forefathers dealt in. The *Fabij* were so denominated from a dung-pit, in which the first of the family was begot by stealth in the way of fornication. A ploughman gave rise to the great family of the *Serrani*, the ladies of which always went without smocks. The *Suilli*, the *Bubulci*, and the *Porci*, were descended from a swine-herd, a cow-herd, and a hog-butcher.—What could be more disgraceful than to call the senator *Strabo*, *Squintum*; or a fine young lady of the house of *Pæti*, *Pigsnies?* or to distinguish a matron of the *Limi*, by the appellation of *Sheep's-eye?*—What could be more dishonourable than to give the surname of *Snub-nose* to P. *Silius*, the proprætor, because his great-great-great-grand-father had a nose of that make? Ovid, indeed, had a long nose, and therefore was justly denominated *Naso*: but why should Horace be called *Flaccus*, as if his ears had been stretched in the pillory: I need not mention the *Burrhi*, *Nigri*, *Rufi*, *Aquilij*, and *Rutilij*, because we have the same foolish surnames in England; and even the *Lappa*; for I myself know a very pretty miss called *Rough-head*, tho' in fact there is not a young lady in the Bills of Mortality,[29] who takes more pains to dress her hair to the best advantage. The famous dictator whom the deputies of Rome found at the plough, was known by the name of *Cincinnatus*, or *Ragged-head*. Now I leave you to judge how it would sound in these days, if a footman at the play-house should call out, "*My Lady Ragged-head's coach. Room for my Lady Ragged-head.*" I am doubtful whether the English name of *Hale* does not come from the Roman cognomen *Hala*, which signified *stinking-breath*. What need I mention the *Plauti, Panci, Valgi, Vari, Vatiæ*, and *Scauri*; the *Tuditani*, the *Malici, Cenestellæ*, and *Leccæ*; in other words, the *Splay-foots, Bandy-legs, Shamble-shins, Baker-knees, Club-foots, Hammer-heads, Chubby-cheeks, Bald-heads*, and *Letchers*.—I shall not say a word of the *Buteo*, or *Buzzard*, that I may not be obliged to explain the meaning of the word *Triorchis*,[30] from whence it takes its denomination; yet all those were great families in Rome. But I cannot help taking notice of some of the same improprieties, which have crept into the language and customs of this country. Let us suppose, for example, a foreigner reading an English news-paper in these terms: "Last Tuesday the right honourable *Timothy Sillyman*, secretary of state for the Southern department, gave a grand entertainment to the nobility and gentry at his house in *Knaves-acre*.[31] The evening was concluded with a ball, which was opened by Sir *Samuel Hog* and Lady *Diana Rough-head*.—We hear there is purpose of marriage between Mr. Alderman *Small-cock* and Miss *Harriot Hair-stones*,[32] a young lady of great fortune and superlative merit.—By the last mail from Germany we have certain advice of a compleat victory which General *Coward* has obtained over the enemy. On this occasion the general displayed all the intrepidity of the most renowned hero:—by the same canal we are informed that Lieutenant *Little-fear* has been broke[33] by a court-martial for cowardice.—We hear that *Edward West*, Esq; will be elected president of the directors of the *East-India* company for the ensuing year. It is reported that Commodore *North* will be sent with a squadron into the *South-Sea*.—Captains *East* and *South* are appointed by the Lords of the Admiralty, commanders of two frigates to sail on the discovery of the *North-west* passage.[34]—Yesterday morning Sir *John Summer*, bart. lay dangerously ill at his house in *Spring-garden*:[35] he is attended by Dr. *Winter*: but there are no hopes of his recovery.—Saturday last *Philip Frost*, a dealer in *Gunpowder*, died at his house on *Snow-hill*,[36] of a high fever caught by overheating himself in walking for a wager from *No Man's Land* to the *World's End*.[37]—Last week Mr. *John Fog*, teacher of astronomy in Rotherhith,[38] was married to the widow *Fair-weather* of *Puddledock*.[39]—We hear from Bath, that on Thursday last a duel was fought on Lansdown,[40] by Captain *Sparrow* and *Richard Hawke*, Esq; in which the latter was mortally wounded.—Friday last ended the sessions at the Old Bailey,[41] when the following persons received sentence of death. Leonard *Lamb*, for the murder of *Julius Wolf*; and Henry *Grave*, for robbing and assaulting Dr. *Death*, whereby the said *Death* was put in fear of his life.

Giles Gosling, for defrauding *Simon Fox* of four guineas and his watch, by
subtle craft, was transported for seven years; and *David Drinkwater* was ordered to be set in the stocks, as an habitual drunkard. The trial of *Thomas
Green*, whitster[42] at Fulham,[43] for a rape on the body of *Flora White*, a mu-
latto, was put off till next sessions, on account of the absence of two material
evidences, viz. *Sarah Brown*, clear-starcher[44] of *Pimlico*,[45] and *Anthony Black*,
scarlet-dyer of Wandsworth."[46] I ask thee, Peacock, whether a sensible foreigner, who understood the literal meaning of these names, which are all
truly British, would not think ye were a nation of humorists, who delighted
in cross-purposes and ludicrous singularity? But, indeed, ye are not more
absurd in this particular, than some of your neighbours.—I know a Frenchman of the name of *Bouvier*, which signifies *Cow-keeper*, pique himself upon
his noblesse; and a general called *Valavoir*,[47] is said to have lost his life by the
whimsical impropriety of his surname, which signifies* *Go and see.*—You may
remember an Italian minister called *Grossa-testa*,[48] or *Great-head*, though in
fact he had scarce any head at all. That nation has, likewise, its *Sforzas, Mal-
atestas, Boccanigras, Porcinas, Giudices*; its *Colonnas, Muratorios, Medicis*, and
*Gozzi; Endeavours, Chuckle-heads, Black Muzzles, Hogs, Judges, Pillars, Masons,
Leeches*, and *Chubby-chops*. Spain has its *Almohadas, Girones, Utreras, Ursinas*,
and *Zapatas*; signifying *Cushions, Gores, Bullocks, Bears*, and *Slippers*.[49] The
Turks, in other respects a sensible people, fall into the same extravagance,
with respect to the inheritance of surnames. An Armenian merchant, to
whom I once belonged at Aleppo, used to dine at the house of a cook whose
name was *Clock-maker*; and the handsomest Ichoglan in the Bashaw's
seraglio[50] was surnamed *Crook-back*.—If we may believe the historian *Buck*,
there was the same impropriety in the same epithet bestowed upon Richard
III.[51] king of England, who, he says, was one of the best-made men of the age
in which he lived: but here I must contradict the said *Buck*, from my own
knowledge. Richard had, undoubtedly, one shoulder higher than the other,
and his left arm was a little shrunk and contracted: but, notwithstanding the
ungracious colours in which he has been drawn by the flatterers of the house
of Lancaster,[52] I can assure thee, Peacock, that Richard was a prince of a very
agreeable aspect, and excelled in every personal accomplishment; neither was
his heart a stranger to the softer passions of tenderness and pity. The very

---

*The general taking a solitary walk in the evening, was questioned by a sentinel, and
answered "*Va la voir.*" The soldier taking the words in the literal sense, repeated the challenge: he
was answered in the same manner; and being affronted, fired upon the general, who fell dead on
the spot.

night that preceded the fatal battle of Bosworth,[53] in which he lost his life, he went in disguise to the house of a farmer in the neighbourhood, to visit an infant son there boarded, who was the fruit of an amour between him and a young lady of the first condition.[54] Upon this occasion, he embraced the child with all the marks of paternal affection, and doubtful of the issue of the approaching battle, shed a flood of tears at parting from him, after having recommended him to the particular care of his nurse, to whom he gave money and jewels to a considerable value. After the catastrophe of Richard this house was plundered, and the nurse with difficulty escaped to another part of the country; but as the enemies of Richard now prevailed, she never durst reveal the secret of the boy's birth; and he was bred up as her own son to the trade of brick-laying, in which character he lived and died in an advanced age at London.[55]—Moreover, it is but justice in me, who constituted part of one of Richard's yeomen of the guard, to assure thee that this prince was not so wicked and cruel as he has been represented. The only share he had in the death of his brother Clarence, was his forbearing to interpose in the behalf of that prince with their elder brother king Edward IV. who, in fact, was the greatest brute of the whole family:[56] neither did he poison his own wife; nor employ assassins to murder his two nephews in the Tower. Both the boys were given by Tyrrel[57] in charge to a German Jew, with directions to breed them up as his own children, in a remote country; and the eldest died of a fever at Embden,[58] and the other afterwards appeared as claimant of the English crown:—all the world knows how he finished his career under the name of Perkin Warbeck.[59]—So much for the abuse of surnames, in the investigation of which I might have used thy own by way of illustration; for, if thou and all thy generation were put to the rack, they would not be able to give any tolerable reason why thou shouldest be called *Peacock* rather than *Crablouse*.—But it is now high time to return to the thread of our narration. Taycho, having considered the list of officers, without finding one name which implied any active virtue, resolved that the choice should depend upon accident. He hustled[60] them all together in his cap, and putting in his hand at random, drew forth that of Hob-nob;[61] a person who had grown old in obscurity, without ever having found an opportunity of being concerned in actual service. His very name was utterly unknown to Fika-kaka; and this circumstance the orator considered as a lucky omen; for the Cuboy had such a remarkable knack at finding out the least qualified subjects, and overlooking merit, his new collegue concluded (not without some shadow of reason) that Hob-nob's being unknown to the prime minister, was a sort of negative presumption in favour of his character. This officer was accordingly placed at the head of an armament, and sent against the island of Thin-quo, in the conquest of which he was to be supported by a squadron of Fune already in those latitudes, under the command of the chief He-Rhumn.[62]

The voyage was performed without loss: the troops were landed without opposition.[63] They had already advanced towards a rising-ground which commanded the principal town of the island, and He-Rhumn had offered to land and draw the artillery[64] by the mariners of his squadron, when Hob-nob had a dream which disconcerted all his measures. He dreamed that he entertained all the islanders in the temple of the White Horse; and that his own grand-mother did the honours of the table.—Indeed he could not have performed a greater act of charity; for they were literally in danger of perishing by famine. Having consulted his interpreter on this extraordinary dream, he was given to understand that the omen was unlucky; that if he persisted in his hostilities, he himself would be taken prisoner, and offered up as a sacrifice to the idol of the place. While he ruminated on this unfavourable response, the principal inhabitants of the island assembled, in order to deliberate upon their own deplorable situation. They had neither troops, arms, fortifications, nor provision, and despaired of supplies, as the fleet of Japan surrounded the island. In this emergency, they determined to submit without opposition; and appointed a deputation to go and make a tender of the island to general Hob-nob. This deputation, preceded by white flags of truce, the Japonese commander no sooner descried, than he thought upon the interpretation of his dream. He mistook the deputies with their white flags for the Bonzas of the idol to which he was to be sacrificed; and, being sorely troubled in mind, ordered the troops to be immediately reimbarked,[65] notwithstanding the exhortations of He-Rhumn, and the remonstrances of Rha-rin-tumm,[66] the second in command, who used a number of arguments to dissuade him from his purpose. The deputies seeing the enemy in motion, made a halt, and, after they were fairly on board, returned to the town, singing hymns in praise of the idol Fo, who, they imagined, had confounded the understanding of the Japonese general.[67]

The attempt upon Thin-quo having thus miscarried, Hob-nob declared he would return to Japan; but was with great difficulty persuaded by the commander of the Fune and his own second, to make a descent upon another island belonging to the Chinese, called *Qua-chu*,[68] where they assured him he would meet with no opposition. As he had no dream to deter him from this attempt, he suffered himself to be persuaded, and actually made good his landing: but the horror occasioned by the apparition of his grand-mother, had made such an impression upon his mind, as affected the constitution of his body. Before he was visited by another such vision, he sickened and died;[69] and in consequence of his death, Rha-rin-tumm and He-Rhumn made a conquest of the island of Qua-Chu,[70] which was much more valuable than Thin-quo, the first and sole object of the expedition.—When the first news of this second descent arrived in Japan, the ministry were in the utmost confusion. Mr. Orator Taycho did not scruple to declare that general Hob-nob had misbehaved; first, in relinquishing Thin-quo, upon such a frivolous pretence as the supposed apparition of an old woman; secondly, in attempting the conquest of another place, which was not so much as mentioned in his instructions. The truth is, the importance of Qua-chu was not known to the cabinet of Japan. Fika-kaka believed it was some place on the continent of Tartary, and exclaimed in a violent passion, "Rot the block-head, Hob-nob; he'll have an army of Chinese on his back in a twinkling!" When the president Soo-san-sin-o assured him that Qua-chu was a rich island at an immense distance from the continent of Tartary, the Cuboy insisted upon kissing his excellency's posteriors for the agreeable information he had received.[71] In a few weeks arrived the tidings of the island's being totally reduced by Rha-rin-tumm and He-Rhumn.—Then the conquest was published throughout the empire of Japan with every circumstance of exaggeration. The blatant beast brayed applause. The rites of Fakku-basi were celebrated with unusual solemnity; and hymns of triumph were sung to the glory of the great Taycho. Even the Cuboy arrogated to himself some share of the honour gained by this expedition; inasmuch as the general Rha-rin-tumm was the brother of his friend Mr. Secretary *No-bo-dy*.[72] Fika-kaka gave a grand entertainment at his palace, where he appeared crowned with a garland of the *Tsikkburasiba*, or laurel of Japan; and eat so much of the soup of *Joniku*[73] or famous *Swallow's-nest*, that he was for three days troubled with flatulencies and indigestion.

In the midst of all this festivity, the emperor still growled and grumbled about Yesso. His new ally Brut-an-tiffi had met with a variety of fortune, and even suffered some shocks, which orator Taycho, with all his art, could not keep from the knowledge of the Dairo.—He had been severely drubbed by the Mantchoux, who had advanced for that purpose even to his court-yard:[74] but this was nothing in comparison to another disaster, from which he had a hair-breadth 'scape.[75] The Great Khan had employed one of his most wily and enterprising chiefs to seize Brut-an-tiffi by surprize, that he might be brought to justice, and executed as a felon and perturbator of the public peace. Kunt-than,[76] who was the partisan pitched upon for this service, practised a thousand stratagems to decoy Brut-an-tiffi into a careless security; but he was still[77] baffled by the vigilance of Yam-a-Kheit,[78] a famous soldier of

fortune, who had engaged in the service of the outlawed Tartar. At length the
opportunity offered, when this captain was sent out to lay the country under
contribution. Then Kunt-than marching solely in the dead of night, caught
Brut-an-tiffi napping. He might have slain him upon the spot; but his orders
were to take him alive, that he might be made a public example; accordingly,
his centinels being dispatched, he was pulled out of bed, and his hands were
already tied with cords, like those of a common malefactor, when, by his
roaring and bellowing, he gave the alarm to Yam-a-Kheit, who chanced to be
in the neighbourhood, returning from his excursion.—He made all the haste
he could, and came up in the very nick of time to save his master. He fell
upon the party of Kunt-than with such fury, that they were fain to quit their
prey: then he cut the fetters of Brut-an-tiffi, who took to his heels and fled
with incredible expedition, leaving his preserver in the midst of his enemies,
by whom he was overpowered, struck from his horse, and trampled to
death.[79] The grateful Tartar not only deserted this brave captain in such
extremity, but he also took care to asperse his memory, by insinuating that
Yam-a-Kheit had undertaken to watch him while he took his repose, and had
himself fallen asleep upon his post, by which neglect of duty the Ostrog had
been enabled to penetrate into his quarters. 'Tis an ill wind that blows no-
body good:[80]—the same disaster that deprived him of a good officer, afforded
him an opportunity to shift the blame of neglect from his own shoulders to
those of a person who could not answer for himself.[81]—In the same manner,
your general A——y acquitted himself of the charge of misconduct for the
attack of T——a, by accusing his engineer, who, having fallen in the battle
could not contradict his assertion.[82] In regard to the affair with the Mantchoux,
Brut-an-tiffi was resolved to swear truth out of Tartary[83] by meer dint of
impudence. In the very article[84] of running away, he began to propagate the
report of the great victory he had obtained. He sent the Dairo a circumstantial detail of his own prowess, and expatiated upon the cowardice of the
Mantchoux, who he said had vanished from him like quick-silver, at the very
time when they were quietly possessed of the field of battle, and he himself
was calling upon the mountains[85] to cover him. It must have been in imitation
of this great original, that the Inspector, of tympanitical memory, assured the
public in one of his lucubrations, that a certain tall Hibernian was afraid of
looking him in the face; because the said poltroon had kicked his breech the
night before in presence of five hundred people.[86]

Fortune had now abandoned the Chinese in good earnest. Two squadrons
of their Fune had been successively taken, destroyed, or dispersed, by the
Japonese commanders Or-nbos and Fas-khan;[87] and they had lost such a

number of single junks, that they were scarce able to keep the sea. On the coast of Africa they were driven from the settlement of Kho-rhé, by the commander Kha-fell.[88] In the extremity of Asia, they had an army totally defeated by the Japonese captain Khutt-whang,[89] and many of their settlements were taken. In Fatsisio, they lost another battle to Yan-oni,[90] and divers strong holds. In the neighbourhood of Yesso, Bron-xi-tic, who commanded the mercenary army of Japan on that continent, had been obliged to retreat before the Chinese from post to pillar, till at length he found it absolutely necessary to maintain his position, even at the risque of being attacked by the enemy, that outnumbered him greatly. He chose an advantageous post, where he thought himself secure, and went to sleep at his usual time of rest.[91] The Chinese general resolving to beat up his quarters[92] in the night, selected a body of horse for that purpose, and put them in motion accordingly. It was happy for Bron-xi-tic that this detachment fell upon a quarter where there happened to be a kennel of Japonese dogs,[93] which are as famous as the bull-dogs of England. These animals, ever on the watch, not only gave the alarm, but at the same time fell upon the Chinese horses with such impetuosity, that the enemy were disordered, and had actually fled before Bron-xi-tic could bring up his troops to action. All that he saw of the battle, when he came up, was a small number of killed and wounded, and the cavalry of the enemy scampering off in confusion, tho' at a great distance from the field. No matter;—he found means to paint this famous battle of Myn-than[94] in such colours as dazzled the weak eye-sight of the Japonese monster, which bellowed hoarse applause through all its throats; and in its hymns of triumph equalled Bron-xi-tic even to the unconquerable Brut-an-tiffi, which last, about this time, received at his own door another beating from the Mantchoux,[95] so severe that he lay for some time without exhibiting any signs of life; and, indeed, owed his safety to a very extraordinary circumstance. An Ostrog chief called Llha-dahn,[96] who had reinforced the Mantchoux with a very considerable body of horse before the battle, insisted upon carrying off the carcase of Brut-an-tiffi, that it might be hung up on a gibbet *in terrorem*,[97] before the pavilion of the great Khan. The general of the Mantchoux, on the other hand, declared he would have it flayed upon the spot, and the skin sent as a trophy to his sovereign. This dispute produced a great deal of abuse betwixt those barbarians;[98] and it was with great difficulty some of their inferior chiefs, who were wiser than themselves, prevented them from going by the ears together. In a word, the confusion and anarchy that ensued, afforded an opportunity to one of Brut-an-tiffi's partisans to steal away the body of his master, whom the noise of the contest had just roused from his swoon. Llha-dahn perceiving he was gone, rode off in disgust with all his cavalry; and the Mantchoux, instead of following the blow, made a retrograde motion towards their own country, which allowed Brut-an-tiffi time to breathe.[99] Three successive disasters of this kind would have been sufficient to lower the military character of any warrior, in the opinion of any public that judged from their own senses and reflexion: but, by this time, the Japonese had quietly resigned all their natural perceptions, and paid the most implicit faith to every article broached by their apostle Taycho. The more it seemed to contradict common reason and common evidence, the more greedily was it swallowed as a mysterious dogma of the political creed. Taycho then assured them that the whole army of the Mantchoux was put to the sword; and that Bron-xi-tic would carry the war within three weeks, into the heart of China; he gave them goblets of horse-blood from Myn-than; and tickled their ears and their noses: they snorted approbation, licked his toes, and sunk into a profound lethargy.

From this, however, they were soon arroused by unwelcome tidings from Fatsisio. Yaff-rai had proceeded in his route until he was stopped by a vast lake,[100] which he could not possibly traverse without boats, cork-jackets, or some such expedient, which could not be supplied for that campaign. Ya-loff had sailed up the river to Quib-quab, which he found so strongly fortified by nature, that it seemed rashness even to attempt a landing, especially in the face of an enemy more numerous than his own detachment. Land, however, he did, and even attacked a fortified camp of the Chinese; but, in spite of all his efforts, he was repulsed with considerable slaughter. He sent an account of this miscarriage to Taycho, giving him to understand, at the same time, that he had received no intelligence of Yaff-rai's motions; that his troops were greatly diminished; that the season was too far advanced to keep the field much longer; and that nothing was left them but a choice of difficulties, every one of which seemed more insurmountable than another.[101] Taycho having deliberated on this subject, thought it was necessary to prepare the monster for the worst that could happen, as he now expected to hear by the first opportunity, that the grand expedition of Fatsisio had totally miscarried. He resolved therefore to throw the blame upon the shoulders of Ya-loff and Yaff-rai, and stigmatize them as the creatures of Fika-kaka, who had neither ability to comprehend the instructions he had given, nor resolution to execute the plan he had projected. For this purpose he ascended the rostrum, and with a rueful length of face opened his harangue upon the defeat of Ya-loff. The Hydra no sooner understood that the troops of Japan had been discomfited, than it was seized with a kind of hysteric fit, and uttered a yell so loud and horrible, that the blind-fold Dairo trembled in the most internal recesses of his palace: the Cuboy Fika-kaka had such a profuse evacuation, that the discharge is said to have weighed five Boll-ah,[102] equal to eight and forty pounds three ounces and two penny-weight averdupois of Great-Britain. Even Taycho himself was discomposed.—In vain he presented the draught of yeast, and the goblet of blood:—in vain his pipers soothed the ears, and his tall fellows tickled the nose of the blatant beast. It continued to howl and grin, and gnash its teeth, and writhe itself into a thousand contortions, as if it had been troubled with that twisting of the guts called the iliac passion.[103] Taycho began to think its case desperate, and sent for the Dairo's chief physician, who prescribed a glyster[104] of the distilled spirit analogous to your Geneva; but no apothecary nor old woman in Meaco would undertake to administer it on any consideration, the patient was such a filthy, aukward, lubberly, unmanageable beast.—"If what comes from its mouths (said they) be so foul, virulent, and pestilential, how nauseous, poisonous, and intolerable must that be which takes the other course?"—When Taycho's art and foresight were at a stand, accident came to his assistance. A courier arrived, preceded by twelve postilions blowing horns; and he brought the news that Quib-quab was taken.[105] The orator commanded them to place their horns within as many of the monster's long ears, and blow with all their might, until it should exhibit some signs of hearing. The experiment succeeded. The Hydra waking from its trance, opened its eyes; and Taycho seizing this opportunity, hollowed in his loudest tone, "Quib-quab is taken." This note being repeated, the beast started up; then, raising itself on its hind legs, began to wag its tail, to frisk and fawn, to lick Taycho's sweaty socks: in fine, crouching on its belly, it took the orator on its back, and proceeding through the streets of Meaco, brayed aloud, "Make way for the divine Taycho! Make way for the conqueror of Quib-quab!"—But the gallant Ya-loff, the real conqueror of Quib-quab, was no more.—He fell in the battle by which the conquest was atchieved, yet not before he saw victory declare in his favour. He had made incredible efforts to surmount the difficulties that surrounded him. At length he found means to scale a perpendicular rock, which the enemy had left unguarded, on the supposition that nature had made it inaccessible. This exploit was performed in the night, and in the morning the Chinese saw his troops drawn up in order of battle on the plains of Quib-quab. As their numbers greatly exceeded the Japonese, they did not decline the trial; and in a little time both armies were engaged. The contest, however, was not of long duration, tho' it proved fatal to the general on each side.[106]— Ya-loff being slain, the command devolved upon Tohn-syn,[107] who pursued the enemy to the walls of Quib-quab, which was next day surrendered to him by capitulation. Nothing was now seen and heard in the capital but jubilee, triumph, and intoxication; and, indeed, the nation had not for some centuries, seen such an occasion for joy and satisfaction. The only person that did not heartily rejoice was the Dairo Got-hama-baba. By this time he was so Tartarised, that he grudged his subjects every advantage obtained in Fatsisio; and when Fika-kaka hobbled up to him with the news of the victory, instead of saluting him with the kick of approbation, he turned his back upon him,[108] saying "Boh! boh! What do you tell me of Quib-quab? The damned Chinese are still on the frontiers of Yesso." As to the beast, it was doomed to undergo a variety of agitation. Its present gambols were interrupted by a fresh alarm from China. It was reported that two great armaments were equipped for a double descent upon the dominions of Japan:[109] that one of these had already sailed north about for the island of Xicoco,[110] to make a diversion in favour of the other, which, being the most considerable, was designed for the southern coast of Japan. These tidings, which were not without foundation, had such an effect upon the multitudinous monster, that it was first of all seized with an universal shivering.[111] Its teeth chattered so loud, that the sound was heard at the distance of half a league; and for some time it was struck dumb. During this paroxysm it crawled silently on its belly to a sand-hill just without the walls of Meaco, and began to scratch the earth with great eagerness and perseverance. Some people imagined it was digging for gold: but the truth is, the beast was making a hole to hide itself from the enemy, whom it durst not look in the face; for, it must be observed of this beast, it was equally timorous and cruel; equally cowardly and insolent.—So hard it laboured at this cavern, that it had actually burrowed itself all but the tail, when its good angel Taycho whistled it out, with the news of another compleat victory gained over the Chinese at sea, by the Sey-seo-gun Phal-khan, who had sure enough discomfited or destroyed the great armament of the enemy.[112] As for the other small squadron which had steered a northerly course to Xicoco, it was encountered, defeated, taken, and brought into the harbours of Japan, by three light Fune, under the command of a young chief called Hel-y-otte,[113] who happened to be cruising on that part of the coast.—The beast hearing Taycho's auspicious whistle, crept out with its buttocks foremost, and having done him homage in the usual stile, began to react its former extravagances. It now considered this demagogue as the supreme giver of all good, and adored him accordingly. The apostle Bupo was no longer invoked. The temple of Fakkubasi was almost forgotten; and the Bonzas were universally despised. The praise of the prophet Taycho had swallowed up all other

worship.—Let us enquire how far he merited this adoration:[114] how justly
the unparalleled success of this year was ascribed to his conduct and sagacity.
Kho-rhé was taken by Kha-fell, and Quib-quab by Ya-loff and Thon-syn. By
land, the Chinese were defeated in Fatsisio by Yan-o-ni; in the extremity of
Asia, by Khutt-whang; and in Tartary, by the Japonese bull-dogs, without
command or direction. At sea one of their squadrons had been destroyed by
Or-nbos; a second by Fas-khan; a third was taken by Hel-y-otte; a fourth was
worsted and put to flight in three successive engagements near the land of
Kamtschatka, by the chief Bha-kakh;[115] and their grand armament defeated
by the Sey-seo-gun Phal-khan. But Kha-fell was a stranger to orator Taycho:
Ya-loff he had never seen:[116] the bull-dogs had been collected at random from
the shambles of Meaco: he had never heard of Yan-o-ni's name, till he distinguished himself by his first victory; nor did he know there was any such
person as Khutt-whang existing. As for Or-nbos, Fas-khan, Phal-khan, and
Bha-kakh, they had been Sey-seo-guns in constant employment under the
former administration; and the youth Hel-y-otte owed his promotion to the
interest of his own family.[117]—But it may be alledged, that Taycho projected
in his closet those plans that were crowned with success.—We have seen how
he mutilated and frittered the original scheme of the campaign in Fatsisio, so
as to leave it at the caprice of Fortune. The reduction of Kho-rhé was part of
the design formed by the Banyan Thum-khumm-qua, which Taycho did all
that lay in his power to render abortive. The plan of operations in the
extremity of Tartary, he did not pretend to meddle with;—it was the concern
of the officers appointed by the trading company there settled: and as to the
advantages obtained at sea, they naturally resulted from the disposition of
cruises, made and regulated by the board of Sey-seo-gun-sealty,[118] with
which no minister ever interfered. He might, indeed, have recalled the chiefs
and officers whom he found already appointed when he took the reins of
administration, and filled their places with others of his own choosing. How
far he was qualified to make such a choice, and plan new expeditions, appears
from the adventures of the generals he did appoint; Moria-tanti, who was
deterred from landing by a perspective view of whiskers;[119] Hylib-bib, who
left his rear in the lurch; and Hob-nob, who made such a masterly retreat
from the supposed Bonzas of Thin-quo.—These three were literally commanders of his own creation, employed in executing schemes of his own projecting; and these three were the only generals he made, and the only military
plans he projected, if we except the grand scheme of subsidizing Brut-an-tiffi,
and forming an army of one hundred thousand men in Tartary, for the
defence of the farm of Yesso.—Things being so circumstanced, it may be

easily conceived that the Orator could ask nothing which the Mobile would venture to refuse; and indeed he tried his influence to the utmost stretch; he milked the dugs[120] of the monster till the blood came. For the service of the ensuing year, he squeezed from them near twelve millions of obans, amounting to near twenty-four millions sterling, about four times as much as had ever been raised by the empire of Japan in any former war.[121] But, by this time, Taycho was become not only a convert to the system of Tartary, which he had formerly persecuted, but also an enthusiast in love and admiration of Brut-an-tiffi, who had lately sent him his poetical works in a present.[122] This, however, would have been of no use, as he could not read them, had not he discovered they were printed on a very fine, soft, smooth Chinese paper made of silk, which he happily converted to another fundamental purpose.[123] In return for this compliment, the Orator sent him a bullock's horn bound with brass,[124] value fifteen pence, which had long served him as a pitch-pipe when he made harangues to the Mobile;—it was the same kind of instrument which Horace describes; *Tibia vincta orichalco*:[125] and pray take notice, Peacock, this was the only present Taycho ever bestowed on any man, woman, or child, through the whole course of his life, I mean out of his own pocket;[126] for he was extremely liberal of the public money, in his subsidies to the Tartar chiefs, and in the prosecution of the war upon that continent. The Orator was a genius self-taught without the help of human institution.[127] He affected to undervalue all men of literary talents; and the only book he ever read with any degree of pleasure, was a collection of rhapsodies preached by one Ab-ren-thi, an obscure fanatic Bonza, a native of the island Xicoco.[128] Certain it is, Nature seemed to have produced him for the sole purpose of fascinating the mob, and endued him with faculties accordingly.

Notwithstanding all his efforts in behalf of the Tartarian scheme, the Chinese still lingered on the frontiers of Yesso.[129] The views of the court of Pekin exactly coincided with the interest of Bron-xi-tic, the mercenary general of Japan. The Chinese, confounded at the unheard-of success of the Japonese in Fatsisio and other parts of the globe, and extremely mortified at the destruction of their fleets and the ruin of their commerce, saw no other way of distressing the enemy, but that of prolonging the war on the continent of Tartary, which they could support for little more than their ordinary expence; whereas Japan could not maintain it without contracting yearly immense loads of debt, which must have crushed it at the long-run. It was the business of the Chinese, therefore, not to finish the war in Tartary by taking the farm of Yesso, because, in that case, the annual expence of it would have been saved to Japan; but to keep it alive by forced marches, prædatory excursions, and undecisive actions; and this was precisely the interest of general Bron-xi-tic, who in the continuance of the war enjoyed the continuance of all his emoluments. All that he had to do, then, was to furnish Taycho from time to time with a cask of human blood, for the entertainment of the blatant beast; and to send over a few horse-tails,[130] as trophies of pretended victories, to be waved before the monster in its holiday processions. He and the Chinese general seemed to act in concert. They advanced and retreated in their turns betwixt two given lines, and the campaign always ended on the same spot where it began. The only difference between them was in the motives of their conduct; the Chinese commander acted for the benefit of his sovereign, and Bron-xi-tic acted for his own.

The continual danger to which the farm of Yesso was exposed, produced such apprehensions and chagrin in the mind of the Dairo Got-hama-baba, that his health began to decline.[131] He neglected his food and his rattle, and no longer took any pleasure in kicking the Cuboy. He frequently muttered ejaculations about the farm of Yesso: nay, once or twice in the transports of his impatience, he pulled the bandage from his eyes, and cursed Taycho in the Tartarian language. At length he fell into a lethargy, and even when roused a little by blisters and caustics,[132] seemed insensible of every thing that was done about him. These blisters were raised by burning the moxa[133] upon his scalp. The powder of *menoki* was also injected in a glyster; and the operation of acupuncture, called *Senkei*,[134] performed without effect. His disorder was so stubborn, that the Cuboy began to think he was bewitched, and suspected Taycho of having practised sorcery on his sovereign. He communicated this suspicion to Mura-clami, who shook his head, and advised that, with the Orator's good leave, the council should be consulted. Taycho, who had gained an absolute empire over the mind of the Dairo, and could not foresee how his interest might stand with his successor,[135] was heartily disposed to concur in any feasible experiment for the recovery of Got-hama-baba: he therefore consented that the mouths of the council should be unpadlocked *pro hac vice*,[136] and the members were assembled without delay; with this express proviso, however, that they were to confine their deliberations to the subject of the Dairo and his distemper. By this time the physicians had discovered the cause of the disorder, which was no other than his being stung by a poisonous insect produced in the land of Yesso, analogous to the tarantula, which is said to do so much mischief in some parts of Apuglia, as we are told by Ælian, Epiphanius Ferdinandus, and Baglivi. In both cases the only effectual remedy was music;[137] and now the council was called to determine what sort of music should be administered. You must know, Peacock, the Japonese are but indifferently skilled in this art, tho', in general, they affect to be connoisseurs. They are utterly ignorant of the theory, and in the practice are excelled by all their neighbours, the Tartars not excepted.[138] For my own part, I studied music under Pythagoras at Crotona. He found the scale of seven tones imperfect, and added the octave as a fixed, sensible, and intelligent termination of an interval, which included every possible division, and determined all the relative differences of sounds:[139] besides, he taught us how to express the octave by $\frac{1}{2}$, &c. &c. But why should I talk to thee of the antient digramma, the genera, &c. of music, which with their colours, were constructed by a division of the diatessaron. Thou art too dull and ignorant to comprehend the chromatic species, the construction of the tetrachord, the Phrygian, the Lydian, and other modes of the antient music:[140] and for distinction of ear, thou mightest be justly ranked among the braying tribe that graze along the ditches of Tottenham-court or Hockley-i'the-hole.[141] I know that nothing exhilarates thy spirits so much as a sonata on the salt-box, or a concert of marrow-bones and cleavers.[142] The ears of the Japonese were much of the same texture; and their music was suited to their ears. They neither excelled in the melopœia, and rythm or cadence; nor did they know any thing of the true science of harmony, compositions in parts, and those combinations of sounds, the invention of which, with the improvement of the scale, is erroneously ascribed to a Benedictine monk. The truth is, the antients understood composition perfectly well. Their scale was founded upon perfect consonances: they were remarkably nice in tempering sounds, and had reduced their intervals and concords to mathematical demonstration.[143]

But, to return to the council of Twenty-eight, they convened in the same apartment where the Dairo lay; and as the business was to determine what kind of music was most likely to make an impression upon his organs, every member came provided with his expedient. First and foremost, Mr. Orator Taycho pronounced an oration upon the excellences of the land of Yesso, of energy (as the Cuboy said) sufficient to draw the moon from her sphere; it drew nothing, however, from the patient but a single groan: then the Fatzman caused a drum to beat, without producing any effect at all upon the Dairo; tho' it deprived the whole council of their hearing for some time. The third essay was made by Fika-kaka; first with a rattle, and then with tongs and gridiron, which last was his favourite music; but here it failed, to his great surprize and consternation. Sti-phi-rum-poo brought the crier of his court to promulgate a decree against Yesso, in a voice that is wont to make the culprit tremble; but the Dairo was found Ignoramus.[144] Nin-kom-poo-po blew a blast with a kind of boatswain's whistle, which discomposed the whole audience without affecting the emperor. Fokh-si-rokhu said he would try his imperial majesty with a sound which he had always been known to prefer to every other species of music; and pulling out a huge purse of golden obans, began to chink them in his ear.—This experiment so far succeeded, that the Dairo was perceived to smile, and even to contract one hand:[145] but further effect it had none. At last Gotto-mio starting up, threw a small quantity of *aurum fulminans*[146] into the fire, which went off with such an explosion, that in the same instant Fika-kaha fell flat upon his face, and Got-hama-baba started upright in his bed. This, however, was no more than a convulsion that put an end to his life; for he fell back again, and expired in the twinkling of an eye.[147]—As for the Cuboy, tho' he did not die, he underwent a surprising transformation or metamorphosis, which I shall record in due season.

Taycho was no sooner certified that Got-hama-baba had actually breathed his last, than he vanished from the council in the twinkling of an eye, and mounting the beast whose name is Legion, rode full speed to the habitation of *Gio-gio*, the successor and descendant of the deceased Dairo.[148]—Gio-gio was a young prince who had been industriously sequestered from the public view, and excluded from all share in the affairs of state by the jealousy of the last emperor.[149]—He lived retired under the wings of his grand-mother,[150] and had divers preceptors to teach him the rudiments of every art but the art of reigning. Of all those who superintended his education, he who insinuated himself the farthest in his favour, was one *Yak-strot*,[151] from the mountains of Ximo, who valued himself much upon the antient blood that ran in his veins, and still more upon his elevated ideas of patriotism.[152] Yak-strot was honest at bottom, but proud, reserved, vain, and affected.[153] He had a turn for nick-nacks and gim-cracks, and once made and mounted an iron jack and a wooden clock with his own hands. But it was his misfortune to set up for a connoisseur in painting and other liberal arts, and to announce himself an universal patron of genius.[154] He did not fail to infuse his own notions and conceits into the tender mind of Gio-gio, who gradually imbibed his turn of thinking, and followed the studies which he recommended.—With respect to his lessons on the art of government, he reduced them to a very few simple principles.—His maxims were these:[155] That the emperor of Japan ought to cherish the established religion, both by precept and example; that he ought to abolish corruption, discourage faction, and balance the two parties by admitting an equal number from each, to places and offices of trust in the administration: that he should make peace as soon as possible, even in despite of the public, which seemed insensible of the burthen it sustained, and was indeed growing delirious by the illusions of Taycho, and the cruel evacuations he had prescribed: that he should retrench all superfluous expence in his houshold and government, and detach himself intirely from the accursed farm of Yesso, which some evil genius[156] had fixed upon the breech of Japan, as a cancerous ulcer thro' which all her blood and substance would be discharged. These maxims were generally just enough in speculation, but some of them were altogether impracticable;—for example, that of forming an administration equally composed of the two factions, was as absurd as it would be to yoke two stone-horses[157] and two jack-asses in the same carriage, which, instead of drawing one way, would do nothing but bite and kick one another, while the machine of government would stand stock-still, or perhaps be torn in pieces by their dragging in opposite directions.—The people of Japan had been long divided between two inveterate parties known by the names of *Shit-tilk-ums-heit*, and *She-it-kums-hi-til*,[158] the first signifying *more fool than knave*; and the other, *more knave than fool*. Each had predominated[159] in its turn, by securing a majority in the assemblies of the people; for the majority had always interest to force themselves into the administration; because the constitution being partly democratic, the Dairo was still[160] obliged to truckle to the prevailing faction.—To obtain this majority, each side had employed every art of corruption, calumny, insinuation, and priest-craft; for nothing is such an effectual ferment[161] in all popular commotions as religious fanaticism.—No sooner one party accomplished its aim than it reprobated the other, branding it with the epithets of traitors to their country, or traitors to their prince; while the minority retorted[162] upon them the charge of corruption, rapaciousness, and abject servility. In short, both parties were equally abusive, rancorous, uncandid, and illiberal. Taycho had been of both factions more than once.—He made his first appearance[163] as a *Shi-tilk-ums-heit* in the minority, and displayed his talent for scurrility against the Dairo to such advantage, that an old rich hag, who loved nothing so well as money, except the gratification of her revenge, made him a present of five thousand obans, on condition he should continue to revile the Dairo till his dying-day.[164]—After her death, the ministry, intimidated by the boldness of his tropes, and the fame he began to acquire as a mal-content orator, made him such offers[165] as he thought proper to accept; and then he turned *She-it-kums-hi-til*.—Being disgusted in the sequel,[166] at his own want of importance in the council, he opened[167] once more at the head of his old friends the *Shi-tilk-ums-hitites*; and once more he deserted them[168] to rule the roast, as chief of the *She-it-kums-hi-tilites*, in which predicament[169] he now stood. And, indeed, this was the most natural posture in which he could stand; for this party embraced all the scum of the people,[170] constituting the blatant beast, which his talents were so peculiarly adapted to manage and govern. Another impracticable maxim of Yak-strot, was the abolition of corruption, the ordure of which is as necessary to anoint the wheels of government in Japan, as grease is to smear the axle-tree of a loaded waggon.[171] His third impolitic (tho' not impracticable) maxim, was that of making peace while the populace were intoxicated with the steams of blood, and elated with the shews of triumph. Be that as it will, Gio-gio, attended by Yak-strot, was drawing plans of windmills,[172] when Orator Taycho, opening the door, advanced towards him,[173] and falling on his knees, addressed him in these words: "The empire of Japan (magnanimous prince!) resembles at this instant, a benighted traveller, who by the light of the star Hesperus[174] continued his journey without repining, until that glorious luminary setting, left him bewildered in darkness and consternation: but scarce had he time to bewail his fate, when the more glorious sun, the ruler of a fresh day, appearing on the tops of the Eastern hills,[175] dispelled his terrors with the shades of night, and filled his soul with transports of pleasure and delight. The illustrious Got-hama-baba, of honoured memory, is the glorious star which hath set on our hemisphere.—His soul, which took wing about two hours ago, is now happily nestled in the bosom of the blessed Bupo;[176] and you, my prince, are the more glorious rising sun, whose genial influence will chear the empire, and gladden the hearts of your faithful Japonese.—I therefore hail your succession to the throne, and cry aloud, Long live the ever-glorious Gio-gio, emperor of the three islands of Japan." To this salutation the beast below brayed hoarse applause; and all present kissed the hand of the new emperor, who, kneeling before his venerable grandame, craved her blessing, desiring the benefit of her prayers, that God would make him a good king, and establish his throne in righteousness.[177] Then he ascended his chariot, accompanied by the Orator and his beloved Yak-strot, and proceeding to the palace of Meaco, was proclaimed with the usual ceremonies, his relation the Fatz-man[178] and other princes of the blood assisting[179] on this occasion.

The first step he took after his elevation, was to publish a decree, or rather exhortation, to honour religion and the Bonzes; and this was no impolitic expedient: for it firmly attached that numerous and powerful tribe to his interest.[180] His next measures did not seem to be directed by the same spirit of discretion. He admitted a parcel of raw boys, and even some individuals of the faction of *Shi-tilk-ums-heit* into his council; and though Taycho still continued to manage the reins of administration, Yak-strot was associated with him in office,[181] to the great scandal and dissatisfaction of the Niphonites, who hate all the Ximians with a mixture of jealousy and contempt.[182]

Fika-kaka was not the last who payed his respects to his new sovereign, by whom he was graciously received, altho' he did not seem quite satisfied; because when he presented himself in his usual attitude, he had not received the kick of approbation.[183] New reigns, new customs: This Dairo never dreamed of kicking those whom he delighted to honour.[184]—It was a secret of state which had not yet come to his knowledge; and Yak-strot had always assured him, that kicking the breech always and every-where implied disgrace, as kicking the parts before, betokens ungovernable passion. Yak-strot, however, in this particular, seems to have been too confined in his notions of the *etiquette*: for it had been the custom time immemorial for the Dairos of Japan to kick their favourites and prime ministers. Besides, there are at this day different sorts of kicks used even in England,[185] without occasioning any dishonour to the *Kickee*.—It is sometimes a misfortune to be *kicked* out of place, but no dishonour. A man is often *kicked up* in the way of preferment, in order that his place may be given to a person of more interest.[186] Then there is the amorous kick, called *Kick 'um, Jenny*,[187] which every gallant undergoes with pleasure: hence the old English appellation of *Kicksy-wicksy*,[188] bestowed on a wanton leman[189] who knew all her paces. As for the familiar kick, it is no other than a mark of friendship: nor is it more dishonourable to be cuffed and cudgelled. Every body knows that the *alapa* or box o' the ear, among the Romans, was a particular mark of favour by which their slaves were made free; and the favourite gladiator, when he obtained his dismission from the service, was honoured with a sound cudgelling; this being the true meaning of the phrase *rude donatus*.[190] In the times of chivalry, the knight when dubbed, was well thwacked across the shoulders by his god-father in arms.— Indeed, *dubbing* is no other than a corruption of *drubbing*. It was the custom formerly here and elsewhere, for a man to drub his son or apprentice as a mark of his freedom, and of his being admitted to the exercise of arms. The Paraschistes, who practised *embalming* in Ægypt, which was counted a very honourable profession, was always severely drubbed after the operation, by the friends and relations of the defunct;[191] and to this day, the patriarch of the Greeks once a year, on Easter-eve, when he carries out the sacred fire from the holy sepulchre of Jerusalem, is heartily cudgelled by the infidels, a certain number of whom he hires for that purpose; and he thinks himself very unhappy and much disgraced, if he is not beaten into all the colours of the rain-bow.[192] You know the Quakers of this country think it no dishonour to receive a slap o' the face;[193] but when you smite them on one cheek, they present the other, that it may have the same salutation.[194] The venerable father Lactantius falls out with Cicero for saying, "A good man hurts nobody, unless he is justly provoked;" *nisi lacessitur injuria. O,* (cries the good father) *quam simplicem veramque sententiam duorum verborum adjectione corrupit!—non minus enim mali est, referre injuriam, quam inferre.*[195] The great philosopher Socrates thought it no disgrace to be kicked by his wife Xantippe; nay, he is said to have undergone the same discipline from other people, without making the least resistance, it being his opinion that it was more courageous, consequently more honourable, to bear a drubbing patiently, than to attempt any thing either in the way of self-defence or retaliation.[196]— The judicious and learned Puffendorf, in his book *De Jure Gentium & Naturali,* declares, that a man's honour is not so fragile as to be hurt either by a box on the ear, or a kick on the breech, otherwise it would be in the power of every saucy fellow to diminish or infringe it.[197]—It must be owned, indeed, Grotius *De Jure Belli & Pacis,* says, that charity does not of itself require our patiently suffering such an affront.[198] The English have with a most servile imitation, borrowed[199] their *punto,*[200] as well as other modes, from the French nation. Now kicking and cuffing were counted infamous among those people for these reasons. A box on the ear destroys the whole œconomy of their *frisure,* upon which they bestow the greatest part of their time and attention;[201] and a kick on the breech is attended with great pain and danger, as they are generally subject to the piles. This is so truly the case, that they have no less than two saints to patronize and protect the individuals afflicted with this disease. One is St. *Fiacre,* who was a native of the kingdom of Ireland. He presides over the blind piles. The other is a female saint, *Hæmorrhoissa,* and she comforts those who are distressed with the bleeding piles.[202] No wonder, therefore, that a Frenchman put to the torture by a kick on those tender parts, should be provoked to vengeance; and that this vengeance should gradually become an article in their system of punctilio.

But, to return to the thread of my narration.—Whatever inclination the Dairo and Yak-strot had to restore the blessings of peace, they did not think proper as yet to combat the disposition and schemes of Orator Taycho; in consequence of whose remonstrances, the tributary treaty was immediately renewed with Brut-an-tiffi,[203] and Gio-gio declared in the assembly of the people, that he was determined to support that illustrious ally, and carry on the war with vigour.[204]—By this time the Chinese were in a manner expelled from their chief settlements in Fatsisio, where they now retained nothing but an inconsiderable colony, which would have submitted on the first summons:

but this Taycho left as a nest-egg to produce a new brood of disturbance to the Japonese settlements, that they might not rust with too much peace and security.[205] To be plain with you, Peacock, his thoughts were entirely alienated from this Fatsisian war, in which the interest of his country was chiefly concerned, and converted wholly to the continent of Tartary, where all his cares centered in schemes for the success of his friend Brut-an-tiffi. This freebooter had lately undergone strange vicissitudes of fortune. He had seen his chief village possessed and plundered by the enemy; but he found means, by surprize, to beat up their quarters in the beginning of winter, which always proved his best ally, because then the Mantchoux Tartars were obliged to retire to their own country, at a vast distance from the seat of the war.[206]—As for Bron-xi-tic, who commanded the Japonese army on that continent, he continued to play booty[207] with the Chinese general, over whom he was allowed to obtain some petty advantages,[208] which, with the trophies won by Brut-an-tiffi, were swelled up into mighty victories, to increase the infatuation of the blatant beast.—On the other hand, Bron-xi-tic obliged the generals of China with the like indulgences, by now and then sacrificing a detachment of his Japonese troops, to keep up the spirits of that nation.[209]

Taycho had levied upon the people of Japan an immense sum of money for the equipment of a naval armament, the destination of which was kept a profound secret. Some politicians[210] imagined it was designed for the conquest of Thin-quo, and all the other settlements which the Chinese possessed in the Indian ocean: others conjectured the intention was to attack the king of Corea,[211] who had, since the beginning of this war, acted with a shameful partiality in favour of the emperor of China, his kinsman and ally.[212] But the truth of the matter was this: Taycho kept the armament in the harbours of Japan ready for a descent upon the coast of China, in order to make a diversion in favour of his friend Brut-an-tiffi, in case he had run any risque of being oppressed by his enemies. However, the beast of many heads having growled and grumbled during the best part of the summer, at the inactivity of this expensive armament, it was now thought proper to send it to sea in the beginning of winter: but it was soon driven back in great distress, by contrary winds and storms;—and this was all the monster had for its ten millions of Obans.[213]

While Taycho amused the Mobile with this winter expedition, Yak-strot resolved to plan the scheme of œconomy[214] which he had projected. He dismissed from the Dairo's service about a dozen of cooks and scullions; shut up one of the kitchens, after having sold the grates, hand-irons,[215] spits and sauce-pans; deprived the servants and officers of the houshold of their breakfast; took away their usual allowance of oil and candles; retrenched their tables; reduced their proportion of drink; and persuaded his pupil the Dairo to put himself upon a diet of soup-meagre thickened with oat-meal.[216] In a few days there was no smoke seen to ascend from the kitchens of the palace; nor did any fuel, torch, or taper blaze in the chimnies, courts, and apartments thereof, which now became the habitation of cold, darkness, and hunger. Gio-gio himself, who turned peripatetic philosopher[217] merely to keep himself in heat, fell into a wash-tub as he groped his way in the dark through one of the lower galleries. Two of his body-guard had their whiskers gnawed off by the rats, as they slept in his antichamber; and their captain presented a petition declaring, that neither he nor his men could undertake the defence of his imperial majesty's person, unless their former allowance of provision should be restored. They and all the individuals of the household were not only punished in their bellies, but likewise curtailed in their clothing, and abridged in their stipends. The palace of Meaco, which used to be the temple of mirth, jollity, and good cheer, was now so dreary and deserted, that a certain wag fixed up a ticket on the outward gate with this inscription: "This tenement to be lett, the proprietor having left off house-keeping."[218]

Yak-strot, however, was resolved to shew, that if the new Dairo retrenched the superfluities of his domestic expence, he did not act from avarice or poorness of spirit, inasmuch as he should now display his liberality in patronizing genius and the arts. A general jubilee was now promised to all those who had distinguished themselves by their talents or erudition. The emissaries of Yak-strot declared that Mæcenas was but a type[219] of this Ximian mountaineer; and that he was determined to search for merit, even in the thickest shades of obscurity. All these researches, however, proved so unsuccessful, that not above four or five men of genius could be found in the whole empire of Japan, and these were gratified with pensions[220] of about one hundred Obans each. One was a secularized Bonza from Ximo;[221] another a malcontent poet of Niphon;[222] a third, a reformed comedian of Xicoco;[223] a fourth, an empiric, who had outlived his practice;[224] and a fifth, a decayed apothecary,[225] who was bard, quack, author, chymist, philosopher, and simpler[226] by profession. The whole of the expence arising from the favour and protection granted by the Dairo to these men of genius, did not exceed seven or eight hundred Obans per annum, amounting to about fifteen hundred pounds sterling; whereas many a private Quo in Japan expended more money on a kennel of hounds. I do not mention those men of singular merit, whom Yak-strot fixed in established places under the government;[227] such as architects, astronomers, painters, physicians, barbers, &c. because their salaries were included in the ordinary expence of the crown: I shall only observe, that a certain person who could not read, was appointed librarian to his imperial majesty.[228]

These were all the men of superlative genius, that Yak-strot could find at this period in the empire of Japan.

Whilst this great patriot was thus employed in executing his schemes of œconomy with more zeal than discretion, and in providing his poor relations with lucrative offices under the government,[229] a negociation for peace was brought upon the carpet by the mediation of certain neutral powers; and Orator Taycho arrogated to himself the province of discussing the several articles of the treaty.[230]—Upon this occasion he shewed himself surprizingly remiss and indifferent in whatever related to the interest of Japan, particularly in regulating and fixing the boundaries of the Chinese and Japonese settlements in Fatsisio, the uncertainty of which had given rise to the war: but when the business was to determine the claims and pretensions of his ally Brut-an-tiffi, on the continent of Tartary, he appeared stiff and immoveable as mount Athos.[231] He actually broke off the negotiation, because the emperor of China would not engage to drive by force of arms the troops of his ally the princess of Ostrog, from a village or two belonging to the Tartarian free-booter, who, by the bye, had left them defenceless at the beginning of the war, on purpose that his enemies might, by taking possession of them, quicken the resolutions of the Dairo to send over an army for the protection of Yesso.[232]

The court of Pekin perceiving that the Japonese were rendered intolerably insolent and overbearing by success, and that an equitable peace could not be obtained while Orator Taycho managed the reins of government at Meaco, and his friend Brut-an-tiffi found any thing to plunder in Tartary; resolved to fortify themselves with a new alliance. They actually entered into closer connections with the king of Corea, who was nearly related to the Chinese emperor, had some old scores to settle with Japan, and because he desired those disputes might be amicably compromised in the general pacification, had been grossly insulted by Taycho, in the person of his ambassador. He had for some time dreaded the ambition of the Japonese ministry, which seemed to aim at universal empire; and he was, moreover, stimulated by this outrage to conclude a defensive alliance with the emperor of China; a measure which all the caution of the two courts could not wholly conceal from the knowledge of the Japonese politicians.[233]

Mean while a dreadful cloud big with ruin and disgrace seemed to gather round the head of Brut-an-tiffi. The Mantchoux Tartars, sensible of the inconvenience of their distant situation from the scene of action, which rendered it impossible for them to carry on their operations vigorously in conjunction with the Ostrog, resolved to secure winter-quarters in some part of the enemy's territories, from whence they should be able to take the field, and act against him early in the spring. With this view they besieged and took a frontier fortress belonging to Brut-an-tiffi, situated upon a great inland lake which extended as far as the capital of the Mantchoux,[234] who were thus enabled to send thither by water-carriage all sorts of provisions and military stores for the use of their army, which took up their winter-quarters accordingly in and about this new acquisition. It was now that the ruin of Brut-an-tiffi seemed inevitable. Orator Taycho saw with horror the precipice to the brink of which his dear ally was driven. Not that his fears were actuated by sympathy or friendship. Such emotions had never possessed the heart of Taycho. No; he trembled because he saw his own popularity connected with the fate of the Tartar. It was the success and petty triumphs of this adventurer which had dazzled the eyes of the blatant beast, so as to disorder its judgment, and prepare it for the illusions of the Orator: but, now that Fortune seemed ready to turn tail to Brut-an-tiffi, and leave him a prey to his adversaries, Taycho knew the dispositions of the monster so well as to prognosticate that its applause and affection would be immediately turned into grumbling and disgust; and that he himself, who had led it blindfold into this unfortunate connexion, might possibly fall a sacrifice to its resentment, provided he could not immediately project some scheme to divert its attention, and transfer the blame from his own shoulders.

For this purpose he employed his invention, and succeeded to his wish. Having called a council of the Twenty-eight, at which the Dairo assisted in person, he proposed, and insisted upon it, that a strong squadron of Fune should be immediately ordered to scour the seas, and kidnap all the vessels and ships belonging to the king of Corea, who had acted during the whole war with the most scandalous partiality in favour of the Chinese emperor, and was now so intimately connected with that potentate, by means of a secret alliance, that he ought to be prosecuted with the same hostilities which the other had severely felt.[235] The whole council were confounded at this proposal: the Dairo stood aghast: the Cuboy trembled: Yak-strot stared like a skewered pig. After some pause, the president Soo-san-sin-o ventured to observe, that the measure seemed to be a little abrupt and premature: that the nation was already engaged in a very expensive war, which had absolutely drained it of its wealth, and even loaded it with enormous debts; therefore little able to sustain such additional burthens as would, in all probability, be occasioned by a rupture with a prince so rich and powerful. Gotto-mio swore the land holders were already so impoverished by the exactions of Taycho, that he himself, ere long, should be obliged to come upon the parish.[236] Fika-kaka got up to speak; but could only cackle. Sti-phi-rum-poo was for proceeding in form by citation.[237] Nin-kom-poo-po declared he had good intelligence of a fleet of merchant-ships belonging to Corea, laden with treasure, who were then on their return from the Indian isles; and he gave it as his opinion, that they should be way-laid and brought into the harbours of Japan; not by way of declaring war, but only with a view to prevent the money's going into the coffers of the Chinese emperor.[238] Fokh-si-rokhu started two objections[239] to this expedient: first, the uncertainty of falling in with the Corean fleet at sea, alledging as an instance the disappointment and miscarriage of the squadron which the Sey-seo-gun had sent some years ago to intercept the Chinese Fune on the coast of Fatsisio:[240] secondly, the loss and hardship it would be to many subjects of Japan who dealt in commerce, and had great sums embarked in those very Corean bottoms.[241] Indeed Fokh-si-rokhu himself was interested in[242] this very commerce. The Fatz-man sat silent. Yak-strot, who had some romantic notions of honour and honesty,[243] represented that the nation had already incurred the censure of all its neighbours, by seizing the merchant-ships of China, without any previous declaration of war: that the law of nature and nations, confirmed by repeated treaties, pre-scribed a more honourable method of proceeding, than that of plundering like robbers, the ships of pacific merchants, who trade on the faith of such laws and such treaties: he was, therefore, of opinion, that if the king of Corea had in any shape deviated from the neutrality which he professed, satisfaction should be demanded in the usual form; and when that should be refused, it might be found necessary to proceed to compulsive measures. The Dairo acquiesced in this advice, and assured Taycho that an ambassador should be forthwith dispatched to Corea, with instructions to demand an immediate and satisfactory explanation of that prince's conduct and designs with regard to the empire of Japan.[244]

This regular method of practice would by no means suit the purposes of Taycho, who rejected it with great insolence and disdain. He bit his thumb at the president; forked out his fingers[245] on his forehead at Gotto-mio; wagged his under-jaw at the Cuboy; snapt his fingers at Sti-phi-rum-poo; grinned at the Sey-seo-gun; made the sign of the cross or gallows to Fokh-si-rokhu; then turning to Yak-strot, he clapped his thumbs in his ears, and began to bray like an ass: finally, pulling out the badge of his office,[246] he threw it at the Dairo, who in vain intreated him to be pacified; and wheeling to the right-about, stalked away, slapping the flat of his hand upon a certain part that shall be nameless. He was followed by his kinsman the Quo Lob-kob,[247] who worshipped him with the most humble adoration. He now imitated this great original in the signal from behind at parting, and in him it was attended by a rumbling sound; but whether this was the effect of contempt or compunction,[248] I could never learn.

Taycho having thus carried his point, which was to have a pretence for quitting the reins of government, made his next appeal to the blatant beast.[249] He reminded the many-headed monster of the uninterrupted success which had attended his administration; of his having supported the glorious Brut-an-tiffi, the great bulwark of the religion of Bupo, who had kept the common enemy at bay, and filled all Asia with the fame of his victories. He told them, that for his own part, he pretended[250] to have subdued Fatsisio in the heart of Tartary: that he despised honours, and had still a greater contempt for riches; and that all his endeavours had been solely exerted for the good of his country, which was now brought to the very verge of destruction. He then gave the beast to understand that he had formed a scheme against the king of Corea, which would not only have disabled that monarch from executing his hostile intentions with respect to Japan, but also have indemnified this nation for the whole expence of the war; but that his proposal having been rejected by the council of Twenty-eight, who were influencd by Yak-strot, a Ximian mountaineer without spirit or understanding, he had resigned his office with intention to retire to some solitude, where he should in silence deplore the misfortunes of his country, and the ruin of the Buponian religion, which must fall of course[251] with its great protector Brut-an-tiffi, whom he foresaw the new ministry would immediately abandon.

This address threw Legion into such a quandary, that it rolled itself in the dirt, and yelled hideously. Mean while the Orator retreating to a cell in the neighbourhood of Meaco,[252] hired the common crier to go round the streets and proclaim that Taycho, being no longer in a condition to afford any thing but the bare necessaries of life, would by public sale dispose of his ambling mule and furniture, together with an ermined robe of his wife, and the greater part of his kitchen utensils.[253] At this time he was well known to be worth upwards of twenty thousand gold Obans;[254] nevertheless, the Mobile discharging this circumstance entirely from their reflection, attended to nothing but the object which the Orator was pleased to present. They thought it was a piteous case, and a great scandal upon the government, that such a patriot, who had saved the nation from ruin and disgrace, should be reduced to the cruel necessity of selling his mule and his houshold furniture. Accordingly they raised a clamour that soon rung in the ears of Gio-gio and his favourite.

It was supposed that Mura-clami suggested on this occasion to his country-man Yak-strot, the hint of offering a pension to Taycho,[255] by way of remuneration for his past services. "If he refuses it, (said he) the offer will at least reflect some credit upon the Dairo and the administration; but, should he accept of it, (which is much more likely) it will either stop his mouth entirely, or expose him to the censure of the people, who now adore him as a mirrour of disinterested integrity." The advice was instantly complied with: the Dairo signed a patent for a very ample pension to Taycho and his heirs;[256] which patent Yak-strot delivered to him next day at his cell in the country.[257] This miracle of patriotism received the bounty as a turnpike-man receives the toll, and then slapped his door full in the face of the favourite:[258] yet, nothing of what Mura-clami had prognosticated, came to pass. The many-tailed mon-ster, far from calling in question the Orator's disinterestedness, considered his acceptance of the pension as a proof of his moderation, in receiving such a trifling reward for the great services he had done his country; and the gener-osity of the Dairo, instead of exciting the least emotion of gratitude in Tay-cho's own breast, acted only as a golden key to unlock all the sluices of his virulence and abuse.[259]

These, however, he kept within bounds until he should see what would be the fate of Brut-an-tiffi, who now seemed to be in the condition of a criminal at the foot of the ladder.[260] In this dilemma, he obtained a very unexpected reprieve. Before the army of the Mantchoux could take the least advantage of the settlement they had made on his frontiers, their empress died, and was succeeded by a weak prince, who no sooner ascended the throne than he struck up a peace with the Tartar freebooter, and even ordered his troops to join him against the Ostrog,[261] to whom they had hitherto acted as auxili-aries. Such an accession of strength would have cast the balance greatly in his favour, had not Providence once more interposed, and brought matters again to an equilibrium.

Taycho no sooner perceived his ally thus unexpectedly delivered from the dangers that surrounded him, than he began to repent of his own resignation; and resolved once more, to force his way to the helm, by the same means he had so successfully used before. He was, indeed, of such a turbulent disposi-tion as could not relish the repose of private life, and his spirit so corrosive, that it would have preyed upon himself, if he could not have found external food for it to devour. He therefore began to prepare his engines,[262] and pro-vide proper emissaries to bespatter, and raise a hue-and-cry against Yak-strot at a convenient season; not doubting but an occasion would soon present itself, considering the temper, inexperience, and prejudices of this Ximian politician, together with the pacific system he had adopted, so contrary to the present spirit of the blatant beast.

In these preparations he was much comforted and assisted by his kinsman and pupil Lob-kob, who entered into his measures with surprizing zeal; and had the good luck to light on such instruments as were admirably suited to the work in hand.[263] Yak-strot was extremely pleased at the secession of Taycho, who had been a very troublesome collegue to him in the administration, and run counter to all the schemes he had projected for the good of the empire. He now found himself at liberty to follow his own inventions, and being naturally an enthusiast, believed himself born to be the saviour of Japan. Some efforts, however, he made to acquire popularity, proved fruitless. Perceiving the people were, by the Orator's instigations, exasperated against the king of Corea, he sent a peremptory message to that prince demanding a categorical answer; and this being denied, declared war against him, according to the practice of all civilized nations: but even this measure failed of obtaining that approbation for which it was taken.[264] The monster, tutored by Taycho and his ministers, exclaimed, that the golden opportunity was lost, inasmuch as, during the observance of those useless forms, the treasures of Corea were safely brought home to that kingdom;[265] treasures which, had they been interrupted by the Fune of Japan, would have payed off the debts of the nation, and enabled the inhabitants of Meaco to pave their streets with silver. By the bye, this treasure existed no where[266] but in the fiction of Taycho and the imagination of the blatant beast, which never attempted to use the evidence of sense or reason to examine any assertion, how absurd and improbable soever it might be, which proceeded from the mouth[267] of the Orator.

Yak-strot, having now taken upon himself the task of steering the political bark, resolved to shew the Japonese, that altho' he recommended peace, he was as well qualified as his predecessor for conducting the war. He therefore, with the assistance of the Fatzman, projected three naval enterprizes;[268] the first against Thin-quo,[269] the conquest of which had been unsuccessfully attempted by Taycho; the second was destined for the reduction of Fanyah,[270] one of the most considerable settlements belonging to the king of Corea, in the Indian ocean; and the third armament was sent to plunder and destroy a flourishing colony called Lli-nam,[271] which the same prince had established almost as far to the southward as the Terra Australis Incognita. Now the only merit which either Yak-strot, or any other minister could justly claim from the success of such expeditions, is that of adopting the most feasible of those schemes which are presented by different projectors,[272] and of appointing *such* commanders as are capable of conducting them with vigour and sagacity.

The next step which the favourite took was to provide a help-mate for the young Dairo; and a certain Tartar princess of the religion of Bupo, being pitched upon for this purpose, was formally demanded, brought over to Niphon, espoused by Gio-gio, and installed empress with the usual solemnities.[273] But, lest the choice of a Tartarian princess should subject the Dairo to the imputation of inheriting his predecessor's predilection for the land of Yesso, which had given such sensible umbrage to all the sensible Japonese who made use of their own reason; he determined to detach his master gradually from those continental connexions, which had been the source of such enormous expence, and such continual vexation to the empire of Japan. In these sentiments, he with-held the annual tribute which had been lately payed to Brut-an-tiffi;[274] by which means he saved a very considerable sum to the nation, and, at the same time, rescued it from the infamy of such a disgraceful imposition.—He expected the thanks of the public for this exertion of his influence in favour of his country; but he reckoned without his host.[275] What he flattered himself would yield him an abundant harvest of honour and applause, produced nothing but odium and reproach, as we shall see in the sequel.

These measures, pursued with an eye to the advantage of the public, which seemed to argue a considerable share of spirit and capacity, were strangely chequered[276] with others of a more domestic nature, which savoured strongly of childish vanity, rash ambition, littleness of mind, and lack of understanding. He purchased a vast ward-robe of tawdry cloaths, and fluttered in all the finery of Japan: he prevailed upon his master to vest him with the badges and trappings of all the honorary institutions of the empire, altho' this multiplication of orders in the person of one man, was altogether without precedent or prescription.[277] This was only setting himself up as the more conspicuous mark for envy and detraction.

Not contented with engrossing the personal favour and confidence of his sovereign, and, in effect, directing the whole machine of government, he thought his fortune still imperfect, while the treasure of the empire passed through the hands of the Cuboy,[278] enabling that minister to maintain a very extensive influence, which might one day interfere with his own. He therefore employed all his invention, together with that of his friends, to find out some specious pretext for removing the old Cuboy from his office; and in a little time accident afforded what all their intrigues had not been able to procure.

Ever since the demise of Got-hama-baba, poor Fika-kaka had been subject to a new set of vagaries. The death of his old master gave him a rude shock:[279] then the new Dairo encroached upon his province, by preferring a Bonze without his consent or knowledge:[280] finally, he was prevented by the express order of Gio-gio from touching a certain sum out of the treasury, which he had been accustomed to throw out of his windows at stated periods, in order to keep up an interest among the dregs of the people.[281] All these mortifications had an effect upon the weak brain of the Cuboy. He began to loath his usual food, and sometimes even declined shewing himself to the Bonzes at his levee; symptoms that alarmed all his friends and dependants.[282] Instead of frequenting the assemblies of the great, he now attended assiduously at all groanings[283] and christenings, grew extremely fond of caudle,[284] and held conferences with practitioners, both male and female, in the art of midwifry. When business or ceremony obliged him to visit any of the Quos or Quanbukus of Meaco; he, by a surprising instinct, ran directly to the nursery, where, if there happened to be a child in the cradle, he took it up, and if it was foul, wiped it with great care and seeming satisfaction. He, moreover, learned of the good women to sing lullabies, and practised them with uncommon success: but the most extravagant of all his whims, was what he exhibited one day in his own court-yard. Observing a nest with some eggs, which the goose had quitted, he forthwith dropped his trowsers, and squatting down in the attitude of incubation, began to stretch out his neck, to hiss and to cackle,[285] as if he had been really metamorphosed into the animal whose place he now supplied.

It was on the back of[286] this adventure that one of the Bonzes, as prying, and as great a gossip as the barber of Midas,[287] in paying his morning worship to the Cuboy's posteriors, spied something, or rather nothing, and was exceedingly affrighted. He communicated his discovery and apprehension to divers others of the cloth; and they were all of opinion that some effectual inquisition should be held on this phænomenon, lest the clergy of Japan should hereafter be scandalized,[288] as having knowingly kissed the breech of an old woman, perhaps a monster or magician. Information was accordingly made to the Dairo, who gave orders for immediate inspection; and Fika-kaka was formally examined by a jury of matrons.[289] Whether these were actuated by undue influence, I shall not at present explain; certain it is, they found their verdict, The Cuboy *non mas*;[290] and among other evidences produced to attest his metamorphosis, a certain Ximian, who pretended to have the second sight, made oath that he had one evening seen the said Fika-kaka in a female dress, riding through the air on a broom-stick.[291] The unhappy Cuboy being thus convicted, was divested of his office, and confined to his palace in the country;[292] while Gio-gio, by the advice of his favourite, published a proclamation, declaring it was not for the honour of Japan that her treasury should be managed either by a witch or an old woman.

Fika-kaka being thus removed, Yak-strot was appointed treasurer and Cuboy in his place, and now ruled the roast with uncontrouled authority. On the very threshold of his greatness, however, he made a false step, which was one cause of his tottering, during the whole sequel of his administration. In order to refute the calumnies and defeat the intrigues of Taycho in the assemblies of the people, he chose as an associate in the ministry Fokh-si-rokhu, who was at that instant the most unpopular man in the whole empire of Japan;[293] and at the instigation of this collegue, deprived of bread a great number of poor families, who subsisted on petty places which had been bestowed upon them by the former Cuboy.[294] Those were so many mouths opened to augment the clamour against his own person and administration.

It might be imagined, that while he thus set one part of the nation at defiance, he would endeavour to cultivate the other; and, in particular, strive to conciliate the good-will of the nobility, who did not see his exaltation without umbrage. But, instead of ingratiating himself with them by a liberal turn of demeanour; by treating them with frankness and affability; granting them favours with a good grace; making entertainments for them at his palace; and mixing in their social parties of pleasure; Yak-strot always appeared on the reserve, and under all his finery, continually wore a doublet of buckram,[295] which gave an air of stiffness and constraint to his whole behaviour. He studied postures, and, in giving audience, generally stood in the attitude of the idol Fo;[296] so that he sometimes was mistaken for an image of stone. He formed a scale of gesticulation in a great variety of divisions, comprehending the slightest inclination of the head, the front-nod, the side-nod, the bow, the half, the semi-demi-bow, with the shuffle, the slide, the circular, semi-circular, and quadrant sweep of the right foot. With equal care and precision did he model the œconomy of his looks into the divisions and sub-divisions of the full-stare, the side-glance, the pensive look, the pouting look, the gay look, the vacant look, and the stolid look. To these different expressions of the eye he suited the corresponding features of the nose and mouth; such as the wrinkled nose, the retorted[297] nose, the sneer, the grin, the simper, and the smile. All these postures and gesticulations he practised, and distributed occasionally, according to the difference of rank and importance of the various individuals with whom he had communication.[298]

But these affected airs being assumed in despite of nature, he appeared as aukward as a native of Angola, when he is first hampered with cloaths; or a Highlander, obliged by act of parliament to wear breeches.[299]—Indeed, the distance observed by Yak-strot in his behaviour to the nobles of Niphon, was imputed to his being conscious of a sulphureous smell[300] which came from his own body; so that greater familiarity on his side might have bred contempt. He took delight in no other conversation but that of two or three obscure Ximians,[301] his companions and counsellors, with whom he spent all his leisure time, in conferences upon politics, patriotism, philosophy, and the Belles Lettres. Those were the oracles he consulted in all the emergencies of state; and with these he spent many an Attic evening.[302]

The gods, not yet tired of sporting with the farce of human government, were still resolved to shew by what inconsiderable springs a mighty empire may be moved. The new Cuboy was vastly well disposed to make his Ximian favourites great men. It was in his power to bestow places and pensions upon them; but it was not in his power to give them consequence in the eyes of the public. The administration of Yak-strot could not fail of being propitious to his own family, and poor relations, who were very numerous.[303] Their naked backs and hungry bellies were now clothed with the richest stuffs, and fed with the fat things[304] of Japan. Every department civil and military was filled with Ximians. Those islanders came over in shoals to Niphon, and swarmed in the streets of Meaco, where they were easily distinguished by their lank sides, gaunt looks, lanthorn-jaws, and long sharp teeth.[305]—There was a fatality that attended the whole conduct of this unfortunate Cuboy. His very partiality to his own countrymen, brought upon him at last the curses of the whole clan.

Mr. Orator Taycho and his kinsman Lob-kob were not idle in the mean time. They provided their emissaries, and primed all their engines. Their understrappers[306] filled every corner of Meaco with rumours, jealousies, and suspicions. Yak-strot was represented[307] as a statesman without discernment, a minister without knowledge, and a man without humanity. He was taxed with insupportable pride, indiscretion, pusillanimity, rapacity, partiality, and breach of faith. It was affirmed that he had dishonoured the nation, and endangered the very existence of the Buponian religion, in withdrawing the annual subsidy from the great Brut-an-tiffi: that he wanted to starve the war, and betray the glory and advantage of the empire by a shameful peace: that he had avowedly shared his administration with the greatest knave in Japan: that he treated the nobles of Niphon with insolence and contempt: that he had suborned evidence against the antient Cuboy Fika-kaka, who had spent a long life and an immense fortune in supporting the temple of Fak-ku-basi:[308] that he had cruelly turned adrift a great number of helpless families, in order to gratify his own worthless dependants with their spoils: that he had enriched his relations and countrymen with the plunder of Niphon: that his intention was to bring over the whole nation of Ximians, a savage race, who had been ever perfidious, greedy, and hostile towards the natives of the other Japonese islands. Nay, they were described as monsters in nature, with cloven feet, long tails, saucer eyes, iron fangs and claws, who would first devour the substance of the Niphonites, and then feed upon their blood.

Taycho had Legion's understanding so much in his power, that he actually made it believe Yak-strot had formed a treasonable scheme in favour of a foreign adventurer who pretended to the throne of Japan, and that the reigning Dairo was an accomplice in this project for his own deposition.[309] Indeed, they did not scruple to say that Gio-gio was no more than a puppet moved by his own grandmother and this vile Ximian, between whom they hinted there was a secret correspondence which reflected very little honour on the family of the Dairo.[310]

Mr. Orator Taycho and his associate Lob-kob left no stone unturned to disgrace the favourite, and drive him from the helm. They struck up an alliance with the old Cuboy Fika-kaka, and fetching him from his retirement, produced him to the beast as a martyr to loyalty and virtue.[311] They had often before this period, exposed him to the derision of the populace; but now they set him up as the object of veneration and esteem; and every thing succeeded to their wish. Legion hoisted Fika-kaka on his back, and paraded through the streets of Meaco, braying hoarse encomiums on the great talents and great virtues of the antient Cuboy.[312] His cause was now espoused by his old friends Sti-phi-rum-poo and Nin-kom-poo-poo, who had been turned adrift along with him, and by several other Quos who had nestled themselves in warm places under the shadow of his protection:[313] but it was remarkable, that not one of all the Bonzes who owed their preferment to his favour, had gratitude enough to follow his fortune, or pay the least respect to him in the day of his disgrace.[314]—Advantage was also taken of the disgust occasioned by Yak-strot's reserve among the nobles of Japan. Even the Fatz-man was estranged from the councils of his kinsman Gio-gio, and lent his name and countenance to the malcontents,[315] who now formed themselves into a very formidable cabal, comprehending a great number of the first Quos in the empire.

In order to counterballance this confederacy, which was a strange coalition of jarring interests, the new Cuboy endeavoured to strengthen his administration, by admitting into a share of it Gotto-mio, who dreaded nothing so much as the continuation of the war, and divers other noblemen, whose alliance contributed very little to his interest or advantage. Gotto-mio was universally envied for his wealth, and detested for his avarice:[316] the rest were either of the She-it-kum-sheit-el faction, which had been long in disgrace with the Mobile; or men of desperate fortunes and loose morals,[317] who attached themselves to the Ximian favourite solely on account of the posts and pensions he had to bestow.

During these domestic commotions, the arms of Japan continued to prosper in the Indian ocean. Thin-quo was reduced almost without opposition;[318] and news arrived that the conquest of Fan-yah was already more than half atchieved.[319] At the same time, some considerable advantages were gained over the enemy on the continent of Tartary, by the Japonese forces under the command of Bron-xi-tic.[320] It might be naturally supposed that these events would have, in some measure, reconciled the Niphonites to the new ministry: but they produced rather a contrary effect. The blatant beast was resolved to rejoice at no victories but those that were obtained under the auspices of its beloved Taycho; and now took it highly amiss that Yak-strot should presume to take any step which might redound to the glory of the empire. Nothing could have pleased the monster at this juncture so much as the miscarriage of both expeditions, and a certain information that all the troops and ships employed in them had miserably perished. The king of Corea, however, was so alarmed at the progress of the Japonese before Fan-yah, that he began to tremble for all his distant colonies, and earnestly craved the advice of the cabinet of Pekin touching some scheme to make a diversion in their favour.

The councils of Pekin have been ever fruitful of intrigues to embroil the rest of Asia. They suggested a plan to the king of Corea, which he forthwith put in execution. The land of Fumma,[321] which borders on the Corean territories, was governed by a prince nearly allied to the king of Corea,[322] although his subjects had very intimate connexions in the way of commerce with the empire of Japan, which, indeed, had entered into an offensive and defensive alliance with this country.[323] The emperor of China and the king of Corea having sounded the sovereign of Fumma, and found him well disposed

to enter into their measures, communicated their scheme, in which he immediately concurred. They called upon him in public, as their friend and ally, to
join them against the Japonese, as the inveterate enemy of the religion of Fo,
and as an insolent people, who affected a despotism at sea, to the detriment
and destruction of all their neighbours; plainly declaring that he must either
immediately break with the Dairo, or expect an invasion on the side of Corea.
The prince of Fumma affected to complain loudly of this iniquitous proposal;
he made a merit of rejecting the alternative; and immediately demanded of
the court of Meaco, the succours stipulated in the treaty of alliance, in order
to defend his dominions. In all appearance, indeed, there was no time to be
lost; for the monarchs of China and Corea declared war against him without
further hesitation; and uniting their forces on that side, ordered them to enter
the land of Fumma, after having given satisfactory assurances in private, that
the prince had nothing to fear from their hostilities.[324]

Yak-strot was not much embarrassed[325] on this occasion. Without suspecting the least collusion among the parties, he resolved to take the prince of
Fumma under his protection, thereunto moved by divers considerations.
First and foremost, he piqued himself upon his good faith: secondly, he knew
that the trade with Fumma was of great consequence to Japan; and therefore
concluded that his supporting the sovereign of it would be a popular measure:
thirdly, he hoped that the multiplication of expence incurred by this new
war, would make the blatant beast wince under its burden, and of consequence reconcile it to the thoughts of a general pacification, which he had
very much at heart. Mean while he hastened the necessary succours to the
land of Fumma, and sent thither an old general called Le-yaw-ter,[326] in order
to concert[327] with the prince and his ministers the operations of the campaign.

This officer was counted one of the shrewdest politicians in Japan, and
having resided many years as ambassador in Fumma, was well acquainted
with the genius of that people. He immediately discovered the scene which
had been acted behind the curtain.[328] He found that the prince of Fumma,
far from having made any preparations for his own defence, had actually
withdrawn his garrisons from the frontier places, which were by this time
peaceably occupied by the invading army of Chinese and Coreans: that the
few troops he had, were without cloaths, arms, and discipline; and that he
had amused[329] the court of Meaco with false musters, and a specious account
of levies and preparations which had been made. In a word, though he could
not learn the particulars, he comprehended the whole mystery of the secret
negotiations. He upbraided the minister of Fumma with perfidy, refused to

assume the command of the Japonese auxiliaries when they arrived, and returning to Meaco, communicated his discoveries and suspicions to the new
Cuboy. But he did not meet with that reception which he thought he deserved for intelligence of such importance. Yak-strot affected to doubt; perhaps, he was not really convinced; or, if he was, thought proper to temporize;
and he was in the right for so doing. A rupture with Fumma at this juncture,
would have forced the prince to declare openly for the enemies of Japan; in
which case the inhabitants of Niphon would have lost the benefit of a very
advantageous trade. They had already been great sufferers in commerce by
the breach with the king of Corea, whose subjects had been used to take off
great quantities of the Japonese manufactures, for which they payed in gold
and silver; and they could ill bear such an additional loss as an interruption of
the trade with Fumma would have occasioned. The Cuboy, therefore, continued to treat the prince of that country as a staunch ally, who had sacrificed
every other consideration to his good faith; and, far from restricting himself
to the number of troops and Fune stipulated in the treaty, sent over a much
more numerous body of forces and ships of war; declaring, at the same time,
he would support the people of Fumma with the whole power of Japan.

Such a considerable diversion of the Japonese strength could not fail to
answer, in some measure, the expectation of the two sovereigns of China and
Corea; but it did not prevent the success of the expeditions which were actually[330] employed against their colonies in the Indian ocean. It was not in his
power, however, to protect Fumma, had the invaders been in earnest: but the
combined army of the Chinese and Coreans had orders to protract the war;
and, instead of penetrating to the capital, at a time when the Fummians, tho'
joined with the auxiliaries of Japan, were not numerous enough to look them
in the face, they made a full-stop in the middle of their march, and quietly
retired into summer quarters.[331]

The additional incumbrance of a new continental war, redoubled the
Cuboy's desire of peace; and his inclination being known to the enemy, who
were also sick of the war, they had recourse to the good offices of a certain
neutral power, called Sab-oi, sovereign of the mountains of Cambodia.[332]
This prince accordingly offered his mediation at the court of Meaco, and it
was immediately accepted.—The negotiation for peace, which had been
broke off in the ministry of Taycho, was now resumed; an ambassador plenipotentiary arrived from Pekin; and Gotto-mio was sent thither in the same
capacity, in order to adjust the articles, and sign the preliminaries of peace.[333]

While this new treaty was on the carpet, the armament equipped against
Fan-yah under the command of the Quo Kep-marl, and the brave admiral,

who had signalized himself in the sea of Kamtschatka, reduced that important place, where they became masters of a strong squadron of Fune belonging to the king of Corea, together with a very considerable treasure, sufficient to indemnify Japan for the expence of the expedition.[334] This, though the most grievous, was not the only disaster which the war brought upon the Coreans. Their distant settlement of Lli-nam was likewise taken by general Tra-rep, and the inhabitants payed an immense sum in order to redeem their capital from plunder.[335]

These successes did not at all retard the conclusion of the treaty, which was indeed become equally necessary to all the parties concerned.[336] Japan, in particular, was in danger of being ruined by her conquests. The war had destroyed so many men, that the whole empire could not afford a sufficiency of recruits for the maintenance of the land-forces. All those who had conquered Fatsisio and Fan-yah, were already destroyed by hard duty and the diseases of those unhealthy climates: above two-thirds of the Fune were rotten in the course of service; and the complements of mariners reduced to less than one half of their original numbers. Troops were actually wanting to garrison the new conquests. The finances of Japan were by this time drained to the bottom. One of her chief resources was stopped by the rupture with Corea; while her expences were considerably augmented; and her national credit was stretched even to cracking. All these considerations stimulated more and more the Dairo and his Cuboy to conclude the work of peace.

Mean while the enemies of Yak-strot gave him no quarter nor respite. They vilified his parts,[337] traduced his morals, endeavoured to intimidate him with threats which did not even respect the Dairo, and never failed to insult him whenever he appeared in public. It had been the custom, time immemorial, for the chief magistrate of Meaco to make an entertainment for the Dairo and his empress, immediately after their nuptials, and to this banquet all the great Quos in Japan were invited.[338] The person who filled the chair at present, was Rhum-kikh,[339] an half-witted politician, self-conceited, head-strong, turbulent, and ambitious; a professed worshipper of Taycho, whose oratorial talents he admired, and attempted to imitate in the assemblies of the people, where he generally excited the laughter of his audience. By dint of great wealth and extensive traffick he became a man of consequence among the mob, notwithstanding an illiberal turn of mind, and an ungracious address;[340] and now he resolved to use this influence for the glory of Taycho and the disgrace of the Ximian favourite. Legion was tutored for the purpose, and moreover, well primed with a fiery caustic spirit[341] in which Rhum-kikh was a considerable dealer. The Dairo and his young empress were received by him and his council with a sullen formality in profound silence. The Cuboy was pelted as he passed along, and his litter almost overturned by the monster, which yelled, and brayed, and hooted without ceasing, until he was housed in the city-hall, where he met with every sort of mortification from the entertainer as well as the spectators. At length Mr. Orator Taycho, with his cousin Lob-kob, appearing in a triumphal car at the city-gate, the blatant beast received them with loud huzzas, unharnessed their horses, and putting itself in the traces, drew them through the streets of Meaco, which resounded with acclamation. They were received with the same exultation within the hall of entertainment, where their sovereign and his consort sat altogether unhonoured and unnoticed.[342]

A small squadron of Chinese Fune having taken possession of a defenceless fishery belonging to Japan, in the neighbourhood of Fatsisio, the emissaries of Taycho magnified this event into a terrible misfortune, arising from the mal-administration of the new Cuboy: nay, they did not scruple to affirm, that he had left the fishing-town defenceless on purpose that it might be taken by the enemy.[343] This clamour, however, was of short duration. The Quo Phyl-Kholl,[344] who commanded a few Fune in one of the harbours of Fatsisio, no sooner received intelligence of what had happened, than he embarked what troops were at hand, and sailing directly to the place, obliged the enemy to abandon their conquest with precipitation and disgrace.

In the midst of these transactions, the peace was signed, ratified, and even approved in the great national council of the Quos, as well as in the assembly of the people.[345] The truth is, the minister of Japan has it always in his power to secure a majority in both these conventions, by means that may be easily guessed; and those were not spared on this occasion. Yak-strot, in a speech, harangued the great council,[346] who were not a little surprised to hear him speak with such propriety and extent of knowledge; for he had been represented as tongue-tied, and in point of elocution, little better than the palfrey[347] he rode. He now vindicated all the steps he had taken since his accession to the helm: he demonstrated the necessity of a pacification; explained and descanted[348] upon every article of the treaty; and finally, declared his conscience was so clear in this matter, that when he died, he should desire no other encomium to be engraved on his tomb, but that he was the author of this peace.

Nevertheless, the approbation of the council was not obtained without violent debate and altercation. The different articles were censured and inveighed against by the Fatzman, the late Cuboy Fika-kaka, Lob-kob, Stiphi-rum-poo, Nin-kom-poo-poo, and many other Quos; but, at the long-run, the influence of the present ministry predominated. As for Taycho, he exerted himself in a very extraordinary effort to depreciate the peace in the assembly of the people. He had for some days pretended to be dangerously ill, that he might make a merit of his patriotism by shewing a contempt for his own life, when the good of his country was at stake. In order to excite the admiration of the public, and render his appearance in the assembly the more striking, he was carried thither on a kind of hand-barrow, wrapped up in flannel, with three woollen night-caps on his head, escorted by Legion, which yelled, and brayed, and whooped, and hollowed, with such vocifera-tion, that every street of Meaco rung with hideous clamour. In this equipage did Taycho enter the assembly, where, being held up by two adherents, he, after a prelude of groans to rouse the attention of his audience, began to declaim against the peace as inadequate, shameful, and disadvantageous: nay, he ventured to stigmatize every separate article, though he knew it was in the power of each individual of his hearers, to confront him with the terms to which he had subscribed the preceding year, in all respects less honourable and advantageous to his country.[349] Inconsistencies equally glaring and absurd he had often crammed down the throats of the multitude: but they would not go down with this assembly of the people, which, in spite of his flannel, his night-caps, his crutches, and his groans, confirmed the treaty of peace by a great majority.[350] Not that they had any great reason to applaud the peace-makers, who might have dictated their own terms, had they pro-ceeded with more sagacity and less precipitation.[351] But Fokh-si-rokhu and his brother undertakers,[352] having the treasure of Japan at their command, had anointed the greatest part of the assembly with a certain precious salve,[353] which preserved them effectually from the fascinating arts of Taycho.

This Orator, incensed at his bad success within doors, renewed and re-doubled his operations without. He exasperated Legion aganst Yak-strot to such a pitch of rage, that the monster could not hear the Cuboy's name three times pronounced without falling into fits. His confederate Lob-kob, in the course of his researches, found out two originals admirably calculated for executing his vengeance against the Ximian favourite.[354] One of them, called Llur-chir,[355] a profligate Bonze, degraded for his lewd life, possessed a won-derful talent of exciting different passions in the blatant beast, by dint of quaint rhimes, which were said to be inspirations of the dæmon of obloquy, to whom he had sold his soul. These oracles not only commanded the pas-sions, but even influenced the organs of the beast in such a manner, as to occasion an evacuation either upwards or downwards, at the pleasure of the operator. The other, known by the name of Jan-ki-dtzin,[356] was counted the

best marksman in Japan in the art and mystery[357] of dirt-throwing. He possessed the art of making balls of filth,[358] which were famous for sticking
and stinking; and these he threw with such dexterity, that they very seldom
missed their aim. Being reduced to a low ebb of fortune by his debaucheries,
he had made advances to the new Cuboy,[359] who had rejected his proffered
services, on account of his immoral character: a prudish punctilio, which but
ill became Yak-strot, who had payed very little regard to reputation in choosing some of the colleagues he had associated in his administration.[360] Be that
as it may, he no sooner understood that Mr. Orator Taycho was busy in
preparing for an active campaign, than he likewise began to put himself in a
posture of defence.[361] He hired a body of mercenaries, and provided some
dirt-men and rhymers. Then, taking the field, a sharp contest and pelting-
match ensued: but the dispute was soon terminated. Yak-strot's versifiers
turned out no great conjurers, on the trial. They were not such favourites of
the dæmon as Llur-chir. The rhimes they used, produced no other effect
upon Legion, but that of setting it a-braying. The Cuboy's dirt-men, however, played their parts tolerably well. Though their balls were inferior in
point of composition to those of Jan-ki-dtzin, they did not fail to discompose
Orator Taycho and his friend Lob-kob, whose eyes were seen to water with
the smart occasioned by those missiles: but these last had a great advantage
over their adversaries, in the zeal and attachment of Legion, whose numerous
tongues were always ready to lick off the ordure that stuck to any part of
their leaders; and this they did with such signs of satisfaction, as seemed to
indicate an appetite for all manner of filth.

Yak-strot having suffered wofully in his own person, and seeing his partisans in confusion, thought proper to retreat. Yet, although discomfited, he
was not discouraged. On the contrary, having at bottom a fund of fanaticism[362] which, like camomile, grows the faster for being trod upon,[363] he
became more obstinately bent than ever upon prosecuting his own schemes
for the good of the people in their own despite. His vanity was likewise
buoyed up by the flattery of his creatures,[364] who extolled the passive courage he had shewn in the late engagement. Tho' every part of him still tingled
and stunk from the balls of the enemy, he persuaded himself that not one of
their missiles had taken place;[365] and of consequence, that there was something of divinity in his person. Full of this notion, he discarded his rhymsters
and his dirt-casters as unnecessary,[366] and resolved to bear the brunt of the
battle in his own individual.[367]

Fokh-si-rokhu advised him, nevertheless, to fill his trowsers with gold

Obans, which he might throw at Legion in case of necessity, assuring him
that this was the only ammunition which the monster could not withstand.
The advice was good; and the Cuboy might have followed it, without being
obliged to the treasury of Japan; for he was by this time become immensely
rich, in consequence of having found a hoard in digging his garden:[368] but
this was an expedient which Yak-strot could never be prevailed upon to use,
either on this or any other occasion.[369] Indeed, he was now so convinced of
his own personal energy, that he persuaded his master Gio-gio to come forth
and see it operate on the blatant beast. Accordingly the Dairo ascended his
car of state, while the Cuboy, arrayed in all his trappings, stood before him
with the reins in his own hand, and drove directly to the enemy, who waited
for him without flinching. Being arrived within dung-shot of Jan-ki-dtzin, he
made a halt, and putting himself in the attitude of the idol Fo,[370] with a
simper in his countenance, seemed to invite the warrior to make a full discharge of his artillery. He did not long wait in suspence. The balls soon
began to whizz about his ears; and a great number took effect upon his person. At length, he received a shot upon his right temple which brought him
to the ground. All his gewgaws fluttered, and his buckram doublet rattled as
he fell. Llur-chir no sooner beheld him prostrate, than advancing with the
monster, he began to repeat his rhymes, at which every mouth and every tail
of Legion was opened and lifted up; and such a torrent of filth squirted from
these channels, that the unfortunate Cuboy was quite overwhelmed. Nay, he
must have been actually suffocated where he lay, had not some of the Dairo's
attendants interposed and rescued him from the vengeance of the monster.
He was carried home in such an unsavoury pickle, that his family smelled his
disaster long before he came in sight; and when he appeared in this woeful
condition, covered with ordure, blinded with dirt, and even deprived of
sense and motion, his wife was seized with *hysterica passio*.[371] He was immediately stripped and washed, and other means being used for his recovery, he
in a little time retrieved his recollection.

    He was now pretty well undeceived, with respect to the divinity of his
person: but his enthusiasm took a new turn. He aspired to the glory of martyrdom, and resolved to devote[372] himself as a victim to patriotic virtue.
While his attendants were employed in washing off the filth that stuck to his
beard, he recited in a theatrical tone, the stanza of a famous Japonese bard,
whose soul afterwards transmigrated into the body of the Roman poet
Horatius Flaccus, and inspired him with the same sentiment in the Latin
tongue.

Virtus repulsæ nescia sordidæ
Intaminatis fulget honoribus;
Nec sumit, aut ponit secures
Arbitrio popularis auræ.[373]

His friends hearing him declare his resolution of dying for his country,[374] began to fear that his understanding was disturbed. They advised him to yield to the torrent, which was become too impetuous to stem; to resign the Cuboyship quietly, and reserve his virtues for a more favourable occasion. In vain his friends remonstrated: in vain his wife and children employed their tears and intreaties to the same purpose. He lent a deaf ear to all their sollicitations, until they began to drop some hints that seemed to imply a suspicion of his insanity, which alarmed him exceedingly; and the Dairo himself signifying to him in private, that it was become absolutely necessary to temporize, he resigned the reins of government with a heavy heart,[375] though not before he was assured that he should still continue to exert his influence behind the curtain.[376]

Gio-gio's own person had not escaped untouched in the last skirmish. Janki-dtzin was transported to such a pitch of insolence, that he aimed some balls at the Dairo,[377] and one of them taking place exactly betwixt the eyes, defiled his whole visage. Had the laws of Japan been executed in all their severity against this audacious plebeian, he would have suffered crucifixion on the spot:[378] but Gio-gio, being good-natured even to a fault, contented himself with ordering some of his attendants to apprehend and put him in the public stocks, after having seized the whole cargo of filth which he had collected at his habitation for the manufacture of his balls.[379] Legion was no sooner informed of his disgrace, than it released him by force, being therein comforted and abetted by the declaration of a puny magistrate, called Praffpatt-phogg,[380] who seized this, as the only opportunity he should ever find of giving himself any consequence in the commonwealth. Accordingly, the monster hoisting him and Jan-ki-dtzin on their shoulders, went in procession through the streets of Meaco, hollowing, huzzaing, and extolling this venerable pair of patriots as the *Palladia*[381] of the liberty of Japan.

The monster's officious zeal on this occasion, was far from being agreeable to Mr. Orator Taycho, who took umbrage at this exaltation of his two understrappers, and from that moment devoted Jan-ki-dtzin to destruction. The Dairo finding it absolutely necessary for the support of his government, that this dirt-monger should be punished, gave directions for trying him according to the laws of the land.[382] He was ignominiously expelled from the assembly of the people, where his old patron Taycho not only disclaimed him, but even represented him as a worthless atheist and sower of sedition: but he escaped the weight of a more severe sentence in another tribunal, by retreating without beat of drum, into the territories of China, where he found an asylum, from whence he made divers ineffectual appeals to the multitudinous beast at Niphon.

As for Yak-strot, he was every thing but a down-right martyr to the odium of the public, which produced a ferment all over the nation. His name was become a term of reproach. He was burnt or crucified in effigy[383] in every city, town, village, and district of Niphon. Even his own countrymen, the Ximians, held him in abhorrence and execration. Notwithstanding his partiality to the *natale solum*,[384] he had not been able to provide for all those adventurers who came from thence in consequence of his promotion. The whole number of the disappointed became his enemies of course;[385] and the rest finding themselves exposed to the animosity and ill offices of their fellow-subjects of Niphon, who hated the whole community for his sake, inveighed against Yak-strot as the curse of their nation.

In the midst of all this detestation and disgrace, it must be owned for the sake of truth, that Yak-strot was one of the honestest men in Japan, and certainly the greatest benefactor to the empire.[386] Just, upright, sincere, and charitable; his heart was susceptible of friendship and tenderness. He was a virtuous husband, a fond father, a kind master, and a zealous friend. In his public capacity he had nothing in view but the advantage of Japan, in the prosecution of which he flattered himself he should be able to display all the abilities of a profound statesman, and all the virtues of the most sublime patriotism. It was here he over-rated his own importance. His virtue became the dupe of his vanity. Nature had denied him shining talents, as well as that easiness of deportment, that affability, liberal turn, and versatile genius, without which no man can ever figure at the head of an administration. Nothing could be more absurd than his being charged with want of parts and understanding to guide the helm of government, considering how happily it had been conducted for many years by Fika-kaka, whose natural genius would have been found unequal even to the art and mystery of wool-combing.[387] Besides, the war had prospered in his hands as much as it ever did under the auspices of his predecessor; though, as I have before observed, neither the one nor the other could justly claim any merit from its success.

But Yak-strot's services to the public, were much more important in another respect. He had the resolution to dissolve the shameful and pernicious engagements which the empire had contracted on the continent of

Tartary. He lightened the intolerable burthens of the empire: he saved its credit when it was stretched even to bursting. He made a peace, which, if not the most glorious that might have been obtained, was, at least, the most solid and advantageous that ever Japan had concluded with any power whatsoever; and, in particular, much more honourable, useful, and ascertained,[388] than that which Taycho had agreed to subscribe the preceding year;[389] and, by this peace, he put an end to all the horrors of a cruel war, which had ravaged the best parts of Asia, and destroyed the lives of six hundred thousand men every year. On the whole, Yak-strot's good qualities were respectable. There was very little vicious[390] in his composition; and as to his follies, they were rather the subjects of ridicule than of resentment.

Yak-strot's subalterns in the ministry, rejoiced in secret at his running so far into the north of Legion's displeasure.[391] Nay, it was shrewdly suspected that some of their emissaries had been very active against him in the day of his discomfiture. They flattered themselves, that if he could be effectually driven from the presence of the Dairo, they would succeed to his influence; and in the mean time would acquire popularity by turning tail to, and kicking at, the Ximian favourite, who had associated them in the administration in consequence of their vowing eternal attachment to his interest, and constant submission to his will. Having held a secret conclave to concert[392] their operations, they began to execute their plan, by seducing Yak-strot into certain odious measures of raising new impositions on the people,[393] which did not fail, indeed, to increase the clamour of the blatant Beast, and promote its filthy discharge upwards and downwards; but then the torrents were divided, and many a tail was lifted up against the real projectors of the scheme which the favourite had adopted. They now resolved to make a merit with the Mobile, by picking a german quarrel[394] with Strot, and insulting him in public. Gotto-mio caused a scrubbing-post[395] to be set up in the night, at the Cuboy's door.—The scribe Zan-ti-fic[396] presented him with a scheme for the importation of brimstone into the island of Ximo:[397] the other scribe pretended he could not spell the barbarous names of the Cuboy's relations and countrymen, who were daily thrust into the most lucrative employments. As for Twitz-er the Financier,[398] he never approached Yak-strot without clawing his knuckles in derision. At the council of Twenty-Eight, they thwarted every plan he proposed, and turned into ridicule every word he spoke. At length they bluntly told the Dairo, that as Yak-strot resigned the reins of administration in public, he must likewise give up his management behind the curtain; for they were not at all disposed to answer to the people for measures dictated by an invisible agent.[399] This was but a reasonable demand, in which the emperor seemed[400] to acquiesce. But the new ministers thought it was requisite that they should commit some overt act of contempt for the abdicated Cuboy. One of his nearest relations had obtained a profitable office in the island of Ximo; and of this, the new cabal insisted he should be immediately deprived.[401] The Dairo remonstrated against the injustice of turning a man out of his place for no other reason but to satisfy their caprice; and plainly told them he could not do it without infringing his honour, as he had given his word that the possessor should enjoy the post for life. Far from being satisfied with this declaration, they urged their demand with redoubled importunity, mixed with menaces which equally embarrassed and incensed the good-natured Dairo. At last Yak-strot, taking compassion upon his indulgent master, prevailed upon his kinsman to release him from the obligation of his word, by making a voluntary resignation of his office. The Dairo fell sick of vexation: his life was despaired of; and all Japan was filled with alarm and apprehension at the prospect of an infant's ascending the throne: for the heir apparent was still in the cradle.[402]

Their fears, however, were happily disappointed by the recovery of the emperor, who, to prevent[403] as much as possible the inconveniences that might attend his demise, during the minority of his son, resolved that a regency should be established and ratified by the states of the empire.[404] The plan of this regency he concerted in private with the venerable princess his grandmother, and his friend Yak-strot; and then communicated the design to his ministers, who knowing the quarter from whence it had come, treated it with coldness and contempt. They were so elevated by their last triumph over the Ximian favourite, that they overlooked every obstacle to their ambition; and determined to render the Dairo dependant on them, and them only. With this view they threw cold water on the present measure; and to mark their hatred of the favourite more strongly in the eyes of Legion, they endeavoured to exclude the name of his patroness the Dairo's grandmother, from the deed of regency, though their malice was frustrated by the vigilance of Yak-strot, and the indignation of the states, who resented this affront offered to the family of their sovereign.[405]

The tyranny of this junto became so intolerable to Gio-gio,[406] that he resolved to shake off their yoke, whatever might be the consequence: but before any effectual step was taken for this purpose, Yak-strot, who understood mechanics, and had studied the art of puppet-playing,[407] tried an experiment on the organs of the cabal, which he tempered with[408] individually without success. Instead of uttering what he prompted, the sounds came out quite altered in their passage. Gotto-mio grunted; the Financier Twitz-er bleated, or rather brayed; one scribe mewed like a cat; the other yelped like a jackall. In short, they were found so perverse and refractory, that the master of the motion[409] kicked them off the stage, and supplied the scene with a new set of puppets[410] made of very extraordinary materials. They were the very figures through whose pipes the charge of mal-administration had been so loudly sounded against the Ximian favourite. They were now mustered by the Fatzman, and hung upon the pegs of the very same puppet-shew-man against whom they had so vehemently inveighed. Even the superannuated Fika-kaka appeared again upon the stage as an actor of some consequence; and insisted upon it, that his metamorphosis was a meer calumny. But Tay-cho and Lob-kob kept aloof, because Yak-strot had not yet touched them on the proper keys.[411]

The first exhibition of the new puppets, was called *Topsy-turvy*,[412] a farce in which they overthrew all the paper houses which their predecessors had built: but they performed their parts in such confusion, that Yak-strot inter-posing to keep them in order, received divers contusions and severe kicks on the shins, which made his eyes water; and, indeed, he had in a little time reason enough to repent of the revolution he had brought about. The new sticks of administration proved more stiff and unmanageable than the former; and those he had discarded, associating with the blatant Beast, bedaubed him with such a variety of filth, drained from all the sewers of scurrility, that he really became a public nuisance. Gotto-mio pretended remorse of conscience, and declared he would impeach Yak-strot for the peace which he himself had negotiated. Twitz-er snivelled and cried, and cast figures[413] to prove that Yak-strot was born for the destruction of Japan; and Zan-ti-fic lured an incendiary Bonze called Toks,[414] to throw fire-balls[415] by night into the palace of the favourite.

In this distress Strot cast his eyes on Taycho the monster-tamer, who alone seemed able to over-ballance the weight of all other opposition; and to him he made large advances accordingly; but his offers were still inadequate to the expectations of that Demagogue, who, nevertheless, put on a face of capitula-tion. He was even heard to say that Yak-strot was an honest man and a good minister:[416] nay, he declared he would ascend the highest pinnacle of the highest pagod[417] in Japan, and proclaim that Yak-strot had never, directly nor indirectly, meddled with administration since he resigned the public office of minister. Finding him, however, tardy and phlegmatic in his proposals, he thought proper to change his phrase, and in the next assembly of the people swore, with great vociferation, that the said Yak-strot was the greatest rogue that ever escaped the gallows. This was a necessary fillip to Yak-strot, and operated upon him so effectually, that he forthwith sent a charte blanche to the great Taycho,[418] and a treaty was immediately ratified on the following conditions: That the said Taycho should be raised to the rank of Quanbuku, and be appointed conservator of the Dairo's signet:[419] that no state measure should be taken without his express approbation: that his creature the lawyer Praff-fog should be ennobled and preferred to the most eminent place in the tribunals of Japan;[420] and that all his friends and dependants should be provided for at the public expence, in such a manner as he himself should propose.[421] His kinsman Lob-kob, however, was not comprehended in this treaty, the articles of which he inveighed against with such acrimony, that a rupture ensued betwixt these two originals.[422] The truth is, Lob-kob was now so full of his own importance, that nothing less than an equal share of administration would satisfy his ambition; and this was neither in Taycho's power nor inclination to grant.

The first consequence of this treaty was a new shift of hands, and a new dance of ministers. The chair of precedency was pulled from under the antiquated Fika-kaka, who fell upon his back; and his heels flying up, discovered but too plainly the melancholy truth of his metamorphosis.[423] All his colleagues were discarded, except those who thought proper to temporize and join in dancing the hay,[424] according as they were actuated by the new partners of the puppet-shew. This coalition was the greatest master-piece in politics that ever Yak-strot performed. Taycho, the formidable Taycho! whom in his single person he dreaded more than all his other enemies of Japan united, was now become his coadjutor, abettor, and advocate; and, which was still of more consequence to Strot, that Demagogue was forsaken of his good genius Legion.

The many-headed Monster would have swallowed down every other species of tergiversation[425] in Taycho, except a coalition with the detested favourite, and the title of Quo, by which he formally renounced its society:[426] but these were articles which the mongrel could not digest. The tidings of this union threw the Beast into a kind of stupor, from which it was roused by blisters and cauteries applied by Gotto-mio, Twitz-er, Zan-ti-fic, with his understrapper Toks, now reinforced by Fika-kaka, and his discarded associates: for their common hatred to Yak-strot, like the rod of Moses,[427] swallowed up every distinction of party, and every suggestion of former animosity; and they concurred with incredible zeal, in rousing Legion to a due sense of Taycho's apostacy. The Beast, so stimulated, howled three days and three nights successively at Taycho's gate; then was seized with a convulsion, that went off with an evacuation upwards and downwards, so offensive, that the very air was infected.

The horrid sounds of the Beast's lamentation, the noxious effluvia of its filthy discharge, joined to the poignant remorse which Taycho felt at finding his power over Legion dissolved, occasioned a commotion in his brain; and this led him into certain extravagancies, which gave his enemies a handle to say he was actually insane.[428] His former friends and partizans thought the best apology they could make for the inconsistency of his conduct, was to say he was *non compos*;[429] and this report was far from being disagreeable to Yak-strot, because it would at any time furnish him with a plausible pretence to dissolve the partnership, at which he inwardly repined: for it was necessity alone that drove him to a partition of his power with a man so incapable of acting in concert with any collegue whatsoever.

In the mean time Gotto-mio and his associates left no stone unturned to acquire the same influence over Legion, which Taycho had so eminently possessed: but the Beast's faculties, slender as they were, seemed now greatly impaired, in consequence of that arch empiric's practices[430] upon its constitution. In vain did Gotto-mio hoop and hollow: in vain did Twitz-er tickle its long ears: in vain did Zan-ti-fic apply sternutatories,[431] and his Bonze administer inflammatory glysters; the monster could never be brought to a right understanding, or at all concur with their designs, except in one instance, which was its antipathy to the Ximian favourite. This had become so habitual, that it acted mechanically upon its organs, even after it had lost all other signs of recognition. As often as the name of Yak-strot was pronounced, the Beast began to yell; and all the usual consequences ensued: but whenever his new friends presumed to mount him, he threw himself on his back, and rolled them in the kennel[432] at the hazard of their lives.

One would imagine there was some leaven[433] in the nature of Yak-strot, that soured all his subalterns who were natives of Niphon; for howsoever they promised all submission to his will before they were admitted into his motion, they no sooner found themselves acting characters in his drama, than they began to thwart him in his measures; so that he was plagued by those he had taken in, and persecuted by those he had driven out. The two great props which he had been at so much pains to provide, now failed him. Taycho was grown crazy, and could no longer manage the monster; and Quam-ba-cundono the Fatzman, whose authority had kept several puppets in awe, died about this period.[434] These two circumstances were the more alarming, as Gotto-mio and his crew began to gain ground, not only in their endeavours to rouse the Monster, but also in tampering with some of the acting puppets, to join their cabal and make head against their master. These exoterics[435] grew so refractory, that when he tried to wheel them to the right, they turned to the left about; and, instead of joining hands in the dance of politics, rapped their heads against each other with such violence, that the noise of the collision was heard in the street; and if they had not been made of the hardest wood in Japan, some of them would certainly have been split in the encounter.

By this time Legion began to have some sense of its own miserable condition. The effects of the yeast potions which it had drank so liberally from the hands of Taycho, now wore off. The fumes dispersed; the illusion vanished; the flatulent tumor[436] of its belly disappeared with innumerable explosions, leaving a hideous lankness and such a canine appetite as all the eatables of Japan could not satisfy. After having devoured the whole harvest, it yawned for more, and grew quite outrageous in its hunger, threatening to feed on human flesh, if not plentifully supplied with other viands. In this dilemma Yak-strot convened the council of Twenty-Eight, where, in consideration of the urgency of the case, it was resolved to suspend the law against the importation of foreign provisions, and open the ports of Japan[437] for the relief of the blatant Beast.

As this was vesting the Dairo with a dispensing power unknown to the constitution of Japan, it was thought necessary at the next assembly of the Quos and Quanbukus that constitute the legislature, to obtain a legal sanction for that extraordinary exercise of prerogative,[438] which nothing but the *salus populi*[439] could excuse. Upon this occasion it was diverting to see with what effrontery individuals changed their principles with their places. Taycho the Quo, happening to be in one of his lucid intervals, went to the assembly,[440] supported by his two creatures Praff-fog, and another limb of the law, called Lley-nah, surnamed Gurg-grog, or Curse-mother;[441] and this triumvirate, who had raised themselves from nothing to the first rank in the state, by vilifying and insulting the kingly power, and affirming that the Dairo was the slave of the people, now had the impudence to declare in the face of the day, that in some cases the emperor's power was absolute, and that he had an inherent right to suspend and supersede the laws and ordinances of the legislature.[442]

Mura-clami, who had been for some time eclipsed in his judicial capacity by the popularity of Praff-fog, did not fail to seize this opportunity of exposing the character of his upstart rival.[443] Though he had been all his life an humble retainer to the prerogative, he now made a parade of patriotism, and in a tide of eloquence bore down all the flimsy arguments which the triumvirate advanced. He demonstrated the futility of their reasoning, from the express laws and customs of the empire; he expatiated on the pernicious tendency of their doctrine, and exhibited the inconsistency of their conduct in such colours, that they must have hid their heads in confusion, had they not happily conquered all sense of shame, and been well convinced that the majority of the assembly were not a whit more honest than themselves. Muraclami enjoyed a momentary triumph; but his words made a very slight impression; for it was his misfortune to be a Ximian; and if his virtues had been more numerous than the hairs in his beard, this very circumstance would have shaved them clean away from the consideration of the audience.

Taycho, opening the flood-gates of his abuse, bespattered all that opposed him. Lleynah, alias Curse-mother, swore that he had got into the wrong-box;[444] then turning to Praff-fog, "Brother Praff, (cried he) thou hast now let down thy trowsers, and every rascal in Japan will whip thy a—se!" Praff was afraid of the Beast's resentment; but Taycho bestrid him like a Colossus,[445] and he crept through between his legs into a place of safety. This was the last time that the Orator appeared in public. Immediately after this occurrence it was found necessary to confine him to a dark chamber,[446] and Yak-strot was left to his own inventions.

In this dilemma he had recourse to the old expedient of changing hands;[447] and as a prelude to this reform, made advances to Gotto-mio, whom he actually detached from the opposition, by providing his friends and dependants with lucrative offices, and promising to take no steps of consequence without his privity and approbation. A sop was at the same time thrown to Twitz-er; Zan-ti-fic, lulled with specious promises, discarded Toks the incendiary Bonze; Lob-kob signed a neutrality, and old Fika-kaka was deprived of the use of speech:—in a word, the ill-cemented confederacy of Strot's exoteric foes fell asunder; and Legion had now no rage but the rage of hunger to be appeased. But the Ximian favourite was still thwarted in his operations behind the curtain; for he had so often chopped and changed the figures that composed his motion, that they were all of different materials; so wretchedly sorted and so ill-toned,[448] that when they came upon the scene, they produced nothing but discord and disorder.

The Japonese colony of Fatsisio had been settled above a century, and in the face of a thousand dangers and difficulties raised themselves to such consideration, that they consumed infinite quantities of the manufactures of Japan, for which they payed their mother-country in gold and silver, and precious drugs, the produce of their plantations. The advantages which

Japan reaped from this traffic with her own colonists, almost equalled the amount of what she gained by her commerce with all the other parts of Asia. Twitz-er, when he managed the finances of Japan, had in his great wisdom planned, procured, and promulgated a law saddling the Fatsisians with a grievous tax to answer the occasions of the Japonese government; an imposition which struck at the very vitals of their constitution, by which they were exempt from all burthens but such as they fitted for their own shoulders.[449] They raised a mighty clamour[450] at this innovation, in which they were joined by Legion, at that time under the influence of Taycho, who, in the assembly of the people, bitterly inveighed against the authors and abettors of such an arbitrary and tyrannical measure.[451] Their reproach and execration did not stop at Twitz-er, but proceeded, as usual, to Yak-strot, who was the general butt at which all the arrows of slander, scurrility, and abuse, were levelled. The puppets with which he supplied the places of Twitz-er and his associates, in order to recommend themselves to Legion, and perhaps, with a view to mortify the favourite, who had patronized the Fatsisian tax,[452] insisted upon withdrawing this imposition, which was accordingly abrogated,[453] to the no small disgrace and contempt of the law-givers: but when these new ministers were turned out, to make way for Taycho and his friends, the interest of the Fatsisians was again abandoned. Even the Orator himself declaimed against them with an unembarrassed countenance,[454] after they had raised statues to him[455] as their friend and patron; and measures were taken to make them feel all the severity of an abject dependance upon the legislature of Japan.[456] Finally, Gotto-mio acceded to this system,[457] which he had formerly approved in conjunction with Twitz-er; and preparations were made for using compulsory measures, should the colonists refuse to submit with a good grace.

The Fatsisians, far from acquiescing in these proceedings, resolved to defend to the last extremity those liberties which they had hitherto preserved; and, as a proof of their independence, agreed among themselves to renounce all the superfluities with which they had so long been furnished, at a vast expence, from the manufactures of Japan,[458] since that nation had begun to act towards them with all the cruelty of a step-mother. It was amazing to see and to hear how Legion raved, and slabbered, and snapped its multitudinous jaws in the streets of Meaco, when it understood that the Fatsisians were determined to live on what their own country afforded. They were represented and reviled as ruffians, barbarians, and unnatural monsters, who clapped the dagger to the breast of their indulgent mother, in presuming to save themselves the expence of those superfluities, which, by the bye, her cruel impositions had left them no money to purchase. Nothing was heard in Japan but threats of punishing those ungrateful colonists with whips and scorpions.[459] For this purpose troops were assembled and fleets equipped;[460] and the blatant Beast yawned with impatient expectation of being drenched with the blood of its fellow-subjects.

Yak-strot was seized with horror at the prospect of such extremities; for, to give the devil his due, his disposition was neither arbitrary nor cruel; but he had been hurried by evil counsellors into a train[461] of false politics, the consequences of which he did not foresee. He now summoned council after council to deliberate upon conciliatory expedients; but found the motley crew so divided by self-interest, faction, and mutual rancour, that no consistent plan could be formed: all was nonsense, clamour, and contradiction. The Ximian favourite now wished all his puppets at the devil, and secretly cursed the hour in which he first undertook the motion. He even fell sick of chagrin, and resolved, in good earnest, to withdraw himself intirely from the political helm,[462] which he was now convinced he had no talents to guide. In the mean time, he tried to find some temporary alleviation to the evils occasioned by the monstrous incongruity of the members and materials that composed his administration. But before any effectual measures could be taken, his evil genius, ever active, brewed up a new storm in another quarter, which had well-nigh swept him and all his projects into the gulph of perdition.[463]

FINIS.

NOTES TO THE TEXT

Volume 1

1. "these ticklish times . . . plague of prosecution": The "advertisement" bears a strong resemblance to the "cover story" in the correspondence between Jonathan Dustwich and the bookseller that opens *Humphry Clinker*: both display exaggerated concern over prosecution for libel; both are ironic, though for different reasons. For Smollett's own views see *Continuation*, 5:120. See also *CR* 20 (1765): 45–49; Basker, 273–74, attributes the review of *A Digest of the Laws Concerning Libels* to Smollett. For discussion of the state of the libel laws see Carl R. Kropf, "Libel and Satire in the Eighteenth Century," *Eighteenth-Century Studies* 8 (1974): 153–68. From John Wilkes's election for Middlesex in March to Smollett's final departure from England in the autumn, the year 1768 was marked by frequent mob violence and rioting; many feared revolution. See Rudé, 38–74.

2. "the 7th of March . . . 1748": This precautionary or ironic predating may be connected with the title-page dating of "MDCCXLIX" in some copies of the first issue, though the latter may also have been an accidental error. See O M Brack, Jr., "*The History and Adventures of an Atom*, 1769," *PBSA* 64 (1970): 336–38. The *Continuation*, to which the *Atom* may be considered a parodic-satiric parallel, begins with the year 1748.

3. "Bombazine": A twilled dress material of silk and worsted, much used for mourning; the connotation would be "respectable widow."

4. "Old-street": In the central city area, commercial and unfashionable in Smollett's time.

5. "Peacock": In *CR* 10 (August 1760): 159, James Peacock's translation of Virgil's first pastoral is reviewed with great severity.

6. "Islington": North of central London, rural in Smollett's time; Goldsmith and other literary figures lived there. The church is probably Saint Mary's, Islington, still extant.

7. "tristich": Any poetic unit of three verses.

8. "*Hic, hæc, hoc*": L. The beginning of the declension of the demonstrative pronoun would represent an illiterate's stab at a Latin epitaph.

9. "the White House": The White Conduit House, mentioned by Goldsmith in *The Bee*, no. 2 (13 October 1759) and no. 3 (20 October 1759), and in Letter 122 of *The Citizen of the World* (1762), where citizens eat hot rolls and butter "with solemnity." The *Gentleman's Magazine* 31 (May 1760): 242 says that on Sunday at the White House "indiscriminate the gaudy beau / And sloven mix."

10. "Kempfer": Engelbert Kaempfer (1651–1715), a Dutch physician, was in Japan in 1690–92 as medical officer to the Dutch trading company at Nagasaki. His

History of Japan (English translation, 2 vols., 1728), together with various accounts compiled by Jesuit missionaries, furnished the material for the section on Japan in the *Universal History*; see below, n. 11.

11. "the Universal History": This vast compilation, published by a booksellers' combine and written by numerous hands, began to appear in 1730; the "Ancient Part" was completed in 1744. Smollett was "responsible for nearly a third of *The Modern Part*" (Martz, 8); various volumes were enthusiastically noticed by Smollett in the *Critical Review* as they appeared (Basker, 225–28). In 1763, Smollett took with him to Nice the fifty-eight octavo volumes that had appeared up to that point; he continued to work on the project in various ways for the rest of his life (Martz, 105). Volume 9 of the "Modern Part" contains the account of Japan (pp. 1–169); this volume was reviewed at length in *CR* 8 (September 1759): 189–99. Smollett derived from it virtually all of his Japanese material. See the introduction, pp. xliii–xliv; and see below, the key. See also Martz, 90–103.

12. "chamber-council": An attorney who does not plead in court but merely advises clients in his chambers.

13. "the Vision of Ezekiel, or the Lamentations of Jeremiah the prophet": Both Ezekiel (chapters 2–24) and Jeremiah (chapters 1–25) bewail the corruption and presumption of Jerusalem and prophesy its destruction and the Babylonian captivity.

14. "purchased the copy": Purchased the text of the work, together with the right to publish it.

15. "Bucklersbury": An unfashionable commercial area in the city, adjoining Cheapside. Bucklersbury was known for its grocers and apothecaries and for its numerous taverns.

16. "S. ETHERINGTON": *CR* 10 (August 1760): 137–44 includes an enthusiastic review of a book on the cure of fevers written by the Rev. G. Etherington.

17. "*Vivant Rex & Regina*": L. Long live the king and queen. This expression is appropriate for the year 1769 (George III had married in 1761) but not for 1749, since Caroline, queen to George II, had died in 1737.

18. "the parish of St. Giles": Located at what is now the eastern end of Oxford Street, the area was thoroughly disreputable, with its pawnshops, petty criminals, and prostitutes; it was the traditional antithesis of Saint James's, scene of the court and its fashionable milieu. *An Apology for the Ministerial Life*, a pro-Bute pamphlet of 1766, says scornfully that "the neighbourhood of St. Giles's now possesses a right of debating on the formation of our laws" (p. 17); and in *CR* 4 (November 1757): 470, Smollett berates the *Monthly Review* for having characterized the *Critical* as breathing "the true spirit of St. Giles's—ask mine a--e." Smollett then inquires, "How came you so well acquainted with the spirit of St. Giles's?" See Basker, 224, 240–41.

19. "haberdasher": Haberdashers sold hats, thread, ribbons; they were thus dealers in trifles. *CR* 13 (January 1762): 66 refers to Sterne's Rabelaisian "haberdash-

ery," and Smollett's friend Alexander Carlyle wrote a pamphlet in ironic dispraise of Pitt, *Plain Reasons for Removing a Certain Great Man* (1759), under the name of "O. M., haberdasher."

20. "three pair of stairs": Three flights of stairs; Peacock is a "garreteer politician."

21. "sublunary enjoyment": An allusion to the idea in Ptolemaic cosmology that all things below the sphere of the moon are subject to time and decay.

22. "a shrill, small voice": In 1 Kings 19:12, God tells the despairing Elijah in a "still small voice" to return to his homeland and anoint kings and prophets. Martz, 91, cites an allusion to John Hawkesworth's *Adventurer*, no. 5 (21 November 1752), in which a transmigrating soul, like Smollett's atom, dictates a paper to the author in a "small shrill voice."

23. "pericranium": The membrane surrounding the skull.

24. "citation": A formal summons to appear in court. Legal jargon often forms part of Peacock's "high style."

25. "adjured": Solemnly called upon; put on oath.

26. "an atomy": In Smollett's time the word could mean a skeleton or anatomical preparation, an atom or particle, or a tiny being like the "little atomies" of Mercutio's Queen Mab speech in *Romeo and Juliet* 1.4.57.

27. "fear and trembling": 2 Corinthians 7:15, Ephesians 6:5, Philippians 2:12.

28. "conceit": Notion, idea.

29. "the handwriting on the wall": An allusion to God's warning of the downfall of Babylon at Belshazzar's feast in Daniel 5:5, 24–28.

30. "My knees . . . cold sweat": This is the Smollettian trademark, the "stereotype of fear," occurring almost verbatim in all of the novels. See Albrecht B. Strauss, "On Smollett's Language," *Style in Prose Fiction: English Institute Essays, 1958*, ed. Harold C. Martin (New York: Columbia University Press, 1959), 29–32.

31. "for a season entranced": "The hand of the Lord is upon thee, and thou shalt be blind, not seeing the sun for a season" (Acts 13:11).

32. "White-livered caitiff": Cowardly wretch; probably an echo of "milk-livered man," *King Lear* 4.2.50. The phrase "white-livered" occurs in *Henry V* 3.2.32 and *Richard III* 4.4.464.

33. "unsavoury odour": At the end of Charles Johnstone's *Chrysal* (1760–65), the Spirit of Gold, which has been narrating the book's "secret histories," disappears in disgust when his amanuensis involuntarily farts. *Chrysal*, the most probable direct source for the *Atom*'s fictional framework, was reviewed enthusiastically in *CR* 9 (May 1760): 419 and in *CR* 11 (April 1761): 336.

34. "art": Human skill and wisdom, as opposed to "nature."

35. "steam from a dunghill": "Steams from Dunghills . . . furnish as comely and useful a vapour, as incense from an altar" (Swift, *Tale of a Tub* 9).

36. "odoriferous gale": "Of gentlest gale *Arabian* odours fann'd" (*Paradise Lost* 2.264). A gale was a sudden but not violent wind.

37. "excoriated . . . plain Spanish": Abraded or raw from coarse snuff. *CR* 12 (July

1761): 76 includes a review of *Cautions Against the Immoderate Use of Snuff* (1761),
by Dr. [John] Hill, which mentions this dangerous abrasion.

38. "embarrass": Hamper, hinder.

39. "the pineal gland": A gland resembling a pine cone in shape and located at the
base of the brain. Descartes, as Smollett doubtless knew, considered this gland
the seat of the soul.

40. "promulge": Formally publish a law or decree.

41. "revolutions": In the older sense of changes or alterations.

42. "British ministers": Technically, heads of government departments; but "the
minister" usually meant the first lord of the Treasury, in effect the head of
government.

43. "fantastic undulation of a disturbed brain": The celebrated "mad-doctor" William Battie proposed in *A Treatise on Madness* (1757) the mechanistic theory that
madness was caused by irregular vibrations of the particles of brain tissue. Smollett is the author of a qualified but respectful review of Battie's treatise in *CR* 4
(December 1757): 509–16 (Basker, 224, 240–41). See Richard A. Hunter and
Ida Macalpine, "Smollett's Reading in Psychiatry," *Modern Language Review* 51
(1956): 409–11.

44. "preferred": Presented, sent up.

45. "orison": Prayer.

46. "fruition": Enjoyment, possession, or both.

47. "phantasma or hideous dream": *Julius Caesar* 2.1.65.

48. "*alpha* privativa, and *temno* to cut": In Greek grammar the letter alpha functions
as a "privative" or negative particle or prefix. The atom's etymology is thus
correct.

49. "a learned physician of my acquaintance": Dr. Thomas Thompson (c. 1700–
1763), a noted society physician and London eccentric. Smollett calls Thompson "a meddling, prating, blundering, busy dunce" in *Reproof*, line 186, mentions his false etymologies in *CR* 5 (March 1758): 224 (Basker, 224, 243), and
pokes fun at him in *Roderick Random* (as Dr. Wagtail) and elsewhere. See Robert
Adams Day, "When Doctors Disagree: Smollett and Thomas Thompson,"
Etudes Anglaises 32 (1979): 312–24.

50. "Theophrastus": A pupil and successor of Aristotle, Theophrastus (c. 370–288/5
B. C.) wrote on many subjects; the doctor would think of him as a botanist.

51. "Aretæus": Greek physician, first century A. D. His *De causis morborum*, on diseases, was still a standard medical text in the eighteenth century, notably as
translated into Latin by the great Dutch physician Hermann Boerhaave in 1731.

52. "chemical specifics": Drugs for particular diseases or parts of the body.

53. "Foggien": The eighteenth century; see key. Smollett's footnote is based on a
confusion of *UH*, 108, 126; see Martz, 97.

54. "Firando": Later Hirado, now Nagasaki; see key. At the time when Smollett

wrote, the Dutch were the only foreigners allowed to trade in or enter Japan, and they had to remain in virtual house arrest at Firando.

55. "scorbutic": Connected with scurvy, which in consequence of dietary deficiencies was very common among seamen.

56. "cordwainers": Shoemakers, from "cordovan" leather. The "feast" would be the annual banquet of the shoemakers' guild or company.

57. "animalcule": Microscopic animal. According to a popular theory of reproduction, each spermatozoan contained a *homunculus* or perfect though microscopic human being, the mother providing merely a medium for growth; "*animal*cule" is thus the atom's sneer at Peacock. Sterne amused himself with the same theory in *Tristram Shandy*, volume 1, chapter 1; see Louis A. Landa, "The Shandean Homunculus," in *Restoration and Eighteenth-Century Literature: Essays in Honor of Alan Dugald McKillop*, ed. Carroll Camden (Chicago: University of Chicago Press, 1963), 49–68.

58. "three large islands": See the introduction, pp. xliii–xliv, for Smollett's fascination with the parallels between Great Britain and Japan in geographical formation and placement and in politics and national character. He developed these parallels at length in his review of Volume 9 of the "Modern Part" of the *Universal History*, *CR* 8 (September 1759): 189–99. See also Martz, 94–96.

59. "such inconsistent, capricious animals": The long passage that follows, though of course satirical in its treatment of the English character, is a free variation on the comparison of Japanese and Chinese traits with those of the English and the French in the review mentioned above, n. 58. The passage also may owe something to the character of Zimri (Buckingham) in Dryden's *Absalom and Achitophel* (lines 544–62), and to Pope's *Epistle to a Lady*, especially the character of Narcissa (lines 63–64). Accounts of contrasting Japanese traits, very similar in wording, are found in *Present State*, 2:214–15, and in *Voltaire*, 6:153–54.

60. "copans": A Japanese coin (*UH*, 57–58) worth one-tenth of an oban (see below, n. 269). Now *kopan, koban*.

61. "their constitution . . . liberty and property": Since the revolution of 1688 these three terms had been shibboleths for both parties, and indeed were fundamental clichés of eighteenth-century English political thought. For a recent treatment of their ubiquity, see Garry Wills, *Inventing America* (New York: Doubleday, 1978), 228–39. See also H. T. Dickinson, *Liberty and Property: Political Ideology in Eighteenth-Century Britain* (New York: Holmes and Meier, 1977).

62. "practicable": Capable of being used or exploited.

63. "the Cuboy, or minister": See key. The first minister is always meant by the term "Cuboy."

64. "tall fellows": In the opposing senses of "tall" as "valiant" and "dexterous."

65. "a pipe . . . particular pitch": Smollett apparently alludes to *Tale of a Tub* 9, where Swift compares the inflaming of an audience to the sympathetic vibra-

tions of musical instruments. There is also an echo of *Briton*, no. 16 (11 September 1762): 92: "We shall find [in history] the people of Athens led about by every turbulent orator in their turns, like an ill-tamed monster, from vanity to vice . . . from the lowest depth of despondence, to the most giddy height of elation." The exact source of the "bullock's horn" has not been traced, though Horace Walpole writes to John Chute on 29 September 1755, "Mr. Pitt is scouring his old Hanoverian trumpet"; see Walpole, *Correspondence*, 35:89.

66. "Dairo": The British sovereign; see key.

67. "this emperor . . . the inactive Dairo": *UH*, 27, thus describes the *shōguns* or military dictators, the real rulers of Japan from the late middle ages to the mid-nineteenth century: "it was by one of these cubo's that the dairo's were stripped of their whole civil authority . . . ." Smollett refers to the relative practical limitations upon the powers of the Hanoverian kings imposed during the ministries of Sir Robert Walpole and his successors; see Speck, 11–30. He had earlier discussed the question of the inactive monarch in *Voltaire*, 6:153–54, and in *Briton*, no. 25 (10 November 1762): 149: "I would have the K[ing] of E[nglan]d like . . . the Dairo of Japan . . . . They enjoyed the nominal honours . . . the power, the influence and authority resided in . . . the cubay."

68. "not a lineal descendant": Queen Anne, the last of the Protestant Stuart line, had no surviving children, and the Act of Settlement (1701) declared the electress Sophia of Hanover heir to the throne as granddaughter of James I. Sophia did not live to become queen, but her son was crowned George I of England in 1714, after the death of Anne.

69. "*Bupo*": George I; see key.

70. "Fakkubasi": The "worship" of Hanover; see key. Smollett's phrasing ("Fak-kubasi . . . horse") is copied from a reference to Kaempfer at the bottom of page 113, *UH*.

71. "white horse": The Saxon white horse, which figured as a representation of Hanover in the royal arms of Brunswick-Lüneburg, on medals, and in many satirical prints.

72. "culture": Cult, worship, homage, as in the modern French *culte*.

73. "still": In the older sense of always, constantly.

74. "the Cuboy, who gratified this sordid passion": Sir Robert Walpole may have been somewhat cynical in supporting the Hanoverian preoccupations of the first two Georges; but Newcastle was by conviction the upholder of an early version of the "balance of power" doctrine, which could not be maintained without constant British-Hanoverian intervention in Continental power politics. See Browning, 156–58.

75. "Pythagoras, a philosopher of Crotona": Greek philosopher, c. 582–c. 507 B.C., who founded a religious brotherhood committed to a belief in the transmigration of souls and in the numerical basis of all physical relationships in the universe.

76. "the convocation": The synod of the province of Canterbury, having upper and

lower houses; the ecclesiastical equivalent of Parliament. Prorogued by George I in 1717, the synod met only once again in the century, in 1741, when it was again prorogued before any business of importance could be transacted. See Speck, 93; see also Norman Sykes, *Church and State in England in the Eighteenth Century* (Cambridge: The University Press, 1934), 313.

77. "bate": Withdraw, retract.

78. "the stake at Smithfield": At the site of the present Saint Bartholomew's Hospital, Smithfield was in Smollett's time famed for slaughterhouses and Bartholomew Fair. The Protestant martyrs were executed there under Mary I; burnings occurred as late as the 1650s.

79. "verily . . . thee": Uttered by Jesus for emphasis on many occasions recorded in the gospels.

80. "remove": Moving, as from one residence to another; also, a step in a process: here, transmigration.

81. "plexus . . . venison and turtle": A plexus is a bundle of fibers, in this instance nerve fibers. Venison and turtle are symbolic of aldermanic luxury, as traditionally served at the annual banquet of the lord mayor of London.

82. "*Peter Gore* . . . Croton": This reference has not been traced; perhaps it is to a contemporary farce.

83. "a type . . . unveiled": A symbolic figure as well as a historical personage, not yet explained and understood. Smollett uses *type* in its theological sense, as when Moses is seen as a "type" of Christ. The statements following in this passage, the first of the *Atom*'s Rabelaisian-Sternean learned digressions, can be traced partly to the early standard biography of Pythagoras, *Peri tou Pythagorikou biou*, L. *Vita Pythagoræ*, by Iamblichus, a Neoplatonist who died c. A.D. 333; partly to the many fantastic extrapolations from this biography; and partly to legends about Pythagoras that arose in antiquity.

84. "circumstances . . . learned world": Smollett acknowledges the character of Pythagoras as celebrated by Iamblichus. On metempsychosis, or transmigration of souls, see Iamblichus, chapter 14; see also *Peregrine Pickle*, chapter 47: "Pythagoras affirmed the spirit of Euphorbus had transmigrated into his body." The "harmonies" alluded to are those of music; see Iamblichus, chapter 26. Iamblichus claims that Pythagoras also developed theories of the "motion of the earth" (chapter 27), that he described the "elements of geometry and arithmetic" (chapter 29), that he imposed five years of "silence" upon his followers during their discipleship (chapter 17), and that he required them to follow a vegetarian diet (chapter 24).

85. "veneration . . . his life": According to Iamblichus, chapter 24, Pythagoras ordered his disciples to abstain from eating beans as well as meat; an ox, similarly admonished, likewise abstained from beans (chapter 13). Iamblichus reports (chapter 31) that several Pythagoreans were killed by enemies in a bean field because they would not flee for fear of touching the beans. The historian

Diogenes Laertius (fl. third century A. D.) tells the same story of Pythagoras himself in "Lives, Teachings, and Sayings of Famous Philosophers," 8.39.

86. "his golden thigh . . . truths are concealed": Iamblichus states (in chapters 19, 28) that Pythagoras showed one of his thighs, which was of gold, both to the audience at the Olympic games and to Abaris, the sage of the north. The Roman grammarian Aulus Gellius, in *Noctes atticæ* 4.11.14, reproduces fragments from the Greek writers Dicearchus and Clearchus claiming that at one time Pythagoras transformed himself into "a beautiful courtesan named Alco." The "golden verses" are a collection of fifty-odd gnomic fragments existing in innumerable editions and commentaries; these fragments are usually attributed to Pythagoras and are specifically identified as his by both Iamblichus and Diogenes Laertius. The Greek αὐτὸς ἔφα, or "*ipse dixit*," is a proverbial expression supposedly originating with Pythagoras; in *Humphry Clinker*, Matthew Bramble writes to Dr. Lewis, London, June 2, "the *ipse dixit* of this new Pythagoras." Among the other legends surrounding Pythagoras were those of his birth to the supposed virgin Pythias (from the Pythian oracle) or Parthenis (*parthenos*, or virgin) and his "descent into hell," where he met Homer and the poet Hesiod; see Iamblichus, chapter 2, and see Diogenes Laertius 8.21, 38, 41, 45, which cites "Hieronymus" as the source for the story of Pythagoras in Hades.

87. "Philip Tessier": The *Grand dictionnaire historique* (1674) of Louis Moréri, a standard reference work much used by Smollett (probably in the fourteenth edition, Amsterdam, 1717) when annotating historical allusions, states in the entry on "Pythagore" that at Béziers in 1682 the Carmelite Père Philippe Tessier presented a thesis contending that Pythagoras and his disciples, together with the Gauls and the Druids, were Carmelites. The thesis was condemned at Rome two years later.

88. "*Utrum Pythagoras . . . Carmelita*": "Whether Pythagoras was a Jew, or a Carmelite Monk." This work, an account of the thesis of Tessier, is mentioned by Moréri as written by "J. Frid. Meyer."

89. "Waving": Waiving, giving over.

90. "circumcised": Saint Ambrose (Epistle 28, to Irenæus) argued that Pythagoras, voyaging by way of Mount Carmel, served as a Jewish intermediary between Moses and Plato. The possible source of Ambrose's argument is the biography by Iamblichus, chapter 3, which describes Pythagoras as traveling to Egypt. *Tristram Shandy*, volume 5, chapter 27, also refers to the circumcision of Pythagoras by the Egyptians.

91. "eleusinian mysteries": The rites of the goddess Demeter at Eleusis were never divulged in detail throughout antiquity, but were generally thought to have involved a symbolic rebirth for the initiates.

92. "Dryden's translation . . . Æneid": In this translation of 1697 Aeneas's father, Anchises, whom he encounters in his journey to the underworld, explains that souls are purged there and sent back to earth to inhabit better or worse creatures

according to their deserts (lines 923–24, 974–1020). The atom assumes that Peacock has no Latin.

93. "diversorium": L. Temporary lodging or shelter.

94. "crasis": L. Mixture of elements, in this case of the soul or spirit.

95. "a goat, a spider": Traditional emblems of lust and of self-engendered poison, respectively.

96. "intuition, or communication of ideas": The modes by which angelic beings were thought to derive knowledge.

97. "Mercury": Patron of games and entertainments, but also of thieves and tricksters.

98. "the period Foggien . . . at peace with all her neighbors": The War of the Austrian Succession had ended in 1748 with the Peace of Aix-la-Chapelle; the hostilities leading to the Seven Years' War began in 1754. See below, n. 317.

99. "article": Critical point or moment.

100. "*a posteriori*": L. From the rear; hence, anally.

101. "the appetite of the mother": Smollett probably alludes to a scandalous episode involving Count Königsmarck, the lover of Sophia Dorothea of Celle (1666–1726), consort to the elector of Hanover and mother of George II. The count was murdered on 1 July 1694; the elector divorced the princess, who was then imprisoned in her father's castle of Ahlden for the remainder of her life. See Hatton, 55–62.

102. "animalcule": See above, n. 57.

103. "inspired": In the Latin sense of breathed in, absorbed.

104. "Got-hama-baba": George II of England; see key.

105. "his last character": His previous incarnation or mode of existence.

106. "slavering bib": Smollett elsewhere evoked the same image for satiric purposes. *Briton*, no. 38 (12 February 1763): 225 depicts the duke of Newcastle with "a cap and bells upon his head, a slavering-bib under his chin, and a rattle in his hand." See also *CR* 8 (November 1759): 420: "procure a slavering bib; for none but an ideot could utter such a wretched rhapsody."

107. "a blind attachment to . . . Fakku-basi": See key; and see above, n. 70. Since George II was also elector of Hanover and had lived there continuously until he was past thirty, his attachment to his German domains is entirely understandable; but the "Continental connection" is Smollett's *bête noire* throughout all of his political and historical writings.

108. "kicking the breech . . . in private": A reference to the first minister's daily audiences in the king's Closet, or private study. George II's rudeness and temper tantrums were notorious and much satirized. He once kicked Dr. "Spot" Ward when the latter was examining an inflamed royal thumb, and sometimes kicked his own hat and wig around the room. See Mack, 130–31, 139, 143; and see below, vol. 2, nn. 184–88. Smollett's most probable direct source is the spurious part 2 of *Candide*, chapter 4 (*Voltaire*, 18:157): "The monarch . . . conducted

[Candide] back to the guardroom, with several sound kicks on the posteriors; at which the courtiers were ready to burst for envy. . . . no person had ever received such signal marks of his majesty's favour in this way as Candid."

109. "a little after the conception . . . a future Cuboy": George II was in fact ten years older than Newcastle, "the future Cuboy," who was born in 1693.

110. "changling soul": A fickle, inconstant, or changeling spirit. Smollett alludes to the popular belief that the fairies stole human infants and left their own in exchange. In another familiar sense, the changeling is an idiot or imbecile.

111. "dottril": Also spelled "dotterel"; a variety of plover, a bird proverbial for its stupidity.

112. "cow-boy": Not, of course, in the American sense; a term of mockery deriving from the nature of the cow-boy's task and signifying a loutish, stupid youth.

113. "Quanbuku": Duke; see key. Newcastle was in fact the son of a baronet. His father was created Baron Pelham in 1703, and he himself was not created a duke until 1713. See Browning, 2, 9.

114. "We at different times": This sentence strongly echoes the wording of Pope's *Essay on Man* 2:165–202, on the "ruling passion."

115. "the same spirit": In the double sense of "the same soul in two successive bodies" and "the same inclination in different persons."

116. "cried up in an Hector": Extolled, praised. Hector is proverbial for dauntless courage.

117. "a patriot to harangue": Given the context, doubtless an allusion to William Pitt; see key, TAYCHO. On Pitt as "patriot" see Brewer, *Party*, 96–111.

118. "ungrateful": Scanty; unresponsive to tillage.

119. "Fika-kaka": Thomas Pelham-Holles, duke of Newcastle; see key.

120. "an immense fortune": Newcastle was enormously wealthy; see below, n. 144.

121. "a total absence of pride . . . upon negatives": This is an accurate summary of Newcastle's character; see Browning, 80–88.

122. "œconomy": Prudence in managing one's private affairs in general, and especially one's financial affairs.

123. "no retention": In two senses: "lacking self-restraint" and "lacking a retentive memory."

124. "profuse": Extravagant, spendthrift.

125. "leaky": Unable to keep a secret; also, not retentive of memory. Smollett describes himself to the Rev. Alexander Carlyle as "weak and leaky"; see *Letters*, 11.

126. "He appeared . . . all day": Probably an echo of Lord Wilmington's *mot*, "The Duke of Newcastle always loses half an hour in the morning, which he is running after the rest of the day without being able to overtake it"; see Walpole, *George II*, 1:107.

127. "animal spirits": In pre-modern medical theory, vapors arising from the organs or blood, which transmitted energy and movement to the body.

128. *"Lusus Naturæ"*: L. Trick of nature; monstrosity.

129. "original": In the pejorative sense of being ridiculously eccentric in unheard-of ways.

130. "administration . . . consigned": Newcastle was effectively first minister, alone or in tandem with Pitt, from 1754 to 1762. See key.

131. "dancing bareheaded . . . Bonzas . . . Cambadoxi": See key. What Smollett intends is uncertain, but he clearly alludes to Newcastle's intense interest in religious matters and his obsessive desire throughout his career to be in total control of ecclesiastical preferment. See Browning, 78–79, 186–88.

132. "a certain treaty with the Chinese": The Treaty of Utrecht, ratified in 1713, ended the War of the Spanish Succession and made peace with France.

133. "queen Syko": Queen Anne; see key.

134. "so ignorant of geography": Newcastle's alleged abysmal ignorance of geography is a favorite topic of Smollett, who alludes to it several times in the *Atom* and again in *Humphry Clinker*, Jery Melford to Sir Watkin Phillips, London, June 2. Smollett always has in mind an incident recorded by Walpole, *George II*, 2:16: Newcastle is supposed to have said to Lord Ligonier, the army commander, during a council of war, "Certainly we must fortify Annapolis [the town in Nova Scotia]. Where is Annapolis?" See Williams, 1:252, and Paul-Gabriel Boucé, "The Duke of Newcastle's Levee in Smollett's *Humphry Clinker*," *Yearbook of English Studies* 5 (1975): 137–41.

135. "fourteen sects of religion . . . Japan": These are mentioned and then listed in the *Universal History*'s account of Japan (*UH*, 9). Smollett perhaps intends a satirical reference to the various dissenting sects and to the Methodists, of whom he disapproved.

136. "a superstitious devotion . . . white horse." See key. To Smollett's intense disgust, Newcastle was from first to last a confirmed advocate of the idea that maintaining a balance of power in Europe was of paramount importance; he thus vigorously promoted Britain's entanglements in Continental politics. It has been maintained that Newcastle's attempts after 1749 to bribe or persuade the imperial electors into designating a king of the Romans (who would automatically succeed to the German empire) was a basic cause of the Seven Years' War. See Reed Browning, "Newcastle and the Imperial Election Plan," *Journal of British Studies* 7 (1967): 28–47.

137. "alarmed": With a disturbed or alarmed look.

138. "embarrassed": Clogged, confused.

139. "perplexed": Complicated, unclear.

140. "the Chinese language . . . at court": George II was trilingual and proud of his English, though he spoke with a heavy German accent. He always wrote in French, and he also used French in conversation with foreign diplomats and ordinarily with members of the royal family. See Hatton, 131–32.

141. "cooks from China . . . expence": The duke's French chef, Cloué or Clouet, was

much satirized, as were his magnificent plate and extravagant banquets. On Cloué, see Print 2684*; on Newcastle's extravagance, see Print 3476. See also Romney Sedgwick, "The Duke of Newcastle's Cook," *History Today* 5 (1955): 308–16.

142. "drank huge quantities . . . flimsy texture": Newcastle was no drunkard, but he was far from abstemious; see Browning, 82.

143. "an involuntary discharge . . . intestines": Newcastle actually suffered from constipation, not diarrhea; see Browning, 85.

144. "a prodigious estate": The combined inheritance from his father and his maternal uncle, John Holles, first duke of the second creation, gave Newcastle as a young man an annual income of at least £32,000; thus at the start of his career he was among the wealthiest men in England. But he was not "entitled by his birth"; see Browning, 4–5, and see above, n. 113.

145. "connected with all the great men": Newcastle married Lady Harriet Godolphin, granddaughter of the first duke of Marlborough and of Queen Anne's lord treasurer. He held various court offices uninterruptedly from 1717 onward. See Browning, 12, 13.

146. "their souls being congenial": Though for various reasons they constantly saw one another, George in fact never liked Newcastle, and there were serious breaches between the two, especially in 1717, 1746, and 1757. See Davies, passim, and Browning, 19 and passim.

147. "twin particles . . . ever after": The wording of this passage suggests that Smollett is deliberately echoing the atomic theory of Democritus as outlined by Lucretius in *De rerum natura* (c. 55 B.C.).

148. "the most eminent offices of the state": Newcastle was a member of the cabinet, except briefly in 1756–57 and from 1762 to 1765; he was secretary of state, Southern Department, including the colonies, 1724–54; for seven years he served as first lord of the treasury, an office that made him first minister.

149. "the dignity of Cuboy, or chief minister": Newcastle became first lord of the treasury in 1754, succeeding his deceased brother Henry Pelham. See John B. Owen, *The Rise of the Pelhams* (London: Methuen, 1957).

150. "who could not write": Newcastle wrote voluminously, but the style of his thousands of letters and documents is ungraceful and often extremely confused.

151. "never could balance accounts with his own butler": This statement is literally true. Newcastle was perpetually on the verge of ruin and by the end of his life had mortgaged away the bulk of his vast estate. See Ray Kelch, *Newcastle: A Duke Without Money* (London: Routledge and Kegan Paul, 1974); and see Browning, 40–43, 123–29, 328–29.

152. "magnificence": In the Latin sense, combining munificence with splendor of living.

153. "Meckaddo . . . mysteries of his religion": For all proper names in this passage, see key. "Tensco-Dav-dsin" is listed in *UH* (103, n. A) as the first of five ter-

restrial gods; "Shi-whang-ti" sent three hundred youths and three hundred maidens to Japan in quest of the universal medicine (*UH*, 112); "Fo-hi," according to Smollett's *Compendium of Voyages*, 7:72, was the legendary Yellow Emperor who discovered the universal medicine.

154. "Bonzas or clergy": See key, BONZA.

155. "the university Frenoxena*": Cambridge; see key. Smollett's footnote is simply copied, as a "Japanese" detail, from *UH*, 38, n. e.

156. "chose him their supreme director": Newcastle was elected high steward of Cambridge in 1737 and chancellor in 1748; see Browning, 80, 170–71, and *Continuation*, 1:36. Unlike Oxford, which was often considered disaffected or even Jacobite, Cambridge enjoyed the reputation of being "Whig," or pro-administration.

157. "every morning . . . worship": A reference to Newcastle's regular formal morning receptions, or levees, at which he was attended by a throng of petitioners and hangers-on. For descriptions of these see above, n. 134.

158. "Nem-buds-ju": The Jews; see key.

159. "he himself . . . the operation": Print 3205*, "The Circumcised Gentiles," attacks Newcastle and his brother, the first minister Henry Pelham, for their support of the Jewish Naturalization Bill of 1753, commonly known as the "Jew Bill." See below, n. 162.

160. "a slight scarification": Probably a reference to Newcastle's embarrassment at having to move for repeal of the "Jew Bill," which he had promoted; see below, n. 162.

161. "a valuable consideration": Print 3206 repeats the widespread accusation that Newcastle and his brother had accepted a bribe of £500,000 offered by the Jews in exchange for their support of the Naturalization Bill.

162. "a law was promulgated . . . the measure": In June 1753 Parliament enacted the Jewish Naturalization Bill, permitting Jews (though at an expense few of them could afford) to be naturalized by private bills in Parliament without taking the customary Christian oath of allegiance. The measure met with little or no resistance in the House of Lords; when it passed the Commons and became law, the Opposition seized the opportunity to foment and make political capital of popular anti-Semitism. The resulting tumults so terrified Newcastle (who was mocked as "King of the Jews" at Cambridge) that in November, with an election approaching, he took the embarrassing step of moving and securing repeal of the bill. See Thomas W. Perry, *Public Opinion, Propaganda, and Politics in Eighteenth-Century England: A Study of the Jew Bill of 1753* (Cambridge: Harvard University Press, 1962); Tuvia Bloch, "Smollett and the Jews," *American Notes and Queries* 6 (1968): 116; Ian Campbell Ross, "Smollett and the Jew Bill of 1753," *American Notes and Queries* 16 (1977): 54–56; *PH*, 14:1365–1432, 15:91–163; Walpole, *George II*, 1:238–45.

163. "the most placid resignation": While this statement is greatly exaggerated,

Smollett refers primarily to Newcastle's firm support of the king's determined views concerning the costly preservation of Hanover. Newcastle, who was in constant terror of the king, perpetually complained about his rude treatment in the Closet.

164. "the podex": The rump or buttocks.

165. "Dr. Woodward": John Woodward (1665–1728), an eminent physician, naturalist, and antiquary, wrote many works on diverse subjects and was embroiled in numerous controversies. See Joseph M. Levine, *Dr. Woodward's Shield* (Berkeley: University of California Press, 1977).

166. "*immanis* αιδοῖων *pruritus*": L. and Gr. Immoderate itching of the private ("shameful") parts. Smollett takes this phrase from the review cited below, n. 167.

167. "colluctations with oil, &c.": Colluctations: strife, opposition. This passage is based on the quoted matter in Smollett's sarcastic review of Woodward's *Select Cases and Consultations in Physick* (1757), *CR* 3 (January 1757): 24–30. "Mrs. Harry of Lime-house" was afflicted with the itching (p. 29) and had "great redundance of salts"; the phrase "break the colluctations with oil" appears on page 26. See Basker, 223.

168. "the celebrated Fan-sey": See key.

169. "informed": Gave shape and life to, as the soul was supposed to give shape and life to the body.

170. "balsamics, and sweeteners": Soothing preparations and antacids.

171. "Gargantua": The giant-hero of medieval folk literature whom Rabelais portrayed as the son of Grandgousier and father of Pantagruel in *Gargantua and Pantagruel* (1532–64). In the passage that follows, Smollett alludes directly to an episode in chapter 12 of the popular translation of Rabelais by Sir Thomas Urquhart, *The Works of Mr. Francis Rabelais* (1693; many subsequent editions); the same episode is mentioned by him in *CR* 4 (October 1757): 376 (Basker, 224, 239).

172. "pillow-bier . . . the portion of the son of Grangousier": A "pillow-bier" is a pillowcase; "poke" means bag; a "pannier" is a basket shaped so as to hang on the side of a horse's saddle; the "lamprey," a primitive fish resembling an eel, was considered a table delicacy in antiquity and during the middle ages; a "lure" is a cluster of feathers attached to a long cord, used in training falcons to strike. The French "*volupté merifique au trou de cul*," meaning a wondrous delight at the anus, is from the Urquhart translation of Rabelais, as quoted by Smollett in *CR* 4 (October 1757): 376; see above, n. 171.

173. "boar-cat": Tomcat.

174. "cackling like a hen in labour": A sarcasm on Newcastle's mannerisms; see below, vol. 2, n. 282.

175. "glandula pinealis": The pineal gland; see above, n. 39.

176. "run distracted . . . gadfly": Io, loved by Zeus, was turned into a cow by the jealous Hera, who sent a gadfly to sting and pursue her over the whole earth.

177. "mystery and revelation": Smollett uses the terms in their Christian and doctrinal sense.

178. "lamb's wool": A drink made of hot ale, spices, sugar, and apple pulp. Smollett doubtless echoes Dryden's satiric reference in *Absalom and Achitophel* (lines 575–76) to Lord Howard of Escrick, the "canting *Nadab*" who cynically took the sacrament in lamb's wool.

179. "the Ebro": The Spanish river of Toledo, a city celebrated for the production of superbly tempered sword blades.

180. "perineum": The area between the anus and the genitals.

181. "great gut": The colon and rectum.

182. "meer": Mere, in the older sense of pure, absolute.

183. "simple, independent ideas . . . definition": This phrase echoes Locke's *Essay Concerning Human Understanding* (1690), book 3, chapter 4, "Of the Names of Simple Ideas."

184. "nervous papillæ": Minute nipple-like protuberances, as on the tongue, receiving sensations of taste and touch.

185. "whether by irritation . . . vibration": Smollett's probable source, David Hartley's *Observations on Man* (1749), discusses these possible modes for the transmission of sensory impulses through the nerves. In chapter 2, section 1, Hartley refers to "sentient Papillæ" (pp. 116–17) and remarks that itching of the *glans penis* is "given a Check" by "a Pressure made *in Perinæo*" (p. 129).

186. "subaltern": Subsidiary, secondary.

187. "but the other day . . . composition of light": Newton's *Principia* appeared in 1687, his *Opticks* in 1704.

188. "reptile": In the older sense of "creeping thing."

189. "Categories . . . ὑποκείμενον": In Scholastic philosophy the "categories" underlay all definition of a thing, were ten in number, and were the subject of much dispute; they included substance, quality, quantity, relation, place, and time. The "Organum," or "instrument of reasoning," was the blanket title of some half-dozen of Aristotle's works involving logic, among them the *De interpretatione* and the *Analytics*. The Greek words cited by Smollett are technical terms of philosophy: οὐσια, substance or essence; ὕλη, matter; ὑποκείμενον, the subject to which attributes are assigned, that is, the "substance" or essential part of any thing, which underlies its "accidents" or nonessentials.

190. "diurnal incense": Newcastle's daily levee; see above, n. 157.

191. "cabinet": Private study or office.

192. "abstersive": Cleansing or purgative.

193. "verriculum": Sieve, net, bunch of fibers; a medical term.

194. "black": Here in the older sense of brunette.

195. "posterior rite of worship": Arse-kissing as a metaphor for sycophancy is found as early as Swift's Yahoos, and is prevalent in anti-Walpole satire. See Mack, 148.
196. "calcitration": Kicking with the shod foot, from *calceus*, shoe or sandal. See below, vol. 2, nn. 184–88.
197. "digitation": Touching with the finger or toe, therefore with the unshod foot.
198. "hebetude": Dullness, lethargy.
199. "close-stool": Commode, containing a chamberpot.
200. "offices": Services, kindnesses.
201. "one he shook . . . horse-laugh": On Newcastle's mannerisms see Browning, 83; on Smollett's depiction of them in *Humphry Clinker* see above, n. 134.
202. "the negative particle": The word "no" or the word "not".
203. "a computable chance of performance": See Browning, 83. Smollett's statement is not inaccurate, but he may be echoing Swift's satire on the shortness of ministerial memories in *Gulliver's Travels*, part 3, chapter 6.
204. "he promoted a great number of Bonzas": Newcastle arranged the appointment of twenty-six bishops during his years of power. For a summary of his ecclesiastical policies, which were by no means disreputable in their time, see Browning, 186–87. See also Norman Sykes, "The Duke of Newcastle as Ecclesiastical Minister," *English Historical Review* 67 (1942): 59–84.
205. "preferred": The usual term for ecclesiastical promotion.
206. "demulcent": Soothing, reducing irritation.
207. "a phosphorus": A bearer or emitter of light.
208. "apotheosis": G. Deification; a visible ascent into heaven.
209. "Pontifex Maximus": L. Literally translated "greatest bridge-builder," the phrase was used for the chief priest of pagan Rome and is used at present for the pope. The context suggests the possibility of reference to successive archbishops of Canterbury: John Potter (1737), Thomas Herring (1747), Matthew Hutton (1757), and Thomas Secker (1758). More probably, Smollett is merely embroidering his satirical theme.
210. "philosophy": Natural philosophy; the exact sciences.
211. "immersions and emersions": Astronomical terms meaning entrance into and emergence from eclipse.
212. "Saturn . . . the planets": The existence of the three most remote planets, Uranus, Neptune, and Pluto, was unknown; the discovery of Uranus by Sir William Herschel did not take place until 1781.
213. "Sti-phi-rum-poo . . . the Dairo's personal regard": A reference to Philip Yorke, earl of Hardwicke, whose father was an attorney of Dover. The Yorke family was prosperous and of some consequence, but of no "birth"; see below, n. 249. Hardwicke served as lord chancellor from 1737 to 1756. For explanation of the phrase "*Quo*, or nobleman," see key.
214. "interest": Influence through personal connections.

215. "inclosures": Restrictions, limitations.

216. "avarice and cruelty": Prints 3412, 3416*, 3502, and 3558, among others, depict Hardwicke as a vulture clutching moneybags.

217. "The appearance of cruelty . . . open rebellion": In 1746 and 1747 Hardwicke was made lord high steward to preside in the House of Lords at the trials of the Scottish lords Cromartie, Kilmarnock, Balmerino, and Lovat, who were charged with treason for leading the Jacobite insurrection of the "Forty-Five" in an attempt to place the Pretender, James Francis Stuart, on the English throne. See *PH*, 13:1422, 1438–46.

218. "sentence of death by self-exenteration*": The Japanese custom of *seppuku*, or ritual suicide by disembowelment, is described in *UH*, 33, 35. Kilmarnock, Balmerino, and Lovat were beheaded, and Smollett conflates their fate with the hanging, drawing, and quartering of other rebel officers; see below, n. 268.

219. "a dastardly heart . . . liberal sentiment": Hardwicke, in conducting the trials, allowed himself to be guided by the extreme violence of English sentiment against the rebel leaders. As subsequent passages of the *Atom* make clear, Smollett never overcame his indignation at the treatment of the Scottish rebels.

220. "purblind": The word has several applicable senses; the most probable here are "virtually blind" or "blind in one eye."

221. "making speeches . . . seasons of the year": The sovereign's speech from the throne at the opening of Parliament outlines the administration's legislative program for the ensuing session. Beginning in 1744 and for many years afterward, Hardwicke drafted all or nearly all of these highly significant addresses. See Browning, 123.

222. "qualified to ease him . . . government": Until Hardwicke's death Newcastle constantly consulted him on even the smallest matters (often to his intense irritation), referred to him as "my sheet-anchor," and in return steadily promoted his career. See Browning, 18–19, 80–81, 298.

223. "a subfuscan hue": Dark brown or gray.

224. "initiated in the mysteries of the cabinet": A member of the House of Commons from 1719, Yorke was created Baron Hardwicke in 1733; he was appointed lord chancellor (and thus a cabinet member) in 1737. In 1754 he was created earl of Hardwicke.

225. "nobilitation": Advancement to the nobility.

226. "glutæi muscles": The three large muscles forming each of the buttocks.

227. "Nin-kom-poo-po": George, Baron Anson; see key.

228. "*Fune*, or navy of Japan": Navy, or ship(s). *UH*, 128: "*Fune*, or men of war." The modern word is *fune* or *hune*.

229. "bred to the sea from his infancy": Anson, born in 1697, began his naval service as a midshipman in 1712.

230. "pacific service": Peacetime service.

231. "jonkh": Junk, ship; man-of-war or merchant vessel. The word, derived from

the Javanese *djong* (ship), had passed into common usage in Western languages by the eighteenth century. See *Present State*, 8:57.

232. "a crew of pyrates . . . treasure": Captain Anson circumnavigated the globe in 1740–44 with a squadron of four ships, of which one, the *Centurion*, survived to return to England. On 20 June 1743, off Cape Espiritu Santo on the Philippine island of Samar, Anson surprised the Spanish treasure galleon *Nuestra Señora de Cabadonga*, which was headed for Manila from Acapulco, and captured cargo variously estimated in value at £350,000–£500,000. "Corea" is Spain; see key.

233. "the transports of the people . . . produced": Anson returned to London in triumph on 15 June 1744; he was ennobled and decorated after his victory in the battle of Finistère, 1747. Smollett, unlike most historians, gives Anson scant credit. In the *Compendium of Voyages*, 8:366 he comments at length on Anson's good fortune; in *Voltaire*, 8:53 he says that Anson's thirty-two wagonloads of treasure were not enough to defray the costs of his expedition; and in the *Complete History*, 4:654 he remarks that Anson became an "oracle," though but for the accidental capture of the treasure he would have been superannuated. "Meaco" is London; see key.

234. "five kisses": A notorious mannerism of Newcastle; see Browning, 83.

235. "Sey-seo-gun": See key. Anson was made first lord of the admiralty in 1751.

236. "a strict alliance": In 1748 Anson married Lord Hardwicke's daughter, Lady Elizabeth Yorke.

237. "the whole management of the *Fune* . . . his hands": Except for a brief interlude in 1756–57, Anson directed naval operations from 1751 to the end of the Seven Years' War in 1763.

238. "Salamander . . . live in fire": A tradition going back to Pliny's *Historia naturalis* (A.D. 77) holds that the salamander is so cold by nature that it can live in fire. Addison's *Spectator*, no. 198 (17 October 1711) associates the creature with impotence or frigidity. Smollett may be alluding to Swift's "Description of a Salamander" (1705), a savage attack in similar terms on Lord Cutts.

239. "a mere fable": Contemporary satirical prints throw light on Smollett's allegations in the passage here concluded. Print 3394* alludes to Anson's love of gambling, showing him with a dice-box; in Print 3412 he is "Anser," a duck or goose; Print 3522, "Null Marriage," refers to his frigidity, or impotence; in Print 3493* he is shown as a sea lion; Print 3395, in another allusion to his gambling, represents him as the knave of diamonds.

240. "affected to establish new regulations": Naval historians generally praise Anson for his revision of naval regulations, his reorganization of the marines, his establishment of the Articles of War, and his administration of the naval dockyards. See Stanley W. C. Pack, *Admiral Lord Anson* (London: Cassell, 1960); but see also below, n. 244.

241. "seemed to take pleasure in denying a request": This phrase raises the possibility

that Smollett's view of Anson had its roots in a real or fancied personal slight, a favor sought and denied.

242. "this vain creature . . . trinkets of pewter": The *DNB* characterizes Anson as cold and selfish. Walpole, *George II*, 1:129, 2:164 calls him "reserved and proud" and notes that "his incapacity grew the general topic of ridicule; he was joined in all the satiric prints with his father-in-law, Newcastle, and Fox."

243. "assessors . . . co-adjutors": The admiralty board.

244. "the care of the scribe . . . repelling each other": The "scribe" was John Cleveland (c. 1707–63), secretary of the admiralty throughout Anson's period of service, 1751–63. Clevland, an indefatigable supporter of the administration in Parliament and a lifelong career man in naval administration, acquired such control of the navy as to generate "a vulgar opinion that Clevland is Lord High Admiral"; see Romney Sedgwick, *The House of Commons, 1715–1754* (London: H. M. Stationery Office, 1970), 2: 220–21. *A Letter to the Right Honourable Lord A----* (1757) accuses Anson of entirely turning over the admiralty to Clevland, who is said to be practicing wholesale corruption, sending out confusing instructions, and generally wrecking the navy. Anson himself was frequently charged with excessive gambling, shady financial dealings, and unethical conduct of his office.

245. "Amphisbæna": According to tradition, a serpent with a head at each end.

246. "Foksi-Roku": Henry Fox, Lord Holland; see key.

247. "interested": On the alert for personal gain.

248. "latitudinarian": Ordinarily used to mean flexibility or tolerance in religious doctrine; here used to mean "unprincipled."

249. "without the advantages of birth": Fox, however, was the son of Sir Stephen Fox, a wealthy and eminent political figure; he was able to marry a sister of the duke of Richmond. "Birth" for Smollett is explained by a passage in *Ferdinand Count Fathom*, chapter 48, which refers to persons identifiable as Hardwicke and Fox, the one "sprung from the loins of an obscure attorney" and the other "grandson of a valet de chambre."

250. "interest": Influential friends or family connections; Fox in fact had both, abundantly.

251. "projecting": Inventive; fertile in projects.

252. "high offices . . . a wicked administration": By 1755 Fox was leader of the Commons and secretary of state, southern department; in 1757 he became paymaster general of the armed forces, the most lucrative post in the government. He amassed a huge fortune and barely escaped trial as a "public defaulter of millions." Smollett's characterization of Fox as "detested by the people" is accurate, though not everyone agreed that the administration he served was "wicked."

253. "m——y": Ministry. The "gutting" or "castration" of such words (as with "ad[ministratio]n," in the following paragraph), was customary in periodicals,

pamphlets, and books; see Kropf, "Libel and Satire in the Eighteenth Century." In the *Continuation*, 5:200, Smollett remarks of pamphlets regarding the controversial Cyder Tax of 1763 that "The usual caution of not printing names at length was now laid aside." Given the circumstances of the *Atom*'s composition, Smollett may in the present passage be satirizing the ridiculous convention of gutting; alternatively, the printer may have automatically gutted certain words written out in the manuscript.

254. "uncertainty of his attachment": Throughout his career Fox was completely and openly opportunistic about shifting his political alliances for his greatest personal advantage.

255. "another knot of competitors . . . army": A reference to the fluctuating attachment of Fox and others to William Augustus, duke of Cumberland, second surviving son of George II and commander-in-chief of land forces after 1745; see key, QUAMBA-CUN-DONO. Cumberland, who enjoyed his father's complete confidence and favor until 1757 (see below, n. 581), was a member of the council of regency whenever the king was in Hanover; he was thought by many, including Fox, to be willing if not eager to establish a military dictatorship. Cumberland would in any case have become regent if the king, an elderly man by eighteenth-century standards, had died before his grandson (the future George III) attained his majority. See Browning, 172–74, 196–97.

256. "Fatzman . . . eminence": A reference to Cumberland's corpulence; see key, and see Prints 3441* and 3613*. Smollett's footnote cites Kaempfer's *Amœnitatum Exoticarum* (1712), a work on natural history called "Amœnit. Japan" in *UH*, 99; see Martz, 99. The Greek phrase (its literal meaning is *"par excellence"*) quoted and translated by Smollett possibly was taken from a satirical novel, *Memoirs and Adventures of Tsonnonthouan*, favorably reviewed in *CR* 15 (May 1763): 378–88. The reviewer, possibly Smollett himself, remarks that the Indians "have distinguished all [Governor Montgomery's] successors κατ' ἐξοκὴν, by the same denomination" (p. 378). See James R. Foster, "A Forgotten Noble Savage, Tsonnonthouan," *MLQ* 14 (1953): 348–59.

257. "greatest in his mind": Smollett probably intends not only an irony, but also a suggestion that Cumberland thought himself the "greatest."

258. "your Shakespeare . . . than other men": "Thou seest I have more flesh than another man, and therefore more frailty" (*1 Henry IV* 3.3.166–68).

259. "bowels": Pity, compassion, sympathy.

260. "sentimentize": To produce "sentiments," that is, weighty thoughts or sayings; to experience tender feelings.

261. "poultice of brain": Smollett may have taken the idea and wording from the *Memoirs and Adventures of Tsonnonthouan*, 23; see above, n. 256.

262. "many glorious exploits . . . on the continent": Cumberland distinguished himself in the War of the Austrian Succession; he was wounded at Dettingen, 1743,

and he displayed great gallantry at Fontenoy, 1745, though he was criticized for using poor judgment in the latter battle. See Davies, 210–11.

263. "he was sent . . . disaffection": In December 1745 Cumberland took command of the army against the Jacobites, who were attempting to place the Stuart Pretender on the throne. On 16 April 1746 the rebels were decisively defeated at Culloden Moor and the rebellion was effectively crushed. "Ximo" is Scotland; see key.

264. "his humanity emerged": This passage appears to describe what Cumberland should have done but did not do. Smollett first voiced his lifelong indignation at the aftermath of Culloden in the widely circulated ballad *The Tears of Scotland* (1746). In *Voltaire*, 1:72, 8:43 he went out of his way to allude to Cumberland's brutality, and in the *Complete History*, 4:673–74 he remarked: "One cannot reflect upon such a scene, without grief and horror." These passages caused much indignation in England. Horace Walpole wrote, in *George III*, 1:140: "an abusive Jacobite writer . . . [Smollett] had spoken most scurrilously of the Duke of Cumberland for suppressing the rebellion." But Cumberland's measures (massacres, burned houses, wholesale evictions, destruction of cattle) caused widespread revulsion. He was called "The Butcher"; see Print 2843*, and see W. A. Speck, *The Butcher* (Oxford: Basil Blackwell, 1981).

265. "voluntarily taxed themselves . . . the hero Quamba-cun-dono": On 4 June 1746 Parliament voted £25,000 per annum to Cumberland and his heirs.

266. "mercy is surely no attribute of the Japonese": While Smollett of course means the English, *UH*, 36 makes the same remark; see also *CR* 9 (September 1760): 190: "Travelers charge the Japanese with *cruelty*, and a *vindictive* disposition: all the world well knows that the English are *merciful* and *forgiving*."

267. "even as a hen gathereth her chickens": "O Jerusalem . . . how often would I have gathered thy children together, even as a hen gathereth her chickens under her wings, and ye would not!" (Matthew 23:37, the "*improperia*").

268. "crucifixion . . . exenteration": See *UH*, 40:367: "seventeen officers of the rebel army were hanged, drawn, and quartered at Kennington Common . . . nine were executed in the same manner at Carlisle, and eleven at York." See also *Present State*, 2:175: "a disgrace to humanity executed literally with every circumstance of barbarity."

269. "Obans . . . sterling": The oban, a Japanese coin, was "worth between 42 and 43 shillings sterling" (*UH*, 58).

270. "harrigals": Scottish dialect. Viscera.

271. "pope's eye": A gland, covered with fat, found in the middle of a leg of mutton.

272. "those animals . . . their own country": Smollett, while noting the poverty of Scotland, is imitating the satiric technique of Swift's *Modest Proposal* (1729), which advises cannibalizing the Irish.

273. "hard meat": Grain (for fattening) as opposed to grass or hay.

274. "You dog . . . liver": In *Roderick Random*, chapter 11, Captain Weazel says, "I'll have his liver for my supper."
275. "Americans": American Indians.
276. "Shakespear's cauldron . . . Jew": The Third Witch in *Macbeth* 4.1.26 mentions this ingredient.
277. "loathed . . . dead or alive": Smollett probably refers to the future animosity between Newcastle and Lord Bute.
278. "Gotto-mio . . . Xicoco": John Russell, duke of Bedford; see key. Bedford was made lord lieutenant of Ireland in 1756.
279. "his fortune": Bedford was one of the wealthiest men in England.
280. "declined . . . a kicking": In the autumn of 1755 Bedford declined the cabinet office of lord privy seal, which involved virtually no power or emolument.
281. "the council of Twenty Eight": The cabinet, in which Bedford held several posts at one time or another. *UH*, 29 describes the Japanese council. In Smollett's time the English cabinet was informally constituted, unlike the far less powerful privy council; the usual maximum number of members was from ten to fourteen, and there was often an "inner cabinet" or "conciliabulum" of four to six members. See below, vol. 2, n. 14; and for a table of cabinet incumbents, 1742–70, see Betty Kemp, *Sir Francis Dashwood* (London: Macmillan, 1967), 196–200.
282. "his œconomy so sordid": Horace Walpole says of Bedford, in *George III*, 4:163: "he ruined his tradesmen, paid nobody, and sold a place that was *not* vacant, during only six weeks that he was Lord Lieutenant of Ireland."
283. "a cross . . . Kow-kin": Richard Rigby; see key. See also *Complete History*, 3:125–26: "a gibbet was erected for one gentleman in particular"; and see Walpole, *George II*, 3:87: "their greatest fury was intended against Rigby. . . . The mob prepared a gallows, and were determined to hang Rigby on it: but, fortunately, that morning he had gone out of town to ride, and received timely notice not to return."
284. "his patron soon followed him": Bedford returned to England, here called Niphon (see key), in May 1758.
285. "Soo-san-sin-o": John Carteret, Earl Granville; see key. Carteret was lord president of the cabinet from 1751 until his death in 1763.
286. "macerated in one alembic": Softened or digested by soaking together in a single retort or distilling vessel.
287. "The Dairo . . . in private": Carteret, a man of great charm who spoke fluent German, regularly accompanied George II on his visits to Hanover. He virtually directed foreign policy until 1744, when Newcastle and his brother Henry threatened wholesale resignations, thereby forcing the king, much against his will, to dismiss Carteret as secretary of state. Early in 1746, after mass resignations and at the king's urging, Carteret vainly tried to form a government. Thereafter he kept apart from ministerial quarrels, but maintained a close and friendly relationship with the king; he may be said to have replaced Queen

Caroline, who died in 1737, as George's principal confidant. See Basil Williams, *Carteret and Newcastle* (London: Frank Cass, 1966).

288. *"ex officio"*: As an entitlement of his office.

289. "laughed and quaffed": In later life Carteret had the deserved reputation of being a frivolous drunkard.

290. "the celebrated table of Cebes": Cebes, a disciple of Socrates, figures in the Platonic Dialogues. The *pinax* or table attributed to him, a staple of teaching in both elementary Greek and moral doctrine for the eighteenth century, is an elaborate *ekphrasis* or systematic rhetorical description of an imaginary picture, in this case filled with allegorical figures. The table is divided into three "courts": the lowest, "the sensual life," contains the gate of birth and the individual's directing genius, along with Delusion, Fortune, lewdness, avidity, punishment, anguish; the second court, "the studious life," includes wisdom and fancy together with seducers of and aids to wisdom; the third, "the virtuous life," exhibits knowledge, fortitude, health, temperance. See Earl Wasserman, "Johnson's *Rasselas*: Implicit Contexts," *JEGP* 74 (1975): 1–26, for a detailed description of the table of Cebes and an account of how thoroughly its figures informed conventional wisdom in Smollett's time.

291. "what was objected to the philosopher": Smollett apparently refers to criticism of Cebes' table for its lack of organization; the nature and source of such criticism have not been traced.

292. "invention": In classical rhetoric, the first step in composition: selection of topics to treat or arguments to use.

293. "sauntering, strolling, vagrant": Smollett here appropriates the legal terminology used to describe beggars, unattached actors, and other itinerant undesirables.

294. "All was bellowing . . . uproar": Smollett echoes Pope's *Dunciad* 2.237–42.

295. "the ΔΑΙΜΩΝ, or Genius": The tutelary spirit accompanying each newborn soul in the table of Cebes; here also in the sense of intelligence or ingenuity.

296. "the round stone": The ball or globe on which Fortune emblematically totters.

297. "καλῶς μηνύει φῦσιν αὐτῆς": Gr. Fairly shows her nature.

298. "Deception tendering the cup of ignorance": The figure is so depicted in the table of Cebes, though Smollett may be remembering the beginning of Pope's analogous portrayal of Sir Robert Walpole in *Dunciad* 4.517: "With that a Wizard old his cup extends."

299. "groupe of true education . . . grove of happiness": "Groupe" is a variant of "group," but in the spelling Smollett uses here the word was frequently understood as a technical term in painting. The "groupe" and the "grove" are represented in the table of Cebes as within the topmost court of the virtuous life.

300. "two factions . . . council": Smollett alludes to the factions of Newcastle-Hardwicke-Anson and of Cumberland-Fox-Bedford, who divided both "council" and "counsel."

301. "as St. Paul saith . . . things not seen": "Now faith is . . . the evidence of things not seen" (Hebrews 11:1). See also below, n. 676.

302. "without hesitation, or mental reservation": This language suggests the terminology of an imposed oath certifying the religious orthodoxy of ordinands or candidates for office.

303. "I believe in the White Horse": The passage that follows parodies both the Athanasian Creed, as in the Book of Common Prayer, and the language of the Thirty-Nine Articles.

304. "Jeddo, which is the land of promise": Jeddo is Continental Europe; see key, JEDDO, and also YESSO. The phrase "land of promise" echoes Hebrews 11:9, "[By faith Abraham] dwelt in the land of promise"; see also Numbers 14:20 and Deuteronomy 9:28, 19:8.

305. "begot by a black mule": Mules are sterile.

306. "hoofs are of brass": A favorite material for the thighs (Daniel 2:32), hoofs (Micah 4:13), or feet (Revelations 1:15) of biblical creatures of prophecy. Allusions to brass were commonly used to represent ministerial impudence, especially in many earlier anti-Walpole political satires; see Mack, 131–32.

307. "that he eats gold . . . diamonds as dung": A reference to the vast sums consumed by Hanover. Print 3592 shows a white horse evacuating coins, while Print 3069* pictures the horse feeding on the blood of Britannia.

308. "the people of Jeddo . . . litter": Smollett often uses "Jeddo" to mean Hanover as well as Europe or Germany.

309. "practically": In fact, feasibly.

310. "devoting": Setting aside for sacrifice or religious uses.

311. "tenets . . . thirty-nine articles": Smollett refers to eighteenth-century controversies arising from cases of conscience or of possible unscrupulousness among clergy expected to subscribe to the articles. Some refused; some who subscribed were thought to have done so hypocritically. Here "glib" means smoothly, without obstruction.

312. "to philosophize like H——e, or dogmatize like S——tt": Smollett refers to the *History of Great Britain* (1754–57), by David Hume, and to his own *Complete History*. Both works were accused of Tory or even Jacobite bias; see, for example, the review by Owen Ruffhead in the *Monthly Review* 18 (April 1758): 289–305. Hume puzzled the critics of his day by introducing social and cultural history, by writing to exemplify his own political philosophy, and by taking into account the influence of political psychology on events; see Duncan Forbes, ed., *Hume: The History of Great Britain* (Harmondsworth: Penguin, 1970), 14–16. A very favorable review of both histories appeared in *CR* 13 (January 1762): 60, but it was not without echoes of such objections: Hume's "sometimes paradoxical positions, extreme refinement, and philosophising talent, gave offence"; Smollett is "more varied in style" and reminds one of Seneca, but "is disagreeably sententious."

313. "Taliessin and Geoffrey of Monmouth": Taliessin, the perhaps legendary bard supposed to have flourished c. A.D. 550, is associated with early Welsh heroic poems; Geoffrey (d. 1155) introduced King Arthur and King Lear into history with his *Historia regum Britanniæ* (c. 1140), a work almost devoid of value as "history" in the modern sense.

314. "The whole world . . . six good historians": Smollett's short digression on historians may have been inspired by a similar parodic list in the fifth of John Arbuthnot's *John Bull* pamphlets, *Lewis Baboon Turned Honest* (1712), which mentions Herodotus, Thucydides, Livy, Tacitus, Davila, and Sarpi, or "Fra. Paulo." See Alan W. Bower and Robert A. Erickson, eds., *John Arbuthnot: The History of John Bull* (Oxford: Clarendon Press, 1976), 93, 236–67.

315. "Herodotus is fabulous . . . Sarpi, truth": Smollett, with some irony, apparently expects his reader's responses to the Atom's views of these several historians to vary. Herodotus (c. 480–c. 425 B.C.), the "father of history," reports many fantastic things but is scrupulous in giving his sources and estimating their credibility. Thucydides (c. 460–c. 400 B.C.), the historian of the Peloponnesian War, has a dense but precise style, here called "perplexed," or complicated; Smollett possibly plays upon a review of his own *Complete History* in *CR* 3 (June 1757): 482: "Smollett has imitated Thucydides in weight and conciseness of diction." Polybius (c. 204–c. 122 B.C.), the historian of Rome, was regarded in antiquity as unimaginative, unpolished, and too colloquial in style, though reliable. Livy or Titus Livius (59 B.C.–A.D. 17), was considered elegant but inaccurate; *CR*, in the review already cited, praises Smollett as richly descriptive, imitating "Livy in painting." Cornelius Tacitus (c. A.D. 55–c. 117) is proverbial for elliptical concision. Smollett's characterization of Tacitus is ironic; Johnson's *Dictionary* defines a coxcomb as "a superficial pretender to knowledge or accomplishments." Francesco Guicciardini (1483–1540) was the author of an important history of Italy, a translation of which (attributed to Oliver Goldsmith) received extravagant praise, along with an acknowledgment of Guicciardini's reputation for tediousness, in a review in *CR* 8 (August 1759): 89–95; the earlier review of Smollett's *Complete History* noted its successful imitation of Guicciardini in "drawing characters." Enrico Davila (1576–1631), who wrote a history of the civil wars in France, was criticized in *CR* 4 (December 1757): 473–74 for a style "harsh and embarrassed" and "often tediously circumstantial"; Smollett offers a similar objection here with his remark that Davila wants "digestion," or proper ordering and condensation. Paolo Sarpi (1552–1623), author of a famous history of the Council of Trent, was of a pronounced anti-papal bias; Smollett shared this bias, and his suggestion that Sarpi wants "truth" is thus clearly ironic.

316. "one hundred and fifty four": 1754, the year of the first overt hostilities between the French and British colonists in North America.

317. "the incroachments of the Chinese . . . ridicule and contempt": For Smollett's

comments on the hostilities as a historian, see *Continuation*, 1:173–78, *Voltaire*, 6:71, and *British Magazine* 1 (January 1760): 45–47, "The History of the Present War." In contravention of agreements, the French had begun to build a chain of forts along the Ohio. At the end of 1753 Governor Dinwiddie of Virginia sent Major George Washington with a message of protest to the commandant of a fort near Lake Erie, but without result. See Fortescue, 271.

318. "some skirmishes . . . various success": Washington had been sent to destroy Fort Duquesne, located at the point where the Monongahela and Allegheny rivers join to form the Ohio. He won the first engagement but was defeated in the second, at Fort Necessity (Great Meadows), May 1754. See Fortescue, 272–73, and Walpole, *George II*, 2:18.

319. "When the tidings . . . fear and confusion": The news of Washington's defeat at Great Meadows reached London in August 1754; for the reactions in the government, and especially for Newcastle's reaction, see Browning, 207.

320. "the island of Fatsissio": North America, or more properly its northeast areas; see key.

321. "only three members . . . empire of Japan": While secretary of state for the southern department in the 1740s, Newcastle had fostered a policy of "salutary neglect" toward the American colonies; see Browning, 301. Throughout Smollett's nonfictional writings he inveighs at every opportunity against such indifference, as he saw it, to valuable commercial resources.

322. "Fika-kaka . . . kissed him . . . council": This is a version of the "Cape Breton is an island" incident figuring in *Humphry Clinker*, Jery Melford to Sir Watkin Phillips, London, June 2. On the subject of Newcastle's ignorance of geography, see above, n. 134.

323. "the law of nature and nations": A translation of the title of Samuel Pufendorf's classic treatise *De jure naturae et gentium* (1672). See below, vol. 2, n. 197.

324. "intercepting the succours . . . Fatsissio": On 27 April 1755 Admiral Boscawen was dispatched to head off the French fleet, which had left Brest and Rochefort for America. He was also instructed to attack any French ships he might encounter. See Corbett, 1:43–44. As is clear from this passage, Smollett strongly disapproved of privateering; he expresses similar views at several points in the *Continuation*.

325. "Koan . . . selected for this service": Koan is General Edward Braddock; see key. Braddock, a man of sixty at the time (1755), had been promoted chiefly on seniority; his only service of note had been at the siege of Bergen-op-Zoom, 1746.

326. "he let loose . . . prisoners": By the end of 1755 British ships had taken some three hundred French merchant ships and some eight thousand crewmen; see Corbett, 1:83.

327. "the Chinese exclaimed . . . astonishment": See *Continuation*, 1:346–48 for Smollett's "official" attitude, which, despite his objections to privateering, was decidedly anti-French.

328. "to cruise in the open sea . . . winter night": In May 1755 Boscawen's fleet proceeded to the vicinity of Newfoundland to prevent the French from landing troops at Louisbourg; see Corbett, 1:43–44.

329. "General Koan . . . unseen enemy": Braddock, a favorite of Cumberland, was well known as a haughty martinet. Although his orders warned of the possibility of ambush, he insisted on marching as though on an open plain; his Indian scouts had already deserted in disgust. On 9 July 1755, seven miles from Fort Duquesne, his troops were ambushed and slaughtered by French and Indian snipers in an engagement lasting two hours. Braddock died of wounds on 13 July. See Fortescue, 274–87. Here "shambles" means slaughterhouse.

330. "changing their course . . . distemper": Admiral de la Motte went into the Saint Lawrence by Belle Isle Strait, a somewhat unusual route. He thus eluded Boscawen, though on 10 June the British took the French ships *Alcide* and *Lys*, thus beginning formal naval hostilities. Typhoid decimated the British fleet, and news of the disaster reached London in July. See Corbett, 1:53–57.

331. "like a goose disturbed": Newcastle, not the king, was often depicted in the prints as a goose, partly because of his association with Fox. See Prints 3330 ("A Goose of old did save a State"), 3398, 3412, 3469.

332. "congelation": Freezing so as to cause numbness. The term was often used to describe the numbness of paralysis.

333. "Day": Nobleman; see key.

334. "the fish called Torpor": The electric ray or electric eel, also called "torpedo." See *Compendium*, 7:343–44: "whoever happens to touch this fish, feels an instantaneous numbness diffuse itself through his whole body." The same fish is mentioned in Admiral Anson's narrative, *A Voyage Round the World* (1748), 266.

335. "adopted by Fahrnheit": The scale of temperature measurement and the mercury thermometer of Daniel Fahrenheit (1686–1736) were rapidly adopted in England during and after the 1720s. Smollett mentions Fahrenheit in Letter 24 of his *Travels* (p. 197).

336. "The Dairo consoled himself . . . glory of Japan": George II, the last English monarch to lead troops into battle (at Dettingen, 17 June 1743) and a man of physical courage, was notorious for his delight in uniform design, in parades, and in classical military evolutions. Throughout his reign he insisted on maintaining personal supervision of the army, including promotions, and he enjoyed the smallest military details.

337. "The Fatzman assured him . . . troops formed under my direction": Cumberland was devoted to classical military theory, and was much criticized for introducing Continental discipline and procedures into the English army. Extremely unimaginative, he was firmly convinced that colonial troops had no discipline and were worthless. See Browning, 230.

338. "hollow square . . . potence": The military formation of the hollow square was retained in the British army throughout the nineteenth century. The potence was a formation created by a line of troops standing at right angles to the main body.

339. "we shall be . . . another occasion": Smollett perhaps echoes Braddock's dying words, "Another time we shall know better how to deal with them." See Davies, 301.

340. "a number of bloodhounds . . . impediments": A reference to Cumberland's stubborn resistance to the unorthodox use of Indian scouts and irregular colonial troops.

341. "the bed of honour": The battlefield.

342. "several conquests in Fastsissio": Indians, incited by the French, made incursions into Virginia, Maryland, and Pennsylvania. On 14 August 1756 General Montcalm took Oswego in New York, of vital importance because of its location. See *Continuation*, 1:360–61.

343. "specious remonstrances . . . perfidy and piracy": See above, n. 327.

344. "Motao . . . in a former war": Motao is Minorca; see key. Spain had ceded the island to England by the Treaty of Utrecht, 1713.

345. "repeated advices . . . Japan": On 25 February 1756 an intercepted dispatch from Bunge, the Swedish minister to Paris, alerted the government to the threat against Minorca, but ships were not sent out until 1 April; see Corbett, 1:84–85. British naval forces were inadequate, and an invasion of southern England was also feared; see Browning, 232–33.

346. "infatuation": In the sense of "utter folly."

347. "Americans": American Indians.

348. "the ephod, the urim and the thummim": The ephod was a sleeveless garment slit at the sides, worn by Hebrew priests. The urim and thummim, part of the high priest's regalia, apparently were decorations (perhaps jewels) worn on the breastplate. See Exodus 28.

349. "a new law . . . the keys": Hardwicke's Marriage Act of 1753, intended to correct many abuses, required banns, licenses, and witnesses for a valid marriage and prevented clandestine, abductive, or coercive unions. The legislation was violently opposed. See Print 3336, "Hymen Fettered"; see also *PH*, 15:1–86, and John Shebbeare's novel, *The Marriage Act* (1754). For Smollett's views see *Continuation*, 1:145–49.

350. "sea-lion . . . golden gudgeons": An allusion to Admiral Anson's avarice and passion for gambling. The gudgeon, a small freshwater fish, was known for its eagerness to swallow anything; hence the term "gudgeon" as proverbial for a person easily cheated. "Golden," or "Chinese gudgeon," was also the standard term at the time for goldfish. See Prints 3394*, 3424, 3535.

351. "*One did laugh . . . murder*": *Macbeth* 2.2.20, the scene in which Macbeth tells of Duncan's grooms.

352. "felt the teeth . . . Bonza": If Newcastle's dream has a specific as well as a general satiric point, it may refer to events of May 1757 when the king, exasperated with the duke's dawdling in forming a new government, took revenge by making ecclesiastical appointments without consulting him. See Browning, 259.

353. "places, and reversions": Places were government posts, often lucrative sinecures, offered as political rewards; reversions, the rights to such posts after
they were vacated by incumbents.

354. "laid fast hold on the trunk-breeches of the Cuboy": In September 1755 Fox was
rewarded for expediting Commons business by being made secretary of state,
southern department. At the time this appointment was erroneously considered
dangerous to Newcastle's power and indicative of his capitulation to the Fox-
Cumberland faction. See Browning, 227.

355. "fundamentals": The genitals.

356. "Foutao": Gibraltar; see key, and see below, n. 359.

357. "Bihn-goh . . . any act of valour": Bihn-goh is Admiral John Byng; see key.
Byng's naval career, though long, had been spent entirely in routine duties.
Anson favored him, though Newcastle was unhappy with the choice. See
Browning, 233.

358. "ill manned . . . fleet of China": Byng was given only ten ships, primarily
because of other priorities and the inadequate size of the navy at the time.

359. "orders sent . . . obeyed": Nob-o-di is Viscount Barrington; see key. In the
Continuation, 1:348–53, Smollett comments at length on the confusion of orders,
reproducing four letters sent to Lieutenant-General Thomas Fowke, the military governor of Gibraltar, 21 March–12 May 1756. These letters indicate that a
battalion was to be detached for Byng if invasion of Minorca seemed likely;
Fowke, knowing that the French had already landed several thousand troops on
the island, maintained that he could not detach troops for Byng and retain a
sufficient force to defend Gibraltar.

360. "invested": Cut off and besieged.

361. "Both commanders . . . by consent": Admiral de la Galissonnière, the French
commander, was as indecisive as Byng. On 20–21 May 1756, one English division attacked the French but the rest did not; Byng, after hesitating for hours
while the French ships made off, at last sailed in pursuit, but too late for any
possibility of overtaking them. He then returned to Gibraltar. See Continuation,
1:319–22.

362. "Fi-de-ta-da . . . Chinese general": Fi-de-ta-da is General William Blakeney,
then governor of Minorca; see key. After a valiant defense of seventy days,
Blakeney surrendered Fort Saint Philip on 28 June 1756. On his return to
England he was celebrated as a popular hero, made a knight of the Bath, and
created a baron.

363. "on the back of": Immediately following.

364. "the ministry had almost sunk . . . had been betrayed": Smollett does not exaggerate here; see Browning, 235–36, and Prints 3367–3396.

365. "the terror of an invasion": See Continuation, 1:307–14. The French had fortified
Dunkirk and ordered British subjects to leave, while concentrating troops and
ships at Brest. At the end of March 1756, Parliament approved the use of Hes-

sian troops for defense and Fox asked for further authorization to use twelve battalions of Hanoverians.

366. "trunk hose": Underdrawers.

367. "postern of his microcosm": The rear or private "door" to the body seen as a miniature of the universe; hence, the anus.

368. "barbal abstersion": Cleaning, wiping, or purging with the beard. Smollett may have borrowed the phrase from the *Memoirs and Adventures of Tsonnonthouan*, 33; see above, n. 256.

369. "a dissertation on trousers or trunk breeches": Smollett doubtless alludes both to Walter Shandy's learned researches into breeches on his son's behalf and to the absurdly pedantic *De re vestiaria veterum* ("On the Clothing of the Ancients"), by Rubenius, son of the painter Rubens; see *Tristram Shandy*, volume 6, chapter 19. The word περίζωματα (actually "girdles" but used by Sterne so as to suggest "codpiece") occurs in "Slawkenbergius's Tale" at the beginning of *Tristram Shandy*, volume 4.

370. "called by the Greeks . . . bra-ak": Except for the fabricated Japanese word, these are reasonably correct approximations of the terms used in the various languages for breeches, long trousers, or leggings.

371. "Περιζωματα and Ζωνιον γυναιχεῖον": Gr. Girdle and woman's girdle, or sash.

372. "cingulum muliebre": L. Woman's girdle.

373. "orgia": L. Equally "secret ceremonies," or "orgies."

374. "pro tempore": L. For the occasion.

375. "shim . . . black ladies in Guinea": A shim is a smock; the term itself, according to Wright, is a shortened form of *chemise*. *UH*, 13:460–61 refers to the loincloths worn by women in Guinea, but gives their name as "paan."

376. "Persius . . . porticus": Aulus Persius Flaccus (A.D. 34–62) writes in his third satire of "the portico painted with trousered Medes" (lines 53–54). The Stoa, or Painted Portico (where the Stoics taught), was decorated with scenes of the wars of Athens against the Medes and Persians.

377. "Gomanaus": Almost certainly a misprint for "Gomerians." See *UH*, 4:314, 315, 329, and William Maitland, *The History and Antiquities of Scotland* (1757), 1:33. According to these sources the Gomerians were a tribe descended from Gomer, eldest son of Japhet; the historian Josephus (in *Antiquitates Judaicæ*, A.D. 93/4) claimed that the Celtæ descended from Gomer; and Old Celtic, or Gomerian, was still spoken in the mountains of Scotland.

378. "Jamblychus . . . Abaris . . . wore long trousers": Jamblychus, or Iamblichus, was the author of a life of Pythagoras; see above, n. 83. In chapter 28 of the life Iamblichus says that Abaris was a Scythian, priest of Apollo among the Hyperboreans; he does not say that Abaris wore long trousers. Smollett may have had in mind John Toland's posthumous *History of the Druids* (1740), 215; Toland identified Abaris as a Scottish druid and repeated a claim by the orator Himerius (c.

A. D. 310–90) that Abaris wore trousers reaching from the soles of his feet to his waist. A review by Smollett of James Macpherson's *Fingal* (1761) in *CR* 12 (December 1761): 407 refers to "the famous Hyperborean philosopher *Abaris*, supposed to have been a Highlander, celebrated by Herodian, Diodorus Siculus, Jamblichus." See Basker, 227, 266–67.

379. "expose their posteriors to the wind": By wearing kilts.

380. "unbreeched by the Romans": Conquered and therefore obliged to adopt Roman dress; but also made effeminate.

381. "Brigantes, *quasi Brigantes . . . Brag-Brag*": The Latin name "brigantes" was given to the northernmost British tribes subdued by the Romans. This passage is a learned spoof, though it does not depart significantly from many serious conjectural etymologies of Smollett's day. "Brag-brag," according to Wright, was a vulgar challenge of defiance; clapping the hands to one's buttocks was a common obscene gesture, as many of the period's satirical prints indicate.

382. "the shield of Ajax . . . Dutch skipper": *Iliad* 7.245 (Pope's translation):

> Huge was its orb, with seven thick folds o'ercast,
> Of tough bull-hides.

Dutch breeches were either padded or made with several layers of fabric.

383. "Cloacina . . . this kingdom": Cloacina was a name originally given to Venus as patroness of purification, but early associated with *cloaca*, sewer; hence, for the eighteenth century the name denoted a goddess of defecation and privies, as in Gay's *Trivia* and Pope's *Dunciad*. Smollett's joking reference to the differing rites of worship in north and south echoes the common canard that the Scots (and Irish) did not use privies. See Print 3988*, "Sawney in the Bog-House," and see also *Briton*, no. 15 (4 September 1762): 86: "I expect to see the nobles of this land appearing at court without breeches, like so many Highland chiefs . . . there will not be one single temple of Cloacina left in England . . . ."

384. "*sed . . . locus*": L. "But this is not the place for these matters." Quoted (inaccurately) from Horace *Ars Poetica* 19. Smollett may be thinking of Swift's device, in *Tale of a Tub*, of suddenly breaking off just as he is about to "solve" a profound mystery.

385. "Linschot . . . the Chinese": Jan Huygen van Linschoten was a sixteenth-century explorer and geographer. Smollett's mistake about the name shows the closeness of his dependence on the *Universal History*, whose error he repeats; see *UH*, 104, n. a, "Vide LINSCHOT. itiner.," and 105, n. (c), "*Linschott*." Smollett playfully reverses the *Universal History* interpretation of Linschoten's theory.

386. "Dr. Kempfer . . . Babel": Kaempfer, *History*, 1:86–87, 90–92 makes this conjecture, which is quoted and dismissed in *UH*, 105. "Confusion": the confusion of tongues, followed by the dispersion of the builders of Babel; see Genesis 11.

387. "*Braccatorum filii . . .* progenitors": The Latin phrase means "sons of the

breeched ones." See *UH*, 60, for a description of Japanese men as they were dressed in the formal kimono (still worn today): the lower part of the kimono made them appear to "wear wide breeches like the Chinese."

388. "the face and attitude . . . the Dutch taste": When the apostle Paul was summoned before the Roman governor Felix he defended himself with such force that "Felix trembled"; see Acts 24:24–25. On 27 November 1754 Pitt confronted William Murray, the future Lord Mansfield, in a famous attack certainly well known to Smollett, accusing Murray of having harbored Jacobite sentiments; see key, MURA-CLAMI. On this occasion Pitt exclaimed, making a slight error, "Methinks Judge Festus trembles"; see Williams, 1:273. Smollett may have been drawn to Hogarth's famous print by a personal connection, for the minor character Tertullus is said to be Hogarth's caricature of Alexander Hume Campbell, with whom Smollett had quarreled; see *Letters*, 21. Hogarth, having executed a large painting of the subject for the Inns of Court, exhibited it for the benefit of a charity. The tickets for the exhibition included a print caricaturing the same scene, called "Paul Before Felix Burlesqu'd," in which Felix has clearly beshit himself and various spectators are holding their noses; see Print 3173*. Smollett writes in *Sir Launcelot Greaves*, chapter 12, of "the same unsavory effects, that are humourously delineated by the inimitable Hogarth in the print of Felix on his tribunal, done in the Dutch stile." The epithet "Dutch" indicated a contrast to the grand, or Italian style, and suggested low or trifling subject matter or preoccupation with petty details.

389. "a long tube": Probably a sarcastic reference to the well-known lorgnon or quizzing-glass constantly used by Newcastle. See Prints 3371*, 4159*.

390. "Daygos": Nobles; see key. Smollett may be attempting a mock version of the conventional address to "Dukes, Marquesses, Earls, and Barons."

391. "watched and fasted": "Watch and pray that ye enter not into temptation: the spirit indeed is willing but the flesh is weak" (Matthew 26:41). See also Mark 13:33, 14:38.

392. "my chief cook": The famous Cloué; see above, n. 141, and see Print 2684.

393. "olio à la Chine": A stew, ragout, or casserole, highly seasoned. Smollett again derides Newcastle's fashionable taste for French cookery, perhaps with a reminiscence of *Tale of a Tub* 9, "A Digression on Digressions."

394. "have watched . . . should sleep": The other sense of the phrase is found in *Tale of a Tub* 10, where Swift refers to his reader, "for whose benefit I wake when others sleep and sleep when others wake." The joke is that Swift, like Newcastle, is putting others to sleep by his dullness. The ultimate source for both Swift and Smollett is Lucretius *De rerum natura* 1:141–42, where the poet tells of staying at his task late into the night so that his patron might be enabled to understand the complexities of the Epicurean philosophy and thus enjoy sleep untroubled by fear.

395. "fasted that they should feed": Smollett, *Advice* (1746), lines 15–16:

> When sage *Newcastle*, abstinently great,
> Neglects his food to cater for the state. . . .

396. "ejaculated": A triple pun. As used here the word suggests a short prayer suddenly uttered, a sexual ejaculation, and Newcastle's habitual manner of speech.

397. "Matsuris . . . religious rites": Smollett translates the Japanese word. No specific reference is intended, though Smollett alludes to Newcastle's abiding interest in ecclesiastical affairs. *UH*, 122 refers to "*Matsuri's*, or solemn feasts and religious processions." The modern word is the same.

398. "headed the multitude . . . ragamuffins in Japan": Newcastle's alleged wholesale bribery and lavish entertainments at borough elections were the subject of much ridicule; see Browning, 28–35, 183–88. "Headed" probably refers to managing the Commons.

399. "O happy nation . . . ha! ha! ha!": The parody of Newcastle's incoherent speech here reaches its climax.

400. "*ab anteriori*": L. From before. The implication is that Newcastle could utter nothing more from his mouth but could still "speak" through his anus. A review of volumes 5 and 6 of *Tristram Shandy*, *CR* 13 (January 1762): 68 compares Sterne to Rabelais and remarks: "'tes paroles sont brayes.' That is, not a language spoken *ab anteriori*."

401. "The Dairo . . . bring it up": The king's undignified pugnacity was much satirized. On one occasion in December 1736, anxious to return from Hanover, he was delayed in the royal yacht by a storm and kicked his hat about the deck in a paroxysm of rage. See Mack, 130; and see Print 2326, "Aeneas in a Storm."

402. "big": Pregnant.

403. "suffered severely . . . a former occasion": In September 1747 at the Lichfield races, during a riot by Jacobite sympathizers and their opponents, Bedford was horsewhipped by an attorney named Hector Humphrey while his aide Rigby was cudgelled. See Print 2863, and see *Continuation*, 1:37.

404. "a many headed monster": The "Hydra of Faction" was an eighteenth-century satirical cliché for the mob; the image derived from the monster slain by Hercules, its heads redoubling as fast as cut off. Here, Smollett probably makes a punning reference to Pope, *Epistle to Augustus*, line 305, on the mob as theater audience: "the many-headed Monster of the Pit." Smollett regarded Pitt as the chief manipulator of the mob.

405. "Cerberus . . . sop": Cerberus, the triple-headed dog that guarded the gate of Hades, could be temporarily diverted by a sop, as in *Aeneid* 6:417 or in the legend of Cupid and Psyche.

406. "a whale . . . amusement": A well-known figure; the *locus classicus* is the preface

to Swift's *Tale of a Tub*. Smollett employed the figure in *Continuation*, 1:323, referring to Byng as scapegoat. Here and elsewhere in the *Atom* Smollett uses "amusement" in the sense of diverting someone's attention from something with which he or she should be concerned.

407. "brief let me be": Spoken by the Ghost in *Hamlet* 1.5.59.

408. "solemn promises . . . justice shall be done": Perhaps an allusion to the notorious occasion when Newcastle, in a state of panic, babbled to a deputation from the city of London that Byng "shall be tried immediately—he shall be hanged directly." See Browning, 236, and Walpole, *George II*, 2:166.

409. "let us employ . . . continual fuel": Most of this passage consists of verbatim transcriptions or paraphrases of the wording of *Continuation*, 1:323. The description of Bihn-goh, or Byng, as a "devoted" officer is ironic in that the word also implies "set aside for sacrifice."

410. "Bihn-goh . . . close prison": On 26 July 1756, when he arrived in England, Byng was arrested and confined to Greenwich Naval Hospital.

411. "Agents were employed . . . burn him in effigie": This sentence reproduces almost verbatim material in the *Continuation*, 1:323, and *CR* 2 (October 1756): 257 (by Smollett; Basker, 222).

412. "a public trial . . . recommended to mercy": Byng's court martial, conducted by members appropriate to his rank, lasted from 28 December 1756 to 27 January 1757. The court found him guilty of failing to do his duty according to the provisions of the twelfth article of war, for which the punishment was death. Having found no cowardice or disaffection, the court recommended mercy. Although a great controversy arose over the issue of capital punishment for mere misconduct, the king, in the absence of recommendations to the contrary from the administration, refused mercy. Pitt, pleading for Byng's life, was brutally snubbed by the king. For details of these events see Browning, 257, Davies, 315–17, and *PH*, 15:803–27.

413. "crucified for cowardice . . . heroic courage": At noon on 14 March 1757 Byng was shot on the quarterdeck of the *Monarque*. At first he refused to be blindfolded, but on being told that the firing squad would be disconcerted he permitted it, himself giving the signal to fire. *Continuation*, 1:470–80, gives a detailed and indignant account of the trial and its sequels. See also *CR* 6 (August 1758):109: "Crucifying is a very common punishment among them at Japan." This passage is from a review by Smollett of John Entick's *A New Naval History* (Basker, 224, 245); Smollett, Basker finds, wrote most or all of the *Critical*'s reviews of materials concerning the Byng case.

414. "that Bihn-goh had bribed . . . in his stead": This apparently fantastic report may be based on Smollett's remembering the doctrines of the Basilidian heresy; see below, n. 705.

415. "calculated . . . Japonese populace": The phrase "calculated for the meridian," meaning precisely designed to appeal to a given person or persons, is a favorite

locution of Smollett. The judgment here echoes Smollett's account of a famous remark concerning Byng made by Voltaire, who said that the English "kill an admiral from time to time to encourage the others": "we have heard this in twenty companies"; see *Voltaire*, 18:54.

416. "the Chinese . . . an invasion": On the invasion scare see *Continuation*, 1: 307–13.

417. "the Tartars of Yesso": The inhabitants of Hanover; see key, YESSO.

418. "brought them over . . . dominions": In April 1756 several thousand Hanoverian and Hessian mercenaries arrived to supplement the inadequate British armed forces; see *Continuation*, 1:310–13, and Browning, 231.

419. "nursed among them": George II was thirty when he saw England for the first time in 1714, the year of his father's accession to the throne.

420. "His father . . . farm in that country": George I became elector of Hanover in 1698. Pitt, during his anti-Hanoverian episodes in Parliament, sarcastically referred to Hanover as "the Farm"; see John Timbs, *Anecdote Biography* (London: R. Bentley, 1860), 134. Smollett, an early admirer of Pitt, would have been familiar with his characterization of Hanover.

421. "a cabin": The electoral palace and estate of Herrenhausen, which in fact were very large, impressive, and famed for their beauty. See *Present State*, 4:247–48; see also Davies, 1–2, and Hatton, 47–48, 97–98. To the consternation of their advisers both George II and his father insisted on spending several months of the year in Hanover when circumstances did not positively preclude such visits; a council of regency had to be set up each time.

422. "manners": Customs, habits.

423. "mustachios": An allusion to George II's fondness for "spit-and-polish." Moustaches at the time were worn almost exclusively by Continental military men, as many contemporary prints indicate.

424. "at first, they were received . . . look in the face." This passage is a heightened version of the account in *Continuation*, 1:312.

425. "artists": Artisans; "those skilled at a particular [manual] art" (Johnson, *Dictionary*).

426. "caught the Tartar": Proverbial phrase: an intended victim proves formidable and can neither be controlled nor got rid of.

427. "wolves . . . sheep": An allusion to a fable of Aesop.

428. "bell-weather": Bellwether, a castrated ram wearing a bell, the leader of the flock; hence Newcastle.

429. "sent home in disgrace": The mercenaries returned to Germany in January 1757.

430. "tribunal of the populace": The House of Commons.

431. "one Taycho": William Pitt; see key.

432. "college": In the sense of a collective body or assembly.

433. "an unabashed countenance": After lengthy and violent opposition to various

administration measures, Pitt was made joint vice-treasurer of Ireland on 22 February 1746. On 8 April he rose in defense of the administration's proposal to hire 18,000 Hanoverians for duty in Flanders, blandly saying that he could speak with "an unembarrassed countenance." In the same year Sir Charles Hanbury Williams published a widely circulated satirical ballad with Pitt's phrase as its title. Pitt's speech also gave rise to a political cartoon; see Print 2854*. For full discussion of the speech see Davies, 248–49, and Williams, 1:147–48.

434. "an intrepidity of opposition . . . Cuboy": Smollett remarks in *Continuation*, 1:424 that Pitt had "upon sundry occasions, combated the gigantic plan of continental connections with all the strength of reason, and all the powers of eloquence."

435. "personal sarcasms . . . Dairo himself": Pitt's sarcastic treatment of George II, considered very daring, provoked a detestation that abated only when, in 1759, the king was won over to Pitt's policies and conduct of the Seven Years' War. The *Gentleman's Magazine* 14 (1744) quotes Pitt's remark that "[Britain] is considered only as a province to a despicable Electorate" (p. 77), adding his mocking comment on the king's "yearly visits to that delightful country [Hanover]" (p. 119). Pitt, according to the *Gentleman's Magazine*, opposed an address of thanks to the king after the battle of Dettingen, "more than insinuated" that reports of the king's personal courage there were untrue, and derided the king's "ridiculous, ungrateful, and perfidious Partiality [for Hanover]" (p. 119).

436. "he generally happened to be on the right side": Smollett was a fervent admirer of Pitt until about 1760, when he finally became convinced that Pitt was hopelessly committed to the Continental connection. See Lewis M. Knapp, "Smollett and the Elder Pitt," *Modern Language Notes* 59 (1944): 250–57.

437. "this Cerberus . . . sop": See above, n. 405. In addition to being vice-treasurer of Ireland, Pitt was made paymaster of the forces (considered the most lucrative post in the government) in May 1746 on the death of Sir Thomas Winnington, the incumbent. Pitt vastly enhanced his reputation for incorruptibility by depositing the funds entrusted to him instead of following the usual custom of investing them at will until they were called for and then keeping the interest as a perquisite. See Williams, 1:147, 151–57.

438. "shake his chains . . . cry": The figure of Pitt as a dog is continued. "Open" and "cry" are technical terms for the yelping of foxhounds on the trail.

439. "North Britain": Scotland. The term was used by those who wished to emphasize the Union and minimize prejudice against Scots.

440. "the strum-strum": A primitive guitar.

441. "his former fickleness and apostacy": *Briton*, no. 36 (30 January 1763) is largely devoted to a running account of Pitt's numerous reversals of position: "he seems never to have had any set of fixed principles at all" (p. 215). See also Brewer, *Party*, chapter 6.

442. "Mura-clami": William Murray, earl of Mansfield; see key.

443. "no idea . . . humanity": Smollett's view of Mansfield was colored by the fact that the latter had presided at his trial for libeling Admiral Knowles, had denied his appeal for clemency, and had sentenced him to a fine and a prison term. See Knapp, 218, 230–37.

444. "the maxims of his family . . . from inclination": Members of Murray's family had been implicated in the service of the Old Pretender, to whom his brother James was "prime minister." It was alleged that in the year 1732, at the house of one Mr. Vernon, a Jacobite mercer in Ludgate, Murray and two others "drank the health of the Pretender on their knees." See C. H. S. Fifoot, *Lord Mansfield* (Oxford: Clarendon Press, 1936), 38. Though Murray was acquitted by the privy council, similar charges haunted him throughout his career and were debated as late as 1770. See above, n. 388; see also Browning, 189, 214, Sedgwick, xxvii–xxix, and Walpole, *George II*, 1:196.

445. "fought a good battle with orator Taycho": From their student days Murray and Pitt maintained a lifelong personal rivalry. After 1754 Murray consistently defended the Newcastle administration against Pitt when necessary; after 1760 he supported Bute.

446. "more easy to inflame than to allay": "[Our] intention is . . . not to inflame but to allay" (*Briton*, no. 1 [29 May 1762]: 1).

447. "snuffed up the excrementitious salts": See *Briton*, no. 4 (19 June 1762): 21: "the base illiberal herd . . . greedily snuff up the fumes of scandal, even to intoxication." The ammonia for smelling salts was often obtained by distilling urine: see *Humphry Clinker*, Jery Melford to Sir Watkin Phillips, Hot Well, April 18, where Dr. Linden recommends excrement as more effective than "volatile salts."

448. "citizen of Edinburgh . . . perfumer." The smell of excrement in Edinburgh had become proverbial, and Smollett often commented on it. See *Present State*, 2:115–16; *Humphry Clinker*, Matthew Bramble to Dr. Lewis, July 18, and Win. Jenkins to Mrs. Mary Jones, July 18; and *Travels*, Letter 5: "I could give you some high-flavoured instances, at which even a native of Edinburgh would stop his nose" (p. 33).

449. "Philippics of Demosthenes and Tully": Smollett's age referred to Marcus Tullius Cicero (106–43 B.C.) as Tully. Demosthenes (384–322 B.C.), by his famous denunciations of Philip of Macedon (359–336 B.C.), created the generic term for fiery invectives.

450. "A man feels . . . rascal": The language here, and continuing for the remainder of the paragraph, recalls Swift's account of the effects of satire in the preface to *Tale of a Tub*.

451. "the Pharisaical consolation . . . publican": "The Pharisee stood and prayed thus with himself, God, I thank thee, that I am not . . . as this publican" (Luke 18:11). A publican was a tax-collector, despised by the Jews as a servant of Rome.

452. "he proposed measures . . . Fatsissio": Murray was an advocate of vigorous military action in America as early as the autumn of 1754, but Newcastle was irres-
olute and timid and little was done; see Browning, 210–11.

453. "Brut-an-tiffi . . . rapine": Brut-an-tiffi is the rapacious Frederick the Great of
Prussia; see key. *Briton*, no. 7 (10 July 1762): 39 characterizes him as "a royal
free-booter." The "Kurd" are the Prussians; see key.

454. "Of all mankind . . . could have made his own": George II, Frederick's maternal
uncle, had quarreled with Frederick's father when both were children, and the
two royal families maintained a personal feud from that time; see Davies, 6,
104–5. Hanover's complete lack of any natural barriers against neighboring
states made it dangerously vulnerable. Smollett's sentence echoes *Continuation*,
1: 375–76.

455. "between hawk and buzzard": In a cruel dilemma; proverbial, from Aesop.

456. "He had, indeed . . . attended by rapine": See *Briton*, no. 9 (24 July 1762): 51–
52: "in the last war . . . Great Britain supported the house of Austria, and his
Prussian Majesty was strictly attached to the French King then at war with
England . . . . [In 1744] on the back of the treaty of Breslaw, by which he
engaged to preserve a strict neutrality . . . he suddenly entered Bohemia . . .
[and] reduced the cities of Prague, Tabor, Budweis." Smollett's characterization
of Frederick conspicuously includes the familiar charge of his "scoffing" at
religion. Frederick's writings, his association with Voltaire, and the religious
tolerance of the Frederician Code for Prussia suggest that he was in fact a free-
thinker or atheist.

457. "granted a large subsidy . . . whenever it should be attacked": In September
1755 George II signed an agreement with the Czarina Elizabeth by which
England would pay Russia £100,000 per year; in return Russia would maintain a
force of 50,000 troops in Livonia to defend Hanover in the event of an attack.
When a condition of war existed the subsidy would rise to £500,000 per year.
See *Continuation*, 1:280–82. The phrase "Mantchoux Tartars" refers to the Russian people; see key.

458. "Ottoman Porte . . . most Christian king": The government of the Ottoman
Empire at Constantinople was commonly known as the Ottoman Porte; the king
of France was formally titled "most Christian king."

459. "a plan of usurpation": A reference to the conquests that Frederick would
attempt during the Seven Years' War.

460. "He gave the Dairo to understand . . . irruptions of the Chinese": The eventual
results of the negotiations between the governments of George and Frederick
were the Treaty of Westminster (January 1756) by which Britain and Prussia
mutually pledged to keep foreign troops out of the German empire, and the first
of the annually renewable subsidiary treaties (April 1758) by which, to insure
Prussian cooperation, Britain agreed to furnish Frederick £670,000 (four million

Prussian crowns) per year. See Asprey, 414–16; see also Richard Lodge, *Great Britain and Prussia in the Eighteenth Century* (Oxford: Clarendon Press, 1923; reprint, New York: Octagon Books, 1972).

461. "Taycho . . . among the mob": A reference to Pitt's speeches in Parliament against the plans to defend Hanover; for details see Williams, 1:267–71.

462. "pelting farm": A characterization of Hanover as paltry and contemptible. Smollett alludes to the famous speech of John of Gaunt in *Richard II* 2.1.60, which describes England as leased out "like to a tenement or pelting farm."

463. "like Aaron's rod": A reference to Aaron and the magicians of Pharaoh, Exodus 7:12: "For they cast down every man his rod, and they became serpents; but Aaron's rod swallowed up their rods."

464. "He expatiated . . . to perdition": A reference to Pitt's famous speech of 13 November 1755, in which he said that a policy promoting a Continental war "would hang like a millstone about the neck of any minister and sink him along with the nation"; see Speck, 262. Later, when Pitt reversed his position, Fox twitted him by alluding to this speech; see Walpole, *George II*, 2:214. In his speech Pitt had echoed the words of Jesus, Matthew 18:6: "Whoso shall offend one of these little ones . . . it were better for him that a millstone were hanged about his neck, and that he were drowned in the depth of the sea." See *PH*, 15:535–38.

465. "withdrew the garrison . . . adjoining to the farm": On 6 April 1757 Frederick pulled his troops out of the frontier towns of Wesel and Gueldres, which were immediately occupied by the French; see *Continuation*, 2:68–69.

466. "played at foot-ball with his imperial tiara": On the king's hat-kicking, see above, n. 401. George had in fact accepted a challenge to a duel with Frederick's father in 1729. See Davies, 105, 186; and see Prints 2326, 2862.

467. "a commission of lunacy": A body officially appointed to determine whether an individual should be considered legally insane.

468. "flat-bottomed junks": A reference to the threat of an invasion by the French. In Letter 5 of his *Travels*, Smollett mentions seeing "a dozen of those flat-bottomed boats, which raised such alarm in England, in the course of the war" (p. 31, n. 4). See above, n. 365, and below, vol. 2, n. 109; see also Print 3679, the subject of which is another invasion scare in July 1759.

469. "The Fatzman offered . . . motions of the enemy": Frederick had asked that Cumberland command an "army of observation," and George approved. Cumberland, dubious of his own abilities and violently opposed to Pitt (then secretary of state, southern department), refused to go while Pitt remained in office. Pitt was dismissed on 6 April 1757; Cumberland left for the Continent on 9 April. See Corbett, 1:158.

470. "sunk . . . ocean": The satirical ballad by Sir Charles Hanbury Williams mocking Pitt's "unembarrassed countenance" speech of 8 April 1746 contains a refer-

ence to "digging Hanover quite into the sea"; see above, n. 433. It is clear that
Williams echoes a phrase from Pitt himself. See Davies, 248–49, and Timbs,
Anecdote Biography, 143.

471. "weighing": Raising, as in weighing an anchor.

472. "Taycho's head nodding from a window": On 26 October 1756 the king was told
that a cabinet post for Pitt was absolutely essential for the preservation of Hanover, as nothing less than such an appointment would put a stop to his opposition; see Williams, 1:282–83. Smollett probably alludes to the nodding man-
darin figurines, imported from China, which had become popular bibelots in his
day.

473. "motion": Bowel movement, in the medical terminology of the day.

474. "occasional": Temporary, improvised for the occasion.

475. "The first step . . . Fatsissio": This passage is a satirical allegory of Smollett's
view (partially correct) that Pitt largely owed his success to the firm support of
the substantial merchants and financial interests in the city of London. For a
detailed analysis of the nature and fluctuations of Pitt's support in the city see
Marie Peters, *Pitt and Popularity* (Oxford: Clarendon Press, 1980). City aldermen
represented the companies that were the survivors of the medieval guilds; the
objects of their trade often figured in their coats of arms. Thus the "fig-box"
refers probably to grocers; the "nightman's bucket" suggests the scavengers who
removed the contents of privies at night; "hempseed" denotes halter-makers but
possibly also hangmen, whose ropes were made from hemp; the "kilderkin," a
cask for liquor or fish, indicates the wine merchant or fishmonger; "bag of soot"
refers to the chimney-sweep; "hard wood" suggests carpenters but perhaps also
alludes to logwood (a source of dye and thus an emblem of the dyer's trade) and
to mahogany, two woods so valuable that the rights to cut them figured in the
Treaty of Paris that ended the war.

476. "varnished lettered post . . . crazy hogshead": The post may be a barber's pole
or, more probably, a column or kiosk on which booksellers' wares and quack
medicines were advertised. The hogshead is Alderman William Beckford, Pitt's
staunchest and most powerful supporter; see key, RHUM-KIKH. "Crazy"
means cracked, but Smollett also uses the word in its modern sense to mean
insane. See *Briton*, no. 37 (5 February 1763): 219: Scipio Africanus, to whom
Pitt is compared, did not "climb upon the shoulders of the mob to the first
offices of the state."

477. "climax": In the Latin and Greek sense of "ladder."

478. "a *capias*": L. A magistrate's order to make an arrest.

479. "Bagshot heath": In Woking, Surrey, twenty-six miles from London on the
Great Western Road; the name was a byword for armed robbery of passengers in
coaches or on foot.

480. "finisher of the law": Jocular slang for the hangman.

481. "noddled": Nodded quickly or slightly. In this scene Smollett conflates Pitt's first and second entries into cabinet office, December 1756 and June 1757.

482. "that many-headed hydra the mob": See above, n. 404. The satirical cliché of the "hydra of faction" was used by all parties in the period; see Print 4024. Smollett used the phrase in various ways to refer sometimes to the House of Commons, sometimes to the "City interest" of London merchants, sometimes to the people as a whole. See *Briton*, no. 31 (25 December 1762): 181: "The heads of Hydra faction are now cut off . . . ."

483. "had treated his person with indecent freedoms": See above, n. 435, and below, n. 494.

484. "turned his own back upon the Cuboy": This characteristic and undignified gesture of displeasure by the king was notorious. He is pictured in a print, "The Festival of the Golden Rump," as a satyr turned away from his worshipers; see Print 2327*, and see Mack, 138–47. There was a "Rump Steak Club" composed of those on whom the king had turned his back in this manner; see Mack, 130, n. 6.

485. "the Stagyrite": Aristotle, so called because he came from Stagyra in Chalcidice.

486. "ἡ ὀργή . . . no equal": Smollett translates the Greek, quoted from book 12, chapter 54 ("How Aristotle Succeeded in Recalling the Enraged Alexander to Mildness") of *De varia historia libri xiii*, by Claudius Ælianus (third century A. D.). Smollett's characterization of Aristotle's statement as a "syllogistical sophism" is accurate: the statement is in syllogistic form but is a sophism because Aristotle does not say that Alexander has no superiors, or that we may not be angry at our inferiors.

487. "no other way of saving the farm . . . Taycho": See Davies, 309–10, 320, for discussion of the negotiations which brought the king to admit that he would have to buy off Pitt's opposition with a cabinet post.

488. "the clouds . . . compelled": Smollett recalls Pope's epithet for Dulness in *Dunciad* 1.80, "cloud-compelling queen," which in turn echoes the Homeric epithet for Zeus, *nephelegereta*.

489. "he consented . . . introduction": George II overcame his opposition to Pitt and appointed him secretary of state, southern department, on 4 December 1756.

490. "sung a solemn Palinodia": A palinode is an ode or other poem written in recantation of an earlier poem. See *Continuation*, 1:193: "Some of [the opposition] had prudently sung their palinodia to the ministry, and been gratified with profitable employments."

491. "repeated . . . creed": The Athanasian Creed and a statement of assent to the Thirty-Nine Articles had to be repeated and signed as a legal requirement for ordination.

492. "like a tame bear to the stake": As in the sport of bear baiting, for which a bear was tied to a stake and set upon by dogs. Smollett uses the same phrase in *Peregrine Pickle*, chapter 9, and in *Sir Launcelot Greaves*, chapter 22.

493. bending the body . . . buttock": Smollett doubtless alludes to the grotesque posture for taking oaths in Lilliput (*Gulliver's Travels*, part 1, chapter 3), as well as to the common eighteenth-century gesture of derision.

494. "recapitulation . . . growling to his den": See *Briton*, no. 5 (26 June 1762): 28: "The K[ing] himself was so incensed by the unmannerly freedoms [Pitt] had taken, that all the servility of his m[inisteria]l compliance, when he afterwards forced himself into the c[a]b[ine]t, could not overcome the disgust he had occasioned by his former virulence." See also Davies, 205–6, on Pitt's personal slurs against the king.

495. "lugged": Hauled out roughly by the ears, as in bear baiting; see *King Lear* 4.3.42, "the head-lugg'd bear."

496. "exalting his voice": A favorite locution of Smollett. See *Briton*, no. 4 (19 June 1762): 22, addressing John Wilkes: "you will exalt your throat in general invectives against B[ut]e"; see also *Briton*, no. 6 (3 July 1762): 31. The probable source is 2 Kings 19:22: "Against whom hast thou exalted thy voice? . . . even against the Holy One of Israel."

497. "cabalistical": Mysterious, magical; from the Hebrew *kabbalah*, a corpus of mystical interpretation of scripture.

498. "sideling, . . . cobbling": Sidling, gobbling.

499. "*os sacrum*": L. The bone at the bottom of the spine constituting the center of the pelvis.

500. "indenture tripartite": A mutual triple covenant. In legal documents for such covenants the tops of copies were identically serrated ("indented") for identification and security. In the ensuing description Smollett conflates two sets of events: Pitt first became secretary of state in December 1756, but was forced by the king to resign in April 1757; after an eleven-week interval during which the king tried in vain to form a government without him, he was brought back with full powers on 29 June.

501. "his levees": Namier, *England*, 76–77, cites descriptions of Newcastle's levees by Chesterfield and Lord Fitzmaurice: they were "his pleasure, and his triumph; he loved to have them crowded"; he "accosted, hugged, embraced, and promised everybody"; after his accommodation with Pitt he had "undisturbed enjoyment of the whole patronage of the Crown," he was "abundantly content," and he "enjoyed full levees."

502. "places": Here meaning control of sinecures as a means of political influence.

503. "chief scribe": Secretary of state.

504. "the blatant beast whose name was Legion": The House of Commons. The image of the Blatant Beast, with a hundred tongues that speak falsehood, is from Spenser's *Faerie Queene*, books 5 and 6. In Mark 5:9 the unclean spirit says, "My name is Legion, for we are many"; see also Luke 8:30. Smollett may be alluding to Swift's famous satire on the Irish House of Commons, *The Legion Club* (1736).

Pitt's role, in which he was eminently successful, was to steer the administration's war measures (now largely his own) through Parliament.

505. "kidney": Character, nature, disposition.

506. "infatuation": In the older, literal sense of being made a fool of.

507. "a free gift": On 17 May 1757 Parliament ratified the Convention (or Treaty) of Westminster, granting a large sum for the equipping of Hanoverian and Prussian troops; see above, n. 460, and see also *Continuation*, 1:425–26.

508. "winked so hard": Chose to overlook.

509. "his apostacy": *Continuation*, 1:424–25 gives an account of how Pitt, immediately upon gaining office, reversed himself and urged generous support for the Continental campaign. He spoke on 13 and 18 February 1757, urging an appropriation of £200,000 in support of Hanover and Prussia. In response Fox reminded him of his "millstone" speech of 13 November 1755; see above, n. 464.

510. "to all Europe": This reference may be taken as evidence that Smollett did not revise his manuscript carefully; consistency would require "to all Asia."

511. "Qamba-cun-dono . . . a point of termination": Cumberland left to take command of the Army of Observation on 9 April 1757. Smollett here alludes sarcastically to his disastrous defeat at the end of July; see below, n. 575.

512. "drench them with mandragora or geneva": To drench is to administer a liquid medication, especially to animals. Mandragora is a narcotic made from the mandrake. Geneva is gin; see *Briton*, no. 8 (18 July 1762): 47: "a drench of geneva." The word *geneva* is a corruption of the French *ginièvre*, juniper; its English connotation in the eighteenth century was of a vile intoxicant for the lowest classes of society, as in Hogarth's *Gin Lane* (1751).

513. "a yearly tribute to Brut-an-tiffi": A reference to a clause in the Second Treaty of Westminster, the annual subsidy to Prussia of £670,000. The treaty was first voted on 11 April 1758 and was renewed three times; see above, n. 460.

514. "seven times the value of the lands": So Smollett declared in *Briton*, no. 7 (10 July 1762): 40.

515. "wagged its tail . . . intire satisfaction": In *Continuation*, 1:425–26, Smollett comments more mildly (but still sarcastically) on the docility of Parliament.

516. "fritter on Shrove Tuesday": The day before the commencement of Lent was traditionally an occasion for London apprentices to feast on pancakes.

517. "juggler in politicks": *Sir Launcelot Greaves*, chapter 10, refers to a "Germanized minister" as "a juggler."

518. "cat in pan": To "turn the cat in the pan" is to be a traitor or turncoat; the phrase seems to be a corruption of the French *tourner le coté en peine*.

519. "κατα παν": Gr. Roughly equivalent to "all things to all men."

520. "perspective": Telescope, opera glass.

521. "an unblemished hero": After Frederick's victory over the Austrian army at Rossbach on 5 November 1757 he became widely popular in England. There

were illuminations on his birthday, 24 January 1758, and he was lauded as the "Protestant champion." *Continuation*, 4:158–59 contains a long passage condemning the view of Frederick as hero.

522. "fascinate": In the Latinate sense of tying up or rendering incapable.

523. "*Quos Jupiter . . . dementat*": L. "Those whom Jupiter would destroy he first makes mad." The saying, attributed to Publilius Syrus (first century B.C.), is also applied to "Fortune" or "the gods." The caption to Print 4163* repeats the saying, doubtless with reference to Pitt's periods of madness or depression.

524. "Pol-hassan-akousti": Augustus, king of Poland and elector of Saxony; see key, and see Davies, 126–28.

525. "a most beautiful colony . . . a minute's warning": Frederick demanded free passage for his troops through Saxony. He took Dresden on 8 September 1756, Leipzig on 20 September. The Saxon army capitulated in October, and Frederick requisitioned the entire revenues of the Saxon crown. See Asprey, 427–28.

526. "compelled the domestics . . . banditti": The Saxon troops were compelled to serve under Frederick.

527. "plundered his house . . . gentlewoman his wife": The royal family of Saxony were put under guard at Dresden in their palace, which was systematically plundered. Frederick dismissed all court officers and set up a commission to rule Poland. He further demanded the surrender of the Saxon state archives and, after agreeing that they should be put under seal, sent officers to seize them. The queen herself blocked the door leading to the archives, but finally admitted the officers when orders from Frederick threatened her removal by force. See *Continuation*, 1:388–89, and *Voltaire*, 18:122.

528. "dispersed a manifesto": This manifesto, entitled *A Vindication of His Prussian Majesty's Conduct* (1756), was reviewed severely by Smollett in *CR* 2 (November 1756): 315–26: "The respect which has been paid to the person of the queen of *Poland*, is, to be sure, a convincing proof of the invader's gallantry and greatness of mind. It was by dint of the most suitable representations only, that she was prevailed upon to suffer some papers to be taken out of the state-paper-office in *Dresden*. The representations were doubtless very cogent . . . . What pain, what anxiety, what agony, it must have produced in the bosom of this tender-hearted monarch, to be under the necessity of driving *Augustus* out of his own country! He must also have felt severely for the distress of the unhappy queen of *Poland*. We hope the illustrious conqueror will not suffer in his health from the humanity of his affections" (pp. 318, 319). Frederick is further censured in Smollett's review of a reply to his *Vindication* by the Austrian archduchess Maria Theresa, *CR* 3 (February 1757): 153–54. See Basker, 222, 223, 233–34.

529. "sequester the rents": Impound the royal revenues.

530. "the Spaniard . . . your own good": The anecdote repeated here, though apocryphal, was widely circulated and believed. The source appears to be a letter

written by the French wit Saint-Évremont criticizing the policy of Cardinal Mazarin and comparing him to the executioner, for which Saint-Évrémont was forced to flee into lifelong exile in England. The story is told at some length in Smollett's review of volumes 20–22 of the *Universal History* in *CR* 10 (August and September 1760): 81–90, 161–78; the true version of the events is given on p. 166 (Basker, 226, 259). It is mentioned again in *Voltaire*, 5:11, where Smollett criticizes Voltaire for repeating it. The same story figures in a controversial pamphlet, *Thomsonus Redivivus* (1746), probably written by Smollett; see Robert A. Day, "When Doctors Disagree: Smollett and Thomas Thompson," *Etudes Anglaises* 32 (1979): 312–24.

531. "the politeness of Gibbet in the play": Gibbet is a comic highwayman with pretensions to gentility in George Farquhar's *The Beaux' Stratagem* (1700). The episode alluded to occurs in act 5, scene 2. The review of Frederick's *Vindication* in *CR* (see above, n. 528) remarks of that prince's conduct toward the royal family of Saxony: "this circumstance puts us in mind of a scene in the play, called The Beaux's Stratagem, which the reader will excuse us for not particularizing" (p. 318).

532. "fair and fertile province . . . house of Ostrog": The reference is to Bohemia, roughly equivalent to modern Czechoslovakia, then under the rule of Maria Theresa, queen of Hungary and archduchess of Austria. See key, OSTROG.

533. "fleshed": Inured to bloodshed.

534. "a sudden irruption . . . Amazonian princess": Because of the condition of the roads, troop movements of any size, and therefore campaigns, were rarely attempted except in summer. Austria had treaties of defense with France, Russia, and Sweden.

535. "the great Cham . . . princess of Ostrog": Francis I, Holy Roman Emperor, was the husband of Maria Theresa.

536. "Inspired by these projects . . . reign of desolation": The Prussian invasion of Bohemia was stopped at Lobositz, 1 October 1756, by Austrian troops under the command of Count George Browne, an expatriate Irish general. Frederick retreated with his army into Saxony, wintering in Dresden.

537. "a general assembly": Smollett conflates the Aulic Council, meeting at Vienna, and the Imperial Diet, meeting in more or less permanent session at Ratisbon, or Regensburg. George II, as elector of Hanover, maintained a minister at the Diet.

538. "a deputy . . . universally condemned": See *Continuation*, 1:378–79. Just before the invasion of Saxony in 1756, George II ordered his minister at Ratisbon to protest that the first Treaty of Westminster (see above, n. 460) was not aimed at the Catholic religion and was purely defensive in nature.

539. "apprehended a sentence of outlawry from the Cham": The edict that George II feared was promulgated in August 1757, but in much weakened form. See *Continuation*, 1:396–97, 2:318.

540. "a piteous clamour": See *Continuation*, 1:396–408. In 1756 Frederick presented to the Imperial Diet a memorial based on the papers he had seized at Dresden, to the effect that Russia, Austria, and Poland were conspiring to reduce his territories and restore Silesia (taken by him in 1741) to Maria Theresa. Smollett, in his historical account, points to faults on both sides.

541. "conjuration": Mutual oath. This oath, or agreement, is printed in Frederick's *Vindication*; see above, n. 528.

542. "a former occasion . . . best provinces": The emperor Charles VI, Maria Theresa's father, had died in 1740. Although Charles had tried to secure the succession of the Hapsburg line to the imperial throne (the "Pragmatic Sanction"), Frederick immediately took advantage of the unsettled state of affairs to annex Silesia, starting the War of the Austrian Succession with the battle of Mollwitz in 1741. In 1745 Silesia, among other territories, was ceded to Frederick in return for his support of Maria Theresa's husband, Francis I of Lorraine, as Holy Roman Emperor. See Davies, 182–83, 202, 229; and see Asprey, 347.

543. "He publicly taxed . . . his conquests": In *Continuation*, 2:170 Smollett discusses and reproduces in a footnote a letter to George II in which Frederick "taxes him with having instigated him to commence hostilities."

544. "the Serednee Tartars": The Swedes; see key.

545. "a decree of outlawry and rebellion": In 1757 the Aulic Council placed Frederick under the ban of the empire. He was to leave Saxony, and all the states were to refuse him troops or other aid. Although many formal diplomatic negotiations took place before the decree, Frederick regarded it as the farce that it was. See above, n. 539.

546. "the Amazon herself opposed him": *Continuation*, 1:379: "The court of Vienna formed two considerable armies in Bohemia and Moravia."

547. "magazines": Storage depots.

548. "The Serednee . . . operations of the war": An allusion to efforts by the French to start a Swedish war with Prussia. At this same time, in 1756, internal conspiracies (the "intestine divisions" alluded to in the text) had made King Adolphus threaten to abdicate, and a revolution in Sweden seemed likely. See *Continuation*, 1:377.

549. "a strong barrier . . . Chinese": The Army of Observation under Cumberland marched to the southwestern border of Hanover, where it faced territories occupied by the French.

550. "rehearse": Relate, repeat.

551. "under the middle size": Frederick, at five feet six inches tall, was not so diminutive as Smollett suggests. The remainder of his description is either quite accurate or not greatly exaggerated. See Asprey, 351–52.

552. "the character of Gibbet . . . expressive feature": See above, n. 531. During Smollett's London years Gibbet was played by no less than twenty-five actors,

but the person most probably meant is Edward Shuter (1728–76), who took the part more frequently than anyone else and was noted for his ability to distort his face. Shuter's move in 1753 from Drury Lane to Covent Garden and "higher" or more serious roles would have made him a "late" comedian. See *The London Stage*, pt. 4, ed. George Winchester Stone (Carbondale: Southern Illinois University Press, 1962).

553. "With respect to religion . . . contempt": Voltaire, the probable source of Smollett's portrait, declared that Frederick lived without religion; see *Memoirs of the Life of Voltaire*, 3d ed. (1785), 91.

554. "He pardoned a criminal . . . through all his dominions": Frederick, pardoning a cavalryman convicted of bestiality with a mare, observed that the best punishment would be to transfer him to the infantry. According to Voltaire, *Memoirs*, 91–92, Frederick permitted "free liberty of opinion, and of **** [sexual behavior] . . . throughout his territories." Smollett, by his use of the word *prosecute*, suggests that Frederick actually promoted freethinking and aberrant sexuality. See Asprey, 145.

555. "He had studied the Chinese language": Frederick's numerous writings were in French, and he took pride in their stylistic elegance. Voltaire, during his residence at the Prussian court, was employed to criticize and improve Frederick's prose and verse; he complained that this task left him little time for his own work. See Asprey, 395–97.

556. "buskins": Riding boots.

557. "embraced him . . . so long absent": Frederick's intimates were the constant victims of his capriciousness and his often cruel practical jokes. The incident alluded to by Smollett has not been traced; it may be a distorted version of what happened to Voltaire when he left the Prussian court for the last time, carrying with him a privately printed copy of poems Frederick wished to keep out of circulation. Voltaire's letter describing his treatment was published in *Babouc* (1748), a work well known in England as early as 1754, when it was translated by W. Owen. See Asprey, 403–4.

558. "occasionally": As the occasion required.

559. "capital": Chief, principal.

560. "a musical instrument . . . Tartars": Frederick was an accomplished performer on the transverse or "German" flute; he also composed chamber music and frequently played in ensembles. See Asprey, 21.

561. "conversing . . . philosophers": Among the intellectuals who stayed at Frederick's Potsdam palace of Sans Souci were Voltaire, the Marquis d'Argens, La Mettrie, Maupertuis, and Count Algarotti.

562. "no communication with the female sex": Frederick was homosexual. See Asprey, 404.

563. "participation of his pastime": Sharing in his leisure activities.

564. "Chinese refugees": Most of the French intellectuals at Frederick's court were in

temporary or permanent exile as a result of opinions and writings considered dangerous at home.

565. "They wrote systems . . . his own": Smollett exaggerates here, but Voltaire is known to have spent much time "improving" and praising Frederick's works; see above, n. 555.

566. "a Western hero . . . Quintus Curtius": Raskalander is Alexander the Great, perhaps conflated by Smollett with Peter the Great of Russia; see key. Quintus Curtius Rufus (first century A.D.) wrote a life of Alexander entitled *Historia Alexandri Magni*. Voltaire calls the translation of Curtius by Vaugelas (1646) "the first well-written book" in French; see *Voltaire*, 9:3.

567. "fired with the ambition . . . Raskalander": Smollett's intention here is unclear. Frederick is known to have admired and aspired to emulate not Alexander, but Peter the Great; he would surely have read Voltaire's *Histoire de l'empire de Russie sous Pierre le Grand* (1759) and his *Anecdotes* of Peter the Great (1760). See *Voltaire*, 9:20, 21, and 10:14–34.

568. "Alexander deposited . . . precious casket": Plutarch relates this episode in his life of Alexander.

569. "sophistication": Fraudulent alteration of a product or work; adulteration.

570. "Tum-ming-qua . . . Yan": These names may be complete fabrications; see key.

571. "He now took the field . . . end of the campaign": Frederick again invaded Bohemia in late April 1757; he defeated Marshal George Browne at the battle of Prague on 6 May and then besieged the city of Prague.

572. "another old, experienced commander": Leopold Joseph, Count von Daun; see key, KUNT-THAN.

573. "gave him battle . . . disgrace": An allusion to the disastrous defeat suffered by Frederick at Kolin, 18 June 1757. He was afterward obliged to abandon the siege of Prague.

574. "A separate body . . . with great loss": Smollett refers to two critical engagements: the defeat of General Winterfeld by the Austrians at Gorlitz, 7 September 1757, and the retreat of the Prussians from Norkitten a week earlier, on 30 August. Winterfeld died at Gorlitz, and Frederick wept over his loss; the retreat from Norkitten came after a bloody battle during which the victorious Russian forces suffered even greater casualties than the Prussians. See Asprey, 465–66.

575. "The Fatzman of Japan . . . a terrible disaster": Cumberland arrived in Hanover on 16 April 1757. After various skirmishes he began to retreat, crossing the Weser (the boundary of Hanover) on 18 June. The French crossed the same river unopposed on 10–11 July, soundly defeated Cumberland at Hastenbeck, and then occupied Hanover and Hesse. Cumberland retreated farther, and at the end of August he was completely hemmed in at Stade. On 8 September, with the king of Denmark acting as mediator, Cumberland signed the Convention of Klosterseven, by which his remaining troops were to disperse and return home; forty thousand men were thus put out of action. Smollett's "official" account of

these events in the *Continuation*, 2:98–117 is no less sarcastic than the description offered here. He severely criticizes Cumberland for marching 150 miles in a circle instead of 100 miles in a straight line, arguing that he should have crossed the river Leine instead of the Weser. Smollett's criticism may not be entirely fair, for it appears that Cumberland's army was seriously undermanned through no fault of his own; see Browning, 266. For a general account of this and further campaigns by British forces, see Sir Reginald Savory, *His Britannic Majesty's Army in Germany During the Seven Years' War* (Oxford: Clarendon Press, 1966).

576. "a compound impulse": In Newtonian physics, the resultant of several gravitational forces acting upon a body from different directions.

577. "five stone of suet": Seventy pounds of fat.

578. "all the damage . . . cause to regret": This passage echoes Smollett's sentiments as expressed in the *Continuation*, 2:109–10 and in *Briton*, no. 22 (22 October 1762): 130.

579. "the tribe of Ostrog . . . intimately connected": The son of Louis XV, the dauphin Louis (d. 1765), was married to Maria Theresa's niece, Maria Josepha of Saxony.

580. "raised a hideous clamour . . . country of Yesso": For the details of Frederick's charges against Cumberland see *Continuation*, 2:169–72.

581. "He dismissed the Fatzman": Cumberland returned to England on 11 October 1757 and resigned his commands effective four days later, 15 October. Numerous sources record the king's remark, "Here is my son, who has disgraced himself and ruined me." See Davies, 323.

582. "hills of heath . . . wastes of sand": *Present State*, 4:222 describes Hanover as having "much sandy, marshy, heathy, barren ground."

583. "freestone": A fine-grained sandstone or limestone.

584. "turnep-garden": Hanover was much ridiculed as producing nothing better than turnips; see Prints 3610, 3615.

585. "black cattle": An archaic Scotticism for "cattle."

586. "houseless sides": Adapted from *King Lear* 3.4.30: "houseless heads and unfed sides."

587. "fill your hungry bellies . . . good things": "He hath filled the hungry with good things, and the rich hath he sent empty away" (Luke 1:53, the "*Magnificat*").

588. "larded the lean earth with thy carcase": "Falstaff sweats to death, and lards the lean earth as he walks along" (*1 Henry IV* 2.2.108–9). In *Humphry Clinker*, Jery Melford quotes this passage in his letter to Sir Watkin Phillips, London, June 10.

589. "uncovered": In the military sense of being unprotected by artillery, troops, garrisons.

590. "like a partridge on the mountains": "The king of Israel is come out to seek a flea, as when one doth hunt a partridge in the mountains" (David, minimizing his threat to Saul, 1 Samuel 26:20).

591. "dotterel": See above, n. 111.

592. "Go home to your own palace": Probably an allusion to Newcastle's temporary disgrace during the first short Pitt administration, December 1756 to April 1757, when the duke retired to his estate at Claremont; see Browning, 254–55.

593. "Most gracious . . . Boh": With these ludicrous words of address Smollett launches a passage in which he parodies the excessively florid style typical of Pitt's oratory.

594. "apparent": In the literal sense of evident, visible.

595. "embalm": Anoint, perfume.

596. "the rivers Jodo and Jodogava": See key. Smollett here begins a sustained allusion to the most famous flower of Pitt's rhetoric. On 13 November 1755, after Parliament had been sitting for eleven hours, Pitt electrified the members with a speech of an hour and a half, during which he developed the celebrated "millstone" simile (see above, n. 464). Denouncing the treaties for Hessian and Russian subsidies, Pitt sarcastically compared the newly formed alliance of Fox and Newcastle with the confluence of the Rhone and the Saône: "this a gentle, feeble, languid stream, and though languid, of no depth—the other, a boisterous and impetuous torrent. They meet at last; and long may they continue united, to the comfort of each other, and to the glory, honour, and security of this nation." See Walpole, *George II*, 2:69–73; see also *PH*, 15:660–64.

597. "Meaco . . . bay of Osaca": Meaco is London; see key. Osaca is Osaka, though the equivalent to the "bay" would be the Thames estuary.

598. "Kugava": See key; possibly a reference to a river flowing near Osaka.

599. "a jewel in an Æthiop's ear": Juliet "hangs upon the cheek of night / Like a rich jewel in an Ethiop's ear" (*Romeo and Juliet* 1.5.45–46).

600. "It shall hang . . . perdition": Another reference to Pitt's "millstone" simile.

601. "the center": The center of the earth and thus, in the Ptolemaic system, the center of the universe.

602. "your faithful Taycho . . . firmament": An echo of Hotspur's huffing speech in *1 Henry IV* 1.3.201–5:

> By heaven, methinks it were an easy leap,
> To pluck bright honour from the pale-fac'd moon,
> Or dive into the bosom of the deep,
> Where fathom-line could never touch the ground,
> And pluck up drowned honour by the locks.

603. "imposition": Imposition of taxes.

604. "Pekin": Paris, the French court; see key.

605. "the trade of blood": The policy by which subjects were obliged to serve in the armies of foreign powers in return for subsidies. Hesse was notorious throughout Europe for its extensive use of such a policy.

606. "more free and ample than the road to Hell": An allusion to Milton's description of the causeway built by the devils, *Paradise Lost* 7.577: "A broad and ample road, whose dust is gold." The Miltonic pentameter mocks Pitt's oratorical style.

607. "the mighty beast whose name is Legion": See above, n. 504.

608. "Lance-presado": An archaic term for the British rank of lance-corporal, the lowest grade of noncommissioned officer, corresponding to the American private first class. Pitt had been a "cornet" (equivalent to a modern second lieutenant) in the Blues; in February 1735, when he entered Parliament for the pocket borough of Old Sarum, his immediate and violent opposition to Sir Robert Walpole caused the minister to exclaim, "We must muzzle this terrible cornet of horse." Pitt's commission was revoked in 1736, and he made much political capital of the incident, calling it an example of ministerial tyranny. See Davies, 141, and Williams, 1:66–68.

609. "cabinet": Private chamber.

610. "perinæum": See above, n. 180.

611. "pervaded": Became diffused or absorbed.

612. "instead of a heart": Smollett doubtless alludes to Mansfield's refusal to grant his appeal in the Knowles libel case; see above, n. 443.

613. "viscus": Medical term for any soft, hollow internal organ, such as the bladder.

614. "would infallibly incur disgrace": Mansfield was a lifelong rival of Pitt; see above, n. 445. Horace Walpole shared Mansfield's view that, as Walpole put it in a letter to Sir Horace Mann (13 November 1756), Pitt could be expected to ruin himself in one way or another "if he Hanoverizes"; see Walpole, *Correspondence*, 21:17.

615. "Success began to dawn . . . Fatsisio": See below, n. 618.

616. "Brut-an-tiffi . . . the Ostrog": Smollett alludes to two spectacular victories that made Frederick a popular hero. On 5 November 1757 he won the battle of Rossbach against the French general Soubise; on 5 December, opposing the Austrian army under Count von Daun at Leuthen, he obtained the surrender of Breslau. See above, n. 521.

617. "Ian-on-i": General Sir William Johnson; see key.

618. "repulsed a body . . . fortified": In the summer of 1755, at Lake George in New York, General Johnson captured a French encampment and took the French general Dieskau prisoner, thus saving the colony from a full-scale invasion. For his achievement Johnson was made a baronet. See Fortescue, 288–90. Smollett makes light of Johnson's victory in the *Continuation*, 1:264–69, and in *Voltaire*, 8:77.

619. "knew their trim": A nautical term for familiarity with the steering and ballasting idiosyncrasies of a particular vessel. *Briton*, no. 38 (12 February 1763): 227 remarks of Pitt that he "had got the trim of all on board."

620. "an old tub": In the satiric literature of Smollett's day, a standard contemptuous

figure for the pulpit of a dissenting or fanatical preacher or demagogue, as with "Henley's gilt tub," *Dunciad* 2.2, or the contemporary illustrations to Swift's *Tale of a Tub* 1.

621. "exordium": The introductory part of a formal oration.

622. "Bartholomew-fair": Held in Smithfield for three days in the summer, this London fair with its puppet-shows, jugglers, monsters, strong men, and farces had become a type for vulgar entertainment, as in Pope's *Dunciad* or Ben Jonson's *Bartholomew Fair*.

623. "the Japonese empire": The lengthy passage here concluded is in effect a summation of the arguments in Israel Mauduit's *Considerations on the Present German War* (1760), a pamphlet that seems to have crystallized Smollett's growing disapproval of Pitt because of his support for the German war. A most enthusiastic review of the pamphlet, no doubt by Smollett, appeared in *CR* 10 (November 1760): 403–4; and in *Continuation*, 4:155–73 Smollett summarizes Mauduit's arguments at length, saying that they are identical with his own sentiments. In *Sir Launcelot Greaves*, which first appeared in the *British Magazine* during 1760 and 1761, Ferret launches into a harangue emphasizing that the "mountebanks" have made the nation delirious and pro-German (chapter 10). The *Atom* allowed Smollett a latitude of expression which earlier works did not, but in the *Continuation*, 2:434, he wrote boldly of the subsidy treaty of 1758: "This was perhaps the most extraordinary treaty that ever was concluded; for it contains no specification of articles, except the payment of the subsidy: Every article was left to the interpretation of his P[russia]n m[ajest]y."

624. "like the vitriol acid . . . stronger attraction": If iron is immersed in a solution containing copper sulphate and sulphuric acid, ferric sulphate will be formed and pure copper will be deposited. Paracelsus and Newton had both noticed the phenomenon and speculated that it might represent the transmutation of elements. According to a letter printed in the *Philosophical Transactions* of the Royal Society, volume 47 (1751–52), the phenomenon had been observed in the mines of Wicklow, Ireland. Smollett's source here is his review in *CR* 4 (September 1757): 242–43 of John Rutty, M.D., *A Methodical Synopsis of Mineral Waters* (1757); see Basker, 223, 238–39. See George S. Rousseau, "Smollett and the Eighteenth-Century Sulphur Controversy," in *Tobias Smollett: Essays of Two Decades* (Edinburgh: T. & T. Clark, 1982), 144–57.

625. "amuse": Beguile; divert from the essential facts or issues of an argument.

626. "concrete and abstract terms . . . mood and figure": Smollett refers to the most elementary Aristotelian logical operations, which a beginner would study. Genus and difference: the class and the distinguishing characteristics of an individual; copula: the verb connecting subject and predicate in grammar or logic and governing their relationship; mood: the classes (nineteen in number) into which figures are subdivided; figure: the forms determined by the different positions of the middle term in the premises of a syllogism.

627. "ring the changes": From bellringing; perform variations by altering the sequence of the notes rung.

628. "opposition . . . damned fulsome": The oppositions here are consistent except in the instance of "a shameful rascal or a shameful villain." One suspects an error in Smollett's manuscript. The pattern of the sentence as a whole would seem to call for "shameful . . . shameless," though that would be problematical since, in this intended opposition only, Smollett varies the nouns without introducing contrast. His sources for the overall sequence of oppositions are probably two. The satirical novel *Memoirs and Adventures of Tsonnonthouan* (see above, n. 256) contains a chapter on word-twisting, "Of the Indian Idiom of Speech," with examples like these. But virtually the same passage occurs in Charles Johnstone's *Chrysal*, 4th ed. (1765), 2:2: "The horse, that wins the match, goes damn'd fast; as the one that loses, goes *damn'd* slow." For reference to other relations between the *Atom* and Johnstone's *Chrysal*, see above, n. 33.

629. "He knew how . . . infamous apostate": Pitt's sarcastic manner was famous and dreaded, as numerous anecdotes testify. Smollett retaliates here.

630. "an iron machine and a wooden instrument": The eighteenth-century rotisserie, or spit, was powered by various means, including small dogs; a boot-jack secured the heel in pulling off boots. Smollett here parodies the fanciful etymologies of his day.

631. "*ultima lex*, or *ultima ratio regum*": L. The ultimate law, the final method or argument of kings. The cannon of Louis XIV bore the latter insignia, which Frederick the Great adopted for his artillery.

632. "the sect of Ali": Ali, the cousin and son-in-law of Mohammed, founded the Shi'a or Shi'ite sect of Islam.

633. "*good man* . . . benevolence": Smollett possibly alludes to *Merchant of Venice* 1.3.10–17 and Shylock's play upon words denoting solvency and virtue in describing Antonio as a "good man"; he certainly alludes to Johnstone's *Chrysal*, 2:2: "On the *Royal-Exchange* he is a *good man*, who is worth ten thousand pounds, and pays his bills punctually, by whatever private and public frauds he has amassed that sum. . . . At the politer end of the world, *goodness* assumes another appearance." By fanaticism Smollett means rigid Presbyterian orthodoxy; his own religious opinions were liberal.

634. "at O—— and C——": Oxford and Cambridge. Cambridge in Smollett's time was reliably Whig, or of the "Court party"; Oxford was thought to be Tory, Country, or even Jacobite. See *Continuation*, 1:34–36.

635. "the Cocoa-tree in Pall-mall": This coffeehouse was the unofficial headquarters of the Tories, especially while Lord Bute was in power, 1761–63.

636. "Garraway's in Exchange-alley": Stocks were traded at this Whig coffeehouse in Cornhill, a center for the mercantile and financial interests of the city.

637. "a Mile-end assembly": Mile-end was in Stepney, east of Whitechapel, and distinctly unfashionable. The assemblies or dances held there were open to the

public by the purchase of tickets; Smollett describes scenes from such assemblies in *Roderick Random*, chapter 47, and in *Humphry Clinker*, Jery Melford to Sir Watkin Phillips, Bath, April 30.

638. "the cow-heel . . . come, eat me": An allusion to *Don Quixote*, part 2, chapter 59. Smollett here echoes the wording of the passage in his own translation of *Don Quixote* (1755), volume 2, book 4, chapter 7: "Come, eat me: come, eat me." In *Sir Launcelot Greaves*, chapter 4, the cowheel cries, "Come cut me, come cut me." Cowheel is prepared by stewing the foot of a cow or ox.

639. "agreeing to maintain an army . . . the farm of Yesso": A reference to the electoral army of Hanover, established in violation of the Convention of Klosterseven (see above, n. 575), which George II had repudiated. The army was organized in November 1757 and was reinforced by English troops. See *Continuation*, 2:174–76.

640. "to prolong the annual tribute . . . Brut-an-tiffi": A reference to the first renewal of the subsidiary treaty with Prussia; see above, n. 460.

641. "This new general": Duke Ferdinand of Brunswick; see key, BRON-XI-TIC.

642. "address": Adroitness.

643. "Every article . . . they had undertaken": Smollett gives a comparable account of these corruptions in *Continuation*, 3:227–28, where he is understandably much more cautious in his wording, even hinting that he dare not be too severe; his reason was the marriage in 1764 between Prince Charles of Brunswick and the English Princess Augusta, sister of George III. An anonymous pamphlet, *Anecdotes Relative to Our Affairs in Germany* (1762), provides substantially the same account; Smollett no doubt knew this pamphlet, as it was favorably reviewed in *CR* 13 (June 1762): 452. The reported expense of forage was enormous; in 1759 a member of Parliament holding the military rank of major-general was sent to investigate, but met with so little cooperation and so much obstruction that he soon returned to England.

644. "exceeded the whole expence . . . of the empire": See *Briton*, no. 6 (3 July 1762): 33: "Great Britain now expends annually, more than the amount of the whole yearly supply, which was granted in the reign of Queen Anne, when we subsidised almost all the princes of Germany, brought above two hundred thousand men into the field, and maintained a mighty war against Lewis XIV. in the zenith of his power and glory."

645. "The money expended . . . the subjects of Japan": See *Briton*, no. 6 (3 July 1762): 34: a "great part" of English ready money "was conveyed to Germany, from whence it never can return."

646. "stretching the bass-strings of the mobile": A recurrence of the musical figure from Swift; see above, n. 65. *Mobile* is here used in the Latinate sense recalling *mobile vulgus*, "the fickle populace"; Smollett thus accuses Pitt of playing upon the baser instincts of the public.

647. "a cask of water . . . at the long-run": See *Briton*, no. 22 (22 October 1762): 131:

"If any person would undertake to fill a cask that leaked six gallons in an hour, with a pipe that runs no more than two in the same time, would not every hearer perceive at once, and own the folly of the undertaker?"

648. "Japan . . . obans every year": Smollett's "Japanese" sum is accurate; he estimates England's annual expenditure for the war at £6,000,000.

649. "were it put up to sale . . . of the sum": An echo of the captain's words in *Hamlet* 4.4.20–22, on the value of the land Fortinbras goes to conquer.

650. "the annual ballance . . . *two* millions": *Briton*, no. 22 (22 October 1762): 131 estimates that if England should retain all its acquisitions of territory during the war there would be "an addition of three or four millions to our annual revenue."

651. "in profile": In outline.

652. "A former Cuboy . . . in this kingdom": As chancellor of the Exchequer, Sir Robert Walpole in 1717 proposed measures to consolidate the national debt at a rate of five percent and to divert surplus revenue into a sinking fund to reduce the principal. Smollett mentions this fiscal innovation in *Voltaire*, 15:21, and in *Complete History*, 4:519–22.

653. "national debt . . . an enormous burthen": Smollett never tired of pointing out, as in *Briton*, no. 22 (22 October 1762): 130, that the national debt had grown in his day to £136,000,000: "Great Britain is adding yearly twelve millions sterling to her national debt, already so oppressive, that she can hardly stagger under the enormous burthen." See also *Briton*, no. 28 (4 December 1762): 167.

654. "inhanced": Made more expensive; the word was commonly used as an intransitive, "to rise in price."

655. "the price of labour . . . a more moderate expence": Smollett laments the crisis in wages and pricing in *Continuation*, 1:409–10, 443–44, 2:32.

656. "Chaldean manuscripts": Literally, manuscripts written in the language of the Semitic Chaldeans, an ancient people of southern Babylonia. A Chaldean suggested one versed in astrology, the occult, or sorcery.

657. "Hermes Trismegistus . . . of all metals": This digression on alchemy may have been inspired in part by Walter Shandy's admiration for the name Trismegistus; see *Tristram Shandy*, volume 4, chapter 12. Several of the alchemical writers Smollett mentions are found in Chambers, one of Sterne's favorite sources for learned lore. Hermes Trismegistus ("Thrice-Great Hermes") seems to have been a Greek name for the god Thoth, Egyptian inventor of arts and sciences and the subject of a body of legend deriving from his reputed authorship of numerous works of occult wisdom. Geber was an Arabian alchemical writer of the seventh century, earlier mentioned by Smollett in chapter 1 of *Sir Launcelot Greaves*. Zosimus the Panapolite wrote in the early fifth century; Olympiodorus, called an alchemist by the Greek scholar Photius, was a fifth-century historian of Thebes. Heliodorus, bishop of Tricca in the late fourth century, was the supposed author of a poem on the art of making gold. Agathodæmon (dates

unknown) was an Alexandrian who made maps to accompany Ptolemy's work on geography. Morienus wrote on alchemy in the twelfth century, and Albertus Magnus (1200–80), a pioneer of scientific thought, was considered a magician in medieval times. Roger Bacon (1220–92), an English monk, is of great importance to the history of science; but the doctrine of mercury and sulphur was a commonplace of alchemy. See Lynn Thorndike, *A History of Magic and Experimental Science* (New York: Macmillan, 1929–41), 2:617–87.

658. "Swartz . . . a monk of Westminster": The discovery of gunpowder is usually dated in the late fourteenth century and credited to Berthold Schwarz. Smollett may be right to date the discovery earlier and attribute it to Bacon, but the evidence is inconclusive.

659. "the Philosopher's stone . . . Alkahest": In alchemical lore the philosopher's stone was a substance which, if found, would convert base metals into gold. The term *Alkahest*, from the Arabic, refers to the supposed universal solvent sought by alchemists, though it has sometimes been confused with the philosopher's stone.

660. "Van Helmont . . . Archidoxa": Jean-Baptiste Van Helmont (1577–1644), a Flemish physician and chemist, was noted for his *Ortus medicinæ* (1648). The charge of plagiarism against him here is taken almost verbatim from the great Dutch physician, Hermann Boerhaave (1668–1738), whose *Elementa chemiæ* (1732), a history of chemistry, was translated by P. Shaw and E. Chambers and published in two volumes as *A New Method of Chemistry* (London, 1735); the translation must have been included in Smollett's reading as a medical student. Boerhaave argues (trans., 1:27) that there is no universal solvent and that Van Helmont's remarks on it were taken from the *Archidoxa Medicinæ* (1570). Ferret's harangue in chapter 10 of *Sir Launcelot Greaves* mentions "the alkahest of that mad scoundrel Paracelsus" and the "archæus of that visionary Van Helmont." For Paracelsus see below, n. 662.

661. "occiput": The back of the head; loosely, the skull.

662. "Aureolus . . . de Hohenheim": The full name of the alchemist Paracelsus (1493–1541).

663. "scrapings . . . the itch": Sulphur, or brimstone, was supposed to cure the itch; see below, vol. 2, nn. 300, 397.

664. "Tickets . . . circulation of Japan": Banknotes, not in general use in England until the middle of the eighteenth century, were far from being universally negotiable.

665. "It was a country . . . e'er returned": *Hamlet* 3.1.78–79. Smollett adapts lines on death from Hamlet's "To be, or not to be" soliloquy. See *A Second Letter from Wiltshire to the Monitor* (1759), 12: "all this Money must be sent to a Country, *from whose Bourne*, like that of Death in Shakespeare, no British Guinea ever returned." Similar phrasing occurs in *Briton*, no. 6 (3 July 1762): 34, and no. 17 (18 September 1762): 101.

666. "engrossed": Monopolized.

667. "a method to save the expence of solid food": Smollett here begins a variation on the events described in the *Continuation*, 4:193–98, 215: in December 1760 Parliament voted £12,000,000 for the expenses of the war, with the money to be raised by a continuation of the salt tax and by additional taxes on ale and beer; Smollett considers these fiscal policies dangerous (pp. 194, 198) and reports that there were riots over the beer tax (p. 215). *Briton*, no. 6 (3 July 1762): 33–34 remarks upon the perilous state of public credit early in 1761; high premiums at the time tempted everyone to buy government securities, while there was a disastrous cash drain to Germany and America. *CR* 22 (August 1766): 149, reviewing a pamphlet on Pitt, observes that he was thought to be "the author of the tax upon beer"; but in fact Pitt prudently avoided meddling with any Treasury matters.

668. "as the dog was blown up . . . Cervantes": A reference to the prologue, second part of *Don Quixote*. See *CR* 15 (January 1763): 20, a review by Smollett of a novel entitled *The Peregrinations of Jeremiah Grant, the West Indian* (1763): "We would recommend to the serious perusal of this writer . . . the apologue of Cervantes concerning the practice of dog-blowing." See Basker, 228, 271.

669. "*os magna sonaturum*": Horace *Satires* 1.4.43–44:

> ingenium cui sit, cui mens divinior atque os
> magna sonaturum, des nominis huius honorem.

"If one has inborn gifts, if one has a divine soul and tongue of noble utterance, to such give the honor of that name [poet]."

670. "He strutted . . . systems": A probable echo of Swift's description of the blown-up Aeolists or fanatical prophets in *Tale of a Tub* 8.

671. "barm goblets": Barm is the yeasty froth on ale or beer. In Print 3913*, "Sic Transit Gloria Mundi," Pitt blows bubbles to deceive the mob. One bubble is labeled "BEER."

672. "passenger": Passerby.

673. "eructation": Belching. Swift praises belching in *Tale of a Tub* 8.

674. "He equipped . . . Fatsisio": From February to April 1757 four fleets were dispatched to American waters, and in September the Rochefort expedition took place (see below, n. 675).

675. "The commander . . . wild grapes": See *Continuation*, 2:8–14. On 23 September 1757, at the outset of the expedition to capture Rochefort, the British fleet under Admiral Hawke took the half-finished fortifications on the small island of Aix near the mouth of the river Charente in Saintonge; Rochefort lay upriver. The garrison at Aix numbered six hundred men, but there was little fighting; the rest of the expedition was a failure. Smollett appears to have used two sources for the atom's satiric characterization of its inauspicious beginning. In Numbers 13:23

the Israelite spies sent into Canaan bring back an enormous bunch of grapes; there is dispute concerning whether Israel is strong enough to invade Canaan, and the spies report that they have seen giants in the land. Print 3616*, suggesting that the naval war should be prosecuted in the Caribbean instead of on the French coast, depicts a man on the island of Oléron shouting to the fleet through a trumpet, "Take what Grapes you please, so you let us have your Rice, Tobacco, Indigo, sugars, &c. &c." See Robert A. Day, "*Ut Pictura Poesis?* Smollett and the Graphic Arts," *Studies in Eighteenth-Century Culture*, vol. 10, ed. Harry C. Payne (Madison: University of Wisconsin Press, 1981), 297–312. Smollett was not alone in his sarcastic treatment of the Rochefort expedition. Samuel Johnson wrote, in *Idler*, no. 5 (13 May 1758), "I cannot but think that seven thousand women might have ventured to look at Rochefort, sack a village, rob a vineyard, and return in safety." Johnson further remarked, in an essay published posthumously in the *Gentleman's Magazine* 55 (October 1785): 764–65, "Caligula once marched to the sea-coasts and gathered cockle-shells; our army went to the coast of France, and filled their bellies with grapes" (p. 764).

676. "parapets of sand . . . naked eye": Numerous pamphlets and reports appeared in print to justify the conduct of the officers in charge of the expedition. Several of these were reviewed scathingly in *CR* 4 (December 1757): 468, 550–51 and in *CR* 5 (January 1758): 81–87. The atom's reference to parapets of sand echoes a passage in the January 1758 review essay: "our generals proceed upon the *evidence* of *things not seen*, and therefore [must be counted] among the number of the *faithful*" (p. 87). See above, n. 301; see also *Continuation*, 2:21.

677. "ascertain": Reconnoiter.

678. "Homer's account of the Cyclops": See *Odyssey* 9.190–93: this giant was *pelorios*, "monstrous"; "he was not like a man . . . but like a wooded peak of lofty mountains."

679. "commissary": Quartermaster; the person or department in charge of furnishing supplies.

680. "perspectives": Telescopes.

681. "Pho-beron-tia": The word is Greek and means "things to be dreaded," or bugbears, bugaboos.

682. "posteriors of an old woman": Smollett bases this fantastic scene on Print 3625*, "Sʳ Jnᵒ Suckling's Bugg-a-Boh's," in which a naval officer on board ship (Suckling was commander of the frigate *Viper*) contemplates through a telescope a group of women on shore who derisively expose their buttocks to him. He cries, "I am sure they are the Swiss Guards. I know them by their Broad Faces & their Whiskers." For fuller details see Day, "*Ut Pictura Poesis?* Smollett and the Graphic Arts."

683. "*sub dio*": L. A commonplace form of *sub divo*, under the open sky, in the open air (*OED*). The form is, in the strictest sense, an error. In *Travels*, Letter 24, Smol-

lett commits the same error: Nice is so dry that "you may pass . . . the whole night, *sub Dio*, without feeling the least dew" (p. 196). In *Humphry Clinker*, Matthew Bramble repeats the error in his letter to Dr. Lewis, London, May 29.

684. "a trading town . . . called Sa-rouf": Fort Fouras; see key. This fort, located at the mouth of the Charente where the river emptied (or "disembogued") into the sea, had to be taken before the British could sail upriver and lay siege to Rochefort. See Paul-Gabriel Boucé, "Smollett and the Expedition against Rochefort," *Modern Philology* 65 (1967): 33–38; and Boucé, "The 'Chinese Pilot' and 'Sa-rouf' in Smollett's *Atom*," *English Language Notes* 4 (1967): 273–75.

685. "admiral of the Fune": Admiral Edward Hawke; see key, PHAL-KHAN.

686. "Sel-uon": Admiral Sir Charles Knowles; see key.

687. "let": Impediment, hindrance.

688. "A Chinese pilot . . . nor be offended": The pilot's name was Joseph Thierry. Smollett's account is only slightly exaggerated. For details see the two essays by Boucé cited above, n. 684; and see *Continuation*, 2:15.

689. "Sey-seo-gun": Admiral; see key.

690. "a council of war was held": There were three councils. The first, on 25 September 1757, resolved to call off the landing; the second, on 28 September, determined to carry on with the original plan; the third, on 29 September, lasted for three hours (while the troops waited in landing craft) and concluded with a decision to cancel the attack. The fleet went home, arriving at Spithead on 6 October. See Corbett, 1:216–21.

691. "*re infecta*": L. With the task unperformed.

692. "the beast called Legion . . . Taycho lulled it": The failure of the Rochefort expedition caused considerable but brief controversy. Pitt quickly overcame the controversy by rhetorical bravado and parliamentary manipulation. General Mordaunt, commander of the expedition, was court-martialed; though judged innocent of disobeying the king's orders he was censured and dismissed from the service. See Fortescue, 313–15. The Atom treats these events and the controversies surrounding them cryptically; in the *Continuation*, 2:17–30, Smollett attacks Pitt severely but surreptitiously, attributing criticism to the minister's enemies.

693. "It growled at the . . . paradoxes of Sel-uon": This is the nearest Smollett comes in the *Atom* to acknowledging his own involvement with Admiral Knowles. In a review of Knowles's *The Conduct of Admiral Knowles on the Late Expedition Set in a True Light* (1758), *CR* 5 (May 1758): 438–39, he characterized the admiral as "ignorant, assuming, officious, fribbling . . . conceited as a peacock, obstinate as a mule, and mischievous as a monkey." The resulting libel suit, tried by Lord Mansfield, led to a fine of £100 and a term in the King's Bench prison. See Knapp, 218, 230–37.

694. "The other armament . . . disgrace and destruction": In early August 1757 the commanders of the fleet sent to attack the city of Louisbourg on Cape Breton

Island discovered through intercepted dispatches that the French troops, stores, and ships provided for the city's defense greatly exceeded those available to the British. The commanders at Halifax then canceled the operation.

695. "They demolished some forts . . . colonies of Japan": Smollett refers principally to the massacre at Fort William Henry, after which the British abandoned the territory of the Five (Iroquois) Nations. See *Continuation*, 2:41–43; see also Fortescue, 311–12.

696. "bubbles": In this familiar eighteenth-century usage the word means swindles, deceptions, frauds.

697. "victories over the Chinese and Ostrog": On 20 April 1757, in two separate engagements, Frederick's troops defeated the Austrians at Reichenberg and the French near Prague.

698. "blowed the gay bubbles . . . eyes": Print 3913* shows Pitt, clay pipe and bowl of soapsuds in hand, blowing bubbles to divert the mob.

699. "the ease and pleasure . . . that magician": Newcastle shared in the political benefits of the honeymoon period enjoyed by Pitt's new coalition government; see Browning, 261–64.

700. "Many a time and often": *Merchant of Venice* 1.3.106. The allusion is to a speech by Shylock to Antonio, who formerly abused the Jew for his money and his "usances" but, in need of his help, has begun to court and flatter him.

701. "profuse temper": Spendthrift nature; the reference is to Newcastle, not Pitt.

702. "principal": The actual party to a contract, rather than an agent. In this instance the "principal" is Pitt.

703. "turning the sieve and sheers": A popular method of divination, like "dowsing," but supposed to detect thieves; the shears, stuck into the sieve, would dip when they pointed to the guilty party. Congreve mentions this practice in *Love for Love* 2.1.108. There is a further allusion to the same scene later in the *Atom*; see below vol. 2, n. 37. Smollett had Congreve's play with him at Nice; see Knapp, 249.

704. "reading prayers backwards": The standard method of summoning the devil.

705. "*Abrasax Adonai*": *Adonai* is Hebrew for "Lord"; *Abrasax* was a name for God used by the followers of Basilides, a Gnostic teacher who lived in Roman Alexandria during the reigns of Hadrian and Antoninus Pius in the second century, A.D. The Basilidians were still active as a sect in the fourth century; among their beliefs was the idea that a substitute took the place of Christ upon the cross.

706. "goody . . . Camberwell": Goody, or goodwife, was a patronizing generic term for an old woman of the lower classes; Camberwell was in Smollett's time a fairly rural district in Surrey.

707. "Norway . . . conventicle": Lapland, the region of far northern Europe including Norway, was synonymous with witchcraft; a conventicle was a more or less clandestine religious meeting. Smollett refers sarcastically to a coven of witches.

708. "*De volucri arborea*": The title means "On the Tree-Bird." This treatise, pub-

lished in Frankfurt in 1619, is by Count Michael Maier (1568–1622), physician, occultist, alchemist, and private secretary to the German emperor Rudolph II. Maier wrote seventeen Latin works on such occult subjects as "natural magic." *De volucri arborea* is not concerned with sorcery, but is instead an extremely confusing discussion of the barnacle goose and other anomalies of nature as demonstrations of the wonders of God's power. For an account of Maier's argument see Robert A. Day, "Joyce, Stoom, King Mark: 'Glorious Name of Irish Goose,'" *James Joyce Quarterly* 12 (1975): 221–22, 247–48.

709. "the Rosicrucian society . . . chastity": Whether or not such a group as the Rosicrucians ever existed, numerous writings about or allegedly by its members appeared in the sixteenth and seventeenth centuries. The Rosicrucians were supposed to possess ancient wisdom and to be powerful magicians; Pope alludes to their requirement of strict chastity in *The Rape of the Lock* 1.67–68. Thieving-Lane, now Great George Street in Westminster, was inhabited in Smollett's day by dealers in secondhand goods, by pawnbrokers, and therefore also by the thieves who supplied both trades.

710. "three divisions of magic . . . diabolical": These divisions of magic were traditional; descriptions of them were available in many sources, including Chambers, under "Magic." They are mentioned in Smollett's *British Magazine* 6 (1762): 173–74.

711. "Pharmacopola": G. A dealer in drugs.

712. "the glass sphere . . . Albertus Magnus": The "artificial" devices of magic mentioned here were included in many standard lists of ancient wonders. Smollett could have found the first five in Defoe's *A System of Magick* (1727), 60. Archimedes (287–212 B.C.) made a glass sphere that showed the movements of the heavenly bodies. The second-century Latin compiler Aulus Gellius, in *Noctes atticæ* 9.12, mentions a flying wooden dove made by Archytus, a Greek statesman and philosopher (c. 400 B.C.). On the emperor Leo, Smollett appears to be in error. He has evidently conflated two quoted passages in his review of Abbé de Marigny, *History of the Arabians* (1750; trans. 1758), *CR* 5 (March–April 1758): 136–44, 177–88: "Mamon wrote to Emperor Michael the stammerer [sic], 'send to me the most learned philosopher Leo. . . .' [Mamon's court had] a tree of massy gold . . . eighteen large principal branches . . . birds of gold and silver . . . warbled out various notes" (pp. 185–86); see Basker, 224, 242. Boethius (A.D. 480–524), author of *De Consolatione philosophiæ* (c. 520), is said by the historian Cassiodorus (c. A.D. 480–575) to have made a sundial and a waterclock, but no source for the birds or serpents has been traced. Albertus Magnus, in addition to his many authentic achievements in science and philosophy, was reputed to have made an iron man that could speak.

713. "the magicians of Pharaoh": Exodus 7:11–12 tells of how the pharaoh's magicians cast down their rods and, with their "enchantments," turned them into serpents, as Aaron had done.

714. "that conjurer . . . deprived of all motion": An allusion to Casparus Peucerus, *Commentarius: De Præcipuis divinationum generibus*, "Commentary: On the Principal Varieties of Divination" (Frankfurt, 1606). In the course of a chapter treating the close resemblances between devilish and divine miracles, Peucerus includes the "wonderful" story of a female harper of Bologna (p. 14). Smollett's allusion is an exact translation from the Latin original.

715. "according to St. Isidore . . . enemies": Saint Isidore of Seville (c. A.D. 560–636) was the author of the voluminous *Etymologiæ*, a compendium of knowledge. Smollett refers to a passage in book 8, "De ecclesia et sectis diversis" ("On the Church and Various Sects"), chapter 9, "De Magis" ("Of Magicians"), paragraph 9, "Magi sunt qui . . ." ("They are magicians who . . ."). See *Patrologia Latina*, 82: col. 311.

716. "Cato . . . *coeunt, &c.*": Marcus Porcius Cato, or Cato the Elder (234–149 B.C.), gives the charm for healing a dislocation in *De agri cultura* ("On Farming," or "On Agriculture"), section 159. One splits a reed, lays it on the dislocation, and chants: "*motas væta daries dardares astataries dissunapiter*" (Loeb text) until the parts come together. The words of the chant are meaningless; the idiosyncratic corruptions of the Latin as repeated by Smollett indicate that his source was a transcription of a particular medieval manuscript.

717. "the virtues of ABRACADABRA": See *Briton*, no. 4 (19 June 1762): 20: the word *Scotsman* "shall have no more efficacy than the ABRACADABRA, or any other talisman that ever necromancy contrived." See also *Briton*, no. 38 (12 February 1763): 226: party slogans, "like the cabalistical terms *Abraxas* and *Abracadabra*, will, I hope, be the more efficacious, the less they are understood."

718. "Wendelinus . . . hexameter verse": Gottfried Wendelin (1580–1660), or "Wendelinus," was an important seventeenth-century cosmographer. Julius Caesar Scaliger (1484–1558) was a celebrated classical scholar and writer on botany and zoology. Claude de Saumaise (1588–1653), or "Salmasius," was the most noted classical scholar of his time. Athanasius Kircher, S.J. (1601–80), wrote extensively on both conventional and occult science. Quintus Sammonicus Serenus (d. A.D. 212) wrote *De medecina præcepta saluberrima*, a didactic poem in hexameters arguing that the efficacy of "abracadabra" as an amulet for the treatment of ague is a childish superstition. Serenus includes a diagram of the "disposition" of the word, which can be formed into the sides of a triangle of letters reading the same in any direction. Chambers, "Abracadabra," may have been Smollett's source, but the same material is also included in Montfaucon, *Antiquity Explained*, 2:224–27, 240–41; see below, n. 722.

719. "Αβρασαξ . . . days in the year": For Basilides, see above, n. 705. The numbers of the letters of Αβρασαξ, or "Abrasax," as they are placed in the Greek alphabet, can be made to add up to 365 if they are properly manipulated.

720. "Baronius . . . Annals": Cardinal Caesar Baronius (1538–1607) was the author of the huge and learned *Annales ecclesiastici* (1588), long the standard work on

church history. Smollett refers to the *"gemma ex amethysto,"* a figure of a man holding a spear and a shield on which is written the word "ABRASAX." The figure first appears in volume two of the *Annales*, second edition (Antwerp, 1597), and Baronius declares (p. 65) that the talisman had been found since the publication of the first edition. In any case Smollett errs; that Baronius discusses the talisman at all means that it was discovered in the sixteenth century, not the seventeenth.

721. "the figure of St. George": *CR* 14 (September 1762): 216–22 includes a generally unfavorable review of John Pettingal, *A Dissertation on the Origin of the Equestrian Figure of the George and of the Garter* (1753): "Such is the substance of this learned, ingenious, and very useless dissertation . . . the author misspent talents which might be employed more to the advantage of literature." For the Atom's long account of the history and lore of the Saint George figure Smollett took most of his material, including nearly all of the quotations, directly from Pettingal's work, from the review, or from both, transposing the position of phrases in a very complicated manner.

722. "Montfaucon . . . Sig. Capello": Bernard de Montfaucon (1655–1741), a cleric and scholar of immense industry, devoted himself to a reconstruction of antiquity from statuary, inscriptions, and gems. His ten-volume work, *Antiquity Explained, and Represented in Sculptures* (1719, 1724), was translated by David Humphreys 1721–25; the second volume of the translation includes a long section on "The Abraxas" in part 2, book 2. Montfaucon's *Antiquities of Italy* (1702), translated by John Henley (2d ed., 1725), was one of the sources Smollett used when writing his *Travels*; see Martz, 86–87. The work includes an account of the antique gems in the collection of "Antonis Capelli." Capelli, or Capello, a Venetian senator, was thought to own the largest collection of such gems in his day. Both Pettingal (p. 25) and the review of his work in *CR* (p. 219) mention Capelli's collection. The abraxas "exhibited" by Montfaucon appears as figure 21 of plate 53 in the second volume of the Humphreys translation of *Antiquity Explained*.

723. "crusards": Crusaders. The *OED* cites only one instance of this word, from the English translation of Voltaire's *Micromégas* (1752). The translation was attributed to Smollett by Ralph Griffiths, in the *Monthly Review* 8 (November 1752): 376. In the *Travels*, Letter 10, Smollett uses the variant spelling "croisards" (p. 83).

724. "Constantine's labarum": The imperial standard of Constantine (A.D. 285–337), marked with a cross. At the crucial battle of the Mulvian Bridge in the year 312, a cross was said to have appeared to Constantine in the heavens along with the words *in hoc signo vinces*, "in this sign you shall conquer." The episode is supposed to have caused Constantine, and Rome, to convert to Christianity. See *CR* 14 (September 1762): 219.

725. "George the Arian": George of Cappadocia, an Arian or disbeliever in the trinity. In A.D. 355 he ousted Bishop Athanasius from Alexandria; his purification

of the temple occurred in the year 361, shortly before his murder. Smollett's account of George the Arian, following, combines details from Pettingal, *Dissertation*, 34, and from the review of Pettingal, *CR* 14 (September 1762): 220.

726. "I kiss your hilt": Smollett's intention, though unclear, is doubtless obscene; according to Wright, "hilt" can mean flesh or skin.

727. "the mystical words . . . Greek character of termination": Verbatim from Pettingal, *Dissertation*, 24, as repeated in the review of Pettingal, *CR* 14 (September 1762): 219.

728. "De Croy . . . *Gnostics*": Jean de Croi or "Croius" (?–1659), a French Protestant theologian, published his *Specimen conjecturarum et observationum in quædam Origenis, Irenæi, et Tertulliani loca* at Geneva in 1632. The *Specimen* is a prospectus for a commentary on the authors mentioned in the title and on the so-called thirty aeons of Valentinus, a Gnostic who taught in Rome, A.D. 135–160. The "aeons" or ages, which Valentinus maintained were deities, are apparently what Smollett refers to as "genealogies."

729. "Grabius": Johann Ernst Grabe (1666–1711) came to England in 1695 from Königsberg. He settled at Oxford and took orders, attracting extensive patronage for his voluminous and learned publications in theology. His edition of Irenæus, *S. Irenæi contra omnes hæreses libri quinque* (Oxford, 1702), prints de Croi's *Specimen* at the end, separately paginated. The *Specimen* makes no mention of *abrasax*. Since the *Specimen* is neither cited nor quoted in Pettingal's *Dissertation*, Smollett may have taken the trouble to look at the work himself; perhaps he intended to lead the curious reader on a wild-goose chase.

730. "Albertus Magnus . . . difficulty": See above, n. 712. Smollett misrepresents Albertus, who in fact said that he had been able to learn something even from persons in these despised professions.

731. "Henry Cornelius Agrippa . . . *Ceremoniis*": The German Agrippa (1486–1535), like many early students of science, was thought to deal in black magic. *De occulta philosophia* (1531) is one of his works; *De cæcis ceremoniis* (the actual title is *De ceremoniis magicis*, 1533) is spurious.

732. "who kept his demon . . . immediately disappeared": Smollett takes the story of Agrippa's dog from a review of Peter Whalley's edition of the works of Ben Jonson, *CR* 1 (June 1756): 462–72. The review censures Whalley's pedantic erudition in the notes to his edition, citing as a specimen of it his irrelevant digression on Agrippa's dog to illustrate a line in Jonson about affixing a charm to a dog's collar. The story is from the Italian historian Paulus Jovius, *Elogium doctorum vivorum* (1577); the Latin reads, "Go, damned beast, that hast entirely damned me" (p. 469). The river is the Arar or *Araris*, Latin for the Saône; "Soame" may be a printer's error.

733. "Don't we read . . . the devil?": For the magicians of Pharaoh see above, n. 713. Manasses, or Manasseh, "used enchantments, and dealt with familiar spirits and

wizards," 2 Kings 21:6. The witch of Endor raised up the spirit of Samuel for Saul, 1 Samuel 28:7–25. Simon, a sorcerer of Samaria, was converted by Philip, Acts 8:9–13. Paul blinded the sorcerer Barjesus at Paphos, Acts 13:6–11; he cast out the devil from the body of the sorceress, Acts 16:16–19.

734. "the fathers": The fathers of the church, or Christian writers of antiquity.

735. "particularly in Scotland . . . sorceries": King James conducted the first witch trials at North Berwick in 1590; between that year and 1704, more than four thousand witches were burned. In 1563 witchcraft was made a capital crime in Scotland and remained so until 1736; see Christina Larner, *Enemies of God: The Witch Hunt in Scotland* (Baltimore: Johns Hopkins University Press, 1981).

736. "the havock that was made . . . those diabolical delinquents": Increase Mather (1639–1723) and his son Cotton (1663–1728) were closely involved in the Salem witch trials; both wrote works on witchcraft in 1693. Cotton's admiring biography of Sir William Phips (1697), included in his famous *Magnalia Christi Americana*, observes in chapter 16: "divers were Condemned, against whom the *chief Evidence* was founded in the *Spectral Exhibitions.*" Phips or Phipps, made governor of the Massachusetts Bay colony by King William in 1691, appointed a bigot named Stoughton director of a special commission responsible for the trials of witches. In 1695 Phipps was recalled to England to answer for his conduct. *CR* 25 (January 1768): 34, reviewing the second volume of Thomas Hutchinson's *History of Massachusetts Bay Colony* (1768), charges Phipps with "Horrid barbarities . . . disgraceful to humanity."

737. "Urban Grandier . . . *Achas*": Canon Grandier, whose downfall actually resulted from writing lampoons against Cardinal Richelieu, died at the stake in August 1634. Smollett, in *Voltaire*, 6:193, says that Grandier was found guilty on the "evidence" of the same devils named here in the *Atom*, "in other words, by the Ursulines, supposed to be possessed by those devils." Grandier in fact was known to have engaged in sexual misconduct with the Ursuline nuns to whom he was confessor.

738. "king James's History . . . in his breech": James's *Demonologie* (1597) does not contain these details. Smollett's source, if any, has not been traced; it seems probable that he has conflated three elements that recur in numerous descriptions of witches' sabbaths: lewd dances; the use of candles, often black; and the practice of saluting the devil by kissing his breech. See, for example, Boguet, *Discours des sorciers* (1608), in Montague Summers, *The History of Witchcraft and Demonology* (New York: Alfred Knopf, 1926), 132–43.

739. "the earl of Gowry's conspiracy . . . characters were removed": On 5 August 1600 John Ruthven, earl of Gowry, allegedly attempted the king's life after trapping him alone in an upper room of a castle. The circumstances were mysterious, and Gowry may have been "framed." The story of the amulet is in Maitland, *The History and Antiquities of Scotland*, 2:103–4, and is reproduced in the

review of Maitland in *CR* 3 (April 1757): 298–99. The "certain person" was one Weemys, a gentleman of the bedchamber to James; Weemys reported hearing that Gowry had studied magic in Venice.

740. "old women . . . agent of the devil": A reference to the bench of bishops, who were usually slavish followers of the administration when voting in the House of Lords.

741. "inference . . . risque of being annihilated": In this passage Smollett may be referring to the religious crisis experienced by Newcastle in his last years; see Browning, 329–30. The doubts and anxieties attributed to Newcastle, however they may strike us, were taken very seriously by such contemporaries of Smollett as Samuel Richardson and Samuel Johnson.

742. "assembled . . . nature of the soul": The scene that follows is undoubtedly based on an episode in chapter 7 of Voltaire's *Micromégas*; see above, n. 723. In this episode the two giants from Sirius question earthly philosophers on the nature of the soul and receive wildly conflicting answers. Some of the answers given, though derived from philosophers as different as Plato, Aristoxenus, Malebranche, and Leibniz, seem to come from Voltaire's *Elements of Newton's Philosophy*, chapter 7, "Of the Soul," in *Voltaire*, 19:114–22.

743. "*accident*": In scholastic philosophy, any characteristic that differentiates an individual from other members of its class.

744. "ay, there's the rub": *Hamlet* 3.1.64. A rub is an impediment or hindrance.

745. "back-friends": This ambiguous term can mean supporters or backers, but more usually it refers to pretended or false friends. Print 3487 is entitled "The Mirrour: Or the British Lion's Back Friends Detected."

746. "the centurions, the decuriones": In Roman military terminology, leaders respectively of one hundred and of ten soldiers; here, persons controlling groups of borough electors.

747. "concoct": Cook; hence, digest and assimilate.

748. "vague promises . . . soul and body": In addition to equating Newcastle's promises with his farts, Smollett may be alluding to Pope's picture of Jove at stool, wiping himself with petitions; see *Dunciad* 2.83–96. The phrase "eruptive crudities" refers to undigested matter bursting out.

749. "recalled the general . . . Fatsisio": Early in 1756 General William Shirley was recalled as commander-in-chief in America. He was to be replaced by the earl of Loudon, who did not arrive until May. See *Continuation*, 1:342.

750. "Abra-moria": General James Abercromby; see key.

751. "having reconnoitred . . . considerable slaughter": General Abercromby arrived at Albany in June 1756 and promptly lost forts Ontario and Oswego to the French and Indians; see *Continuation*, 1:358–61. The details mentioned here suggest that Smollett has conflated these events with Abercromby's disastrous defeat at Ticonderoga in July 1758. See *Continuation*, 2:286–90; see also below, vol. 2, n. 82, and see Davies, 332–33, and Fortescue, 328–38.

752. "Yaf-frai and Ya-loff": Generals Jeffrey Amherst and James Wolfe; see key.
753. "a strong Chinese fortress . . . Fatsisio": On 26 July 1758 Amherst and Wolfe took Louisbourg on Cape Breton Island.
754. "a factor . . . commercial settlement": Ka-liff is Robert, Lord Clive; see key. A factor was a member of the third grade of East India Company employees; senior and junior merchants ranked above factors, writers below. Fla-sao is Plassey, a village in west Bengal. Clive's decisive victory there on 23 June 1757 helped to establish British rule in India; see Fortescue, 423–31. The "trading company" is the East India Company, which, by the mid-1750s, had virtually acquired the status of an independent state in the region of Calcutta and in other parts of India. See Lucy S. Sutherland, *The East India Company in Eighteenth-Century Politics* (London: Oxford University Press, 1952).
755. "Taycho was an utter stranger . . . end of Tartary": Smollett misrepresents the historical facts. Clive had been active in the fighting in India since the siege of Pondichéry in 1748; Pitt characterized him in Parliament as "that heaven-born general." Pitt also promoted Amherst to the rank of major general and, over some opposition, gave Wolfe a brigade in 1758. Though Pitt was able to make these appointments, it appears that his wishes were often frustrated by the king's stubborn insistence on seniority as the prime factor in promotions and assignments; see Williams, 1:366–67, 2:24. In this passage Smollett echoes the account he had given earlier in *Briton*, no. 37 (5 February 1763): 221, where he observed that while Pitt had made three disastrously bad choices of officers, the victorious military leaders had all been in service before Pitt's arrival on the scene. This particular argument against Pitt is perhaps Smollett's weakest and least justifiable.
756. "the Isle Ka-frit-o": Cape Breton; see key.
757. "Yaf-frai has slain . . . ten thousands": "Saul hath slain his thousands, and David his ten thousands" (1 Samuel 21:11).
758. "The emperor of China . . . the army of China": Smollett records these events in *Continuation*, 2:109, 310, 322–23, adding (to the credit of France) that the French government acted to replace the duc de Richelieu in Hanover, where he had been guilty of inhumane conduct while serving as military governor.
759. "One of his generals . . . claimed the victory": At Zorndorf on 25 August 1758 Frederick's army compelled the Russians to retreat. The Russians lost ten thousand troops, the Prussians eleven thousand.
760. "Another of his leaders . . . Ostrog": At Hochkirch on 14 October 1758 Prince Francis of Brunswick was defeated by the Austrians, with nine thousand killed.
761. "he repulsed the Chinese army with considerable loss": On 3 October 1758 Frederick raised the siege of Neiss, but at the cost of heavy casualties.
762. "a victory over the general of the Ostrog": On 10 November 1758 Frederick recaptured Dresden, forcing Count von Daun to retreat into Bohemia.
763. "Bron-xi-tic . . . farm of Yesso": Bron-xi-tic is Ferdinand, duke of Brunswick;

see key. Ferdinand took charge of the combined forces not under the direct command of Frederick at the end of November 1757. On 23 June 1758 he defeated the French at Krefeld, but by mid-August the disposition of his troops had become so fluid that he recognized an impasse and withdrew to Hanover. See *Continuation*, 2:178, 326–32, 334.

764. "Tzin-khall . . . Terra Australis": Tzin-khall is Senegal; see key. "Terra Australis" is the older name for Australia. The geography of the eastern hemisphere as used by Smollett is a mirror image of his real subject, the West; Australia thus equals Africa.

765. "Banyan": Quaker; see key.

766. "conjured": Earnestly entreated.

767. "Thum-Khumm-qua": Thomas Cumming; see key.

768. "solemnly promising . . . all his forces": The Moorish emir of Senegal promised to grant an English monopoly of trade if the French could be driven out of his country. Smollett took great interest in Senegal and in the story of the British campaign there. *Briton*, no. 27 (27 November 1762): 162 argues at length for the value of Senegal and its exports. *Continuation*, 2:270–78 describes the campaign, the story of which is also told in the *British Magazine* 1 (April 1760): 179–81. The campaign and Cumming's part in it inspired a book and a pamphlet, both of which were reviewed in *CR*; see below, n. 774.

769. "interesting": From the point of view of profit.

770. "a precious gum . . . exorbitant price": Gum senega, a variety of gum arabic, was widely used as a filler or stiffener for fabrics. See *Briton*, no. 27 (27 November 1762): 162: "we expended, for this gum, a yearly sum not less than one hundred thousand pounds . . . during the war, this money, thro' the medium of the Dutch, was paid to our enemies."

771. "Taycho at length . . . according to his prediction": Though Smollett was firmly convinced that fault for the delay rested with Pitt, opposition in fact came from Cumberland and Lord Ligonier, commander-in-chief of the land forces. Cumming and a colleague, Touchet, proposed their Senegal campaign in 1756, and in February 1757 they received a letter from Pitt promising a monopoly of the Senegal trade if they succeeded. They finally got under way in March 1758; and on 1 May Fort Louis, the French headquarters on the island of Goree at the mouth of the Senegal, capitulated to the British troops. See *The Jenkinson Papers*, ed. Ninetta S. Jucker (London: Macmillan, 1949), 106.

772. "magnified": Praised, extolled.

773. "Taycho . . . flung the door in his face": In fact Pitt received Cumming with joy, but informed him that a mistake had occurred; the promised monopoly, proving to be illegal, could not be conferred. See *The Jenkinson Papers*, 106.

774. "Such was the candour . . . carried into execution": *CR* 14 (December 1762): 478 unfavorably reviews *A Letter to a Merchant at Bristol* (1762), written in defense of

Pitt, arguing instead that Cumming should have a monopoly of the Senegal trade because he was solely responsible for the British conquest there. *CR* 6 (September 1758): 252, in a review of an earlier book (*In Honour to the Administration. The Importance of the African Expedition Considered*, 1758, by Malachy Postlethwayt, Esq.), observes that the expedition "was undertaken at the remonstrance of *Friend Cumming*. We have undoubted reason to believe the ministry ascribe to him, and to no other, that scheme. . . . They consulted him . . . they followed his advice . . . no doubt they will reward him in proportion to the national advantage . . . [for] the great expence, loss of time and trade he has been at." A "projector" is one who proposes or undertakes to perform a project; an entrepreneur.

775. "renounced by the whole sect of the Banyans": According to the *DNB* there is no evidence that the Quakers cast out or repudiated Cumming.

776. "found favour with a subsequent minister." On 18 November 1761, after the earl of Bute had come to power, Cumming was granted a pension of £500 per year for thirty-one years on the Irish Establishment. See *Calendar of Home Office Papers, 1760–65* (London: Longmans, 1878) under that date. The pension was also recorded in the *Gentleman's Magazine* 33 (November 1763): 541.

777. "The other . . . in the beginning": Here Smollett begins an account of the expedition in the summer of 1758 against several targets in Brittany: Saint Malo, Cherbourg, and Saint Cas. The expedition was very costly, involving a huge fleet and over twelve thousand men, and one of Pitt's main intentions was to divert substantial French forces to Brittany from the German front; in this the expedition was ineffective. See *Continuation*, 2:246–65, where Smollett treats the expedition with great severity, appending "reflections on war in general." Smollett may have written, and reviewed, a pamphlet castigating the officers who led the expedition for incompetence; see Paul-Gabriel Boucé, "A Note on Smollett's *Continuation of the Complete History of England*," *Review of English Studies*, n.s., 20 (1969), 57–60.

778. "considerable damage . . . the windows of the enemy": Smollett's fantasy in his account of this episode is complex. He refers to the prank, frequent among "Mohocks" or riotous young men of fashion, of breaking windows (then far more costly than now) by throwing heavy coins; he alludes to the game of ducks and drakes, or skipping stones over water, thus accusing the government of idly throwing away or squandering money; and he echoes a current witticism about the conduct and the objectives of the expedition. Horace Walpole wrote to Sir Horace Mann on 18 June 1758: "The French have well said, 'Les anglais viennent nous casser les vitres avec des guinées'"; see Walpole, *Correspondence*, 21:213–14. Smollett observed in *Briton*, no. 38 (12 February 1763): 228: "Here we continued tilting among rocks, mispending our time, consuming our provision, making ducks and drakes of our broad pieces [guineas], and expend-

ing our ammunition in shooting sea-mews." *Briton*, no. 12 (14 August 1762): 68 refers to "petty excursions along the coast of France . . . breaking glass-windows, and alarming fishermen." The Saint Malo landing took place at Cancale, 6–8 June; there was no engagement with French troops. See Fortescue, 348–52.

779. "forces were landed . . . streets in procession": In August 1758 Cherbourg was demolished by the British, who met no resistance. Stores and ships (including, importantly for the war effort, numerous privateers) were burned; twenty-one French cannon were brought back to England and carried in a parade from Hyde Park to the Tower. See *Continuation*, 2:265.

780. "Hylib-bib": General Edward Bligh; see key. Bligh, aged seventy-three in 1758, had been appointed a lieutenant-general four years earlier, largely by seniority; at that time he had had little combat experience.

781. "he advanced some leagues into the country": On 8 September 1758 Bligh marched inland from Saint Malo to Saint Cas.

782. "he depended upon . . . an engineer": Bligh, who had been reluctant to command the expedition, depended heavily on the advice of his quartermaster-general, Colonel Robert Clarke (or Clerk), who may well have been totally incompetent; see Corbett, 1:294, 299.

783. "rusty": Rancid.

784. "motions were so slow . . . three miles": On 10 September 1758 Bligh received intelligence that a French army was near. At 2:00 A.M. the next morning he sounded the *generale* on the drums and retreated to the coast, taking until 9:00 A.M. to cover three miles. See *Continuation*, 2:258, 264.

785. "his van . . . massacred or taken": Bligh took ship with his forward troops, or van, abandoning the rest of his men to distract the enemy. Smollett here paraphrases the account of this episode given in *Continuation*, 2:261.

786. "these notes of discontent": *CR* 6 (November 1758): 435 slashingly attacks a pamphlet (*A Letter from . . . B[li]gh to . . . P[it]t*, 1758) purportedly written by Bligh in justification of his conduct: "the loss of seven or eight hundred men is a circumstance hardly worth mentioning . . . but surely we have reason to complain, if a thousand of our choice troops were unnecessarily sacrificed." *Briton*, no. 12 (14 August 1762): 68 refers scornfully to "great officers who, at the approach of the enemy, would have wisely declined a battle, without having taken precautions for a retreat, and left the whole rear of [their] army to be cut in pieces, or carried into captivity."

787. "keeping sheep on the island of Xicoco": Shortly after the Saint Cas debacle Bligh resigned his offices and retired to his estates in Ireland.

788. "engineer . . . mountains of Ximo": Colonel Clarke retired to Scotland. Smollett once again refers scornfully to Clarke's "excellent nose," implicitly comparing him to the dogs and pigs used to hunt and dig up truffles.

Volume 2

1. "turn tail": Abandon, desert.

2. "province": Department, area.

3. "the president": Granville was lord president of the cabinet; see above, vol. 1, n. 285. Here Smollett intends no specific reference.

4. "a two-penny trumpet . . . a sword . . . a rattle for my lord Cuboy": They are to occupy themselves with military trivia; for the rattle, see above, vol. 1, n. 106.

5. "animal spirits": See above, vol. 1, n. 127.

6. "exercitations": Habitual exercises.

7. "a total privation of eye-sight": Smollett may have intended a retaliation against Print 3886, which represents George III as blindfolded and being led about by his mother and Lord Bute.

8. "to entail . . . latest posterity": To entail is, legally, to ensure that property may not be disposed of, but inherited in irrevocable succession. Latest: last. Smollett's fear of eternal indebtedness was basic and pervasive; see Sekora, 135–50.

9. "brought to market . . . in its defence": A paraphrase of *Hamlet* 4.4.20–22: see above, vol. 1, p. 59 and n. 649. *Briton*, no. 7 (10 July 1762): 40 remarks: "I hope the Elector of H——r will never again have influence enough with the K——g of G——t B——n, to engage him in a war for retrieving it, that shall cost his kingdom annually, for a series of years, more than double the value of the country in dispute."

10. "I quit the reins of administration": See below, n. 246.

11. "the dog that returns to its vomit": See Proverbs 26:11: "As a dog returneth to his vomit, so a fool returneth to his folly." See also 2 Peter 2:22.

12. "delegation": Delegation of powers.

13. "hæmorrhoids . . . great disturbance": Smollett may be alluding to the fits of gout and of acute depression which on several occasions totally incapacitated Pitt, as in November 1756 when he was about to assume office as secretary of state. See Williams, 1:284, 290, 307.

14. "annihilated all opposition in the council of Twenty-eight": By 1758 the cabinet numbered about seventeen. The full cabinet met rarely, despite the protests of many members. Newcastle had formed an *ad hoc* "conciliabulum" consisting of himself, Pitt, Granville, Legge (chancellor of the exchequer), and one or two others; this group convened more regularly than the cabinet. See Brooke, *Chatham*, 13.

15. "parade . . . coast of China": The implication is that naval operations off the French coast were wasteful and useless.

16. "the original, and the most natural scene of the war": The war had begun with skirmishes between English and French troops along the Ohio. Smollett argued constantly in the *Briton* that only the American war had any value for Britain.

17. "Quib-quab": Quebec; see key.
18. "a broad . . . river": The Saint Lawrence.
19. "two different avenues . . . the same instant of time": This passage echoes and slightly intensifies the sarcastic commentary on Pitt's Canadian plans in *Continuation*, 3:171–73. On the campaign as a whole see Fortescue, 364–94.
20. "Yaff-ray . . . Ya-loff": Generals Amherst and Wolfe; see key. Wolfe had earned Pitt's admiration by a critique of the operation at Rochefort; he appeared to have been the only officer there who had shown good sense. See Corbett, 1:209–22.
21. "art": Human as opposed to natural agency.
22. "one Chinese general": The chevalier de Bourlamaque, who had his headquarters at Ticonderoga.
23. "the route which was to be followed by Yaff-rai": In the summer of 1759 Amherst executed a concentric advance on Montreal with three bodies of troops. The first, led by Wolfe, moved up the Saint Lawrence to capture Quebec; the second advanced west from Fort Niagara, which was reduced on 24 July; the third marched northwest from Albany by way of Ticonderoga and Crown Point, which Amherst fortified in August. Further advance seemed impossible at the time.
24. "another commanded a separate corps": The marquis de Montcalm had encamped with his troops between the Saint Charles and the Montmorency, seven miles to the east; see Corbett, 1:419.
25. "another darling scheme": The invasion of Martinique. On Pitt's plans for this invasion see Williams, 1:380.
26. "Thin-quo": Martinique or "Martinico"; see key.
27. "a body of forces": Land forces, soldiery.
28. "*cognomina*": L. Family names. The following digression on surnames had the distinction of being reprinted by Edmund Burke in the *Annual Register* for 1769 (pt. 2, pp. 193–96). Smollett's source, if there is a single source, has not been traced, though William Camden's *Remains Concerning Britain* (1605) is a possible stimulus; the 1674 edition of Camden's work contains a section of 140 pages concerning English names and their origins, beginning (pp. 193–94) with Roman names of ridiculous derivation, all of which Smollett includes in his digression. Smollett alternates between received and fantastic, or conjectural, etymologies of names; some of the Roman names are *cognomina*, some not. The following list of glosses on the names in Smollett's digression relies on *A Greek-English Lexicon*, ed. Henry G. Liddell and Robert Scott, rev. ed. (Oxford: Clarendon Press, 1968); *A Latin Dictionary*, ed. Charlton T. Lewis and Charles Short (1879; reprint, Oxford: Clarendon Press, 1962); and Iiro Kajanto, *The Latin Cognomina* (Helsinki: Finnish Academy of Sciences, 1965).

Xenophon: Smollett's etymology is correct. Xenophon (428/7–364 B.C.), a general in the Persian wars, was a prolific and varied writer.

Pythagoras: The name is probably related etymologically to Pythian Apollo, though the root *pyth-* has to do with rotting or decay.

Heraclitus: "The glory of Herakles." The founder of metaphysics, Heraclitus (540–475 B.C.) was called "weeping" because of his solitary life and scorn for mankind.

Pisones: *Piso*, a mortar; hence, grinder or miller.

Cicerones: From *cicer*, chickpea or "vetch"; both Pliny and Plutarch are inclined to this derivation.

Lentuli: Slow, sluggish; probably not from *lens*, lentil.

Fabij (Fabii): From *faba*, bean; but also "pellet," as of goat dung.

Serrani: From *serra*, saw; possibly from *serere*, to sow.

Suilli: Smollett's etymology is correct.

Bubulci: Smollett's etymology is correct; found in Pliny.

Porci: *Porcellus*, *porcilla*, piglet.

Strabo: Squinting. Strabo (64/3 B.C.–21 A.D.) was a Roman historian and geographer. But "senator" suggests an allusion to Smollett's political antagonist John Wilkes, M.P. (see key, JAN-KI-DTZIN). Wilkes squinted badly, as in Hogarth's famous print; see Print 4041*.

Squintum: This epithet had been given currency in Samuel Foote's farce *The Minor* (1760), which lampoons the Methodist evangelist George Whitefield.

Pæti: Having leering eyes, prettily blinking; an epithet of Venus.

Pigsnies: Archaic term for darling, sweetheart.

Limi: Probably from *lima*, a file, though *limus* means leering or looking sideways.

P. Silius: Propraetor of Bithynia in 51–50 B.C., a recipient of letters from Cicero. *Silo*, *silus*, snubnosed.

Ovid: The poet Publius Ovidius Naso (43 B.C.–A.D. 17). *Naso*, large-nosed; *ovis*, sheep.

Horace: The poet Quintus Horatius Flaccus (65–8 B.C.). *Flaccus* means flabby or flap-eared.

Burrhi: From *pyrrhus*, Greek for red.

Nigri: Black (hair).

Rufi: Red-headed.

Aquilij (Aquilii): Having swarthy skin; Smollett may be thinking of the similarity with *aquila*, eagle.

Rutilij (Rutilii): Red-headed.

Lappa: A burr, as in the name Burr.

Cincinnatus: With curly hair. Lucius Quinctius Cincinnatus is supposed to have been called from plowing his fields to the military dictatorship of Rome in an emergency of 458 B.C.

Hala: No such *cognomen* is known, though the prefix *hal-* is associated with both breath and odors.

Plauti: Flatfooted.
Panci: No such *cognomen* is known; Smollett may have had in mind Sancho
    Panza, or belly, paunch.
Valgi: Bowlegged.
Vari: Derived from *varo*, knock-kneed.
Vatiæ: Bowlegged or knock-kneed.
Scauri: With swollen ankles.
Tuditani: From *tudes*, hammer, mallet; hence, driving or beating.
Malici: No such *cognomen* is known.
Cenestellæ: Possibly an error for *Fenestella*, one of the smaller gates of Rome.
Leccæ: No such *cognomen* is known.

29. "the Bills of Mortality": Official records of baptisms and burials, kept by the
clerks of 109 parishes in and around London, were published weekly. The "bills
of mortality" thus included most of the greater metropolitan area.

30. "the *Buteo*, or *Buzzard . . . Triorchis*": See Francis Willughby, *The Ornithology of
Francis Willughby* (1678), 71: "That sort of hawk (as Pliny witnesseth) which the
Romans named *Buteo*, was by the Grecians called Triorchis, from the number of
its stones [testicles]." Smollett certainly refers to Lord Bute, his "perfidious
patron."

31. "*Knaves-acre*": From Old English, "land assigned to young men or servants."
Three such plots, none of them in London, are listed in John Field, *English Field
Names* (Newton Abbott: David & Charles, 1972).

32. "*Hair-stones*": A reference to testicles is probably intended.

33. "broke": Deprived of his commission.

34. "discovery of the *North-west* passage": Efforts to find a North American polar sea
route from the Atlantic to the Pacific began in the late sixteenth century and still
continued in the 1760s. A route was finally discovered by a British expedition
under Robert McClure in 1853–54, during a search for the lost exploring party
of Sir John Franklin.

35. "*Spring-garden*": The "old" Spring Garden (closed about 1660) was between
Saint James's Park and Charing Cross; its entertainments were soon transferred
to the "new" Spring Garden, located at Vauxhall in Lambeth.

36. "*Snow-hill*": The highway through the disreputable and rundown area lying
between Holborn Bridge and Newgate.

37. "*No Man's Land* to the *World's End*": Regarding No Man's Land see Samuel
Lewis, *A Topographical Dictionary of England* (London, 1849), 3:417: "An extra-
parochial liberty in Wiltshire; containing 149 inhabitants, and comprising 18
acres." World's End: The name for a passage and tavern located off King's
Road, Chelsea, in an area of dubious respectability that Smollett knew well.
Congreve refers to the same location in *Love for Love* 2.1.448, 456, and may have

provided Smollett with a literary source for his allusion; see above, vol. 1, n. 703.

38. "Rotherhith": A dockyard and warehouse area in Surrey, between Bermondsey and Deptford; Gulliver's "Redriff."

39. "*Puddledock*": Located on Upper Thames Street, Blackfriars, in the old city area.

40. "Lansdown": A square and crescent in Bath.

41. "the Old Bailey": The central criminal court of London and Middlesex, still located near Covent Garden.

42. "whitster": Bleacher.

43. "Fulham": A borough of southwest London.

44. "clear-starcher": One who starches clothes. Clear starch is colorless.

45. "*Pimlico*": A district in southwest Westminster.

46. "Wandsworth": In Smollett's time, a town some miles southwest of central London.

47. "a general called *Valavoir*": The identity of this person has not been traced.

48. "an Italian minister called *Grossa-testa*": The identity of this person has not been traced.

49. "*Sforzas* . . . and *Slippers*": All of these Italian and Spanish names are correctly if idiomatically rendered.

50. "Ichoglan in the Bashaw's seraglio": Page in the pasha's harem.

51. "the historian *Buck* . . . Richard III.": Sir George Buc or Buck (d. 1623) was an apologist for Richard III. In his posthumously published *History of the Life and Raigne of Richard the Third* (1646), 79, 80, he quotes descriptions of Richard from the chronicler Stow and another unnamed source: "he was of bodily shape comely enough, only of low stature . . . of an even and well disposed structure"; "the speciall patterne of Knightly prowesse . . . [was] in the lineaments of his body and in the favour of his visage."

52. "the flatterers of the house of Lancaster": The Tudor historians, who united in denigrating Richard. Early in 1768 Horace Walpole's *Historic Doubts on the Life and Reign of Richard III* appeared; *CR* 25 (February 1768): 116–26 censured Walpole's work severely as "historic fribblism," and this passage in the *Atom* seems to satirize Walpole's attempt to rehabilitate Richard. Smollett's own opinion of Richard III was uniformly severe. He condemned Richard's character vehemently in the *Complete History*, 2:451, and agreed with the negative physical and mental picture of him represented in *Voltaire*, 3:240–45.

53. "the fatal battle of Bosworth": The scene of Richard's death in 1485.

54. "the first condition": The highest rank.

55. "the secret of the boy's birth . . . an advanced age in London": The sentimental story of Richard's son is entirely apocryphal. By repeating it here Smollett appears to mock Walpole's trusting account in *Historic Doubts*, already discredited by the review in *CR*: "Mr. Walpole has touched . . . upon the ridiculous

story of Richard III's supposed natural son, Richard Plantagenet the bricklayer
. . ." (p. 126). The same story is mentioned earlier in *British Magazine* 16 (August
1767): 423.

56. "The only share he had . . . the whole family": See *Voltaire*, 3:240. Smollett
does not dissent from Voltaire's statement that the cruel Edward IV had
Clarence drowned in a barrel of wine.

57. "Tyrrel": Sir James Tyrrel (d. 1502), the supposed assassin of the princes in the
Tower.

58. "Embden": An important seaport in Hanover; now spelled Emden.

59. "Perkin Warbeck": Pretender to the English throne. Risings in favor of Warbeck
(1474–99) took place from 1491 to 1497; Henry VII imprisoned him in the
Tower and then executed him. Voltaire claimed that Warbeck was the son of a
Jewish broker of Antwerp; see *Voltaire*, 3:248. *CR*, in its review of Walpole's
Historic Doubts, took the work to task for skimming over the fact that James IV of
Scotland believed Warbeck to be the rightful heir (pp. 125–26).

60. "hustled": Shuffled.

61. "Hob-nob": General Peregrine Hopson; see key. The actual reason for Hopson's
appointment was the king's stubborn insistence on military seniority; see Corbett, 1:376–77.

62. "He-Rhumn": Admiral Sir John Moore; see key.

63. "The voyage . . . without opposition": Hopson landed at Martinique on 16 January 1759. Despite every prospect of success the expedition failed; Smollett
gives a disgusted account of it in *Continuation*, 3:132–44.

64. "draw the artillery": Attract the fire.

65. "ordered the troops . . . reimbarked": Hopson, elderly and timid, believed the
report of a French deserter who claimed that the ground was mined.

66. "Rha-rin-tumm": Colonel (later General) John Barrington; see key.

67. "the deputies . . . the Japonese general": Smollett observes in *Continuation*,
3:134 that the inhabitants of Martinique could scarcely believe they saw the
English troops departing. The "idol Fo" apparently refers only to the "idol-
atrous" Catholicism of the French; but see Key. *Present State*, 7:65 remarks upon
the large number of people belonging to the "third sect" in China, "which is that
of the idol Fo, or Fohi, the founder of the Chinese nation . . . ."

68. "*Qua-chu*": Guadeloupe; see key.

69. "he sickened and died": Hopson died of a tropical fever at Guadeloupe, 27 February 1759; see Corbett, 1:382.

70. "made a conquest of . . . Qua-Chu": Guadeloupe finally surrendered on 1 May
1759.

71. "the importance of Qua-chu . . . information he had received": This passage
develops another variation on Smollett's theme of Newcastle's ignorance concerning geography: see above, vol. 1, n. 134.

72. "Mr. Secretary *No-bo-dy*": William Wildman Barrington, secretary of war, 1755–61, and brother of Colonel John Barrington; see key, NO-BO-DI.

73. "*Tsikkburasiba . . . Joniku*": The source of these Japanese terms has not been traced; Smollett probably intends no specific reference, but is evidently using the word *tsukimurashiba*, which roughly means a bunch (or wreath) of the twigs of the *tsuki* (botanical genus *Zelkova*), a tree resembling the laurel. By *joniku* he may intend to signify the celebrated "bird's-nest-soup," since the Japanese *niku* means "meat," and *choniku* or *joniku* means "the flesh of birds."

74. "severely drubbed by the Mantchoux . . . courtyard": On 23 July 1759 Russian troops defeated the Prussian General Wedel at Züllichau, and shortly afterwards succeeded in taking Frankfurt.

75. "a hair-breadth 'scape": *Othello* 1.3.135–36:

> Of moving accidents by flood and field,
> Of hair-breadth 'scapes . . . .

76. "Kunt-than": Field Marshal Count von Daun; see key.

77. "still": In the older sense of "always."

78. "Yam-a-Kheit": Field Marshal James Keith; see key.

79. "the opportunity offered . . . trampled to death": Smollett alludes at length to the battle of Hochkirch, 14 October 1758. Frederick had chosen a position of which Keith disapproved; at 5:00 A.M., while the latter was on a foraging expedition, the Austrians under von Daun attacked. Frederick was nearly captured but was rescued by the forces of Keith, who was then killed in battle. See *Continuation*, 2:354–57; and see Asprey, 501–6.

80. "'Tis an ill wind that blows no-body good": A common proverbial expression.

81. "a person who could not answer for himself": See *Continuation*, 2:357–60; in a long footnote Smollett strenuously defends his fellow Scot against "the calumny industriously circulated" in England suggesting that Keith died because he was surprised in his tent, "naked and half-asleep." Smollett blames Frederick for the rumors. A brief laudatory biography of Keith appeared in *British Magazine* 1 (February 1760): 81–83.

82. "general A——y . . . contradict his assertion": Abercromby suffered a major defeat at Ticonderoga in July 1758; see above, vol. 1, n. 751. The engineer was George Augustus, fourth Viscount Howe, whom Smollett praises in *Continuation*, 2:287. See Davies, 332, and Corbett 1:330–31.

83. "swear truth out of Tartary": A coinage of Smollett adapted from the proverbial expression "swear the devil out of hell" and similar phrases.

84. "In the very article": At the very moment.

85. "calling upon the mountains": "Then shall they begin to say to the mountains, Fall on us; and to the hills, Cover us" (Luke 24:30).

86. "the Inspector . . . five hundred people": John Hill (1716?–75), an eccentric author, botanist, and herb-doctor, conducted a daily gossip column, "The Inspector," in the *London Daily Advertiser and Literary Gazette*, 1751–53. On 30 April 1752 Hill lampooned an Irishman, Mountefort Brown, and refused to retract. On 6 May, at the pleasure-garden of Ranelagh, Brown pulled off Hill's wig and kicked and caned him. In his column Hill claimed that Brown was hiding from his vengeance, and on 9 May he announced that his doctors had diagnosed an "empyema" as the result of his injuries. The incident was widely caricatured in prints and pamphlets; see Henry Fielding, *The Covent-Garden Journal*, ed. Gerard E. Jensen (New Haven: Yale University Press, 1915), 1:72–75. On Hill in general see G. S. Rousseau, "John Hill, Universal Genius Manqué: Remarks on his Life and Times, with a Checklist of his Works," in *The Renaissance Man in the Eighteenth Century* (Los Angeles: William Andrews Clark Memorial Library, 1978), 45–139; and see Rousseau, ed., *The Letters and Papers of Sir John Hill* (New York: AMS Press, 1982). Tympanitical: swollen or dropsical.

87. "Or-nbos and Fas-khan": Admirals Henry Osborne and Sir Edward Boscawen; see key. In the spring of 1758 Osborne, through massive destruction of French shipping, gained control of the Mediterranean; and in mid-August 1759 Boscawen destroyed most of Admiral de la Clue's fleet off Lagos, Portugal. See Williams, 1:370, 2:5–6.

88. "Kho-rhé . . . Kha-fell": Kho-rhé is the island of Goree at the harbor of Dakar, Senegal; Kha-fell is Commodore Augustus Keppel. See key. In late December 1758 Keppel bombarded and captured Goree; see *Continuation*, 2:297. For consistency Smollett should have located Goree in "Terra Australis"; see above, vol. 1, n. 764.

89. "Khutt-whang": Colonel (later General) Sir Eyre Coote; see key. The surrender of Wandewash in January 1760 and of Pondichéry a year later meant the total defeat of the French forces in India. See Corbett, 2:129–30, 134–35, and Fortescue, 471–83.

90. "lost another battle to Yan-oni": A reference to the battle of Niagara, 24 July 1759, won by Major-General Sir William Johnson. See key, IAN-ON-I; and see Fortescue, 375–76.

91. "Bron-xi-tic, who commanded . . . time of rest": Bron-xi-tic is Ferdinand, duke of Brunswick; see key. Smollett here begins an account of the crucial battle of Minden, described at much greater length in *Continuation*, 3:229–35. During June and July 1759 Ferdinand had retreated by degrees from Lipstadt to Minden. See Fortescue, 493–506.

92. "beat up his quarters": Arouse, break in upon. The French began firing at 3:00 A.M. on 1 August; see *Continuation*, 3:231.

93. "a kennel of Japonese dogs": Six regiments of English infantry and two battalions of Hanover guards were among Ferdinand's troops. *Voltaire*, 7:130 quotes the military leader Count Solmes, referring to English troops as "English bull-dogs."

94. "this famous battle of Myn-than": Myn-than is Minden; see key. The English troops routed the French cavalry and the fighting was over by noon. Smollett here minimizes the importance of the battle (see, for comparison, *Continuation*, 3:235), and it is notable that he makes no mention of the one flaw in the English triumph, the misconduct of Lord George Sackville. Sackville refused to bring up his troops and was later cashiered for this decision; Smollett was almost alone among journalists of the time in defending him. See Robert Donald Spector, *English Literary Periodicals and the Climate of Opinion During the Seven Years' War* (The Hague: Mouton, 1966), 56–61; see also Basker, 225, 254, and Philip J. Klukoff, "Smollett and the Sackville Controversy," *Neuphilologische Mitteilungen* 69 (1968): 617–28.

95. "another beating from the Mantchoux": At the battle of Kunersdorf, 12 August 1759, Frederick was soundly defeated by the Austrians and Russians and barely escaped capture. See *Continuation*, 3:251–55.

96. "Llha-dahn": Field Marshal von Laudohn; see key.

97. "*in terrorem*": As a warning or deterrent example.

98. "abuse betwixt those barbarians": The account of the battle of Kunersdorf given in the *Continuation*, 2:251–56 reports that Frederick fiercely attacked the Russians under Saltykov, who retreated. The Russians rallied; against the advice of his generals, Frederick renewed his attack and was routed with great slaughter. As night fell he sent a dispatch to Berlin advising the queen that the city should be evacuated. To his great astonishment, however, Laudohn retired and Saltykov withdrew to join von Daun's troops in Lusatia. *Continuation*, 3:255–56 speculates that the action was abandoned because of high-level jealousy between the Austrians and Russians; Vienna disliked the prospect of Russian troops in Brandenburg. See Asprey, 514–21.

99. "time to breathe": Smollett echoes his own phrase in *Continuation*, 3:256.

100. "Yaff-rai" . . . a vast lake": After retaking Crown Point and Ticonderoga, Amherst arrived in October 1759 at Lake Champlain, where he had to halt. See Davies, 340.

101. "Ya-loff had sailed . . . more insurmountable than another": At the end of June 1759 Wolfe sailed up the Saint Lawrence, and at the end of July he was repulsed on the Montmorency; to pursue the campaign seemed hopeless, as he wrote to Pitt. The news reached London on 2 September, causing long and widespread consternation. See *Continuation*, 3:196, and Williams, 2:8–10.

102. "five Boll-ah": According to Wright, the boll was an archaic Scottish measure that varied locally from two to six bushels; it was also a measure of weight for flour, ten stone or 140 pounds.

103. "the iliac passion": An old term for colic, or ailments arising from intestinal obstruction.

104. "glyster": Clyster, enema; a frequent feature in political cartoons, as in Print 3917*, where Smollett, as a quack doctor, gives Britannia a clyster.

105. "Quib-quab was taken": Quebec fell on 13 September 1759, though the official surrender came on 18 September. The news of the victory did not reach London until mid-October, when a day of thanksgiving was proclaimed. See *Continuation*, 3:197–98. On 21 October 1759 Horace Walpole wrote to George Montague, "Our bells are worn threadbare with ringing for victories" (*Correspondence*, 9:251).

106. "The contest . . . fatal to the general on each side": Wolfe was killed in action on the Heights of Abraham, which the British troops had scaled during the night; his death is depicted in the famous painting by Benjamin West. Montcalm received fatal wounds during the battle. A French retreat, ordered at nine in the evening, turned into a rout. (Smollett contributed an "Ode to the Late General Wolfe" to the February 1760 number of the *British Magazine*; see Basker, 286.)

107. "Tohn-syn": Brigadier George Townshend; see key.

108. "turned his back upon him": An allusion to the king's habit of "rumping"; see above, vol. 1, n. 484. Smollett misrepresents the interview; George was in fact "radiantly happy" over the victory in Quebec. See Davies, 355.

109. "It was reported . . . the dominions of Japan": The report was true, and was taken so seriously that in late May 1759 the king sent messages to both houses of Parliament; the militia was activated, and four English squadrons watched the French coast. See *Continuation*, 3:109–13, Davies, 336–38, and Corbett, 2:92–93; see also *PH*, 15:940–41. The invasion was scheduled for August, but in July Admiral Rodney destroyed the French fleet's flat-bottomed landing craft while bombarding Le Havre.

110. "one of these . . . Xicoco": Ships under the command of the formidable privateer Thurot were sailing to the north of Scotland for an attack on the coast of Ireland; see Corbett, 2:88–92.

111. "These tidings . . . universal shivering": The episode that follows may be intended as an elaborated reference to Pitt's very successful efforts to rally the English people and protect the country by organizing the militia and volunteer troops. See Williams, 1:403–7.

112. "another compleat victory . . . armament of the enemy": Phal-khan is Admiral Edward Hawke; see key. On 20–21 November Hawke won the resounding victory of Quiberon Bay, virtually ending the power of the French navy; see Corbett, 2:65–70, and *Continuation*, 3:116–19.

113. "Hel-y-otte": Captain John Elliot; see key. In October 1759 Thurot's fleet escaped to Göteborg and Bergen; its remnants attempted a landing at Carrickfergus in Ireland in February, but were repulsed; the fleet was finally destroyed by Elliot off the Isle of Man on 28 February 1760. See *Continuation*, 3:394–95; *British Magazine* 1 (April 1760): 207 gives a short biography of Elliot.

114. "Let us enquire . . . this adoration": The long passage that follows is a paraphrase of *Briton*, no. 37 (5 February 1763): 221, a general attack on Pitt in which Smollett argues that the victorious land and sea campaigns owed nothing to Pitt

himself and also that, on the contrary, the disasters were embarked upon at his insistence.

115. "Kamtschatka . . . Bha-kakh": Kamtschatka is India; Bha-kakh is Admiral Sir George Pocock. See key. Pocock fought several engagements with the French commodore d'Aché (or d'Apché) off Madras in March, August, and September 1758. After 26 September the British were totally in control of the coast of India. See Corbett, 2:120–22, 125–26, 139–40.

116. "Ya-loff he had never seen": Directly contrary to fact; see Williams, 1:395–97.

117. "the youth Hel-y-otte . . . his own family": Elliot was the son of a judge, Lord Minto, and the brother of Sir Gilbert Elliot, an influential Scots M.P. and a lord of the treasury. See *British Magazine* 1 (April 1760): 207.

118. "the board of Sey-seo-gun-sealty": The admiralty board, which directed naval operations.

119. "Moria-tanti . . . view of whiskers": Moria-tanti is General Sir John Mordaunt; see key. Smollett refers to the Rochefort expedition of September 1757. In the earlier episode devoted to the expedition he makes no reference to Mordaunt; see above, vol. 1, pp. 61–62 and nn. 674, 675, 682.

120. "dugs": Teats, nipples; usually in reference to animals.

121. "For the service . . . any former war": Smollett's sources for these figures are *Briton*, no. 6 (3 July 1762): 33, and *Briton*, no. 28 (4 December 1762): 167.

122. "Brut-an-tiffi . . . poetical works in a present": Frederick was very proud of his poetry, which he caused to be elaborately printed. On several occasions he took care to have his personal admiration and gratitude privately conveyed to Pitt, but what Smollett intends here is obscure. He may have in mind Frederick's widely circulated remark about Pitt, "England hat lange in schweren Wehen gelegen, aber endlich hat es einen Mann geboren" ("England has long been in hard labor, but it has finally borne a man"). Probably he refers to Prince Charles of Brunswick's incognito visit to Pitt's estate at Hayes in late January 1764. In *Continuation*, 5:296–97 Smollett speculates that the prince had been especially commissioned by Frederick to convey his personal thanks to Pitt. See Williams, 1:306.

123. "he could not read them . . . fundamental purpose": Frederick's poems were written in French, which Pitt, like most educated Englishmen of his day, could read; see Williams, 1:212. Smollett plays on "fundament" as a euphemism for "backside" or more properly the anus. The reviewer (no doubt Smollett) of a satirical pamphlet on Lord George Sackville's conduct at Minden, where Sackville is said to have been at stool when the attack occurred, recommends that the pamphlet be used as a "much more soft, commodious, and comfortable *detersorium* than the hard stiff paper used for cartridges"; see *CR* 8 (September 1759): 257.

124. "a bullock's horn bound with brass": Presumably Pitt's "Hanoverian trumpet" (see above, vol. 1, n. 65), in the sense that his oratory, formerly directed against

any British expenditures in Germany, was now wholly at Frederick's service.

125. "*Tibia vincta orichalco*": Horace *Ad Pisones* (*De Arte Poetica*) 202–3: "tibia non ut nunc orichalco vincta tubaeque / aemula, sed tenuis simplexque" ("the flute, not as now bound with brass and a rival of the trumpet, but slender and simple").

126. "the only present . . . his own pocket": Compare *Briton*, no. 7 (10 July 1762): 38: "avarice, which indeed I never took to be part of [Pitt's] character."

127. "a genius self-taught . . . human institution": Pitt graduated from Eton, but left Trinity College, Oxford, without taking a degree. His reading was limited, though he read Demosthenes, Bolingbroke, Barrow's sermons for their style, and Bailey's Dictionary; his sister said that he knew no literary work thoroughly except the *Faerie Queene*. See Williams, 1:31–39, 212–15.

128. "Ab-ren-thi . . . island Xicoco": Ab-ren-thi is the Reverend John Abernethy, an Irish Presbyterian clergyman; see key. Neither Smollett's source nor his reason for this characterization of Abernethy has been traced.

129. "The Chinese still lingered . . . Yesso": The passage following paraphrases the arguments of *Briton*, no. 7 (10 July 1762): 40–42: "[Ferdinand of Brunswick is] a soldier of fortune, whose interest is to husband the war . . . to insult, to oppress, to embezzle. . . . France will be able to protract the war in that country, without . . . adding to her national encumbrances, while Great Britain will run every year in debt, more than the whole amount of the French revenue, until all her resources are drained, and her credit utterly extinguished."

130. "horse-tails": Emblems of the dignity of a pasha among the Turks, these serve as the "Oriental" equivalent of captured battle standards sent as trophies. Smollett mentions horse-tails again in *Humphry Clinker*, Jery Melford to Sir Watkin Phillips, London, June 5.

131. "his health began to decline": The king was much gratified by the later progress of the war, but in his last years Newcastle found him to be emotionally unstable, plaintive, and inclined to weep. He also suffered from deafness and cataracts. See Browning, 270, and Davies, 348–49, 355.

132. "blisters and caustics": Treatment with counter-irritants applied to the skin was standard medical practice for a great variety of ailments.

133. "moxa": Dried moss, still so called, and still used in Japanese medicine; a pinch of the powdered moss is ignited on the skin to produce a blister, as a counter-irritant. See *UH*, 41, quoted in *CR* 8 (September 1759): 193.

134. "*menoki* . . . *Senkei*": According to *UH*, 42, abdominal disorders are cured in Japan by a "powder which is only sold in the village of *Menoki*." Smollett misreads another passage in *UH*, which says that "a kind of endemic cholicky disorder . . . by them called *Senki*, is *cured* by acupuncture" (p. 39). Shimada's key (see reference, below, p. 250) says that *senki* means lumbago.

135. "could not foresee . . . successor": Although Pitt had flirted from time to time with Leicester House (the court of the future George III), by 1760 he was totally out of favor there, largely because of his shifts on various questions of policy.

Prince George referred to him as "that snake in the grass." See Williams, 1:186–88, 2:63–66; Namier, *England*, 105–9; Sedgwick, lvii.

136. *"pro hac vice"*: L. For this particular occasion.

137. "a poisonous insect . . . remedy was music": See *Briton*, no. 22 (22 October 1762), 127: "One would imagine the people of this metropolis . . . like those who have been bit by the tarantula . . . have suffered from the stings of certain mischievous insects . . . such virulent poison . . . as produces a temporary delirium." See also *Briton*, no. 32 (1 January 1763): 188: "this venerable patrician [Newcastle, has] fits of melancholy despondence, from which nothing can rouse him but the sound of marrow-bones and cleavers. This has nearly the same effect upon him, as the fiddle has upon those who are bit by the Tarantula." These passages probably are derived from an essay on the tarantula in *British Magazine* 1 (April 1760): 185–87, presumably by Smollett, which tells of a specimen "at Salter's coffee-house at Chelsea," citing the three authorities mentioned in the *Atom*. Apuglia: Apulia, a province of southern Italy. Ælian: see above, vol. 1, n. 486. Epiphanius Ferdinandus: according to the essay in the *British Magazine*, an Apulian physician. Baglivi: Giorgio Baglivi (1668–1703), an Apulian doctor and professor of anatomy at Rome; his works include a Latin dissertation on the tarantula. *CR* 10 (October 1760): 249 (see below, n. 143) also alleges that the frantic dancing (or convulsions) of the tarantula's victims is curable by music.

138. "indifferently skilled . . . Tartars not excepted": The second number of the *British Magazine* (February 1760), 74–76, contains an article by Goldsmith on the various schools of music, slighting England. The April number includes a "rejoinder," also by Goldsmith, defending and praising "English" musicians, among them Handel and David Rizzio, the favorite of Mary Queen of Scots. Smollett perhaps echoes the two essays by Goldsmith here. Interestingly, the rejoinder (pp. 181–84) precedes Smollett's contribution on the tarantula.

139. "He found . . . differences of sounds": This passage is taken verbatim from the review of a translation of *L'Arte armonica* (1760) by Giorgio Antoniotto, *CR* 11 (January 1761): 18–19.

140. "besides, he taught . . . the antient music": This is a rearrangement of the passage immediately following that cited in the previous note. The reviewer, citing the life of Pythagoras by Iamblichus, 26 (see above, vol. 1, nn. 83, 84), attributes these additional contributions to him. Digramma: an error (copied by Smollett) for *diagramma*, the tablature or scale used in Greek musical notation; colours: chromatics; diatessaron: the interval of a fourth; tetrachord: a scale of four notes, half an octave; Phrygian and Lydian modes: the ancient equivalents of musical scale systems, each having a specific quality and emotional effect.

141. "Tottenham-court . . . Hockley-i'the-hole": Tottenham Court, located north of central London, was associated with boxing exhibitions and low entertainment. Hockley-in-the-hole, north of the city in Clerkenwell, was the site of a bear

garden mentioned in Pope's imitation of the Satires of Horace, book 2, 1.1.49: "Fox loves the Senate, Hockley-hole his Brother." Smollett mentions the two places in a similar derogatory fashion in *Roderick Random*, chapter 27.

142. "a sonata on the salt-box . . . marrow-bones and cleavers": *OED*: "in burlesque music, the salt-box has been used like the marrow-bones and cleaver, tongs and poker" to make the "cacophonous music of the vulgar." A description of Ferret in *Sir Launcelot Greaves*, chapter 4, alludes to "a solo on the salt-box or a sonata on the tongs and gridiron."

143. "in the melopœia . . . mathematical demonstration": This passage comes almost verbatim from *CR* 10 (October 1760): 250, in a review of *Harmonics* (1760), by R. Smith; Smollett adds only one new sentence: "The truth is . . . perfectly well." Melopœia: the art of composing melodies. Benedictine monk: Guido of Arezzo (c. 990–1050), who developed modern musical notation with the staff; he is mentioned also in *Voltaire*, 3:40. Consonances: harmonies. Nice: precise. Tempering: tuning. Intervals: distances between tones. Concords: harmonies.

144. "was found Ignoramus": Smollett continues the legal imagery of "crier of his court . . . culprit." In British law the term *ignoramus* means to dismiss an indictment for lack of evidence; thus, no evidence of life could be "found" in the sense of a legal finding.

145. "a sound . . . contract one hand": The king's petty avarice was notorious. On one occasion a court lady is supposed to have exclaimed, "If your majesty does not stop counting those coins, I shall leave the room"; she presently did so. See Davies, 69.

146. "*aurum fulminans*": Detonating or explosive gold; the gold salt of fulminic acid. Smollett possibly alludes to the *aurum potabile* or drinkable gold (an actual medical preparation) which Queen Caroline is shown administering to the king as an enema in Print 2327*, "The Festival of the Golden Rump."

147. "expired in the twinkling of an eye": George II did in fact die suddenly on the morning of 25 October 1760, but of hemorrhage caused by a ruptured right ventricle; see *Continuation*, 4:111.

148. "he vanished . . . deceased Dairo": For a description of the actual events see below, n. 173. Gio-gio is George III; see key. The eldest grandson of George II, he was "successor and descendant" because his father, Frederick Prince of Wales, had died in 1751.

149. "a young prince . . . the last emperor": George III was twenty-two at his accession. George II had certainly resisted various attempts (including the prince's own) to bring him forward into public life. His mother, Augusta of Saxe-Gotha, dowager Princess of Wales (1719–72), was anxious to prevent his incurring political debts that would have to be paid; with the assistance of Lord Bute and young George's natural diffidence, she virtually ensured that he would be "hermetically shut up." See Sedgwick, li–lvii, and Brooke, *George III*, 40–49.

150. "his grand-mother": His mother.

151. *"Yak-strot"*: John Stuart, earl of Bute; see key.
152. "his elevated ideas of patriotism": The actual political opinions of the young king and of Bute have been much disputed by several eminent twentieth-century historians. Smollett, however, as the *Briton* and the *Continuation* show, evidently felt that something like a Bolingbrokian "patriot king" was potentially present in the young man. See Robin Fabel, "The Patriotic Briton: Smollett and English Politics," *Eighteenth-Century Studies* 8 (1974): 100–114; and see Donald Greene, "Smollett the Historian: A Reappraisal," in *Tobias Smollett: Bicentennial Essays Presented to Lewis M. Knapp*, ed. G. S. Rousseau and P.-G. Boucé (New York: Oxford University Press, 1971), 25–56.
153. "Yak-strot was honest . . . affected": Smollett's portrait of Bute, essentially a reworking of *Continuation*, 5:119–21, is fair and accurate when judged against modern accounts. See Brooke, *George III*, 47.
154. "an iron jack and a wooden clock . . . patron of genius": Bute dabbled in a number of arts, crafts, and sciences, notably botany; he was chiefly responsible for founding Kew Gardens. On Bute's "patronage of genius" see below, pp. 102–3 and nn. 220–25, 227–29. Smollett may have felt, as Pope did in the *Dunciad* (book 4, lines 585–604), that banausic hobbies were unworthy in a nobleman and damaging to the state.
155. "His maxims were these": The passage following is a fairly accurate summary of Bute's (and the king's) principles as the reign began. See Sedgwick, lvi–lix; Namier, *England*, 94–105; *Continuation*, 5:121; Brooke, *George III*, 55–66.
156. "evil genius": Demon.
157. "stone-horses": Horses retaining their "stones," or testicles; stallions. Smollett observed similar teams of ill-matched draft animals in France; see *Letters*, 125, and *Travels*, Letter 8 (p. 67).
158. *"Shit-tilk-ums-heit*, and *She-it-kums-hi-til"*: Tories and Whigs; see key.
159. "Each had predominated": The passage following makes clear that the stereotype of Smollett as a "Tory" is without foundation. See Fabel, "The Patriotic Briton."
160. "still": Always.
161. "ferment": Cause of fermentation.
162. "retorted": Cast back.
163. "He made his first appearance": Pitt began his parliamentary career in opposition to Walpole and the court party; hence he was nominally "Tory." See above, vol. 1, n. 608; and for a concise summary of Pitt's political veerings and their causes see Brewer, *Party*, 96–111.
164. "an old rich hag . . . his dying-day": Sarah, dowager duchess of Marlborough, who died in 1744, was violently anti-Walpole; she left Pitt £10,000 and made him co-heir presumptive to half of her estates for "his defence of the laws of England" and "his efforts to prevent the ruin of his country." When Pitt reversed himself and entered the administration, a satirical print (2786*) was

issued portraying the appearance of the duchess's ghost to him. The print was followed shortly by a pamphlet, *A Letter from the Duchess of M---gh, in the Shades, to the Great Man,* and then by a second pamphlet in defense of the first; reviews in *CR* 7 (June 1759): 557, and in *CR* 8 (August 1759): 164–65, observed that both pamphlets contained "melancholy truths."

165. "the ministry . . . made him such offers": A reference to the "unembarrassed countenance" interlude of 1746 (see above, vol. 1, n. 433), when Pitt was made vice-treasurer of Ireland and later paymaster of the forces, upon which he became what we should call chief whip in the Commons. See Davies, 248–49.

166. "Being disgusted in the sequel": Pitt was for some years quiet and cooperative after being made paymaster in 1746. In March 1754, with the death of the first minister, Henry Pelham, a general administrative reorganization was indicated. Newcastle and Hardwicke led Pitt to believe that the king could be persuaded to give him a cabinet post, but the appointment did not materialize. Beginning in late 1754, Pitt went into violent opposition to all of the government's measures, including the Russian and Prussian subsidiary treaties; he continued in this posture without interruption until he entered the cabinet in 1756. See Brewer, *Party,* 98; and see Marie Peters, *Pitt and Popularity* (Oxford: Clarendon Press, 1980), 32–79.

167. "he opened": Used of foxhounds; to give tongue, to begin to cry when on the scent.

168. "once more he deserted them": The coalition with Newcastle, Pitt serving as secretary of state, began in November 1756. Pitt was firmly in control of the Commons.

169. "predicament": In the philosophical sense merely of "situation."

170. "party . . . scum of the people": Smollett was firmly opposed to the mercantile and financial interests that supported Pitt and the Whigs, as against the land-owning "country" party; see Sekora, 174–84, 321–23. For a more thorough analysis of Pitt's supporters than would have been available to Smollett, see Marie Peters, *Pitt and Popularity.*

171. "the abolition of corruption . . . loaded waggon": See *Continuation,* 1:iv, "To the Public": "We have also lived to see the fallacy of a pernicious and spurious maxim, adopted by some late ministers, that the machine of government could not be properly moved, unless the wheels were smeared with corruption." By a striking coincidence this sentence closely parallels a remark in Swift's short satire entitled *An Account of the Court and Empire of Japan,* a work much resembling the *Atom.* Swift's *Account* could hardly have been a source for the *Atom* as a whole, since it was not published until 1765. But Smollett may well have echoed this passage in the introduction to the complete *Continuation* in five volumes, which he dates 1 July 1765; and the *Account* is cited in a review of Deane Swift's edition of Swift's posthumous works, *CR* 19 (May 1765): 350. See Herbert

Davis, ed., *The Prose Works of Jonathan Swift* (Oxford: Oxford University Press, 1939–68), 5:106.

172. "drawing plans of windmills": This of course refers to Don Quixote's tilting at windmills, but Smollett may have known of the young king's considerable talent as an architectural draftsman, a talent Bute shared; see Print 4043. Johnson said, as reported by William Shaw, "[Bute] had taught [the king] to *draw a tree*"; see *The Early Biographies of Samuel Johnson*, ed. O M Brack, Jr., and Robert Kelley (Iowa City: University of Iowa Press, 1974), 171. As early as 1759 the prince and Bute were making fairly detailed plans for the new reign; see Sedgwick, lvi–lix.

173. "Orator Taycho . . . advanced towards him": To announce the death of George II, as he does in the speech that follows. In fact the prince, who had informants at court, knew of the event within an hour or two after it happened. Pitt, informed by the dead king's mistress, the countess of Yarmouth, asked Princess Amelia if he should attend the new king. She was noncommittal; Pitt saw Bute before he could see his master, and nothing was said at the audience beyond formal condolences and compliments. See Walpole, *George III*, 1:5. *Continuation*, 4:145 has Pitt going to Kew to make the official announcement to the king, which it would have been his normal duty to do. See Brooke, *George III*, 74.

174. "the star Hesperus": The evening star. Smollett here renews his mimicry of Pitt's florid style.

175. "the tops of the Eastern hills": See *Hamlet* 1.1.166–67:

> But look, the morn, in russet mantle clad,
> Walks o'er the dew of yon high eastward hill.

176. "in the bosom of the blessed Bupo": In the parable of Dives and Lazarus (Luke 16:22), the happy in death repose in "Abraham's bosom." The same biblical expression is used in *Richard III* 4.3.38.

177. "establish his throne in righteousness": The archbishop of Canterbury's ritual exhortation to the newly crowned sovereign, dating back to William the Conqueror, contains the same words; they occur seven times in the Bible. Given Smollett's opinions, he probably thought of Proverbs 25:5: "Take away the wicked from before the king, and his throne shall be established in righteousness."

178. "his relation the Fatzman": Cumberland was George III's uncle.

179. "assisting": In the French (and Scottish) sense of "being present."

180. "The first step he took . . . to his interest": On 31 October 1760 George III issued a royal proclamation "for the encouragement of piety and virtue, and the preventing and punishing of vice, profaneness, and immorality"; see *Continuation*, 4:147.

181. "a parcel of raw boys . . . associated with him in office": Bute told Newcastle

that the king intended to retain his grandfather's cabinet for six months; see Namier, *England*, 146. However, Bute was immediately made groom of the stole and thus a cabinet member, and five Tories were appointed to the bedchamber. Interestingly, these latter appointments were made on Pitt's advice; see Brewer, *Party*, 47. In March 1761 Bedford was made lord privy seal and Bute secretary of state, northern department. Other minor appointments, though not Tory, considerably lowered the average age of the cabinet.

182. "the Niphonites . . .jealousy and contempt": On contemporary anti-Scottish feeling see *Continuation*, 5:117–20. There is no doubt that the opposition to Bute in pamphlets, newspapers, and prints constituted the heaviest propaganda barrage in English history to that date; see Brewer, "Misfortunes."

183. "he was graciously received . . . approbation": Newcastle met with chilly politeness; the king said, "My Lord Bute is your very good friend; he will tell you my thoughts at large." See Browning, 272.

184. "delighted to honour": A phrase frequently used in connection with the conferring of titles.

185. "different sorts of kicks . . . England": Smollett here begins a digression on kicking, the idea for which he most probably took from several issues of the periodical *Common Sense* for 1737 (19 March, 26 March, 11 June, and 17 September). These contain very daring satire against Walpole, George II, and Queen Caroline, presented in the form of learned essays on kicking, rump-worship, and turning one's back. They further contain numerous phrases and ideas that closely parallel Smollett's, not only here but throughout the *Atom*. For a description of the satires in *Common Sense* see Mack, 137–48, 160–61.

186. "*kicked up* . . . interest": To be "kicked up" to "preferment" exactly corresponds to the modern bureaucratic phrase "kicked upstairs." Here "interest" refers to political connections or influence.

187. "*Kick'um, Jenny*": The title of a popular, amusing, and very obscene ballad that appeared in 1733, with eleven more editions in the next four years. Jenny tells Roger that if he will kiss her breech she will marry him. He does as she requests, and then proceeds to extremities; Sir John and his lady, watching through a cranny, respectively cry "Kick him, Jenny" and "F--k her, Roger." All ends happily.

188. "*Kicksy-wicksy*": Baby-talk for wife or sweetheart, as in *All's Well That Ends Well* 2.3.280.

189. "leman": Archaic term for lover; here a euphemism for prostitute.

190. "the favourite gladiator . . . *rude donatus*": See *Briton*, no. 9 (24 July 1762): 49: "It was a custom among the ancients to discharge the superannuated gladiator, by giving him a rod or cudgel, hence he was called *rude donatus* or *rudiarius*." Horace uses the phrase in *Epistles* 1.1.2; the *rudis* was a wooden sword used in gladiatorial practice.

191. "the Paraschistes . . . the defunct": The embalmer who made the first incision

in a dead body for the removal of the viscera was cursed and stoned by the bereaved to absolve them of the guilt of injuring the corpse. This information is provided by the historian Diodorus Siculus (first century B. C.) in his *Bibliotheca historica*, but Smollett may have seen it in the "Ancient Part" of *UH*, 1:240.

192. "the patriarch of the Greeks . . . the rain-bow": Many sources as late as the early twentieth century comment on the rioting that erupted during this ceremony when the faithful (not the infidels) mobbed the patriarch so as to be first to light their candles from the holy fire. See the entry on "Easter," *The New Schaff-Herzog Encyclopedia of Religious Knowledge*, ed. Samuel M. Jackson et al. (New York: Funk and Wagnalls, 1908–14). Smollett's specific source has not been traced.

193. "Quakers . . . slap o' the face": Smollett may be alluding to Swift's account of the fanatical Jack's behavior in *Tale of a Tub* 11.

194. "when you smite them . . . salutation": Matthew 5:39; Luke 6:29.

195. "Lactantius . . . *quam inferre*": Lucius Cecilianus Firmianus Lactantius (c. A. D. 250–c. 330), in book 6 of his *Divine Institutes*, chapter 18 ("*De quibusdam Dei mandatis et patientia*," "Of Certain Commands of God, and of Long-suffering"), takes issue with Cicero's statement in book 2 of *De officiis*: "Oh, what a simple and true sentiment he has corrupted by the addition of two words! For it is no less evil to return an injury than to do it" (*Patrologia Latina*, tom. 6, col. 700).

196. "Socrates . . . retaliation": Diogenes Laertius (third century A. D.), in his life of Socrates, section 17, gives five anecdotes of Socrates' meekness, including this one.

197. "Puffendorf . . . infringe it": A reference to Samuel Puffendorf (or Pufendorf), 1632–94, whose book of 1672 (*Of the Law of Nature and Nations*) was a classic, familiar to Smollett from his university days; see Knapp, 16. The work appeared in a fifth edition in 1749. Smollett alludes to a statement in book 2, chapter 5, section 12 ("Of a Box on the Ear. Of Self-Defence"), and he borrows verbatim the words "in the power of . . . infringe it" (5th ed., p. 191).

198. "Grotius . . . affront": An allusion to Hugo van Groot (1583–1645), whose earlier work of 1625 (*On the Law of War and Peace*) had equal status with Pufendorf's treatise. Pufendorf quotes the words "charity . . . affront" in the same passage (p. 190) from which Smollett borrows in the preceding sentence. Smollett may have been led to both Grotius and Pufendorf by his three-part review of T. Rutherforth, *Institutes of Natural Law* (1756), in *CR* 2 (September, October, November 1756): 160–81, 227–43, 299–315, which mentions (p. 178) a box on the ear as considered in their works. See Basker, 222.

199. "The English have . . . borrowed": The passage following contains material that appeared in Letters 7 and 15 of Smollett's *Travels*; both letters are addressed to a lady, and both deal with French affectations or absurdities of manners. Since it is likely that much of the *Atom* and the *Travels* were composed at the same time (see Martz, 72–73), Smollett may have borrowed from either for the other, or may have decided to work the same material into both.

200. *"punto"*: Small point of behavior; punctilio. *Travels*, Letter 15: Henri IV, who patronized dueling, established "a *punto*, founded in diametrical opposition to common sense and humanity" (p. 135).

201. "A box on the ear . . . time and attention": Letter 7 of the *Travels* ridicules the amount of time Frenchmen spend on their hair, and observes that a French gentleman will as a matter of course help a lady to arrange her hair, "like a friseur" (p. 58).

202. "One is St. *Fiacre* . . . bleeding piles": In the *Travels*, Letter 4, Smollett remarks that Saint Veronica may be identical with "St. *Hemorrhoissa*, the patroness of those who are afflicted with the piles, who make their joint invocations to her and St. Fiacre, the son of a Scotch king" (p. 28). Saint Fiacre is authentic; he was an Irish anchorite who became an abbot in France and died c. A.D. 670. The "blind piles" are closed piles, those which do not bleed.

203. "the tributary treaty . . . Brut-an-tiffi": On 12 December 1760 Parliament renewed the Second Treaty of Westminster (1758), which provided for an annual subsidy to Frederick of Prussia. See above, vol. 1, n. 513; and see *PH*, 15:996–98.

204. "Gio-gio declared . . . with vigour": A reference to the new king's first address from the throne, 18 November 1760. This was the famous speech in which George "gloried in the name of Britain." *Continuation*, 4:174 gives the word as "Briton," as do many subsequent accounts; but the manuscript of the speech, now displayed in the British Library, clearly reads "Britain." See *PH*, 15:981–85. Smollett directly echoes *Continuation*, 4:177, where the king is said to have declared that he was "determined . . . to prosecute this war with vigour."

205. "an inconsiderable colony . . . peace and security": The colony was Louisiana. Smollett frequently commented on its importance and its neglect by Pitt: see *Continuation*, 4:264, 321; *British Magazine* 1 (February 1760): 85–86; *Briton*, nos. 5 (26 June 1762), 6 (3 July 1762), 17 (18 September 1762). Numerous references occur in the *Critical Review*.

206. "his chief village possessed . . . the seat of the war": Berlin was taken by Russian and Austrian troops in October 1760, but on 3 November of the same year Frederick, with forty-four thousand troops, defeated Count von Daun's army of fifty thousand at Torgau near Dresden. See Corbett, 2:288, and Asprey, 540–44.

207. "to play booty": To join with a confederate in a game to cheat another player.

208. "some petty advantages": On Ferdinand's engagements in the summer of 1760 at Corbach, Erdorf, Werbourg, and Campen, see *Continuation*, 4:37–57.

209. "now and then sacrificing . . . that nation": Another echo of Voltaire's remark on the execution of Byng; see above, vol. 1, nn. 413, 415.

210. "politicians": Dabblers in politics, amateur political analysts.

211. "Corea": By this reference to Spain Smollett continues to develop his geographical mirror-image of Europe. As Spain is a peninsula bordering France, the two

countries sharing dynastic ties, so Korea borders China, the two countries likewise dynastically linked.

212. "shameful partiality . . . his kinsman and ally": Charles III (1716–88), who had
been king of Naples and was crowned king of Spain in 1759, was a "kinsman" in
that his brother had married Louise Elisabeth, daughter of Louis XV. Moreover, the Spanish Bourbon monarchs were descended from Philip V of Spain,
who was a son of Louis XIV of France. On the "Family Compact" between
France and Spain see below, n. 233.

213. "it was now thought proper . . . ten millions of Obans": Smollett refers to the
expedition against Belle-Isle, in the Atlantic off the coast of Brittany. After
months of expensive secret preparations, the expedition was to have started in
November 1760, but was postponed until June 1761, when Belle-Isle was taken.
Primarily intended to divert French troops from the German front, the expedition did not succeed in this aim. Most of the cabinet disapproved of the plan,
and military historians consider it a serious error of judgment on the part of Pitt.
Smollett's bitter disapproval is expressed in *Continuation*, 4:251–64; see also Corbett, 2:154–63, and Fortescue, 530.

214. "the scheme of œconomy": See Walpole, *George III*, 1:36. In March 1761 Lord
Talbot was appointed steward of the household and immediately began
retrenchment. Kitchens were closed, cooks dismissed; the maids of honor complained about their breakfasts, and the king and queen were later said to live on
mutton and turnips. Talbot's economies were ironically praised in *North Briton*,
no. 12 (21 August 1762), and Talbot attempted a duel with its author, John
Wilkes. See Rudé, 21.

215. "hand-irons": Andirons.

216. "soup-meagre . . . oat-meal": Soup-meagre (Fr. *soupe maigre*) is any thin soup of
vegetables or fish. The "oat-meal," of course, makes reference to Bute as a Scot.

217. "peripatetic philosopher": The Aristotelian school of philosophy was so called
because its founder allegedly taught while walking up and down with his disciples in the ambulatory of the Lyceum at Athens.

218. "a certain wag . . . house-keeping": Probably a reference to Print 3990*, "A
Catalogue of the Kitchen Furniture of JOHN BULL Esqr. leaving of House-
keeping now selling by AUCTION."

219. "Mæcenas . . . a type": The wealthy supporter of Horace and Virgil was
emblematic for a generous patron of the arts. The persons and events of the Old
Testament were "types," or imperfect anticipations, of Christ and his life.

220. "these were gratified with pensions": The passage that follows echoes *Continuation*, 5:27–28, where Smollett discusses with considerable venom the pensions
granted by Bute.

221. "a secularized Bonza from Ximo": John Home (1722–1808) was the author of the
immensely popular play *Douglas* (1756); the Kirk of Scotland forced his resigna-

tion for the scandal of being a playwright. Home's pension of £300, augmented by a £300 sinecure in Scotland, owed much to the fact that he was private secretary to Bute.

222. "a malcontent poet of Niphon": Samuel Johnson, who had originally been violently anti-Walpole and had vigorously expressed his opposition to the colonial war; his £300 pension came at the suggestion of Thomas Sheridan and others, including Bute's influential friend Alexander Wedderburn. See James L. Clifford, *Dictionary Johnson* (New York: McGraw-Hill, 1979), 165–87, 262–77.

223. "a reformed comedian of Xicoco": Thomas Sheridan (1719–88), actor and manager in Dublin and London, friend of Johnson, and father of the dramatist Richard Brinsley Sheridan. His pronouncing dictionary had established him as an authority on language in the opinion of many; he received a pension of £300.

224. "an empiric, who had outlived his practice": Dr. Thomas Thompson; see above, vol. 1, n. 49. Thompson was a hanger-on of Bute's adherent George Bubb Dodington, now Lord Melcombe, through whom his pension of £300 was awarded. An empiric was a practitioner who allegedly or in fact relied merely on experience, rather than on the classical precepts of medicine.

225. "a decayed apothecary": "Sir" John Hill; see above, vol. 2, n. 86. Hill is not included in the *Continuation* account of Bute's pensions; conversely, the *Atom* omits a number of deserving persons mentioned in the *Continuation* as receiving smaller stipends. Smollett was aware that Bute was rewarding Hill lavishly for his works on botany; see the *British Magazine* 6 (March 1765): 110–15.

226. "simpler": One who gathers and administers herbal remedies, or simples.

227. "established places under the government": It was customary for a new administration to dismiss many persons holding court sinecures and to replace them with new appointees as a way of paying political debts; but since Bute appointed a number of Scots, the barrage of criticism was intense. The lords of the bedchamber increased from twelve to eighteen, as Wilkes complained in *North Briton*, no. 12 (August 1762). On what was sometimes called the "Scotch invasion" see Print 3823*, "We are all a-comeing."

228. "a certain person . . . to his imperial majesty": Smollett alludes to Mr. (later Sir) Frederick Augusta Barnard (1743–1830). It was Barnard who presented Samuel Johnson to the king in the famous encounter in the royal library. He was long believed to have been George III's illegitimate half-brother; but John Brooke, in "The Library of George III," *Yale University Library Gazette* 52 (1977): 33–45, has shown that he was in fact the son of John Barnard, a page of the backstairs, whose family had been royal servants for several generations. Prince Frederick and Princess Augusta were probably his godparents, as his Christian names indicate.

229. "providing his poor relations . . . government": Charles Churchill, in a note to an early issue of *The Prophecy of Famine* (1763), an anti-Scottish and anti-Bute satire, observed that according to the official *Gazette* there were eleven Stuarts

and four Mackenzies among sixteen promotions. Stuart was Bute's family name; the Mackenzies were closely connected to the Stuart clan.

230. "a negociation for peace . . . articles of the treaty": In March 1761 France made overtures for peace through Spain, the Hague, and the Russian ambassador; see *Continuation*, 4:291–324, where Smollett discusses at length the terms of the overtures and Pitt's reactions to them. The phrase "upon the carpet," meaning "under discussion," was a favorite locution of Smollett. A literal rendering of the French *sur le tapis*, the phrase occurs in the passage from the *Continuation* already cited and in numerous other places as well.

231. "mount Athos": Probably Smollett's error for Ossa in Thessaly, proverbial in classical literature as that which cannot be moved.

232. "He actually broke off . . . protection of Yesso": After a French memorial of 13 September 1761 refusing to agree to the removal of Austrian troops from the border towns of Wesel and Gueldres, the negotiating ministers were recalled. See *Continuation*, 4:313–23; and on Frederick's earlier withdrawal from Wesel, see above, vol. 1, n. 465.

233. "The court of Pekin perceiving . . . Japanese politicians": A detailed account of the matters treated in this paragraph, with documents and particulars of negotiations, is given in *Continuation*, 4:353–63. Secret dealings between Paris and Madrid ended in the signing of the "Bourbon Family Compact" at Paris on 15 August 1761. Pitt's brusque treatment of the Spanish ambassador Fuentes, with regard to his misleading official account of the negotiations, led to Fuentes's recall; Pitt had been notified very early of the Family Compact by Marshal Keith. On Newcastle's views of the situation see Browning, 280–81.

234. "they besieged and took . . . the capital of the Mantchoux": In August 1761 Russian troops attacked the fortress of Colberg on the Baltic; the fortress surrendered on 17 December. See *Continuation*, 4:289–90.

235. "Having called a council . . . had severely felt": The account here agrees with that given in *Continuation*, 4:324–27. At a cabinet meeting on 18 September 1761, Pitt presented evidence that the Family Compact had been concluded and asked for an immediate declaration of war on Spain. Only his brother-in-law Lord Temple supported him, and the cabinet finally voted to temporize. See Namier, *England*, 342, and Browning, 281.

236. "Gotto-mio . . . come upon the parish": Bedford's enormous wealth and avarice were common knowledge; see Print 3892. Walpole, *George III*, 1:54, 61–62, says that Bedford was the only cabinet member who generally opposed Pitt's dictatorial ways, and that he "was clamorous against a Spanish war." "Come upon the parish": Paupers in Smollett's time were maintained by the parish in which they were registered.

237. "proceeding in form by citation": According to legal procedure, by consulting precedents.

238. "Nin-kom-poo-po declared . . . the Chinese emperor": In *Continuation*, 4:324

Smollett attributes this proposition to Pitt. Anson pointed out that the British navy lacked the strength to face both the French and Spanish fleets; see Browning, 281.

239. "Fokh-si-rokhu started two objections": See *Continuation*, 4:326, where the objections are not ascribed.

240. "miscarriage of the squadron . . . Fatsisio": A reference to Boscawen's failure; see above, vol. 1, nn. 324, 330.

241. "bottoms": Commercial metonymy for ships.

242. "was interested in": Had investments in. The source of this remark about Fox has not been traced.

243. "Yak-strot . . . honour and honesty": The sentence that follows corresponds to *Continuation*, 4:325, where Smollett presents the same argument but in his own voice.

244. "The Dairo acquiesced . . . empire of Japan": The ambassador was Lord Bristol, though he was not ordered to "demand" but rather to explore; see Browning, 281.

245. "forked out his fingers": The traditional gesture indicating a cuckold.

246. "pulling out the badge of his office": Secretaries of state and certain other cabinet members formally resigned by "giving up the seals" or surrendering to the crown the seals officially used in certifying their executive orders. Pitt resigned on 5 October 1761 after a stormy cabinet meeting three days earlier (on 2 October), at which most of the members offered cogent objections to his demand for immediate war. It was on this occasion that he made the famous statement, "I will be responsible for nothing that I do not direct." The king was far from reluctant to have him go. Bute, however, was apprehensive of the consequences; see Karl W. Schweizer, "Lord Bute and William Pitt's Resignation in 1761," *Canadian Journal of History* 8 (1973): 111–25. See *Continuation*, 4:327–30, and Browning, 280–82. The scene here resembles that described in *Briton*, no. 8 (18 July 1762): 44.

247. "his kinsman the Quo Lob-kob": Lord Temple; see key, LOB-KOB. Temple was Pitt's brother-in-law, and for some years slavishly adhered to his policies.

248. "the effect of contempt or compunction": Temple, lord privy seal (a largely honorific office), resigned on 9 October 1761. *Briton*, no. 8 (18 July 1762): 45 reports that he "threw many a long look behind, in hopes of an invitation to return."

249. "his next appeal to the blatant beast": A reference to Pitt's famous letter explaining his conduct to Alderman William Beckford (see key, RHUM-KIKH), his most prominent and faithful supporter. The text and Beckford's reply are given in *Continuation*, 4:330–32, where Smollett also provides a cautious discussion of Pitt's motives (pp. 327–30).

250. "pretended": Claimed, took credit for.

251. "of course": In the natural or probable course of events.

252. "a cell in the neighbourhood of Meaco": Pitt's estate at Hayes in Kent, near London. See Williams, 2:169–71.

253. "hired the common crier . . . kitchen utensils": Pitt ostentatiously advertised for sale his coach-horses and harness (here "furniture"), alleging poverty; see Print 4121*, and see Williams, 2:126. The "ermined robe" represents an allusion to the fact that Pitt's wife was created Baroness Chatham in her own right the day after his resignation; the two events were announced simultaneously in the official *Gazette*, 10 October 1761. Thus a peerage was secured to Pitt's descendants, while he could remain in and control the Commons.

254. "twenty thousand gold Obans": The £10,000 from the duchess of Marlborough (see above, vol. 2, n. 164), together with £3,000–£4,000 a year from Pynsent, had made Pitt a rich man. See Williams, 1:125–26, 2:170.

255. "Mura-clami . . . a pension to Taycho": In fact it was Hardwicke, not Mansfield, who suggested the pension; see Robert R. Rea, *The English Press in Politics, 1760–1774* (Lincoln: University of Nebraska Press, 1963), 19.

256. "the Dairo . . . Taycho and his heirs": A pension of £3000 was settled on Pitt for his life and for the lives of his wife and eldest son.

257. "Yak-strot delivered . . . his cell in the country": Smollett is thinking of a later and more famous private visit to Pitt at Hayes, that of Cumberland; see below, n. 411, and see also Print 4121*.

258. "slapped his door . . . face of the favourite": *Briton*, no. 3 (12 June 1762): 18 describes Pitt as "kicking his heels in the face of his benefactor."

259. "The many-tailed monster . . . virulence and abuse": Pitt's acceptance of the pension, considered by many a triumph for the court, caused consternation in London and was widely discussed in print; but his letter to Beckford calmed the turmoil and left him at least as strong as before. See Walpole, *George III*, 1: 63–65. *Briton*, no. 7 (10 July 1762): 38: "I never supposed avarice to be part of his character, and was the more surprised when he accepted of a pension."

260. "at the foot of the ladder": That is, about to ascend the ladder leading to the gallows.

261. "their empress died . . . against the Ostrog": Elizabeth of Russia died on 5 January 1762. Her successor Peter III, who was feeble-minded or insane, ordered his troops on the same day to fight under the command of Frederick; he returned East Prussia and other conquered territories to Frederick and removed Swedish troops from Pomerania. After Peter was deposed and murdered (June–July 1762), the empress Catherine recalled her troops but maintained peace with Frederick. See Asprey, 551–55.

262. "engines": Devices, instruments.

263. "much comforted and assisted . . . work in hand": On the propaganda campaign against Bute, see below, pp. 119–21 and nn. 354–55, 358, 361. Pitt himself avoided direct connection with the campaign, which was largely directed by Lord Temple, though the latter carefully avoided showing his hand and

worked through his chief assistant John Wilkes and others; see *Continuation*, 5:115–17.

264. "he sent a peremptory message . . . for which it was taken": Late in 1761 conversations between Lord Bristol and the Spanish ambassador Fuentes proved fruitless, and Britain declared war on 4 January 1762. See *Continuation*, 4:350–55, and *PH*, 15:1129–30.

265. "the treasures of Corea . . . to that kingdom": The Atlantic treasure fleet reached Spain in October 1761.

266. "this treasure existed no where": It was in fact immensely rich.

267. "proceeded from the mouth": "Man shall not live by bread alone, but by every word that proceedeth out of the mouth of God" (Matthew 4:4).

268. "projected three naval enterprizes": Early in January 1762, by which time Bute was a secretary of state, a secret committee was formed to make the plans Smollett describes in the passage following; see Sedgwick, 78.

269. "Thin-quo": Martinique; see above, vol. 2, nn. 25, 26.

270. "Fan-yah": Havana; see key. The expedition to Havana was in fact Lord Anson's project.

271. "Lli-nam": Manila; see key. Smollett here locates Manila properly, forgetting his mirror-image geography.

272. "different projectors": In this case the planning staff. In fact, *contra* Smollett, Pitt had maintained the most constant and detailed supervision of all military operations since assuming office.

273. "The next step . . . with the usual solemnities": On 8 September 1761 the king married Charlotte Sophia of Mecklenburg-Strelitz (1744–1818). As elector of Hanover, George was a vassal of the empire, and he was thus legally required to make a royal marriage. The double coronation was held on 22 September.

274. "he with-held the annual tribute . . . Brut-an-tiffi": In April 1762 the cabinet voted to discontinue the Prussian subsidy of £670,000 per annum; see Browning, 285, and Karl W. Schweizer, "The Non-Renewal of the Anglo-Prussian Subsidy Treaty, 1761–1762: A Historical Revision," *Canadian Journal of History* 13 (1978): 383–98.

275. "reckoned without his host": Miscalculated, in the sense of reckoning up one's own bill without considering what an innkeeper may decide to charge.

276. "chequered": Variegated, as a chessboard.

277. "to vest him with the badges . . . prescription": Bute, who was extremely vain of his personal appearance (particularly of his shapely legs), had been invested with the Order of the Thistle by George II. On 22 September 1762, in a single ceremony, George III installed his brother Prince William and Bute as knights of the Garter. Though Bute had begged on 5 May to decline the honor, the king insisted; see Sedgwick, 98–99. The storm of protest was violent; at least fifty prints show Bute's Garter, notably 3843, 3848, and 3896. Wilkes's *North Briton*, no. 2 (12 June 1762) is largely devoted to the topic.

278. "treasure of the empire . . . the hands of the Cuboy": Newcastle had been first lord of the treasury (except for a brief interval in 1756–57) since 1754. He was constantly accused of bribery and corruption. The accusations were accurate in the sense that he did everything he could to control parliamentary elections; but Namier, *Structure*, 173–234, assembles a mass of material that casts doubt on charges of any extensive misuse of funds other than the duke's personal fortune. The king and Bute had been anxious to displace Newcastle since well before the accession, and they proceeded to impede his work at the treasury and elsewhere as early as 1761; see Browning, 284–89, and Brewer, *Party*, 126.

279. "The death . . . rude shock": See Browning, 271, and Namier, *England*, 134. The shock was personal as well as political, however, as is clear from Horace Walpole's famous account (in a letter to George Montague, 13 November 1760) of Newcastle at the old king's funeral; see *Correspondence*, 9:322–33.

280. "preferring a Bonze . . . consent or knowledge": In October 1761 Bute translated Bishop Hayter of Norwich instead of Bishop Thomas of Lincoln to the see of London, saying to Newcastle, "If Thomas is such a favorite with your Grace, why did you not promote him when you had the power?" (Walpole, *George III*, 1:57). Newcastle wrote of Hayter: "a man . . . who has acted so ungratefully to me, who made him every thing, that he *ever was* . . . with difficulty I swallow it" (Namier, *England*, 333). Hayter had been Prince George's tutor.

281. "he was prevented . . . dregs of the people": Newcastle was forbidden to use secret service funds in conducting the election of March 1761. See Namier, *Structure*, 208, and Walpole, *George III*, 1:31.

282. "symptoms . . . friends and dependants": The passage that follows reflects familiar mocking characterizations of Newcastle. Because of his long career, combined with his irresolution and timidity, Newcastle had long been pictured in the political prints as an old woman or old nurse; see Prints 3385, 3373, 3394*, 3342, 4133*. *Briton*, no. 30 (18 December 1762): 175 opens with a mock dissertation on sex-change in antiquity and the term *matronisatio*, a "form or ceremony" of the Romans for "such of their countrymen as grew to be old women." The reference to Newcastle's "incubation" may be in retaliation for Bute's being pictured similarly in Print 4164*, but the same image occurs in the review of a book on cockfighting, *CR* 14 (August 1762): 155; the review condemns the sport itself as barbarous and says of the author, "His cares extend to the earliest period of incubation; and so explicit are his rules, that we cannot help thinking he has devoted some part of his time to the very act of hatching." The political allusions in the passage are to the period when Newcastle was systematically frustrated in his conduct of the treasury by those intent upon forcing his resignation; see Browning, 287–89.

283. "groanings": Lyings-in.

284. "caudle": A sweet spiced gruel for women in childbed.

285. "began . . . to hiss and to cackle": Political prints sometimes depicted Newcastle

as a goose, partly because of his association with Fox; see, for example, Print 3589.

286. "on the back of": Immediately after.

287. "the barber of Midas": Midas, for judging the satyr Marsyas a better musician than Apollo, was given ass's ears. These he concealed under a Phrygian cap; but his barber, unable to refrain from gossip, whispered the secret to the reeds, which whispered it to the world.

288. "scandalized": Disgraced by being made the subject of scandal.

289. "a jury of matrons": Such juries had sometimes been used in cases of disputed virginity, as with the widowed Catherine of Aragon before her marriage to the future Henry VIII; Catherine had been married to Henry's elder brother, Prince Arthur.

290. "*non mas*": L. Not a man. Smollett devoted much effort to attacking Archibald Bower's *History of the Popes* (1748–66); see Knapp, 16n. In a review of the fourth volume of Bower's work, *CR* 7 (January 1759): 46–47, he ridiculed the story of Pope Joan and the legend that thenceforth the youngest cardinal deacon inspected the privates of the pope-elect through a perforated seat and proclaimed, "*Mas est; Deo gratias.*" See Basker, 225, 249.

291. "a certain Ximian . . . on a broom-stick": Here Smollett possibly retaliates against Print 3852*, an obscene depiction of Bute riding on a broomstick toward the dowager princess of Wales, the king's mother.

292. "divested of his office . . . in the country": Newcastle resigned on 26 May 1762 and retired to his estate at Claremont. See *Continuation*, 5:33–34: the king had "no very high idea of the d-ke's management and capacity." See also Browning, 289–90.

293. "the most unpopular man . . . empire of Japan": Bute induced Fox, because of his abilities in managing Parliament, to desert the Whigs and lead the Commons. He was to be continued as paymaster-general, "the most lucrative place under the British government." Fox agreed to the arrangement on 12 October 1762, and joined the formal cabinet. *Continuation*, 5:21: "Mr. F-x, who was, undoubtedly, next to himself [Bute], the most unpopular man in the whole kingdom."

294. "deprived of bread . . . the former Cuboy": A reference to the so-called "massacre of the Pelhamite innocents" in December 1762, when numerous petty appointees of the government were dismissed. *Continuation*, 5:34–35 observes that the episode "gave umbrage to the whole Whig party." Williams, 2:150, characterizes those dismissed as "clerks, schoolboys, widows, servants, and old pensioners," their stipends, given by Newcastle, going to Fox's dependents; Namier, *England*, 468–83, finds that many of them were not so innocent.

295. "a doublet of buckram": A coarse cloth, stiffened with gum; by Smollett's time the phrase had begun to imply a stiff, exaggeratedly formal manner. Shakespeare refers to doublets of buckram in *1 Henry IV* 2.4.193, 204–5, 219.

296. "the attitude of the idol Fo": See above, vol. 2, n. 67; nothing is meant here beyond hieratic stiffness.

297. "retorted": Turned up.

298. "these postures and gesticulations . . . communication": The source of this characterization of Bute's mannerisms has not been traced. Smollett may be parodying a manual for actors, or echoing such a parody as that of Addison on the management of the fan, *Spectator*, no. 102 (27 June 1711).

299. "a Highlander . . . breeches": After the suppression of the rebellion of the "'Forty-Five" Hardwicke drafted and Parliament passed legislation forbidding the wearing of Highland dress. The intention was to dissipate the cohesiveness and loyalty of the clans. The measure became law in June 1746. See *PH*, 14:269–315.

300. "a sulphureous smell": One of the calumnies against Scots was that they were all afflicted with the itch, for which sulphur was used as a cure. See Prints 3823*, 3946*.

301. "two or three obscure Ximians": These were Sir Henry Erskine, M.P., poet and soldier (he rose to the rank of lieutenant-general); Thomas Worseley, M.P., surveyor-general of the Board of Works; and John Home, Bute's private secretary, author of the play, *Douglas*, and former tutor to the king. See Walpole, *George III*, 1:28–29.

302. "an Attic evening": An evening of refined conversation in the manner of the Greeks. Smollett is perhaps thinking of the learned *Noctes Atticæ*, by the Roman writer Aulus Gellius, a compendium of recondite information.

303. "his own family . . . very numerous": Bute's bestowal of places and favors upon family and friends represented little more than standard practice at the time. His conduct in this matter was vastly exaggerated by his opponents, and Smollett, having failed to receive the consulship he had hoped for, was emphatic about his dissatisfaction; see *Letters*, 110–11.

304. "fat things": The best parts or choicest portions. The phrase is used frequently in the Bible; see, for example, Isaiah 25:6.

305. "Those islanders came . . . long sharp teeth": Smollett echoes many literary and pictorial satires, as Churchill's *Prophecy of Famine* (1763) and Print 3823*, "We are all a-comeing."

306. "understrappers": This word for subordinate or assistant is a trademark of Smollett; it occurs throughout his work, from *Roderick Random* to the *Briton*.

307. "Yak-strot was represented": The accusations repeated in the passage that follows are substantially those of numerous anti-Bute pamphlets and especially Wilkes's *North Briton*. See Brewer, "Misfortunes," and Nobbe.

308. "that he had suborned . . . Fak-ku-basi": This charge was basically true. Bute obtained "inside financial information that might be damaging to Newcastle" (Browning, 287); and Newcastle had vastly depleted his own fortune in promoting the policies he supported. See above, vol. 1, n. 151.

309. "a treasonable scheme . . . his own deposition": Bute was a distant relative of the Stuart pretender to the English throne. *Briton*, no. 4 (19 June 1762): 22–23, and the entirety of no. 19 (2 October 1762), are devoted to vindicating the earl, the Stuarts, and the Scots in general from such charges.

310. "Gio-gio was no more than a puppet . . . family of the Dairo": The first of these charges was very frequent, to the extent that mobs burned a boot and a petticoat, symbolizing Bute and Princess Augusta; Bute was often compared to Sejanus, the all-powerful favorite of the emperor Tiberius. The second accusation was more guardedly expressed in print, but a widely circulated adaptation of the old play *The Fall of Mortimer* (1763) featured a weak king, a wicked queen-mother, and a scheming lover. The political prints were less inhibited. Many showed the two "lovers," often obscenely, and some depicted them as controlling the king. See *Continuation*, 5:115–16; Brewer, "Misfortunes," 7, 10; Prints 3823, 3978, 3852*, 3849*, 3940, 4149; and Herbert M. Atherton, *Political Prints in the Age of Hogarth* (New York: Oxford University Press, 1974), 208–27.

311. "They struck up . . . loyalty and virtue": The alliance was formal and was made public at a dinner at Devonshire House in March 1763; Pitt and Newcastle thereafter acted in concert against Bute. See Browning, 295. *Humphry Clinker* comments on Newcastle's being "extolled as a pattern of public virtue" (Jery Melford to Sir Watkin Phillips, London, June 2).

312. "Legion hoisted . . . antient Cuboy": This procession is a version of that described in *Briton*, no. 38 (12 February 1763): 225.

313. "His cause was now espoused . . . his protection": Hardwicke and Anson had resigned their offices shortly after Newcastle's departure.

314. "not one of all the Bonzes . . . disgrace": Newcastle had made twenty-six bishops, but only one, Cornwallis of Lichfield, attended his last levee in office. The duke is said to have remarked: "Bishops, like other men, are apt to forget their maker." See Browning, 290.

315. "Even the Fatz-man . . . malcontents": Cumberland, victor at Culloden but disgraced at Klosterseven in 1757 (see above, vol. 1, n. 575), began to regain his popularity because of anti-Scots sentiment. He disliked Fox and felt that the Peace of Paris was too lenient. All of these circumstances led the opposition to woo him, with success, though Cumberland took no office.

316. "Gotto-mio . . . his avarice": On Bedford see above, vol. 1, nn. 278–80, 282. Bedford was anxious to secure peace (he was made British representative for the forthcoming Peace of Paris), and was lord privy seal in Bute's cabinet.

317. "desperate fortunes and loose morals": This phrase probably refers to the rakish and incompetent Sir Francis Dashwood, of "Hell-Fire Club" notoriety. Dashwood became chancellor of the exchequer; he had been a good friend of Bute's late influential hanger-on, George Bubb Dodington, Lord Melcombe. See *Continuation*, 5:121–22.

318. "Thin-quo . . . without opposition": Martinique surrendered on 14 February 1762.

319. "the conquest of Fan-yah . . . atchieved": Havana was not finally taken until 13 August 1762.

320. "some considerable advantages . . . Bron-xi-tic": See *Continuation*, 4:272. The most important of these "advantages" was Ferdinand's defeat of the French generals de Broglie and Soubise at Kirch-Denkern, 16 July 1761.

321. "Fumma": Portugal; see key.

322. "a prince . . . king of Corea": The king of Portugal had married the sister of Charles III of Spain.

323. "intimate connexions . . . alliance with this country": See *Continuation*, 5:45–66, for an account of the affairs of Portugal and of the incidents described in the passage that follows. Relations between England and Portugal had been close since Charles II had married Catherine of Braganza, and the Portugal trade (fostered by the Methuen Treaty of 1704) came to £1,000,000 per year.

324. "monarchs of China and Corea . . . hostilities": Early in 1762 Spanish troops approached the Portuguese border, and Lisbon appealed to London. On 16 March France and Spain asked Portugal to renounce the British alliance and join the "Family Compact," allowing four days for an answer; the alternative was an invasion. The king of Portugal refused to comply, and another demand followed on 1 April. Portugal declared war on Spain on 23 May, and British troops were immediately dispatched.

325. "embarrassed": Perplexed; hampered by bewilderment.

326. "Le-yaw-ter": Lord Tyrawley; see key.

327. "concert": Plan cooperatively.

328. "discovered . . . curtain": In the theatrical sense of "revealed by opening the curtain." The account that follows is a paraphrase of *Continuation*, 5:53–55.

329. "amused": Deceptively engaged.

330. "actually": In the French sense of "at this or that time."

331. "the combined army . . . summer quarters": Smollett comments in *Continuation*, 5:60 that the French-Spanish advance had been so slow that collusion seemed likely.

332. "Sab-oi . . . Cambodia": Charles Emmanuel III of Savoy, king of Sardinia; see key.

333. "an ambassador plenipotentiary . . . preliminaries of peace": Beginning in September 1762 the duc de Nivernais conducted discussions in London; the preliminaries were signed at Fontainebleau on 3 November by Bedford for England, Choiseul for France, and Grimaldi for Spain.

334. "Kep-marl . . . expence of the expedition": Admirals George Keppel (see key, KEP-MARL) and Pocock took the surrender of Havana on 13 August 1762. A treasure of £2,000,000 was recovered, and the Spanish navy was effectively put

out of commission. See *Continuation*, 5:124–35; the words "indemnify . . . expedition" are taken verbatim from p. 134. The "sea of Kamtschatka" is the Indian Ocean.

335. "general Tra-rep . . . plunder": "Tra-rep" is General Sir William Draper; see key. Draper took and sacked Manila on 6 October 1762; see *Continuation*, 5:146. The city agreed to a ransom of four million dollars, which was not paid; see Corbett, 2:365.

336. "These successes . . . parties concerned": The paragraph that follows is a version of the arguments presented in *Briton*, no. 17 (18 September 1762): 97–102.

337. "parts": Abilities, capacities, talents.

338. "It had been the custom . . . were invited": A reference to the lord mayor's annual banquet, held in the Guildhall, to which the sovereigns were traditionally invited as guests of the city of London.

339. "Rhum-kikh": Alderman William Beckford; see key. The banquet referred to was held, however, on 9 November 1761, and Beckford did not become lord mayor until a year later; the incumbent at the time was Sir Samuel Fludyer. Smollett's error probably resulted from his reliance upon a passage concerning Beckford in the *Continuation*, 5:115.

340. "an ungracious address": Uncouth manners.

341. "a fiery caustic spirit": Rum.

342. "The Dairo and his young empress . . . unhonoured and unnoticed": This account is only slightly exaggerated. The royal couple met with the bare minimum of politeness; although Bute had prudently provided himself with a bodyguard of "butchers and bruisers," including several well-known boxers, his coach was mobbed and he was in considerable danger. The crowd, which had been hired by Beckford to applaud Pitt and Lord Temple as they "appeared in a chariot," erupted into a riot; see Brewer, "Misfortunes," 5. For a contemporary account see Walpole, *George III*, 1:69–70.

343. "A small squadron . . . by the enemy": On 24 June 1762 a French squadron under Admiral de Ternay took Saint John's in Newfoundland; see *Continuation*, 5:40–41. Smollett minimizes the incident in *Briton*, no. 12 (14 August 1762): 69: "The French have surprised some fishing vessels, destroyed a few old wooden stages, taken one or two inconsiderable places that were never thought tenable."

344. "the Quo Phyl-Kholl": Admiral Alexander Colville; see key. Colville retook Saint John's on 18 September 1762; see *Continuation*, 5:152–54.

345. "the peace was signed . . . assembly of the people": The preliminaries of 3 November 1762 were ratified by Parliament on 9 December. The Peace of Paris was formally signed on 10 February 1763. See *PH*, 15:1240–79. The "great national council of the Quos" is the House of Lords; the "assembly of the people" is the House of Commons.

346. "Yak-strot . . . harangued the great council": On 9 December 1762 Bute addressed the Lords on the subject of the peace. Smollett's description of the

speech, following, resembles accounts given earlier in *Continuation*, 5:161–62 and in *Briton*, no. 32 (1 January 1763): 188–89. Walpole, *George III*, 1:103, says of an earlier speech by Bute: "his admirers were in ecstasies; the few who dared sneer at his theatric fustian did not find it quite so ridiculous as they wished."

347. "palfrey": A small, gentle horse, suitable for ladies.

348. "descanted": Discoursed upon.

349. "In this equipage . . . advantageous to his country": Pitt, suffering from gout, entered the Commons on 9 December 1762 supported in the arms of two friends. He received permission to address the members while sitting, and spoke for two hours on the separate articles of the peace; for him the speech was an unusually poor effort. See Williams, 2:146–49. In *Briton*, no. 32 (1 January 1763): 189 Smollett writes of Pitt's "flannel gown, the frowzy badge of courted popularity"; and in *Continuation*, 5:161–62 of his having "agreed to articles [in the abortive 1761 negotiations] much less advantageous to Great Britain." See *PH*, 15:1259–71.

350. "by a great majority": The vote in the Commons was 319 to 65.

351. "Not that they had . . . less precipitation": See *Continuation*, 5:186–91, where Smollett specifically identified some of the inadequacies of the treaty as he saw them: the French were allowed fishing rights in the Gulf of Saint Lawrence and off Newfoundland; Guadeloupe, Goree, and the trading stations in India were restored to French control; the British once again failed to recognize the importance of Louisiana.

352. "undertakers": Those who undertake to perform an enterprise.

353. "anointed . . . a certain precious salve": Fox, in return for the promise of a peerage, had agreed to steer the Peace of Paris through the Commons. He was universally believed to have engaged in wholesale bribery. Rumor had it that in one morning at a window in the Pay Office a sum amounting to £25,000 was paid out to M.P.'s who came there publicly to receive their bribes; see Print 4079, and see Walpole, *George III*, 1:156–57. Namier, *Structure*, 181–84, challenges the rumor. The "massacre of the Pelhamite innocents," however, was in part a retaliation carried out as punishment for those who had voted against the peace; see above, vol. 2, n. 294.

354. "Lob-kob . . . vengeance against the Ximian favourite": Walpole, *George III*, 1:144 observes: "[The propagandists] had a familiar at their ear, whose venom was never distilled at random . . . Earl Temple, who whispered them where they might find torches, but took care never to be seen to light one himself. [He thus enjoyed] vengeance, and a whole skin." Smollett uses the term "originals" in the pejorative sense of "like no one who ever lived."

355. "Llur-chir": Charles Churchill; see key. Although he was in orders and even held curacies in various parishes, Churchill's drunkenness and sexual adventures soon led to his resignation. *The Rosciad* (1761), a verse satire on actors, made him famous, and at the time he was England's most celebrated poet. Many of his

satires touch on Bute and the Scots; *The Prophecy of Famine* (1763) is wholly devoted to them. Churchill was co-author, with Wilkes, of the *North Briton*; and in *The Author* (London, 1763), 250, 254 he characterized Smollett as a "vile pensioner of State": "And what makes SMOLLETT write, makes JOHNSON dumb."

356. "Jan-ki-dtzin": John Wilkes; see key.

357. "art and mystery": Technical skill and knowledge; a formula used for the indenturing of apprentices.

358. "making balls of filth": *Briton*, no. 14 (29 August 1762): 82, a satire on Wilkes in the manner of the popular "Arabian tale," is the source for the idea of throwing filth. Wilkes was the proprietor and usually the author of the *North Briton*, by far the most effective weapon in the arsenal of the anti-Bute forces.

359. "made advances to the new Cuboy": Through his connections with Pitt and Temple, Wilkes had unsuccessfully solicited from Bute the ambassadorship to Constantinople and the governorship of Quebec; see Print 4041*.

360. "prudish punctilio . . . his administration": Smollett alludes to Fox and to the notorious rakes Sir Francis Dashwood and the earl of Sandwich; see *Continuation*, 5:121, 211–12.

361. "Be that as it may . . . posture of defence": The passage that follows presents an account of the paper war waged between the ministry and its opposition. On the course of these hostilities see *Continuation*, 5:119–22; Nobbe; Brewer, *Party*; and Peters, *Pitt and Popularity*. The *Briton* and Arthur Murphy's *Auditor* opposed the *North Briton* and the *Monitor* by frequently satirizing Pitt, Temple, and Newcastle; they met with little success.

362. "having at bottom a fund of fanaticism": In a letter of 1770 Smollett writes of "the absurd Stoicism of Lord Bute, who set himself up as a Pillory to be pelted by all the Blackguards of England, upon the Supposition that they would grow tired and leave off" (*Letters*, 139). In *Continuation*, 5:118–19, he remarks: "All this torrent of abuse the earl of Bute sustained with a degree of fortitude that bordered upon stoicism, and might have been very easily mistaken for insensibility. . . . This very extraordinary person was really an enthusiast in patriotism. . . . He was of the opinion that virtue, by its own intrinsic efficacy, would in the end triumph over all opposition; therefore, he did not think it necessary to reinforce it by means of any temporizing art, auxiliary law, or other precaution." See also *CR* 15 (January 1763): 60–62, 69. Bute was neither so naive nor so passive as Smollett thought; on his hack writers and secret service network see Brewer, *Party*, 226.

363. "like camomile . . . trod upon": Smollett echoes Falstaff's mock-Euphuistic speech to Prince Hal in *1 Henry IV* 2.4.400–401.

364. "his creatures": His dependents; beings whom he had "created."

365. "taken place": Hit the mark.

366. "he discarded . . . as unnecessary": Both Smollett's *Briton* and Murphy's *Auditor* were discontinued shortly after the signing of the Peace of Paris, which was

Bute's chief objective as minister. On Bute's early troubles in connection with these papers see Brewer, *Party*, 222.

367. "in his own individual": In person.

368. "immensely rich . . . digging his garden": Bute's father-in-law, Edward Wortley Montagu (estranged husband of Lady Mary), died on 22 January 1761, leaving his daughter coal fields and estates in Yorkshire and Cornwall valued at £1,300,000. "Hoard" perhaps refers to the notorious stinginess of the Montagus; see Pope's imitation of Horace, *Satires*, book 2, 2.49–60.

369. "an expedient . . . any other occasion": Smollett may have received little or no monetary compensation for writing the *Briton*; and though he may have applied to Bute for a pension and certainly did apply for consulships, he got nothing. See *Letters*, 110–11.

370. "the attitude of the idol Fo": See key, FO. Smollett here appears to mean that Bute strikes the pose of the Buddha, indicating tranquil resignation.

371. "*hysterica passio*": L. Hysterics. Smollett echoes *King Lear* 2.4.57. The intention of this scene is obscure, but since it involves the foulest besmirching of Bute it may refer to the constant innuendoes that Bute and Princess Augusta were lovers. Bute was said to have contrived a secret passage between his villa at Kew and the royal apartments; see Prints 4131 and 4177, "A View of Lord Bute's Erections at Kew." Smollett always alludes to the insinuations about Bute and the princess with the greatest delicacy.

372. "devote": Dedicate.

373. "*Virtus . . . auræ*": Horace *Odes* 3.2.17–20: "True worth, that never knows ignoble defeat, shines with undimmed glory, nor takes up nor lays aside public office at the fickle mob's behest." This passage is the motto for *Briton*, no. 6 (3 July 1762).

374. "dying for his country": The same Horatian ode identified in n. 373 contains (line 13) the famous "*Dulce et decorum est pro patria mori*": "it is sweet and fitting to die for the fatherland."

375. "the Dairo himself . . . heavy heart": In actuality, Bute had always been more cautious and reluctant than the king wished regarding his advancement to high office. In addition to the obloquy he suffered, he was on several occasions in grave physical danger; see Brewer, "Misfortunes," 5–9. According to Walpole, *George III*, 1:201–2, Bute had long intended to resign as soon as the Peace of Paris was achieved. Like Horace Walpole's father Sir Robert, he actually stepped down in the midst of a relatively trivial affair, the parliamentary difficulties over the passage of an excise tax on cider; see below, n. 393.

376. "influence behind the curtain": A familiar phrase constantly used, from at least as early as the time of Sir Robert Walpole's fall from power in 1742, to refer to the secret manipulation of policy by a favorite of the king. The phrase occurs regularly in prints, pamphlets, and private correspondence. Until at least 1770 Bute was firmly believed by the vast majority, high and low (including Smollett),

to be the real ruler of England; see Brewer, "Misfortunes," and see also Print 4049*.

377. "he aimed some balls at the Dairo": The famous Number Forty-Five of the *North Briton* (23 April 1763) dealt with the king's speech closing Parliament; see *PH*, 15:1321–31. In his paper Wilkes daringly used language which could be interpreted as calling the king a liar and characterizing him as the mere mouthpiece of Bute. Arguably constituting treason and *lèse-majesté*, his remarks were taken at the time as a direct insult to the king; *Continuation*, 5:212 describes them as "indecent to His Majesty's probity as well as his person." See Nobbe, 207–13; and see *PH*, 15:1331–36.

378. "Had the laws of Japan . . . on the spot": A close paraphrase of a passage in *Continuation*, 5:120; as early as *Briton*, no. 32 (1 January 1763): 190, Smollett had said that the libelers of Bute and the king deserved branding and the pillory.

379. "Gio-gio, being good-natured . . . balls": On 26 April 1763 a general warrant for the "authors, printers, and publishers" of *North Briton*, no. 45 was issued by the secretaries of state; on 30 April Wilkes was taken to the Tower and his house was searched for incriminating evidence. See *Continuation*, 5:211–18; and see *PH*, 15:1336–40.

380. "Praff-patt-phogg": Chief Justice Charles Pratt; see key. Pratt released Wilkes with a writ of *habeas corpus* on the grounds of his parliamentary privilege, the dubious legality of the search and seizure in his case, and the lack of specificity in the general warrant. See Brewer, *Party*, 170, and *Continuation*, 5:215–16.

381. "*Palladia*": From the statue of Pallas supposed to protect Troy; thus, national talismans, or objects on which the safety of the state depends. Wilkes and Pratt became national and colonial heroes; both received the freedom of many cities, and variations upon "Wilkes and the Forty-Five" or "the number forty-five" remained familiar slogans for years.

382. "The Dairo . . . laws of the land": On 15 November 1763 the king sent a message to the Commons requesting that Wilkes be tried. On 23 November, during the ensuing debate (which included the question of general warrants), Pitt called Wilkes "a blasphemer of his God and a libeller of his King." On 15 November Parliament had ordered the public burning of *North Briton*, no. 45; the burning was attempted on 3 December in the Royal Exchange, but a rioting mob prevented it (see Walpole, *George III*, 1:219–21, 223, 243–56). Wilkes fled to France in December and was expelled from Parliament on 20 January 1764. Meanwhile his obscene *Essay on Woman*, with notes foisted onto the formidable Bishop Warburton, had been found in Wilkes's house. The Lords therefore tried him for obscene and seditious libel of a peer in February 1764; he was found guilty and, since he had fled the country, was outlawed. See Rudé, 22–36; *Continuation*, 5:219–36; *PH*, 15:1346–1413. Adrian Hamilton, *The Infamous Essay on Woman* (London: Andre Deutsch, 1972), reproduces the *Essay* and many contemporary documents pertaining to the case, with detailed discussion.

383. "He was burnt or crucified in effigy": This is substantially true. See Brewer, "Misfortunes," 6–9.

384. *"natale solum"*: L. Native soil or land; from Ovid *Metamorphoses* 7:52, 8:184. The phrase is used in *Briton*, no. 34 (15 January 1763): 201.

385. "of course": As might be expected; in the natural course of events.

386. "one of the honestest men . . . empire": The ensuing balanced portrait of Bute echoes *Continuation*, 5:121, and is consistent with modern estimates; it is kinder than Walpole's representation in *George III*, 1:15–17, 42, 132–35.

387. "wool-combing": The carding of wool.

388. "ascertained": Made precise and guaranteed.

389. "Taycho . . . the preceding year": See *Continuation*, 4:294–313 on the abortive peace articles of 1761.

390. "vicious": Faulty.

391. "running . . . displeasure": An echo of *Twelfth Night* 3.2.26–27; a similar echo occurs in chapter 100 of *Peregrine Pickle* and in a review of James Boswell's *Rodondo*, *CR* 15 (February 1763): 130.

392. "concert": Coordinate.

393. "certain odious measures . . . impositions on the people": A reference to the Cider Tax, proposed by Sir Francis Dashwood, chancellor of the exchequer, to obtain much-needed revenues. The proposal raised a great popular uproar reminiscent of that which had forced Sir Robert Walpole to withdraw his excise taxes some thirty years earlier; it brought about Bute's downfall. At the opening of the parliamentary session on 25 November 1762, Bute was assaulted and nearly killed in his sedan-chair; see Brewer, "Misfortunes," 5–6. The Cider Bill passed the Lords on 30 March 1763, and the city unsuccessfully petitioned the king not to sign it; Bute incautiously promised a City delegation that he would have the legislation repealed at the next session, and the resulting publicity made him resign. See *Continuation*, 5:195–202; Walpole, *George III*, 1:199–201; *PH*, 15:1307–16, 1321–30.

394. "a german quarrel": In modern French, *querelle d'allemands*: groundless and deliberately provoked.

395. "a scrubbing-post": The Scots, said to be afflicted with the itch (see above, vol. 2, n. 300), were thus also said to have a continual need to scratch their backs against a post, as swine do. See Prints 3823*, 3946*.

396. "the scribe Zan-ti-fic": The earl of Sandwich; see key. From 23 April to 9 September 1763 Sandwich was first lord of the admiralty in the Grenville cabinet, which succeeded Bute's; he was then secretary of state, northern department, until 11 July 1765.

397. "brimstone . . . Ximo": Another allusion to the Scotch itch, which was supposedly cured by brimstone, or sulphur. An anti-Bute pamphlet called *The True Flower of Brimstone* appeared in 1763. ("Flower" means "flour," *i.e.*, powdered.)

398. "Twitz-er the Financier": George Grenville, first lord of the treasury and chan-

cellor of the exchequer; see key. The abrupt introduction of the two characters of Sandwich and Grenville as though they had been described before suggests that at this point, when his personal involvement with the story ceased, Smollett laid his manuscript aside in Nice and then took it up again at Bath in 1765. The additional and equally sudden reference to "the other scribe" indicates that Smollett was thinking of the two secretaries of state, Sandwich and the earl of Halifax.

399. "they bluntly told the Dairo . . . invisible agent": On 23 May 1765 Grenville and others informed the king that they must resign unless he gave his word never to have any further communication with Bute on matters of policy or public business. The king reluctantly consented. See Sedgwick, 240, and Brewer, *Party*, 124–25. The date of this event, coupled with the fact that in the *Atom* Smollett scarcely touches on significant events of 1764, when he was in Nice, makes it very likely that in 1765, when he was completing the *Continuation*, he was continuing the *Atom* merely as a version of its chronicle. On Smollett's activities at Bath in 1765, when he was working up for publication the text of his *Travels*, also written at Nice, see Martz, 71.

400. "seemed": In the older sense of "pretended to, gave the appearance of."

401. "One of his nearest relations . . . deprived": James Stuart Mackenzie, Bute's brother, had been made lord privy seal of Scotland and given control of all Scottish patronage, previous to Bute's resignation; Grenville now demanded his removal. He had been promised a life appointment on the king's word of honor, but resigned to save the king the embarrassment of having to dismiss him. See Walpole, *George III*, 2:125.

402. "The Dairo fell sick . . . in the cradle": The king had a mysterious and dangerous illness from 12 January 1765 through the month of March. It was certainly a severe cold or influenza; it may or may not have involved the first onset of the porphyria that produced his later "madness," but there is no evidence that he was deranged at this time. See Ida Macalpine and Richard A. Hunter, *George III and the Mad Business* (London: Allen Lane, 1969), 176–91; and on Smollett's alleged posthumous involvement in the matter (the supposed suppression of *Continuation*, 5 by the authorities), see Peter Miles, "Bibliography and Insanity: Smollett and the Mad-Business," *The Library*, 6th ser., 31 (1976): 205–22. The Prince of Wales had been born on 12 August 1762.

403. "prevent": Forestall.

404. "a regency . . . states of the empire": On 24 April 1765 the king asked Parliament for a bill authorizing him to appoint as regent the queen or "a person of the royal family usually residing in Great Britain." See *PH*, 16:52–58. The "states of the empire" are the estates of the realm, or the Lords and Commons.

405. "they endeavoured to exclude . . . of their sovereign": According to Walpole, Smollett, and others, the ministers raised the question of whether the Dowager Princess Augusta was legally a member of the royal family as a pretext for telling

the king that the regency bill would not pass the Commons unless she were excluded. The king appealed to Grenville, then first minister, who concurred with the others; but the Commons insisted that Princess Augusta be specifically included, and passed the bill on 9 May 1765. See *Continuation*, 5:444–49. The passage of the regency bill is the last event of political importance recorded in the *Continuation*, the conclusion to which is dated "July 1, 1765." The actual negotiations over the regency were very complex and involved several factors unknown to any except the king and a few others; see Brooke, *George III*, 110–13. See also Derek Jarrett, "The Regency Crisis of 1765," *English Historical Review* 85 (1970): 282–316.

406. "the tyranny of this junto . . . Gio-Gio": The king intensely disliked the cabinet as constituted after the removal of Bute, with Grenville chiefly in power, seconded by Bedford and Sandwich. See Sedgwick, 209–38.

407. "the art of puppet-playing": The satiric image of the minister as puppeteer goes back at least as far as Pope's comment on Sir Robert Walpole's manipulation of George II through Lord Hervey: "And as the prompter breathes, the puppet squeaks" (*Epistle to Dr. Arbuthnot*, line 318). Bute is satirically represented as a puppeteer in Prints 4186, 4230, and 4049*, "The S[cotch] Puppitt Show," in which he is made to say, "Tho I am out tis known for Certain / I prompt 'em still behind the Curtain."

408. "tempered with": Smollett uses an archaic but still familiar spelling for *tampered* (*OED*). He may be punning through conflation of meanings carried by both common spellings of the word. To temper (with): to mix in proper proportions, to tune (*i.e.*, an instrument); to tamper (with): to meddle or interfere (with), so as to alter, misuse, corrupt, or pervert.

409. "motion": Archaic term for a puppet-show or similar exhibition.

410. "a new set of puppets": The Rockingham ministry of July 1765–July 1766. The duke of Cumberland, though without formal office, presided at cabinet meetings and acted as liaison with the king; he was in effect first minister until his death at the end of October 1765. Newcastle was lord privy seal, while the marquess of Rockingham served as first lord of the treasury; the remaining ministers (including the duke of Grafton) were for the most part new to cabinet office. The king had used Cumberland as an intermediary in forming the new cabinet, since protocol prevented him from soliciting potential members in person. See Paul Langford, *The First Rockingham Administration, 1765–1766* (London: Oxford University Press, 1973).

411. "Taycho and Lob-kob . . . proper keys": The king realized the vital importance of Pitt in securing parliamentary support; he approached Pitt through Lord Temple, who proved an obstacle. So anxious was the king to secure Pitt's services that he sent the prematurely aged and obese Cumberland down to Hayes to plead with him in person. Pitt stubbornly refused to take office unless Temple was in the cabinet; but Temple twice declined an offer of the treasury because he

wanted to form a ministry including his brother George Grenville, whom the
king by now detested for personal as well as political reasons. See Williams,
2:162, 172–77, 196; Brewer, *Party*, 124; and Print 4121*. An informative general work dealing with the personal and political history of the Grenville family
is Lewis M. Wiggin, *The Faction of Cousins: A Political Account of the Grenvilles,
1733–1763* (New Haven: Yale University Press, 1958).

412. "The first exhibition . . . *Topsy-turvy*": From this point onward Smollett's treatment of occurrences and persons becomes increasingly patchy and occasionally
appears confused; it is at times difficult to determine what specific events, if any,
he has in mind, and their chronology is not always maintained. He seems to
have been erroneously convinced that Lord Bute continued to be more or less
firmly in control of political developments, but this was in fact the general opinion, extending even to those in close contact with the court and the cabinet; see
Jucker, *The Jenkinson Papers*, 393–400, for evidence on this point. It may be
conjectured that the remainder of the *Atom* was completed hastily in manuscript
shortly before Smollett left England in the autumn of 1768, since the events run
through the summer of that year.

413. "cast figures": Made charts, specifically astrological charts. Smollett may allude
here to the Grenville administration's frequent boasting of its frugal fiscal policies, as compared with Bute's extravagance, and of the increased yield of customs duties; see the *Annual Register* for 1764, 31–32.

414. "an incendiary Bonze called Toks": The Rev. Dr. James Scott; see key. Walpole,
George III, 2:191: "Sandwich had set up a most virulent and scurrilous paper,
called *Anti-Sejanus*, written by one Scott, an hireling parson, and chiefly levelled
at Lord Bute." See also Brewer, *Party*, 234.

415. "fire-balls": Projectiles filled with explosives or combustibles.

416. "heard to say . . . good minister": Pitt's favorable references to Bute were made
in speeches of 14 January and 4 March 1766. See Brewer, *Party*, 106–7, *PH*,
16:98, and Brooke, *George III*, 106–7.

417. "pagod": Pagoda.

418. "a charte blanche . . . Taycho": In July 1766 the Rockingham ministry was in
total collapse, and Pitt was offered virtually anything he desired in an effort to
persuade him to form a government. See Brooke, *Chatham*, 5–19, and Brooke,
George III, 134–37.

419. "the rank of Quanbuku . . . the Dairo's signet": On 30 July 1766 Pitt was created earl of Chatham and appointed lord privy seal, an office which gave him
cabinet rank but involved no burdensome duties, thus ensuring his complete
freedom to control Parliament.

420. "his creature . . . tribunals of Japan": Charles Pratt had been created Baron
Camden in 1764; in 1766 he became lord chancellor in Pitt's cabinet.

421. "all his friends . . . himself should propose": Pitt asked for ten offices in all; see
Walpole, *George III*, 2:247.

422. "Lob-kob . . . these two originals": In July 1766 Temple quarreled with Pitt, foreseeing that without his brother Grenville in the cabinet he would be "a capital cypher"; and for a third time he refused the treasury. He thereafter began a pamphlet war against Pitt which lasted until 1768, and in which he also employed James Scott. See Williams, 2:208–10.

423. "The chair of precedency . . . metamorphosis": Since Pitt was now lord privy seal, Newcastle finally retired from politics, or at least from office. See Browning, 314–16. For Newcastle's "metamorphosis" (into an old woman) see above, vol. 2, n. 282.

424. "dancing the hay": A country-dance involving the changing of places. Smollett's source for the metaphor may be Print 4147*, "The New Country Dance."

425. "tergiversation": Backsliding; apostasy; forsaking a cause or party.

426. "the title of Quo . . . renounced its society": The reaction to Pitt's peerage, by which the Great Commoner "formally renounced" the Commons and thereby lost his power, was violent. Walpole, *George III*, 2:254, remarks that "the fatal title blasted all affection . . . he could not have sunk lower in public esteem."

427. "the rod of Moses": Smollett means the rod of Aaron; see above, vol. 1, n. 463. His confusion perhaps resulted from the fact that the rod of Moses also turned into a serpent; see Exodus 4:2–3.

428. "certain extravagancies . . . actually insane": Pitt suffered frequent bouts of severe and incapacitating depression. The worst and longest of these began early in 1767; in March Pitt went into seclusion, refusing to take any action whatever in spite of frantic pleas from the king, including several personal letters. An article in the *British Magazine* 8 (May 1767): 257–59 gives the opinion of the eminent Dr. Williamson that Pitt was evidently insane. See Williams, 2:238–47, and Brooke, *George III*, 138–41.

429. "*non compos*": L. *Non compos mentis* is the legal term for "of unsound mind."

430. "that arch empiric's practices": By "empiric" Smollett here means "quack" or unqualified practitioner.

431. "sternutatories": Drugs to cause sneezing and thus clearing of the air passages.

432. "kennel": Gutter or trench running in the center of the street.

433. "leaven": Yeast, fermenting agent.

434. "the Fatzman . . . died about this period": Cumberland died on 31 October 1765, at the age of forty-four.

435. "exoterics": Uninitiated persons; outsiders.

436. "flatulent tumor": Swelling produced by gas.

437. "it was resolved . . . open the ports of Japan": An act of Charles II permitted the export (not importation, as Smollett mistakenly or playfully has it) of wheat and wheat flour when its price was below a certain level. In the summer of 1766 the shortage of grain was so severe, and profiteers were so greatly increasing it by exports, that a royal proclamation of 26 September (when Parliament stood prorogued) put an embargo on such shipments. Throughout the year 1767 the *Crit-

ical Review (volume 22) printed reviews of many pamphlets discussing grain prices, the embargo, and the constitutional questions it raised; the *Annual Register* for 1767 discusses the matter at length (pp. 39–48).

438. "it was thought necessary . . . exercise of prerogative": When Parliament opened in the autumn of 1766, debate began immediately on proposed legislation that would indemnify those who had obeyed the embargo and would ratify the right of the crown to make the proclamation, which amounted to a royal abrogation of a Parliamentary act. See *PH*, 16:243–313.

439. "*salus populi*": *Salus populi suprema lex esto*; L. "Let the welfare of the people be the supreme law" (Cicero, *De legibus*, bk. 3, chap. 3, sect. 8). Walpole reports, *George III*, 2:264, that Pratt (now Lord Camden) cited this precept in the parliamentary debate. See Print 4151; and see *Briton*, no. 7 (12 July 1762): 40, where the same phrase occurs.

440. "Taycho . . . went to the assembly": A reference to Pitt's maiden speech in the Lords as earl of Chatham, 11 November 1766. See Walpole, *George III*, 2:263.

441. "Lley-nah . . . Curse-mother": Robert Henley, earl of Northington; the "surnames" allude to Henley's reputation for drunkenness and profanity. See key.

442. "this triumvirate . . . of the legislature": Both Henley and Pratt had distinguished themselves by their attacks on royal prerogative in the debate over general warrants in the Wilkes case; see Rudé, 29–30. Now Henley argued that the king's embargo proclamation was both legally and morally justifiable; Pratt reasoned that there had been "at most a forty days' tyranny." See Walpole, *George III*, 2:264.

443. "Mura-clami . . . his upstart rival": Mansfield maintained that an embargo act would be illegal and that there was no such thing as prerogative. Camden twitted him on his "new Whiggism"; he was daunted and retracted his remarks. See Walpole, *George III*, 2:264.

444. "got into the wrong-box": Worked himself into an untenable position.

445. "Taycho bestrid him like a Colossus": Smollett combines two Shakespearean echoes: "Why, man, he doth bestride the narrow world / Like a colossus" (*Julius Caesar* 1.2.135–36); and "Hal, if thou see me down in the battle, and bestride me, so; 'tis a point of friendship" (*1 Henry IV* 5.1.121–23). Pitt was sometimes depicted as a colossus; see Print 4162*, and see *Briton*, no. 8 (18 July 1762): 47, which refers to "the great Colossus P-tt."

446. "necessary to confine him to a dark chamber": By March 1767 Pitt had gone into what seemed to be a totally incapacitating and permanent depression; he literally remained "in a dark chamber" for more than two years. During this period the duke of Grafton, first lord of the treasury in the Chatham administration, was in effect first minister. See Williams, 2:238–47.

447. "this dilemma . . . expedient of changing hands": For an account of the complex negotiations alluded to in the passage that follows see Browning, 323–26, and Brooke, *George III*, 141–43.

448. "ill-toned": Out of tune; poorly harmonized.

449. "Twitz-er . . . their own shoulders": Here Smollett looks back to 1765, when the government was desperate for funds in the aftermath of the war; Grenville, as first lord of the treasury, proposed the notorious Stamp Tax, which the Commons passed unanimously on 5 February 1765. The colonies of course had no "constitution," but the question of Parliament's right to tax them was at once raised. See *Continuation*, 5:420–24; Walpole, *George III*, 2:49–53; *PH*, 16:34–40; and, for an extended and detailed historical treatment, P. D. G. Thomas, *British Politics and the Stamp Act Crisis: The First Phase of the American Revolution, 1763–1767* (Oxford: Clarendon Press, 1975). See also John L. Bullion, *A Great and Necessary Measure: George Grenville and the Genesis of the Stamp Act* (Columbia: University of Missouri Press, 1983).

450. "a mighty clamour": In 1765 British ships were seized by the colonists, stamps were burned, and the houses of revenue officers were pillaged. See Gipson, 101–11; and see *PH*, 16:111–36.

451. "Taycho . . . arbitrary and tyrannical measure": In January and February 1766 Pitt spoke against the Stamp Act and the Declaratory Act, though he did assert the technical right of Parliament to tax the colonies. For details of these speeches see Ian R. Christie, "William Pitt and American Taxation: A Problem of Parliamentary Reporting," *Studies in Burke and His Time* 17 (1976): 167–79.

452. "the favourite, who had patronized the Fatsisian tax": See Print 4118*; Bute received much of the blame for the Stamp Act.

453. "this imposition . . . abrogated": The Stamp Act was repealed on 4 March 1766. For details of the debate see Walpole, *George III*, 2:211–18, and *PH*, 16:177–206.

454. "the Orator himself . . . an unembarrassed countenance": Precisely what Smollett intends is difficult to determine. The evidence is clear concerning Pitt's contention that Parliament had no power over the colonies' internal taxation, but that it did have the power to impose external taxes such as port duties and tariffs for the regulation of commerce; see Christie, "William Pitt." An article entitled "The History of Party During the Present Reign," *London Magazine* 38 (April 1769): 203–4, indicates that there were those who blamed Pitt for his conduct with respect to taxation of the colonies: "Through caprice, [Pitt] ruined all . . . . the justice which was done to the colonies, Mr. P--- looked upon as a favour . . . the administration imagined that our fellow subjects beyond the Atlantic might . . . bear a new oppression . . . the colonies . . . appearing very much dissatisfied . . . the ministry accused them of the most scandalous ingratitude . . . and prepared by an armed force to gain that submission from them." See *PH*, 16:103–10. For explanation of the phrase "an unembarrassed countenance" see above, vol. 1, n. 433.

455. "after they had raised statues to him": The colonies gave Pitt the chief credit for the repeal of the Stamp Act; statues were raised to him in a number of cities, including New York, Charleston, South Carolina, and Dedham, Massachusetts. See Williams, 2:206–7.

456. "measures were taken . . . legislature of Japan": In August 1767 Parliament

passed the Townshend Act, introduced by Charles Townshend, chancellor of the exchequer, imposing port duties on glass, paper, paints, and tea. In addition, a board of commissioners of customs was established; and an act was passed suspending the New York legislature until it complied with the provisions of the Quartering Act for the billeting of troops. See Gipson, 173–76.

457. "Gotto-mio acceded to this system": In December 1765 Bedford spoke in favor of government enforcement of obedience by the colonies; shortly afterwards he signed a protest against the repeal of the Stamp Act.

458. "agreed among themselves . . . manufactures of Japan": In 1767 Massachusetts determined not to import English manufactured goods; other colonies followed suit, and many addresses to the king were prepared. See Gipson, 181–89.

459. "whips and scorpions": See 1 Kings 12:11, 14; and 2 Chronicles 10:11, 14. Rehoboam says: "My father [Solomon] hath chastised you with whips, but I will chastise you with scorpions."

460. "troops were assembled and fleets equipped": In the summer of 1768 two regiments and seven ships were sent to Boston to strengthen the forces there; see Gipson, 190.

461. "train": A series or sequence.

462. "withdraw himself . . . political helm": In fact Bute had engaged much earlier to resign as keeper of the privy purse and to abstain entirely from political affairs. He did so in September 1763, and retired to the country; see Sedgwick, 236. Smollett probably refers here to Bute's departure, in August 1768, to take the waters at Barèges in France; he did not reside in England, except very briefly, for some years.

463. "a new storm . . . perdition": Smollett's precise meaning here has not been established. John Wilkes returned from his exile in France on 6 February 1768; on 11 March Parliament was dissolved and warrants were issued for a general election. Wilkes was elected to Parliament for the borough of Middlesex by an overwhelming majority. In April he submitted to arrest, going into the King's Bench Prison; in June Chief Justice Mansfield reversed his sentence of outlawry on a technicality, but sentenced him to a fine and to imprisonment for twenty-two months. In the aftermath of Mansfield's decision, with Wilkes in prison, widespread rioting broke out. Newcastle feared that "we must be either governed by a mad, lawless mob, or the peace preserved only by a military force, both of which are unknown to our constitution" (Brooke, *George III*, 150). On 10 May the "massacre of St. George's Fields" had taken place. Anti-Scots sentiment reached new heights, and though it was focused on Bute, Scots in general (doubtless including Smollett) had good reason to fear for their personal safety; see Rudé, 40–46, 57. Bute's house was attacked, and when he departed for France in August he was in grave danger from a mob at Dover; see Brewer, "Misfortunes," 6, 8. So prevalent were the disorders that many feared the outbreak of a revolution. On 12 October 1768 Pitt resigned from the government

for reasons of ill health and refused to reconsider. It was at this time, in the autumn, that Smollett departed from England for "perpetual exile" (*Letters*, 136).

The tumults, however, did not subside. On 3 February 1769 Parliament deprived Wilkes of his membership, a measure of which the king had written in January that it was one "whereon almost my crown depends" (Brooke, *George III*, 150). On 16 February Wilkes was re-elected for Middlesex, declared incapable of sitting by Parliamentary resolution, re-elected yet again, and finally replaced by his defeated opponent, Colonel Henry Luttrell, on the technical grounds (again by Parliamentary resolution) that the latter was the "qualified" candidate with the most votes. The *Atom* was thus published in an atmosphere of constitutional crisis, continuing political chaos, and social unrest; but Smollett was now safe in Italy.

KEY

Many eighteenth-century copies of the *Atom* contain manuscript "keys," or identifications of characters, in the margins or endpapers. None of these is complete, and many entries are erroneous. The same is true, though to a lesser extent, of the printed keys that accompany various modern reprints, largely because until now the text has not been thoroughly studied. (For example, all keys identify the character "Toks" with John Horne Tooke, the radical political writer and philologist; but Horne did not assume the name Tooke until some years after Smollett's death.)

In contriving pseudo-Oriental names to disguise his characters and augment the narrative's "Japanese" element, Smollett relied chiefly upon two processes: ingenious distortions of real English names or of epithets by means of anagrams, phonetic approximations, or complex puns, sometimes multilingual; and modifications of names, most of them from the list of emperors he found in the section on Japan in the *Universal History*, volume nine. (He had reviewed this volume of the *Universal History* in the *Critical Review* for September 1759, and the entire work accompanied him to France in 1763.) The authentic Oriental names, however, reached him in forms often very unlike their modern equivalents. The pronunciation of Japanese has changed from the sixteenth century to the present day almost as radically as that of English between Shakespeare's time and ours; pronunciation varied greatly among dialects and social levels; and the missionaries and merchants from whose accounts the *Universal History*'s essay on Japan was derived, writing in Latin, Portuguese, or Italian, used arbitrary combinations of letters to designate unfamiliar sounds (which often they could hardly pronounce). More than three-fifths of Smollett's Oriental names, however, are derived from authentic Japanese names. These are given here with their modern equivalents and other relevant information, showing to what extent and with what ingenuity Smollett manipulated his source in the *Universal History*, where he also found remarkable parallels to his own views of European geography, politics, and personalities.

The list that follows includes in alphabetical order all persons, places, and (in a very few instances) topics referred to in the *Atom* by "Oriental" names. For the convenience of the reader, important variant spellings of the names are given in parentheses immediately after the entry heading. Each key entry provides the following: the real person, place, or topic meant by the name, with dates and major biographical, topographical, or other relevant information; a brief statement regarding the pertinence of the name to Smollett's satire (although details and more particular dates are furnished in the notes); identification of Smollett's source, or the process by which the name was produced; the actual reference of the original name; and its modern, usually Japanese, equivalent. The abbreviation *UH*, with numbers indicating pages, refers to the account of Japan in the *Universal History* presumably used by Smollett—pages 1–169 of the ninth volume of the "Modern Part" in the octavo edition of 1759.

The reader who may wish to consult other keys available in print is referred to the following:

William Davis, "A Key to Smollett's *History and Adventures of an Atom*," in *A Second Journey Round the Library of a Bibliomaniac* (London: W. Davis, 1825), 115–18.

Lewis M. Knapp, "The Keys to Smollett's *Atom*," *English Language Notes* 2 (December 1964): 100–102.

Takau Shimada, "Key to the Japanese Names in *The History and Adventures of an Atom*," *English Language Notes* 23 (June 1986): 24–31.

ABRA-MORIA. Major-General James Abercromby (1706–81). Disastrously defeated at Ticonderoga, 1758. "Aber" is converted to the pseudo-Arabic "Abra," familiar from Moorish characters in the heroic drama, and added to "Moria" (*UH*, 117), now *Mononobe no Moriya*, who tried to extirpate idols in the sixth century A.D. *Moria* is also Greek for "folly."

AB-REN-THI. John Abernethy (1680–1740), an Irish Presbyterian clergyman, author of numerous sermons and tracts arguing for religious toleration and against religious tests for office. His most noted work was the posthumously published *Discourses Concerning the . . . Perfections of God* (1742–43). Smollett distorts a phonetic spelling of Abernethy's name.

AMI, Lake of. Lake Biwa (so called because its shape is that of a *biwa*, or lute). The lake is located in the province of Ōmi; Smollett's source (*UH*, 84) mistakenly calls it "the lake Oomi."

BANYAN. A Quaker. The word, from Gujarati by way of Arabic and Portuguese, was used for any Hindu; but because of the Hindu abstinence from meat it had gathered the adjectival force of "one of austere religion." Smollett says in *Roderick Random*, chapter 25: "banyan [meatless] days [on shipboard] take their denomination from a sect of devotees in some parts of the East Indies, who never taste flesh."

BHA-KAKH. Admiral Sir George Pocock (1706–92). Renowned for naval victories at Madras and Havana; made knight of the Bath, 1761. Smollett phonetically approximates "Pocock."

BIHN-GOH (BYN-GOH). Admiral the Hon. John Byng (1704–57); son of a famous admiral, the earl of Torrington. Byng, though undistinguished, became commander-in-chief in the Mediterranean in 1747. After an inconclusive engagement with a French fleet in May 1756 he was blamed for the loss of Minorca. The public clamor against him resulted in his execution. "Byng" is converted into "Bin-go," a possible combination of Japanese syllables.

BONZA (BONZE). An Anglican clergyman, though Smollett virtually always uses the term to mean "bishop." Probably derived through the Portuguese, the term was common in Smollett's time for a Buddhist priest; it probably originates in the Japanese *bonzō* (*bōzu*), a religious or cleric (*UH*, 63).

BRON-XI-TIC. Ferdinand, duke of Brunswick (1721–92), commander of the allied German and English armies from 1757 to 1763. His most notable victories were at Krefeld and Minden. The name is a distortion of "Brunswick."

BRUT-AN-TIFFI. Frederick the Great (1712–86); succeeded to the throne of Prussia in 1740. "Brut" may suggest "brute," "Brut-an" "Prussian," and "tiffi" "tiff"; thus, "the brutal, quarrelsome Prussian." But Smollett may also be thinking of a character in his translation of *Gil Blas*, the German nobleman Brutandorff; or of the fact that in official (Latin) documents "Prussia" was rendered as "Borussia."

BUPO. George I (1660–1727). Elector of Hanover from 1698, George ascended the throne of Great Britain in 1714. Bupo is mentioned (*UH*, 112) as having "landed in *Japan*, from the *Indies* . . . on a white horse." The white horse figuring in the arms of Hanover was much used in political prints to represent the Hanoverian interests; Smollett thus adopted a familiar symbol. "Bupo" is apparently a corruption of *buppō*, a contraction of the Japanese *butsu*, the Buddhist law.

CAMBADOXI. The use of the syllable "Cam" suggests that this word may mean Cambridge University, of which the duke of Newcastle was chancellor. But Smollett speaks of Newcastle dancing at the "festival of Cambadoxi," and may have intended no more than a picturesque Oriental detail. Cambadoxi (*UH*, 16–17) was a "bonza" who invented writing and is venerated at an annual festival; the modern equivalent is *Kōbo Daishi*, credited with the invention of *kana*, or phonetic characters. A third possibility for the meaning of the term is the Cambridge ceremony for conferring degrees, at which Newcastle would have presided as chancellor, or the duke's official visitations in that capacity.

CAMBODIA. Sardinia (see SAB-OI).

CHAM. The Holy Roman or German emperor (see KHAN). The word was in common use for the Mongol and Manchu emperors of China and for the ruler of "Tartary."

CHINA. France.

COREA. (Korea.) Spain.

CUBOY (CUBO). The first minister: successively (during the period of the *Atom*'s coverage) Newcastle, Pitt, Bute, George Grenville, and the Marquess of Rockingham. There being no "prime minister" in the modern sense, Smollett refers to the cabinet member in effective control of the administration at any time. His source (*UH*, 27–29) tells how the cuboys, since A.D. 1188, have usurped the emperor's power, for Smollett an obvious parallel with the relatively limited powers of the Hanoverian monarchs. *Kubō*, the modern equivalent, means "court," hence "master of the palace"; the usual term is *shōgun* or military governor. The *shōguns* were the effective rulers of Japan from 1188 until the nineteenth-century Meiji restoration.

DAIRO. George II and George III (see GOT-HAMA-BABA, GIO-GIO). The *dairo* (*UH*, 19, 27–29) was both the ecclesiastical and the temporal ruler of Japan (as the British sovereign was and is also head of the Church), but since ancient times he had been the puppet of his chief minister. The modern *dairi* means the imperial palace; the writers on whose work the *UH* was based had been given a reverential circumlocution for "emperor" (see *UH*, 109, where this fact is understood).

DAY, DAYGO. A nobleman; a peer (*UH*, 109, 123); but Smollett may have confused the title with "Day-Go," the sixtieth emperor. *Dai* is "great [person]"; *daimyō*, "magnate."

FAKKUBASI. "Or the temple of the white horse." Hanover, the House of Hanover, or more properly the interests of Hanover against those of Britain; Smollett presents the support of Hanover as amounting to a religion. The running white horse, actually from the arms of Brunswick-Lüneburg, was incorporated into the British royal arms on the accession of George I and remained until Hanover was separated from Great Britain in 1837, on Victoria's accession. It was worn on the caps of Hanover grenadiers and was often used in political prints as a derogatory symbol of Hanover. *UH*, 113 mentions the temple (see BUPO); the modern equivalent is *hakuba-ji*. Alternatively, *fakkubasi* would have been the Japanese equivalent of the Chinese *Pai-ma-ssu*, the miraculous white horse on which the Buddhist scriptures were said to have been brought to Loyang in China during the first century A.D. by the Indian sage Dharmaraksa. The *dharma* of this sage's name refers to the Buddhist law of the created universe, or in Japanese *buppō* (see BUPO); he was also known as Gobharana, which may be the source of the name "Kobot" (see KOBOT).

FAN-SEY. Probably no reference to an actual person is intended. The name is that of the nineteenth emperor of Japan (*UH*, 114; in modern Japanese, *Hanshō*); but there is doubtless also a pun on "fancy," in the sense of a whimsical idea.

FAN-YAH. Havana. Smollett approximates the sound of the Cuban city's name.

FAS-KHAN. Admiral the Hon. Edward Boscawen (1711–61). Boscawen served continuously in the navy from 1726, was a member of Parliament, and had several victorious engagements to his credit. The sound of his name is approximated, with the inclusion of the Oriental title "Khan."

FATSISSIO (FASTSISSIO, FATSISIO). North America, represented as an island. *UH*, 34 describes it as an island used for the banishment of political prisoners of high rank (Smollett regarded the administration's early neglect of the North American colonies as scandalous). The actual Japanese island, now *Hachijō*, is south of Tokyo.

FATZMAN. The duke of Cumberland (see QUAMBA-CUN-DONO), who became grotesquely fat in later life and was frequently caricatured. As commander-in-chief of the army he could be connected with "*Fatsman*, the *Mars* of the *Japanese*" (*UH*, 125), in modern Japanese *Hachiman*, the god of war.

FI-DE-TA-DA. General William Blakeney (1672–1761). An ensign in Flanders in 1702, in 1747 lieutenant-general and lieutenant-governor of Minorca. Surrendering to the French in 1756 after a siege of seventy days, he became a popular hero and was made knight of the Bath and created

Baron Blakeney. Fide-tada, the thirty-third shōgun (*UH*, 148), besieged
and executed the remnants of the persecuted Japanese Christians in 1638,
thus extirpating Christianity in Japan; the siege lasted for three months.
The modern equivalent is *Hidetada*.

FIKA-KAKA (FIKA-KA, FIKA-KAHA, FIKA-KIKA). Thomas Pelham-Holles
(1693–1768), first duke of Newcastle-upon-Tyne of the third creation, and
first duke of Newcastle-under-Lyme. Member of the privy council from
1717; of the cabinet, in one office or another, 1724–56, 1757–62, 1765–66;
secretary of state (southern department), 1724–54; first lord of the treasury,
1754–56, 1757–62. Except during Pitt's periods in power, Newcastle was
effectively the first minister, 1754–62. Smollett may have used the name
Go-Fikakusa (*UH*, 129), eighty-eighth emperor (now *Go-Fukakusa*); but he
certainly intended a pun on two Italian words, *fica* and *caca*, suggesting
"cunt-shit." Newcastle is represented throughout as the most contemptible
figure in the *Atom*.

FIRANDO. A small island near Nagasaki, to which the members of the Dutch
"factory," the only foreign trading mission allowed in Japan in Smollett's
day, were confined at all times. In current Japanese, *Hirado*.

FLA-SAO. Plassey, where Robert Clive (see KA-LIFF) won a decisive victory
in the Indian campaign. Smollett approximates the sound of "Plassey."

FO. Sometimes Catholicism, sometimes "an idol." *UH*, 13 (and elsewhere) is
equally ambiguous, referring to "the worship of *Fo*." "Fo" is in fact the
Chinese pronunciation of the character read in Japanese as *Butsu*, "Buddha,
Buddhism."

FOGGIEN. The eighteenth century, in about "the middle of" which the action
of the *Atom* takes place. In the reign of Gossii-Rakava (now *Go-shirakawa*)
occurred "a bloody and destructive war . . . called *Foggieno Midarri*, or *The
desolation of the Foggien æra*" (*UH*, 126). The word is now *Hōgen*.

FOKSI-ROKU (FOKH-SI-ROKHU, FOKSI-ROKHU). Henry Fox, first Baron
Holland (1705–74). A member of the privy council from 1747, at various
times a cabinet member as secretary for war, secretary of state, leader of
the Commons, and paymaster-general. Fox constantly shifted his political
alliances and was regarded as the most unscrupulous and corrupt politician
in Britain, though of formidable power. The name is formed from "Fox,
foxy" and Roku-Dsio (now *Rokujō*), the seventy-ninth emperor (*UH*, 126).

FOU-TAO. Gibraltar. Source unidentified; the Chinese *fo-tao*, however, means "the Way of Buddha."

FRENOXENA. Cambridge University, of which Newcastle was chancellor. The name refers to a great academy in Japan about ten miles from the capital (*UH*, 38, n. U). In modern Japanese, *Hiei-no-yama*, a large monastery northeast of Kyoto.

FUMMA. Portugal. Source unknown; perhaps improvised by Smollett, though he possibly had encountered the Chinese phonemes *fu ma* (which may have various meanings, since Chinese is rich in homonyms).

GIO-GIO. King George III (1738–1820), who came to the throne in 1760. The name is a faintly contemptuous variation on "Geo."

GOT-HAMA-BABA. George II (1683–1760) succeeded to the throne in 1727. The name is derived from the eighty-second emperor Go-ta-ba (in modern Japanese *Go-Toba*), during whose reign the first cuboy (see CUBOY) to usurp the imperial power gained ascendancy (*UH*, 127–28). Smollett may also have intended overtones of "Gautama Buddha" and of "Gotham" (England); one might conjecture "God-damned baby."

GOTTO-MIO. John Russell, fourth duke of Bedford (1710–71). Immensely rich and very unpopular, Bedford nevertheless occupied at one time or another nearly all cabinet offices and was one of the signers of the Peace of Paris, ending the Seven Years' War. Go-Kwo-Mio (now *Gō-Komyō* or *Gōtomyō*), "commonly styled Gotto-mio" (*UH*, 136), was the 111th emperor. One is tempted to see a pun by way of the Italian on "my God!"

HEL-Y-OTTE. Captain (later Admiral) John Elliot (d. 1808), who destroyed the remnants of a French invasion squadron in the Irish Sea in 1760. The name is a phonetic distortion of "Elliott."

HE-RHUMN. Admiral Sir John Moore (1718–79), who took the island of Guadeloupe in 1759. The name is a distortion of "Moore," reversed.

HOB-NOB. Major-General Peregrine Hopson (d. 1759). After a long and undistinguished career he was transferred from the governorship of Nova Scotia to a Caribbean invasion force, dying at Guadeloupe of fever. The name is a contemptuous derivation from "Hop."

HYLIB-BIB. Lieutenant-General Edward Bligh (1685–1775). In 1758 his incompetence resulted in a massacre of English troops in Brittany. The name is an expanded anagram of "Bligh."

IAN-ON-I (YAN-ONI, YAN-ON-I). Major-General Sir William Johnson (1715–74). A superintendent of Indian affairs for the colonies, Johnson lived with the Indians and developed an expertise at wilderness fighting that gained a series of important victories. The name is a variation on "John."

JACKO. The archbishop of Canterbury; Smollett does not intend a specific person. The mid-eighteenth-century incumbents were John Potter, Thomas Herring, Matthew Hutton, and Thomas Secker (all protegés of Newcastle). Smollett's source for the name is *UH*, 38: "*Xacco*, or *Jacko*, or head pontiff of all the bonzas." The word is probably a distortion of *Shaka*, the name of Gautama Buddha.

JAN-KI-DTZIN. John Wilkes (1727–97), radical politician. Elected M.P. for Aylesbury in 1757, his sensational career in the 1760s made him the most famous or notorious man in England; many feared (or hoped) that he would lead a revolution. In the *Briton*, no. 14 (29 August 1762) Smollett had lampooned Wilkes in a pseudo-Arabian fable as "Jahia Ginn," "Jahia" being Yahya, an enemy of the historical Harun al-Rashid, and "Ginn" referring to the profitable liquor business operated by Wilkes's father. "Dtzin" is evidently a development of "Ginn," and "Jan-ki" is "Johnny."

JAPAN. The British Isles. Smollett was fascinated by the remark in *UH*, 2 that "Were *South* and *North Britain* divided by an arm of the sea, *Japan* might be most aptly compared to *England, Scotland*, and *Ireland*." He quoted the remark in his review of *UH* in the *Critical Review* and again in *Present State* and the *Atom*, and it is most probably the germ of his idea to give the *Atom* a Japanese setting.

JEDDO. Variously Hanover, Germany, and the European continent, but generally the last. *UH*, 78 refers to "Jeddo, Jedo, or Yeddo, the other metropolis of Japan [besides the capital]"; elsewhere it is "the land of Jesso" (p. 48), or "the large continent of Jedzo . . . on the north, the southern parts of which are subject to the emperor" (p. 71). "Yesso," which Smollett always uses to mean Hanover (see YESSO), is given as an alternate spelling for "Jedso" (p. 150). The modern spelling for the city is *Edo* or *Yedo*; it is the older designation for Tokyo.

JODO, JODOGAVA. No specific reference to European rivers is intended. *UH* refers to the "*Jedogawa* . . . about as broad as our *Thames* at *London* bridge" (p. 84) and to the "*Askagava* [which] affords their poets and orators elegant allusions" (p. 6). The two rivers are the same, the suffix *-gawa* meaning "river," in this case the Yodo river near Osaka. See Martz, 102, n. 47, for a discussion of the probable geographical confusion into which Smollett was led here by consulting maps of Japan.

KA-FRIT-O. Cape Breton Island, Nova Scotia: "Ca[pe]-Bret-o[n]." The island was taken by New England colonists in 1745, ceded to France in 1748, and captured by English troops in 1758.

KA-LIFF. Robert, Lord Clive (1725–74), hero of the British campaigns in India. He distinguished himself at Pondichéry (1748) and in the defense of Arcot (1751), and his decisive victory at Plassey (see FLA-SAO) established the English as rulers of Bengal, of which he became governor for the East India Company. Smollett approximates the sound of "Clive."

KAMSCHATKA. India.

KEP-MARL. George Keppel, third earl of Albemarle (1724–72). General of the forces sent against Havana under Admiral Pocock, he captured the city in August 1762 and was made knight of the Bath in 1764. Smollett joins the first syllable of "Keppel" with the last of "Albemarle."

KHA-FELL. Admiral Augustus Viscount Keppel (1725–86), brother of George Keppel, earl of Albemarle (see KEP-MARL). An expedition under Admiral Keppel's command captured the fort at Goree in 1758, giving the English control of Senegal. The sound of "Keppel" is approximated.

KHAN. Francis Stephen of Lorraine, grand duke of Tuscany (1708–65); later Francis I, Holy Roman or German emperor. Consort of the archduchess Maria Theresa of Austria (see OSTROG), he was elected emperor in 1745. See CHAM.

KHO-RHÉ. Goree (now Dakar). A fortified island commanding the harbor of Dakar, Senegal, an important center of the slave and gum trade. See KHA-FELL.

KHUTT-WHANG. General Sir Eyre Coote (1726–83). After a series of victories in India (Plassey, Arcot, Wandewash), Pondichéry surrendered to him in January 1761; in April he received the total surrender of the French in

India. To "Coote" is added the Chinese *whang*. *UH*, 112 tells of the Chinese emperor "*Shi-whang-ti*"; he is actually *Ch'in-shih huang-ti*, the last two syllables forming the epithet usually translated "Son of Heaven," applied to all emperors.

KIO. Possibly a vague reference to the doctrine that Continental connections were for England's benefit. *UH*, 112: Bupo (see BUPO), "from a foreign country, brought with him . . . a book called Kio, containing the mysteries of his religion." The word (now *kyō*) means a sutra, or book of Buddhist scripture.

KOAN. Major-General Edward Braddock (1695–1755). Relatively inexperienced in battle, he was supreme commander in America, 1754; his crushing defeat near Fort Duquesne in July 1755 (he was fatally wounded) was the first in a series of major disasters for British forces that began the Seven Years' War. Koan was the sixth Japanese emperor; under his reign "there happened a great eclipse of the sun" (*UH*, 111).

KOBOT. Another name for Bupo (see BUPO). Smollett's source (he quotes verbatim from *UH*, 112) is evidently confused; the syllable "bot" seems to be related to *butsu*, or Buddhist law. See also FAKKUBASI.

KOW-KIN. Richard Rigby (1722–88), secretary and political agent to the duke of Bedford (see GOTTO-MIO). Rigby represented a pocket borough in Parliament for thirty years, became paymaster-general, and was widely detested as one of the most cynical, powerful, and corrupt politicians of the age. The name is that of the eighth Japanese emperor (*UH*, 111–12); the modern equivalent is *Kōgen*.

KUGAVA. No specific reference to a European river intended. Martz, 102, n. 47, conjectures that Smollett took the name from a map which shows the river "Dsusu Kugava" (now *Suzuka-gawa*) near Osaka.

KUNT-THAN. Leopold Joseph, Count von Daun (1705–66), Austrian field marshal. Able and experienced, he fought at Kolin (1757), Hochkirch (1758), and Maxen (1759); he was wounded in the defense of Torgau (1760), after which he performed staff duties. The name approximates "Count Daun."

KURDS. Prussians. Smollett knew the Kurds as fierce, barbarous nomadic warriors.

LE-YAW-TER. James O'Hara, second Baron Tyrawley (1690–1773). Field marshal and ambassador to Portugal, 1728–41. In 1762 he was again sent to Portugal as ambassador plenipotentiary and head of a military mission; he returned in 1763. The name is an anagram of "Tyrawley."

LLEY-NAH. Robert Henley, first earl of Northington (1708–72). A protegé of Pitt, he was attorney general in 1756, lord chancellor in 1761, president of the council in 1766. A heavy drinker who used profanity on the bench, he was known as "Surly Bob." The name is an anagram of "Henley."

LLHA-DAHN. Ernst Gideon Laudon or Loudon, Freiherr von Laudohn (1717–90), Austrian field marshal. He led Imperial troops in most of the major engagements with Frederick the Great in the Seven Years' War. The name approximates the sound of "Laudohn."

LLI-NAM. Manila, captured by an English fleet in October 1762 and then sacked; Spain agreed to a ransom (never paid) of four million dollars for its return. The name is an obvious anagram.

LLUR-CHIR. The Rev. Charles Churchill (1731–64). Ordained in 1756, he resigned as curate of Saint John's, Westminster, in January 1763 and thereafter performed no clerical functions. Churchill became the most celebrated satirical poet of his day; he was a close friend of John Wilkes, with whom he collaborated in anti-administration propaganda. *The Apology* (1761) and *The Prophecy of Famine* (1763), both by Churchill, contain violent attacks on Smollett. The name is an anagram.

LOB-KOB. Richard Grenville-Temple, Earl Temple (1711–79). Member of the Commons before coming to his title in 1752. Temple's political fortunes followed those of Pitt after his sister Hester married Pitt in 1754. He was first lord of the admiralty, 1756; lord privy seal, 1757; knight of the Garter, 1760. Temple resigned from the cabinet with Pitt in 1761 and was the principal patron and director of attacks on the Bute administration in newspapers and pamphlets. He later quarreled with Pitt and left politics. "Lob-Kob" seems to have no source, but suggests uncouthness; Temple's appearance and manner earned him the nickname of "Squire Gawkee."

MANTCHOUX. Or "Mantchoux Tartars." Smollett uses the term with reference to Russia or the Russians. The modern form is *Manchu.*

MEACO. London. "Meaco . . . the antient metropolis of the whole empire" (*UH*, 74). The modern *Miyako* means "capital city" and was the designation of Kyoto, the seat of government in eighteenth-century Japan.

MECKADDO. No contemporary reference intended. *UH*, 110: "The *Mikaddos*, or original Emperors of Japan." Mikado means "emperor."

MORIA-TANTI. General Sir John Mordaunt (1697–1780). No more than competent as a soldier, he commanded the troops in an amphibious expedition against the French coast in 1757. In October, after a week of inconclusive councils of war, he returned to England without having attacked. A court-martial found him not guilty of disobeying the king's orders. Smollett approximates "Mordaunt" by combining "Moria" or "folly" (see ABRA-MORIA) with (perhaps) a pun on the French *tante*, aunt or old woman.

MO-TAO. Minorca. The island, ceded to Britain by the Treaty of Utrecht in 1713, was conquered by the French in 1756 (see BIHN-GOH, FI-DE-TA-DA). Its loss, regarded as a national disaster, hastened the fall of the Newcastle administration and the rise of Pitt. The source of the name has not been traced; the syllables are apparently Chinese, and may mean "the Way of Mo-tzu," an ethical system based on the teachings of this sage.

MURA-CLAMI. William Murray, first earl of Mansfield (1705–93). A brilliant lawyer and politician, friend of Pope and Bolingbroke, he became lord chief justice and a member of the cabinet in 1756. He was created Baron Mansfield in 1756, Earl Mansfield in 1776. A lifelong rival of Pitt, whom he often opposed in Parliament, he was renowned for elegance and eloquence in speaking but was perpetually accused of having secret Jacobite sympathies. He presided in 1759 at Smollett's trial for libeling Admiral Knowles. The name, playing on "Murray" and perhaps on "clammy" (Smollett characterizes Mansfield as cold), derives from the sixty-second emperor, Murakami (*UH*, 124).

MYN-THAN. The battle of Minden, 1 August 1759, in which Ferdinand of Brunswick (see BRON-XI-TIC) led Prussian and English troops to a decisive victory against the French. The sound of "Minden" is approximated.

NEM-BUDS-JU. The Jews. According to *UH*, 76, the *Dainembudsiu* (probably *nembutsu-shū*, a sect devoted to Amida Buddha), with but 289 members, represent the smallest of the "fourteen sects of religion" in Japan. Smollett may equate "ju" (-*siu*, -*shū*) with "Jew."

NIN-KOM-POO-PO (NIN-KOM-POO-POO). George, Baron Anson (1697–1762). After his capture of a Spanish treasure ship while circumnavigating the globe, 1740–44, he became a national hero. A leading Whig politician, Anson was first lord of the admiralty from 1751 to 1762 (except for one year); he considerably reorganized the administration of the navy and directed operations throughout the Seven Years' War. He was held to be principally responsible for the loss of Minorca in 1756. The cause of Smollett's specific animosity (as indicated by the name) is unknown; Anson may have refused a favor Smollett thought was his due.

NIPHON. Great Britain (as distinct from the British Isles), "from the largest island belonging to [Japan]" (*UH*, 1). The modern word is *Nippon*, "the land of the rising sun."

NOB-O-DI. William Wildman Barrington, second Viscount Barrington (1717–93). Secretary of war, 1755–61 and later. As the name indicates, Smollett evidently regarded Barrington as a nonentity.

OR-NBOS. Admiral Henry Osborne (1698?–1771). He blockaded and destroyed a French squadron in the Caribbean in March 1758. The name is an anagram.

OSACA. The city of Osaka. No specific topical reference intended.

OSTROG. Austria. The "House of Ostrog" is the Hapsburg dynasty; the "Tartar princess of the house of Ostrog" or the "Amazon of Ostrog" is Maria Theresa, daughter of the Emperor Charles VI. Maria Theresa (1717–80) became queen of Hungary and Bohemia and archduchess of Austria on her father's death in 1740; in 1745 she ceded Silesia to Frederick the Great in return for his recognition of her consort Francis I (see CHAM, KHAN) as Holy Roman Emperor. The Russian *ostrog*, a stockade or fortified town, is used for its resemblance in sound to "Austria."

PEKIN. Paris, since China represents France.

PHAL-KHAN. Edward Hawke, Lord Hawke, admiral of the fleet (1705–81). After a long and successful naval career, Hawke effectively destroyed French naval power at the battle of Quiberon Bay in November 1759, prevented an invasion of England, and virtually terminated the war at sea. The name approximates the sound of "falcon," a pun on "Hawke."

PHYL-KHOLL. Admiral Alexander Colville, seventh Baron Colville of Culross (1717–70). A French squadron had taken Saint John's, Newfoundland, in June 1762; in September Colville drove out the French fleet and the town surrendered. The name approximates the sound but reverses the syllables of "Colville."

POL-HASSAN-AKOUSTI. Frederick Augustus III, king of Poland and elector of Saxony (1696–1763). Frederick the Great took his cities of Dresden and Leipzig in September 1756, to Smollett's great indignation. The name combines "Pol" from "Poland," the Arabic *Hassan* (handsome, generous, noble), and a distortion of "Augustus"; thus, "Augustus the noble of Poland."

PRAFF-PATT-PHOGG (PRAFF-FOG). Charles Pratt, first Earl Camden (1714–94). Chief justice of the Court of Common Pleas, 1761; member of the privy council, 1762; lord chancellor, 1766. After John Wilkes had been arrested on a general warrant, Pratt granted him *habeas corpus* and freed him from the Tower, 6 May 1763. Laying down the principle that general warrants were unconstitutional, Pratt became a popular idol. The name suggests "Pratt," "fog," and perhaps "fart."

QUA-CHU. The island of Guadeloupe, taken by a British fleet in February 1759. The name seems to be improvised, a distant approximation of the sound of "Guadeloupe."

QUAMBA-CUN-DONO. William Augustus, duke of Cumberland (1721–65), second surviving son of George II. A military man, Cumberland fought gallantly and was wounded at Dettingen (1743) and distinguished himself at Fontenoy (1745); he crushed the Young Pretender's troops at Culloden (1746). Commander-in-chief and a member of the Council of Regency during the king's frequent absences in Hanover, he commanded the Army of Observation in Germany in 1757. In the political crisis of 1765 he was instrumental in forming an administration. *UH*, 144 mentions "Quamba-cundono" as a nephew of "Fide-josi" (Hideyoshi, who in the late sixteenth century became supreme ruler of Japan). The former was "disgraced, and . . . ordered to rip up his own bowels"; Smollett may have connected this episode with Cumberland's disgrace in 1757. The modern equivalent of "Quamba-cun-dono" is not a name but a title, *Kampaku-dono*, meaning "regent," the suffix *-dono* merely signifying "lord." "Quambacundono" sounds not unlike "Cumberland." See FATZMAN.

QUANBUKU (QUAMBUCU). Smollett uses this title to mean "duke." *UH*, 134 says that "the dignity . . . was then the next to that of the *Dayro*" (see DAIRO). The modern Japanese word is *Kanpaku, kampaku*, "regent."

QUIB-QUAB. Quebec, taken by the British in September 1759; its surrender marked the effective end of the land war in North America. Smollett repeats the distorted first syllable.

QUO. A nobleman (*UH*, 109); the modern word is *kō*.

RASKALANDER. Peter the Great of Russia. Smollett's intention is unclear, but he evidently wishes the reader to think of "Alexander the Great" and "rascal." Smollett, like Defoe, and like his contemporaries Richardson (in *Clarissa*) and Fielding (in *Jonathan Wild*), had come to regard military conquerors, of whom Alexander was the classic example, as enemies of the human race.

RHA-RIN-TUMM. General John Barrington (1729–1800). Brother of the second Viscount Barrington (see NOB-O-DI), he served with great distinction throughout the Seven Years' War, and (a colonel at the time) captured the islands of Guadeloupe and Marie-Galante in 1759. Smollett approximates "Barrington."

RHUM-KIKH. William Beckford (1709–70). An immensely rich owner of plantations in Jamaica, dealer in sugar and rum, and father of the novelist, he became an M.P. in 1753 and lord mayor of London in 1762. In effect Beckford represented the powerful mercantile interests of the City; a turbulent politician in perpetual enmity with the crown, he was Pitt's firmest supporter, and Pitt owed him much of his power. Smollett says (*Continuation*, 5:115): "B--k---d, lord mayor of London, a native of Jamaica, proud, violent, and obstinate, who, by means of an ample fortune and extensive commerce, had acquired considerable influence in the city, without any personal address, or any superiority of understanding." "Rhum-kikh" suggests "rum keg"; Beckford was frequently satirized as "Alderman Rumford" and "Rumbo." Smollett, in *Briton*, no. 15 (4 September 1762): 89, speaks of "a wretch like Rumford" and calls him a "negro-driver."

SAB-OI. Charles Emmanuel III of Savoy, king of Sardinia (1730–73). His minister to the Court of Saint James, Count de Viry, was a very important secret go-between among Pitt, Newcastle, Bute, and the French government from the mid-1750s; several abortive attempts at peace discussions and the preliminaries of the Peace of Paris resulted in the king's being the formal mediator between France and Great Britain in 1762. The name is a variation on "Savoy."

SA-ROUF. Fort Fouras, at the mouth of the Charente in the province of Saintonge, now Charente-Maritime. One of the targets of the amphibious operation against Rochefort in September 1757, the fort was erroneously believed by Admiral Knowles (see SEL-UON) to be invulnerable to attack; his failure to reduce it contributed to the abandonment of the expedition. The name is an anagram of "Fouras."

SEL-UON. Admiral Sir Charles Knowles (1704?–77). He served at Porto Bello (1739) and Carthagena (1741); an engagement with the Spanish fleet in 1749 led to his being court-martialed. Knowles was second in command in the expedition against Rochefort (see SA-ROUF); his pamphlet defending his conduct there was severely reviewed in the *Critical Review* in May 1758, the result being his successful libel suit against Smollett. The name is an anagram of "Noules."

SEREDNEE TARTARS. The Swedes, Sweden. The name apparently derives from the Russian *srednyi*, "middle."

SEY-SEO-GUN. First lord of the admiralty, specifically Lord Anson (see NIN-KOM-POO-PO), 1751–56 and 1757–62. *UH*, 127n., says that "*Sei-seogun* . . . meant the generalissimo of the emperor's forces," the modern *shōgun*.

SEY-SEO-GUN-SIALTY. The admiralty (see SEY-SEO-GUN).

SHIT-TILK-UMS-HEIT; SHE-IT-KUMS-HI-TIL (SHI-TILK-UMS-HEIT, SHI-TILK-UMS-HITITES; SHE-IT-KUM-SHEIT-EL, SHE-IT-KUMS-HI-TILITES). Tories and Whigs. Smollett seems to have invented the names with the idea of making them as grotesque as possible; but it should be noted that both play upon the word *shit* and that they are very close to being anagrams of each other, suggesting Smollett's view of the nature of the two parties. Smollett probably has in mind Swift's "*Tramecksan* and *Slamecksan*," the Lilliputian political parties in *Gulliver's Travels*; in *Briton*, no. 35 (22 January 1763): 206–7 he remarks that the names "Whig" and "Tory" are meaningless, the parties having constantly switched tenets; they are "terms invented by knaves, and adopted by fools." For Smollett the Tories were more "fools" than "knaves."

SHI-WANG-TI. No reference intended. A Chinese emperor, mentioned in *UH*, 112 (see under KHUTT-WHANG). Smollett, observing in the *Atom* that Shi-Wang-Ti was "possessed of the universal medicine," confuses him with the legendary Chinese "Yellow Emperor."

SOO-SAN-SIN-O. John Carteret, Earl Granville (1690–1763). Lord president of the council, or presiding officer of the cabinet, from 1751 until his death. He had been secretary of state for the northern department (including Germany) in 1742–44, and was a great favorite of George II, partly because of his fluent German; ousted in a political coup, he remained the king's confidential adviser until the latter's death in 1760. Learned and of elegant manners, he had a reputation for frivolity and drunkenness. The name is taken directly from the alternative name of the sixth *shōgun* (*UH*, 140); no word-play seems to be involved.

STI-PHI-RUM-POO. Philip Yorke, first earl of Hardwicke (1690–1764). Named solicitor-general as early as 1720, he joined the privy council in 1723 and became lord chancellor in 1737. Though he resigned in 1756 with the fall of Newcastle's administration, Newcastle constantly sought his advice on even the smallest matters until Hardwicke's death; he thus had a very large share in the government's decisions. He presided over the trials of the Jacobite rebel lords in 1746 and had a reputation for cruelty and avarice; he was frequently shown as a vulture in satirical prints. There appears to be no source for the name, unless we wish to find in it the words *stiff*, *rump*, and *poo*.

SYKO. Queen Anne (1665–1714); acceded 1702. The name is chosen because Syko (Suiko) was an empress in her own right (*UH*, 118).

TARTARY. The German empire, by geographical analogy.

TAYCHO. William Pitt, later first earl of Chatham (1708–78). Generally regarded as the savior of his country and widely considered the greatest orator of the age, Pitt had a reputation comparable to that of Winston Churchill in the twentieth century, but was unquestionably an opportunistic politician. Smollett's warm admiration for him began to cool about 1760. "Taycho" (*Taikō*), or "sovereign lord" (*UH*, 144), was a title assumed on retirement by "Fide-Josi" (Hideyoshi), who was "the first that deserved the title of secular emperor . . . sprung from the lowest rank . . . vice-gerent of the empire" (*UH*, 141–44). "Neither the antient dairo's nor modern emperors, except this taycho, were known ever to aim at making any conquests abroad" (*UH*, 30n.); he eliminated opposition by sending turbulent princes to fight abroad, "exhausting their strength and treasure against the warlike *Tartars*" (*UH*, 143).

TENSIO-DAI-SIN. According to *UH*, 108, "the first founder of the Japanese monarchy." Smollett quotes directly from this source; no specific contemporary reference is intended. *Tenshō-daijin* or *Tenshōkō-daijin* is the goddess *Amiterasu-no-kami*, from whom the imperial line derived.

THIN-QUO. Martinique. The island was captured by a British force in 1762. The name is a distortion of "-tinico," from "Martinico," as the island was also designated.

THUM-KUMM-QUA. Thomas Cumming (d. 1774), the "fighting Quaker." As a merchant Cumming had established friendly relations with an African king who promised an English monopoly on trade if the French could be expelled from his dominions; Cumming persuaded the government to sponsor an expedition under his direction. The French were forced to capitulate, and in April 1758 the British were in possession of Senegal. Smollett took much interest in Cumming, discussing him in the *British Magazine* 1 (April 1760): 179–81, in the *Continuation*, 2:271–78, and in *CR* 6 (September 1758): 252. The name adds an "Oriental" syllable to "Thom. Cumm."

TOHN-SYN. General George Townshend, fourth Viscount and first Marquess Townshend (1724–1807). On the death of General James Wolfe (see YA-LOFF) he took command of the troops besieging Quebec and received the city's surrender in September 1759. The name approximates "Townshend."

TOKS. The Rev. Dr. James Scott (1733–1814). In 1765, sponsored by the earl of Sandwich (see ZAN-TI-FIC), Scott began a violent and extended attack on Bute (see YAK-STROT) in the *Public Advertiser*, under the signature "Anti-Sejanus." At first he eulogized Pitt, but attacked him vehemently after he received a title; in 1769, under the signature "Old Slyboots," Scott resumed his polemics. The name is a reversal of "Scott."

TRA-REP. General Sir William Draper (1721–87), who captured Manila from Spain in October 1762. The name distorts "Draper."

TUM-MING-QUA. *UH*, 8:7 remarks: "[the Chinese] added likewise some pompous title to the *qua* [*kuo* in modern romanization], which signifies a kingdom; such as, *Tum-ming-qua*, the kingdom of brightness, or perfection."

TWITZ-ER. George Grenville (1712–80), member of a powerful political family, brother of Lord Temple (see LOB-KOB) and brother-in-law of Pitt, influential member of the Commons. In 1762–63 he became in rapid succession secretary of state (northern department), first lord of the admiralty, chancellor of the exchequer, and first lord of the treasury, remaining first minister until mid-1765. His financial measures laid the foundation of the American Revolution; George III disliked him intensely; Pitt was instrumental in securing the repeal of his Stamp Act. There seems to be no source for the name. It may be a variation on "Twister," perhaps suggesting tormentor of the king and extractor of taxes; Johnson's *Dictionary* gives for "twister" the additional meaning of "vacillator."

TZIN-KHALL. Senegal. See KHO-RHÉ, KHA-FELL, THUM-KUMM-QUA. The name is an approximation of "Senegal."

WHEY-VANG. No specific contemporary reference intended. *UH*, 108: "the seventeenth emperor of the *Chew*, or third Chinese dynasty." The historical person is *Hui Wang*, "Gracious Sovereign" of the *Chou* dynasty, c. 700–600 B.C.

XICOCO. Ireland. *UH*, 71: "*Xicoco*, the smallest of the three [islands of Japan]." The modern Japanese name is Shikoku.

XIMO. Scotland. *UH*, 71: "*Ximo*, the next [island] in bigness." The Japanese *shima*, however, merely means "island"; the island referred to is now called Kyushu.

YAF-FRAI (YAFF-RAY, YAFF-RAI). General Jeffrey Amherst, Baron Amherst (1717–97). Pitt promoted him to major-general; in 1758 he took Ticonderoga and Crown Point and then Louisbourg; he became governor-general of North America and knight of the Bath in 1761. The name approximates "Jeffrey."

YAK-STROT. John Stuart, third earl of Bute (1713–92). A favorite of George III's father, Frederick, Prince of Wales; on Frederick's death in 1751 Bute became in effect the governor of the adolescent prince as well as his closest friend and advisor in all matters. Bute was made groom of the stole and a member of the cabinet immediately upon George's accession in 1760; in 1761 he became secretary of state, northern department, and he was named first lord of the treasury on 29 May 1762. Violent attacks on him from all quarters produced his resignation in April 1763; but he was firmly and generally believed as late as 1770 to be the secret ruler of England. "Yak" is presumably "Jack"; "Strot" seems to combine "Stuart" and "strut," the latter in reference to Bute's notorious vanity about his physical appearance and his pompous, affected manner in public. He is called "Jack Scot" in the parable in *Briton*, no. 26 (20 November 1762), and Smollett may also allude to the character of Lord Strutt in John Arbuthnot's famous Queen Anne satire, *The History of John Bull* (1712).

YA-LOFF. General James Wolfe (1727–59). He distinguished himself at Dettingen and Culloden; his zeal in the disastrous Rochefort expedition made the king promote him to colonel. Pitt advanced him to major-general and put him in command of the attack on Quebec; his heroic death during the successful attack made him a national hero. The name is a distortion of "Wolfe."

YAM-A-KHEIT. Marshal James Keith (1696–1758). Fleeing England after the Jacobite rebellion of 1715, he saw service in Spain and became a Russian general in 1747. Entering service with Frederick the Great, Keith became his most valued officer; he fought at Lobositz, Prague, Leipzig, Rossbach, Olmutz, and Hochkirch, where he was killed in action while saving Frederick's life. As a fellow Scot, Smollett was tender of Keith's reputation. The name anagrammatizes "Keith" and adds the Japanese *yama*, "mountain."

YAN. No reference intended. The source of the name has not been traced.

YAN-ONI. See IAN-ON-I.

YESSO. Hanover, to which George I and George II were in Smollett's view catastrophically partial as electors. Hanover is called "Jeddo" (see JEDDO) in the early pages of the *Atom*, "Yesso" in the latter pages. *UH*, in a geographically vague appendix (pp. 150–62), describes "the land of Jedso" (probably Hokkaido and Sakhalin) as a "vast tract of land lying on the north side . . . of *Japan* . . . commonly looked on as part of that empire, and subject to it"; the appendix gives "Yesso" as an alternate spelling.

ZAN-TI-FIC. John Montagu, fourth earl of Sandwich (1718–92). An army officer and naval administrator, he was first lord of the admiralty in 1748–51 and briefly again in 1763; he was then for two years secretary of state, northern department. Notorious for his love of sport and debauchery, he was nicknamed "Jemmy Twitcher" (an allusion to a character in John Gay's *Beggar's Opera*), after denouncing Wilkes in the House of Lords and reading aloud Wilkes's obscene *Essay on Woman*. The name is a distortion of "Sandwich."

PRINTS

The Festival of the Golden Rump (2327)

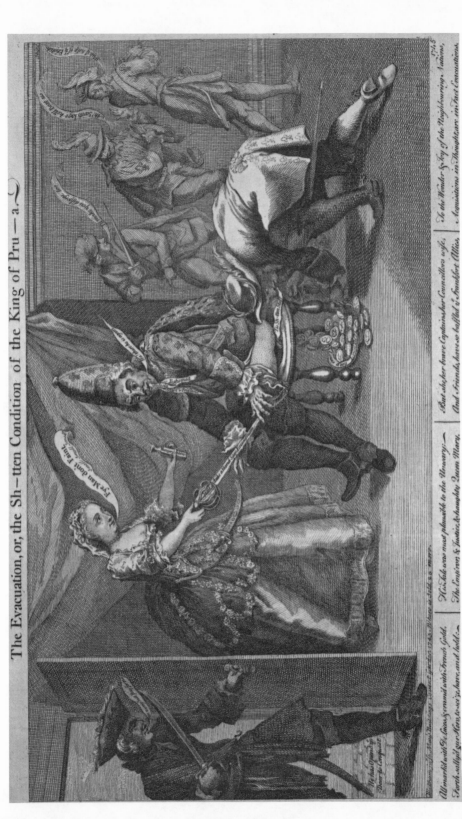

The Evacuation, or the Sh-tten Condition of the King of Pru——a (2601)

The Duke of N——le and His Cook (2684)

The Ghost of a Duchess to William Pitt, Esq. (2786)

The Butcher,
Taken from y̌ Sign of a Butcher in y̌ Butcher Row.

Old Esop who in Morals did surpass,   The Tray's a Breast-Plate to ward off their blows,
Wrapt in a Lion's Skin produc'd an Ass;   His Axe, Knives, Clever is prepar'd for fight,
And sure as fit a Cloathing we provide,   And Death & Slaughter are his sole delight.
Who dress a Butcher in an Oxe's Hide,   Thus arm'd he Terror all arou(n)d d[...]
The Candle serves his Foe-men to disclose, Hath he not borrow'd from a Calf his Head.

Decem: 29. 1746

The Butcher (2843)

This is the Unembarrass'd Countenance or, an Irish Post Face (2854)

Honour in the Breech is lodg'd, | Because a Kick in that Part, more
As wise Philosophers have Judg'd | Hurts Honour, than deep wounds before

The Spy (2857)

The Conduct, of the twoB*****rs.

O England, how revolving is thy State!
How few thy Blessing! how severe thy Fate
O destin'd Nation, to be thus betray'd
By those, whose Duty 'tis to serve and aid!
A griping vile degenerate Viper Brood,
That tears thy Vitals, and exhausts thy Blood.

A varying Kind, that no fixt Rule pursue,
But often form their Principles anew;
Unknowing where to lodg Supreme Command
Or in the King, or Peers, or People's Hand.
Oh Albion, on these Shoulders ne'er repose
These are thy dangerous intestine Foes.

The Conduct of the Two Br——s (3069)

PAUL BEFORE FELIX

Design'd & Etch'd in the ridiculous manner of Rembrant, by Wm Hogarth. Published according to Act of Parliament, May 1.st 1751.

Paul before Felix (3173)

The Circumcised Gentiles, or a Journey to Jerusalem (3205)

The Pillars of the State (3371)

Punch's Opera with the Humours of Little Ben the Sailor (3394)

The Devil Turnd Drover (3416)

The Cole Heavers (3423)

Gloria Mundi (3441)

The Downfall (3480)

MORES HOMINES ⌒

The Sea Lyon (3493)

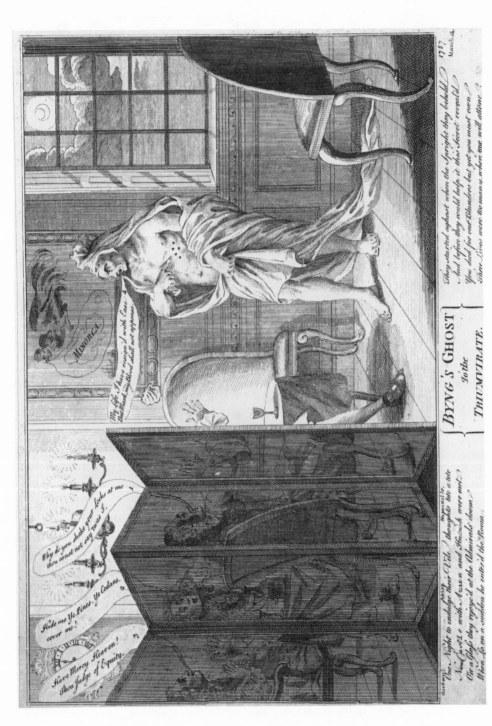

Byng's Ghost to the Triumvirate (3570)

The Treaty or Shabears Administration (3608)

THE DREAM. *1757*

The Dream (3613)

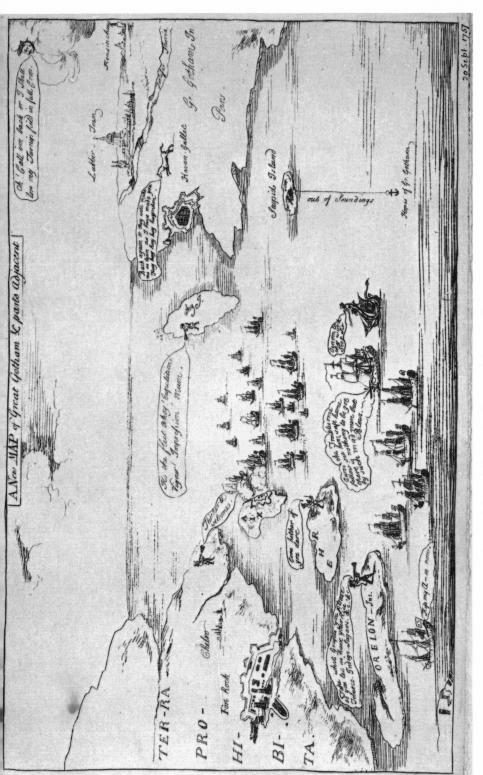

A new Map of Great Gotham and Parts Adjacent (3616)

(3619)

The Whiskers or Sir Jno. Sucklings Bugg-a-Bohs (3625)

We are All a Comeing or Scotch Coal for Ever (3823)

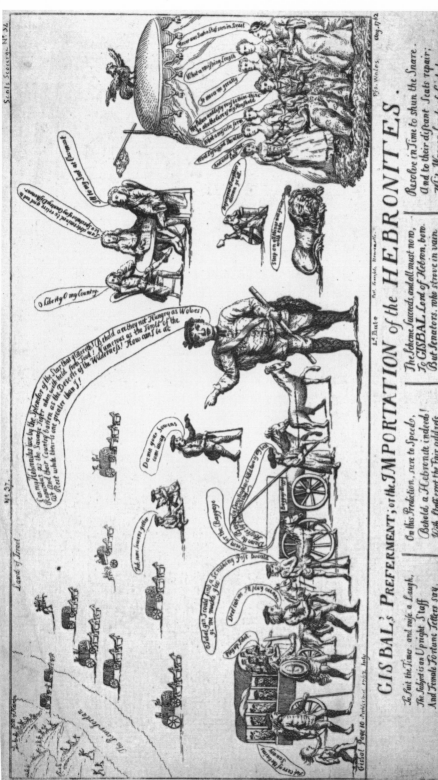

Gisbal's Perferment, or the Importation of the Hebronites (3849)

The Scotch Broomstick & the Female Besom, A German Tale,
by Sawney Gesner (1852)

The Fishermen (3875)

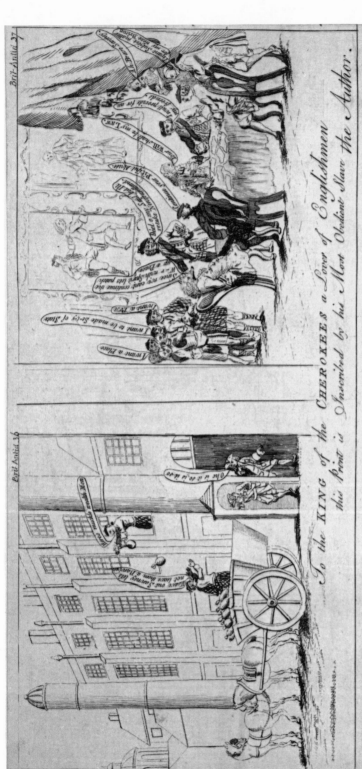

Brit:Antid: 36

Brit:Antid: 37

To the KING of the CHEROKEES a Lover of Englishmen
this Print is Inscribed by his Most Obedient Slave the Author.

WITHOUT

With Shame O BRITONS here behold!
Sly SAWNEY Pocketing your Gold ⸺
While we who got it for his use ⸺
Are forc'd to Pocket the Abuse ⸺⸺
But having throw to laugh that now ⸺
Lets see what Tricks are play'd within ⸺⸺

WITHIN

See here the STATE turn'd upside down
The BONNET triumphs o'er the ⸺
The half starv'd CLANS in hopes of Prey
Come o'er the Hills and far away ⸺
But let us still our Rights maintain ⸺
And drive the LOCUSTS home again ⸺⸺

Web: at Webb's (60¢)

1762

John Bull's House Sett in Flames (3890)

Sic Transit Gloria Mundi (3913)

The Evacuations (3917)

The Scrubbing Post (3946)

The Tempest or Enchanted Island (3958)

The Jack-Boot Kick'd Down or English Will Triumphant. A Dream (3965)

Tit for Tat, or Kiss my A——e is No Treason (3978)

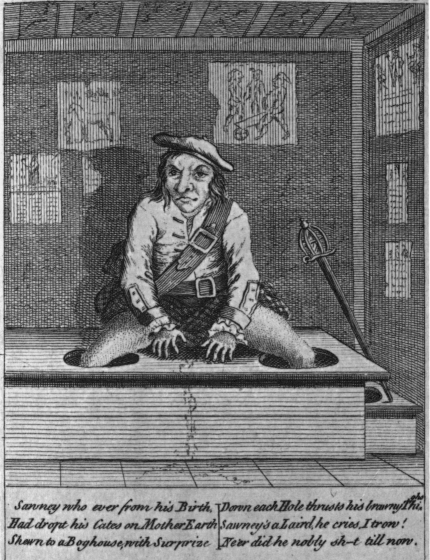

Sawney who ever from his Birth, | Down each Hole thrusts his brawny Thigh.
Had dropt his Cates on Mother Earth | Sawney's a Laird, he cries, I trow!
Shewn to a Boghouse, with Surprize | Neer did he nobly sh—t till now.

Sawney in the Bog-House (3988)

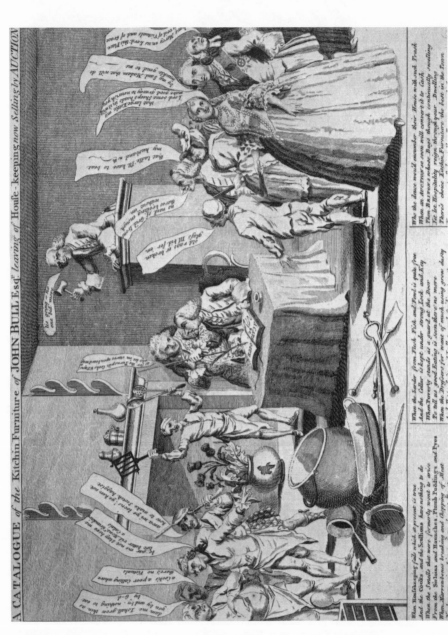

A Catalogue of the Kitchin Furniture of John Bull Esqr. Leaving of House Keeping Now Selling by Auction (3990)

Representing the Heroes of the Times Supposed to be Concern'd in the
Grand Political Uproar (4037)

[Hogarth's Caricature of John Wilkes] (4041)

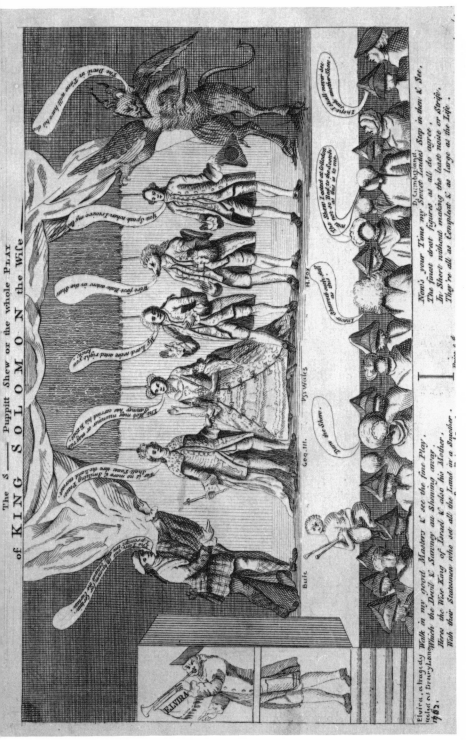

The S—— Puppitt Shew or the Whole Play of King Solomon
the Wise (4049)

The Last Shift (4118)

THE COURIER

Bute

The Road to Hayes
The Road to Hayes

Popularity
The Glory of Mᵗ Pᵗᵗ

Hectore Qui!   Quantum Mutatus ab illo

D of Cumberland, went to Hayes May. 1785.

The Courier (4121)

The State Nursery (4133)

The WORLD turned upside down,
OR
The OLD WOMAN taught WISDOM.

GOODY Bull and her Daughter together fell out, Both squabbled and wrangled, and made a damn'd Rout; But the Cause of their Quarrel remains to be told, Then lend both your Ears and the Tale I'll unfold. *Derry Down, &c.* The old Lady it seems, took a Freak in her Head, That her Daughter, grown Woman, might earn her own Bread, Self applauding her Scheme, she was ready to Dance, But we're often too sanguine in what we advance. *Derry Down, &c.* For mark the Event: thus by fortune we're crost, Nor should any one reckon without a good Host: The Daughter was sulky, and wou'd n't come to, And pray what in this Case could the Old Woman do?

In vain did the Matron hold forth in the Cause, That the young one was able, her Duty, the Laws, Ingratitude vile, Disobedience far worse; But, she might e'en as well have sung Psalms to a Horse. *Derry Down, &c.* Young, froward and sullen, and vain of her Beauty, She turtly reply'd, that she well knew her Duty, That other Folk's Children were kept by their Friends, And that some Folks lov'd People but for their own Ends. *Derry Down, &c.* She sobbed and blubber'd, she bluster'd and swore, If her Mother persisted, she'd turn common Whore, The old Woman thus threaten'd fell down in a Fit, And who in the Nick should hop in but Will P--tt, *Derry Down, &c.*

Zounds! Neighbour, quoth he, what the Devil's the Matter, A Man cannot rest in his House for your Clatter, Alas! cries the Daughter, here's dainty fine Work, The old Woman's grown harder than Jew or than Turk. *Derry Down, &c.* She be d---nd, cries the Farmer, and to her he goes, First roars in her Ears, then tweaks her old Nose, Holla, Goody, what ails you? Wake Woman, I say, I am come to make Peace in this desperate Fray. *Derry Down, &c.* Adsooks ope thine Eyes, what a pother is here, You have no right to compel her, you have not I swear, Be rul'd by your Friends, kneel down and ask Pardon, You'd be sorry I'm sure, should the walk Covent Garden. *Derry Down, &c.*

Alas! cries the old woman, and must I comply, But, I'd rather submit than the Hussy should die, Pooh, prithee be quiet, be friends and agree, You must surely be right, if you're guided by me, *Derry Down, &c.* Unwillingly aukward, the Mother knelt down, While the absolute Farmer went on with a Frown, Come kiss the poor Child, then come kiss and be friends, There kiss your poor Daughter, and make her amends. *Derry Down, &c.* No thanks to you Mother; the Daughter replied; But Thanks to my Friend here, I've humbled your Pride, Then pray leave of this Nonsense, 'tis all a meer Farce, As I've carried my point, you may now kiss my — *derry down, &c.*

The World Turned Upside Down or, The Old Woman
Taught Wisdom (4142)

The Patriot Unmaskd or the Double Pensioner being Billy Pynsents
Last Shift (4146)

The New Country Dance, as Danced at Court (4147)

The Precipice. 1766 (4153)

Prosperity to the County of Sussex with 3 Huzza's (4159)

[Caricature of Pitt by Townshend] (4160)

The Colossus (4162)

Pitt and Proteus, or a Political Flight to the Moon (4163)

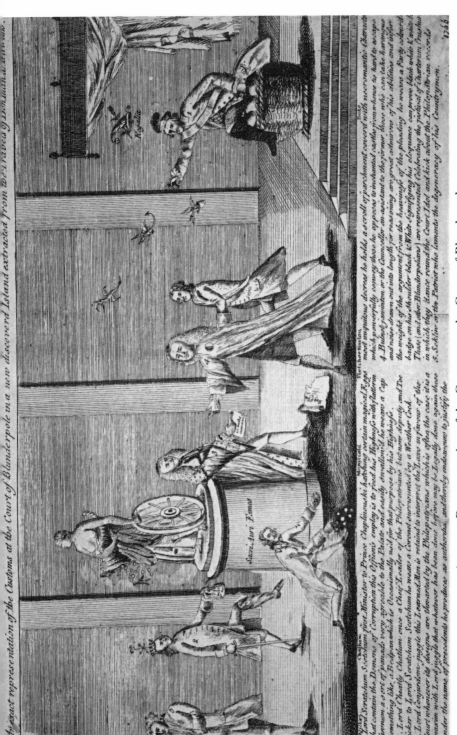

An exact Representation of the Customs at the Court of Blunderpole
in a new Discoverd Island extracted from the Travels of
Don Juan Telltruth (4164)

TEXTUAL COMMENTARY

PUBLICATION HISTORY

In the *London Chronicle*, *London Evening Post*, and *Whitehall Evening Post* for 6–8 December and 8–10 December 1768, *The History and Adventures of an Atom* was announced as to be published "in a few days," printed for J. Almon opposite Burlington House in Piccadilly. In February 1769 the *Atom* was again announced as to be published "in a few days," but this time for G. Kearsly, No. 1, Ludgate Street. This announcement appeared in *Lloyd's Evening Post*, 8 February; *London Chronicle*, 9 February; *St. James's Chronicle*, 9 and 11 February; and *Whitehall Evening Post*, 9 and 11 February. Then the work was announced again, this time as forthcoming on Saturday, 1 April 1769, printed for Robinson and Roberts, No. 25, in Paternoster Row.[1]

The bibliographical description given below (p. 341) for the Almon imprint also fits those copies bearing the Robinson and Roberts imprint, which are nothing more than the sheets printed for Almon with canceled half-title and title pages. Sheets H–L in volume one and the sheets in volume two contain a large scroll watermark. As expected, the original A gatherings often contain this watermark, but the canceled leaves are printed on paper watermarked with a fleur-de-lis and countermarked with a Roman numeral IV.[2] A number of copies of volume one with the Robinson and Roberts imprint, too tightly bound to see that A1 and A2 are conjugate, have gathering A with both watermarks, clearly indicating that A1, 2 were printed on different paper from A3, 4. Apparently when the half titles and titles were being printed, someone discovered that the "X" was on the left of the "L" rather than on the right and this was changed.[3]

One can only speculate about the complicated publishing procedures for one printing of Smollett's satire. It seems certain that John Almon had the work printed and ready for sale in December 1768. (The title pages bearing Almon's imprint are reproduced in the present edition.) After a few copies had been sold, Almon either became afraid that the contents of the *Atom* would lead to his being sued for libel, or he discovered (or had it pointed out to him) that it contained an attack on his friend John Wilkes. In any case, rather than take a loss on the work, Almon canceled the half-title and title pages and sold the sheets, or bound copies, or both, to George Kearsly (or Kearsley). Why the printer of the *North Briton* decided to publish the *Atom* is difficult to understand; it seems probable, however, that he too discovered the nature of the satire after having advertised the work, as no copies appear to have been issued with his imprint.[4] The work was finally accepted, for reasons unknown, by George Robinson and John Roberts and was published 1 April 1769 with canceled half-title and title pages.

In May 1769 a Dublin edition appeared, but another London edition was apparently not needed until 1778.

EDITORIAL PRINCIPLES

As is the case with so many other eighteenth-century works, the autograph manuscript of the *Atom* has disappeared. In fact, no printer's copy for any of Smollett's works has survived. The nature of the manuscript can only be deduced from letters, never intended for publication, and from an examination of manuscript revisions the author made in a copy of the 1766 first edition of *Travels through France and Italy* for a new edition that did not appear.[5] The revisions for the *Travels* include additions, translations of passages in foreign languages, and corrections to the printed text. It might be argued that Smollett, by the mid-1760s largely free from his numerous editorial tasks, had new leisure to correct the *Travels*; but an examination of other works he saw through the press shows much the same care, for he left uncorrected only the kinds of errors that none but the most exacting proofreaders might have caught.[6]

The revisions to the *Travels* are written in Smollett's neat hand, which, after more than two centuries, can be read with ease. A compositor, then, would have had no difficulty reading the author's manuscript of the *Atom*, but in the process of setting the type an overlay of normalization no doubt occurred. As John Smith notes in *The Printer's Grammar* (1755), "By the Laws of Printing, indeed, a Compositor should abide by his Copy, and not vary from it. . . . But this good law is now looked upon as obsolete, and most Authors expect the Printer to spell, point, and digest their Copy, that it may be intelligible and significant to the Reader; which is what a Compositor and the Corrector jointly have regard to, in Works of their own language." The compositor peruses his copy but, before beginning to compose, "should be informed, either by the Author, or Master, after what manner our work is to be done; whether the old way, with Capitals to Substantives, and Italic to Proper names; or after the more neat practice, all in Roman, and Capitals to Proper names and Emphatical words," and nothing "in Italic but what is underscored in our Copy." When composing from printed copy and "such Manuscripts as are written fair," we "employ our eyes with the same agility as we do our hands; for we cast our eyes upon every letter we aim at, at the same moment we move our hands to take it up; neither do we lose our time in looking at our Copy for every word we compose; but take as many words into our memory as we can retain."[7] Since the *Atom* and the *Travels* are printed in what Smith describes as "the more modern and neater way," numerous changes must have occurred between the manuscripts and the printed books, including some normalization of spelling.

In the lengthy manuscript additions to Letter 11 of the *Travels*—the English translation of a Latin letter to Antoine Fizes and the professor's reply in French—Smollett followed the old practice, though somewhat inconsistently, of capitalizing nouns and some adjectives. Schooled to capitalize substantives, he continued in his habitual way.[8] But he certainly knew that his capitalization and his use of the ampersand for "and" would be brought into conformity with the rest of the book. He seems to have accepted the new style, or at least acquiesced. In the printed text of the *Travels* he corrected such small matters as a transposed letter, "muscels" (the bivalve mollusc) to "muscles," and a verb tense "affords" to "afford"; at the same time he allowed to stand variant spellings such as "paltry"–"paultry," "ake"–"ach," and so on.[9] Smollett was not consistent in his spelling, although he did have a preferred spelling for some words; but the compositors, by taking as many words into their memory as they could retain, sometimes introduced their preferences. Smollett appears to have been content with the resulting inconsistencies in spelling as long as they were correct, and he did not attempt to restore his capitalization and punctuation.

The 1769 first edition of the *Atom*, printed from Smollett's lost autograph manuscript, or a fair copy made from it, is the only authoritative text and has been chosen as copy-text for this edition. The possibility that Smollett saw proofs of the *Atom* is slight, as he was traveling on the Continent. He left England for the last time in the fall of 1768, reaching Pisa by the end of March 1769. Nothing is known of his activities during this period.[10] Dr. John Armstrong seems the most likely person to have seen the work through the press; at least he knew about it before it was published 1 April 1769.[11]

In the present edition no attempt has been made to achieve a general consistency in spelling, punctuation, or capitalization, because in the absence of the manuscript one cannot determine whether Smollett or the compositor was responsible for their variations. Hence the spelling, punctuation, and capitalization of the 1769 first edition have been retained except when they are clearly in error, or when they obscure meaning or distract the attention of the reader. All emendations to the copy-text have been made on the authority of the textual editor. Hyphenated words at a line-end have been adjusted according to the usual practice of the first edition insofar as that practice could be ascertained from other appearances or parallels. Only the following changes have been made silently: all turned letters or wrong fonts have been corrected, the long *s* has been replaced by the modern letter *s*, and "ae" and "oe" have been treated as digraphs. Display capitals have not been exactly reproduced. Quotations have been indicated according to modern practice, and the punctuation in relation to the quotation marks has been normalized. The length of dashes and the space around them have also been normalized according to modern practice.[12]

APPARATUS

A basic note in the list of emendations provides the page-line reference and the emended reading in the present text. Except for the silent alterations described above, every editorial change in the first edition copy-text has been recorded. Following the square bracket is the earliest source of emendation and the history of the copy-text reading up to the point of emendation. Emendations marked "W" are the responsibility of the present edition. A wavy dash (~) is substituted for a repeated word associated with pointing, and an inferior caret (∧) indicates pointing absent in the present text or in the edition from which the variant was drawn. The form of the reading both to the right and the left of the bracket conforms to the system of silent alterations, and there is no record of any variations except for the instance being recorded. When the matter in question is pointing, for example, the wavy dash to the right of the bracket signifies only the substantive form of the variant, and any variation in spelling or capitalization has been ignored. Emendations from catchwords are indicated as *cw*. A vertical stroke | indicates a line-end.

Some emendations and decisions to retain the copy-text reading are discussed in the textual notes. All hyphenated compounds or possible compounds appearing at line-ends in the copy-text are recorded in the word-division list. The reader should assume that any word hyphenated at the line-end in the present text, but not appearing in this list, was broken by the modern printer.

COLLATION

The present edition has been printed from the following copies of the 1769 first edition with the Almon imprint: volume one in the Pennsylvania State Uni-

versity Library (T823 Sm79h 1769); volume two in the New York Society
Library. Photocopies of these volumes were compared on the Hinman Collator with two copies at the University of Iowa Library (xPR3694 H5 and
xPR3694 H5 1769a) and photocopies from the University of California at
Berkeley (PR3694 A87 1749), University of Texas at Austin (Wm Sm79
769h), Bibliothèque Nationale (Y2 4261–4262), British Library (12612.dd.9),
and Victoria and Albert Museum (Dyce 17.a.45). No press-variants were
discovered.

Notes

1. Announcements appeared in *Lloyd's Evening Post*, *London Chronicle*, and *St. James's Chronicle*.

2. Not all preliminary gatherings in each copy contain a watermark, of course, since not all would be printed on the portion of the sheet containing it. Originally the four-leaf preliminary gathering in volume one and the two-leaf gathering in volume two were probably printed as part of gathering L of volume one, allowing the printer to fill the entire sheet. In both Huntington Library copies leaf [A]3^r (p. *v*) offset on Leaf L6^v (p. *228*).

3. I have discovered no bibliographical evidence that would suggest the highly unlikely possibility that the date was originally correct and that the date was made incorrect in the process of repairing some damage to the pages of type. I say "pages" because the incorrect date appears on the title page of both volumes one and two. The sets at CU, GEU, PSt, and the Bibliothèque Nationale have the first volume with the Almon imprint and the second volume with the Robinson and Roberts imprint with the incorrect date. The NNS set has the second volume with the Almon imprint and the first volume with the Robinson and Roberts imprint and the incorrect date. Only the copy at PPRF (EL2 .S666at 769 copy 2) has both volumes with the Almon imprint. (Copy 1 has the Robinson and Roberts imprint with the incorrect date in both volumes; the copies have been examined for me.) It was not noticed, however, when the date in the Robinson and Roberts imprint was corrected, that the half title of volume two read "History *an* Adventures" rather than "History *and* Adventures."

4. An extensive search has failed to turn up any copies bearing Kearsly's imprint. Kearsly worked with Almon and Robinson and was not overly scrupulous about which political view he supported, but both Kearsly and Almon had experienced previous difficulties with the authorities and may not have wanted to risk another confrontation. See Barbara Laning Fitzpatrick, "The Text of Tobias Smollett's *Life and Adventures of Sir Launcelot Greaves*, The First Serialized Novel" (Ph.D. diss., Duke University, 1987), 133–35.

5. This copy of the *Travels* is in the British Library, shelf mark C.45.d.20, 21. Apart from the manuscript revisions of the *Travels* and a relatively small number of holograph letters, what survives in Smollett's hand is very little: a one-leaf holograph note on the reign of Edward III in the Berg Collection, New York Public Library, and about a dozen signed receipts and documents. See *Letters*, xvi–xvii.

6. Smollett was content to make small changes because the *Travels*, written at a relatively slow pace, did not require the extensive stylistic revisions of the earlier works. His first three novels were written quickly, but Smollett took the opportunities offered by new editions of *Roderick Random* and *Peregrine Pickle* to make revisions. In the works of his later career, revision seems to have been carried out before publication; by this time he was also a more experienced writer. For discussion of the composition of the *Travels*, see the introduction by Frank Felsenstein, ed., *Travels through France and Italy* (Oxford: Oxford University Press, 1979), xxxv–xli.

7. John Smith, *The Printer's Grammar* (London, 1755), 199, 201–2, 209.

8. Bertrand H. Bronson, *Printing as an Index to Taste in Eighteenth Century England* (New York: New York Public Library, 1958), 17.

9. *Travels*, ed. Felsenstein, 88, 160, 279.

10. Knapp, 276–79.

11. See above, the introduction, pp. liv–lv. For arguments that Dr. Armstrong may have acted as Smollett's agent in London not only for the *Atom* but for *Humphry Clinker* and the second edition of *Ferdinand Count Fathom*, see the Textual Commentary to the Georgia Edition of *Ferdinand Count Fathom*, pp. 445–47.

12. I am grateful to Mary Jane Early for her assistance with the preparation of the text and with the proofreading. I also wish to thank Sidney E. Berger for his work on the Hinman Collator. No edition could be completed without the assistance of librarians, and I wish to thank the following for their unfailing courtesy in answering my queries: Anthony S. Bliss, University of California at Berkeley; Charles Mann, Pennsylvania State University; Clive E. Driver and Leslie A. Morris, The Rosenbach Museum and Library; Ellen Nemhauser, Emory University; Frank Paluka and Robert A. McCown, University of Iowa Library; Mark Piel, New York Society Library.

LIST OF EMENDATIONS

[The following sigla appear in the textual apparatus of the Georgia Edition:
1 (the first edition; London, J. Almon, 1769), W (present edition).]

6.26	voice] W	~, 1
9.21	bullock's] W	bullocks's 1
17.6	beard] W	heard 1
19.2	abrupt] W	abrubt 1
25.25	actually] W	actully 1
38.9	magazine] W	magazines 1
39.17	Kurds] W	Kurd 1
45.22	establish] W	estabish 1
45.30	whom before] W	before whom 1
48.2	with] W	w!th 1
55.29	populace] W	popoulace 1
59.39	become a favourite (cw)] W	become vourite (text) 1
63.5	kept] W	keept 1
63.26	Taycho] W	Tycho 1
67.5	*Achas*] W	*Acbas* 1
70.3	has] W	had 1
80.32	subtracted] W	substracted 1
83.17	*Porcinas*] W	*Por-|Porcinas* 1
105.3	come upon (cw)] W	upon (text) 1
122.16	curtain.] W	~, 1

56.39   a shameful rascal or a shameful villain] The repetition of "shameful" may be an error in Smollett's manuscript or an error introduced by the compositor. One might guess "shameless" in the second instance, but this is problematical since, in a departure from his practice with the other items surrounding it, Smollett varies the noun. Why he has "rascal" and "villain" rather than two of one or the other is not clear. Perhaps this is a sign of haste, a common problem with Smollett, particularly in his earlier writings.

63.26   Taycho] The general policy is not to normalize names, because Smollett rarely shows preference for one form over another. This is true not only in the *Atom*, as a glance at the Key (pp. 249–68) makes clear, but in most of his other works as well. Smollett consistently refers to Pitt, however, as "Taycho," except in this one instance, suggesting that the omission of the "a" is a typographical error.

WORD-DIVISION

I. LINE-END HYPHENATION IN THE GEORGIA EDITION

[The following compounds, hyphenated at a line-end in the Georgia Edition, are hyphenated within the line in the 1769 first edition.]

5.21	White-|livered
7.35	state-|intrigue
15.24	hare-|skin
15.37, 59.6, 84.34, 105.3	Fika-|kaka
18.29	Fakku-|basi
21.1	Nin-kom-|poo-po
21.16, 62.21	Sey-seo-|gun
28.16, 31.28, 118.38	Sti-phi-|rum-poo
32.3	money-|bags
35.15	Sti-|phi-rum-poo
35.36	Bihn-|goh
39.31	Gothama-|baba
40.2, 94.29	Got-hama-|baba
40.16, 40.29, 42.33, 53.28	Got-|hama-baba
45.11	To-|day
45.36	Pol-|hassan-akousti
51.37	mud-|walled
64.24	tripe-|woman
69.24	Ya-|loff
77.13	Soo-san-|sin-o
79.29, 90.35	Quib-|quab
80.9, 89.33	Yaff-|rai
82.22	court-|martial
86.17	Rha-rin-|tumm
88.18	Bron-xi-|tic

91.32	Hel-y-|otte
97.20	priest-|craft
97.34	*She-it-|kums-hi-til*
97.36	*Shi-|tilk-ums-hitites*
98.30	Fatz-|man
104.10	Brut-an-|tiffi
105.17, 125.30, 126.24, 128.10	Yak-|strot
106.10	Brut-|an-tiffi
108.34, 114.28	Fan-|yah
111.32	semi-|circular
120.12	pelting-|match
122.17	Jan-|ki-dtzin
122.27	Praff-|patt-phogg
123.15	fellow-|subjects
130.7	Mura-|clami

2. LINE-END HYPHENATION IN THE 1769 FIRST EDITION

[The following compounds or possible compounds are hyphenated at a line-end in the first edition. The form in which each has been given in the Georgia Edition, as listed below, represents the usual practice of the 1769 first edition insofar as it may be ascertained from other appearances or parallels.]

5.15	handwriting
11.30	hot-headed
12.24	good-humoured
13.1	bareheaded
13.25, 18.15, 24.34, 25.16, 29.26, 31.36, 41.10, 43.10, 111.2	Fika-kaka
14.35, 29.21, 39.31, 40.16,	

43.16, 52.39,	
53.4, 53.28,	
55.15, 78.3,	
94.13, 96.9,	
98.17, 110.3	Got-hama-baba
15.30	boar-cat
17.25, 63.5	overwhelmed
20.5	self-exenteration
21.18, 28.16,	
31.28, 35.15,	
95.37, 113.31	Sti-phi-rum-poo
22.8, 92.26	Sey-seo-gun-siality
23.26	malcontents
25.3	Quamba-cun-dono
25.29, 77.13,	
104.27	Soo-san-sin-o
28.19, 31.31,	
32.10, 32.14,	
95.39, 105.9,	
113.31, 118.39	Nin-kom-poo-po
29.24, 31.28,	
77.12, 114.8	Gotto-mio
30.35, 108.32,	
118.38	Fatzman
32.3, 77.13	Foksi-roku
32.23, 36.14,	
36.17	Bihn-goh
37.18	bell-weather
40.4, 40.32,	
44.31, 47.16,	
50.11, 56.6,	
58.13, 70.14,	
70.18, 88.31,	
88.38, 100.35,	
101.15, 103.16,	
106.25	Brut-an-tiffi
40.34	dumbfounded
41.27	oyster-women

92.10	Kha-fell
92.11	bull-dogs
94.25, 130.7	Mura-clami
95.36	gridiron
96.2, 105.10, 111.13, 119.23	Fokh-si-rokhu
97.14, 97.28, 97.37, 98.37	*Shit-tilk-ums-heit*
97.32	dying-day
98.8, 113.39	Gio-gio
101.39	sauce-pans
102.3	soup-meagre
102.10	antichamber
102.13	household
104.34, 105.37, 112.7, 112.20, 117.23, 119.28, 120.7, 120.13, 124.9, 124.21, 126.11, 127.1, 128.29	Yak-strot
105.20	merchant-ships
111.31	side-nod
111.35	full-stare
112.26	lanthorn-jaws
114.10	She-it-kum-sheit-el
114.15	Thin-quo
118.2	overturned
118.15	mal-administration
119.7	hand-barrow
119.33	Llur-chir
122.29	commonwealth
125.11	good-natured
125.22	grandmother
126.28	monster-tamer
127.7	Praff-fog
128.36	Quam-ba-cundono
132.11	self-interest

3. SPECIAL CASES

[The following compounds, or possible compounds, are hyphenated at a line-end in both the Georgia Edition and in the 1769 first edition.]

69.29	Abra-|moria's	(Abra-moria's)
82.3	*stinking-|breath*	(*stinking-breath*)
96.26	nick-|nacks	(nick-nacks)
101.6	free-|booter	(free-booter)
102.23	Yak-|strot	(Yak-strot)
130.13	wrong-|box	(wrong-box)

BIBLIOGRAPHICAL DESCRIPTIONS

1. THE FIRST EDITION
THE | HISTORY | AND | ADVENTURES | OF AN | ATOM. | IN TWO
VOLUMES. | VOL. I. | [*printer's ornaments*] | LONDON: | Printed for J.
ALMON, opposite Burlington-House, | in Piccadilly. MDCCLXIX. |
Half title: THE | HISTORY | AND | ADVENTURES | OF AN | ATOM. |
VOL. I. |

Volume 2: Title page as in volume I except "VOL. II." substituted for
"VOL. I." Half titles as in volume I except "VOL. II." substituted for
"VOL. I."

Collation: 12° (190 x 110 mm. uncut). Volume I: [A]⁴ B–K¹² L⁶. Pp. *i* half
title, *iii* title, *v*, vi–viii Advertisement, *1*, 2–227 text, *228 blank*. Volume II:
[A]² B–I¹². Pp. *i* half title, *iii* title, *1*, 2–190 text, *191–92 blank*.

Press figures: Volume I: 4–5, 46–5, 50–2, 72–5, 87–3, 109–3, 143–4, 157–2,
167–8, 182–7, 213–2, 214–1, 222–7, 224–4. Volume II: 15–1, 24–7, 34–6,
45–8, 52–1, 63–4, 86–2, 118–2, 130–6, 133–7, 167–8, 178–6, 181–7.

Typography: Volume I: 87 in some copies = 78. Running head page 74 and
= ana. Catchwords: *1* cock,] ~. 140 ting∧] ding, 179 a fa-] vourite. No
catchwords 38, 65, 126, 133. Volume II: Volume registers at foot of $1
incorrectly for C and D "Vol. 1.," correctly for all others "Vol. II." Catchwords: 22 *cinas*,] *Porcinas*, 63 ley] ley- 96 come] upon 113 periods,] riods,
136 admiral∧] ~, 144 atention] attention.

Copies: Textually collated CU (PR3694 A87 1749), IaU (xPR3694 H5 and
xPR3694 H5 1769a), NNS, PSt (T823 Sm79h 1769), TxU (Wm Sm79
769h), Bibliothèque Nationale (Y2 4261-4262), British Library (12612.dd.9),
and Victoria and Albert Museum (Dyce 17.a.45). Additional copies bibli-
ographically collated CSmH (39048 and 124651), CaOTU (B-10 5124 and
B-10 5125), CtY (Im Sm79 769, Im Sm79 769b, and Tinker 1932), ICN
(Case Y 155 .S662), IU (x823 Sm7ad 1769 and Nickell x823 Sm7ad 1769),
NH (*EC75 Sm792 769h and *EC75 Sm792 769ha), TxU (PR3694 H5
1749), British Library (1208.b.22), Bodleian (Hope 8/o 14,15), and Cambridge University Library (S727.d.76.6).

INDEX